BORROWED TIME

VOLUME 1

Infinity Books

Ramirez & Clark
PUBLISHERS

DÄNNA WILBERG

About the Author

"The best secrets are the most twisted."

Sarah Shepard's quote from 'Twisted' best describes author Dänna Wilberg's quest to unravel life's mysteries with every keystroke, on every page. Her series, *The Red Chair*, *The Grey Door,* and *The Black Dress* featuring psychotherapist Grace Simms, pose the question: "What do we *really* know about a person?"

Dänna's paranormal *Borrowed Time* series, about a woman who acquires a psychic gift after a near-death experience, is filled with gems from Dänna's experience producing and hosting TV show "Paranormal Connection" for over fifteen years. Her background as an award-winning script-writer and film-maker further add to the magic of her storytelling.

Wilberg resides in Northern California with her family. She loves her children, grandchildren, traveling the world, and karaoke. She loves to dance, cook, make short films, dabble in her garden, and great music. Her mantra is reach for the stars.

Visit Dänna's website: dannawilberg.com

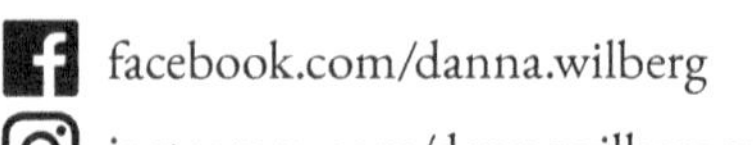

ISBN: 978-1-955171-48-9

A Few Words From Suzanne Cash

"I remember him pulling me close, his iron grip, his hot breath in my ear, goosebumps skittering up my body...and when he clamped his hand over my mouth, and pressed the gun to my back...my first thought was... *why*?

"Waking up in a hospital bed with tubes snaking up my arms was alarming to say the least. I didn't know why I was there, and I won't lie, I was scared. And then when I saw Detective Sam Metzger standing by my bed, I knew something bad had happened."

"The visions didn't come immediately, but it felt as though I had an electrical current running through my body. *I knew things*. Random things that didn't make sense. I kept seeing my dead fiancé in my dreams...and in my room. In my dreams he took me places...and at first, I welcomed the memories...we were so in love...but then he began taking me to places I didn't recognize, and showing me things I didn't want to see...dead bodies of young women who had been brutally murdered."

"Sam didn't believe in the paranormal. Psychics defied logic, reasoning, and his code of ethics. But when he couldn't deny the accuracy of the information popping out of my mouth like a hiccup, or knowledge gained during my fugue or altered state, he was left with no other choice than to trust me."

"I don't always get it right. My psychic friend, Linda Schooler, and other gifted friends help me put puzzle pieces together when I get stumped. But as time goes on, my abilities grow stronger, and I can rely on one thing...the universe has a plan...and everything *does* happen for a reason."

BOOK 1: BROKEN PROMISES

Contents

BORROWED TIME

BOOK 1 - BROKEN PROMISES

Infinity Books

DÄNNA WILBERG

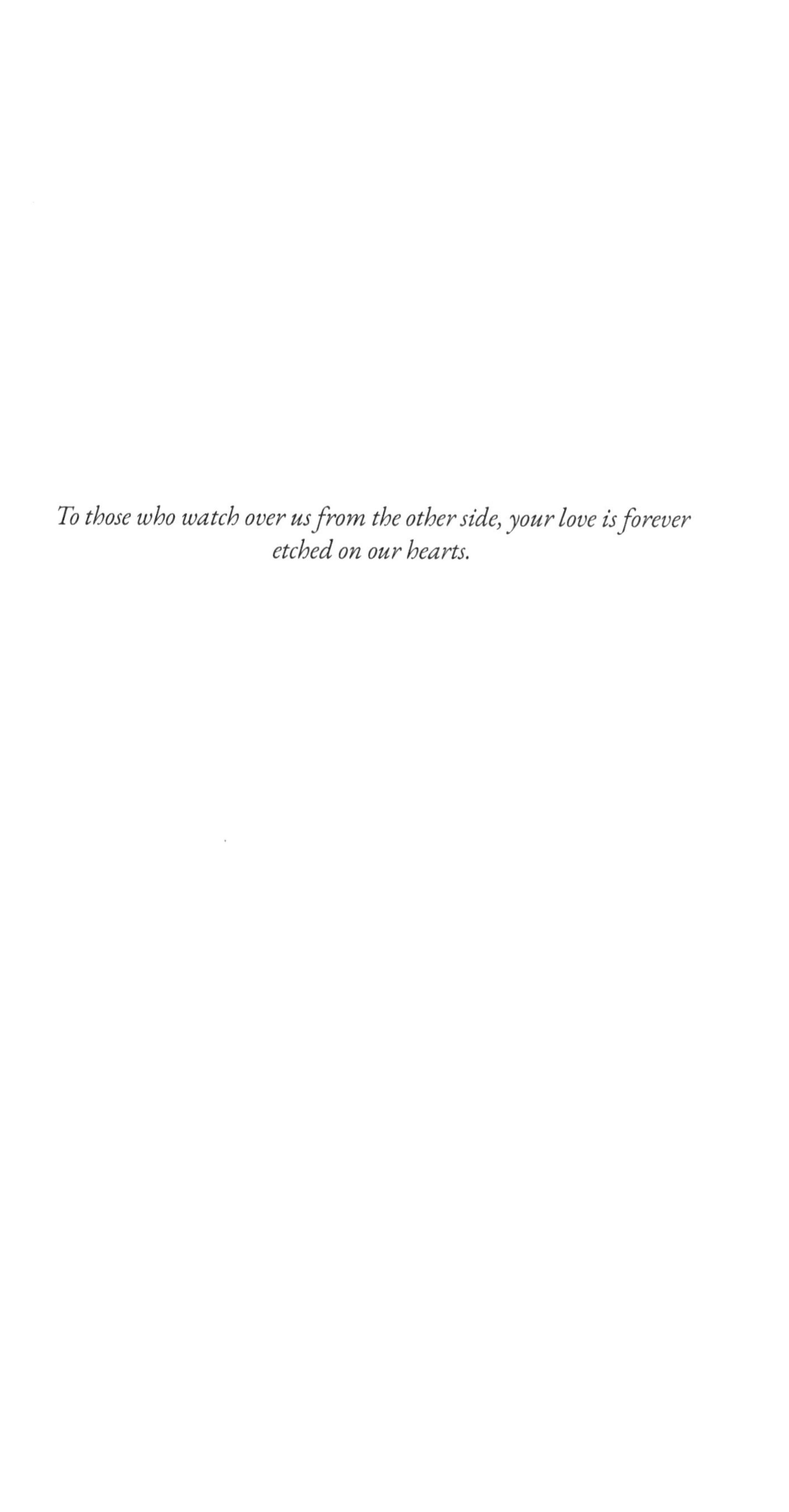

To those who watch over us from the other side, your love is forever etched on our hearts.

Prologue

Amy Fitzpatrick sucked in her stomach, straightened her shoulders, and turned toward the Tabby cat sprawled across her bed. “What do you think, Rex?” Twelve weeks ago, she criticized her muffin top and super-sized chest. Today she relished the change. *Crossfit*. By summer’s end, her abs never looked better, her arms and legs, defined. *Thank God for pull-ups and squats.*

She slipped into a pair of stone-washed jeans, a silky white tank top, and scooted her feet into strappy sandals. “Too plain?” But Rex didn’t respond. He licked one paw and swiped it across his left ear. “I hope my date shows more interest than you, my friend,” she said, brushing her long cinnamon colored hair.

Amy thought about her date, an older guy she’d met online thirty pounds ago. He said he was coming to town and wanted to meet her in person. His name was Jeff, and he suggested dinner. *Sushi, my favorite.*

She sometimes wished she could go back in time. Reset the clock. She didn’t date much in high school, she preferred books to broken promises. When she graduated college and applied for a position at a local broadcasting company, she had no idea taking the job meant giving up the best years of her life. She ate her way through lonely nights and weekends. Starbucks became her new best friend, and she discovered Venti Frappuccino’s with double whip. Coupons, received in the mail for pizza or buy one hamburger, get one free, upgrades for supersize fries with a large soft drink purchase, gave her something to look forward to. Until one day she looked in the mirror and no longer recognized herself.

Joining the dating site gave her a new lease on life. Whittling her weight down from a size 10 to a size 6 improved her confidence. She was ready for a relationship. “You know, Rex,” she said, “if this guy works out, you may find your lazy ass sleeping on the floor.”

Rex yawned and stretched.

At 7:48 p.m., Amy pulled into a parking structure on 11th and K Streets. She drove to the designated level and parked near the elevator as Jeff instructed. She thought the directive was odd and wondered why he didn’t agree to meet at the restaurant. *Maybe he wants to check you out before he wastes his evening wining and dining you?* She took one last look in her visor mirror. *Don’t be silly.*

A handsome, dark-haired man stood near the elevator door. She recognized him immediately from his photo.

“Hello, Jeff.”

He flashed a Hollywood smile. “Amy? Is that you?”

“Surprised?” Amy twirled around.

His lips puckered, and he whistled low. “Damn, you are even more beautiful in person!”

They rode the elevator to the ground floor and navigated their way through a courtyard with clusters of people enjoying Labor Day weekend. “This way,” he said, ducking into the first doorway they came to. “I reserved a table for us in the corner—where it’s quiet.” His hand rested at the base of her spine. “We can get better acquainted.”

The restaurant was nothing extravagant, but the food was spectacular. Jeff surpassed all expectations, and she wondered, *could he be the one*?

“This photo was taken last Thanksgiving,” he said, sliding his phone across the table. “That’s my grandma—she’s 86, but boy can she dance up a storm. She’s holding my fur baby, Penny.”

Amy smiled at the photo, wondering if Penny and Rex would hit it off. She was getting ahead of herself, but he seemed to have all the qualities she dreamed of: funny, charming, attentive, talented and handsome. A career, family values–assets most girls put high on their wish list. *Almost too good to be true.* “Why are you still single?”

"Why are you?"

"I'm a workaholic?"

"I think we're in the same boat. I love my job."

"Does that mean we're destined to be alone?"

"Let's go to my place, we can talk about it there." His eyes traveled to her breasts and back.

"No. I don't think—"

His smile faded. His eyes turned cold. He slapped his hands on the table. "Hey, no worries," he said.

Amy needed a moment to assess his mood swing and excused herself to the restroom. She wasn't ready to have sex on their first date. Then again, maybe she was over-thinking the way he looked at her. A cartoon image of a wolf licking his chops came to mind. Maybe her mother had been right, maybe online dating wasn't such a good idea. When they connected on the dating site, she thought he'd be more mature than guys she dated in college, because of his age. *Less pushy.*

When she returned to the table, Jeff had ordered more Saki.

"I have to get up early, Jeff, I don't think I should—"

"Please, one more drink. I don't want the evening to end. I'm sorry if I rushed things, but I really like you."

He held her in his gaze until...

"Okay–I'm sure one more won't hurt."

———

Amy felt dizzy. Unsteady. Nauseous. "Where are we?" she asked. She didn't understand why her limbs were filled with cement, why bees swarmed in her head. *I only took a few sips.* "I don't feel right."

Jeff pushed a key into the lock.

"I have work tomorrow," she slurred, leaning against the heavy wooden door frame.

"I know. This won't take long," he whispered.

———

JACK

"Let's put it over there," said events coordinator Suzanne Cash, pointing to the blank wall across the hotel ballroom. Julien, her assistant, dragged a gigantic cardboard cut-out of a bunny peeking out of a top hat across the room and lifted it as high as his five-foot-seven frame could stretch. Suzanne nodded and clapped her hands. "Perfect."

"Are you sure?" he asked, holding the cut-out in place.

"I'm sure."

"You were sure the last *two* times. Are you positive this is where you want it?"

"One hundred percent positive."

"You know these kids aren't going to care if the purple letters in ABRACADABRA clash with the wall sconces or the carpet, they're coming to see the *magic*."

She buried her hands in the pockets of her maxi skirt. "Geez, Julien–don't the kids deserve perfection in their imperfect world?"

"They're kids. Not experts in Feng Shui."

Suzanne brushed past Julien. "Did you get the black curtains I asked for?"

"Sure did. They will be hung tonight before I leave."

"We have to be finished with the stage decorations and the props by three o'clock tomorrow afternoon. Catering starts their set-up at four. Doors open six o'clock sharp. Can you check the weather again? Someone mentioned rain."

"Nothing until next week. We may be in for a wet Halloween."

"Damn, I still have my dress to collect from the cleaners."

"The kids are going to love you no matter what you wear. And I promise you, we will be done. Now scoot. You look bitchy with puffy eyes."

Suzanne smirked. "Do you need anything before I go?"

"No. Get some rest. Recharge your batteries."

She didn't argue. Her eyes *were* puffy, her long auburn hair needed washing, and her make-up had melted off hours ago. She was beat. Her feet throbbed; she couldn't remember the last time she had eaten. She was oblivious to everyone around her. Her bones yearned for bed. *I hate when he's right.*

The wind stirred leaves along the walkway. The sun, long gone, left the moon in charge. *Nothing looks familiar.* She turned to go back inside the hotel only to find the door locked. Frustrated, she walked towards a fenced area, noticing the hotel marquee in the distance. "Making Magic for Wish Kids."

After tomorrow night she'd get her life back. *No hurry there.* She loved her work. Whether the kids went into remission, or journeyed into the next astral plane, she rallied for every dime that went towards helping them forget their illness, pain, and struggle.

Suzanne walked toward the pool area and paused. *Presto!* The moon disappeared behind the clouds. *Now you see it, now you don't.* It was dark. *Too dark.* She must've gotten turned around. She stopped to listen. *Footsteps?* "Don't be paranoid," she mumbled, and inched her way towards the pool's eerie glow. She reached inside her purse for her phone, about to dial Julien, when an arm snaked around her neck and a large hand covered her mouth. Something hard pressed beneath her right shoulder blade. His hot breath seethed in her ear. "You shouldn't've meddled."

Then came a pop, and searing, hot, pain impaled her. A blow to the back of her head sent her reeling. She saw stars, heard a splash. Cold. Falling. Plumes of blood escaped her body as she descended to the bottom of the pool, her arms flailing like *snow angels.* Loving eyes acknowledged her despair. Tender arms enfolded her. She closed her eyes and listened to the familiar voice. “Don’t fight it,” he whispered, “relax.”

There was no mistaking the voice. *Jack.*

No longer falling. *Floating.*

Jack...my first love.

Sam

Samson Metzger picked up the phone on the fifth ring. He hated being called in the middle of the night. Sleep was a commodity, not to be wasted. The desk sergeant's voice shattered the final fragments of his REM state. "He's at it again."

"Son-of-a—" Sam grumbled, pulling himself upright. "Where?"

"Diamond Springs, 515 Afton Street. I called the coroner. Johnson and Schuster are already on the scene. Dixon wants you there. Now."

"Fine." Sam plunked the phone back on its receiver. Twenty minutes later, he ducked under the yellow tape securing the scene. He flipped his badge at the officer standing vigil and donned the gear he had tucked under his arm. Once he was gowned from head to toe, he wiggled his fingers into a pair of nitrile gloves, dreading what lie ahead. He was well acquainted with the smell of death.

"What do we have?"

Rob Schuster lowered his mask. The camera around his neck dangled from a thick black strap. "If it isn't sleeping beauty."

"Not in the mood, Rob." Sam stood in the doorway to the living room of the rundown Victorian performing his usual overview of the crime scene. Starting at the far corner of the room, he began working in sections. "Same guy?"

"Looks like it," Rob said, holding up an evidence bag.

"Orange twine?"

"Yep. We'll know more once we get all the samples collected. Johnson's in the other room with the body." Before Rob reseated his mask, he added, "She's been here awhile."

Sam navigated his way down the hall. When he reached the bedroom, he pulled his mask over his nose and mouth. Inside, Dove Johnson, Goldorado County's finest crime scene investigator and forensic specialist, stood over the body of a young woman. Sam cleared his throat, and Dove jerked his head around.

"Hey partner–"

"Where's Dixon?"

"It's Friday night, probably bangin' some cheerleader." Dove shook his head. "Who knows? He said he'd be here. That was over an hour ago." Dove maneuvered his way around the body like a ninja. He lifted the dead girl's hand and carefully extracted an orange fiber embedded in her wrist. "This one fought like a hellion, just like the others."

Sam scanned the room. "No signs of struggle here in the house?"

"Nope—drop off, just like the Wheeler girl. I imagine when we find the scene of the crime it'll be horrific."

Sam squatted next to Dove. His eyes traveled the girl's body assessing decomposition and lividity. "How long?"

"Three to four weeks, give or take a few days."

"What kind of sick fuck does this?"

"The kind we'd better catch quickly." Dove nodded toward the girl's pelvic area. "I extracted the broom handle for prints."

Sam's stomach clenched. He moved away from Dove and tore at his mask. "When can I expect a report?"

"I'll be finished here in a couple hours. I should have something for you by midmorning."

Sam reached his hand in his pocket and pulled out the cell phone vibrating against his thigh. A grimace flashed across his face. "Detective Metzger."

"Just got a call from Mercy," Kelly, Goldorado County's bubbly dispatcher announced. "They pulled a body from the pool at the Marriott. She's still alive. Dixon wants you to check it out."

"It's freaking 2:00 a.m."

"I'm just the messenger—he said to get over there ASAP."

"O.D.? Suicide?"

"Not unless she shot herself in the back first."

"Jesus H. Christ," Sam hissed, flipping a page on his notepad. "Who called it in?" He scribbled the info on the page. "All right, I'll get over there as soon as I finish here." Sam clicked his phone off and slipped it in his pocket. "Like they say, no rest for the wicked," he said, slapping Dove's back. He took a last glance at the body. The girl was about his sister Audra's age. He shuddered.

On his way out, Sam approached Schuster, who was down on his knees photographing the Persian rug. He squatted beside him. "Anything?"

"One hundred-seventy-eight knots per square inch. Doesn't match the rest of the décor."

Sam noticed the furniture in the house was mismatched, shabby or broken. He lifted one corner of the rug. "The floor isn't faded," he said.

"No." Schuster snapped a series of photos. "Our guy carried the body here inside the rug, then staged the body in the bedroom."

Sam balled his mask inside his fist. "I got another call. I'll check in later."

Suzanne's brother, Steven, perched on the edge of her hospital bed and held her hand. "Hey Suz, you had us all worried."

Across the room, her husband Ben sat engrossed in a magazine. He'd barely lifted his eyes when she regained consciousness.

"Hurts," she whispered. She felt weak, her head pounded, pain radiated from her back in places she couldn't pin-point. Brightly colored scrubs swam across her vision, poking and prodding her body. Pliable tubing snaked from an IV pole to the PICC line delivering medication directly to her heart. Tiny lights flitted into black space and pulsated along her peripheral vision. She struggled to keep herself from falling back into the abyss.

"Do you know where you are Mrs. Cash?" a woman's voice came from the blur of colors above her head.

She tried to speak.

Steven lifted her hand to his cheek. "You're at Mercy Folsom," he said. "They brought you in last night." His voice quivered, "You were shot, found floating in the pool at the Marriott." He paused, choking back tears. "We thought we lost you."

Suzanne's fingers closed around his.

Ben circled to the other side of the bed and loomed over her fragile form. She tried to turn in his direction but couldn't. Her head spun. She felt nauseated.

Steven covered her hand with his. "The doctor said you're gonna be fine. You were in surgery for a good part of the night. The bullet nicked an artery. A centimeter to the left and—" Steven cleared his throat. "The Doc said you were lucky, the wound was clean, he said it would heal in no time. He also said you have a nasty concussion. I asked him how he could tell."

Suzanne couldn't laugh. Her brother always teased her about being the only "dizzy" brunette on the planet.

"What were you doing at that hotel?" Ben's tone turned Suzanne's blood to ice. Her eyes shifted to her brother, hoping he would intervene.

"How about if we go get some coffee Ben," he said. "Let Suzanne get her beauty sleep. We'll be back to check on you later, Sis."

Suzanne's lids closed, and she began to dream...

She was fifteen. A leaden sky, not unusual for December in Chicago, promised at least six more inches of snow. Suzanne trudged home from school. Three months into her sophomore year, and she wasn't doing well. A misfit with poor grades, not a good start. Her dad worked long hours, her mom worked part time, but between Rotary Club meetings and bake sales, mother-daughter time dwindled. When Suzanne's older brother, Steven, needed a favor he was her best friend, otherwise she didn't exist. Destined to be invisible.

She didn't notice the Chevy parked on the street in front of her bungalow until it was too late. Upon impact, Suzanne was jolted from one type of pain into another. A goose egg formed on her knee-cap, and she swore under her breath, "Dammit God! Why me?" Suddenly, large wet flakes tumbled from the sky. "Oh great. Just what I needed," she said and tromped inside the house.

"You're all wet," said the stranger sitting at the kitchen table.

"Is that YOUR stupid car out there?" Suzanne pulled at the torn fabric stretched across her knee. "My tights are ruined."

"I'd hate to see the other guy," he said and bent down to touch her throbbing knee.

His touch took her breath away. It was gentle, soothing, contradictory to his tough guy appearance. His sagging jeans and worn leather jacket made her wonder if he was trouble. Trouble wasn't her type.

While Suzanne assessed his shaggy blond hair, the boy glanced up. She inspected his face; warm eyes, one brown, one green; dark lashes; faint freckles splashed across a nicely structured nose; a full mouth, centered on a square jaw. "I'm going to have a fat bruise," she said. The hand touching her knee had little nicks and cuts; the fingernails embedded with black grease. Casualties of maintaining the Chevy? Perhaps, but when their eyes connected, she felt kindness, generosity, and sensed a desire to know her better. The pain in her knee vanished.

"Who *are* you?"

"I'm Jack. And you–"

Suzanne examined her knee as if she were part of a hoax. "How did you do that?"

"Energy healing. You know, physician heal thyself?"

"Aren't you a little old to be playing doctor?"

Steven appeared from his room toting a classic car magazine. He flipped through pages, rattling off features of the new Mustang without acknowledging Suzanne's presence until his friend spoke up.

"You didn't tell me you had a sister," Jack said, nodding towards Suzanne.

"Oh, yeah. Jack, meet Suzanne."

She recognized the tone in Steven's voice as her cue to leave the kitchen. She gathered her things and started for her room when Jack blocked her path.

"Drop something?" he asked, dangling a glove from his pinky finger.

"Are you flirting with me?"

She grabbed the glove, and brushed past him, grazing his thigh with the back of her hand. A soft moan rumble in his throat.

Later that evening the storm let up, but high winds and drifting snow made it impossible to drive. Jack didn't seem to mind being stranded. Jack, Steven, and Suzanne bundled up and went outside to shovel the steps, walkways, and driveway.

The boys were piling the last hour's accumulation on the side of the drive when Suzanne threw the first snowball, hitting Jack on his right shoulder. It was war. Suzanne hid behind the mound of snow closest to the back door, and bombarded the boys, clearly having an advantage. Jack shielded his face against the onslaught of loosely packed ammunition.

"Wait till I get a hold of you," he yelled.

She screamed, throwing snow quickly.

"Did you really think a little thing like *you* was going to stop *me*?" he asked, holding a handful of snow inches from her face.

"You underestimate me," she said, batting the snow out of his hand.

"And you, young lady, underestimate me."

"Steven, help," she cried, knowing her brother wouldn't come. *Don't fight.* She pretended to weaken, but when Jack relaxed his grip, she pushed hard, sending him reeling into a deep drift of snow.

"I give up," he said, brushing himself off.

"You want to call a truce?"

"Come," he said, reaching for her hand. She didn't resist. Something about him made her feel spontaneous, *daring*.

He led her to a patch of flat ground. "Turn around," he said.

Suzanne stood with her back to the virgin snow, arms stretched wide.

Jack turned to her; his eyes filled with a promise of something more —*a future*. "Ready?" he asked. "On my count—1-2-3."

"Mrs. Cash?"

Suzanne didn't recognize the voice. Her eyes refused to open.

"Mrs. Cash, I'm sorry to bother you," the voice insisted. "I'm Detective Samson Metzger with the Goldorado County Sheriff's Department. I'd like to talk to you about what happened."

Suzanne's ears strained to hear.

"Mrs. Cash, we're losing time. We need to catch the person who did this to you. If you could answer some questions for me, I'll be as brief as possible." Sam pulled a chair next to her bed. "You were found in the pool at the Marriott, do you remember being there?"

She couldn't speak. Caught between worlds, she chose the past.

It was her sixteenth birthday. She was on the swing at the playground of her grammar school. Jack pushed her from behind. She pumped her legs to go higher.

"Go steady with me," he said.

"Steady?" She gasped.

He released the swing and planted himself in her path.

She gripped the chains. "What are you doing?" She dragged her feet until she skidded to a stop. Dust and gravel sprayed on Jack's shoes.

"I'm not moving until you give me your answer."

"Why should I go steady with you?"

"Because I love you," he replied. "I've loved you from the moment I saw you. I love everything about you." His thumb brushed a strand of hair from her cheek. "Don't you love me? Don't you want to be my girl?"

"Of course, I do."

Jack pulled his class ring from his finger and slipped it on hers. The ring was huge and wouldn't stay on her finger. Jack pulled orange twine from his pocket and wound it around the shank of the ring. He slipped it back onto Suzanne's finger and kissed her tenderly. "I will always, always, love you," he vowed.

"Mrs. Cash? Can you hear me?"

"Orange twine?" she mumbled weakly. *Funny. Why would Jack wrap orange twine around his class ring? He was a mechanic's apprentice. He always carried black tape.*

"Orange what?" The detective's voice sounded urgent. "Can you speak up? Were you meeting someone there?" Metzger pressed on. Suzanne's eyes fluttered. She fought to stay awake. "Tell me what happened, ma'am," he said. "Who did you go there to see?"

"Ki–" The word wouldn't form on her tongue. She wasn't making any sense.

"Were you there to meet a friend?"

She sensed his impatience. "Ki–" She repeated.

"Kids?" he said, remembering something about Wishes For Kids on the hotel marquee. "Is this about the fundraiser?"

She nodded.

"Did you *see* the person who attacked you?"

"Dark." As much as she wanted to cooperate, she couldn't describe the pictures in her head. She couldn't figure out if the drugs they were pumping into her system were the cause of her wooziness, or if her injured brain insisted on defaulting to sleep-mode. She wanted to explain to the detective that all the exits looked alike—somehow, she ended up in the rear of the building by the pool. *I needed to get home—on my feet all day. Lost.* She envisioned her attacker's arm wrapped around her neck; the muzzle of his gun pressed between her shoulder blades. She remembered his foul breath, his accusing words—

"British accent," she whispered, as a final "bang" rang out in her recall. Fear and exhaustion sucked her into an abyss.

Suzanne barely heard the detective rise from his chair. "I'll be back when you're feeling better," he said. "If there is *anything* you remember from last night, please have one of the nurses contact me immediately. I'll leave my card by the phone. You get some rest now." His hand touched hers. "Take care."

The sound of trays rattling on a metal cart in the hallway jarred Suzanne's senses. The smell of food wafted into the room. A woman's voice hummed a soulful tune. She heard rustling near her bed. The humming stopped.

"Mrs. Cash? My name is Veronica. I'm going check your dressing. Is there anything I can get for you? How is your pain, sweetheart?"

Suzanne saw Jack standing in the corner of the room, dressed in his Army uniform. *He looks so young*. He had that smile on his face, the kind that made her melt, and she wanted him to come closer. *Why is he here?* She raised her hand to beckon him, but plastic tubing restricted her movement. A beeping sound pierced her brain.

The nurse began yelling. "Mrs. Cash? Suzanne, look at *me.*"

Another nurse rushed into the room. The blood pressure cuff squeezed Suzanne's arm. She felt a slight tug on her PICC-line. A warm sensation rushed over her, but she couldn't take her eyes from the corner of the room. *Falling*. She willed Jack to come with her and he did.

They were walking back to her house from the playground. Jack was kissing her hand, admiring his class ring on her finger. "One day," he said, "you'll be wearing a diamond."

"A diamond?" she said, although she couldn't imagine being any happier than she was at that moment.

"I'm going to take good care of you Suz. We'll live in a nice house, have a bunch of kids." When she gasped, he gave her a nudge. "Okay, how about two?"

Suzanne didn't answer. Something was wrong. "This isn't my house." She turned to Jack, expecting him to explain. She'd never seen him look so intense.

"You have to go in there with me, Suzanne. We need to find out what happened. Don't be afraid, I'll be with you." The three numbers below the porch light caught her attention. *515*. Panic rose before her hand touched the handle on the door. Her heart pounded in her chest, each beat–too hard, too fast. She knew what waited on the other side.

The girl's body wasn't cold yet.

"Suzanne, it's Steven." She opened her eyes. "How are you'?" he asked.

What's with the scruffy beard? The last time she saw him he was clean shaven.

"You've been knocked out for the past couple of days."

Days? She was here a few minutes ago with– "Where's Ben?"

"Who knows, I'm sure he'll stop by later. You're pale again." Steven poured water into a glass from the pitcher on the nightstand.

"Nightmare—" She shuddered. "It seemed so real."

"Here, drink this," he said, handing her the cup.

"What day is it?"

"Tuesday. Detective Metzger is still hanging around the hospital, says it's imperative he talk to you. Are you up to it? The last thing you need is stress. The doctor said your heart's been acting wacky. I can tell Metzger to go away if you want."

"He'll have to wait," she said, her voice cracking. "I need to tell you something." She took a sip of water.

Concern wrinkled Steven's brow. "What is it, Sis?"

"I saw Jack. He was here, in my room–I saw him as clear as day. He was in the pool too."

"That's impossible, Jack's been gone since—" he said, choking down his emotion. "He was my best friend. I would know if...he died in Iraq."

"But he was there." Suzanne pointed, "Standing in the corner."

"Jack? A ghost? No way. You're hallucinating—must be the morphine."

"Maybe," she said. Seeing Jack did seem preposterous. Still, *I know what I saw.* What she couldn't figure out was why Jack had been with her since the night at the Marriott, she hadn't thought of him in years. Head trauma and morphine could cause hallucinations. "He saved my life. How do you explain that?"

"I can't–I–I'm just glad you survived."

As if her physical pain wasn't enough, she reflected on Jack's last night on leave–the two of them together, his promise to write the moment he got to Iraq. Weeks went by without word. At first, she worried, and then she felt foolish. Weeks stretched into months and she wondered if he had jilted her. She convinced herself their love-making was something they needed to get out of their system, nothing more. She wrote to him every day, desperate for him to love her the way she loved him. When he didn't respond, she knew it was over. Three days after she mailed her farewell, the news came. Jack had been killed in an explosion. Three months later, she married Benjamin Cash at City Hall.

She remembered their marriage started on shaky ground, Ben, a wanna-be rock star, struggled with undiagnosed anger issues. She still silently grieved for Jack, the love of her life. Ben put up with her moodiness—she patched holes in the walls. Ben bounced from one band to another. She buried herself in charity work. Dysfunction took its toll on their relationship. They separated many times but reunited because *that's what dysfunctional people do.* Fifteen years of resentment and disappointment shaped their roles as husband and wife.

Steven interrupted her thoughts. "Ben off his medication again?" Her frown confirmed his suspicions. "Want me to have a talk with him?"

"Asenapine changes his pH, he doesn't like the way it makes him smell. I don't know, maybe he'll listen to you. I'm not up for one of his tantrums."

Steven nodded, "The detective asked him a few questions, now he's obsessing about what you were doing at the Marriott." Steven searched her face. "If you were—I mean, who could blame—you'd tell me, right?"

Her eyes grew large. "What?"

Steven knew better than to push. "Have you seen the doctor today?"

"Apology accepted, and no, I haven't talked to the doctor. But the nurse explained the results of my MRI, and the tear in my artery."

"Good news?"

"Yes, I'm healing nicely," she said. Suzanne's focus shifted to the corner of the room. "Scary. I don't remember having any tests. They said the pain will go away eventually, but what about my memory lapses?"

"Concussions take time to heal, Suz. In a few weeks, when the swelling is gone, you'll be back to eh, normal."

Suzanne touched the stitches on the back of her head. They were stiff and rubbed against the pillowcase when she moved. "I want to go home. Do you think you can arrange that for me?"

"I'll see what I can do. What about Metzger? He has a toothbrush tucked in his breast pocket. He's not going away."

Suddenly she remembered. "The event! I'm the committee chairman for the Wish Kid Foundation, I need to call Elaine."

"She called Ben, he explained what had happened."

"Did she say how it went? Did the kids have fun? Did we reach our goal?"

Steven crossed the room and peeked through the blinds. "Looks like we're in for a storm."

"It took months to put it together. The kids were excited about wearing masks. The mystery we chose was brilliant—the pledges—all those prizes? Steven, you're my brother, tell me—what happened?"

"Ben didn't say much, only that some lady named Elaine left a hundred messages on the answering machine and used up all the recording space. He was pissed, he erased 'em all. You know how he is."

"I need to call—"

"Knock-knock." Suzanne and Steven turned to face the man in the doorway. His voice was deeper than his stature called for. "Do you remember me? Detective Metzger. Samson Metzger. Sam. I've been waiting to speak with you, Mrs. Cash. I hope now is a good time."

Suzanne waved him forward. Salt and pepper hair framed a face etched with laugh lines, complexity, and at least forty years of sunshine. Bright blue eye, fringed with black lashes sparkled beneath nicely shaped brows. His tone dipped another register, "Sorry for the interruption, but the last time we spoke, well, we really didn't speak, I did most of the talking. You were heavily sedated." He re-introduced himself to Steven and shook his hand. When he turned back to Suzanne, images flashed in her mind; cathedrals, palaces, cliffs, a winding river...a feeling of contentment came over her. It was as if she had known him all her life. "Your father--he's German descent, he migrated to Austria after the war," she blurted. "Your mother was born in Sicily."

Sam took a step back. "Whoa. Thought I was the one running background checks around here."

"Sorry. That popped into my head. I don't know what came over me."

"I checked with the Wish Kid Foundation," he said. "I was thinking how ironic it was that the person responsible for organizing a 'Magical Mystery' event is now subject to a mystery of her own. Can you tell me more about the man with the accent?"

How did he know? "Did I *say* he had an accent?"

"You don't remember?" He moved closer. Spice, vanilla, and a hint of peppermint lingered in the air. "I want to find the person who tried to kill you *before* the town goes vigilante. People tend to freak out when the body count goes up."

"515." The number came out of her mouth like a hiccup. The detective moved closer still.

Steven stood up, ready to intervene, but Sam held up his hand.

"Say again?"

When Suzanne repeated the number, the detective pulled a notepad from his pocket and began to write. "What about 515, Mrs. Cash?"

"I don't know." She felt confused. "In the nightmare, it wasn't my house–" Her stomach began to pitch. The color red flooded her vision. "515" flashed neon in her mind. She was caught in a series of violent images and gore.

"Tell me what you're seeing."

"A wooden floor. She's face-down," she heard herself say, "Her hands and feet are bound with orange twine. Her clothes, crumpled in a ball."

"Go on," the detective insisted, but it wasn't him talking any more–it was Jack. He was there, like he had promised.

"What else do you see?"

"Blood," she cried. "I see bloodstains on a white blouse, on faded jeans."

The hospital door burst open, spitting Sam to the curb. Twenty years on the force, and *never* had he experienced anything like that. *Who the hell is she? What does she know about Amy Fitzpatrick?* More women had been found brutally murdered over a course of eight months: Twila Averose, Melinda Carlisle, Dillyn Wheeler, and Amy Fitzpatrick. The only people privy to the details found at the crime scenes were guys he had worked with for years. Nobody leaked a case. *Nobody.* How did she know about his father? His mother? *Austria*?

To make matters worse, she had an effect on him. Even in her injured state, she was beautiful. He dipped his hand in pocket and grasped the sobriety coin. *Ten years. Don't blow it now.*

Alcohol had kept the demons at bay. Numbed his heart. Served as a catalyst between reality and the underworld. And then one day he was called to a scene, a child had been severely beaten, set on fire, and thrown into a dumpster. After dowsing his anger with a fifth of whiskey, he had an epiphany. You can't medicate a conscience.

"Nooo," Suzanne cried out. The kink in her IV sounded an alarm. Jack hovered near the edge of the bed. His eyes sad.

"Mrs. Cash, calm down. *Shhhhh,*" the nurse said, patting Suzanne's hand. "I'm Belinda. You had a bad dream, that's all."

"I saw her—she's—" Suzanne said, catching her breath. "Is Detective Metzger still here?"

"No, I haven't seen him all morning."

"Morning?"

"Yes, Mrs. Cash it's morning."

"Can you call Detective Metzger for me? It's urgent."

Belinda called the number on the card Detective Metzger had placed on Suzanne's nightstand and handed her the phone. "Her name is Amy. I see her with a man, a dark-haired man. She's in trouble."

"I'll be right there."

"I don't understand, why come here? Find her before it's too—"

"She's already dead."

"But she can't be I just saw her—"

"Her body was found at 515 Afton Street."

Suzanne dropped the phone. A small voice echoed in the distance, "Mrs. Cash? Mrs. Cash, are you there?"

Sam pulled up a chair and drew his pad from his shirt pocket. "Tell me what you saw."

Suzanne ached more for the dead girl, than she did from her gunshot wound. "I saw her getting ready for her date. She lost thirty pounds and was excited about fitting into her new jeans. After dinner, he took her to a place—the hallway had green carpet with sort of a diamond pattern in the center. Small sconces lined the walls—she was wobbly."

Metzger stopped scribbling on his pad, his gaze, hard around the edges.

Suzanne hiked her cover up an inch or two. "You think I'm making it up?"

"I'm trying to wrap my head around what you're telling me. Go on."

Suzanne felt sick inside. "What good is this information if she's dead?"

"Amy Fitzpatrick died weeks ago. She was found in an abandoned house on Afton Street."

"But I saw —"

"We did a thorough exam of the crime scene. She was murdered somewhere else. Green fibers were found beneath her fingernails. The house on Afton had hardwood floors."

Suzanne's scalp tingled from the top of her head to the nape of her neck. Her stomach knotted. Jack appeared in the corner of the room; his arms tight across his chest.

"Have you talked to anyone else about your dreams, Mrs. Cash?"

"Suzanne, please."

"Deal, if you call me Sam."

"No, I didn't tell anyone about the girl," she said, diverting her gaze.

"There's more?"

"You'll think I'm insane."

"Try me."

"I have been seeing my dead boyfriend from long ago in these dreams."

"I see. And?"

"And—I see him here, in my room."

Sam raised one eyebrow. "And?"

"And–he's standing behind you."

While Sam took an incoming phone call into the hallway, Suzanne dozed. She dreamt of the summer she turned sixteen, she and Jack were cleaning the pool. Suzanne was a poor swimmer. Jack insisted she learn to float.

"Suzanne, *floating* is part of *swimming.*"

"I'm afraid," she cried.

"Of what?"

"Sinking."

Jack's face softened. "C'mere, let me show you." He pulled her close and turned her around. "Lean back against me," he said, placing one hand at the base of her head, and one on her lower back. "Relax."

She obeyed, closing her eyes to the blazing sun. His touch made her shiver.

"No monkey business, this is serious." His hand moved lower, resting too close to one of her "off limit" zones.

"No tricks—promise?" she said, moving his hand higher up.

"I promise," he said, lowering his mouth to hers. His kiss, gentle at first, grew more urgent. It felt as though he was sucking air from her lungs. She tried to scream. The had sun vanished from the sky. *Darkness*. Suzanne struggled to free herself from the orange twine around her wrists, and feet. Something impeded her movement. Her eyes felt gritty. A damp earthy smell, a scraping noise. Realization hit her. *Buried alive*.

Suzanne woke with a start, tearing at her face, gulping in as much air as her lungs could hold. Sam took her hand. "What's wrong?"

"I can't—I can't breathe."

It didn't take Sam long to understand. "Jennifer Richmond's body was found a half mile from the Kingsvale exit. The Goldorado County coroner determined her death as strangulation by suffocation. The Sheriff's Department withheld news about her being buried. They didn't share little details—like orange twine imbedded in her hands and feet." Sam paced once around the room and returned to Suzanne's bedside. "An autopsy will reveal whether she was still alive when she was put in the ground."

Suzanne winced. "She struggled."

"How can you be sure?"

"I felt—" She gripped the side rails of her bed to steady her hands, she could still recall shovels of dirt filling the hole. "She was still alive."

———

Ben

Ben parked in Calvin's driveway. "Fucker better be home," he grumbled. Calvin Cook headed the band, booked their performances, controlled the money. He dreamed of quitting his job at the hospital—*We'll take the show on the road.* Ben knew better. Calvin talked more crap than a porta-potty, which was okay most of the time. What wasn't okay was cancelling the last few practices.

Calvin still owed the guys money from a gig they'd played Fourth of July weekend. With Suzanne in the hospital, Ben needed money to live on until she could make a deposit into their account. He knew not to force the issue. She'd question money spent on things most people didn't understand.

Ben had met Calvin through Suzanne. They'd worked together on a few projects through the hospital. When Calvin told her he was a musician, Suzanne invited him over for a beer. He brought his guitar and he and Ben jammed. Ben had to admit, at first, he envied Calvin. Calvin was tall, handsome and a smooth talker. When he sang, women couldn't get enough. Especially during their British oldies set, when Calvin sang lead on Herman's Hermits, "Mrs. Brown You've Got A Lovely Daughter," and the Beatles, "Love Me Do." Ben shined more on their hard rock set—AC/DC, Billy Idol. The band was good. *Goin' places.*

Ben knocked on the door and peeked through the window. No answer.

"Calvin? Open the fucking door, man." Ben looked through the window again. It was dark inside. His temper sent a potted geranium smashing on the sidewalk. He needed his *medicine.*

He slammed his car door and peeled out of the driveway. A quarter mile down the road he pulled over to make a call. Calvin wasn't the only game in town.

Two weeks passed before Suzanne was discharged from the hospital. Ben drove her home, then said he was going to work. *Work*. Hanging out in his buddy's basement all day, smoking pot. *Being creative.*

Suzanne fixed herself a cup of tea and turned on the news.

> "Are criminal investigators calling the latest murder part of a crime spree? Is there a serial killer on the loose? Stay tuned for more—"

The cup slipped from her hand and crashed to the floor. Jack stood in front of the 55-inch TV screen, hovering inches from the floor.

"You can't keep scaring me like this, Jack. I don't want you here. You're dead!"

"You know why I'm here. You need to trust me."

"Trust you? I trusted you once—you broke my heart. Now you're filling my head with horror. Why?"

"Come with me."

Suzanne was blindsided by an image of an ax hitting bone. "Stop," she cried, but Jack grabbed her hand, and pulled her into another place, another time.

The house was dim.

Shards of light squeezed between faded draperies. Italian Provincial furniture beneath fine art hanging above a dingy mantle. Papered walls, wooden floors. Blood stained the center of a green, diamond-patterned, ornate rug. The man's back was turned. Legs dangled across his forearms.

She followed unseen, down a flight of stairs. A large wooden table stretched across the width of the room. He laid the body down, careful of her long hair. He fanned her chestnut tresses around her head, turned her palms up, and crossed her bare feet, right over left. A sharp metal object gleamed under florescent light, its wooden handle, stained with blood.

"Stop," Suzanne pleaded.

"You've seen enough, Suz. Come."

Stepping back in time, Jack and Suzanne were in a swimming pool.

"Try it again," he said.

"You're trying to drown me, I know it."

"Why would I hurt you? I love you."

There, he said it. Said the words she had longed to hear. "I love you too, Jack. But if you don't stop trying to drown me, I may change my mind."

"If you're going to learn to swim, you have to learn to float."

Why did he keep saying that?

Before she could object, she was back in her living room. The TV blasted the news.

"—body parts found along the American River."

The feeding frenzy had begun.

She Googled most recent 'brutal murders in Sacramento'. She scrolled down. Twila Averose, Melinda Carlisle, Dillyn Wheeler, Amy Fitzpatrick, most recent, Jennifer Richmond. She grabbed her phone.

"Detective Metzger," she demanded, her hand shaking. The receiver had a hum she didn't remember hearing before her near-death experience. Her senses seemed to be on overload. She smelled flowers that weren't there, perfume, smoke. Doctors chalked it up to her brain injury. She knew different.

When Metzger identified himself on the other end of the phone, she blurted out, "He's setting me up."

"Suzanne? Who's setting you up?"

"Jack."

"You said he's dead, how could he—"

"From the beyond. He's showing me the murders after they happen, but he's teaching me to float, and once I learn to float, he'll teach me to swim, and once I can swim, he'll show me the murders before they happen—can't you see? He's preparing me, setting me up!"

"Take it easy." His voice calmed her. "Want me to stop by? I can be there in fifteen minutes."

"Yes. And Sam? Please tell me I'm not going insane—because it feels like I'm losing my mind."

After they hung up, Suzanne hurried to the kitchen to make a pot of coffee. Sam was a coffee kind of guy. How she knew didn't register.

Fifteen minutes later, the doorbell rang. Suzanne opened the door.

"Is that coffee I smell?"

"Yes, come in." She led him to the kitchen. "Sit," she said. "Sorry. Ben hates when I order him around."

"Nothing wrong with being direct."

He could've taken offense, but he hadn't, and she was beginning to like the way he made her feel comfortable. It had been a long time since she'd been able to be herself. When working with people in charity, she kept her opinions to herself. Charity work was about the cause. The cause always took priority over any feelings she may have had about how the goals were met. She chose her profession to keep sunshine in her life. *Purpose.* If it were up to Ben, he would've sucked the joy out of her life long ago. *Contrast.* As a couple, they were not only opposites, Ben's bipolar disorder kept her on her toes. She watched what she said and learned to walk on eggs without cracking the shells. And then there was Sam...

"Tell me again," he said. "I'm not clear on how Jack is setting you up."

She poured coffee, filling two mugs. "When we were young, Jack promised to teach me how to swim, but he said I had to learn to float first. He believed in taking things one step at a time. I think that's what he's doing—taking it one step at a time. Seeing how much I can take—how long I can float before I sink."

"What did he show you this time? What did you see?"

"An old house, ornate furniture. A tall, husky, man. I couldn't see his face. The woman was maybe early twenties. Long hair, brown." Suzanne shuddered. "I saw an ax."

"Dear God."

She wanted to reach over and touch him. He moved first, taking her hand, holding it in his. *Strong hands.*

"Are you okay?" he asked.

His concern melted her heart. "Yes. No. I threw-up."

"That's not cool." He smiled. "I don't know what to think about all of this 'spooky' stuff—about *you*."

Ben walked in the back door. When he saw them, his face twisted in rage. "What the hell is going on here?"

"Ben, you remember Sa—Detective Metzger?"

Sam rose and extended his hand.

Ben's eyes were wild. "I don't give a fuck who you are— What are you doing sitting in MY kitchen with MY wife?"

Suzanne intervened. "Calm down. Nothing is going on. He came because I asked him to. I don't expect you to understand. I was upset. Detective Metzger was merely consoling me, that's all."

Ben slammed his hand on the table spilling coffee. "Look what you made me do. Clean it up."

"Hey—" Sam stepped between Ben and Suzanne, "Chill. Your wife is instrumental in a murder case I'm working, nothing more. A young woman was found butchered along the American River. Did you hear about it?"

Ben stepped back. "No shit," he said. His eyes, cold, and fathomless, gave Suzanne chills.

Ben retired early. Suzanne sat up, alone in the dark, mulling over conversations with Sam. As foreign as her visions seemed to him, he tried to understand. He couldn't deny that she knew things. Sam didn't judge. Ben did.

And Jack? The visions brought back bittersweet memories she had spent years trying to forget. *Pain.* She let her mind drift back to a time when she questioned his love. She was sixteen, working at a restaurant. Jack and Steven had come in for a bite to eat. Another waitress, whom Suzanne considered a rival, and whom Jack said he detested, made a point to tell him it was her birthday. Suzanne watched as Jack rose from his chair, grabbed the girl's face and kissed her passionately. *I was crushed.* He had laughed at her jealousy, said it was all in fun, but she didn't see it that way. She never fully trusted him after that.

"Why did you agree to marry me then?"

Jack's voice made her flinch. He sat beside her, took her hand and held it to his cheek. "I loved you the moment I saw you. I love you still. The other side doesn't erase the love we feel for those we love when we're alive." He turned her face toward his. "Look at me."

"This is insane—the visions—they're terrifying—"

"I'm sorry, but you're the one. I have to make you see."

In an instant, she saw herself in a hallway. The green diamond-pattern on the carpet was familiar. A man, his back towards her, turned his head, allowing her a partial view of his profile. His ball cap shaded his features. *He's dragging something.*

"No—Please don't!" Suzanne covered her eyes. When she looked up, the figure standing in the doorway was *Ben*. She was back in her living room.

"What the hell is wrong with you?"

"I'm sorry, I didn't mean to wake—"

"Hell if you didn't."

"You're free to go elsewhere if my yelling bothers you so much."

"Why don't you? Maybe that little pissant you were coffee-klatching with today will put up with your shit."

"Go back to bed, Ben." Suzanne sighed. "I'm in no condition to fight with you."

"Serves you right for being at some hotel instead of home, where you belong."

"Leave me alone. We'll talk in the morning."

"The hell we will. I'm DONE, done with your weirdo woo-woo shit. Done with you thinking you can save the world when you can't even save yourself. Look at you—you used to be pretty, you took care of yourself. Now you're like all the other plain Janes fighting for the *cause*. How 'bout the cause at home? When's the last time we had sex?"

"I'm not going anywhere until I'm healed. Stay with your friend, you know–the other rock star, the one you *work* with. I'm sure he has room in his basement for his good buddy."

"Screw you, Suzanne." Ben stormed out of the room. Their fights had progressed over the years. She knew he had mental issues, but she was tired of putting *his* health first. She warned him that going on and off his meds would mess-up his brain chemistry but nagging only escalated his anger.

She got up and went into the kitchen. Tea wouldn't fix things, but it would busy her hands until she calmed down. Reaching for a cup aggravated the stitches in her chest. She plopped down on a kitchen chair and began to cry. A hand reached for hers, startling her.

"Dammit Jack."

"He's a jerk, I hope you plan to leave him."

"Go away."

She was about to sip her tea when she heard a crash upstairs. Something hit the bottom of the stairs with a thud. She peeked around the corner. *My pillow?* Next came her blanket, a shoe, her hair-brush. She prayed he would stop.

Ben barreled down the stairs, his arms filled with clothes from her closet, his eyes wild, his face red. She reached for the phone, ready to dial 911. *He's out of control.*

"Ben, this isn't going to solve anything."

"You think you can leave me? Have at it—here you go." He threw clothes at her, whipping a handful at a time. The zipper on one of her skirts nicked her cheek.

She held the phone tight, her thumb hovering over the 9. The pain in her chest burned. Tiny lights danced in the corner of her eye. It felt as though she were moving, picking up speed. Ben's voice echoed in her brain. His mouth moved in slow motion, he raised his fist, but before he struck her, her world went black and she was gone.

"Can't leave you alone for a minute," Steven teased. "Someone should be down in a bit to take you for your MRI."

"MRI?"

"Doctor thinks you may have another concussion. You hit your head hard when you passed out. He said it's a wonder you didn't crack your skull open. I told him you've always—"

"Been a hard head, I know. Do you ever say anything nice about me? Where's Ben?"

"He's staying with his buddy."

"I'm leaving him. I can't take the abuse anymore. He's going to be the death of me if I stay."

"Where will you go?"

"Your house."

"I thought you'd never ask."

"You're my brother. Brothers look out for their sisters, right?"

"You know you don't have to ask. I'll have Karen prepare the guest room for you."

"I promise, it won't be for long, as soon as I get on my feet, I'll—"

"Quit worrying. With all the traveling I do, Karen will be thrilled to have the company."

"I hope *I* still have a job when I get out of here."

"Elaine can't run that place by herself, and it would take a millennium to train someone to fill your shoes."

A young orderly pushed a wheelchair into the room.

"Ready for a little ride?" The orderly double-checked the name on Suzanne's wristband, and helped her out of bed. After he put terry socks on her feet and placed a blanket over her lap, he wheeled her toward the door.

Suzanne lay on a cold, stainless steel table, her hands pressed to her side. A woman hovered near by.

"You're not claustrophobic, are you?" A young technician donned in turquoise scrubs smiled as she spoke.

"Not that I know of."

"Good. I'm going to strap your head in place. It will prevent you from moving during the MRI. The less you move, the sooner we finish."

Suzanne felt her body being maneuvered into place. "Once you're in the tube, you're going to hear a rat-a-tat-tat noise. Please keep your head as immobile as possible. Feel free to close your eyes, relax. It will be over soon."

She closed her eyes. The table moved. The noise began.

Jack was with her; it was late summer.

"When are we going to the lake?"

"When you can swim."

"I thought I was doing really well."

"You still can't float."

"I can do the breaststroke pretty good."

"I know, you're making progress, but if you get in trouble, you'll need to float."

"What kind of trouble?"

She heard another voice. A man's voice. *Him.* "You're doing just fine Mrs. Cash," she heard him say with a *British accent*, and without warning, she was at the Marriott. It was dark. She stood by the edge of the pool, confused. She didn't know where she was. *All turned around.* Go back? Julian would help. While digging in her purse for her phone she felt his breath on her neck. His words hissed in her ear. "*You shouldn't have meddled.*" Meddle? And then hard, cold, steel pressed against her back, and hot pain seared through her. He hit her in the back of the head with the gun, and she plunged into the water. She heard beautiful music, angels singing. *Jack's voice.* "I'm here." *Cold air on my face.* "Breathe, Suzanne, breathe."

"Mrs. Cash?"

Suzanne's eyes squinted into the light.

"Are you all right?"

"What?" All Suzanne could see was the mid-section of the young woman dressed in turquoise. The table moved forward.

"You stopped breathing. Are you okay?" The technician's eyes expressed her concern.

"I must've—who else is here?"

"Dr. Reynolds was here a bit ago. He got called to the ER. I checked the images," she said, loosening the strap across Suzanne's waist. "Everything looks good. We're finished." She helped Suzanne into a sitting position. "Are you all right?"

"I'm—fine."

An orderly wheeled Suzanne into her room. Steven was on his phone. He placed his hand over the speaker. "It's Metzger."

"Let me speak to him."

Steven handed her the phone.

"Detective Metzger, I know who shot me."

Sam walked in the door ten minutes later and asked, "What do you have to tell me?"

"There's a Dr. Reynolds that works here. He has a British accent. He shot me."

"How can you be sure?"

"I recognized his voice."

"Why would a doctor shoot you?"

"I don't know. But I know it's him."

"I'll check into it." He brushed her hand with his fingertips. A warm sensation reached a part of her she had long forgotten.

"Why are you so nice?" Her M.O., *trust no man*. Too many letdowns. Too many broken promises.

"I like you." His hand reached for hers. She pulled away. "I intend to find the creep who put you here," he said.

"Sounds like you're going to be *very* busy."

"You're worth it."

After the detective left the room, Steven sat beside Suzanne. "What's going on? Are you falling for this guy?"

"Who's falling for who?" Suzanne and Steven turned toward the voice coming from the doorway.

Steven stood up. "Ben, what are you doing here? Don't you think you've put my sister through enough?"

"I'm her husband, asshole, I have a right to be here."

Suzanne grabbed Steven's arm. "Steven asked me if I was falling for the excuses the doctor made—regarding my condition."

"Oh, so now you have a condition?"

Steven stepped between her husband and the bed. "Suzanne is staying with me and Karen until she's back on her feet. Doctors' orders.

She needs full time care, and Karen is happy to play nursemaid. Beats having to pay someone to come to the house."

"You're up to something."

"Dammit, Ben—can't you think of someone besides yourself? I need to be with someone who can care for me, not a ticking time bomb." Suzanne could tell by Ben's expression that he would store this moment and use it against her later. "Karen is home, you're not. I need to rest, not battle with you."

"Fine. Have it your way. You'll regret talking to me like one of your little volunteer twits."

"Please go. Just let me get better."

Ben left.

Steven stood in the doorway. "Tell me you're done taking his abuse."

"When it's right—"

"You've been saying that for the last five years—what's it gonna take? Him beating the crap out you? Slicing your throat?"

"Don't be so dramatic. He's not going to make it easy. Please, let me take care of things my way, in my own time."

"If he gets any crazier, we'll have to put him away."

"You think committing a person is that easy?"

"Fine."

After Steven left, Suzanne closed her eyes. She knew Ben would make her life hell. She remembered how persistent he had been at winning her back when they separated the last time. He'd sent flowers, showed up at the house, then at her office. He was charming, apologetic —*sincere*. When she agreed to give it another whirl it didn't take long for his horns to emerge. The flowers stopped. His phone calls became more frequent. His questions accusing. "Where are you? What are you doing? Who are you with?" By then, she was exhausted. *Dating wasn't my thing; I didn't trust other men.* She knew what to expect with Ben, so she settled, once again.

She thought about Detective Metzger. Wondered what it would be like to live in *his* world. How she longed for normalcy.

Being shot, thrown in a pool, and left to die changed a person. *Not to mention being visited by your dead boyfriend.* Maybe her head injury had knocked some sense into her. She couldn't go back. She couldn't spend another day with Ben. *I'm done.*

Jack stood at the foot of her bed.

"Go away. I'm done with you, too. I'm making changes, and I'm starting with you, Jack. Stay out of my head, my dreams, my—"

Without warning, she saw a house with dingy windows. She smelled urine, mixed with Lysol and bleach. The stench was enough to make her retch— but how could she? *This isn't real. Wake up*!

Jack let go of her hand and she froze. A man busied himself collecting tools from a rack on the wall. A saw. A drill. A large file. She could see a bottle of bleach beneath the bench next to a shoe? *Dear God.* The foot was still attached.

"Mrs. Cash?" Suzanne's lids fluttered. Bile rose in her throat. "Mrs. Cash, wake up."

Jack leaned against the wall; his arms crossed. How many times had she seen that pose? Him waiting patiently for her to *get it*? "Leave me ALONE!"

"Mrs. Cash, calm down. It was just a dream. You're okay. You're safe, now. Do you know where you are?"

"Do you see him? There—in the corner?"

"No ma'am, I don't see anyone. You were having a dream."

"There was a—foot—it was—"

"Shhhh, now. You're at Mercy General, and you are safe. I'm Justine, your nurse this evening, and I am going to make sure nothing bad happens to you. Understand me?"

"Yes," Suzanne whispered, but she knew it was a lie.

Visions

Weeks turned into months. Christmas had come and gone. Budding trees, blossoms, promising spring. And then came summer, almost without notice.

Sam parked on the street and made his way up the winding drive. He checked the address against the paper in his hand. The conversation he had with Dove about Suzanne being spooky played in his head. "If you want to know more about that kind of stuff, ask a psychic. I know a good one." Dove wrote her name and number down and handed it to Sam. "She's the real deal."

He tucked the paper in his pocket and rang the bell.

A face peeked through the crack in the door. "May I help you?"

"I hope so. I'm Detective Samson Metzger, Goldorado County Sheriff's Department. I'd like to talk to you about a case I'm investigating."

"How I can help," the woman asked, inching the door open.

"You're Linda Schooler, the psychic?"

"Yes. Do you want a reading? I only take clients by appointment—"

"I really need your help." Sam presented his badge. "Please?"

"I'm expecting a client shortly. Can we make this quick?"

"I hope so. May I come in?"

The psychic scanned him from head to toe. "Okay, but for just a few minutes—as I said, I am expecting a—"

"Thank you," he said, brushing past her.

The woman closed the door. "Come." Sam followed her into a quaint parlor furnished with a loveseat and two sapphire-blue velvet wingback chairs. She offered him the chair across from her. "What is it you'd like to know?"

"Can people see the dead?"

"Are you seeing dead people, detective?"

"Not me, it's—"

"A friend."

"Yes."

"Does your friend have a name?"

"Suzanne."

The psychic closed her eyes. He watched her eyes move back and forth beneath her lids. Her head moved from side to side.

Her eyes opened and she spoke. "Suzanne is a vessel. What she brings from the beyond is a gift. She lost someone very dear to her, that's the connection. Love. The love they shared was severed. He is gifting her *sight*, showing her things that will propel her journey here on the earth plane. You see, what we undergo on this level is an experience. Once our journey at this level is complete, we move to the next realm. Like a video game. Each level presents a challenge before reaping a reward."

"The 'gift' as you put it, is information. It's not pleasant."

"I see that. Your friend not only wants to shut it out, she fears the unknown. She'll adjust. She needs to believe in her higher self, and let the information flow to its destination, which is— *you*."

"Me?"

"You're in a quandary—there's more to come."

Sam didn't have patience for riddles. "Thank you for your time. How much do I owe you?"

"Nothing. Catch your killer. The world is full of checks and balances. Good cannot exist without evil."

"Tell that to the parents of the murder victims."

"Right. And tell her what's in your heart."

"Pardon me?"

"You're falling in love with her."

Sam drove home dissecting the information he had received from the psychic. How had she pick up on his feelings for Suzanne? *Am I that transparent?* He had spent a lifetime guarding his heart, putting up walls. The last thing he wanted was a complex relationship. He liked women, liked the pleasure they gave him when he was in need, but that was the extent. He'd never been in love, or even cared about a woman long enough to establish more than a casual friendship. Suzanne was different. He loved her eyes, and the way her lips formed words when she spoke. Her beauty, masked behind the stress of her situation, presented itself when she looked his way. *I can't wait to see her again.*

Who was he kidding? His time was eaten up trying to solve a puzzle with too many obscure pieces. Another young woman missing, and he and his men were no closer to catching the killer. The man who shot Suzanne was still at large. No wonder Dixon gave him shit.

Angela Foxworthy stood on her tip-toes, suspended from a beam overhead. Shackles bit into her flesh, pain radiated from her head to her feet, but that was nothing compared to the burning sensation she felt having her skin stapled to the wood pressing against her spine.

She had given up smoking two months ago, now she wondered why. Like the diet her mom went on before she found out she had cancer. All that struggle for nothing. Angela knew she fucked up. She knew she shouldn't have been walking home late at night, but she wanted to go to the party. She thought she had a better chance of getting home safely walking three miles, than riding with one of her drunk friends. When the car slowed, she was apprehensive, but when she saw who it was, she hopped in without a second thought. He offered her a soda. The can was open, but he said he hadn't drunk any yet. She had no reason to doubt him. She was thirsty.

She danced around the sticky blood, screaming each time her skin tore, and fresh blood added to the mix. It seemed as though she had been in and out of consciousness for days. Her captor hadn't returned. No food. No water. *No cigarettes for you.*

She wished she hadn't been so trusting. She wished she could go back, do things differently. She wished he would kill her and get it over with.

Linda

"I'm not hungry." Suzanne pushed her plate away. "The chicken is delicious, Karen. It's my stomach. Must be the meds."

Steven looked up from his meal.

Karen said, "Try and eat another bite or two. You need your strength."

"Okay, Mom."

Steven scowled. "What the hell has gotten into you?"

"I don't know." Suzanne dropped her fork on the table. "I'm going to go lie down."

She closed her bedroom door and laid across the bed, burying her face in her pillow. Words and images, cyclones spinning in her head.

The knock on the door made Suzanne bristle. "What?"

"Can I come in?"

Sam. Shit. Suzanne hadn't thought about brushing her hair. *What's the use*? She opened the door. "Hi."

"Bad time?"

"What makes you say that?"

"The brush you're holding like a led pipe."

Suzanne tossed the brush on the bed. "Let's go outside. Boys aren't allowed in my room."

"Boys?"

"The whole male species, brothers included. Why are you here?"

"I checked out your Dr. Reynolds."

"And?"

"He doesn't exist."

"I heard him—he was there!"

"Someone was there. The nurse collaborated your story, but there is no Dr. Reynolds on staff."

"The nurse called him by name."

"She didn't know him, she identified him by his badge."

"So, who is he?"

"Million-dollar question."

Sam's hand gravitated toward Suzanne's.

"Why do you keep touching me?" she asked.

His smile was sheepish, his voice dropped a notch. "A psychic told me I liked you."

"You talked to a psychic? About me?"

"I needed more info on near death experiences, thought I'd consult an expert."

"And she just happened to mention that you like me?"

"Well, yes, sort of. Have you ever been?" he asked.

"Ever been what?"

"To a psychic?"

"Once. A séance. I thought maybe I could summon Jack— the table shook a little—that's all. It was a long time ago. What else did she say?"

"She said you were given a gift."

———

Suzanne studied the sky, lost in thought. Steven took a lounge chair next to her. "You're acting like a shit, Suz."

"I know, I owe you and Karen a huge apology. I don't know what's come over me." She shrugged. "I don't sleep—may be why I'm so cranky." She heard Steven sigh.

"You were born cranky."

"Thanks."

"Truth hurts, what can I say?"

"You can say you've been through a lot—you deserve a break."

"Mom and dad taught us to suck it up."

"Yeah, well someone didn't shoot them in the back and throw them in the pool to die."

"I'll let you slide this time but take it easy on Karen. She doesn't deserve to be treated like your personal whipping post."

"You're right, I *am* a shit."

"Bygones. What were you and Dick Tracy talking about?"

"Psychics. He talked to a psychic about me."

"I thought he'd consult a psychiatrist, not a psychic. You did hit your head. Who knows what kind of damage you did?"

"The MRI didn't show any tumors, the bleeding has stopped. But the radiologist kept shaking his head while he was reading it."

"Meaning?"

"Meaning whatever he was looking at wasn't the norm."

"I could've told you that."

"Why does everything have to be a joke? These visions scare me."

"How often are you having them?"

"It's been a few days. The last one was while I was in the hospital." Suzanne massaged her temples. "Whenever I see Jack, it happens. It's like watching a horror movie and I–"

"Are you still on that kick?"

"You don't believe me?"

"I thought when you felt better—"

"So, as long as you thought I had brain damage, seeing Jack was acceptable?"

"I just can't wrap my head around it."

"That's what Sam said. Only *he* went to a psychic to try to understand."

"Sam?"

"Stop." Suzanne folded her arms across her chest.

"You want me to go to a psychic?"

"Let's both go."

"No thanks. I don't need to know the extent of your—"

"My what?" Tears welled in Suzanne's eyes.

"Fine," he said. "I'll go with you to see a psychic."

That night Suzanne couldn't sleep. Karen's Pinterest ideas had transformed the guest room into a magazine-worthy retreat. Pale yellow walls trimmed in white, garage sale cast-offs refinished into shabby chic treasures with crystal knobs. Sheer, pale grey panels framing tall transom windows, billowed in the summer breeze. All she had to do was close her eyes and drift away on a moonbeam, but when she closed her eyes, she saw Jack.

"It's okay. Take your time." They were in the pool, Jack's hand supporting her back. "Relax." His hand moved away. *I'm floating*.

Floating. Drifting. Suzanne could feel the sun's heat warming her body. Water droplets sparkled like diamonds on her skin. But before she reached nirvana, clouds bruised the sky and she was tumbling down a flight of stairs.

"Get up you stupid bitch." Leather slapped against denim. "I said, get up!" The whimpering she heard was not hers. She scrambled for a place to hide. From the corner where she crouched, as small, and inconspicuous as possible, she saw a girl, sprawled on the floor, her chin split, and bleeding. Her teeth had gone through her lip when she hit the concrete floor. Blood oozed from her mouth, and she spit out something small and white. The girl crawled on her belly as the leather strap broke the skin on her back.

"Please," she cried. "Help me, dear God, please."

God was not in the room.

Suzanne woke, gasping for air, her hair and nightgown drenched in sweat. The wind whipped the curtains into a frenzy. The air smelled like rain. *It doesn't rain in Sacramento. Not in June*. The wind came to a halt, the grey panels settled in place, and crickets chirped a summer's concerto. The damp smell was gone.

The next morning Suzanne dialed Detective Metzger. "You wouldn't believe the dream I had."

"Good morning to you too."

Suzanne glanced at the clock. *7:08*. "Did I wake you?"

"No, no. I'm up."

Suzanne could tell by the smoky tone of his voice that she woke him up. "Late night?"

"Very. A few bad guys and vampires. What can I do for you?"

"I had another dream."

"Interesting. I don't have any new victims."

"Perhaps I should save it for when you do."

"I didn't mean—tell me about your dream."

"He kicked her down a flight of stairs, I'm assuming she is in a basement. She was bleeding. He whipped her with a belt."

She heard Sam suck in a breath. "California homes typically don't have basements."

"One flight of stairs, the floor was concrete."

"I suppose I could check with my realtor friend to see what's around here."

"I don't think she's in the vicinity."

"Why?"

"I smelled rain." Suzanne closed her eyes remembering the scent.

"It doesn't rain here in June."

"Exactly."

"Do you think the vision is from another time? I can check the almanac, see when we had rain in June and cross reference to our crime data base."

"Sounds like a plan."

Awkward silence fell between them, until he asked, "Did you get any sleep?"

"Not really. I'm becoming quite the bitch. It won't be long before Steven and Karen get out the holy water or start smudging the house."

"What-ing the house?"

"People smudge their house with sagebrush to get rid of evil spirits. Steven said he'd go see a psychic with me. Is it okay if I call yours?"

"Sure. Let me get her number."

She heard him rummaging through stuff while she waited. Ben would've complained, crabbed about the inconvenience.

"916-555-3255, her name is Linda. Linda Schooler."

"Great, I'll let you know what she has to say."

Suzanne checked the address as Steven pulled against the curb. "Do I have to go in?"

"She's a psychic, not a witch. C'mon, Steven, Sam said she's nice. Don't you want to hear what she has to say?"

"Not really. You know how I feel about this stuff. I'm a pragmatic person. I work with numbers. Numbers add up. If they don't, I haven't done my job. Simple explanation, end of story."

"Jack believed."

"Jack believed in a lot of things, flying saucers, little green men."

"I see him."

"I don't. Let's just get this over with."

Linda opened the door wide. "Welcome."

"Thank you. I'm Suzanne, this is Steven."

"Yes, the vessel and the non-believer. C'mon in." She led the two into her parlor and pulled the chain on a Tiffany lamp, filling the room with a soft glow. She placed a deck of Tarot cards on the table. "Just in case."

"Just in case, what?"

"Just in case you run out of questions before our time is up. I read both ways. Your choice."

Suzanne twisted a lock of her hair. "This is my first time. What do I do?"

"What would you like to know?"

"I have a spirit, Jack—he saved my life. Now he appears to me—shows me horrific things. Why?"

Steven snickered.

"A young man is telling me you collected cars." She cocked her head and listened. "He says you can't throw a snowball for shit."

Steven sat back, his eyes big.

"What has Jack got to say about me?"

"He says he loved you when he went to the other side. He loves you still, that's why he is coming to you. You see, on the earth plane we experience emotion. That's our biggest challenge. We all have a job to do before we ascend. Jack is helping you overcome something. You two share a bond— you don't need me to tell you that. You've been together in many lifetimes. Reincarnated. You'll be together in many more." Linda placed her hands flat on the table. "You're special," she said. "You have cheated death because it's not your time. The experience has changed you," she tapped her head, "up here." She placed her hand on her heart, "And here." Linda closed her eyes and listened. "Uh, huh. Yes."

Steven and Suzanne exchanged puzzled glances.

"Yes, I'll tell her." She opened her eyes. "The young man says when you can float, you'll swim."

Steven squeezed Suzanne's hand. "What does he mean?"

"Jack was trying to teach me in my dreams, Steven. You thought I was crazy." Suzanne turned to Linda. "Why is he scaring me?"

"He is not trying to scare you. He is emotionally detached from what is going on in this dimension. His task is to give you the tools you need to do the job you came here to do."

"But I don't want the job—I don't want to see young girls being tortured. I don't want Jack sitting on my bed watching me sleep. I don't care if I ever learn to swim!" Suzanne rose to her feet. Steven grabbed her arm.

"Sit. Let Linda finish."

"What can I do?"

"Set your boundaries—tell Jack what is acceptable, what is not."

"Jack was never one to listen." She thought of Jack insisting she learn to float. And Ben, another controlling male in her life. What was she thinking back then? At this moment love was a four-letter word: DUMB.

"We all have choices," Linda said. "These choices determine how our life plays out, but the destination is often the same no matter which way we go. Lessons are learned on a divine level. Sometimes the choices we make are those that bring the lesson to us in a more friendly or timely fashion." Linda leaned back in her chair.

"You're saying that being shot and almost drowning was part of the plan?"

"Ever read a movie script?"

"No."

"When we watch a movie, we are oblivious to the script, and all it took to bring the story to the screen. To be a part of the process, from start to finish, you come to realize that making a movie is a lot like life. Sometimes it takes several takes to get a scene just right." Linda leaned forward. "Imagine yourself in an episode of CSI. Your character has been chosen to solve the mystery, catch the bad guy. It's that simple. Once he's caught, you can move on to the next episode."

"But why me?"

"On a soul level, you auditioned for the role and got it."

"That's bullshit. What about Metzger? How does he factor into my *episode*?"

"He may be your happy ending."

"Never."

"Love is eternal. We bring it with us each time." Linda paused. "Your friend agrees with me."

"Jack? Tell him to quit scaring me. I'll float when I'm ready."

Linda closed her eyes and listened. "He says *relax*."

Steven held Suzanne's arm and helped her into the car. "That was mind blowing. I don't know what to think."

"Try being on this end."

"I have to say, what she said made sense. I never thought of life in terms of a movie, but I guess that's kinda true."

"Well, you picked 'When Harry Met Sally,' I got stuck with 'Silence of the Lambs.'"

"Let's get some dinner. Karen has yoga tonight."

"How about you pick the place?"

Steven did a quick turn into a diner. Neither one spoke.

Suzanne sat quietly, contemplating Linda's advice. She wondered if Linda had actually seen Jack, or only heard his voice. Perhaps it was less unnerving to be clairaudient than clairvoyant.

Steven interrupted her thoughts. "She saw him, didn't she?"

"How did you—"

"I think that's what she said, you know when we first got there. And she knew I didn't believe in hocus pocus."

"You just read my mind. I was thinking the very same thing."

"Perhaps you read my mind. Don't clairvoyants know stuff *before* it happens?"

"I don't think I want to know."

"Face it—something happened to you. As a result, you have this extraordinary talent. Imagine what this could mean."

"My sanity?"

"Naw, you were a little crazy before the accident."

"It was no accident. Just the kind of support I need from my brother."

"Shouldn't you be able to tune into the guy who shot you?"

"It doesn't work like that."

"How do you know?"

"I just know."

Steven ordered Sushi. Suzanne picked at tempura fried shrimp. The sauce, salty and slightly tangy, reminded her of blood. She gagged.

"You're not becoming anorexic, are you?"

"It's the sauce, it tastes like—never mind."

"Eat the rice. A little iron might help."

"I can't eat. I don't know why, but food—maybe it's the antibiotics. I don't have an appetite."

To add to her misery, Jack was sitting next to Steven. His face, devoid of emotion, gave her the creeps. She glanced at the tempura sauce she had dipped her shrimp in moments ago and saw it was no longer brown. *Red*. She bit her tongue, suppressing the urge to scream.

When they got home, Karen was in the kitchen, toasting bread. "How did things go?"

"Toast smells good, may I?" Suzanne grabbed a plate from the cupboard.

"Help yourself—after you tell me what the psychic said."

Steven said, "She told Suzanne she's been chosen to be a messenger."

Karen looked to Suzanne. "Is that true?"

Her situation felt more like a curse than a gift, yet Karen seemed impressed. "Yes. Basically, that's what she said."

"Now what?"

"I guess I take it as it comes." Suzanne pushed the lever down on the toaster. The heat, and the glowing metal strips reminded her of hell. Music filled her ears. Heavy metal. Raw, unbridled shrieking lost in maniacal chords. *Blood dripped from her eyes.* The lyrics pounded in her brain, *Truth oozed from her lips. Kill me now, I beg of you, kill me quick.* And then she saw her.

"Suzanne?"

She didn't respond. She watched the girl twist and turn, trying to free herself from the chains holding her captive. Chunks of flesh clung to the wall. The man taunted her with a chicken leg.

"Want some, bitch?" He waved the leg under her nose. "Too bad. All mine."

She whimpered, and pulled on the chains, writhing in time to the beat. When he finished tearing the meat from the bone, he flung the chicken bone at her chest and laughed. "Dead girls don't eat."

Suzanne felt strong fingers dig into her armpits, hoisting her from the floor. She felt herself being dragged across the room. "No," she cried, echoing the girl's cries. When she opened her eyes, she was lying on the couch. Steven held a cold cloth on her forehead.

"A warning might be nice."

"Sorry. I saw her and—"

"And what?" Karen sat beside her. "What did you see?"

"Another girl. He's going to kill her."

"I'll call Sam." Steven rushed for the phone. Karen patted Suzanne's hand. The smell of burning toast came from the kitchen.

Sam leaned against the kitchen counter. Suzanne paced the room.

"This time it was different."

"How so?"

"Jack wasn't there."

"What do you think it means?"

"I haven't a clue. One minute I'm mesmerized by the toaster, next

I'm witnessing this—this monster." She hesitated and faced him. "God, how I wish this would stop."

"I haven't heard anything—I mean, no one's been reported missing."

"I guess that's a good thing. Still—I feel something tragic is about to happen."

———

Fired

A month went by since Suzanne moved in with Steven and Karen. Ben still hassled her every chance he got. He refused to move out of the house, and she refused to move back home. Her welcome was wearing thin at her brother's. Karen remained kind, yet distant. She knew it was just a matter of time before she'd get her eviction notice. She needed a plan.

"Your scar looks great. How are you feeling?" The doctor folded his arms and waited for her answer.

"Still getting strange visions. Are you sure I don't have a blood clot? Or a tumor?"

"I assure you, you're fine."

"Does that mean I'm free to go back to work?"

"Sure does. But are you ready?"

"No. But I need to work. I'm not only going stir crazy, the bills are piling up. My husband and I are—well, it's time to take my life back."

"Sounds like you could use some counseling." He jotted the name and address of a psychotherapist he thought would be a good fit. "Grace

Simms understands your kind of trauma. Give her a whirl. Let me know how you're doing."

When she got home, she called Elaine. She didn't expect her tone to be so short. "What did you expect? I tried to reach you—you haven't returned my calls. We had work to do, the accounts payables had to be turned in. I know what happened to you was tragic, and I'm really sorry, but you really didn't think we would just limp along until you came back, did you?"

Suzanne's heart reached her throat. Tears welled in her eyes. "No, Elaine. I get it, thanks. I'll stop by to pick up my things."

"I already dropped off the contents of your desk, didn't Ben tell you?"

"No. No, he didn't."

"Son-of-a-bitch!" She wanted to strangle her husband, throw his sorry ass out in the street. She knew her only recourse was to file for divorce and try to get the house. *But without a job...*

"You okay in there Suzanne?" It was Karen.

Suzanne opened the door. "Sorry. Having some anxiety. Lost my job."

"Oh. Now what?"

"I got my all-clear from the doctor today, guess I'll look for another job."

"How long do you think—"

"Listen, I know you're tired of my crap. I'll be out of here as soon as possible."

"Why are you being so—"

"What? A bitch?"

"I didn't—"

"Of course not. You're too kind." The tears Suzanne had been holding back spilled down her cheeks.

Karen embraced her. "I'm so sorry this is happening to you. Your brother and I care about you. We both want to help. But it's hard sometimes, you're like a wounded animal. We're struggling to communicate with you, but you lash out so easily."

"I know. I'm angry. Some guy is walking around free after devastating my life, my husband is an asshole, my dead ex-boyfriend is scaring the living shit out of me. I 'm being crushed from the inside out and I'm not being fair to you or Steven."

"Come, let's have a glass of wine, sit on the patio, and enjoy the sunset. Steven won't be home 'til late. I have chicken Vesuvio in the crock-pot."

"Okay, I'll meet you outside."

Suzanne ran cold water and submerged a washcloth. The water turned red. She shook off the vision, hoping it was just a misfire in her brain, but the color of the water deepened until it was almost black. She looked around the room for Jack. He wasn't there.

She dipped her hands into the water, grabbed the washcloth and squeezed. The water was clear. *Odd.*

She brushed her hair. The medication she had been prescribed to prevent infection made her hair lackluster. But in the last couple of weeks, the shine had returned. Her eyes seemed brighter, and the redness of the scars on her chest were beginning to fade. She had lost ten or more pounds, which she couldn't afford, but with Karen's cooking she was filling out again. *I may be able to land a decent job if I keep it up.*

She needed to make things right. She vowed to be more civil, and grateful. She heard a familiar voice coming from the patio. *What's he doing here?*

"What brings you out this way, Sam?"

"Thought I'd stop by with an update."

Karen poured three glasses of wine. Suzanne expected Sam to refuse, saying he was on duty, but he claimed to be on his own time.

"I spoke with the X-ray tech who told you the doctor's name. I reviewed the surveillance footage from the camera outside the lab. The man posing as a doctor covered the lower part of his face when he entered and exited the room, but we were able to zoom in on his eyes. I cross-checked his eye pattern with immigration and didn't get a match." He leaned forward. "My hunch? Our guy faked the accent."

"Why bother?"

"I think you know this guy."

"I don't know anyone who would try to harm me except—"

"Except, who?"

"Ben wouldn't be that crazy—or have the balls."

"You said yourself he's unpredictable."

"Volatile, yes—but premeditate something like that? I'd bet a million bucks he's not capable of—" The word *murder* lodged in her throat.

"The nurse's description matches Ben's."

"Ben is a lot of things, but a cold-blooded killer isn't one of them. Besides, what about motive? We can't even separate without him unraveling. Why would he want to kill me?"

"That's the million-dollar question."

"He's sick. He may get violent, but he—" Ben's band played a lot of British oldies. They were good, *authentic*. "I'm sure I would've recognized Ben's voice, accent or not."

"I'm not here to badger you. I'm trying my damnedest to figure out who tried to kill you. I need to eliminate any possibilities." His angst morphed into concern. "Any more visions?"

"Strange you should ask. I'm getting flickers, snippets, nothing that adds up. And Jack is still missing from the equation."

"Maybe he felt you were ready to 'swim'."

"And maybe I should visit your friend, Linda."

"Despite your extraordinary talents, we're no closer to catching your assailant *or* our serial killer. I'm for good ol' fashion detective work."

"Have it your way."

"Let's get back to Ben."

"Trust me, he's not your man."

"Is he yours?"

Sam's eyes smoldered in the glow of the setting sun and she wanted to reach for him. Lose herself in his arms. It was as if their souls mingled in the last remains of the day, and she wanted him. "No. Ben and I are through. It's a matter of formalities, that's all."

"I should be going." He rose. "Early court call. Laundry to do, shirts to press."

"You do your own ironing?"

"I find it therapeutic. I watch a few of my recorded programs, nuke a microwave dinner, or make a sandwich. It's a good life."

"Karen made chicken Vesuvio, perhaps you'd care to join us?"

"Thank you, but I need to get home. Raincheck?"

"Sure."

Stars appeared in the sky. She wished on every one of them.

Sam dialed up the volume on his car radio and sang along to a Beatles tune. "Listen, do you want to know a secret? Do you promise not to tell, whoa, whoa–oh, closer. Let me whisper in your ear, say the words you want to hear— I'm in love with you-ou..." How he loved the oldies. He loved the simplicity, the poetry. Boy meets girl. They fall in love. *Happy ending.*

Sam knew getting involved with Suzanne on a personal level was unwise. He'd seen too many times when a cop fell for a "vic" and got his heart stomped. *Not me.* He concentrated on the British invasion playing on the radio. Why would someone want to kill Suzanne? What was "elaborate" about it? Why the British accent? Because she knows him. Did disguising his voice alleviated some of the guilt? But was it Ben? Suzanne was convinced no. He wasn't so sure.

He began to station surf; "Tears of a Clown," he flipped again, "Will you still love me tomorrow..." He joined in. He didn't have the heart to tell Suzanne about Angela Foxworthy. An elderly couple found her body while on their morning walk. Her body appeared to have been bitten by something, a chicken bone lodged in her throat.

Busted

Ben chugged another beer. He set the empty between two cans, completing the second row of his pyramid. When he reached the top, he planned to take a photo and send it to Suzanne. "See what you made me do?"

His life was in the shitter. Suzanne was gone. The band had kicked him to the curb, and he was flat broke. Out of drugs, out of luck, just plain out of it. The best he could do was a beer buzz. He had pawned his gold wedding band for $160. Not a whole hell of a lot, considering.

Rage ebbed and flowed in his head. He hated the world. He hated Suzanne more. But he'd give his left testicle to have her back. *Why?* He didn't know. That notion came from the sick part of his brain. Why would anyone want a woman who betrayed him? He popped opened another beer. The sound gave him a thrill. The extent of his love song.

Sam clicked his mouse to refresh his screen. Ben Cash. *Run-of-the-mill loser*. High school education. No job in the last eight months. Before that, truck driver, delivery man, 7-11 clerk. One arrest for drunk and disorderly. Six calls for domestic violence, charges dropped each time by spouse. Seven parking tickets, all paid. *Nothing*. The "why" still niggled at his brain. Perhaps a call to Suzanne would help. *Who you trying to kid?* He simply wanted to hear her voice.

Suzanne answered her phone on the second ring. "Hello?" Her tongue felt tacky, like wet paint.

"Did I wake you?"

"Sorta."

"Shall I call back?"

"No, that's okay. The ceiling won't look any different twenty minutes from now."

"Are you okay?"

"I'm fine. Trouble sleeping. What else is new?"

"I'm drawing blanks. I thought maybe you could help."

"I'll try."

"I'm back to motive. You stated the man said you shouldn't have meddled. Do you have any idea why he would've used those words?"

"You asked me before. My answer is still I don't know."

"Tell me about the fund raiser..."

"What's there to tell?" Suzanne cast her mind back to before the fund raiser.

"What kind of people do you come in contact with? Surely there's a little drama now and then."

"Drama? These kids are sick. Drama is not allowed."

"Even behind the curtain?"

"Our donors are solid. Staff is minimal—we love what we do. Or I should rephrase. I loved what I did."

"You quit?"

"Not exactly. I got replaced."

"That must've stung."

"Yeah, big time. Let's move on. Don't want to drown in my sorrows this early in the day."

"Their loss."

"Yep. What's next?"

"Motive. You know something, saw something, or heard something," Sam said.

"What if the guy thought I was someone else?"

"I checked the hotel. There were eight women staying there. One was on business. Blond. 5'7", 210 pounds. Seven were traveling with spouses. None matched your description. What about the people attending the fund raiser? Anyone seem out of place?"

"No. I'm stumped."

Metzger tapped a pen on the blank sheet of paper on his desk. "Me too. If you think of anything..."

"I want the guy caught too Sam, but right now I think you have bigger problems."

"Why's that?"

"I just had another dream."

Suzanne gripped her cup with both hands while Sam busied himself with cream and sugar. "I didn't recognize the area. Or the train. People were speaking in foreign languages. I remember Belvedere Palace. The girl was alive. In fact, she was excited. She was with a man."

Sam sipped his coffee. "What do you make of it?"

She tried to avoid his eyes. "The dream was definitely different from the others. Where is the Belvedere Palace anyway? Is it a new casino or something?"

"There's the Belvedere Palace in Vienna, Austria." He set his cup down slowly. She watched his shoulders sag. "What's wrong?"

"It's creepy enough that you dream about murdered women. Austria is—well it's sacred to me. I vacationed there as a child." He looked away. "I have fond memories of the Belvedere."

"Care to share?"

"My parents had their hands full keeping me from playing in the fountains. My sister and I chased birds and smelled the flowers." His face softened. "I had to know how each bloom was assembled—my mother fussed over grass stains on my trousers."

"How many siblings do you have?"

"My parents were older when they married. Audra came along the day before my eighth birthday, change-of-life baby."

She imagined him having to share his parent's attention with a new baby, a girl no less. Steven had gone through the same thing. But they were only three years apart. They had become closer in later years. "Where is your sister now?"

"Budapest." Sam shifted in his seat, added more sugar to his coffee and stirred. "Tell me more about your dream. Did this man resemble the man in your previous visions?"

"I didn't see his face. He didn't speak."

"Maybe we should pay a visit to Linda Schooler."

"We?"

"It wouldn't serve any purpose me going alone." His fingertips brushed her arm.

"Oh," she said, ignoring the tiny bumps on her skin.

With Sam gone, Suzanne was free to breathe. Why he affected her the way he did was still up for speculation. She didn't want to feel anything for anyone right now. The hole in her chest would heal more quickly than the ache in her heart. Jack hadn't appeared for some time. What if he was a figment of her imagination? The more time that passed, the more time she had to re-evaluate her state of mind. And? *Can't debate the fact that you knew things about the murdered girls.*

"Hey?"

Suzanne jumped. "Steven—you startled me."

"Did I see Sam?"

"He just left. He wants to see Linda Schooler with me."

"I think he has the hots for you."

"Don't be ridiculous. He wants to know more about my crazy dreams."

"Another murder?"

"No. But it was really weird. I was in a foreign country."

"Speaking of foreign, any thoughts about work?"

"Is this the eviction speech?"

"No speech. But when do plan to move out?"

"If Ben would leave—"

"Forget Ben. You've been here eight weeks. Do you have a plan? That's all I'm asking."

"I've been looking at the want ads."

"What about some kind of healing work? I'm sure working with terminally ill children all these years qualifies you for—"

"The jobs I'm qualified to do won't support me."

"Fat chance you'll get alimony."

"Puts me in a pickle, huh?"

"Keep looking. Karen is a saint, but I think she misses our 'us' time."

"I don't blame her." Suzanne's words trailed as she watched her brother leave. "Damn." She collapsed into a chair and dialed Ben.

———

Ben lazed with one leg propped on the arm of the sofa. Black Sabbath competed with the announcer pitching an anti-psychotic drug on TV. Smoke hovered over his head each time he took a drag off the joint, held his breath. His self-entertainment was interrupted when the light on his phone caught his eye. Suzanne's picture made him cringe. He picked up the offending object and examined the pretty face ruining his high. He slid the bar to accept the call.

"What the fuck do YOU want?"

"Ben, we need to talk."

"About what? I thought I made myself perfectly clear. I am not giving you a divorce, and I am not moving out of this house. What more is there to say?"

"How are you?"

"Fucking amazing with you gone."

"I can't stay with Steven forever."

"That's your problem."

"California is a fifty-fifty state. I can force you out."

"Is that right?" He drew on the burning stub between his thumb and forefinger and blew smoke into the phone. "You go ahead and try." He ended the call. Laughter rumbled in his chest. He felt victorious until he closed his eyes and images of Calvin's house filled the blank screen behind his eyelids. "Fucker," he seethed.

He launched himself off the sofa, grabbed his car keys and slammed the back door. "Calvin, you better be home, man."

Ben had no sooner pulled onto the ramp to highway 50 when flashing lights filled his rearview mirror. Tempted to give the law a run for his money, he tapped the accelerator upping his speed.

"Pull over," reverberated into the night.

Ben pulled onto the shoulder, but the black and white flew past. "Holy fuck." He broke into fits of laughter. "Shit, that was close." He pulled back onto the road and headed toward Calvin's.

When he turned onto Calvin's street, he slowed down. Calvin's house was lit up like Christmas. Black and white cars filled the cul-de-sac. Lights swirled everywhere. Neighbors came out of their houses like moths drawn to a flame. "Holy shit. This cannot be good."

Suzanne's phone rang at 11:04 P.M. She stretched one arm across her pillow, resenting the intrusion. She didn't remember falling asleep. Her voice, groggy and weak, managed "Hello." Sam's voice sounded excited.

"Sorry to wake you, Sleeping Beauty, but we need you down at the station. We arrested a guy we're interested in for your case."

"Can it wait until morning?"

"Of course, I just thought—"

"I'm happy you caught him, but I'm in bed and I—"

"No worries. I'll swing by to pick you up at 9:00."

"I can drive myself—"

"I thought maybe we could get a cup of coffee before I take you to the County jail."

"Okay." Silence filled the distance between them.

"Sleeping Beauty? You sounded like you were asleep and—"

"And?"

"Well, the beauty part goes without saying."

"Sam, don't you think you're being—"

"Unprofessional? Forgive me. Go back to sleep, Suzanne. See you in the morning." Suzanne heard the click on the other end of the line. *Mission accomplished. It's all over. He's going to slip out of my life.*

Sam shoved his phone into his pocket. He grabbed the cup of stale coffee he had reheated twice and headed for the interrogation room. It was going to be a long night. Another young woman was reported missing.

Suzanne fluffed her pillows, straightened her covers and took three deep breaths. The fourth exhale caught in her lungs. "Jack. Dammit."

"It's not over."

"Sam said they caught the guy who shot me."

Jack extended his hand. Suzanne pulled the covers to her chin. "No more. I have to move on."

"He's still out there."

"Who? Why can't you just tell me?"

"It doesn't work that way."

"I didn't sign up for this, Jack, never."

"We don't have time to argue the details, look—"

Suzanne couldn't move. Her ears heard a scraping noise. Her legs were frozen beneath something heavy. Pain radiated up her spine and reached her temples. The smell of blood assaulted her nostrils. Her eyes gravitated toward her knees. She screamed. Her legs were gone.

At 7:45 A.M., she awoke to the sound of her alarm. Her hair was damp. Her nightgown clung to her skin. A veil of perspiration covered her face and chest. Panic set in as she reached beneath the covers for her legs. "Thank God," she whispered. She flopped back against the pillows. One hand balled into a fist and pounded the mattress. Jack loomed behind her eyelids. His face held no malice, only the love she saw during the years they spent together. "What do you want from me?" she cried. His face disappeared behind a bright orange glow. She opened her eyes to golden light pouring through her bedroom window. Outside, birds chirped. A breeze stirred the leaves, scattering them across the patio. Although the moment was picture perfect, deep inside She was sad. *The slow death we embrace as part of life feels too close to home.*

Karen was already up, dressed and starting breakfast in the kitchen when Suzanne shuffled toward the coffee pot. Karen's greeting hit her nerves like nails on a chalkboard.

"Good-*morning* Suz*anne*. Sleep *well*?"

Too early for a pissing contest. "I've slept better. How 'bout you? You're up early."

"Work to do."

"Can I help?" Suzanne mustered her best game face.

"Thanks, you wouldn't—"

"Wouldn't what? Now I'm incompetent?"

"God, why do you have to make things so hard?"

"I'll be out of here as soon as I can."

"I didn't—"

"No, Karen, you didn't. I said it for you." Suzanne stomped out of the kitchen and barricaded herself in her bedroom. She flopped down on the bed, intending to get a grip on her anger. Until Jack showed up.

"This is all your fault," she cried, pulling a pillow over her head. "Why can't you leave me alone?"

"You know why."

"Who is this monster? Why can't you show me his face so I can describe him to police and be done with this? How many more have to die?"

"I wish it were that simple."

"Do you see what you're doing to me, Jack?"

"We can't disrupt the circle of life, Suzanne."

"That's bullshit."

"I know. Come."

"No."

"You must see this."

Jack didn't wait for her permission. He snatched her and plopped her in a dank room. She didn't have to see a thing. She knew. Death enveloped her, seeped into her soul.

She sank to her knees. Growling and laughter assaulted her ears. The girl screamed each time he bit into her flesh or carved little semi-circles into her skin and stapled them to the wall. She couldn't move. Her hands dangled from the orange twine securing her to an overhead beam.

He twisted chunks of her long, fawn-colored hair, and stapled them to the beam. She begged him to stop.

Suzanne felt his mood shift from euphoria to anger when blood oozed from between her legs. He dug through his bag. She heard a cracking sound when he shoved a steel pipe down the girl's throat. Next came the saw.

Sam tilted his head. "How long?"

"A day." Dove Johnson handed him a baggie containing orange twine.

"He's getting ballsier."

"He's expediting his kill. The ligature marks were made hours, not days earlier."

"What's the C.O.D.?"

"Suffocation. He shoved something down her throat. Her trach is shattered." Dove squatted beside the body and moved the girl's jaw back and forth.

Sam could see the jaw was unhinged. "Son of a bitch." He wiped his brow. "What else?"

Dove sighed. He scooted on his knees until he was next to the girl's hips. He lifted her T-shirt, exposing bite marks and flesh wounds the shape of a fish on the girl's lower abdomen. "God only knows what this means," he said.

Sam bent down to get a closer look. "None of the others indicate ritual. What are you thinking?"

"Can't say for sure. We'll know more when the M.E. takes a look at her."

"Anything else?"

"Besides her legs missing? She was menstruating. Evidently, our boy found this offensive. She wasn't raped like the others."

"And you're sure we're looking at the same killer?"

"Unless someone else knows about the orange twine—"

"It's hard to imagine one sicko, let alone two."

Both men turned when the door opened and Rob Schuster came in. "Sorry I'm late. Traffic."

"Where's Dixon?"

"Let's see, what day is it?"

"I want that guy's life." Dove peeled off his gloves and sniffed his fingers. "Anyone notice how toxic these smell?"

Sam and Rob exchanged a glance.

Dove pulled another pair of gloves from his pocket, gave them a sniff, grimaced and put them on. "Let's get her ready for transport. I have a movie date with my better half. Dixon will have to catch up on his own time."

"We all can't be a lady's man," Rob said, performing his cat-walk around the victim.

Sam's phone hummed in his pocket. He pulled it half-way out, checked the caller ID and let it drop back into his pocket. "You guys good to go here?"

"Call me Later. Lambert's on call tonight. He's sharp. We should have a C.O.D. report by quitting time."

Sam rushed his goodbyes and hurried to his car, phone in hand. "Suzanne? What's up?"

Her sobs made him shiver. "Shhh. Calm down." He gave her a moment to compose herself. "Suzanne?"

"I'm here," she said. "I need you."

Her soft, breathy words filled holes in Sam's heart he didn't know existed. But the moment shattered into hardcore reality. *She needs your help. Not you*. "What's wrong?"

"There's a girl. Another victim."

Suzanne showered, dressed in navy leggings, an oversize, dusty blue sweater and tan boots. She twisted her long auburn hair into a knot and secured it with an iridescent-blue clam shell clip that complimented her lapis-colored eyes. She had long given up make-up. A swipe of tinted lip balm would have to do. Her reflection confirmed her suspicions. *You need more sleep.*

She didn't wait for Sam to come to the door. When he pulled up, she jumped into the passenger seat of his car. "Drive," she said, looking straight ahead.

Sam stole a side glance as he pulled into traffic.

"He cut off her *legs*."

"I know. I just came from the scene."

Suzanne buried her face in her hands "I can't take this anymore."

Sam pulled into a Starbuck's drive-thru, ordered two Grande black coffees. "I can't imagine how horrific this must be for you," he said. His hand reached for hers, then stopped mid-way. "We haven't identified the victim yet. My team got the call at 4:00 this morning. She was killed some time yesterday."

"I'm sorry," she said. Her fingertips brushed his as she accepted the cup of coffee.

Sam parked the car at the far end of the parking lot, facing the street. He sipped his coffee in silence, but his eyes darted in all directions, like he expected the killer to pop into view.

"There's a place in Raleigh, North Carolina—a research center. They test paranormal stuff. Interested?"

"In what?"

"Perhaps they could help you understand what's going on. Help you control the visions or something. I don't know, just heard about it–thought I'd pass the info along."

"What about Linda Schooler?"

"I just thought maybe..."

"Maybe what? I could get my head shrunk along with an exorcism? I want it to stop. That's all. Just *stop*." She set her coffee in the cup holder and dug through her purse for a tissue.

"Let's take care of business first. Put away the bastard who shot you and worry about the rest later." His compassion proved overwhelming, and she looked away. "I'm not free, Sam."

"Doesn't mean I can't help."

"As long as you keep that in mind."

Calvin

When they arrived at the County jail, they entered a sparsely furnished area adjoining the interrogation room. A heavy glass window separated her from a man dressed in an orange jumpsuit.

"I know him!" Her face lost color. "Calvin Cook shot me? Why?"

"How well do you know this guy?"

"I considered him a friend. He and my husband—" She turned to Sam, "Is Ben involved too?"

"Not at this point. What can you tell me about him?"

"As the event coordinator for Wish Kids, I often had business at the hospital. I met Calvin in the cafeteria, about three years ago. We got to talking. He said he played guitar. After getting to know him better, I introduced him to my husband. They started playing in a band—a British tribute band." Suzanne's mind whirled. What motive would Calvin have to shoot her? *We were friends*. And how had she "meddled"? Why did he accuse her of meddling before he shot her?"

"We are bringing your husband in for questioning. He may be able to fill in the blanks."

"Is that necessary?"

Sam needed a shave. His eyes were tired. "We need to find out the extent of his involvement."

"He should be at home." She touched Sam's arm. "Be careful. He's been off his meds. Calvin was the closest he came to self-medicating."

"How's that?"

"They smoked a lot of marijuana."

"Anything else?"

She remembered a run-in she had had with Calvin at the hospital days before the fundraiser. She had caught him pocketing a patients' meds. When she confronted him, he turned hostile, swore he wasn't stealing, said it wasn't what it looked like. At the time she had so much on her mind. The kids, the banquet, rehearsing magic acts. It all made sense now. "Calvin may have been stealing drugs from the hospital."

"Do you have proof?"

"A couple of days before the event, I was meeting with one of the nurses on the pediatric ward. She had volunteered to dress as a clown and do face painting. I wanted to make sure she was still available. Sometimes shifts change and people have to drop out. I saw Evelyn, that's her name, talking with Calvin. She was the charge nurse that evening, and she was prepping the med cart for rounds. While she and I were talking, I thought I saw Calvin slip a few of the capsules into his pocket. He did it so quickly, I wasn't sure I saw what I saw. When I asked him about it, he not only denied it, he got angry. Later that evening, I asked Evelyn if she had come up short."

"What did she say?"

"She shrugged it off."

"And you took that for a yes?"

"I didn't take it anyway. Like I said, I had a million other things on my mind." She rubbed her temples. "What happens now?"

"We're holding Cook on suspicion of attempted murder and drug charges. His residence proved to be quite the dispensary."

"What about Ben?"

"I sent a couple of my men to the house to pick him up for questioning."

Suzanne covered her face with her hands. Sam pried them away.

"You know I'm going to make sure nothing happens to you, don't you?"

"How are you going to do that?"

"If your husband knew about Calvin's drug activity, that makes him —" Sam reached for her hand.

"Don't."

Sam scooted his chair until his nose was inches from Suzanne's face. She could feel his breath brush her lips. "I won't let him harm you."

"Ben is my problem, not yours."

"If he broke the law, he's mine." Sam pushed himself backwards and rose. Suzanne flinched when the door slammed behind him. She laid her head on her arms. What else could go wrong? She hated the "poor me" voice taunting her. She wanted to trust Sam, trust that the nightmare would be over, but she didn't know him. Her one leap of faith had ended badly when she had married on the rebound. Ben would seek revenge whether he was Calvin's accomplice or not.

Sam wanted to nestle Suzanne close, make her realize how deeply he had come to care for her. *Stubborn*. Would he want her any other way? *No.* She wanted his help, she didn't want him smothering her, he got that. So why did he feel like a buffoon? *Love, buddy. Love does that to a person.* But first he had a job to do. With a serial killer at large, and Calvin to put away, he had no time to ponder his feelings. Besides, Suzanne was married. He suspected leaning on Ben would make him leave town. *One can only hope.*

Accomplice

Ben peeked out the window. The car pulling into the drive wasn't company. He heard car doors slam, footsteps coming up the walkway. When the officers pounded on his door, he broke into a sweat. Not that he had reason to be nervous, *he* had done nothing wrong. Were they here about Calvin?

"Benjamin Cash? Open the door, sir. We need to speak with you."

"What about?'

"Open the door, sir. We don't want any trouble." The officer at the window took a step back and unsnapped his holster. "We just want to ask you some questions."

Ben sorted possibilities in his head. Paranoia flickered between rational thoughts. He hadn't broken any laws. Proving he smoked a little reefer at Calvin's would be difficult. Even if Calvin had ratted on him, it was Calvin's word against his. He reached for the deadbolt, gave it a twist, and opened the door.

When they grabbed his arms, he felt trapped, his adrenaline surged. He kicked at everything within range, but then he was face down on the porch, cold steel circling his wrists.

"We've got Ben in a holding cell." Sam pushed a chair next to Suzanne. "He got feisty, my men had to secure him."

"He's sick, Sam. He's not a monster."

"We'll take that into consideration. Is there anything you need from the house? I can take you."

"When can I leave?"

"You're free to go anytime. I'll give you a lift."

"How long are you going to hold him?"

"Until I'm convinced he had nothing to do with your attempted murder."

"What makes you think he did?"

"Just making sure the facts add up. I'm like that. Especially when it comes to someone I care about."

"Don't let concern cloud your judgement." Suzanne rose. "Can we go now?"

Sam escorted her to his car without words. When he dropped her off, his goodbye was professional. Suddenly she felt *alone*.

Good Idea

Calvin cringed when he saw Ben walk past the interrogation room. *Why is he here*? Ben had issues. Big ones. Calvin knew Ben didn't play with a full deck. Once Ben had lit up a bowl or two, he was as pliable as Silly Putty. Their only disagreements were over money. Okay, so what if Ben was right about him skimming off the top. He did most the work. He picked the songs. He booked the gigs. He called the practices, got everyone "fired" up before a performance. They owed him.

Suzanne. *Bitch*. Why did she have to stick her nose in his business? Copping a few pills now and then didn't raise any red flags with the hospital staff. He suspected he wasn't the only one with his fingers in the pie. Besides, most of those kids were gonna die anyway. Right? Bleeding hearts, like Suzanne, didn't keep them from the pearly gates. Pain? *Part of life*. Get sick? *You die*. His mother, father, two sisters and Aunt Judy had died of cancer. *Nasty shit*. He didn't care one way or another. Here today? Make the most of it. Get high, *stay high*. Cannabis fed his muse–pain meds were a bonus. All work, *no play*— Suzanne had no right to meddle in his affairs. *She deserved to die*. Miss goody-two-shoes. She didn't notice he was following her. A few OxyContin and a six-pack of Abeita "Purple Haze" had helped with his decision to shoot her. *Seemed like a good idea at the time.* "Just wanted to be a rock star," he whispered to the wall.

Ben's 6'2" frame slammed into a chair across from Detective Sam Metzger. "You needn't go to such extremes to sleep with my wife, Detective. Suzanne is her own person. In case you haven't noticed, she's independent to a fault."

"I'll keep that in mind," Sam said. He leaned back in his chair. "Speaking of Suzanne, how do you know Calvin Cook?"

"What's Calvin got to do with my wife?"

"Whose idea was it to kill her? Yours? Or did you two rock stars cook up the scheme together?"

"I don't know what the hell you're talking about. I didn't conspire with anyone to kill my wife."

"So you didn't know Calvin planned to shoot the missus?"

"No!"

"That's not what your buddy Calvin says. He says you blackmailed him into killing your wife. Except, as we both know, Suzanne being independent to a fault, *survived*."

"I want a lawyer."

Jealous

Sam followed the stairs to the basement where Goldorado County's finest were busy gathering data, testing theories and charting "current events." The basement was known as the "war department."

Dove Johnson stood with hands on hips assessing photos of the latest victim. "Mackenzie McElroy. Twenty-three. Reno posted the MP on her this morning. According to her folks, she was in Sacramento visiting a friend. They gave up asking for details when she turned eighteen. Parents said she was a Virgo. Private. The only thing she shared was instructions; water the orchid on Tuesday. Four ice cubes, no more no less."

Sam said, "Maybe it's a Virgo thing."

"Maybe." Dove moved closer to the photo. He pulled a magnifying glass from his lab coat pocket and zeroed in on the mark near the girl's left breast. First impression was the mark was a bite. The possibility of DNA got Dove excited.

"What is it?" Sam asked.

"I know what it's not. Our boy doesn't bite. Could be a hair clip, tongs, or a clamp of some sort. The punctures are cone shaped and symmetrical, not rectangular and irregular like teeth would make."

"We have the guy that shot Suzanne Cash, if that's any consolation."

"Every douche bag we get off the street is a plus. Hey, we on for dinner Friday night? Nancy would love to see you. She asked me to invite Dixon. Should I be worried?"

"Don't tell me you're jealous of Dixon."

"Cautious, that's all. Guy's a babe-magnet."

"Nancy only has eyes for you."

"How do you know?"

Sam shrugged. "I need to get back upstairs. I've got Suzanne's husband on the hot seat."

"He was in on the plan to shoot her?"

"Probably not." Sam shrugged. "His lawyer should be here *sometime* today. Until then, I want to imagine he's guilty."

"Masochist. You'll never get the girl that way."

On his way upstairs, Sam mulled over Dove's reaction to Dixon. The guy was good looking, smart, made good financial decisions and was single. However, he lacked something. A heart. Sam wondered if that's what it took to survive. Not that he didn't consider himself a good catch. He'd never make the cover of GQ, but he cleaned up well. He wasn't a mush, but he was kind. Sobriety helped with the kind part. Once he became sober, he had thought about settling down, raising a family. Somehow, the job always sucked the hours out of his day. Dixon seemed to have plenty of time on his hands. "He does his job, doesn't rock the boat," is what his men had to say. When Dixon didn't show up at a crime scene, they all figured it was because he was getting laid by a woman most men fantasized about. Dixon's social life was filled with women worthy of the red carpet or the cover of Sports Illustrated. *Big deal*. Sam concluded Dixon would never know the true meaning of love.

The warm evening encouraged Suzanne to join Karen on the patio. "The police have the man who shot me in custody."

Karen set her drink down. She rose and closed in for a hug. Suzanne stiffened, but then relented and let the hug ease her pain.

"Doesn't mean it's over. Ben might be involved. Can you believe it?"

"Ben? How?"

"The police brought Calvin Cook in for questioning. Evidently,

Calvin and Ben were doing more than making music. Calvin's house was raided for drugs. We both know Ben's a lot of things, but drug dealer? Murderer? I know he smokes pot, but chemicals? I can't get him to take his medication—"

"What about the money? Ben seemed to be doing okay while you were in the hospital."

"That's because he was stealing from me. I stashed money in the bookcase. He found it. Ben is sick. He's not a killer."

"How do you know? It's not like you kept tabs on the guy. You've always done your thing. He did his. How many times did he say he was going out of town for a gig and come home broke? Then, suddenly he has money to blow."

"I've been giving him an allowance from what's left of my inheritance."

Suzanne reached for Karen's drink, chugged the remnants, and handed her the empty.

Karen examined the glass in the fading light. "Nothing tequila can't fix. Ready for another?"

She disappeared into the house and returned with two tumblers filled with ice, liquor, and extra lime wedges. "Over here." Karen moved their party to a double glider and began to swing. The soothing motion triggered Suzanne's memory of another time. *Jack. Love.* Her dreams ended by war. Now, she was past her prime, jobless, broken, a vessel for nightmares. She swallowed some tequila along with her bitterness. Life was meant to be sweet. Jack had promised her a future. Instead she had ended up with the first person who'd wanted her, sabotaging any chance for happiness.

"Penny for your thoughts." Karen nudged Suzanne's shoulder.

Tequila warmed her words. "What do you think about Sam?"

Accusations

Ben had been sitting in the same room for six hours waiting for a court-appointed lawyer to show. The burger and fries brought to him an hour ago rumbled in his stomach. He wanted to go and smoke a joint. "This is crap," he mumbled. He crumpled the burger wrapper and squeezed it into a tiny ball.

Sam Metzger watched Ben from the other side of the one-way mirror. He wondered what Suzanne saw in the man. He was average looking, barely a high school graduate and didn't have a pot to piss in. Not to mention his bi-polar personality and volatile disposition. But who was he to judge? He wasn't the lady's man Dixon was, rich, powerful—but he was intelligent, kind, good-natured. *I clean up well.*

When Sam entered the room, Ben growled, "How long are you going to keep here?"

"As long as it takes. Seems Calvin is pointing the finger at you."

"I didn't do anything. You can't arrest me for smokin' a little weed. I have a medical condition. Cannabis calms me down. Ask any shrink."

"I'm more concerned with the plot to kill your wife."

"That's bullshit and you know it."

"Not according to Mr. Cook."

"He's lying. I would never hurt my wife."

"You have quite a temper, Ben." Sam slapped a manila down on the table. "These domestic violence reports don't lie. And from what I hear — you still refuse to take the medication prescribed by your doctor."

"That crap makes me sweat, smell funny, and it doesn't do shit. Besides, smokin' weed or getting a little pissed off doesn't make me a murderer."

"Where were you the night your wife was shot?"

"You asked me that at the hospital. You know damn well I had nothing to do with Suzanne being shot. And until my lawyer arrives, I have nothing further to say—" Ben turned toward the mirrored wall. He wanted to be sure he was heard by whoever stood on the other side of the glass. "Except stay away from my wife."

Sheena

Sac State student, Sheena Bradford, hurried along the walkway leading to the parking lot. She had a two-hour window between classes and had been craving a latte since morning. Cravings were becoming more frequent. *Dammit Dixon.* He had the upper hand when it came to condoms. If she wanted him in her bed, she had to stick to his terms.

"Get one of those apps to track your cycle," he insisted. Why she obeyed him wasn't entirely clear. She thought she'd grown past stupid when it came to men. Dixon was different. His eyes, his touch. His love-making. *Best I've had with anyone.* His mouth, capable of pleasure no woman should live without. *Too late for regrets.* She was addicted. She'd do anything to feel his lips on her skin.

Sheena sent Dixon a text. Latte in ten. Join me? She got into her car, started the engine. Her heart sank when he replied.

Busy. Later.

It's just sex, she reminded herself. He never pretended otherwise. Why did she feel dejected? Being a week late contributed to her bleak mood. She wondered how he was going to react. She suspected he had a dark side. *Won't be pretty.*

Any chance of having a relationship with Dixon was merely a figment of her imagination. "You're barely eighteen," he had said, "I have to protect my image, being in the public eye and all—" but in her heart, she knew, *he's a player*. At that moment, the latte she'd been craving didn't sound so good. Sheena opened her car door and forfeited her dignity along with her breakfast.

———

Ben Cash was released by 8:00 p.m.. First stop, his beloved brother-in-law's place to have a chat with Suzanne.

When he arrived, he smelled smoke and heard music coming from the backyard. He used the back gate, rather than ring the bell.

Suzanne and Karen were huddled near the fire pit roasting marshmallows when he interrupted their girl talk. "Shouldn't you two be singing Kumbaya or some shit like that?"

Suzanne jumped to her feet. "What are you doing here?"

"Just wanted to stop by to thank you for siccing your boyfriend on me. Always wanted to spend a day at a police station. Got a free lunch out of it though."

"Perhaps you should think twice about the company you keep."

Ben moved closer. Suzanne smelled his stale breath. "Who introduced us, huh? Calvin was your friend first."

"I tried to help you. Music was the only connection Calvin and I had."

"I had nothing to do with you being shot. If I wanted you dead, dear wife, I would've killed you myself. Seems Calvin fucks everything up."

Karen stepped between them. "Time to leave, Ben. I don't think you want to spend any more time downtown."

Ben's hateful glare frightened her. "Enjoy your evening ladies."

Once the gate closed behind her husband, Suzanne exhaled. "Life keeps getting better."

"Divorce him. Take your power back. Find a job, start over."

Suzanne hugged herself and shivered. "Let's go inside. I'm cold."

Karen rescued the sticks from the fire. "I have a couple of Hershey bars stashed in the pantry. Let's make s'mores and put on a movie."

"Thank you for understanding Karen. I know you and I clash sometimes, but I can never repay you for your kindness."

"We're family. You drive me crazy, but I love you all the same."

Suzanne lounged on the sofa with a fluffy blanket, s'mores and the 1983 movie, "Svengali" starring Jodie Foster and Peter O'Toole.

"I never saw this one," Karen said, settling next to her on the sofa.

Ten minutes into the movie, a voice invaded Suzanne's brain. *Jack.* Jodie Foster morphed into a young brunette, Peter O'Toole no longer her handsome captor. The man was faced away from the young woman on the screen. His words made her flinch. "Get rid of it." The brunette backed away from him. *Beautiful.* She held her breast as if she could no longer bear the pain. Suzanne wondered what he had meant by "Get rid of it" until she heard a baby cry. The woman screamed.

"Suzanne?" Karen shook her.

"He's going to kill her," she cried.

"Who?"

"Him!" She pointed at the TV, but a Ford commercial segued into a Farmers Insurance promo.

"It was just a movie. I can change the channel." Karen pointed the remote at the TV and scrolled down until she found a comedy. "There. All gone. Only funny stuff from now on."

"She's pregnant. I heard a baby cry. He wants her to get rid of it."

"Maybe you should take Detective Metzger's advice and go to Raleigh. They can help you decipher your visions."

"I'd have to dip into my savings. I can't support Ben *and* go to Raleigh."

"Let Ben take care of himself. If he's that sick, let him get professional help. Quit making excuses for him."

"You're right—I'll talk to Sam."

Confession

Calvin Cook signed his confession at 9:15 p.m. Sam helped escort him back to his cell before leaving the station. His stomach grumbled from lack of food. He considered calling Suzanne to reassure her that her assailant was behind bars, ask her to have a bite to eat with him. Dove was right, *masochist*. The more he wanted her, the more it hurt. He dialed her number.

"Sam? It's late."

"I'm calling to give you an update. Cook confessed. He's at County, you're safe."

"Thanks for the good news." Dead air lingered between them. "Are you still at the station?"

"Yeah. Thought I'd grab a bite to eat. Care to join me?"

Suzanne looked at Karen, who had been eavesdropping.

"Give me ten minutes. I was ready for bed."

"See you then." He disconnected the call. His fatigue had faded.

When Sam arrived at Steve and Karen's house, he parked on the street. He walked to the door, his step light. Karen opened the door before he had the chance to ring the bell.

"Suzanne's almost ready." She stepped outside and closed the door behind her. "I wanted to speak with you. She had another episode. I think sending her to Raleigh would be a good idea. Before she loses her mind."

"That bad?"

"We were watching a movie, she blanked out, started screaming. She needs help, Sam."

"It's her call–"

"I have a feeling you can be pretty persuasive. You're good for her."

He wondered if Suzanne would agree. "I'll see what I can do."

Suzanne appeared in the doorway. Sam admired her quick transition from "ready for bed" to ravishing. Her auburn hair tied back in a low pony-tail, showcasing high cheekbones and silver hoop earrings. Her sapphire scoop-neck top revealed a hint of cleavage, tight jeans hugged her petite frame. She flung a charcoal leather jacket over her shoulder.

"Hope you like burgers," he said. "Not much open at this time of night."

"If we're talking Burgers and Brew, you'll make me a happy girl."

"You didn't tell me you read minds."

He followed her to the car, admiring the scenery on the way. The butterflies were back. When he opened the door for her the moon lit her face in an ethereal glow. He wanted to kiss her. But before the thought turned to action, she shut him down.

"This isn't a date."

"No. Dates are off limits. You're married."

"I'm glad we're on the same page."

She's here with you now, be happy with that. "I respect your decision to keep our relationship professional," he said, sliding behind the wheel, "but don't expect me to be a machine. I like you. I like being with you. You're pretty, funny, and intriguing. This isn't about you being a damsel in distress. If I had met you under different circumstances, I would've felt the same. This is new for me. I don't date co-workers, clients, or cousins of co-workers or clients."

"Do you date at all?"

"No. You're the first. Ever." They both laughed, easing the tension. By the time they reached the restaurant, they were talking as if they were old friends.

Over burgers, Suzanne described her vision. Sam listened. "Do you feel the woman is local?"

"Yes. I also think she's pregnant. Which means, they've been together before."

"And it's always the same guy?"

"Yes. I still can't see his face, but I get the impression he's handsome."

"Handsome?"

"Svengali."

"He's the guy who hypnotized his victims, right?"

"Yes, one woman in particular. In the Jody Foster, Peter O'Toole version, he wanted to make her a star."

"You think Peter O'Toole is handsome?"

"He had the power to make Jody Foster believe he was."

"Quite the age difference, don't you think?"

"I get the feeling the monster you're looking for *is* older than the women he targets."

"Interesting. What else?"

"I want to go to Raleigh."

Sam sat back assessing Suzanne's sudden mood change. "Have you looked into the Durham Center?"

"Karen told me about the place. She said it's a great experimental facility. It's more scientific than hoo-doo."

"Let me see what I can arrange. It would be beneficial to the department, but with all the budget cuts lately, I'm not sure if my boss will go for it. If not, I can pick up the tab."

"That's asking too much. I have a little money saved. I'll make it work–best there's no strings."

"Please, let me help. No strings. You have my word."

"Let me check whether I can get in. They may be booked solid."

"I have a sneaking suspicion this is going to work out for you."

"Predicting the future, Detective?"

The urge to kiss her returned. "Hope so."

———

The Test

The next day, Sam dropped by Steven and Karen's to confirm Suzanne's decision to contact the Durham Research Center. She described her visions in the online form provided by the center. When she hit "send," she felt as if she had sent piece of her soul across the country. "I feel silly," she said.

Sam patted her shoulder. "Let's see what happens. In the meantime, I booked us an appointment with Linda Schooler."

"Us?"

"It's easier for me to witness what's going on, than to hear it second-hand."

"What about work?"

"What we're doing *is* work. And I intend to compensate you for your time."

"I don't remember getting on anyone's payroll."

"Whoever this killer is, he's eluded us for over a year. You're the closest we've come to any leads. I consider you a valuable resource, one the department is fortunate to have."

Suzanne slammed her laptop closed. "We had dinner last night. Please don't think that makes me one of the boys. Ben is furious with me as it is. He thinks–"

"I know what Ben thinks–and maybe he's right. Maybe I do have a thing for you–but my feelings will never interfere with this investigation. I intend to conduct myself as a professional. Do we have a deal?"

"Depends."

"On what?"

"How much are you paying me?" The stunned expression on Sam's face made her smile.

When Sam and Suzanne arrived at Linda Schoolers', Linda greeted the couple with a warm welcome. "Gotta new dog, this is Katie," she said, holding the black Lab's leash tight. "Make yourselves comfortable in the parlor, I'll be right there." Linda disappeared with the dog and reappeared with a tray of tea and cookies.

"Sam told me you were interested in the Durham Center—"

"Yes. I filled out the form this morning."

"Would you like to test your gift?" Linda poured tea in three cups and handed one to Suzanne. "We can start with playing cards. It's a fun way to see how intuitive you are."

Suzanne sipped her tea, her eyes taking in the crystal balls and Edgar Cayce books on the shelf across the room. Linda withdrew a deck of cards from her pocket and shuffled them. She laid ten cards in front of Suzanne, face down. "Can you tell me the suit and number of the first card without turning it face up?"

"Jack of hearts."

Linda turned the card over. "Correct. How about the next one?"

Suzanne glanced at Sam.

"Eight of clubs?"

Linda flipped the card. "Eight of diamonds. Try the next."

Suzanne focused on the third card. "Ten of spades."

Linda lifted one corner of the card for a peek before flipping the card. Sam clapped his hands, encouraging Suzanne to go on to the next. When she correctly identified the remaining seven cards, Linda reshuffled the deck and laid out ten more cards. Once again, Suzanne got them all right. "Lucky guess."

Linda rifled through her desk drawer for pens and paper. "I'm going into the other room and I am going to do something, like nod my head, turn around three times, whatever ... I want you to write down on the piece of paper what you see. Sam? Come with me, you're going to witness my actions and write them down as well. When I finish, we can compare notes."

Sam followed the psychic into the other room. Suzanne expected Jack to show up to help her. When he didn't appear, she became unnerved. After all, it was Jack who showed her things. How could she know what was going on in the other room without his help? When Linda shouted "Ready," Suzanne picked up the pen and closed her eyes. She could see Linda's arms extended from her body. *Arm circles*. Suzanne jotted down her answer. When she closed her eyes again, Linda stood motionless. A moment later, she raised her right foot, put it down, and repeated the motion three times. Suzanne saw what she was doing very clearly, however, she couldn't see her face. Once the exercises were over, Linda and Sam returned to join Suzanne.

"Show me your answers," Sam said.

She handed him her paper. His scent was pleasant, clean. "I did this without Jack's help, so I'm not sure..."

Sam glanced at Linda. "You nailed it."

Linda said, "You have a powerful gift, young lady."

"So how do I explain Jack?"

"A mother holds a child's hand when crossing the street until the child is capable of crossing on their own. Those who help us from the other side have an agenda. They come in love, hold our hand until we're no longer in need of their services. You've proved something to yourself today."

"What's that?"

"You've lifted the veil. You're the one in charge. You still have work to do, but I think you understand that these visions are accurate. You are able to tap into certain frequencies and acquire information."

"I couldn't see your face."

"Practice. In time you will." Linda reached for Sam's arm. "Do you need further proof, Mr. Smarty-pants?"

"I guess, I..."

Suzanne said, "At least you know now that I'm not crazy. Not *yet* anyway."

"You're getting closer to the truth, but be careful," Linda advised. "We don't need you ending up in the river next time."

"What do YOU see?"

"I see a young woman who has a real chance at love, if she allows those around her to protect and care for her. Keep in mind, stubbornness delays manifestation."

Suzanne blushed. "Now look who has super powers?"

———

Sam handed Suzanne the keys to his car. "I'll be a moment." Suzanne headed out the door while he paid Linda her fee. "Thank you," he said.

"Take it slow, Sam. Love shouldn't be rushed."

He shook his head "I've never felt like this before."

"Keep a close watch on her. I have a feeling she hasn't seen the worst of it yet.

When he got into the car, he hurried to close the door so her sweet scent didn't escape. "Hungry?"

"I need to get home."

Once again, he stuffed his feelings inside. When he was with her, he begged time to stand still. *Someday*, he vowed. *Some day*.

Suzanne checked her email when she got home. To her delight, she found a response from the Durham Institute.

> "Dear Ms. Cash,
>
> Thank you for contacting us. We have an opening. Please phone us for the date and time.
>
> Sincerely,
> Beverly Klein
> Durham Psychic Institute Administrator
> 1-888-555-1212

Suzanne picked up the phone and dialed.

———

Dixon

Sheena Bradford struggled to get through her morning art classes. She'd managed a few soda crackers and ginger tea without vomiting, but the urge remained, and all she wanted to do was go home and sleep. She intended to stop by the pharmacy and pick up a pregnancy test. She wouldn't dare alert Dixon to the possibility of a baby without proof. She hurried through the parking lot to her car.

"Hey."

She flinched. Dixon leaned against her car his posture self-assured. He was the last person she had expected to see at this time of day, and his presence was unwelcome. Her nausea was getting the best of her. Seeing him sent her over the edge.

"Got the flu, Dix." She popped the trunk, grabbed a grocery bag, opened it, and puked.

"That's disgusting."

"Yeah, well—" The ginger tea left a sweet aftertaste in her mouth.

A gentleman would've turned away or offered assistance. Not Dixon. He made everything about him. Her predicament was not his problem.

"Your tits look bigger," He said, brushing past her.

She watched him walk away. She had never imagined herself as a mother, but an abortion was out of the question. Even if she had to give the baby up for adoption, she would carry the pregnancy to term. Goodbye dreams. So long aspirations of becoming the world's finest female architect. *Hello nine months of big mistake.*

———

Sam hung around the station going through old files. He still felt stuck. Same guy, different methods. Victims came from different counties, social groups, hair and eye color varied–he finger-drummed his frustration on the scarred surface of his desk. One commonality. Their age. He needed Suzanne's help. But first, she had to help herself.

He dialed the number of his bank. He would transfer money into his checking account, then prepay Suzanne's stay at the Durham Institute. She needn't know the money hadn't come from the department. One way or another, she would identify the killer. He prayed it would be before he killed again.

———

Sheena arrived home to find a bouquet of flowers leaning against her doorjamb. She rushed inside to open the card. Maybe Dixon wasn't a dick after-all. She expected an apology, instead his message chilled her to the bone. Watching You. *Why would he say that?*

She dumped the flowers in the kitchen sink, rushed to the bathroom and collapsed on the floor. The room began to spin and she spent the next hour dry-heaving into the porcelain bowl.

She heard a familiar sound in the next room. Her cell phone lay in the bottom of her purse collecting text messages. She peeked inside. Dixon's private number. *He knows.*

———

Dixon strolled through the station around 4:00 p.m., his vibe less approachable. Sam knew attempting to converse with his boss at this time would be pointless. Dixon's behavior seemed rigid at times. A drill sergeant who didn't refrain from kicking your ass when you didn't comply with the rules. *His rules.* One of which was knowing when he required privacy. Unless the building was on fire, or Air Force One landed on the front lawn, Dixon's office was off limits.

Dixon didn't tolerate whining, chit-chat, or bullshit. On the flip-side he could charm the bark off a tree when he wanted. He could make a person feel ten feet tall, or like dog shit on the bottom of his shoe. There wasn't an in-between.

Dixon had a way with the ladies. Sam figured women were no different than men when it came to admiring good looks. Pretty people were desirable, and Dixon rated twenty on the pretty people scale. Perfect build, perfect hair, perfect teeth. His educated, intuitive, savvy demeanor won him lots of votes during election time. Dixon was competent, he got the job done, but as a team player, he remained apart from the rest. He was the Sheriff. He gave the orders. His rules.

Sam was searching for the file on Amy Fitzpatrick when Dixon appeared at his desk.

"Still at it?"

"I'm working with Suzanne Cash, the woman who was found floating in the pool at the Marriott awhile back."

"As I recall, her case has been resolved. What are you doing, Metzger?"

"She's a proven psychic. We need her help."

"Proven by whom?"

"I had her tested. She's going for training. She's an asset." Sam plopped a photo of Amy Fitzpatrick's mutilated body on the stack of papers on his desk. "A person we can count on to help us catch a psycho."

"I don't recall you asking my permission."

"Don't you want to stop the killing?"

"Don't twist my words."

"I realize I haven't brought you up to speed on our last victim, my apologies."

"You going rogue on me, Sam?

"Just doing my job."

"What makes the information this woman provides so useful?" Dixon's argumentative tone riled Sam.

"She actually sees the murders. In time–she'll be able to identify the killer.

"Are you seriously expecting me to believe your woman is tapping into the guy's head?"

"So far she's been accurate with details. The timeline is still off, but she's closing the gap. At first, she saw the murders after they happened. Lately, her visions have gotten closer to the actual time of the crime. The vision she had recently hasn't happened yet."

"What did she see?"

"A young woman in her early twenties, most likely a student. She saw her carrying books. She also believes the girl is pregnant."

Dixon paled. "Is that so?"

———

Sheena decided she'd wallowed enough, vomited enough, cried enough. Time for action. She thought of her cousin who had moved to upstate New York after high school. Renee was two years older and ten years wiser. She would know what to do.

"Renee? It's Sheena. Yes, I'm still alive," Sheena chuckled, "but I need your help."

The conversation had gone better than she expected. Renee had changed jobs recently and moved into a two-bedroom apartment. Renee admitted that although single life was the way to go, hanging out in clubs and bringing home "strays" was getting old. "You'd love it here."

Sheena agreed. A change of scenery and lifestyle would do her good. She pulled a blank sheet of paper from her binder and began a list: sublet apartment, arrange for transcripts to be forwarded. Perhaps she could finish school in New York. Maybe life wouldn't be so bad after all. Renee seemed cool with the idea of her pregnancy but advised her to be sure before she went all wiggy. She grabbed the pregnancy test off the kitchen counter and headed for the bathroom. She was about to pee on the stick when her doorbell rang.

She remained silent, willing her visitor to go away. The bell rang again. And again. She finished her business and stuffed the pregnancy test under the sink behind a stack of Architectural Digest magazines and a box of tampons. She knew who was at the door even before the pounding began.

"Open up," Dixon yelled. A man down the hall opened his door and peered into the hallway. "She's upset with me," Dixon said, rolling his eyes. The man nodded. He understood. "I'm not going away, Sheena. If I have to stay here all night, I will." Dixon put his ear to the door. *Nothing*. His fist came down on the door once more.

The last thing she wanted was let him in. "Dix?" she called her voice weak. "I'm really sick. Can we talk tomorrow?"

He lowered his voice. "What the fuck, Sheena—why haven't you answered me? I've been texting and calling all afternoon."

"I must've crashed, Dix. I have a fever. 103. I ache all over. My head feels like it's breaking in two." She stood by the door waiting for his reply.

"Fine. Call me tomorrow. We have to talk."

"Ok, baby." Sheena pressed her ear against the door. When she thought she could breathe again, she heard him ask. "Did you like the flowers?"

Patti

For Suzanne, time was her nemesis. She had promised Steven she would find a job and move out soon, however, enrolling in the program at the Durham Institute would delay all plans.

"I'll be gone a month," she said.

"I'm happy you decided to go, Steven said. "I'm hoping you come back prepared to move forward."

Karen set aside a pot of pasta and joined the conversation. "Have you told Ben?"

"Not yet." Suzanne opened the fridge and gathered ingredients for a salad.

Steven popped a black olive in his mouth. "California's a 50/50 state. He can't keep what doesn't belong to him. Mom and Dad didn't leave you an inheritance to blow on a deadbeat husband. That money was to provide for your future. Ben will find another woman to squeeze."

"You make it sound oh-so-simple."

"He's a loser, and the sooner you realize that cutting him off doesn't make you a bad person, the better you'll be."

Suzanne placed the vegetables on the counter and walked away. Her appetite was gone. Her self-respect, iffy. She called Sam. Despite her promise not to involve him in her personal life, she needed his positive energy to boost her spirits.

"Hello?" Sam answered Suzanne's call.

"Ever been to Raleigh?"

"No, can't say I have." Sam opened a jar of pickles.

"I don't know what to pack."

"I hear layering is always good."

"I like that suggestion. I imagine the classes are casual dress. Jeans, T-shirts."

"For sure," he said, conjuring her in tight fitting-denim, thin fabric stretched across perfect breasts. "Wear one of those T-shirts with a profound saying on it like, Got Ghosts? or I Know What You're Thinking and I'm Telling Your Mother."

Laughter bubbled through the phone. "When do you leave?"

"Next week. I plan to book my flight tonight."

"Need a ride to the airport?"

"Not sure yet."

"You should be getting a call about the check in the next couple of days."

"Check?"

"The department will be picking up the tab for your enrollment, lodging, and food."

"But I thought–"

"I spoke with Dixon this afternoon. He's all for it."

"Dixon?"

"My boss. You haven't met him yet."

"When did I become one of the boys?"

"You could never be one of the boys. Is that the reason you called?"

"Would you like to join me for a beer?"

"How would you feel about ice cream instead?" Silence stood between him and destiny. "Beer's good too."

"I love ice cream, but it has to be just ice cream."

"Fine. No toppings for you."

Dixon powered on his computer and waited for the monitor to blink into life. One site he dearly loved and had planned to visit again produced a pop-up reminding him what a lonely man he was and invited him to play. He clicked on the link and typed in a credit card he maintained in a fictitious name. Soon, his screen blossomed with naughty teens. Firm breasts and tight assets jiggled and wiggled in hi def. He increased the volume so as not to miss the moaning and dirty talk. He watched two co-eds get it on, while a third critiqued and graded their efforts. The "A" she gave them came with two "Ss". Dixon sighed. The *ménage a trois* bored him before they reached a climax. He'd seen it all. Time to hunt.

He entered the link to one of his favorite dating sites. With a three-day weekend approaching, he could afford to take a little trip. A place where surveillance was minimal, someplace remote.

He scrolled down the list of singles, reading each bio as if he were shopping for a new car. Too shiny, too many miles, bumpers too big, headlights too small. He scrolled through fifteen pages until he spotted the one. *Patti*. Cute, perky tits, slim in the hips. Porterville, California. *Hello, Patti*. Her fresh face didn't fool him one bit. He knew her type. "Oh, Patti. I have a big surprise for you."

His fingers flew across the keyboard. His file held information fabricated from a death certificate he confiscated while working in Fresno. According to his profile, "Jerod Warner" was born in 1991. Dixon attached a photo, sun-bleached hair, muscle shirt showcasing nicely developed biceps with press-on tattoos he picked up at a Dollar Store in Reno. Sunglasses hid his eyes. His square jaw with three days of growth gave him a rugged look. It was an attractive photo, woman loved it. He received twenty-five to thirty e-mails a day from women all over the world wanting to date him. For now, Patti was his one and only.

"Hi, Patti. Love your name. Patti is fun to say. Like *sugar*. Spunky, sweet. Your profile says you're twenty-two, and although you don't *appear* older, your age defies your years. What I mean is that your eyes are soulful, like someone who has accumulated an extra decade in their head. Someone with depth. Quiet intelligence. Beauty and brains. My kind of woman.

"I'll bet you like country music one minute and classical the next. Am I right? If I'm wrong, forgive me. I love it all, so whatever genre you're into, I'm there. I listen to country when I'm grilling a steak, Andrea Bocelli when I'm my creating my special pasta sauce, but I have to admit I go totally old school and put on Luther Vandross when I'm hot tubbing under the stars. I like it all, even Bieber and Taylor Swift.

"I was quite shocked to discover you live in Porterville. My grandmother lives in Bakersfield. I'll be visiting her this weekend. Do you think we can get together for coffee, or dinner? I would love to meet you. Always, Jerod."

He attached his file number and hit send.

Dixon reread his lies, confident his identity could never be traced, he waited. Ten minutes later, Patti responded.

"Hi Jerod. I'm new at this. Am I supposed to make you wait before responding? You're very attractive and no doubt can get any girl you want, so imagine my surprise that you like country music, know who Andrea Bocelli is and like to cook. I would be happy to meet for coffee. P-Ville Coffee Shop is off 99, first freeway exit when you hit town, on your right. Can't miss it. I'm available after 2pm."

Dixon liked the eager beavers.

Patti, Patti, Patti, you made my day. P-Ville Coffee shop it is. I'll look for you at 3pm.

Dixon leaned back in his chair. He imagined little Patti on her knees, pleading in her sweet Patti voice. *Life is good.*

Patti phoned her best friend Christine. "I have a date with a hottie."

"Please don't tell me you met on the internet."

"Don't be a kill joy—I'm not running off to a motel with him."

"I'm serious, Patti. How do you know he won't slip you a roofie, take you over the border, and sell you to some brothel in Tijuana?"

"I'm not some moony sixteen-year-old. I told him to meet me at a coffee shop."

"Let me be a fly on the wall. I can sit in a booth nearby. Just in case."

"Just in case what?"

"I just don't have a good feeling about this."

"So I was safer going home with Ricky what's-his-name last week? I was drunk, I knew him for twelve-and-a-half minutes, and you tossed him my keys."

"I knew people who knew him. That's different."

"I'm a big girl. If I wanted this kind of treatment, I would still be living with my parents."

"Fine. I'll text you every ten minutes. If you don't respond? I'm calling the police."

"You watch too much CSI."

Patti hung up the phone. She and Christine had been best friends since pre-school. She texted,

OK but I don't want to see you!!!

What she really wanted to say was, "I don't want him to see you, because then he'll be more interested in you than *me*."

She gathered her chestnut brown hair in her hand and twisted it into a French knot. She sucked in her cheeks and did fishy kisses at the mirror. She pulled down the front of her T-shirt until she could see the swell of her breasts. She squeezed her arms together making the flesh pop into view. *"Hi Jerod,"* she said in her best Marilyn Monroe voice. *"It's so nice to meet you." Her eyes grew large. "Really? You think I'm pretty?"* She batted her lashes. *"You say the sweetest things."*

Patti turned to examine her backside. Not bad. Cherry-cheeks. Not apple cheeks, like most men liked, but her two little bubbles looked great in Daisy-Duke shorts, and the bra she purchased the other day would give her that Victoria Secret look that men drooled over. She let go of her hair, letting it fall around her shoulders. "Who are you trying to kid?" Her cat, Friskme, gave her the answer. "Meow."

"That's right my little friend. MeOW." She threw herself on the bed and stared at the ceiling. "On the other hand, he may be the man of my dreams."

Disappear

Sheena's insides churned as she ushered her friend Robert into her apartment. She prayed Dixon wasn't keeping an eye on her. She needed to move quickly. Robert was a big guy, capable of throwing a punch, clearing a path at a heavy metal concert, or getting an ignorant skater boy to move his car at 5a.m. when he had blocked Sheena's car, but she wasn't sure how he would measure up to someone like Dixon.

Robert minded his own business, never hit on Sheena, or made her feel uncomfortable in any way. He confessed one night after numerous margaritas that he preferred men, which made him accessible, but unattainable. When Sheena called to inform him of her dilemma, he was at her door in a heartbeat to hatch a plan.

"I know someone who will take the furniture off your hands, put some extra cash in your pocket." Robert ran a beefy palm along the arm of the sofa.

"Do you want my TV? It's two years old. Media friendly."

"I could put it in my spare room, but—"

"I can't take a thing, Rob. You'd be doing me a favor."

"Okay, but if you change your mind—"

"What about my bar stools? Can you use those?"

"Yeah, mine suck."

"Lastly, my bed. Mr. Asshole bought it for me. It's practically new."

"I don't know—I'd feel weird."

"It's all weird. But I'd rather see the bed go to a friend. Mr. Asshole paid a fortune for it."

"Ok. I can turn my den into a second bedroom, put it in there. Maybe even invite my sister to come down from Wisconsin. She's been dying to visit Sacramento."

"It's settled then." Sheena exhaled. "If you take the stuff to your place after I'm gone, that would be great."

"I'm gonna miss you like crazy. You're the only decent person in this shithole."

"I always considered this shithole affordable housing."

"I'd rather just beat the snot out of Mr. Asshole and keep you here."

"Promise me you won't tangle with him."

Robert puffed out his chest. "As long as he doesn't mess with me."

"Chances are he won't. And please, not a word to anyone that I'm gone. My rent is paid until the end of the month. If you move stuff discretely, no one will know I'm gone."

"Are going to let me know how you're doing?"

"In time. For now, you have to trust me. *No one* can know where I am."

"Why don't you just go to the cops?" he asked, throwing up his hands.

"It's complicated. I need to stay off the radar as long as possible."

"Okay. Give me your bags. I'll put them in my trunk and meet you like we planned."

Sheena reached up for a hug. "Thanks for being my friend."

He wrapped his arms around her and squeezed. "I'll see you in a couple of hours."

She watched Robert take the suitcases to the door. In two hours, it would be midnight. He would drive her to Orangevale where an Uber driver would take her to the airport in San Francisco. Her flight to New York was scheduled for 5:04 a.m.

At 11:42 p.m. Dixon did a little housecleaning on his laptop to make sure his history was clean. He picked up his phone and texted Sheena.

> You still sick? Maybe I should come over and take your temperature. From the rear.

Sheena panicked.

> Very funny. Temps down to 101. And my rear? Sprung a leak. Called the advice nurse at Kaiser. It's the flu all right. Want to come over and watch a movie?

Yeah, right. Dixon worked his thumbs.

> "And expose myself to the flu? No thanks. I know plenty of HEALTHY women."

Sheena's eyes welled with tears. How could she have been attracted to such a monster? Yet, she was about to give up everything to carry his child.

Dixon popped open a beer, and flipped through channels on his TV. He subscribed to all the premium channels, but never went beyond the package. He couldn't afford a footprint of lusty purchases on his cable bill. He went over to the closet where he kept an assortment of goodies under the floorboard. He moved his hiking boots and pulled up a wooden floor plank and grabbed a handful of DVDs. He chose the disc labeled "Sheena", slid it into his DVD player and settled into his favorite recliner. He wondered if she ever posed in front of the mirror like she posed for him. When she bent over in the video to give him a better look at her ass, he imagined a sharp object piercing her bowel. "You'd better not be lying to ol' Dix now, darlin'. That would make me very, very, *angry*."

Ice Cream

Although Suzanne usually dressed to please herself, in the back of her mind she remembered Sam mentioning his favorite color. Yellow. She rummaged through the box of clothing she had grabbed last time she had gone to her house and found the perfect top.

The mustard colored swing top worked nicely with her faded denim jeans and camel suede booties. After slipping five silver bangles over her wrist and jangling them, she removed them. Since her "incident," she felt uncomfortable wearing jewelry. Metal made her wrists ache. Rings felt too warm against her skin. Ben had noticed right away that she had stopped wearing her wedding ring.

Suzanne peeked out the window as Sam pulled up in front of the house. *It's just ice cream*, she thought, hoping he hadn't seen her in the window. She ran to the closest mirror to check herself. She brought her hands to her face, as if their coolness could lessen the heat she felt whenever he was near. When the doorbell rang, she took a deep breath. *Just ice cream.*

Sam took in the sight of her. "Wow, you look..."

"I'll grab my purse." She wanted to run, change her clothes, and undo the feeling of wanting to please. She hurried down the hallway and ducked into her room. When her heart slowed, and the lump in her throat disappeared, she picked up her purse and returned to Sam.

"All set?" She tucked her purse under her arm, avoiding his stare. "Sure you don't want to go for a drink?"

"Go to a bar? A noisy one, where intimacy is out of the question? Lose ourselves in the buzz, and not be responsible for fragmented conversation or misguided signals? You're not going to discourage me. And for the record, I don't bite."

"Perhaps you're the one who should be going to Raleigh."

"Being able to read people comes from being a cop. I'm especially good with lying."

"Who's lying? I thought maybe–" *How dare he be right*? "Okay, I'll give you the noisy part."

Sam yearned to tell her how delicious she looked in yellow, but although he sensed her interest in him, he'd play it cool. Suzanne's behavior reminded him of a horse he contended with when he was eleven years old. His Aunt Deb had given him a handful of carrots to make friends with the horse, which he did, at first. Once the carrots were gone, the horse played hard to get. Sam tried daily to win the horse over, but Aunt Deb assured him that the horse had a mind of her own, and that Sam need not take the horse's behavior personally. "She's fickle," his Aunt had said, "We got her that way. Someone must've mistreated her."

From then on, Sam took a different approach. He let the horse come to him. He always greeted her with a carrot but didn't expect her to do more than take the carrot and bolt. One day the horse surprised him. Instead of bolting, she nudged his hand. By the end of the summer, Sam rode her around the dirt track.

When they arrived at the "Ice Palace," Sam opened her door, but didn't offer his hand.

"What are these things?"

"They're little doughy balls, called Bobas. Try some."

Suzanne scrunched her nose. "I don't know—"

"Live dangerously!"

"What are those?" she asked, pointing to a container of colorful candies.

"Peanut butter drops." Sam spooned a few on his ice cream and moved to the next row of treats. He loaded his cup with sprinkles, fresh raspberries, marshmallow bits and chocolate shavings. He drizzled hot fudge and squirted a generous amount of whipped cream on top. Suzanne lagged, investigating each container's contents. She filled her cup with gummi worms and Oreo cookie bits. When she finished, she presented her masterpiece.

"What do you think?"

"You're sure you've never done this before?"

"I swear on my Mother's—" Suzanne paled. Her spoon bounced on the floor.

"What's wrong?" He grabbed her elbow to steady her. He led her to a table and sat her down.

The cashier rushed over. "You have to pay."

Sam handed the cashier a twenty. "Keep the change." He knelt by Suzanne's side.

"It's not her," she said.

"Who?"

"It's not the pregnant girl."

Blind Date

By noon Saturday, Patti had modeled six outfits for Christine. "Here's the plan," she said, pulling a lime green chiffon top over her head. "I'll drop you off in back of the café, then park in front. Give me five minutes before you come in, and for God's sake, don't look at me."

Christine threw a top at Patti. "Oh, that's right, I'm a fuckin' idiot."

"I didn't say–"

"Green doesn't go with your skin tone. Try the orange."

"I didn't mean—"

"I know. Trust me, I won't blow it. Just don't leave me sitting there forever."

"I promise. But just in case, you have an Uber app, right?"

"How many times have I Ubered your drunk ass home?"

Patti slumped on the bed. "What if he doesn't like me?"

"Don't be silly. What's not to like?"

"I'm not *hot* like you."

Christine handed Patti a pair of denim shorts the size of a toaster cover. Tiny rhinestones lined each pocket. "Put these on. You'll be fine."

Dixon circled the parking lot. If he parked near the dumpster in back, his car would be unnoticeable to anyone entering from the highway. The sun cast a shadow across his black sedan, making it almost invisible. He checked the clock. 2:55. Five minutes until show time.

A chartreuse-colored Beetle rounded the corner.

"Drop me off over there." Christine pointed to the far corner of the building. "I can stand in the shade."

"Wish me luck."

"Patti, he's gonna love you, stop worrying."

Dixon watched Christine slam the car door. *What do we have here?* He briefly thought about picking up the blond. Take her for a ride. Instead, he got out of the car and headed toward the café to meet Patti. He spotted her immediately, like a peach, ripened in the sun. *Easy-picking.*

"You must be Patti," he said, sliding into the booth.

"And you must be Jerod. Nice to meet you."

They both turned when Christine walked in and sat across the room. Dixon said, "You're much prettier than your photo."

"And you're much taller than yours."

"Really? Never heard that before."

"I have to say, I'm a bit nervous. You're my second online date, and the first one doesn't count because I had met the guy before. We went to the same high school."

"Lucky for me it didn't work out." Dixon said, "I think it will be different with us."

Patti smiled. "I hope so."

Dixon ordered coffee from the waitress, extra cream, and two glasses of water. "Cute place, never been here, as many times as I've driven past." He scanned the café. His eyes stopped at Christine. She smiled and reached for the sugar, her long hair spilling across her chest. She held his gaze until he looked away.

"You said you were visiting family—" Patti seemed to sense his interest had been pulled in another direction. "Your Grandmother?"

"Yes. She's eighty-three. I try to visit whenever I can."

"How sweet."

"She practically raised me when we lived in the Midwest. My mom worked."

"And your dad?"

"Which one?" He knew women were as attracted to a man with a dysfunctional past as they were to puppies. *How can I fix this?* clearly written on her brow. "It wasn't so bad." His mournful expression buried a hook between her heart and her better senses. All he had to do was reel her in.

"That must've been difficult for you."

"We moved around a lot. That was the only bad part. I liked to play sports. It was hard getting on a team."

"My father was a naval officer. We moved every two years, like it or not."

The waitress set two coffees and a dish with assorted creamers on the table and went back to fetch two waters. When she returned, Dixon took the glasses from her and placed them on the table. He waited until Patti had finished preparing her coffee to put on his clumsy act. As he reached for the creamers, he bumped one of the waters, caught the glass, but not before it had hit Patti's cup, spilling coffee all over the table.

"Oh my God, what a klutz–are you okay?"

Patti gasped when the hot coffee splashed on her lap and dribbled down her leg. She grabbed her napkin.

"I am so sorry." Dixon rose from the table, napkin ready, but Patti held up her hand.

"It was an accident. No worries." She hurried for the bathroom.

Dixon scribbled a number on a sugar packet and walked over to Christine. "You must think I'm a jerk, but I'm not. You are by far the most beautiful woman I have ever seen. Call me."

Dixon slapped a twenty on the abandoned table and walked out the door.

When Patti emerged from the restroom, Christine intervened. "He left. What an asshole. He spills coffee on you and leaves? So much for Prince Charming."

Patti saw the twenty on their empty table. What she didn't see was the sugar packet her friend slipped into her purse.

Christine listened to her friend cry all the way home. Patti was clueless when it came to men. And other things. Like friendship. Christine befriended Patti for one reason only. Patti provided her with a network of people to use. *Like Jerod*?

She thought of his eyes, his stare seductive, naughty. The way he responded to her smile. She imagined him stripping her naked, tracing every inch of her body with his tongue. Patti was right, she didn't stand a chance with a guy like Jerod. He wanted a real woman, one who could teach *him* a few things.

Once Patti was settled in with a deep-dish pizza, a box of chocolates, and a fifth of Captain Morgan, Christine complained of a headache. "My period must be early I never get headaches."

Two shots in, Patti began to unravel. "I don't know what I would've done if you weren't there. I'm such an idiot," she sniffled. "When am I gonna learn? When am I gonna get it through my head that men are cretins, and I'm better off alone?"

Christine nodded, "I know, you deserve better." She hugged Patti. "Don't drink the whole bottle. I'll call you tomorrow."

Christine walked two blocks to her apartment. Before she went inside, she plucked the sugar packet from the zipped compartment in her purse and studied the phone number. After a few seconds of deliberation, she dialed.

"I hope this is the beautiful blonde from the café." The man's voice was low and sexy.

"I'm a bad girl," she said.

"My favorite kind. What's your name bad girl?"

"Christine. My friends call me Chrissy. I know yours. Jerod."

"How did you—"

"Patti couldn't cut it alone. I was her support system—in case you were a creep."

"You ARE a bad girl." Dixon loved stupid women. "Where are you?"

"Twenty minutes from the café. I can Uber there."

Dixon didn't want anyone to be able to track her whereabouts, he appealed to her vanity. "Save your money for a new lip-gloss, or something. I'll pick you up."

"How sweet. Let's meet at the gas station on Meyers and the highway. If you're heading north from the café, it's the third exit. I'll wait for you by the—"

"If you don't want anyone to see you, meet me in the back."

"Yeah, it wouldn't be cool if Patti decided to—"

"*Exactly.* I get it, *bad girl,* see you soon."

Dixon patted the plastic pouch in his pocket. Enough Rohypnol to knock out a horse. *How I love the feisty ones.*

Christine ran up to her apartment for a quick change. She shimmied into a pair of hot pink thong panties, a matching push-up bra, a black mini skirt, and a tight black tank with cut-outs on either side of her mid-section. She lifted her breasts until they peeked over her neckline. She checked her image, sprayed herself with Victoria's Secret body scent and grabbed her purse and jacket. She had three minutes to reach her destination. No time for the phone buzzing in her purse. She was about to get laid and didn't want to spoil the mood with someone else's drama.

When she approached the gas station, she headed to the back, thinking about Jerod's hand up her skirt. She checked her watch. *He's late.* She checked her phone in case he had been trying to call. Sure enough, *1 Missed Call.* The number made her cringe. *Patti.*

Dixon watched Chrissy. People always did interesting shit when they thought no one was looking. For instance, Chrissy snuck a hand under her skirt to make an adjustment, exposing her bare cheeks. Then, she bent forward and scooped up one breast, then the other, until flesh swelled over her top. He wondered if Chrissy's mother ever warned her about guys like him. Did she warn her to be careful, choose wisely, and always have a back-up plan?

His own mom was too busy screwing everyone in the neighborhood to offer advice. And his dad? He didn't know the man, and he never bothered to pursue the issue. He grew up lying about everything, where he lived, who his parents were. Until he went to live with his grandfather, his mother pawned him off on one charitable person or another.

She always found someone to take pity on their situation. Her fictitious family helped out when they could. "Uncle" Joe registered him for school, "Aunt" Bev intercepted phone calls when he got in trouble. Nobody showed him the ropes.

He was on his own. Like now. But he had a plan. First, he intended to ravage her body. Then, he would offer her a drink. The drugs would make her easier to manage until they arrived at his secret hideaway. Then he would get down to business.

Suzanne mulled over her disaster date with Sam. One moment she was eating ice cream, the next moment she was watching a girl being flung down a flight of stairs. Blonde hair caught on a protruding nail, ripping a clump from the girl's scalp. "How old is she? How do you know she's young?" Sam asked her again and again. *I could tell by her scream.* "I couldn't see her face." She couldn't see the man's face either, which frustrated her even more.

"Dammit, Jack." She closed her eyes, willing him to appear. "If you're going to torment me like this, show me their damn faces." She opened her eyes and looked around her bedroom. Silence. "I hate you," she screamed.

Her packed suitcase mocked her from the corner of the room. Who are you trying to kid? You'll never be a *real* psychic. You're getting space junk. Static. Magnetic waves meant for someone more receptive. Someone more committed. *Someone who wants to catch a killer.*

She examined her image in the mirror. *Is that true?* What she saw was too many sleepless nights, deep creases in the middle of her forehead. "I thought you loved me, Jack," she whispered.

Her phone rang just then, ending the pity party. "Hello?" Even her voice sounded beat. If Sam noticed, he didn't say.

"I guess we can try again."

"Try what again?"

"Ice cream."

"My flight is at 2:00."

"I'm driving you, remember?"

"Sure. We can talk on the way."

"What's wrong?"

"I'm not sure I'm cut out for this paranormal stuff."

She hung up the phone feeling low. The last vision had been a doozy. She could almost feel *her* hair being yanked from her scalp. I want to catch this bastard so much I can taste it. So fine—keep your distance, Jack. I'll find him on my own.

———

Sam felt drained. He couldn't insist Suzanne go to Raleigh. What if the institute wasn't the answer? He dialed Linda Schooler.

"Let her go, Sam. It will be good for her to be around like-minded people. She'll get a better understanding of her potential, how to manage it. It's not a gift until you accept it. Right now, seeing young women being tortured and killed is acid to her soul. Once she learns to detach herself from the experience and sees her 'sight' as a tool, she'll be able to get back to herself."

"I'm going to miss her."

"Let her go. She'll come back ready to work, and, perhaps, ready to love."

"Am I doing the wrong thing by asking her to help catch this monster?"

"She was given the gift for a reason. We never get more than we can handle. The universe supplies us with challenges so we may learn and grow. She's a cactus right now. Once she realizes what she's capable of, and follows her path, she'll become a rose."

"Great, one has needles, the other has thorns."

"Both are equally beautiful and need tender loving care."

———

Chrissy

Christine didn't know what hit her. The last time she felt this wasted was in eighth grade when she polished off a bottle of vodka, popped a hit of speed, and smoked two fat bowls of weed. She remembered being in self-destruct mode over Josh Bellner. Josh had asked Kimberly Asay to the graduation dance. *I was the one who gave him a blow job.* Kimberly wouldn't even kiss him, let alone gobble his schlong.

Jerod had brought wine. *I didn't drink that much. Did I have sex?* The ache between her legs answered her question. *That's right.* Jerod sure knew his way around *precious*. And boy, did *precious* love a big strong man taking her *home*. "Six orgasms," she slurred.

"Don't even think about getting sick."

Her head bounced off the passenger window. Jerod's voice wasn't gentle like it had been when they were making love beneath azure skies.

"Where am I?" Her head swam a couple of laps.

"It's a surprise," he said, his tone flat.

Her brain had turned to pudding. She couldn't feel her feet. She must've dosed. The moon was high against a black backdrop. *No cars*, either direction. She willed her hand to reach for her phone, but her hand lay dead in her lap. Words squeezed through the fissures in her mind. *This should be Patti, not me.*

When Suzanne touched down in Raleigh, a sense of foreboding flooded her senses. *No, not here, not now*, she begged the unknown. The feeling lasted the duration of her ride to the hotel, and through the check-in process. The concierge asked her twice if she was okay, and a bellman insisted upon getting her bags. Safely in her room, she began to shiver.

Her knees weak, the room spinning, she collapsed on the bed. The room was dark, with the exception of a small light in the entry. She wanted to tear open the drapes, open a window, get some air, but she felt paralyzed by the night. She was afraid the stars would converge into a monster and swallow her whole.

Her jaw clenched as snippets of horror danced behind her closed eyes. Images taunted her, daring her to make sense of the scene. Blond hair coiled around a pulley, painted toes desperately reaching for the floor, screams melding with painful cries. The sound of a whip. Metal hitting metal.

Suzanne's body jolted upright. She tore at the drapes, unlocked the window, and gasped for air. Below, the street was empty. The night still. The world around her oblivious to the torture unfolding in some Godforsaken place.

Suzanne reached for her phone. "Sam? Call me." Her chin trembled. "Another girl has been taken."

Dixon slipped into the driver's seat and started the engine. The car belonged to a rich man who wanted to stay out of trouble. *No questions asked*. California was a great state to keep secrets. So many dark roads. So many abandoned shacks. His Grandpa had surveyed land back in the seventies. Dixon had been a snot-nosed little varmint who got under everyone's feet. His mom had pawned him off on whomever she could. Dixon tagged along on Grandpa's jobs. When Grandpa wasn't trying to fondle Dixon's genitals, he was teaching him the lay of the land. When Dixon turned twelve, the poor man had an unfortunate accident. *Writhed in the dirt while crows gathered, eager to peck at his eyes.*

Dixon marveled at the stars. Clear nights launched him into a fantasy world where he piloted his rocket ship into the next galaxy. Driving the desolate highway made him feel as though he were in outer space, navigating the Milky Way. Chrissy's screaming and crying left behind...he was *free*. As he drove past the 'P'Ville Café,' the "Closed" sign glared at him. *Damn, I hate that place.*

———

Sam sat behind his desk, a half-eaten burger churned acid in his stomach. His fries resembled boney fingers, his diet soda, now warm and flat. The room was quiet when the call came in, and he resented the interruption.

"Metzger," he growled.

"Sam?"

"Suzanne? Sorry, I didn't realize it was you."

"He's kidnapped another girl."

"Shit," he grumbled. "When?"

"I got the hit on the way to the hotel. I'm not really sure."

"Tell me what you saw." He ripped a sheet of paper from a pad he kept in his desk drawer and penciled in the date and time.

"She's blonde. About 5'5". Her hair is long, thick. I saw shackles. Chains. I can't see her face, or his." She paused. "He has a whip."

"What does the location look like? Is it the same?"

"Stairs. I saw stairs in the other visions."

"We haven't received any missing person reports fitting the description you gave me." He clicked on his browser and scrolled through the missing person alerts from other counties. "Are you okay?" he asked.

"It was all I could do to get to the hotel without passing out."

"I'm glad you made it there safely. What else can you tell me?"

"Stars."

"What about stars?"

"So many stars you feel like you're falling. I don't know what it means."

"I'm going over previous reports. There has to be something we're missing."

"I have a feeling these girls are going with him willingly. He's handsome, charming..."

"Ted Bundy? *Casanova?*"

"Svengali."

Svengali. She had used that reference once before. "You should get some sleep. I'll make sure I check my phone."

"You do the same."

"Goodnight, Suzanne." He ended the call, feeling unfulfilled. He wanted to chat about Raleigh, about her expectations, the food, anything to keep her on the line. He wanted to be there, tucking her in, kissing her goodnight. *What a fool.* He had promised himself he would never fall in love again, and here he was, feeling like a teenager with his first real crush. Cynthia Brightman had broken his heart in college. He had vowed never to endure that kind of pain again. And yet, the mere thought of having Suzanne in his life brought him joy. Once they caught Svengali, he would pursue her the right way.

Dove Johnson poked his head around the corner of Sam's cubicle. "Seen Dixon anywhere?"

"When's the last time you've seen Dixon in the office at this time of night?"

"I called him about an hour ago, his message referred me to the number here at the station, I just thought..."

"Thought what?" Dixon appeared behind Johnson.

"Surprise, surprise." Sam said. "Your date have a curfew?"

"Now Sam, don't gloat–my dates are all consenting adults. You know how I feel about breaking the law."

Dixon's grin said different.

Suzanne lay back on her pillow, her arm shielding her eyes from the bright lights. "Oh, Jack. How I relied on you." *How you broke my heart.* "And now this."

She slid her hand to the empty side of the bed, yearning to feel the warmth of another. *Sam.* She wondered what his touch would feel like against her skin. Would he be gentle? Aggressive? His lips appeared kissable, yet firm. His blue eyes softened at the sight of her. She had filed for divorce, despite Ben's objections. Once the fight was over, and she was free? *Free.* The word niggled in her mind, as if it came out of someone else's mouth.

Christine blinked. *Dark.* Pain radiated throughout her body. Heavy chains weighted her down. Her limbs were too weak to fight against her restraints. Metal circled her neck and ankles. Orange twine bit into her wrists. Her urine-soaked shorts felt cold against her skin. The air was dank. *Suffocating.* Her head pounded. Her ears rang. The welts on her legs pulsated in waves of pain. A stench assaulted her nostrils. Methane? *Cows.*

Her body shook, her teeth chattered. She opened her mouth to call out for help, but the tight metal collar turned her voice into a feeble whisper. She wished she'd never traded places with Patti. Too late. *I'm going to die.*

Raleigh

Morning in Raleigh sparkled. Suzanne stretched in her bed. Time to get up and face the world. Her first workshop began in an hour, just enough time to take a shower and grab breakfast.

Hot water pummeled tender muscles. The discomfort grew until her arms ached and burned. She caught herself running her tongue along her teeth to make sure they were intact. When she looked down, she saw welts on her legs. *How?* She rinsed and stepped out of the shower. The welts disappeared. The smell of methane made her search the room for the source. Nothing. *Am I losing my mind?*

She hurried up the steps of the Durham Parapsychology Institute. As she rounded the corner, juggling a cup of coffee and a bagel wrapped in a napkin, she collided with another student.

"Let me help you," the woman said, holding Suzanne's cup while Suzanne collected herself. "Name's Bunny Amendola. You here for the *woo-woo* classes?"

"I'm Suzanne. Suzanne Cash," she replied, shaking Bunny's free hand. "Woo-woo?"

"The family's been teasing me all my life about seeing stuff. 'There she goes with that *woo-woo* stuff again'" Bunny steered Suzanne down the hallway. "You don't get that from people?"

"I guess, a little. My brother thinks I'm a freak."

"So, what do you do? See ghosts? Bend spoons? What's your specialty?"

Suzanne wasn't sure how to answer.

"That's okay. I get it. It took me awhile to figure it out."

"If you have it all figured out, why are you here?"

"I died in a car accident, according to paramedics. I went from seeing dead people to being one of them, now I have an entourage."

"You have ghosts following you?"

"Spirits, actually."

"What's the difference?"

"Ghosts are more of an imprint in time. They're like stuck. They stay in one place. A spirit, however, can move about the cabin, so to speak. They show up wherever and whenever they please."

"I have—or had—a spirit. My late fiancé. He died in Iraq. He didn't appear until I almost died. Then he began showing me things."

"What kind of things?"

Suzanne broke free from the woman's company. She wasn't ready to divulge her reason for being at the institute.

———

Patti's thumbs worked the keypad on her phone, texting.

where are you? u mad at me?

Patti reread the dozen texts she had sent the day before.

wtf chrissy?? call me!!! thought we were friends. -:(

Patti tossed her phone on the bed. She sat at her desk. She tapped in her passcode and leaned back as her profile appeared on the screen. She scrolled through her messages, searching for a message from Jerod. "Asshole," she muttered. His profile no longer existed. No great loss, but what would she do without Chrissy? *Why can't I be more like her?* She decided to walk over to Chrissy's apartment. *Better to talk face to face.*

When Patti arrived, she noticed her friend's car looked like it hadn't been moved in days. Parking spots were unassigned, as a result, Chrissy took what was available. She never parked in the same place twice.

Patti walked up three flights of stairs and knocked on her friend's door.

"Chrissy? It's Patti." She put her ear to the door. "Chrissy?" She knocked again. "Come on Chrissy. Don't be mad, let me in."

Patti gave up and headed home. She didn't notice the black car parked close by. She didn't see the man watching her.

Dixon sank down into his seat. He watched Patti climb the stairs to Christine's apartment. He wished he could lure her into his car, take her far away where she would no longer pose a threat. He had never let one of them live before. He had taken a big chance with Patti. *Patti. Patti. Patti. Are you becoming a little sleuth?"*

Once she had given up on Chrissy, she walked toward him. He pulled his cap down, bent away from her line of sight, and began rummaging through his glove compartment.

After Patti had climbed into her VW Bug and driven away, Dixon relaxed. *Time is on my side.* He started the ignition and shifted into drive. He had an important meeting to attend. A serial killer was on the loose. *Can't have that can we*?

Christine's bladder burned. Perspiration beaded along her hairline. Occasionally a bead broke loose and trickled down her face. The smell of her own urine mingled with the smell of cows. She struggled against the orange twine digging into her flesh. "Patti!" she screamed. "This is all your fucking fault."

She had no idea how long she had been tied up. The muscles in her ankles and calves spasmed, her head felt like she'd been clobbered with a block of cement. *Stand up. Stretch.* She shifted onto her knees. Leaning forward, she rested her weight on her hands, intending to push herself upright.

"Ouch," she cried, plucking a sharp object from her knee. It was small, white, flat on one end, jagged on the other. "Nooo—" She kicked and screamed, but her memory froze at age eight, when she had placed an object like this one under her pillow. *For the tooth fairy.*

"What do we know?" Dixon settled against a scarred wooden desk, arms crossed, long muscular legs crossed at the ankle. "Who's first? Sam?"

Sam and his team had been working round the clock gathering evidence since the first murder had occurred earlier that year. Since then they had been scouring the internet and calling other precincts, collecting information on missing and murdered girls. One thing the girls had in common was their age. *Young and pretty.*

Sam said, "I've been working with a psychic. She's been providing me with details from the crime scenes. I feel we're getting closer to a description of the killer."

Dixon rolled his eyes. "Christ. That's all you've got?"

"She gets visions, sees the crimes being committed, pin-points details of the scene. I believe we're getting closer to finding the bastard."

"What happened to good ol' police work?"

Dove stepped forward. "Forensics concluded the girls have been brutally raped, beaten, and dumped in locations that are far from the crime scene. The lab verified the orange fibers found embedded in Amy Fitzpatrick's wrists and ankles matched the orange twine used on Jennifer Richmond and Twila Averose, the girl from Georgetown. Although the victims have been tortured using various methods, we believe there is just one perpetrator." Dove stepped back. "That's all I have."

"Why is that?" Dixon scanned the faces he had come to know over the last five years. Faces filled with apathy, defiance, resentment. A band of underachievers. His job was to lead these men, not babysit them. "Kids! How long have we been at this? Six, seven months? What the fuck you guys been doin'?" He turned to his men one by one, challenging them to respond. The room went silent.

"Whoever this guy is," Sam said, "I would bet these girls are not his first victims. From the get-go the crime scenes have been spotless, no prints, no DNA, his only signature is orange twine."

"Where are the profiles on these cases?" Dixon asked, eyeing everyone in the room. "See—this is what I'm talking about boys, do your fucking job!

Dove said, "Each scenario is different. Our perp has moved the bodies from the scene of the crime to a new location. Whatever evidence is being left behind remains a mystery. Until we find the location of where the girls are being murdered, we're stumped."

Dixon's eyes grew large, his voice rose a notch, his words mocking Dove's account. "Do we know HOW they are being taken?"

Dove responded, "All of them tested positive for Rohypnol, GHB, and Ketamine."

"You can't just buy that shit without some sort of trail." Dixon clapped his hands loudly, demanding everyone's attention. "Okay, let's get find out who's got the goods and who they're selling to."

"What about Suzanne?" Sam asked. "I'd like to get her on the payroll full-time. She's good, and once she gets back from the Durham Psychic Institute, she'll be even better."

"Seriously, Metzger, can't you find a better way to get a woman? Do you have to fuck around at the expense of our taxpayers?"

"We can't all be Casanova."

Dixon cocked his head. "Don't you have work to do?"

"Yes, I have work to do," Sam replied. *And I'm starting with you.*

Suzanne climbed the stairs to the exam rooms, following Olivia, the young docent giving the introductory tour. The first room she entered had black, padded walls. Instruments were set up inside the room and outside. "In here we measure the electromagnetic waves coming from your body. When we are in our psychic mode, we give off more waves. Those in healing mode, register off the charts. We have conducted this experiment all over the world, and the results have been quite remarkable."

The group meandered through the room, checking out the equipment. Suzanne closed her eyes and imagined being alone in the dark. She shuddered when she saw two eyes peering at her, like blurred watercolor paintings, yet the eyes remained, flat, deadly. Suddenly a girl appeared behind Suzanne's lids. Images flashed like lightening. *Cold, afraid, blonde.* The girl's knee bled on a concrete floor. Suzanne gasped. A tiny white object glistened in the palm of her hand.

"Hey!" Bunny stepped up behind Suzanne. "You okay? Looks like you saw a ghost or two, they're not mine, are they?"

Suzanne blinked her way back to the moment. "No ghosts. Lack of sleep. I could use a gallon of coffee. When do we break?"

"After the tour, we have three more rooms. Seriously, you okay? You're pale."

"Not a morning person, I guess," Suzanne said. "This is so cool. Are you getting anything?"

Bunny shook her head. "But I keep hoping."

"For what?"

"I'd like to tap into the collective energy of the group, wouldn't that be awesome? All thirty of us channeling together. Group consciousness magnified."

Suzanne wondered if everyone concentrated on finding a serial killer...*would they see what I see?* A man who stood nearby made a sour face. "We focus on *positive* energy," he said, his twisted features contradicting his message. Suzanne shot a smile his way and walked into the next room.

"Are you all familiar with the experiments of Dr. Duncan McDougall?" Olivia asked, her Vanna White gesture sweeping towards a low stainless-steel table hooked up to a digital scale. "His work substantiated that the soul leaves the body when we die. A theme that was explored in the movie, "21 Grams." This table was developed by—please, don't touch, sir," she said. Everyone looked around. No one else saw him but Suzanne. *Jack.* Olivia blinked, and he was gone. She chuckled, "Spirits love to touch the equipment."

Suzanne slipped into the hallway. "Jack," she whispered. For the first time in days, he appeared. "I thought you left me, again."

"You must leave here, Suzanne. Go home. She's not doing well."

"Who?"

"The girl. The blonde girl. Hurry." Before Suzanne could ask more, he vanished.

Suzanne raced back to the hotel, packed her things and booked the next flight home.

Christine ached all over. Her kidneys throbbed and burned. Her bladder felt gritty, her mouth, sticky and dry. If she didn't die today, she'd find a way to end her misery. *Bash your head on the concrete,* taunted the voice sizzling in her mushy brain. She had managed to quiet the voice when she lost consciousness some time during the night, but now it was back with a vengeance. Her screams left her hoarse, parched and swollen. She could barely swallow. Her arms were frozen behind her, her hands and feet numb. No more tears. Chills seared her skin and pulsated up and down her spine. Goosebumps gathered, stinging her skin. Bass drums boomed in her head, Bose speakers, best you can buy. Her vision blurred from the pressure behind her eyes. Hallucinations came and went. A man, his uniform tattered, bloody, his face kind, said, "Hang in there, kid." And she did.

Dixon didn't care about his victims. Once he got what he wanted, he became bored, ending the game. His position as Sheriff gave him certain privileges. How else could he maintain his appetite for killing? He thought about Patti. *Patti, Patti, Patti.* Something lyrical about that name. He smiled to himself. The wheels were turning. And then fate intervened.

"Call on line three, Sheriff. Deputy Chief Ipswich from Fresno says a girl called about her missing friend. Thought you'd like to take this one."

He took the call.

"Hey, Blake Ipswich here, got a call from a young lady, a Patricia Watson. Her friend has been missing a few days. Heard you guys were working on a serial murder case. Thought you'd like to question this girl she may be able to give you something you can use regarding your case up there."

"Thanks, Blake. Can't hurt." Dixon jotted down the information, ended the call and placed another.

"Hello, this is the Sheriff of Goldorado County, Jim Dixon, is this Patricia Watson?"

"Yes. My friend is missing. I haven't seen her for days. Her car is in the lot, she's not answering her door."

"What is your friend's name."

"Christine Bonnevier."

"Tell me about your friend. Is she single? Could she be with a boyfriend?"

"No. Chrissy doesn't have a boyfriend—that's why I can't imagine where she'd be."

"Can I get your information Miss—it is *Miss* Watson?"

"Yes—it's Miss. I'm really worried."

Dixon pictured Patti twirling her hair, a nervous habit she admitted to while chatting with him online. "Does this young woman have family?"

"Yes, but they're in Canada. Chrissy stayed behind when they moved back there."

"Have you contacted them?"

"No. I really don't know much about them. They're not close, I mean Chrissy rarely even talks about them. She's very independent."

"Independent?"

"She does what she wants, but she doesn't disappear or anything like that. We talk every day." Patti paused. Dixon sensed discomfort.

"What is it?"

"Well, we sorta had a fight. Nothing major. I had a meltdown, she left my house. I went to apologize—her car was there. She didn't answer the door. I've gone over to her place several times since then. She doesn't answer her phone *or* texts."

If you only knew. "Let's start with her address, I'll see that a patrolman is dispatched there. What's her apartment number?"

"How did you know she lived in an apartment?"

"You mentioned—"

"Did I?"

"Miss, I don't have time for games."

"I apologize. I'm being paranoid."

"If you can't trust the police, who can you trust?"

"I'm sorry. She lives at 321 Crest Drive, Fresno."

"Can I get your information as well?"

"It's 733 Brisbayne Road, Fresno. My cell number is 209-555-0809.

Dixon delighted in her naivety, *Patti, Patti, Patti.*

Patti hung up the phone feeling uneasy about Chrissy's disappearance. Speaking with the Sheriff made it worse. She expected him to say something comforting like "don't worry, or "I'm sure your friend is fine. Instead his words lacked empathy. Maybe he felt put upon because Christine's case was out of his jurisdiction. Whatever the reason, Patti felt low, and poured herself a glass of wine. *Settle my nerves*, she convinced herself. She mentally replayed her conversation with Dixon. She couldn't recall mentioning that Christine lived in an apartment, and it disturbed her. Something else niggled at the back of her mind. He asked if she were single. Why did that bother her? Perhaps her feelings were still raw from being kicked to the curb. Who does that? Who invites a lady on a date and disappears while she's in the john?

At least he paid the check. Big deal. She deserved better than that, right?

Chrissy always knew what kind of guy she was dealing with before she accepted a date. Of course, she didn't cruise singles sites. Guys gravitated towards her like bugs to a lightbulb. Patti was careful. She selected Jerod from hundreds of single prospects, read his profile, read between the lines. She had a pretty good sense of what was bullshit, what was truth. Being single was the pits. *Single.* Why did Sheriff Dixon want to know if she was single? "It is Miss, isn't it?" It wasn't the question...it was the way he asked it.

Dixon whistled along with Merle Haggard, "That's the Way Love Goes." In two hours and twenty minutes he would face his next victim, Patti. He had two hours and twenty minutes to come up with a story to convince her he was a nice guy, and how difficult it was for cops to date, and how he wanted nothing more than to help her find her friend.

About the conversation he had had with Patti earlier... she had questioned him about the apartment thing. He could've sworn she had mentioned Christine's apartment. What did it matter? Once he had her, his only concern would be how to punish her.

Sometimes he copied the work of the masters. The internet was a treasure trove of documented cases waiting to be recreated, like serial killer Alberto DiSalvo. *The broom stick jammed in Amy Fitzpatrick's vagina was a nice touch.* No, Patti deserved better. *Inspiration. That's all I need.*

———

Sam sat behind his desk reviewing the reports he had collected over the months. He paid close attention to time codes; when the bodies were found, when his men were dispatched, when everyone checked in at the scene, when they checked out. Dixon had rarely made an appearance. He had a phenomenal team working for him, and no one complained about his absence. Dixon had a way of getting things done without exerting much effort. Once in a while he reined everyone in for a shit storm, but for the most part, he was easy going—*if you don't cross him.*

Sam ran his finger down the list of possible characteristics of their unsub. Handsome, gregarious, intelligent—Dixon fit the bill. *So do a million other guys.* He tossed his pen on the pile and leaned back in his chair. He wondered if anyone else noticed Dixon's dark side. *Something in his eyes. Something he hides quite well.*

The dispatcher poked her head in. "Seen Dixon?"

"Earlier this morning, why?"

"He left right after that call came in, and I didn't have a chance to ask him about taking next Thursday off. I have a dental appointment. Root canal."

"Who was the call from?"

"Deputy Chief Ipswich from Fresno. He had some info he wanted to share. May be a connection to the murders. Dixon didn't tell you?"

Sam picked up the phone and dialed.

"Dixon."

"Jim, where you at?"

"Who wants to know?"

"Kelly said you got a lead."

"Kelly is talking out of her ass."

"She said the deputy chief called from Fresno, said he had a lead."

"Some girl reported her friend missing, and he thought it was connected to our guy. Turns out the two girls had a fight, nothing more. Anything else?"

"No, I'm good."

"I'm headed to Tahoe to meet a farmer about some land he owns up there," Dixon said, "What do you think about a shooting range? Maybe set up a virtual site?"

"I'm sure the guys would love it."

"Cool. See you when I get back."

Same distain he always felt when he and Dixon got into a confrontation. The man was a pro at putting people in their place. *One more feature of a coldblooded killer?* Sam's thoughts were interrupted by the vibration coming from his shirt pocket.

"Detective Samson Metzger."

"Sam? It's Suzanne. I'm calling from the Raleigh airport. I'm on my way home."

"What happened? Are you okay?"

"Jack is back. He told me another girl is in danger. He said she's not doing well."

"Did he tell you where she is?"

"No. But I keep seeing cows."

"Cows? There are cows from here to—" Sam's words came to a halt. *Dixon*. He said he was on his way to Tahoe to speak with a farmer. "Call me when you land, I've got to tie up a few loose ends."

What were the chances Dixon was their guy? He dialed a person he could count on to help.

"Dove, it's Sam. I need a phone number tracked."

"What's up?"

"Just a hunch I'd like to eliminate."

"It's not my fortè, but I can run the number."

"I'll be right over."

Dixon made a U-turn and headed for Placerville. He had an inkling that Sam wasn't finished digging. He needed an alibi and a place to stash his phone. *Just in case*.

When he pulled up to the Liar's Bench bar, he saw Laura Hughes leaning against the entryway smoking a cigarette. He parked at the curb, dropped his cell phone into the padded envelope he had tucked away in his glove compartment, and rolled down his window. "Hey darlin', don't you know by law you're supposed to be fifteen feet away from the building if you're going to kill yourself with one of those things?"

"Why Jim Dixon, I didn't know you cared." Laura took a long drag, tossed the butt to the ground, and smashed it with the heel of her boot. She sashayed to the window and bent down, giving Dixon an eyeful of plump flesh. "Where you been, stranger?"

"Around. Miss me?"

"You know it. Got a few minutes for a quick romp?"

"Not today sweetheart, I'm late for a meeting. Thinking about buying some property up here. Just stopped by to say 'hello' and yank your chain a bit."

"You know I like when you're frisky."

"Have you seen Detective Metzger hanging around?"

"Stiff dick?"

"Yeah, that's the one."

"Nope. Should I?"

"He's sniffing out a case. Thought he might start here."

"Any message if he comes by?"

"If he asks, tell him I went to see a man about a horse." Dixon picked up the padded envelope and handed it to Laura. "Will you hang onto this for me?"

"Does it bite?" she asked, pinning his eyes with hers.

"Just a little insurance. Be by later to pick it up. Maybe we can hang out for a while," he said with a wink.

Laura winked back. She reached in her purse, pulled out a cigarette and lit it, blowing smoke toward Dixon's car. He chuckled. *Bad girl.*

———

Christine mumbled a prayer. "Dear Jesus, I promise if you help me out of here, I'll change my ways. I'll be better. Smarter. Kinder." A pain shot from her abdomen to her back and she whimpered. "Please," she begged. "Either save me or let me die."

By the time the sun poured between the cracks in the blackened windows, she was still there, raging fever and all. She tried to open her clenched fists, but her hands were frozen. The tiny white object mocked her. She wondered who the tooth belonged to.

She gagged. Pain in her torso competed with the fire in her brain. Heat radiating from her face warmed the metal around her neck. When she exhaled, her breath felt hot on her chin. Something skittered across her feet. She was too weak to scream.

Patti peeked through the curtain when she heard her doorbell ring. A tall man stood on her stoop his hands shoved in his pockets. He did a little impatient dance as he waited. She couldn't see his face. Before she unlatched the lock, she called out, "Who is it?"

"It's Sheriff Dixon from the Goldorado County Sheriff's Department. I'm here to speak with Miss Patricia Watson."

When Patti opened the door, her jaw dropped. "Jerod?"

Dixon pushed the door open, stepped inside, and closed the door behind him. "This is awkward, Patti. I had no idea."

"What are you doing here? You're a cop?"

"Sheriff." He lowered his eyes and shuffled his feet. "When we spoke on the phone I had a sneaking suspicion it was you, but I wasn't sure. Have you heard from your friend?"

"No. I haven't." Confusion remained on Patti's face.

"Can we sit? I am here on official business, but first, I think I owe you an explanation."

Dixon placed a hand on Patti's shoulder and steered her into the living room. "Sit," he said softly.

She obliged, but her hands clung to each other between her knees.

"It's good to see you again. I feel like such a schmuck for running out on you like that, but I had to. There was someone across the room, a young lady, I picked up for prostitution a while back, and I didn't want to make a scene. It's not easy dating when you're the Sheriff of a small town. I try to keep my social life as private as possible. Sorry for lying to you. I would've confessed if we had had the chance to get to know each other better." Dixon reached out and touched her hand. "But right now, it's important we find your friend."

Patti relaxed. She leaned back against the couch. "I suppose it was my fault. After you left me, I was feeling sorry for myself. I drank too much. Christine isn't used to weakness, she's tough. She doesn't get hurt when she's rejected, as if that would ever happen. She keeps her head. She—she's not like me."

Dixon leaned closer and smiled. "No one expects you to be anyone other than yourself. What do you say we start over, go get a cup of coffee and figure out where to start looking for Christine?"

"Okay," she said, "Let me get a sweater."

Dixon patted the small packets he had tucked away in his shirt pocket. All he needed was an opportunity to slip one in her coffee. Better here than in public. "Hey Patti?"

"Yes?" She appeared in the hallway.

"Let me go get us some coffee. I can bring it back here. It's quiet. Better to talk."

"I can make coffee if you—"

"I saw a Starbucks down the street. I can be back in a flash. What would you like?"

"I like their Ethiopian blend. Two sugars, extra cream."

"How about a pastry or something to go along with your coffee?"

"No thanks. Don't need the extra calories."

He looked her up and down. "Please don't tell me you worry about weight... You're walking perfection."

Patti blushed. "Thank you."

"I'll be right back," he said. Once outside, he grinned. He had her right where he wanted her. *Patti, Patti, Patti.*

Suzanne's head ached. She had taken two aspirin, but the pain didn't go away. *I never get headaches.* She had asked the flight attendant to bring her water three times, and still, her thirst continued. Her kidneys felt tender and her bladder uncomfortable. Every time she closed her eyes, Jack appeared, dressed in fatigues, his pants torn, his jacket tattered. His face was smudged with black, his hair disheveled.

"Find her, she doesn't have much time" he said, blood oozing between his teeth.

Oh, Jack. Don't leave me. I can't do this without you.

Sam called out Dixon's phone number as Dove typed. A map popped up on the screen, giving the men a look at the area where the signal had appeared last. Placerville. *He said he was going to Tahoe.*

Dove clicked on the plus sign, enlarging the area. "Why does this number sound familiar?"

"No need to know that. I'd appreciate if you kept this between us."

"You think this may be our guy?"

"The signal is stationary."

Dove nodded. "Yep. This person isn't moving."

"Is that Main Street?"

Dove increased the size of the area. "Yep. Liar's Bench to be exact."

Sam patted Dove on the back and left the room. He had to check out the situation himself. Dixon wasn't one to hang out in bars. He knew better. Then again, maybe he was meeting the farmer there. *I have to be sure.*

Dixon paid for two coffees and took them to the condiment counter where he discreetly pulled a packet from his pocket and placed it between two sugar packets. He ripped open the tops and poured them all into one of the cups. He added cream, stirred and closed the lid. He added a splash of Hazelnut flavoring to his cup and a generous amount of cream. He stuck a stir stick in the slot on the lid to make sure he didn't get the two cups mixed up.

Christine and Patti. *Best buds reunite, drum roll please.* Should he ravish Patti first? Or wait and take her in front of Christine? *Won't she be the jealous one?* Little Chrissy, who'd thought she could steal the hearts of Patti's suitors with her rockin' body and wicked ways. *Let's see who's wicked now?*

Dixon remembered the way his mother had manipulated men with her stunning looks and voluptuous figure. He wondered how many times good ol' grandpa had dipped his wick in her tight little ass. *Like a dog with a bone, always wanting to bury it somewhere.*

When his mother was old enough to find her own bones to bury, good ol' grandpa turned to him. Shit runs downhill folks. The family legacy lives on, with one slight difference...*I like to torture and kill.*

His thirst for blood had come at an early age. Killing rats, mostly. There were plenty in the hovels he grew up in. Occasionally, his mom would pawn him off on someone who actually had a bed for him to sleep in. *G-L-O-R-I-A, Glor-i-a.*

Gloria Sutter owned a three-bedroom ranch, but she insisted he sleep in her bed. At twelve years old he had filled out and was one of the best-looking boys in town. He was mature for his age—*getting fucked in the ass does that to a kid.*

Round and robust, Gloria tantalized her little house guest with glimpses of her fleshy parts as often as possible during the day, at night she wore a flimsy nightie that crawled up over her bare ass. The first time she cuddled close, Dixon wasn't sure which part of her doughy body was what. When he slipped her his bone, she bumped up against him so hard she knocked him off the bed. After that she cut to the chase and rode him like a bucking bronco. He remembered once her breasts covered his face and he couldn't breathe.

Their little ritual went on for months. Not once did his mother stop by to check up on him or call to see how he was doing. When summer ended, Gloria was bored and sent him home.

Dixon demonstrated his newly acquired skills on a sixth grader named Kelly. At thirteen, her breasts resembled two sugar cones. She was very proud of her blossoming buds and hinted that she wanted him to touch them. One day after school she placed his hands on her chest instructing him, "Move your hands in circles, like this." When he squeezed, she cried. Later, she told her mother what he did, claiming it was his idea. The next day shit hit the fan. Grandpa had to come to school and bail him out. He spent the rest of the day between grandpa's knees sucking his way to redemption.

Memories ignited the rage that burned deep inside of Dixon. Patti would pay the price. *Just like the others.*

Sam parked on Main Street and walked toward the Liar's Bench. He poked his head inside. It was empty with the exception of a curvaceous redhead standing by the door, smoking a cigarette. "Excuse me," he said, "I'm supposed to meet someone here, tall good-looking guy, dark hair, early forties, have you seen anyone fitting that description?"

"You're a cop aren't you?"

"The court house is up the street. I could be a lawyer."

"I know who you are. If you're looking for your Sheriff, he left a while ago, said he was meeting a man about a horse. Or was it horse property?" She dropped the cigarette on the sidewalk and crushed it with her heel. "Any message if he returns?"

"No message, I'll catch up with him later.

———

Patti sipped her coffee as Dixon asked about Christine. "How long have you and Christine been friends?"

"Twenty-two years. We met at pre-school, Chrissy took me under her wing. I–" Patti set her cup on the table. "I can't imagine her taking off without a word."

Dixon took another drink from his cup. "The property manager said her place was empty. There was no disturbance. Maybe she had an emergency?"

"She would've called. She was mad at me, but I know she would've at least texted me that she was leaving." Patti picked up her cup and took a drink.

She began to relax. Her eyes were glazed, her speech dragged. Dixon moved closer to her on the sofa. He kissed her neck, unbuttoned her shirt. She kept talking about Chrissy in words that no longer made sense. Dixon took her to the bedroom. She didn't resist.

———

Patti's mind seemed like it was skipping tracks. Her thoughts kept wadding up in sticky clumps, her body felt detached. She could hear a voice cajoling her to do things she wasn't sure she wanted to do. She wasn't sure of anything, like whether her arm was really floating above her head or if her knees were connected to her legs. Were those her legs, or did they belong to the beast stealing her soul? He's a pretty beast.

Eyes the color of the sky, burning globes piercing her brain with commands. *Move.* What does that mean? Move? She was cement. A sculpture. A Mermaid with shiny green scales and a giant fin.

"Get up," growled the beast.

I want to, I really do. Can you hear me? Her words were clear, but her mouth was frozen to her face. The floor looked so far away. *Where are my clothes?* Firecrackers exploded behind her eyes. *Where are my feet*?

Sam called the office. He needed to check with Dove regarding Dixon's phone. Suzanne was on her way back home, and he had to finish up a few things before he dealt with her. Why had she come back so soon? He hoped he hadn't made a mistake by sending her to Raleigh.

He dug in his pocket for his phone. "Metzger—"

"It's Suzanne. I just landed. Has anything happened?"

"What do you mean?"

"Has another girl disappeared?"

"Not that I know of. Why? What are you getting?"

"She's blond. Young. She's in pain."

"I'll pick you up in twenty minutes."

"I'll be waiting," she said.

Sam swiped his hand over a day's worth of stubble. He was anxious to see her, but now wasn't the best time. He dialed Dove.

"Would we be able to pick up a phone signal if it was out of cell tower range?"

"Not with the equipment we have. Did you hit a dead end?"

"Yeah. The signal stopped at Liar's Bench. The owner wasn't there, but according to a witness, the owner wasn't far away."

"Placerville is spotty, but the signal we had was strong. What makes you think the owner has the phone with him?"

"Can't be sure. The person I spoke with didn't mention that the phone was left there."

"Let me know if I can help," Dove said, ending the call.

Sam stared out his driver's window. His mind executed a run-down of his morning beginning with the conversation he had had with Dixon.

Something wasn't gelling. "I'm watching you," he whispered. He picked up the phone and dialed the dispatcher.

"Kelly, it's Sam. Do you have the message from Ipswich?"

"Sure do," she said. "Want me to text it to you?"

"Yes, please."

"Sending," she said. "Anything else? I was planning on going to lunch."

"A little late for lunch isn't it?"

"I promised HR I'd cover phones for them while they went to lunch. They're short-handed today."

"Have you heard from Dixon?"

"Not a word. Is he missing again?"

"Excuse me?"

"Sheriff Dixon does a great job, he's hard to keep track of sometimes."

"He's not answering his phone."

"Which one? He has a few phones."

"How does he rate a few phones?"

"Uh oh, I let the cat outta the bag, didn't I?"

"No, I'm giving you grief. I'm sure Dixon has good reason for having more than one phone. Do you happen to have the numbers handy? I haven't been able to get a hold of him all day."

"I have to get permission from him before I give those out."

"I understand." Sam started his ignition. "Check me out for the afternoon, I'm meeting with someone about the Fitzpatrick case. If Dixon calls in, have him give me a jingle."

"Sure, Sam."

He rolled down the window. The weather was gorgeous, and he needed a little sunshine in his life. He dialed Chief Ipswich."

"Chief, Sam Metzger from Goldorado County. I understand you received a call from someone claiming her friend was missing."

"Why yes, I spoke with your Sheriff about it this morning. He said he would handle it, is there a problem?"

"No. No problem, I would like to follow up on the call. Do you have a description of the missing girl?"

"I do, hold on."

Sam listened to an instrumental version of "Raindrops Keep Falling on My Head" while on hold.

"Sam? Her name is Christine Bonnevier. She's twenty-seven years old, five foot seven, one hundred twenty pounds, blond hair and blue eyes. She was last seen at Patricia Watson's home in Fresno."

"Patricia Watson is the person who reported her missing?"

"Yes."

"When did she call?"

"Few days ago. She said she thought Christine would show up at home. When she didn't, she got worried."

"Was anyone dispatched to check out Christine's home?"

"I sent an officer there when I got the call. There's no sign of wrongdoing. The lock wasn't busted, her place was immaculate–her car was even covered."

"Her car was in the lot?"

"Yep. A pretty little Mustang. According to my deputy, she takes really good care of it. I spoke with Jim Dixon about this case. He didn't think it was connected to your cases up there. Are you disagreeing with his assessment?"

"No. I wanted to follow up to make sure we didn't miss anything."

"If we find anything, I'll let you know."

"Thanks, I do have one question."

"What's that?"

"Are there many dairy farms close by?"

"Is the Pope Catholic?"

"I kept smelling them, seeing them. Cows everywhere," Suzanne said. "I don't know what it means. And Jack—he wasn't the same as when I first saw him. His uniform, it's tattered, he's hurt." She turned to Sam. "Is this ever going to stop?"

Sam took her bag. "I don't know."

She stared out the window as they drove down the freeway. "Hungry?" Sam asked.

"No. Yes. I don't know."

"Okay, the 'no' gets a burger, the 'yes' gets something a little more substantial, and the 'I don't know' gets a surprise. Which is it?"

"Surprise me."

Sam pulled off at the next exit and wound his way through Folsom. "I hope you like Mexican." He parked and waited until she unfastened her seatbelt before adding, "I'm glad you're back."

They were seated at a booth by the window. "How was Raleigh?"

"Interesting. I met a few nice people. Can't say I made life-long friends. In fact, some were kinda weird." She chuckled. "I guess I fit right in."

"I would never say such a thing about you." He paused, then said, "I missed you."

Suzanne fiddled with her fork. "When this is over, I hope we can remain friends. I do like you..."

"I hear a 'but' coming—"

"But—after we catch our killer, we can talk about how to continue being human. Emotions and all."

"Deal. What are you going to order?"

"She's starving."

"Did you eat on the plane?"

"No, she's starving. She's dehydrated and starving."

He placed the menu aside. "Who is *she*? Can you get a name?"

"Tooth Fairy. I keep hearing 'Tooth Fairy'." She opened and closed her palm. "It's in her hand." Suzanne's face crumbled. Tears sprung from her eyes.

Sam pinched the bridge of his nose. "Amy Fitzpatrick. Many of her teeth were missing."

Suzanne cupped her hand over her mouth.

"What is it?" Sam moved around to sit next to Suzanne in the booth. He gathered her in his arms. "You're safe." He held her wracking body close to his until she stopped shaking. "Shhhh...you're okay, no one is going to hurt you. We'll find the girl. I promise this horror will end."

Dragonflies

Patti's hands were tied behind her back. She felt detached from her body parts, especially the parts between her legs. Images of chickens, beheaded with a dull knife, danced in her head. She hummed a tune. A lifeless drone, driving Dixon to the brink. "Shut up you stupid bitch!" He shouted, but Patti didn't quiet herself. Inside her mind, dragon flies with sharp teeth gathered around the headless chickens. Surely it was their buzzing the beast referred to. She had no power to make them stop. *I always thought dragonflies were vegetarians.* In another part of her brain, tiny feet shuffled through sand on a cement floor. Gritty little slides, moving back and forth, back and forth. *Ch-ch, ch-ch.* Her inner child cried out in pain. Her mother's voice responded. "*You poor thing. You miss the beach don't you? Maybe when your body parts return home, you can visit the beach*"

Patti could feel the hot sun beating on her face. *Where's my bathing suit? Can someone bring me a towel? I'm all wet.*

Dixon forged ahead, despite the urge to pull over and beat Patti bloody. The tape covering her mouth didn't prevent her from droning on and on. Her humming reminded him of good ol' grandpa after he tied one on and fell asleep in his Barcalounger. Time was ticking away. He needed to dump Patti at the house and get back to Placerville before five. *Doesn't leave much time for a reunion celebration.* "Too bad," he whispered. "I was really looking forward to that."

When he arrived at the house, he parked close to the door and dragged Patti out of the car by the hair. He sang a little ditty. "Get 'em by the hair, yes, get 'em by the hair, *cuzzzz*...when you get 'em by the hair they follow you any-where."

Chrissy opened one eye when she heard the car door slam. Fear pumped the last of her adrenaline to her heart, and it beat like a trapped animal. She didn't expect to see what Dixon was pulling behind him. *Patti.* She swallowed her scream afraid he would kill her or worse. Instead she closed her eyes and pretended to be unconscious.

She heard Dixon talk to Patti as he chained her to metal hoops, fastened underneath the staircase. "There," Dixon said, dropping something on the floor. "You ladies don't stay up too late, now." His laughter, nails on a chalkboard

Chrissy heard him mount the steps, slam the door, and start the car. When she heard the spray of gravel, and the sound of the engine fade, she opened her eyes.

Patti stared ahead as if she were alone in the room. Tape hung loose from her cheek. Chrissy whimpered. *We're fucked now. Really fucked! Who's going to save us? You were my only hope. Damn you, Patti Watson. Damn you!*

"Patti," she whispered. Patti's breathing seemed shallow, and Chrissy noticed blood caked above her right eyebrow, and below left her earlobe. The sun would be gone in the next half hour. The light seeping through the cracks would be gone, and they would be left alone in the dark.

"Patti, it's me Chrissy. Look at me. You can't give in to the pain. We have to get out of here."

Patti remained silent.

Suzanne fought for composure. One thing she had learned in her lone workshop in Raleigh is that fear breeds fear. Her visions were interpretations her brain had compiled from the bits of information she was picking up on. She was a receptor for energy traveling through the ether. She was the vessel into which the information flowed. If she could focus on the information and put her feelings aside, she would be able to assimilate the message without experiencing fear. She also knew it took practice to be able to separate the two. Right now, her mind was filled with chatter. And humming. Dappled sunlight. Sand. *Where is Jack*? When she opened her eyes, she realized Sam was staring from across the table.

"I—I am picking up something, but I'm not sure what. It's not the same as–"

Suddenly it all made sense. "Oh, my god. There are *two* girls," she said.

Sam turned to the window.

Suzanne placed her hand on top of his. "You're keeping something from me—"

"We got a call from Fresno this morning. A young woman reported her friend missing. I tried to call her to get more information, but she's not answering her phone. Sheriff Dixon claims he spoke with this young woman, concluded the two girls had had a fight, and there was nothing to be concerned about."

"You're not convinced?"

"I suspect there is more to the story."

"Have you discussed it with the Sheriff?"

Sam faced her. "Dixon's the kind of person you don't contradict unless you have all your facts."

"What do you need?"

"A trip to Fresno. You in?"

"I'm in."

Dixon arrived in Placerville at 5:04 p.m. He entered the Liar's Bench and took a seat at the bar. Within minutes of his arrival, he felt warm hands massage his shoulders.

"Didn't think you were coming back, cowboy." Laura's fingers dug deep into his muscles and he moaned.

"And miss out on the best massage in town?"

"My magic fingers can do wonders for your stress. Lover."

"Who says I'm stressed?"

"Muscles don't lie. Unless you been haulin' sacks of cement all day."

"It's been a long day."

"Then let's get you comfortable and see if we can't loosen you up a bit."

Dixon slid off the stool and followed Laura through the bar to a stairway, left of the kitchen doors. The steep entry smelled musty and old, but he didn't mind. He'd been in worse places, and right now Laura was a welcome reprieve. He knew her mouth was as skilled as her hands, and a blowjob was just what the doctor ordered, but before he took another step he asked, "Where did you put that pouch I gave you?"

"It's upstairs. I kept it safe and sound for you."

When Laura handed Dixon the pouch, he patted her backside and excused himself to the bathroom. He closed the lid to the toilet, sat down, and ripped the envelope open. He poured the phone into his hand and tossed the envelope aside. He pressed the "on" button and waited until his phone came to life. Six voice messages. Two from Sam Metzger. One from dispatch. The other three were from ladies he had met on the internet. He listened to Sam's message first.

"Jim, it's Sam. I'll be picking Suzanne up from the airport today. I would like you to meet her. Can we arrange that soon? Thanks. Bye."

He replayed the message, analyzing Sam's words. The last thing he needed was some stiff-dick monitoring his every move. He pressed the button to return Sam's call.

"Sam–it's Jim. The cell service here sucks. I just got your message, what's up?"

"I wanted to let you know Suzanne is back from Raleigh. You two should meet. I think she's going to be very valuable to our investigation."

"I have this deal I'm working on, and I'm in meetings all week with the Mayor. How about next Thursday?"

"Next Thursday? We're dealing with a serial killer!"

"We haven't got a chance in hell of catching this guy until we get more leads–we've already been on this what–six months? Longer? What the fuck is a week?"

"Do you want an update if we come up with anything sooner?"

"Yes. I expect to be kept in the loop."

"How did the meeting go today? Did the farmer agree to sell his land?"

"After a fifth of whiskey and a million stories about him and Old Blue, he said he'd take my offer into consideration." Dixon paused. "Anything else?"

"No, just curious. The range sounded like a great idea, that's all."

"Good. Go home. I've got a date with a beautiful masseuse."

Dixon checked his teeth in the mirror and stuck out his tongue. *Nope, no lies there.* He pocketed his phone and went to join Laura.

He found her already undressed down to her black lace bra, panties and garter belt. For a woman of fifty plus, she was in fabulous shape. Toned, and large breasted. She arranged her hair at the nape of her neck and patted the bed. "Come here handsome. Let mama take care of you."

Dixon unbuttoned his shirt and dropped his pants. Laura took care of the rest. After bending down to remove his socks, she dipped her hand into his underwear and whispered sweet nothings. By the time he was naked, she had him so aroused, he was ready to explode. He grabbed her hair in his fist and thrust his hips into her face.

"You don't have to play so rough, cowboy," she cried, gagging.

"C'mere," he said, pulling her down on the bed. "Is this what you want?" He slipped his hand between her thighs.

Dixon rolled on top of her and spread her legs. "I have what you want," he said, burying himself deep inside her.

———

Bad News

Chrissy stretched her foot toward Patti, but it wouldn't reach. "Patti? Patti, it's Chrissy. Wake up." Patti's limp body didn't move. She looked like a rag doll, chained to a four-by-four post.

Patti stirred. *Or did she?* The room filled with shadows in the evening light. Did Patti's eyes flutter? *Or am I seeing things?* "Patti?" She moaned, "Patti, we're going to die"

She heard metal scrape the floor.

"Patti? It's me Chrissy. I'm here."

"Chrissy?"

"Yes! Oh God, yes!" Chrissy scooted as far as her chains would allow. Her foot stopped inches from Patti's.

"Chrissy?"

"I'm here. Are you hurt?"

"Chrissy?"

"Patti, save your strength. Try and sleep. Tomorrow morning, when it's light, we'll figure something out."

"Have to tell—"

"Shhh, I know, don't talk—"

"The man, he's a cop."

Urine dribbled down Chrissy's leg. This was not good news.

Fear

Sam felt good riding next to Suzanne. The sunset cast golden rays across her face giving her an ethereal glow. She smelled sweet, like lemon blossoms and summer rain. He wanted to touch her. Hold her. Kiss her soft lips. Bury his face in her hair. *Never let go.*

As if hearing his thoughts, she turned to him. "How have you been?" Her smile, his kryptonite.

"Busy. Trying to figure out this guy's moves."

"Are you taking care of yourself? Eating, sleeping. Listening to great music and smelling the roses?"

"Now that you're back, I think I can check off most things on that list." He glanced her way.

"I missed you." She blushed. "Even though I shouldn't."

"Any developments with your divorce?"

"Ben is fighting to keep the house. It won't happen. He can't afford to pay for the upkeep, and I'd hate to let it go."

"Do you plan to stay in the foothills?"

"I don't know. Is there a reason I should?"

"It would be nice to get to know you better. Is that reason enough?"

"I want to stay as far away from Ben as possible. I hope you understand."

"Yes," he said. He turned up the volume on the radio, allowing each of them time to let their feelings percolate.

"My goal is to get a job and to pay my brother back," she said. "He's been more than generous with me. I hope that that this new acquired gift presents me with opportunities to make a living. It doesn't have to make me rich, but I will have to eat, keep the lights on, take in a movie now and then."

"Fair enough. Let's catch our killer and go from there."

"Deal," she said.

When Sam turned into the drive leading to Patricia Watson's apartment, Suzanne groaned.

"What is it?"

"Patti isn't here." She jumped out of the car and ran for the trees

Jack stood between two tall pines, his face filled with worry. He paced back and forth, but he didn't look her way. "You have to stop him, Suzanne." Suddenly the sky went dark. She heard a clinking sound, metal, hitting metal. The stench of cows filled the air.

"Where are they? Help me find them."

She closed her eyes and let the images flow. A stairway, a dank room, cement floor. Chains hung from the rafters. A tooth. She could hear mewling. A car door slammed. Silence. Then screams. Fear, like smoke, flowed through the cracks in the window, rose high in the sky, circled the sun, and exploded into thin air. Darkness fell like a blanket, smothering, suffocating—*I can't move*. Suzanne fought to free herself.

"Suzanne!" She heard a voice. *Far away*. No trees. No birds. Only tall weeds. A rusted tractor stood sentinel in front of a broken-down shack. A tin roof, collapsed on one side, made the place look uninhabitable. Padlocks on the doors said different. Etched patches of black reminded her of kindergarten artwork. *Windows?* The image shimmered, then quickly dissolved. She saw Jack, paler than before. Sadness touched the handsome face she'd once loved. And then he was gone.

She felt a hand on her shoulder. A warm, loving hand. Sam's hand. Somehow that scared her as much as her vision.

"I saw where the girls are being held. It's a run-down shack, in the middle of nowhere." She rubbed her brow. "How are we going to find it?"

"I have an idea," he said, grabbing her hand and helping her into the car. "There's a café nearby. I brought my laptop, we can check Google Earth, see if you recognize the place."

Three miles later, Sam pulled into parking lot of the P-Ville Café.

Once inside, he placed his laptop on the table. Suzanne ordered two coffees from the waitress and got a Wi-Fi password.

"I'm on," he said, typing in their location.

As they sipped coffee and scanned the area, Suzanne's hopefulness began to wane. "I don't see it," she said, her voice dropping low.

Sam keyed in another area. He moved his finger on the mouse, moving the cursor until he found wide open spaces. "Here, take a look." She moved closer. He breathed in the scent of her hair, studied the curve of her jaw, the shape of her ear. Her lashes were long and thick as she blinked. He imagined waking up to her profile every morning and felt more determined than ever to end this nightmare.

"Let's see if we can get a closer look." He moved the cursor to a deserted area and expanded the view. A herd of cows appeared. He zoomed out and moved the cursor.

"Look for a tractor," she said. "There's an old tractor in front of the shack."

"It's getting dark," he said. "If we don't find it soon, we'll have to try again tomorrow."

"She doesn't have much time."

"The blonde?"

"Yes."

He didn't speak. He kept moving the cursor on the screen, zooming in and out each time he saw a structure, or vehicle.

"Stop!" She leaned forward until her nose about touched the screen. "That's it," she said, poking the screen with her finger. "That's the place."

Orange Twine

Dixon walked into the night, and gazed at the stars. Exhausted from his romp with Laura, he decided to go home rather than drive back to Fresno. A good night's sleep would recharge his batteries, get him ready for more fun with the girls.

Now that the world was quiet, his thoughts took a left turn and dead-ended with Sam Metzger's voice in his head. Why did Metzger feel compelled to check up on him? And what did that bitch psychic know? He'd worked hard covering his tracks. He had the perfect place to take his victims, he mixed things up so he didn't settle into a pattern. His ego allowed him one signature, orange twine.

No one would ever find the house. Grandpa's house. He had brought his first victim there twenty-two years ago. He was eighteen.

Colleen Crosby was sixteen, a runaway from Des Moines. Her childhood sounded similar to his. Crack-whore for a mother, deadbeat dad. Uncles who played hide the banana from the time she was seven. He picked her up hitchhiking on highway 99, she was grateful for the ride. She said she appreciated having someone to talk to in her southern drawl, adding, "You're about my age, aren'tcha?"

Her journey west included truckers from all fifty states. She reeked of sex, pot, and beer. Good thing he had a hose to wash her down before he fucked her three ways to Sunday. Unlike the other girls, she knew how to handle her drugs.

She enjoyed the sex, went with the flow. No freaking out like the others, in fact, the orange twine was her idea. *Tie me up, baby, do me.* Colleen dug the abuse. So much, she laughed in his face when he slit her throat. He knew then he would kill again, not only for the thrill, but because every bitch he killed lowered the number of women who could reproduce. *Can't stamp out the female population, but heck, I sure enjoy trying.*

———

Open Fields

Chrissy lost consciousness. How long, she couldn't say. She awoke to her friend's lifeless silhouette dangling in the dark. She shifted her weight to stimulate circulation in her ankles, but as soon as she separated her knees her bladder spasmed, sending a shooting pain from her groin to her back. Urine wicked across her denim shorts. The fabric soaked up the liquid and clung to her skin. A drop in temperature called for another round of spastic chills. Her body shimmied, her skin burned. Her teeth chattered. "Patti. Patti? Patti–p-p-please—*wake up*."

Sam and Suzanne drove for hours. Miles of open fields, unmarked roads, like searching for a needle in a haystack. Suzanne's head throbbed. She felt as though she_were the victim, the prospect, hard to bear. Sam stole glances her way, his expression as weary as hers. She knew he related to her discomfort but felt helpless. Yet, his warmth was genuine, something she could grow accustomed to. Her soon-to-be-ex-husband Ben lacked emotion. She had convinced herself his compassion deficit was due to his illness, a symptom of bi-polar disorder. And so, she dealt with the void. *Even got used to it.* Sam was a breath of fresh air. She wanted to breathe deeply, but fear of another broken heart kept her from letting go. She was drawn to Sam. He excited her. When she wasn't dreaming of Jack, or dead girls, his handsome face filled her dreams and she imagined living her life by his side. Happy. Fulfilled. *Loved*.

Sam interrupted her thoughts. "Over there. Look familiar?"

She recognized star thistle, mare's tail, and fiddleneck. "Can we get closer?"

As Sam steered his Land Rover down a rutted path, a structure appeared in the distance. A high pitch sound rang in Suzanne's ears. There it was, the shack with the collapsed roof. "Yes. This is it."

Sam slowed down. "I don't want to get too close." He shut off the engine. "Listen."

"I don't hear anything."

"That's good. No dogs." Still, the house could be booby-trapped, and he didn't want to take any chances. If Dixon was their killer, they'd need to be cautious. Sam couldn't imagine him being sloppy. "Stay put. I'm going to take a look." Sam switched off the interior lights and opened the door.

"Don't leave me here. I promise to be careful."

"All right, stay close behind me." As they neared the shack, the pain in Suzanne's head increased. Soft cries filled her brain like swarming wasps. She held her head, but the sound didn't stop; the smell of cows so pungent, she wanted to retch. And although the temperature had only dropped to sixty degrees, it may as well have dropped to thirty.

Chrissy shivered. Wet, feverish, and beyond hunger, her sanity hung by a thread. The only thing keeping her from going down the rabbit hole was Patti. As much as she hated Patti for getting her into this mess, she still hoped that once Patti was in her right mind, she would have a solution. Patti was the Girl Scout. Girl Scouts trumped "easy" girls when it came to safety. "Wake up Patti," she whispered. Again. And again.

Patti's lips were glued shut, weren't they? She imagined what would happen if she tried to talk, the flesh on her mouth would tear and bleed. She heard a voice. *Chrissy?* Why would Chrissy be in the classroom with her? She would've stopped the teacher from bashing her head with a two-by-four–wouldn't she? Then again, Chrissy was mad at her. And pigs don't fly, and frogs taste good when served on a bed of spring mix, garnished with goldfish and cheese puffs. She wished she'd never become a ballerina. She wanted her feet to touch the ground, she wanted the horse to quit kicking her in the crotch. She wanted to go home. She wanted to let go of the monkey bars and swim in the deep blue sea.

Sam drew his gun. The world was quiet, with the exception of an occasional screech from an owl, weeds rustling in the wind, and the sound of his beating heart. He nudged the door with his shoulder. It didn't budge. He was feeling along the ledge for a key. He holstered his gun, and retrieved the penlight in his pocket. The light traced the door frame. He noticed the door was nailed shut. He clicked off the light and motioned to Suzanne to follow him to the back of the house. She walked close behind and stopped. Out of the corner of her eye, she spotted the window she had seen in her vision and reached for Sam.

They crouched down and peered through the blackened panes. Sam shined his flashlight in the window. Suzanne stifled a scream.

Chrissy thought she was dreaming. A light beam danced across her foot. "Here. We're down here!" Her prayers had been answered after all. She heard a man's voice, authoritative, yet kind. He broke the window.

"Christine Bonnevier? I'm detective Samson Metzger, Goldorado County PD, can you hear me?"

"Yes," she said. "Get me out of here."

"Is Patricia Watson with you?"

"Yes. She's not moving–*hurry*."

Sam moved quickly. He discovered a cellar door at the back of the shack. A chain and a padlock held the door closed. Sam reached in his pocket for a pouch containing an assortment of tools. He inserted the pick into the chamber and wiggled it until he heard the chamber click. He pulled the lock away from the chain, removed the chain from door and opened it wide. A musty odor assailed his nostrils mixed with the smell of urine and blood. He choked back the acid rising in his throat and shined his light into the opening. A steep staircase led down into a room. The room was empty. He moved cautiously toward another set of stairs. He stepped gingerly, each board creaking beneath his weight. When he reached the top of the stairs, he realized the door leading inside was locked as well.

Sam steadied the penlight between his teeth and went to work. Within seconds, he had jimmied the lock.

Sam found himself in a parlor. An antique dining set, a settee, and a washbowl stand made the room look livable. A large bed with a canopy top loomed in the corner. Next to the bed was a doorway. Before Sam reached the door, he spotted a picture hanging on the wall. A man in overalls, a small, dark-haired boy on his lap. Looking closer, Sam realized the man's features were shredded, unrecognizable–but the boy in the photo, undeniably, Dixon.

Sam followed the beam of light across the room to another door and another narrow stairway. He regretted not being able to call for back-up but knew he couldn't take the chance of Dixon getting wind of his discovery and bolting. He needed absolute proof in order to put the son-of-a-bitch behind bars. A little boy in a photo would never stand up in court as evidence. He needed a positive ID. He needed the girls alive.

"Christine?" He heard a moan coming from the far corner of the cellar. He moved toward the voice. "It's me, Samson Metzger. Don't be afraid. I'm here to help you." He bent down and examined her bindings. The girl smelled like rotted flesh. Her clothes were torn; her hair matted and covered in blood; her eyes swollen; her face flushed; hot from infection. Her limbs were bruised and crusted with blood. One kneecap appeared dislocated, one ankle, twice the size of the other. Her lips were cracked and bloody. He pulled her trembling body close to his. "You're safe, now."

Chrissy found Sam's hand, and pressed something hard against his palm. He recognized the shape. *Amy Fitzpatrick's tooth.*

"Patti said he's a cop," she said.

Once Christine was in Suzanne's care, Sam grabbed a lantern from his trunk and returned for Patti. When he unlocked the chains shackled to the iron ring under the stairway, Patti slumped against him. He eased her to the floor, smoothed her hair away from her face and lifted each eyelid, checking her pupils. Dilated. She was still drugged, suffered a concussion, or both. Moving her could be dangerous, but he had no choice. He had to take the chance and bring her outside while keeping the crime scene as uncompromised as possible.

They would drive to the main highway, dispatch a helicopter to transport the girls to the hospital, and then he'd return to the shack and secure the crime scene. If he was wrong about Dixon, he could kiss his job goodbye. If he was right? The nightmare would end, and that was a risk he was willing to take.

When Sam carried Patti outside, Suzanne felt as though her true purpose had been revealed. Jack had shown her the way. For the first time since the nightmares had begun, she understood her destiny. *Sam, not Jack.* Together, they would save lives.

She bundled the girls in the blankets Sam had stashed in the back of his vehicle. Chrissy cradled Patti in her arms and rocked her like a baby. Neither girl spoke. Suzanne put her arms around them. "It's over. You and Patti are going to be all right."

"I knew he was my angel," Chrissy whispered.

"Who?"

"The guy in the uniform."

"Jack?"

Chrissy's eyes searched Suzanne's. "Do you know him?"

"He's my angel too."

Sam glanced at his watch. *9:47 p.m.*. He dialed District Attorney George Rader despite the fact he knew the man retired with the sun and woke with the birds. Aside from his job as D.A., George tended forty horses and milked his own cows. Given the man's schedule, Sam anticipated a greeting far from cordial.

"Who the hell is this and what is so important that you felt compelled to interrupt my sleep?"

"George, it's Samson Metzger, sorry to bother you at home, but I need your help."

"You better have a good goddamn reason for calling this late."

Sam explained his dilemma to George Rader, who sounded as if he couldn't get enough air in his lungs to respond. Everyone loved Dixon. He was the town's golden boy. He could do no wrong. "Are you sure?"

"The boy in the photo on the wall—I'm putting my job on the line, sir. It's him."

Once George swallowed the bad news he said, "I'll call the Fresno County Sheriff's Department, you handle things there. We don't want anyone botching our crime scene. This won't go down well in the community. If you can't trust the Sheriff, who can you trust?"

"I understand, sir. Until I can get a statement from the girls, this conversation has to remain airtight. If Dixon finds out we have the girls, he'll disappear. I need to get my forensic team up here first light, and I'll need your help in keeping Fresno's guys out of my hair. I'll need a warrant for Dixon's arrest.

"Let me see what I can do." George paused a moment in silence. "Geez, I still can't wrap my head around this."

Sam hung up the phone and waited for medical help to arrive. When the helicopter landed in a clearing 100 yards from the highway, Sam drove to meet them. Paramedics poured out of the chopper door and rushed toward the Land Rover. Once the girls were strapped onto gurneys, Sam and Suzanne headed for Fresno Surgical Hospital. He hoped to get a statement from the girls before midnight.

Others

Dixon set a cold beer on the coaster beside his computer, removed his shoes, and unbuttoned his shirt. He sat back in his leather chair and scrolled down his list of dating sites. When he found one of interest, he hit enter and signed in. He perused through "new profile listings" while he sipped his beer. *Too tall, too blonde, too pudgy, too fake, too plain, too short, nope, nope, nope.* He clicked on page two, hoping for better results. When he came up blank, he exited out of that site and explored another. He scrolled through photos until he came upon a woman who fit the bill. *Mia,* 5'5," light brown hair. *No tattoos, loves to cook.* He gave her a "wink", sent his photo and asked for her info. He sat back and waited. By 10:32pm, he had his next victim.

Dear Mia,

It was so refreshing to see someone like you posted on this site. I can't tell you how disappointed I've been since I joined. In fact, I was about to give up and become a priest. Then I saw *you*. Now I've not only changed my mind about becoming celibate, I now believe in angels!

I too, love to cook. My specialty is Coq au Vin, however, I'm a grilling aficionado, and love to make my own pasta. (My pear and gorgonzola ravioli are truly exquisite) I come from a long line of chefs and foodies, and appreciate a nice meal, paired with a beautiful woman and a bottle of wine. Conversation is a must. I'm a great talker, but an even better listener. I will be in the Portland area this weekend on business. If you would like to meet and share a meal, let me know. My heart is beating out of my chest. Please say yes.

Affectionately,
Christopher

Dixon moseyed into the kitchen, popped open another beer. He tore open a bag of tortilla chip, and searched for a jar of salsa in the back of the fridge. By the time he poured salsa into a bowl, he heard a "ping" coming from the other room. Snacks in hand, he returned to his computer.

Dear Cristopher,

Thank you for your awesome introduction. I would love to meet you this weekend, however, I will be in Seattle until Monday. Perhaps we can meet another time? I love Coq au Vin, but my favorite is Italian. I think we will get along nicely. I'm off to the gym. Lots of energy to work off! Now that I've met *you* wink, wink.

"Wink, wink, your ass." Dixon threw the bag of chips against the wall.

As the Land Rover sped down the highway, Suzanne closed her eyes. Jack waited in her deepest thoughts. She imagined the feel his breath on her cheek as he whispered, "I love you, Suzanne. Always have, always will." He kissed her hair, held her close. *I wonder if he'll find peace now.*

Sam reached for her hand. "You doing okay?"

"I'm tired, but so relieved. How about you?"

"The girls are safe, but Dixon is still out there. It's going to be tricky bringing him in."

"Why's that?"

"Our only hope is getting a positive identification from the girls, and DNA from the shack. I suspect Dixon was careful not to leave fingerprints." Sam squeezed her hand. "We have to be careful not to alert him. Although we have the girls, this nightmare won't end until he's behind bars."

"There *are* others."

"Others?"

"Not all of the bodies have been discovered, and I still feel there's another who has escaped. She's young. Dark hair. She moves like she's hypnotized." Suzanne closed her eyes for a moment. "Jack is showing me a baby."

Baby, Baby

Sheena Bradford gripped the balcony railing. Wind whipped her long, dark hair around her face. She massaged the bump pushing against the waistband of her yoga pants. *My baby boy*. The city below glittered with lights. Neon signs peppered the streets with artistic flare. She loved living in New York, every day, a new adventure. Soon, she would be exploring the town with her son.

Every night she prayed for her child to be spared the fear she had come to know. She thought moving across the country would make her safe. And, for the most part, she felt protected living with her cousin, Renee. However, there were times when she looked over her shoulder or hid from strangers who resembled Dixon. Soon, she would give birth to his child. Then what? Would her baby grow up feeling deprived of a father? Would he one day search for him? Surely Dixon wouldn't hurt his own flesh and blood. Would he? Sheena wondered. As much as she feared him, she wanted him near. She wanted him to hold her, tell her he loved her, tell her he was wrong about getting rid of the baby, and that he wanted to be a family. Tears filled her eyes. Why couldn't she forget him? Move on? Because—*despite the fact he's toxic, you love him*.

Collections of Photos

Dixon opened a file he kept for those moments when he needed to fill his head with more than a photo of a pretty girl with a dog or lifting some celebratory drinky-poo. Why did women think guys cared about those things? Show me your tits! Bend over–let me see those firm cheeks.

Dixon collected photos of his escapades. Jennifer–her legs spread wide, her pink bud begging to be kissed. The next photo of Jennifer wasn't as pretty, but it excited him, nonetheless. Her eyes were swollen shut. Blood trickled from the corner of her mouth. He felt himself getting hard. He clicked again. The next photo featured his little coed, Sheena. "Now there's a pair of tits," he mumbled, rubbing his crotch. He scrolled down until he found the photo he was looking for. Sheena, naked in the middle of a field, a flower in her hand. She was stunning. *And stupid*. What had made her think she could trap him into marriage with a baby? He recalled how angry he became when he found her apartment empty. *Bitch.* He imagined her flat tummy big, and round. He suspected she was on the east coast. She didn't have family in California, only her cousin in New York. The reason he didn't pursue her was because she knew nothing about him. *Other than I'm the Sheriff and the best fuck she'll ever have.* His little schoolgirl loved sex. She would do anything to please him, and she was a quick study. Too bad she had to go and get knocked up. He hoped she had enough sense to get rid of 'it.' He hated kids. He'd hated being a kid and had no room in his life for one of his own.

Just like my mama.

Emergency Room

Sam and Suzanne waited for the Emergency Room doctor to update them on the girls' condition. Christine and Patti were taken to a private room. A guard was assigned to each girl. No one could enter without an ID.

"Detective Metzger?" A slight Asian man approached.

"Yes." Sam stood and shook the man's hand.

"I'm Doctor Wang. At the moment, both girls are comfortable. We are waiting for MRI results to substantiate the severity of their concussions and CT scans to access their organs. Both girls have suffered fractures to the face, severe contusions and broken bones—Christine Bonnevier is being treated for acute cystitis that has spread from her bladder to her kidneys. Between the drugs, the beatings, repeated rape with unidentified objects, and dehydration, it's a wonder Miss Bonnevier is still alive—I've called in a gynecologist to repair as much of the damage as possible. Miss Watson's trauma is more current. She has five broken ribs and a punctured lung. We've given her antidotal medicine for the drugs in her system. Once she's coherent, we'll go from there." Doctor Wang scratched his brow. "Unfortunately, at this point neither can describe what happened." He shook his head and spoke directly to Sam. "I hope you find the monster who did this, Detective. In my thirty-plus years of practicing medicine, I have never witnessed such brutality. If you had not found them, both girls would have been dead by morning, or soon thereafter."

Sam glanced toward Suzanne. He took the doctor aside. "When will I be able to talk to the girls? Time is critical, Doctor. I can't nail this monster until they identify him."

It was the doctor's turn to show his discomfort. "I can't let you speak with them until we finish our assessment. We are not certain of the magnitude of their injuries. We have barely scratched the surface. Once we get answers pertaining to their medical condition, we will let you get your answers. Until then, let us do our job so you can do yours." The doctor patted Sam's shoulder, turned, and disappeared behind double doors.

Brutus

After Dixon had relieved his sexual frustration, he showered and climbed into bed. Tomorrow he would drive to Fresno. *Have a little fun*. After all, that's what weekends were for. Maybe he'd look-up Sheena. Say "hello" for old time's sake. He closed his eyes and began drifting off until a memory caused him to stir.

His mother took him by the hand, dragged him across the street to a neighbor's house, where they were greeted by an elderly lady and her Doberman, Brutus. The dog towered over Dixon's head. Paws, the size of cow pies, danced around the woman's legs. The dog's low growl and show of teeth didn't faze him. He knew where the woman kept her toolbox. A hammer to the snout would put Brutus in his place, but who would put his mother in *her* place?

He held her hand tight. "Don't leave me, Mommy."

"Shush now. I'll be back before you know it," she said, pulling a tube of lipstick from her purse. "You behave, or that dog will rip your face off." She smiled and peeled his fingers from her wrist. She pushed him through the door and never looked back.

The old woman slapped a newspaper on the edge of her dining table. "Brutus! You be quiet now. The boy is only here for a visit."

"May I use your bathroom?" Dixon asked.

"Of course. You know the way," she said, wagging her finger. "Wash your hands with soap. I don't want dirt on my clean towels."

"Yes, ma'am," he said, backing his way down the hallway. He slipped into the laundry room, climbed up on the washer, and pulled a wooden box from the cabinet. He held the hammer in his little fist, ready to do battle. As he climbed off the washer, he realized too late the dog was underfoot, and landed on Brutus' paw. Jaws clamped down on his thigh before he had a chance to react. He twisted his body and slammed the hammer into the side of the dog's snout. The dog yelped, freeing Dixon's leg. Dixon slid the hammer under his shirt and tucked the shirt inside his pants.

"What's going on?" asked, the old woman.

"I went into the wrong room," Dixon confessed, "I stepped on Brutus' foot. He hung his head, "I'm sorry."

"Get to the bathroom before you wet yourself," she said, swatting him on the back of the head.

Dixon placed the hammer on the top of the toilet tank and slid his pants down to inspect his bite. No blood. Just tiny blue-grey dents, but the area around the bite was red and swollen. He pulled up his pants and returned the hammer to his waistband under his shirt. He planned his first kill at four years old.

Hit The Road Jack

Suzanne woke with a start. "What time is it?"

Sam smoothed the sleeve where Suzanne had rested her head. "A little after 2 a.m. The doctor should give us an update soon."

"How about some coffee. There's a machine down the hall."

"You stay, I'll get it." Sam rose and stretched.

She noticed Sam's physique. His broad shoulders, trim waist, long legs. Resting against him felt natural. Easy. She didn't want to imagine beyond the here and now, but she had no control of her thoughts. The smell of him lingered. She knew they had far to go before they could get to know each other better, but the prospect warmed her soul.

She closed her eyes and Jack appeared.

"You must stop him, Suzanne. More girls will die."

She ran to the ladies' room, grabbed a paper towel and turned the faucet to cold. She dabbed the wet toweling across her forehead and pressed it to her eyes.

When Sam returned to an empty waiting room, he saw the contents of Suzanne's purse spilled on the seat. He set the coffee on an end table, gathered her things, and searched the hallway. He knocked on the door to the ladies' room. "Suzanne?" he called softly. She appeared at the door, her face damp, her cheeks pink, her eyes haunted. "What happened?"

"Jack. He says Dixon needs to be stopped before he kills again."
"Tell Jack we got this."
"I don't know Sam, suddenly I'm not so sure."

New York

Dixon got out of bed and threw on his clothes. Chrissy and Patti awaited. Two hours before first light. "Can't keep the ladies waiting."

He fixed a cup of coffee, poured it into a travel mug, packed a few protein bars, and bottles of water into a canvas bag while he sang, "On the road again, I've got to get out on the road again..."

Before the creatures of the night retreated and a cool breeze swept stars from the sky, Dixon had jumped into his police cruiser and headed west. As he drove down Highway 50, he keyed the name Sheena Bradford into his dash computer. A series of names scrolled down the screen. He heard a ping. Sheena Bradford had used a credit card in New York. "NYC Memorial Hospital Maternity? What the fuck, Sheena?" Dixon pressed "Save" and increased his speed. "You better not be having that fucking baby." He forgot about Chrissy and Patti and headed for Interstate 80, droning an eerie melody, "Start spreading the news, I'm leaving today, ba-da-da da, da-da-da, New York, New York."

Paranoid

Sheena's sleepy eyes fluttered open with the first light. She never tired of welcoming the rosy bloom in the east. Her bedroom window looked out over the city. The Hudson River, gleaming, and golden, snaked in the distance. She sat up, stretched her arms over her head, and settled her hands on her belly. "Morning little one," she whispered.

She hopped out of bed and went to the window. Filmy curtains billowed around her shoulders. Suddenly, she felt a strong sense of unease. A feeling only one person she knew could provoke. *Dixon*. But how? She'd been careful. Her phone was listed in her cousin's name. The only thing she couldn't use a fictitious name for was her new credit card, but the woman at the bank assured her that her information would not be shared publicly. "We're fine," she promised the bump she fought so hard to protect. "Mama's just being paranoid."

Monster

Suzanne sipped coffee, observing Sam in the distance. Light peeking through the blinds of the waiting room's only window highlighted the silver strands running through his dark hair. Daybreak. A fresh new day. How she wished she could spend time strolling through botanical gardens or hiking in the hills. Anything would be better than sitting here *waiting*. Patti and Chrissy were still off limits until later that afternoon. She bristled at the fact that Sam's hands were tied from obtaining a warrant until one of the girls identified Dixon as their captor. At least Jack had given her a break.

She had mixed feelings about Jack. Part of her wanted him to stick around, the other part of her wanted him gone. She had grown weary of the fear, the murders, the helplessness she felt with each clue he dumped in her lap. Training herself as a medium would take time. Interpreting the images would take faith. She wondered if faith was something she still possessed. It seemed her faith had been shattered when Jack died, and Ben did nothing to rebuild it. Then again, she had never given him a chance. She had never stopped loving Jack. She feared she never would. *Until now?*

Suzanne knew once Dixon was behind bars, she would see a different Sam emerge. He could be a positive light in her world. *If you let him.*

The worry on his face dissolved as he drew near. He smiled.

"What's up?" she asked.

"I should get to the station. From there I can at least keep an eye on Dixon."

"It's Saturday."

"I'm going into the office anyway. Maybe it's better if he's not there. I can do a little snooping."

"I have a better idea."

"What's that?"

"Breakfast. My treat."

They arrived at Morning Toast just as the manager unlocked the doors. They sat in a booth next to the window where they could watch an azure blue-sky transition to rose gold. They ordered fresh squeezed orange juice, Mediterranean omelets with sour dough toast and coffee. When their food arrived, Suzanne didn't hasten to slather her toast with whipped butter and homemade Marionberry preserves.

"I can't remember when I've been this famished," she declared.

"It's been quite some time since our last meal." Sam held his fork mid-bite. "Why do I feel so comfortable around you?"

"Please Sam, don't—"

"We're having breakfast. We're talking like we've known each other forever. We're sharing an experience that will haunt us for a lifetime. We're a team. We're on the same page, the same wavelength. We're good together. If you don't want to move to the next step, so be it, but for now, I am going to enjoy every moment I can with you."

Suzanne picked up her juice. "I like you. I like being around you, but for now that has to be enough. I don't know what the future is going to hold. I have two men rocking my boat now, and it's all I can handle."

"Fair enough."

Sam's phone vibrated on the table. "Detective Samson Metzger."

Suzanne could hear the man speaking on the other end of the phone. Doctor Wang. Watching Sam's face process the news, she realized he had found his way into her heart.

"Patti is awake. She's weak, but she's stable. We can see her at noon. The doctor wants to make sure she's strong enough to handle questioning." He grabbed Suzanne's hand and gently squeezed. "I couldn't have cracked this case without you. Thank you."

Patti winced. Her brain fought to process her surroundings. The last thing she remembered was sitting next to Chrissy in a car. Her vision blurred momentarily, adjusting to the figure standing nearby.

"Do you remember me?" Sam pulled a chair close to the bed.

"Not really," she said, struggling to sit up.

"I'm Detective Sam Metzger, this is Suzanne Cash. She's responsible for locating the place you were being held captive."

Suzanne stepped forward. "Hi. I'm happy to see you're awake. How are you feeling?"

Patti turned to Sam. "Where's Chrissy?"

"She's still in critical condition, but the doctor assured me she's going to recover."

"Did you catch the guy yet? He's a cop, you know."

"I need *your* help putting him away. Can you identify him?"

Sam opened his phone, pressed record and opened an app containing photos of six different men. Patti did not hesitate picking Dixon out of the mix.

"That's him. That's the cop." Her finger shook as she pointed at the screen. "*He's* the monster."

Sam had witnessed Dixon's bullying for years, but never imagined he was capable of such evil. He spoke into the recorder. "The witness has identified Sheriff James Dixon from the Goldorado County Sheriff's Department as her captor and assailant."

Suzanne excused herself from the room as Sam continued his questioning. The judge was on his way with a warrant for Dixon's arrest, but Suzanne's gut told her the chase had just begun. Dixon had no plans to return to Goldorado County. He was on his way to claim his next victim. She knew he was not only after the girl he was after something else. *The baby.*

Chicago

Dixon detested sloppy. *You left the girls alive, dumb shit, and now you have to flee.* "That's okay, no one will find them. Besides, I've got another mission." Michael Jackson sang in his head. "Gonna make a change, gonna make it ri-i-ight."

He had ditched his police cruiser outside of Salt Lake City. After bundling up the police scanner, his laptop, and radio, he took a chance on hitchhiking. A lonely truck driver took pity on him, drove him into Bountiful and even bought him breakfast.

The Toyota pick-up he purchased from the used car lot ate up a good deal of his travel time, but he was able to close the transaction using fake I.D.s and credit cards he'd been saving for this very occasion. How easy it was to scam people when you knew the ropes. Law enforcement afforded him a valuable education. And with a whore for a mother, and a pedophile for a grandpa, he had all the encouragement he needed to succeed in life.

In a drugstore outside Chicago, he placed a box of platinum hair color, a pair of hair-cutting sheers, a package of eyelash extensions, and self-tanning lotion in his basket. Next, he picked out a Cubs T-shirt, a baseball cap, a pair of shorts, and flip-flops, adding the items to his "new look." At the check-out counter, he placed a pair of sunglasses on the conveyer belt and pulled out his wallet.

The clerk was slow and chatty. “I tried that hair stuff on my daughter Gwen. Prit-near made her bald. Be careful with that stuff. And if it doesn’t work for your wife, or your girlfriend, you tell’er to bring back the box, and we’ll give her a refund.” With that said, she picked up the self-tanner, examined the box and said, “Remember when people went to the beach to get a tan? Geez, what’s next?”

“You know women, they’ll do anything to make themselves beautiful.” He flashed the woman one of his killer smiles.

“That’ll be $32.56.” She bagged the items with the same slow deliberation she used ringing them up. Dixon placed three tens, and three ones on the counter. He waited for her to count out his forty-four cents. He knew leaving without his change would stick in her pea-sized brain. He had already spent too much time in one place.

He drove to a nearby upscale men’s store to purchase a new wardrobe. Two pairs of designer jeans; a pair of white linen Prada slacks with matching sport jacket; one pair of black dress pants; five shirts in assorted styles and colors; one pair of athletic shoes; and one pair of black dress loafers. Altogether, it set him back $6300. The young man at the register wasn’t impressed. In fact, he didn’t give two shits whether Dixon’s driver’s license matched his credit card. Did he notice Dixon hadn’t removed his sunglasses the whole time he shopped? *No wonder there are so many criminals in the world.*

Saturday morning in Indiana was nuts. It seemed every Hoosier alive was heading somewhere. Cars packed with kids and dogs crawled along Highway 69. He was at ease, having changed his look slightly before he hit the road. He was admiring his haircutting skills in the rearview mirror when a BMW pulled alongside him to the left and stopped, unable to move forward. The pretty girl sitting in the backseat looked his way. Her eyes connected with his. He licked his lips, she licked hers. He wiggled his tongue, she popped her pointer finger in her mouth and pulled it out slowly. She leaned into the window, pressing her breasts against the glass. He slid his hand between his legs and massaged his aching groin. He imagined himself taking her from behind, hearing her beg for mercy as he pounded her flesh and slit her throat. He blinked away the fantasy before he exploded in his only pair of clean jeans. He glanced her way. Her smile, salacious as she winked at him. She tossed her honey colored hair and blew him a kiss. Cars began moving forward, ending their little game.

Dixon pulled off an exit advertising gas, food, and lodging in Canton, Ohio. He checked into a Holiday Express, intending to grab a meal, a shower, and get a couple hours sleep. Not a city he would've chose for a good time, but there she was, the girl in the BMW, lounging by the pool wearing a neon pink swimsuit that left nothing to the imagination. She filled the tiny scraps of material in the most delicious way. Full, perky breasts, a flat stomach, and long, slender legs.

"Well, I'll be damned," she said, bending one leg.

"Must be fate," he said, tilting his sunglasses to get a better look.

"You following me?"

"Should I be?"

"Maybe." She patted the chair next to hers.

He pulled his chair closer to hers. "I thought maybe I was dreaming."

She placed his hand on her knee. "See. I'm real." Her eyes reminded him of the first little bitch he had killed. He liked the feisty ones. They made sex fun, challenging, exciting, which made the kill even better. *It comes as more of a surprise.* His hand inched toward her inner thigh. She slapped his hand.

"What's your name?" she asked, removing his hand from her leg.

"Doug Owens. What's yours?"

"Mikala Morgan. I'm from Peoria. I'm traveling with my brother and his wife to New York. My brother is an author. He has a book signing on Tuesday."

"What genre does he write?"

"Mysteries."

"You like mysteries?"

"I guess they're all right. What about you? Where are you from?"

"Chicago. I'm on my way to Pittsburg. Grandmother's not well."

"I'm so sorry," she said, covering a giggle with her hand.

"That's funny?"

"No. Yes. This whole thing is rather fucked up, wouldn't you say?"

Dixon appreciated her candor. "I like the fuck part."

"You're kinda old for me, aren't you?"

"Am I going to need Viagra?"

She stared at him for a beat. "I suppose my brother won't miss me for an hour or so."

On the way to his room, Dixon counted the security cameras. Two looked active, a third looked iffy. Inside the room, he pulled off his shirt and untied the straps holding her top in place. He bent down to kiss each breast before he found her mouth. She tasted like candy. She smelled like spring. Her honey hair cascaded over tanned shoulders and tumbled to her petite waist. She took the lead, exploring his mouth with her tongue, and slipping her hand into his pants. Soon they were wrestling on the bed, shedding clothes and scraps of neon pink. He flipped her over kneading her buttocks and planting kisses inside her thighs. She bucked like a wild horse wanting to be mounted, but he wasn't ready. He knew once he entered her, he would lose control.

"Hold on," he said, catching his breath. "You want this to be hot?"

"I thought we were getting there." Her face blushed, her brow moist and shiny. She collapsed against the headboard. "What the fuck, city boy?"

"Meet me in the parking lot at 9:00 p.m." Dixon handed her a fistful of neon pink. "Put this on, your brother might think you've been a naughty girl."

"What's at 9:00 p.m.?"

Dixon nuzzled her ear and snuck his hand between her legs. Her wetness confirmed his suspicions.

"You'll just have to trust me now, won't you?" He brushed his thumbs across her nipples.

"Fine." She bounced off the bed and got dressed.

"I'm parked in the back lot near the dumpster. 9:00. Don't be late."

She shimmied into her suit, grabbed her towel and slammed the door.

He counted on her temperament. He also counted on the security cameras catching her departure.

Dixon curled up in bed, a pillow clutched to his chest. He slept for three hours, showered and dressed. He grabbed his duffle bag, the room key, and four miniature bottles of booze from the min-bar.

At 8:00 p.m., he jumped into his car and started the engine. He pulled out of his space and drove to the supermarket a block away. In the parking lot, he switched license plates with a dusty car parked in a far row. Work completed, he munched on a bag of potato chips and a warm cola he had stashed in the trunk. He cracked open one of the miniatures and opened the foil pouch from his pocket. He poured the contents into the dime-size opening and replaced the cap. At 8:55 he drove back to the motel. He saw Mikala waiting by the dumpster, dressed in blue jeans and a crocheted halter top. Her hair, swept to one side, glistened under the sodium lighting. He wondered if she had an inkling that her life was about to end. He pulled into a space obscured from the camera and beeped the horn. She turned and walked towards him. His face was hidden in the shadows, but she didn't hesitate to climb into the car.

"This better be good. I told my brother I left my sunglasses by the pool and would be right back."

Dixon slid his hand from her knee to her thigh. "I assure you, what you're about to experience is going to blow your fucking mind." She moved his hand higher up, anxious to get the party started.

They drove to the back of an abandoned warehouse and parked between the two shipping containers. "We don't have much time," she said removing her halter top and pressing her breasts against his face. "You promised me one helluva fuck."

"Hey, what's the hurry?" He flicked one nipple with his tongue, then the other, his eyes fastened to hers. "Your brother is probably banging his ol' lady and won't miss you for at least an hour." Dixon offered Mikala a swig of the miniature he pulled from his pocket. "Take a sip." While she sipped, he reached beneath the seat with one hand and grabbed a ball of orange twine. His other hand snaked around her waist and drew her near. While he kissed her, and sucked on her tongue, he grabbed her wrists and twisted them behind her back. She couldn't scream with her tongue between his teeth. She bumped his chest with hers, trying to break away as he wrapped the twine around her wrists. He released her tongue and cupped his hand over her mouth. "Shush. I told you— I'm going to blow your mind."

Mikala's eyes filled with fear as Dixon reached for the duct tape he'd stashed earlier, tore off a strip and placed it over her mouth. She kicked him. He slammed her down on the seat and removed her jeans and neon yellow thong. "Cute," he said, pulling the stretchy lace over her head and twisting the fabric around her neck. Mikala's head thrashed as he stretched her panties and wrapped the lace around the door handle.

"There," he said. "Now you won't head butt me." With her head immobilized and her body pinned beneath him, he began nibbling her breasts. He moved down her belly and spread her legs. He wasn't at all surprised when he heard her catch her breath as he tasted her. "Isn't that nice?" he asked. Darting his tongue inside her soft flesh, she relaxed, and began to moan. At the moment her breathing slowed, he bit down, drawing blood. Her snorting and gasping behind the tape made him giggle. He slammed her knees together, grabbed a bare breast in each hand and squeezed until he took her breath away. When he released her breasts, she panted and whimpered like a trapped animal. He looked deep into her eyes, relishing her pain and fear. "I know, little darlin', you're not happy," he said, reaching into the glove compartment, removing the remaining glass bottles, "but this will all be over soon."

One by one, he drank the contents, shattered the bottle tops and set them on the dash, admiring their jagged edges in the moonlight. "Oops, I almost forgot." He reached behind the back seat and grabbed a plastic drop cloth. Mikala tried to scream as he slipped the sheeting beneath her. "If there's one thing I don't like, it's a messy car." Her eyes opened wide in terror. He jammed the jagged opening of two bottles into each orb, and cut her throat with the third.

"Goddammit," he groaned, lifting her body from the front seat. He dragged her to the edge of the shipping container and shoved her underneath. He watched as her blood pooled beneath her head and shoulders. He faced the heavens with a sense of relief. Mikala would be dead in minutes. One more whore removed from the face of the earth.

———

PARIS

For the next several days, Sam kept Suzanne near him. He was sure Dixon was somewhere in the Midwest, but he took no chances, and brought Suzanne to work with him. As they pulled into the lot of the Sheriff's office, Sam knew from Suzanne's expression that she'd just gotten a psychic hit. He leaned over. "What is it?"

"I'm feeling closed in, like I'm trapped beneath something large. I see graffiti everywhere." She closed her eyes. "Jack is showing me a dark highway."

"Can you see where it leads?"

Suzanne closed her eyes. "Thirteen miles to Paris."

"Paris?"

"Yes. Paris." Suzanne opened her eyes and rubbed her temples.

"You saw the word *miles*?"

"Yes."

"Then it must be a town or city in the United States." He withdrew his phone from his pocket and keyed Paris, U.S.A. into Google. "Great. There's a Paris in just about every state."

"I'm sorry. That's all I'm getting for now."

Sam reached for Suzanne's hand. "You never have to be sorry with me. I don't yell, or punch walls. I feel very fortunate to have you by my side, and I hope this ends soon, because I don't know how long I can refrain from kissing you."

Suzanne leaned forward. Her mouth found his. Their lips fit together like puzzle pieces and moved at a gentle pace. Sam circled his arms around her waist and pulled her close. For a moment, time stood still until Suzanne pulled away.

"I shouldn't have done that," she said. "It complicates things."

Dove Johnson knocked on the driver's window. Sam hit the power button.

"Sorry for the interruption, I've been looking for you everywhere. We got DNA results back on the girls. James Earl Dixon. AKA Earl Ray Freeman, and who knows how many other aliases."

Sam shook his head. "Great. Now all we have to do is find him."

"Follow the trail. A body was found a few miles outside Canton Ohio with the same M.O."

"Orange twine?"

"That, and she was about the same age as the other girls.

Sam pulled out his phone and googled Ohio maps. He slid the map around his screen until he found what he was looking for. "Bingo."

Suzanne peered over his shoulder. "There." She pointed to a marker pinpointing Paris, Pennsylvania.

Sam settled back in his seat. "Why Paris?"

"He's going through Paris, not to Paris." Suzanne turned to Sam and Dove. "He's headed for someplace with a large population. People everywhere. Bright lights." Deep inside the chasms of her mind, Jack hummed a tune. "*New York.*"

Dove shook his head. "I still can't believe it. I know he liked young girls and we all kidded him—but this?"

"Did you know any of the girls he dated? Maybe we can get a hit on who's in New York."

"Let me make a few calls. I'll get back to you." Dove said.

"What about the girl, Suzanne? What can you tell me about her?

"I remember she was young, long dark hair—there was something about," she rubbed her stomach, "a *baby.*"

Grandpa

Dixon drove through the town of Paris before dawn. The streets, empty, just like his life. His biggest thrill to date was killing, and even killing seemed mundane after the fact. He needed more excitement. He knew he couldn't return to California. Time to start anew, be someone else. He had plenty of identities to choose from. He had the means to go anywhere and do anything he pleased. "Good planning," his dear ol' Grandpa use to say, mostly while unzipping his fly. "Gotta have a good plan." Too bad Grandpa didn't plan on his "baby boy" slitting his throat.

After a meagerly attended funeral, Dixon discovered Grandpa was a man of his word. He had somehow stashed away $3.5 million in silver certificates and bearer bonds in his shack. According to the collector Dixon contacted, the silver certificates were worth 50 times their face value, due to their rarity and pristine condition. He had no clue where the money came from, and frankly, he didn't care. Being on the road, at night, all alone, dredged up things he had buried. He deserved that money.

He remembered the day he discovered Grandpa's stash. Dear ol' Gramps had him working in the field, picking green beans and turnips. He hadn't seen his mother in months. She was in Vegas with a high-roller named Frederick Fallahey, who drove a Jaguar, and spoke like he shit money. And as much as Dixon loathed her, he prayed she'd show up and whisk him off to anywhere— other than the hell hole his Grandpa called "the farm".

Eating raw green beans in the hot sun, in addition to the sour milk and bug infested cereal he had choked down that morning, made his stomach churn. Diarrhea hit so fast, he had to squeeze his butt cheeks together to keep from messing his one pair of pants. He scrambled into the cellar entrance just in time to see dear ol' Gramps reposition a rusted refrigerator in front of a hole in the wall. Dixon flew passed him yelling, "Gotta go, gotta go." Out of the corner of his eye he caught a glimpse of what appeared to be bundles of cash piled neatly behind the wall.

Dixon sat on the commode until the wooden seat dug a groove into his backside. He was about to flush when he heard footsteps outside the door.

"Whatcha doin' in there, precious?" the ol' man asked. "Churnin' peanut butter? Or making *cream*?" The man's soft chuckle turned Dixon's bowels to water, and he sat back down on the commode, clenching his teeth. He knew by the sound of the ol' man's voice that he was feeling randy, and Dixon knew what would happen once he opened the door.

"Got the squirts, I'll be awhile," Dixon said, groaning for effect. "Ate too many green beans."

"Stupid ass," the ol' man grumbled.

Dixon listened for his grandpa's footsteps to retreat. When they did, he finished his business, and waited until he heard the screen door slam. While he waited, he hatched a plan. Grab a knife from the kitchen and end the madness, right here, right now.

More than thirty years had passed, but he still enjoyed the memory... the shock on the ol' man's face when his baby boy came barreling out the front door wielding a butcher knife, the realization that he was about to die.

After he had slit his Grandpa's throat, he pulled the body out to the yard, placed it beneath the tractor to make it look like he was repairing the axle. He placed a wrench in his Grandpa's hand, started up the tractor and let the vehicle roll over the ol' man's head. The weight of the back tire crushed his skull like a watermelon.

Dixon hitchhiked into town and reported the accident. Grandpa didn't believe in telephones.

It took two days for the County Sheriff's Office to track down his mother in Vegas. Meanwhile, Dixon stayed with the Sheriff's sister Brenda, and her deputy husband, Andrew. Drew for short.

Once Grandpa was buried, his mother dropped him off at the farm, and took off to Canada with Frank. She swore she'd be back in a week, but Dixon knew better. Frank bought him a bicycle, shelled out ten one hundred-dollar bills, and hit the road.

Dixon didn't mind being left on his own. He survived just fine. He cooked his own meals, washed his own clothes, and taught himself how to make phony IDs. By the end of the summer, he was an expert. He paid visits to Drew, and in time, Drew became his role model. Drew taught him how to shoot, hunt, and fish. Hunting skills certainly came in handy. He learned how to skin a squirrel, decapitate a rattler, gut a pig, and bury a dog so other animals wouldn't find it. Skills he put to good use over the years. Unfortunately, Drew died before Dixon was sworn in as an officer of the law. *He would've been proud*.

Dixon pulled off the highway in Wilkes-Barre and snaked his way through a gas station until he found a vacant pump. He filled up his Toyota pick-up using a bogus credit card and drove a little further down the highway until he came upon the Microtel Inn. *Sleep*. He needed enough to keep him centered between the lines, no more, no less. Mid-afternoon sun made him drowsy, and he had things to do. He explained to the desk clerk he had an early call in the morning and paid for his room in full. He walked half a block to a Burger Chef, grabbed a salad and a burger, and retired for the evening.

Back in his room, he decided to bleach his hair. He read the instructions carefully. He didn't need his scalp burnt, or some gaudy color that would attract attention. He mixed the ingredients in the package, applied the goop on his hair, turned on the TV, and waited.

He flipped through stations, bored with game shows and news reports. His finger was over the button, ready to change the channel when his face loomed on the screen. He leaned closer and pumped up the volume. "Nationwide search for forty-two-year-old Sheriff from Goldorado County, California, James Dixon. If you see this man, call the number on your screen. This man is armed and dangerous."

Dixon checked the progress on his hair. His dark mane had turned copper. *Fifteen minutes to go. The things that can be accomplished in fifteen minutes.* When the color lifted to canary yellow, he was feeling optimistic. The advertisement on the box promised platinum blond. He was counting on the ad being truthful. His fake ID depended on it.

He shampooed the dye out of his hair and examined the results. "Nice." *Now for the lashes.* He opened the package he purchased at the drug store, pinched three fine hairs in the tweezers, dipped the ends into the glue, and applied them to his own lashes. *Man—if you had boobs, you'd be the most popular babe on the block.*

Dixon chose a tight black T-shirt and off-white linen pants. The combination was striking with his new hairdo and dreamy eyes. All he needed was a little swish, and a little lisp to make his new identity believable.

He had pulled Jeremy Wentworth over for a routine traffic stop six years ago. Jeremy was as queer as the day was long. No judgement, Dixon didn't give a fig which way the guy swung. What interested him was Jeremy's looks. Other than their hair color, he and Jeremy could've passed for twins. Dixon confiscated the guy's license and looked up his social security number. Later, he pulled a few strings to obtain a copy of Jeremy's birth certificate and opened a checking account under Jeremy's name. Once the account was open, Dixon put in a change of address at the bank and kept the account active. He used the account to deposit "tips" he received for being a good guy and letting all those little scoundrels off of their DUIs, and other charges. The majority of his assets were safe in an account in the Canary Islands under another fictitious name. "Life is good," he mumbled, finger picking the platinum waves. By this time tomorrow, he'd be in New York City. "Lookin' for my *ba*-by."

At nine o'clock, there came a knock on the door. Dixon froze. He listened. The knock persisted. *Shit.* He didn't budge. The knock turned into pounding. "Felicia! Goddammit, open the fuckin' door!" Dixon did just that, startling the man on the other side. "Who the—"

"Do I look like Felicia to you, asshole?"

The man stumbled backwards. "Dude—Sorry, I guess I'm in the wrong wing." He backed away slowly, his hand reaching for whatever he had tucked in his waistband.

Dixon's eyes followed the man's movement. His smirk dared the man to try something stupid. When the man showed both hands, Dixon smiled and said, "No worries. Have a good night." He turned off the TV and went to sleep.

CONFRONTATION

Suzanne returned home late in the afternoon, followed by Sam. A glass of curdled milk sat on the table beside a half-eaten slice of pizza.

Sam slipped into detective mode, gathering information about Suzanne's lifestyle, and Ben's departure. "Did he tell you he was leaving?"

Suzanne dropped her purse on a camel color leather high-back chair. "No. I haven't heard from him. I imagine he wasn't too happy to receive these divorce documents." She gathered the papers scattered on the floor.

"Looks like he isn't about to make life easy for you."

"No–I didn't expect him to cooperate." She viewed the blank signature line. "He's never made things easy for me. Why should he? I never made life easy for him."

"I can't imagine you being difficult to live with."

"Can you imagine being married to someone who is in love with someone else?"

"No. I'd want you all to myself."

"It will never be just 'me,' Sam."

"If you are referring to Jack, I can handle him. He's no threat to me. In fact, I sorta like the guy...in a way. I consider him a silent partner."

Suzanne tilted her head. "A silent partner?" She burst out laughing. "I need a drink." She dumped the glass of milk in the sink, filled the glass with hot soapy water, and tossed the pizza into the trash. She pulled a long stem glass from the cabinet next to the refrigerator and motioned to Sam. "White or red?"

"Nothing for me. I'm driving remember?"

Suzanne's eyes held his for what seemed an eternity.

"If you get bored while I'm packing, help yourself to music or the TV. I'll be as quick as possible."

"Take your time." He checked his watch. "You've got time for a shower if you like. I haven't given you much time to yourself."

"A shower would be nice–"

"You know what? I could use a shower myself, he said." He ran his hand along his scruffy jaw. "How about if I pick you up in an hour? Will you be all right here alone?"

"I have no idea where Ben is, but I don't expect him to show up just because I'm here alone. Besides, it's not like he's physically abusive."

"Keep your phone close by–just in case."

"Okay. See you in an hour."

Suzanne stripped out of her jeans and a yellow blouse that held every wrinkle from the last twenty-four hours. When she passed the mirror, she expected to see an old woman's face. "They're safe," she told the frazzled image. "They're safe because of you. That's all that matters."

She unhooked her bra and stepped out of her panties. Naked felt good. The hot water massaged her knotted muscles. *Better*. She poured a dollop of shampoo into her palm and worked it through her tangled hair. She stood under the shower head, relishing scented bubbles streaming down her skin. Once the water ran clear, she worked on lathering the rest of her body, as if it were possible to scrub away what she had just experienced.

Stepping out of the shower, she wrapped a towel around her petite frame and headed for the sink. Her dripping hair left a trail as she fluffed the heavy mass with her fingers. Suddenly she felt a chill. The door. *I left it open, didn't I?* She listened for movement downstairs. *Ben?* She held her breath. Silence. "Don't start spooking yourself out—no one is here but you."

"Sure about that?" Ben barged into the room.

Suzanne jumped.

"You scared me! Did you forget how to knock?"

"Why should I knock in my own house?"

"How about so you don't scare the crap out of me?"

"Poor baby," he said.

"What do you want? I'm in a hurry."

"Really? Loverboy?"

"Your accusations are not only unfounded, they're annoying."

"Really? Do you think I'm blind?"

"I've been working with the police on a case. I don't expect you to understand, but what happened to me has changed who I am."

"I'll say."

"I see things."

"Cut the bullshit, Suzanne. You've been looking for a way out for years. Do you think I'm so naïve that I don't see what you're doing?"

"The only thing I'm doing is getting dressed. Now if you'll excuse—"

Ben shoved her into the wall.

"Stop! Just go."

"Who's gonna make me?"

"Me."

Ben spun around. Sam had his hand on his holster.

"What are you doing here? Suzanne is *my* wife, and we are in the middle of a discussion, so back off, before I call the Sheriff and tell him you've entered my home without my permission or a warrant."

"Sam has my permission. This is still my home too, and right now, you're the one who needs to leave, not Sam."

Ben leaned toward Suzanne until his face was inches from hers. "This isn't over."

Sam took a step closer. "Sounds like you're making threats."

Ben backed away. "You two think you can ride off into the sunset and live happily ever after? Leave ol' Ben destitute?" He laughed. "Wrong. I'll see you in court, Suzanne. I'm going to take every cent I can from you." He paused. "At least I'll get *something* out of the last fifteen years. God knows you weren't good for anything else." He stormed out of the room.

"How did you know he was here?"

"I saw him walking toward the house as I was leaving."

Suzanne dropped her gaze. Sam pulled her near, but she pushed him away. "Go. Let me get dressed."

Sam didn't speak. He squeezed her hand and left, closing the door behind him.

Suzanne sat on the edge of the tub, holding her head in her hands. Jack appeared behind her closed eyes. He stood on a ledge, the sun set behind him, setting him aglow like an angel in the hand of God. "Oh, Jack. What now?"

Jack's face showed little emotion as he spoke. "A woman under a spell has no moral compass. The child she carries muddles her good senses."

"Great. Just what I needed. Another riddle."

———

The Park

Sheena planned to take the subway to Times Square and draw some sketches. The temperature outside was 72 degrees, and the skies were partly cloudy, making for some delicious light. She regretted not finishing her degree in art at Sac State, but never gave up her passion for drawing, painting, and photography.

After breakfast, she made her bed, and dressed for the day. Yoga pants, a loose tank top, and colorful kimono tied under the bust gave her an artistic appearance. She brushed her hair into a ponytail, wound it into a top knot, and thrust a wooden pick through the middle to hold it in place. She hadn't gained much weight in her pregnancy, but the protruding bump was a dead give-away. She turned sideways in the mirror. There was no denying it. *I'm going to be a mom.*

She thought about her own mom, taken too soon from the world, along with her dad, while traveling in Budapest. The tour bus they were on collided with another bus, exploding into flames, killing them instantly. A tragic memory she chose not to visit too often. Except for times like this, when she yearned to share her predicament, seek advice from one who filled the role she was about to undertake. She could never imagine anyone's mom being a better mom than hers. She swore her mother came to her in her dreams to console her. She'd wake feeling as though they had chatted all night long. But reaching for the phone wasn't an option, and it still made her sad. Her cousin Renée kept her spirits up, tossing around baby names, and checking out the latest nursery décor on Pinterest, but Sheena still missed her mom.

"Stop feeling sorry for yourself." Sheena placed her sketchpad, pencils, and a bottle of water into her Hobo bag, and locked the door behind her.

The elevator delivered her safely to the first floor, where she greeted Simon, the doorman. His ebony skin glistened with perspiration, alerting Sheena to the rise in humidity.

"Morning Simon," she said.

"Morning Miz Bradlee. Where you off to on this glorious day?"

"Thought I'd go sketch in the park."

"You have a good one, now. Stay hydrated. You don't want that baby swimming on dry land." He chuckled. "You got sunscreen with you?"

Sheena dug in her bag to produce a water bottle and a tube of sunscreen. "Thanks for looking out for me"

"Gotta take care of the mothers in the world, they're God's little jewels."

"Thank you, Simon. See you later." To him, she was Bradlee Tipton, a name she pulled from the telephone book.

Dixon glanced at his image in the mirror across the room. He bore no resemblance to Jim Dixon, the wanted criminal from Goldorado County. He turned his head from side-to-side, admiring his profile. "Handsome devil." Platinum hair took ten years off his looks. "See what you've been missing all these years? Time for this blond to have a little *fun.*"

He showered, dressed in his new linen suit and pink shirt, packed his belongings, and dropped the key on the nightstand. Before walking out the door, he wiped his fingerprints off the door handles, TV remote, lamp, and light switches. He shook out the bedding, and tossed it on the floor, then took the aftershave from his bag and sprinkled half the bottle over the heap of linens. *Housekeeping will have to wash the whole kit and kaboodle.* No one wanted to sleep in another person's scent. He rechecked the bathroom for any evidence that could incriminate him, wiped down the faucets, and decided he was in the clear. No one knew where he had disappeared to, and with his new look and ID's to match, chances were, he would never be found.

Eager Student

Suzanne stared out the window on their drive to the Sacramento airport. The plan was to catch a flight to Akron-Canton Ohio, grab a rental car and meet with the crime investigation team working on what could be Dixon's latest victim. Suzanne felt as though she had stuck her finger in a light socket. She feared they were headed toward disaster. Jack persisted, making sure they followed his leads. She closed her eyes. A young, beautiful, dark haired woman, her life filled with expectations, her womb filled with life.

She chewed her thumbnail. A habit she had never acquired. "I never bite my nails," she said, quizzically, turning toward Sam.

"I did when I was in college. Kept me from being a nervous eater. Helped my food budget as well."

"You? Nervous?"

"I'm dyslexic. It was hard for me to get through school. But I managed. It took several years to break the nail-biting habit. Better than smoking." Sam smiled. "Your turn."

"My turn for what?"

"To share something about yourself."

"I'm allergic to tomatoes."

"I love tomatoes, but I don't like green beans."

"Okay. I had to wear orthopedic shoes until I was four years old."

Sam peeked down at her perfect feet clad in strappy shoes. "Hard to believe."

Suzanne followed his gaze. "I was pigeon toed. At night I wore a brace that kept my feet from turning in. Eventually they straightened out. It would've been horrible to be saddled with orthopedic shoes in grammar school. It was bad enough I had buck teeth." She saw Sam's shocked expression. "Too much information?"

"I can't imagine you with buck teeth. You're so beautiful, I figured you were born perfect."

"You have a lot to learn about me."

"I'm an eager student."

They drove through the airport parking structure in silence until she pointed to an empty space. "Over there—"

Sam pulled in and cut the engine. "Ready?"

She bowed her head and closed her eyes. Jack filled the blackness behind her lids. "Yes," she said, opening her eyes and raising her head, "We're ready."

When they boarded the plane, Suzanne took a window seat, and Sam sat on the aisle, setting a small bag on the seat between them.

After take-off Suzanne gestured to the empty seat. "Do you get special privileges or something?"

Sam leaned in. "Nope. Just got lucky," he said. "May I?" He lifted the arm rests between them. "I love taking off and landing the best. The rest of the flight I usually spend snoozing. How about you?"

"I haven't flown much. I've always dreamed of traveling. Maybe I'll visit Europe one day." She turned toward the window. "The clouds look even more amazing from up here."

Sam unfastened his seat belt and moved closer. "Yes, they do." His eyes drifted from the window to Suzanne's lips and back to her eyes. Light played on her blue irises, circled in grey and a ring of black. Her eyes reminded him of a stained-glass window at St. Stephens Cathedral in Vienna he had visited as a boy. He had spent the entire service waiting for the morning sun to turn from cobalt to royal blue. He found the same comfort by her side and wanted more.

It had been years since he had thought about love, and now it snuck between rationality and conviction at every turn. He swore off getting serious later in his career, when he became a detective. Fighting crime was an ugly business. It required one to think like a criminal. Although his sobriety made a difference in his attitude, he still found it taxing to vacillate between being tender and being tough. Through the years, he had witnessed failed marriages and relationships among his peers and decided he'd rather be alone.

Then there was Dixon, who made a sport of using women. And killing them. Between Jack, Ben, and Dixon, he doubted Suzanne would be eager to jump into another relationship any time soon. Just then, the flight attendant interrupted his thoughts. "Cocktails?"

"Not for me, Suzanne?"

"No, not if you're not having one."

They opted for coffee instead.

"It's probably too early for a drink, anyway," she said, pulling down her tray table.

Sam reached in his pocket and pulled out his sobriety coin. He placed it on her tray. "Ten years. Thought you should know."

"Oh," she said, examining the coin. Images sped through her mind, including a pretty young woman with short blond hair. Her face had broken heart written all over it. "The important thing is you recognized you had a problem." She handed the coin back to him. "Besides, it wasn't just your drinking that made her leave."

"How?

"I'm psychic, remember?"

"I needed to tell you. I want everything between us to be out in the open. No secrets. We're partners. Partners in crime." He nudged her shoulder, and she smiled.

"In that case, I have to confess—"

The flight attendant arrived with their drinks. Sam placed Suzanne's coffee on her tray. "You were about to say?" His eyes found hers.

"I forgot what I was about to say."

When their flight landed, they made their way to the rental car counter. Sam filled out forms, retrieved the keys, and they were on their way.

The crime scene was fourteen miles from the airport. Dark clouds loomed overhead. Sam hoped the crime scene was protected, lest they lose evidence. Not that he expected much evidence.

When they arrived, Sam and Suzanne were met by Detective Hal

Jorgensen, from the Akron P.D. "Not what we're used to around here," he said. "A drifter, I guess. We get all kinds because of the interstate."

"Has the girl been identified?" Sam plucked a pen and a note pad from his shirt pocket.

"Her brother is at the morgue right now, identifying her body. They were on their way to New York. He's some mucky-muck author. Mystery writer. Go figure."

"Does he have any idea who could have murdered his sister?"

"No. Said the only time she was out of his sight was when she went to the pool in the afternoon. Right before she disappeared, he said she told him she forgot her sunglasses by the pool. He found the sunglasses in the hotel room. He thought she might have been meeting someone, so he went to the pool to look for her. The rest is history. Damn shame, if you ask me." Jorgensen gave Suzanne the once over. "Who's this?"

"My partner, Suzanne Cash. I'd like to speak with the brother. Can you arrange that? We have witnesses who identified a serial killer back in Sacramento. He's on the move, and it would be helpful if we can connect him to this murder. We think he's headed East."

"I'll escort you myself." Jorgensen turned to his men. "Get the tarps over these spatters here. It's gonna rain like a son-of-a-bitch in the next hour!"

Sam and Suzanne followed Jorgensen into town. Meyers Lake consisted of a small grocer, a Country-Western Bar, McDonald's, a post office, and an assortment of antique and gift stores. Outside of the two-block radius stood open fields.

They pulled behind a cinder-block building painted pea-green. The humidity had made Sam's hair curl, and his temper short. "They can keep this weather."

Suzanne's skin glowed, and the hair that had escaped her ponytail fell in wispy tendrils around her face.

"I've never been in a morgue before," she said, hesitating at the door.

"Would you rather wait out here?"

"Maybe it would be best."

Sam handed her the keys to the rental. "Stay cool, I won't be long." He watched her walk back to the car.

After introducing himself to the Coroner, Sam braced himself for what he was about to see. Another dead girl. The Coroner grabbed the handle of the drawer and pulled. A slender figure, covered in white sheeting, slid into view.

"We're not used to this kind of brutality around here," the Coroner said, his bushy brow cinched together. "The bastard not only slit her throat and left her to bleed to death, he blinded her with broken bottles, and mutilated her vagina." The man paused. "Her hands were tied behind her back with a friggin' piece of orange twine."

Sam said, "That's our guy." He bent forward to examine the girl's wrists. *Same as before.*

Suzanne started the engine. She turned the AC to 'cool' and flipped on the radio. She whipped through the stations, wiped a smudge off of the window, and picked lint off of her aqua green top. It began to rain. The first drops hit the window with a splat. As the drops increased, she peered out the windshield, and saw veins of lightning shatter the sky.

Thunder crashed in the distance. She turned off the air conditioner, rolled down her window, and killed the engine. She leaned back, breathing in the scent of sassafras. Dark clouds danced across the sky, dumping a deluge of rain, and filling potholes in the parking lot. She took it all in. This was not a California rain, this was Mother Nature connecting with the lush overgrowth of Queen Anne's Lace, wild asparagus, day lilies, and pennyroyal, wild ginger, and pigweed. Herbs that she had learned to recognize when Jack was alive. She closed her eyes, recalling fragments of their long talks.

"I believe God put a cure for every ailment the human body manifests; it's just a matter of cracking the code. Once you know what each flower or plant is capable of, you have to figure out how much to give and when."

Suzanne listened carefully to Jack, cherishing his knowledge, and moments shared learning new things. When he died, she tucked their dreams away with the hurt, and the disappointment, and the realization that her future was lost. Ben had no goals, he lived vicariously through others. Perhaps that's why she was drawn to him. The less of her soul she invested in the relationship, the better.

She felt Jack touch her cheek, but when she opened her eyes, it was Sam.

"Didn't mean to startle you," he said, climbing in beside her, his hair wet.

"You missed the good parts," she said, handing him the keys. "Thunder, lightning, the whole bit."

"It looks like the storm is headed east, and so are we. Dixon killed the girl, no doubt about it, unless there is another killer using orange twine."

She shivered. "What now?"

"I'm going to let you tell me."

"New York. He's going to search for the dark-haired girl. And the baby."

"Then that's where we'll head next. Back to the airport."

The next flight to JFK departed in forty-six minutes. Sam and Suzanne returned the car and hurried through the terminal.

"Just made it, the plane boards in eight minutes. We got the last two seats."

"No chance of an empty in the middle this time, eh?"

"No, but if Lady Luck is on my side, perhaps I'll get a seat next to you."

They boarded last, hoping to find two seats together. A woman by the window, held her infant in her lap. The baby wailed, kicked and fussed. Next to the ruckus, two empty seats. Suzanne sat next to the mother, immediately bonding with the fussy infant. Her smile made his teary-eyed face break into a grin.

His mother nodded apologetically and wiped away his tears with her thumb.

"This is Blake's first plane ride. I hope he doesn't disturb you too much." She brushed the boy's hair back. "We're on our way to see daddy."

Blake nestled closer to his mom. "Daddy," he said.

"How old is Blake?" Suzanne asked.

"He's eighteen months. We're on our way to meet his father. Gordy's in the military. He's stationed at NSA in Saratoga Springs for one more year. It's super expensive to live there, so we thought we'd save a little money by remaining in Akron with his mom. He tries to come home as much as possible, but it's tough. We figured Blake was old enough for a plane trip."

Suzanne felt a surge of love when the boy touched her arm. His brown eyes held the secrets of the universe. She heard a whisper deep in her soul, *destined for great things*, and she held out her hand. The boy didn't hesitate, he latched onto her hand and placed it on his head.

"He wants you to pet him. We have a dog at home," his mother said.

Suzanne ruffled his hair, and he squealed in delight. His little pink tongue hung from his mouth, and he panted, like a dog. Suzanne had hoped one day to have children of her own. That ship sailed long ago.

An empty womb can be a hard adjustment for some women. Suzanne filled her void with children who needed more love than most. Her children were ill, and she loved them like they were her own. She hugged them, fought for them, and mourned them when they passed. Not being able to return to her job was the biggest loss of all.

Sam watched the interaction between Suzanne and the child. He imagined her with children of her own. He too had wondered whether he wanted a family. As years passed by, the idea became more distant. He wished he had met Suzanne sooner. Perhaps they would've gotten on the same page and worked toward a goal. Family. He thought about his own Mom, Dad, and sister. He suddenly realized how much he missed them. Suzanne affected him that way, she gave him hope, purpose, opened his heart like a spigot.

By the time the plane landed at JFK, a bond had formed between Suzanne and the young mother. "Blake is destined for great things," she said, touching the boy's cheek. "He's very intelligent, and his purpose is to use his knowledge to help mankind. He's not mainstream, he's beyond. You may have a ball of fire on your hands. But if you let him follow his heart, it will lead to an incredible destiny."

The woman looked at Suzanne like she had two heads. "Wow. My horoscope said I'd receive good news today."

They picked up another rental car and headed to the Marriott Courtyard Hotel. After checking into adjoining rooms, they met in the lobby. "Are you getting anything?" Sam asked. "I feel like we're looking for a needle in a haystack."

"The only thing I'm getting is hungry," Suzanne said. "It's after four. The complimentary peanuts from the plane are wearing off. Can we grab an early dinner?"

Sam glanced at his watch. Although they had lost another hour, he hadn't thought about eating. Their last meal was breakfast. "I guess I'm still on California time. And just for the record—you have to tell me when you're hungry. I keep such crazy hours, food is the last thing on my mind."

"I'll make note of that." She wondered if that was why he wasn't in a relationship. Pretty hard to keep up with dating when you worked 24/7.

He ushered her out the main door and turned to the left. A couple of blocks from the hotel, Sam spotted the One-Forty-Four Restaurant and Grill. "What do you think?"

"It's food. I like it."

They were seated at a table near the bar area. Sam ordered coffee, and Suzanne ordered sparkling water with lime. By the time their drinks arrived, she had decided on grilled salmon over quinoa and mixed vegetables, and Sam ordered roasted chicken with truffle mashed potatoes, and asparagus.

"It's easy to see how one could get swallowed up in this city," Suzanne stated, sipping her drink. "I can't wait to get to Central Park. People watching. It's all about people watching."

Sam's face puzzled. "I didn't realize you'd been here before."

"I haven't."

"Then—"

"I don't know. It just came to me."

"We'll go as soon as we finish dinner," he said. "The faster we get a bead on Dixon, the better."

"The girl–she's an artist." Suzanne squeezed more lime into her drink. "She majored in art."

Sam withdrew his phone and punched in a number. It rang twice before Dove answered.

"Been waiting to hear from you—was it him?"

"Yes. Same M.O. as the others."

"What now?"

"We're in New York. I need a favor."

"Anything."

"Check with Sac State's Art Department—see if there were any sudden drop-outs." Sam did the math. "Three to six months ago. We're looking for a pretty, dark- haired girl, early twenties."

"Got it."

"Our girl is pregnant. How far along, we're not sure."

"Anything else?"

"Yeah. Talk to the teachers. Get names of friends she may have been close to. One way or another, someone must know why she left suddenly."

"I'll get right on it. Keep me posted."

"Thanks." Sam ended the call just in time to be served his meal. He gazed at Suzanne while she ate.

"This is the best salmon I have ever tasted."

"I'm enjoying it vicariously. You look so happy."

"I love food. Mmm. Tomato, basil and cream cheese on an "everything" bagel sounds good right now. Mike's has the best."

Sam stopped mid-bite.

Suzanne put a forkful of quinoa in her mouth and froze. She hadn't noticed that Sam sat still, waiting for her to speak.

"Mike's Bagel's—we have to find Mike's Bagel's."

Sam keyed the name into Google. "We're in luck. There's only one, and it's in Washington Heights. Unfortunately, they close at 5 p.m."

"Let's check out Central Park, see if I can pick up a vibe. We may be able to get her route."

"This is what I love about you. I can starve you, drag you around the country, and we're still on the same page."

"Don't get used to the starving part. I can get quite testy, you know."

"I'll take your word for it. Now, are you up for dessert? I hear New York is THE place for cheesecake."

"Can we share?"

"Absolutely." Sam placed an order for a slice of cheesecake with fresh strawberries and two forks.

After dinner they hailed a taxi.

While driving along Atlantic Avenue, Suzanne processed the scenery. She sensed the girl would've taken public transportation to the park. *She tries to blend in.* But the bagel shop was close to home, where she could satisfy her craving at a moment's notice.

———

Sentinels

Sheena had enjoyed her day at the park, but was anxious to get back to her part of town before Mike's closed at 5 p.m. When she entered the shop, she was greeted by Marta, employee extraordinaire.

"Hello, Brenda." Sheena had felt bad giving Marta a fictitious name, however, she had rebuilt her life in New York to protect herself and her baby. Lying was a sin, but whatever she needed to do to keep herself safe from Dixon was worth going to hell for.

"Hi Marta, can I have—"

"Tomato, basil, cream cheese, hold the lox, on an 'everything' bagel—right?"

"How do you remember everyone's order like that?"

"I have a photographic memory. My mom said I was foolish for wasting it here, but I love people, and remembering orders is a lot more fun than law codes."

"I wanted to be an artist. Not going to happen now."

"Why?"

"I dropped out of school. I won't be able to afford to go back."

"I can see why you may think you're out of the game," she said, her gaze dropping to Sheena's bump, "But being pregnant may just be the ticket you need to finish school. New York frowns on drop-out mothers-to-be."

"Are you saying I might be able to get a grant?"

"Yep."

"Maybe I'll look into that." Sheena knew it wasn't going to happen. In order to get a grant, she would have to give her social security number to register, and then Dixon would be able to find her. She accepted her bagel, handed Marta a five-dollar bill and said. "Thanks for the tip. Have a good day."

Sheena took her time walking back to the apartment. Renee wouldn't be home for another hour, and she hated being alone at this time of day. The apartment filled with shadows at 4 p.m. and she felt depressed. The lack of light reminded her of afternoons with Dixon. He had demanded the shades be pulled down in her apartment after 3 in the afternoon. Sheena had felt as though she missed half of her day. *He sucked more than light from my life. He stole my soul.*

A block from her apartment, Sheena stopped. She examined her surroundings, but all she saw was an old woman with a shopping cart, and a blond man dressed in a white linen suit, with a pink shirt, talking on a cell phone. He tilted his sunglasses and looked right at her. She pulled her kimono tighter to her breast. She glanced his way. The blond man began shouting obscenities into his phone, his high-pitched whine caused passersby to turn.

"What the fuck y'all looking at! Jesus Norman, people are staring at me. Don't you care?"

Sheena picked up her pace.

Something about the man gave her the willies. When she turned onto her street, she looked back to make sure she wasn't being followed, then ducked into her apartment building. To her relief, Simon was no longer on duty. His shift ended at 5 p.m. He would've picked up on her fear, asked a million questions. The man who relieved him was polite, but not nearly as personable. He tipped his hat, opened the door, and held it until she was inside. "Alonzo, has anyone asked about me?"

"No, Miss Bradlee. Are you expecting a guest?"

"No. Should someone ask for me, or describe me to you, please tell them you have no idea who they are referring to. I encountered a strange man on my walk, he may have followed me home."

"I will be sure to steer him away, Miss Bradlee."

"Thank you." Sheena proceeded to the elevator. When she opened the door to her apartment on the twenty-first floor, she rushed inside and locked the door. "You're panicking over nothing," she assured herself. Yet she went to the window and peeked outside. He was there. Across the street.

Sheena moved away from the window. She had changed her appearance, but was it enough? Her hair was shorter, darker. Her body had filled out. *He's not stupid*. If she could change her image, he could have done the same. Although she couldn't imagine him bleaching his hair or wearing pink, she had to believe he would do anything to find her.

The baby inside her responded to her fear with a tiny kick. She reclined on her bed, willing the fear to go away. She massaged her precious bump. "I promise, he will not hurt you."

Dixon stood outside the high-rise counting the floors. Thirty-nine. Sheena could be in any one of them. Thirty-nine high, eighteen across, times two. Over 1400 residents. Don't forget the doorman. *He probably moonlights as a bouncer in a strip club.* The man was 6'3", and at least 350 pounds. His head was so large, his cap sat on top of his head. His coat fit tight across his chest. *You're a bruiser, all right*. Dixon wasn't worried. *All men bleed the same*. All he needed to do was figure out how to get inside. The rest would fall into place.

Urgency

Sam and Suzanne left the cab a block from the park, and walked to 57th Street. Sam kept an eye on pedestrians, Suzanne kept an eye on subject matter. "I can see why she would love to sketch here."

"Definitely a people-watching wonderland."

"Yes. Bright colors, in all directions. Sad faces. Happy faces. Young and old. Look at the trees, they're lovely."

"Look at the drug deal going down on the corner. *Charming*." He looped his arm through hers. "The park is going through a shift change. Hold onto me." He glanced her way. "And keep your purse close to your body. This place is a treasure trove for pickpockets and purse snatchers."

Suzanne sighed. "And here I thought we were enjoying the view."

"You enjoy all you want, just hang on to me, and follow my lead." He nudged her shoulder. "Something you need to know about me—"

"What's that?"

"I'm really a knight in shining armor."

"Does that make me a damsel in distress?"

"I would never call you a damsel."

"What then?"

"Princess."

"Princess?"

Sam stopped. “My queen?”

“Much better,” she replied, stepping closer.

As they walked, snippets of people flashed through her mind. She froze, holding her hand in the air. “A woman, waving to a child.” She spotted a woman, holding a fist full of balloons in her hand. “She drew a woman and child. The child is holding a balloon, the mother is waving.”

“You feel our girl has been here?”

“Yes. She comes here often.” Jack showed her more. “I see a man. Fake eyes, and blond hair. He has a knife. Not just any knife. The knife is meant for hunting. For gutting animals.” *For getting rid of babies.*

———

Dixon sat on a bench across the street and waited. He enlarged Sheena’s cousin’s photo on his phone. He knew all about Renee. She worked as an editor for ABC 7 NY, made a six-figure income, and loved teacup Chihuahuas. When he finally saw Renee walk by, excitement buzzed in his veins. The doorman opened the door to let her in as if expecting her. *He must know everyone.* But how did he get that information? 1400 units—*a lot to keep track of.* Was there a registry with photos and names? Did they all carry some sort of fob that identified them? He wondered. He needed to find out. He waited until Renee was out of sight, then approached the building.

“Excuse me?” Dixon wrapped on the door. The doorman didn’t respond. Dixon knocked again this time harder. “I said, excuse me— I have a question.” This time the doorman sighed and opened the door.

“I just want to know if they’re hiring here. I was a doorman in Portland, and I’m looking for work.” Dixon gave the doorman his “poor me” look.

“I don’t know if they’re hiring, you’d have to check with the office and right now it’s closed.”

“What time do they open in the morning?” Dixon blinked, portraying an innocent.

“Come back at 9:00, ask for Judy.” The doorman handed Dixon a business card.

“Do you have to know everyone here? I mean there’s so many people here—”

"We have a monitor. But I've been here thirteen years, so I know just about everyone."

"I think I know someone who lives here. Renee Caperone."

The doorman grinned. He wasn't giving Dixon more than he already had.

"Actually, Renee's cousin and I are friends." Dixon said. "Did she have that baby yet?"

"Not yet. We're all betting on a baby boy. Miss Bradlee is carrying mighty low."

Dixon cringed. Bad enough she's pregnant. A baby boy would be disastrous. He'd grow up without his daddy, then his mama would go whorin' around. History would repeat itself. "Not gonna happen," he hissed.

"Excuse me?"

The doorman's puzzled expression brought Dixon back from his nightmare.

"I'm not so sure." He placed two fingers in the middle of his forehead. "I'm feeling it's a girl."

The doorman shook his head. "We'll see about that."

The sun hid behind the trees, peeking through bushes and casting shadows across the sidewalk. Suzanne let her mind wander. She gravitated toward a bench occupied by an elderly woman clutching two trash bags and mumbling to herself.

"God has forsaken thee!" she seethed through her toothless maw. "Thou shall be sent back to hell to suffer for eternity."

Suzanne was unnerved by the woman's wandering eye. Yet she stepped closer. The old woman cowered and covered her head with her arm. "My spot," she cried. "Here first."

"May I sit down and visit with you for a moment?" Suzanne asked in her softest voice. "I'm not going to hurt you," she said. "My name is Suzanne. I am looking for my friend. She's an artist."

The old woman uncovered her face, sat upright and patted the space beside her. "Do you have any spare change?"

Suzanne dug through her purse, gathering quarters, nickels, dimes, and pennies. "Here." She placed the coins in the woman's outstretched hand. And moved closer. The woman scooted to her right, making room for Suzanne to sit down as she counted the coins one by one.

"Two more dimes and three pennies," the old woman said, putting the coins in her pocket.

"My friend is young, early twenties," she said, reaching in her purse for a dollar bill. "She has long brown hair. She's pregnant. She comes here to sketch. She sits on this bench. Have you seen her?"

The old woman tucked the bill inside the top of her dingy T-shirt. "Miss pretty. She draws Hanna sometimes." The old woman began to rock.

"Are you Hanna?"

"I'm Hanna. Hanna Banana."

"My name is Suzanne. My mother called me Suzie Snoozy."

The old woman laughed. "Snoozy, Suzie! That's funny."

"I like Hanna Banana better. Did you see my friend today?"

"She told me a secret. Her name isn't Bradlee, it's Sheena. Sheena Beana!" The woman rocked and cackled, pleased with herself.

Suzanne glanced at Sam. Their eyes connected and held. Then he began texting.

"Do you know Sheena's last name?"

"No. She said no last names, or the devil would kill her baby. Hold him over the fire until he's a tiny crispy critter." The woman opened her bag and pulled out a ragged blanket. "You can't stay here," she said, her eyes narrowing.

"I'll go, but first, does Sheena come here every day?"

"Sometimes."

"Do you know where she lives?"

"On the mountain top. Where God can see her."

Suzanne pulled a twenty-dollar bill from her wallet for Hanna, and then joined Sam. "She was here today. I can feel it. What I'm not getting is where she lives, but I think Hanna said something helpful. She said her name is Sheena, not Bradlee, and she lives on the mountaintop where God can keep an eye on her."

Sam was busy checking the text he received from Dove. A list of students who had dropped out in last six months. Sheena Bradford was on that list. Sam then Googled her name, coming up with a Facebook page that hadn't been updated in weeks. The dark-haired girl was as Suzanne had described her. Young, beautiful. Unhappiness shown in her eyes in the last picture she had posted. Sam clicked on her friends and scrolled through the list. No one with the same last name. He sifted through her posts, looking for something to fill the puzzle pieces they needed. "Bingo," he said, holding up his phone. "She has a connection in New York. Renee Caperone."

He Googled Renee Caperone. A woman matching the photo on Sheena's Facebook page posing with the news team at ABC7NY popped up on the screen. Several photos included Renee, but one grabbed Sam's attention. Renee stood in front of a high-rise building giving a thumbs up. The caption read, "Home Sweet Home."

Suzanne's head began to ache. Jack stomped his feet, his arms flailing like a bird learning to fly. "No, no, no!" he screamed. Suzanne tried to understand the meaning behind his outburst.

"What do you want me to do?" she cried.

Sam grabbed her shoulders. "We got this, Suzanne. We have enough information to find her."

Suzanne shook off the image Jack had planted in her mind. A sharp object, with jagged edges. An object meant for hunting, killing, *gutting*. "We need to find her, NOW."

Chick Flicks

Renee unlocked the door. She had worked overtime on a feature one of the newscasters was doing on runaways. She had the piece ready to go when the man decided he wanted a completely different voice over. Once she disassembled and reassembled the soundtrack, he divulged that he didn't have written permission to use three of the photos he provided. Ugh. Repositioning the only photos they could use threw the story line off completely and the dialog needed be redone. A simple two-hour project turned into a nightmare and a screaming match. She didn't take shit from anybody, let alone some namby-pamby wannabe journalist. She yearned to put her feet up, turn on a mind-numbing chick flick, and drink a glass of Merlot.

Sheena came out of her room, her face practically dragging on the floor.

"Hey Cuz, que pasa?"

"There was this guy—"

"How many times have I told you? You're safe here. No one knows who you are. The staff has been instructed to report any unusual activity to me immediately. I pay top bucks for this kind of security. Now come on, sit. Let's watch girl porn. I haven't seen that new one with Reese Witherspoon."

"Reese Witherspoon is doing porn?"

"Chick flicks. Guys like skin, we get off on cute outfits and happy endings." Renee patted the seat beside her on the couch. "Did you go to the park to draw today?"

"Yes."

"Was that crazy lady there? What's her name?"

"Hanna? She was there. I'm almost finished with the shading on her drawing. Do you want to see it?"

"Absolutely! You know I love your stuff. Let's see!"

Sheena went to her room to get the drawing. When she returned, the house phone rang.

"Are you expecting anyone?" Renee crossed the room to pick up the phone.

"No. Are you?"

"No." Renee picked up the phone. "Yes?"

Alonso said, "There's a man and a woman in the lobby. He says he's a police officer from California and he needs to speak with you."

Renee's brow bunched with worry. "Tell them there must be some mistake. And whatever you do, don't let ANYONE up here."

"Yes Ma'am."

Renee hung up the phone and faced Sheena, who stood in the doorway. "All gone."

"Who was it?"

"Probably someone selling something. Alonso got rid of them."

"I'm scared. I felt someone watching me today."

"You're perfectly safe here. You need to concentrate on being a happy girl. For the baby."

Sheena flopped on the couch. "You're right. What are we watching?"

Renee stroked her arm. "This place is a fortress, no one gets past the guard dogs on duty. Alonso is a trained fighter. He works for us. He won't let anyone in that doesn't belong."

"But who even knew to come here? Doesn't that cause a little concern?"

"I think you're overreacting. But if you want, I can work from home the next few days. I could use a break."

"I don't know what I would do without you. You've been like my mom, dad, and cousin rolled into one."

Renee circled her arm around Sheena and pulled her close. "We're all we got, Cuz, we have to stick together."

Sam left the building feeling defeated. Suzanne took his arm. "It's not a dead end. She's here, I know it. And evidentially they know that someone is looking for them, why else would they lie? You saw how uncomfortable the doorman was when he returned. He knew that we knew he was lying. He had guilt written all over his face."

"You're right. Why did I think this was going to be easy?"

"I say we check out of our hotel and check-in someplace closer so we can keep an eye on the girl."

"And Dixon. He may have tried to contact her already, maybe that's why they're lying."

"The good thing is we found her. The next step is to get to her before Dixon does."

"You think like a cop."

"You must be rubbing off on me."

Dixon hid in the shadows, watching Sam and Suzanne. How did they know about Sheena? Maybe he had underestimated Metzger's little psychic friend. How much did they know? But he was ahead of the game. He had an in with the doorman. And tomorrow he might get the key to the castle.

Connections

Sam and Suzanne didn't go back to the hotel immediately. "I'm going to swing by the 34th Precinct, see if I can get more information on Renee Caperone. Her phone number is unlisted, perhaps they can get it for me, or have one of their men call to warn her."

"We don't know that Dixon is here for sure—"

"We don't know that he isn't."

Sam ushered Suzanne into the five-story brick building. They walked past a marble Memorial Wall etched with the names of those who had served the department, dating back to the late 1800's, and towards the desk Sergeant.

"What can I do for you?"

"I'm Detective Sam Metzger from the Goldorado Sheriff's Department in California. We believe a serial killer has traveled to Washington Heights, and that one your residents may be in danger."

The sergeant didn't speak until he had checked Sam's ID and entered his name into his computer. "Do you have the suspect's name?"

"Sheriff James Dixon."

"This some kind of a joke?" The Sergeant looked around, expecting to see a camera. When he realized that Sam was serious, he typed Dixon's name into the computer.

"James Dixon has an APB out on him." The Sergeant turned the screen toward Sam. "This the guy?"

"Yes. However, I doubt he is using that name. We discovered he has several identities."

"Who's the person in danger?"

"We know very little about her. Her name is Sheena Bradford. She was an art student at Sac State. She dropped out six months ago and dropped off the radar. We believe she's hiding out at her cousin's place in Washington Heights. The Belvedere."

"Do you have the cousin's name?"

"Renee Caperone."

"Renee? From ABC7?"

"According to Google—"

"I know Renee. She's friends with my niece. Nice gal."

"We stopped by her apartment to warn her, but—"

"Let me guess," the Sergeant raised his hands to make air quotes, "she wasn't home."

"You guessed it. I wasn't about to argue with the doorman. He looked like he could break my face in a heartbeat."

"Alonso. Yeah, he boxed for quite a few years. He takes his job seriously. We've been called out there a few times. He can be really ugly–but he's there to make sure no one enters the building without permission."

"Well, he's doing a great job. And Ms. Caperone claimed not to be in when we paid her a visit."

Let me text my niece for Renee's number."

Suzanne felt woozy. As if two bodies occupied the same space in her body. She wanted a beer. *I don't drink beer.* She opened her purse and pulled out a compact. She opened it, looked in the mirror, and gasped. Her image was distorted. *Blurry. Blonde.* She blinked her eyes. The image did the same. She felt as though she were morphing into a man's body, yet she felt compelled to do feminine things. *Lipstick.* What is this about? One thing was clear. She did not feel like herself.

"He's disguised himself."

Sam stepped toward her. "This is Suzanne Cash. She's my partner on the case." The reason we've gotten this far is because of this young lady. She's a psychic."

Suzanne expected him to roll his eyes, break out in laughter, but he didn't. Instead he held up his hand and said, "I get it. My Mom believes in all that stuff."

The Sergeant's cell phone beeped. "It's my niece. She gave me Renee's number." He dialed the number and listened. "Renee, this Jerry Veniccio, Lola's uncle calling from the 34th Precinct. I have a Detective Samson Metzger here from California. He says he needs to speak with you right away. Can you call me back please?"

"While we're waiting for a call back, you wanna tell me what this guy is wanted for?"

"He's tortured and killed over a dozen women—that we know of. You have no idea what he's capable of."

"This BOLO doesn't give many details. Let me get this over to my guys."

"Thanks, I appreciate it."

"Grab some coffee, I'll be right back."

Sam poured a cup of coffee in a Styrofoam cup and handed it to Suzanne. "Black, right?"

"Yes, but maybe some cream and sugar this time. You guys like it a little strong."

"It's a wonder I don't bleed caffeine."

"I'm feeling agitated. Jack is racing in my head. Like he has a bus to catch or something." She pressed her palm on her forehead. "I get the feeling that the clock is ticking. That if we don't catch Dixon soon, that baby won't make it to term."

"When we left Sacramento, I thought we were on a wild goose chase. I never dreamed we'd end up this close to the girl. And if we're this close, Dixon can't be far behind."

"Do you have a plan?" Suzanne leaned over to see what Sam was doing on his phone.

"I'm searching for the closest hotel for starters."

On A Mission

Dixon checked into the Hotel Cliff at 7 p.m. He could almost see Sheena's apartment from the window in his room. He wondered what she was doing and realized that he had no idea because he had never taken an interest. He knew she went to Sac State. He knew she had a mole on her left inner thigh. He knew that her mouth was soft, plump, pliable, juicy. He knew he loved her smooth, flawless skin. The way she tossed her hair to the side when she went down on him. Now, those were things to know. But then he remembered she hadn't had her period...they fucked the whole month without interruption. Her breasts had been tender, *fuller*.

His erection strained against his linen pants. He pictured Sheena in her lace bra and panties. She made those Victoria Secret models look like trolls. He imagined her swollen belly, the sound of the knife splitting her taut flesh, *like one of Grandpa's watermelons*. He got off the bed and undressed. He couldn't afford an accident in his one pair of dress trousers. He had a role to play in the morning. Stains were not an option. His plan was to charm the pants off the property manager, get hired as a doorman, and gain access to Sheena.

Full Alert

Renee ignored the call on her cell phone. What she needed most was down time. A rough day at work had her nerves humming, and a headache threatened to develop into a migraine. She was determined to enjoy her glass of wine, a funny movie, and chillax with her favorite person on the planet. She convinced herself that the person who had paid a visit was no danger. *So why is your head throbbing like a MoFo*? Since Sheena had moved in there was always that niggling. What if? What if that asshole decided to track her down? What if he decided he wanted to be the baby's daddy, and haul her cousin back to Sacramento, where she wouldn't be able to watch over her? She cared too much for the girl to let that happen. Soon there would be a little one to dote over, and she didn't want to miss out.

"Let's watch 'Me Before You.' I heard good reviews, and after the day I had, a good laugh would be welcome."

Sheena clicked on the TV and pressed Netflix. She scrolled through the menu until she found the movie. Before she pressed play, she asked, "Is everything okay? You seemed bothered by something."

"Had a rotten day. But—it's over. We're exactly where we need to be."

"I'm still a little freaked out about that guy."

"What guy?"

"The guy across the street."

"It was probably nothing." She'd lived in Washington Heights Terrace for nine years. Never had she felt more vulnerable. Although the staff looked out for their residents, she knew the doormen made a meager living, and wasn't sure if any of them would accept a bribe. She intended to speak with Judy, the property manager, in the morning to make sure the staff was on full alert.

A Dark Place

Sam and Suzanne drove back to the Marriott, checked out and returned to Washington Heights. They found the Hotel Cliff with ease and were checked in within the hour. Sam carried Suzanne's bag to her door.

"I'll be next door if you need anything," he said.

"I'll be fine. Let me know if you get a call."

Sam slid his key card into the slot and turned the handle to enter. Across the hall, an eye peered through the peephole.

"Well I'll be damned," Dixon whispered. "This IS my lucky day."

Suzanne tossed and turned in her bed. Her dreams were laden with snippets from her younger years. *Jack.* They seemed to be in a house of mirrors. Everywhere she looked, he was there. "What do you want from me?" Her voice was hoarse.

"Do you see me," he asked.

"You're scaring me," she cried. But he wouldn't stop.

"Do you see me?", he demanded.

"I see you. Now stop!"

He stood in front of her. The mirror was gone. "Be careful, Suzanne," he said, his voice trailing away.

Suzanne bolted upright. She slowed the stampede in her chest. "It's a warning," she whispered. She felt Dixon's evil intent down deep inside. A dark place. A place where the devil hides in plain sight. She gasped. "He's here."

———

Sam passed his sobriety coin from finger to finger. When his mind was weighed down by stress or worry, he could rely on the trick to reroute his thoughts. It cleared his mind. *Relax.* If he was lucky, sleep would follow.

The red glowing numerals read 2:45. He checked his phone. Renee Caperone hadn't return Sergeant Viniccio's call earlier, so he called her himself and left a message. Was she that scared? Or that naïve? *Why?*

He dozed between 3:09 and 3:30. In his dream, Suzanne lay beside him, her arm, snug around his waist. Her body nestled close to his. Skin to skin. Her heart beating close to his. Her breath whispering across his chest. He wanted to stay in that moment forever. Something jarred him awake.

He heard a muffled noise. He went to the door joining his room to Suzanne's and listened. Nothing. Perhaps she talked in her sleep? He pressed his ear against the door. The wood felt cool against his cheek. When silence prevailed, he got back into bed.

At 5:00 a.m. another sound woke him. His alarm. He showered, dressed, and left his room at 5:30 in search of coffee. At 6:05, he returned with two coffees, and two bagels. He rapped lightly on Suzanne's door. She didn't answer.

———

Alibi

Dixon was propped up on one elbow, his face inches from Suzanne's. He moved a lock of hair away from her cheek and studied her ear. He thought about cutting it off and leaving it under Sam's door, but decided he wanted a little fun first.

How easy it had been to break into her room, chloroform her, and steal her into the night. And the cool part was, no one would know. He made sure he avoided the surveillance camera by covering the lens with a piece of gaffer's tape. Once he had Suzanne, he removed the tape, and jiggled the lens with a coat hanger. Next, he went downstairs to the front desk to establish his alibi. The hotel was so ancient, he doubted the cameras worked at all. But he couldn't take a chance. The young man at the desk was very accommodating and fetched an extra blanket. "I'm sorry you couldn't get through. Our phones are the pits. Is there anything else I can get for you?"

"You been more than helpful," Dixon replied, holding up the blanket. "I almost forgot to ask, is there a flower shop close by? My Grandmother's wake is tomorrow. I want to pick up some flowers. I used to be in the business, and I know what my dear Grandmother would have wanted."

The desk clerk wrote the name of the closest florist.

Dixon smiled. "Thank you, you are too kind."

He left the desk clerk and headed toward the elevator, playing his part all the way up to his room.

He shut the door and sat down on the bed beside Suzanne. "There, my little darling. All done." He snickered. "Won't Sam be surprised to find his personal bloodhound is nowhere to be found?"

He rested his head on Suzanne's breast. He considered fucking the life out of her, but then he'd lose his bartering tool. No, he'd keep her until he had dealt with Sheena. "And then—" he ran his hand along the inside of her thigh, —"then we'll see."

Sam called Suzanne's cell phone. Maybe she was taking a shower. Maybe she was one of those people who could sleep through a mortar attack, an avalanche, or a hurricane. He turned off the ringer on his phone when he needed to sleep. Maybe she did the same. He glanced at the clock. 6:58 a.m. He sipped his coffee. *Give her an hour*. She deserved that much. She'd been up thirty-six hours, maybe more. *She must be exhausted*. His phone rang.

"Detective Metzger, it's Renee Caperone, returning your call. My apologies for calling so early, but I didn't want to talk when my cousin was around. She's still sleeping, I thought now would be a good time. Tell me what this is all about."

"I'm hoping you can fill me in, Ms. Caperone. What we know is that a very dangerous man is on the loose. We think he is in New York, and we think he is after your cousin–and the baby."

"No one knows about the baby."

"Jim Dixon knows."

"How? Sheena didn't tell anyone."

"I don't have that answer. Maybe he figured it out."

"How did *you* find out?"

"I am working with a woman who—" Suddenly everything seemed preposterous. How could he explain Suzanne to this woman? "She's a psychic. She helped us find two girls Dixon had been holding prisoner. Believe me, as farfetched as it may seem, Suzanne has been spot-on with her information." He paused. "She led me to you." Sam heard Renee gasp. "Can we come over and talk?"

"Give us an hour. Sheena is sleeping."

"So is Suzanne. It was a long night for everyone."

"You have the address?"

"Yes. But your doorman is very protective."

"Yes, they all are." Renee said. "We recently lost one of our best. He was sixty-one, ready for retirement. Sudden heart attack. Gone."

"I'm sorry for your loss."

"It means breaking in a new doorman. I'm hoping for someone as dedicated as Clifford was." Renee's voice trailed off. "I'll see you in an hour."

Sam dialed Suzanne's room from the hotel phone twenty minutes later. He could hear the phone ringing in the adjoining room. She didn't answer.

He hung up and knocked on the door connecting the two rooms. "Suzanne," he called, "Are you awake?" No answer. He knocked again this time louder. Still no answer. He called the front desk.

"This is Detective Metzger in room 310. My partner, Suzanne Cash checked into room 312. Have you seen her? Late thirties, five foot-four, petite build, long dark hair. She's not answering her phone.

"I've been at the desk since 5 a.m.. No one has left the building matching that description, but I cannot be certain your partner did not leave before my shift, or during the shift change."

"In that case, please send someone with a house key. I need to be certain she is okay."

"I will send the manager right away."

Dixon opened the bathroom door and grabbed a towel from the rack. "Fuckin' pig," he seethed, mopping up the urine around Suzanne's bottom. He had propped her up against the bathtub, bound her hands and feet with orange twine, and taped her mouth. Once he cleaned up the mess, he removed the tape from her mouth and administered a dose of Ketamine with an eye dropper.

He wasn't expecting her to bite him.

"Goddammit!" He kicked her thigh. "That hurt, bitch!"

She tried to speak, but Dixon tore off a fresh piece of tape and slapped it over her mouth.

"Gotta love the high," he said, checking her bindings. "Now," he said, rising. "I've got a little business to take care of. Do yourself a favor and be a good girl, otherwise I will kill your boyfriend. Understood?"

Suzanne's eyes rolled back. Her head slumped and her body went limp. However, her brain remained active.

She was on a swing. Jack stood behind her pushing, higher, and higher. She touched the sky with her toes.

The sky turned a greenish grey. She let go of the chains. *I'm flying*. Thick, swollen clouds hurried by. Birds flanked her on both sides, their wings flapping hard against their bodies, their beaks chattering in unison. Suzanne could see the down beneath their wings, she sensed the hunger in their eyes. Below, Jack was a tiny speck. She thought she heard him cackling like a crow.

As she soared into the sky, the birds pecked at her body. Drops of blood spattered her arms. She couldn't scream. She had no mouth. *Where did it go*? She touched the place where her lips had been, the surface smooth.

Higher and higher she climbed, until she crashed into something hard. Her head split open like an egg. Her bare legs dangled below her. Blood ran down her face. She reached for her head, but her hands were not her own. *Talons*? If only she could speak. She wanted an aspirin, a band aide to hold her brain in place.

She began to fall.

Art of Deception

Dixon dressed in his new white linen slacks, a pale grey shirt, peach color tie, and white jacket. He checked his appearance. *Looking good.* He glanced over his shoulder at the body slumped on the bathroom floor. *She's out.* Good. He had work to do.

At 8:15 a.m., he entered Washington Heights Terrace. The doorman he had spoken with the day before had been replaced by an elderly gentleman, who appeared to have been a Mafia hit man in a previous life.

"I'd like to speak with Judy."

"Do you have an appointment, Mister—"

"Duane. Duane Cooley."

"Mizz Judy doesn't see walk-ins."

"Alonso told me she was looking for a doorman. He said to come back this morning."

The doorman gave Dixon the once over. "Doorman, eh? I think she was looking for someone with a little more—*muscle*."

Dixon returned the man's smirk. "Should I kick your ass right here?" He swept the room with his hand. "Or are you going to let me see Judy?"

The man studied Dixon's face for a moment. "Absolutely. One moment."

Dixon watched the man's back disappear into the office across from the elevator. As tempted as he was to make a mad dash, he reconsidered. *No, get the job. Get the girl*. He checked his watch. He wondered if Sam had figured out that his sweetie was missing. He wished he could be a fly on the wall for that scene. Maybe I'll let her live. Maybe I won't. Right now, the only thing that mattered was that Sam was detained.

"Mr. Cooley?" A striking woman in her fifties approached Dixon with an outstretched hand. "I'm Judy Wells, can I help you?"

Dixon addressed the woman's shoes. "Jimmy Choo?"

"Why yes, every woman should own at least one pair. What can I do for you Mr. Cooley?"

"I'd like to fill the position you have open for a doorman."

"We haven't advertised, it was only last week that we—how did you hear about the position?"

"Alonso told me. I stopped by yesterday, but you weren't in."

The woman pivoted on her Jimmy Choo's. "Come. We can talk in my office."

Inside Judy's office, Dixon noted the expensive art on the walls. "You have exquisite taste, Ms. Wells."

"Thank you. My husband and I love to travel. I acquire pieces from all over the world. I like the one behind you. Not a collected artist, but I fell in love with his style.

Dixon noticed how she brightened when she said "style." *Probably fucked the guy*. "I can see why. His brush strokes are incredible, and his color choices take your breath away."

"Do you study art, Mr. Cooley?"

"I know what I like," he said.

"Most of our doorman are–how shall I say this without sounding—"

"Ex-thugs?"

"They're trained to be gentlemen, and very good with our residents."

"I agree. Alonso was a prince."

"I have to be honest you don't strike me as the doorman type, Mr. Cooley."

Dixon removed his jacket, rolled up his sleeve, and flexed his muscle.

His steely glare trapped her comment in her throat. "Can't always judge a book by its cover."

Judy's expression changed. "You're right. Might be refreshing to have an employee with a little *culture*." She rose and opened a closet door on the far side of the room. "You look like a 42 long." She produced a red jacket with a Washington Heights Terrace logo stitched across the pocket. "Do you have a white shirt–black pants?"

"Yes."

"Good. Come back at 11:00. If your background checks out, I can get you started then."

Do Not Disturb

Sam stood behind the hotel manager his sobriety coin clenched in his fist. When the man slid his keycard in the slot and opened the door, Sam pushed past him. The room was empty.

"I don't understand," he said. "No one saw her leave?"

"The front desk is always manned, but that's not to say that the employee on duty doesn't step away from time to time. We have security cameras on every floor. No one has reported anything out of the ordinary. Are you sure she didn't just leave?"

"We're working on a case. A very big case. She wouldn't have left without telling me."

"Well, I will have to get in touch with my manager, but I'm sure if she doesn't turn up soon, we can check the security cameras."

Sam glanced at his phone. *Where is she*? "Do what you have to do. I need answers ASAP."

The manager eased his way toward the door. "Probably out for a jog. It's a beautiful day."

Sam looked around the room. He saw the clothes she wore the day before, but not her phone, or her key. *Maybe her phone is on silent?* He checked the closet. Purse. Shoes. "Perhaps you're right. But just to be sure, I'd like to review the tapes."

The manager retreated, closing the door behind him. Sam stood in the middle of the room. What did he really know about Suzanne? What if something had spooked her? What if she had decided this work was too dangerous, not something she wanted to involve herself in, and didn't know how to tell him? What if she had decided to find the girl on her own?

Sam retraced their steps of the previous day. He searched for the homeless woman Suzanne had spoken to and found her collecting cans from the trash one hundred yards from where they spoke.

"Do you remember me from yesterday? I was here with a woman, dark hair, pretty?"

The woman assessed Sam. "Ain't seen nobody this morning." She returned to her can collecting.

"If you see her, please tell her Sam is worried." He dug in his wallet for a twenty-dollar bill. "Please," he said, folding the money into her hand.

When he returned to the hotel, he was met with concerned faces. The hotel manager stepped from behind the desk. "Anything?"

Sam shook his head. "Let's take a look at that footage."

Dixon slipped past Sam and the manager in the lobby. He entered the elevator and held his breath until the door closed. He avoided looking at the camera in the upper righthand corner. When the elevator stopped, he acted as if he had all the time in the world to exit. Once he was back in his room, he opened the door to the bathroom to find Suzanne still passed out. Her phone vibrated across the floor. He wished he had more time to unclothe her, ravish her body, and kill her properly. But, he had a job, and needed to report to work in an hour.

He filled an eyedropper with Ketamine. "Open up, Bitch." Satisfied that she would be flying high for hours, he quickly changed into his new black pants, a white shirt, and black loafers. He closed the door with such force, he didn't notice the "DO NOT DISTURB" sign fall to the floor.

Sam answered his phone on the first ring, trying not to let his disappointment seep into his tone. "Ms. Caperone."

"I thought you said an hour."

"My apologies. Something has come up." He pinched the bridge of his nose. "Is Sheena awake? I'd like to talk with her."

"My cousin came to me for protection, and to get away from any stress that might impede her pregnancy. You can tell me what's going on. I'll assess whether it's essential she speak with you."

"Do you understand the danger she's in? If we don't find Dixon and put him away, your cousin will be his next victim."

"How can you be sure he knows where she is?"

"I'm working with a reputable psychic."

"Your psychic could be wrong."

"He's here."

"How do you know?" She insisted. "How can you be sure?"

For the first time that morning, he understood. "Because—Suzanne is missing."

HELP

Suzanne's world came to a halt. Giant locusts buzzed in her ears. Her blood turned to granite in her veins. Nothing moved. Her eyelashes, heavy ropes that tied her to the floor like *Gulliver's Travels*. How did she end up in Lilliput? It didn't matter. She felt the drops slide down her throat. And before she could say, "None for me, thank you, I've had enough," she spiraled into a dark abyss.

She stood on a rock, fire blazing all around her. She saw Jack on a ledge before her, his outstretched arms seemed suspended in air, his feet crossed in an awkward position. A crown of thorns circled his head. *Jesus*. Blood trickled from one eye.

"I didn't mean to hurt you. It was my duty. My country needed me. It was war."

"I loved you."

"I loved you more."

"You left me behind."

"I'm here now."

"And so am I. Am I dead?"

"No. But if Sam doesn't find you soon—"

"Sam? Where is he?" She ducked, avoiding the beast flying close to her head.

"You have to fight off the demons, Suzanne. There isn't much time."

"Help me, Jack." She ducked again, but this time the beast swallowed her whole.

Privacy

Dixon entered Washington Square Terrace promptly at 11:00 his red jacket, still in plastic, draped over his arm. Simon greeted him with a broad smile and outstretched hand.

"You must me the new guy–the name's Simon."

"Please to meet you, Simon." Dixon's hand went limp on the handshake. His eyes fluttered. "Miss Judy is expecting me." Dixon cocked his hip and jutted his bottom lip.

Simon chuckled. "She's in her office."

Dixon knocked softly.

Judy appeared at the door a phone cradled at her cheek. "Yes, Renee, I know, I know. No worries, in fact I am training another doorman as we speak." Judy winked at Dixon and motioned for him to enter. "Your cousin is safe, we will make sure of it, and if the police have any questions about the security in our building, they can contact me directly." Judy paused, rolled her eyes, and straightened the pile of papers on her desk. "Yes, absolutely. Bye now." She placed the phone on the receiver and sighed. "Welcome to Washington Heights Terrace."

"Sounds like they keep you on your toes."

"Yes. Your timing couldn't be more perfect. We lost Cliff to cancer. He was with us for twenty-six years, and I have barely had time to send flowers."

"I'm so sorry."

"Thank you. As you may have overheard, the safety of our residents is crucial. When we have a situation, and they don't occur very often, my staff is put on high alert until told otherwise. My apologies for casting you into the mix so soon." She leaned against her desk, her tone matter-of-fact, "I have checked your credentials, and the only flaw you have on record is an unpaid parking ticket from 1983. Is there anything else I should be aware of?"

"I'm gay?"

Judy crinkled her nose, "I hope you're computer savvy. It will expedite your training all the faster."

"I know enough to get by. Where do I start?"

"First, let's get these forms filled out and then," she said, "I will give you a tour of the building."

Sam entered the building. Simon tipped his hat. "Morning sir, can I help you?"

"I'm here to see Ms. Caperone. She's expecting me."

Simon picked up the house phone. "Miz Caperone, there is a gentleman here to see you, a Mr.—" Simon paused, his hand covering the receiver. "Who shall I say is calling?"

"Detective Metzger."

"A Detective Metzger is here to see you." Simon glanced at Sam. "Yes, Ma'am, I will send him right up."

Sam saw a man and woman enter the elevator moments before Simon hung up the phone. As the elevator door closed, he glimpsed the man's profile.

"That's Miz Judy. She's the manager here. She must be touring the new hire," Simon said. "He sure gonna make things interesting around here."

Sam cocked his head. "And why is that?"

"Don't get me wrong, Detective, I enjoy every color of the rainbow, but not sure the residents are ready for—"

"For what?"

"My Mama woulda slapped me silly if I sashayed like that in public. Now days, the closet door is off the hinges."

"The new hire is gay?"

"Flame broiled and buttered."

"Interesting." Sam nodded toward the elevator. "Do I need a passkey or something?"

"Oh—almost forgot." Simon walked to the elevator and swiped his badge. "Miz Caperone is in 1308. Thirteenth floor, to your right."

Sam rode to the eleventh floor in a daze. "Where could she be?" he whispered. He caught his image in one of the elevator's four mirrors. He rubbed the stubble on his chin. He hoped Renee Caperone wouldn't judge him by his unkempt look.

He approached 1308 and knocked softly. The door opened to a short woman in her thirties. "Ms. Caperone?"

"Renee," she said extending one hand. "Come in."

Sam eyes soaked in a stunning young lady sitting on a white leather sofa.

"My cousin, Sheena." Renee took the seat beside her.

"I'm Detective Sam Metzger from the Goldorado Sheriff's department in California. I'd like to speak to you about James Dixon."

Sheena's hands went to the bump in her lap. "How did you find me?"

"It really wasn't that hard. Which means Dixon—"

"He can't know where I am. He'll kill me—kill the baby!"

Renee touched Sheena's hand. "Listen–NO one is going to hurt you OR the baby."

Tears gathered in Sheena's eyes. "If this man found me, so can Dixon."

"She's right. Dixon is a pro."

Renee's forehead furrowed. "Pro at what?"

"Dixon is a killer—a cold-blooded killer. He's calculating, maniacal and he'll stop at nothing."

Renee slipped her arm around Sheena and drew her close. "What do we do?"

"Nothing at the moment. Can you stay put for a couple of days?"

"I can work from here, I guess, but how long will we have to be prisoners in our own home?"

"I wish I had the answer to that."

Sheena leaned forward, "Who told you I was here?"

"As I told your cousin earlier, a psychic. Her name is Suzanne."

Sheena turned to her cousin. "Renee, how could you keep this from me? That bastard wanted me to get an abortion."

"I know, but I never thought he was—dangerous."

"He's here because he wants to kill my baby," she cried.

Sam went to window. "The building is secure—right?"

"Yes. Everyone who works here has been checked out thoroughly. Judy is a stickler for background checks. Simon and Alonso are awesome. And Clifford—he was my favorite." Renee paused. "Judy will replace him with someone just as..."

Sheena placed her hand over Renee's. "Judy only hires professionals. Simon and Alonso are both certified to carry weapons and were boxers back in the day. They won't let anyone come near us."

"Nevertheless—keep your doors locked. And if you need anything, call me. I don't care if it's three in the morning."

Both women nodded. Sam stepped toward the door. "Don't get up, I'll find my way out."

As Sam took his leave, he turned to his left. The woman he had seen enter the elevator earlier disappeared into an alcove. Sam heard her say, "This is where our residents can get snacks and sodas. During inclement weather, they change out some of the candy bars for soup. The residents love it."

Dixon saw Sam's back in the hallway. He struggled to focus on Judy's instructions as she led him from the vending area to a lounge with a large flat screen TV and three commercial washers and dryers.

"Each resident has their own unit in their apartment, but the equipment is designed for small loads. We installed commercial grade equipment mainly for comforters, thick blankets, and winter-wear. It does get cold here."

Dixon pictured Judy's pinched features inside the front loader going around and around and around, as the tub filled with her blood. "I'm looking forward to my first snow."

"We pride ourselves on cleanliness, privacy, and protection. New York can be a dangerous city. We get all sorts of riff-raff hanging around our building with the park across the street. Our doormen are the gate keepers."

Dixon nodded. "I totally understand."

"Excellent, Mr. Cooley. I think we are going to hit it off."

"When do I start?"

"Can you be back after lunch?"

"*Perfect,*" he said.

New Guy

Something fleshy kept getting in the way of Suzanne's teeth. She wanted to yank every tooth out of her mouth, feel the smoothness of her gums rubbing against one another. Enjoy the snakes slithering in and out of her mouth. *I don't like scales stuck between my teeth.* She shivered. Cold air blasted her feet and ankles, and she tucked them beneath her as best she could. She pictured herself as an armadillo. Her eyes lids had stopped working, and her head pounded to the beat of Snoop Dog. Stars shattered all around her as she floated into space. *Good-bye cruel world, I'm off to join the circus.* But the circus wasn't a friendly place. The animals had sharp, gnashing teeth that bit through her armor and nibbled at her intestines.

The pounding continued. A *cannon*? *Every good circus has a huge cannon.* She imagined herself being blasted from the barrel. The pounding stopped. *Look at me, I'm flying!*

She heard metal scraping metal, a clicking noise she couldn't define. Warm fuzz settled on her shoulders. A voice echoed in her head. You're not in Kansas anymore, Dorothy. *Gimme back those shoes.*

Dixon hurried through the Hotel Cliff lobby and rode an empty elevator to his floor. He slipped his key into the door slot and turned the handle. As he pushed the door open, he noticed the door hanger had been turned. He flipped the sign back to DO NOT DISTURB.

He entered the room with caution. Seeing the unmade bed relieved his angst. He undressed. *First things first.*

"Hello, darlin'."

Suzanne lay in a fetal position on the bathroom floor. Her eyes fluttered.

"Miss me?" he asked, squatting close to her face. He held two fingers against the artery in her neck, checking her pulse. "Let's see what Sam sees in you." He removed the tape from her mouth, and the orange twine from her ankles. His hand reached for her breast and squeezed. "Nice." She squirmed away from his touch.

Suzanne tried to click her heels three times. "There's no place like home," she heard Jack say. But the face that loomed over her wasn't his. Red glowing eyes, a forked tongue slithered between sharp teeth. The thing touched her, licked her breast. She felt the pressure of its weight settle on top of her. Something hot, molten, seared her cheek. Stars burst in her head and she floated away. When she fell back to earth, she landed on a lamppost. Her body shattered everywhere.

No time to pick up the pieces. The pounding sound returned. Time to get back to the circus—clean up the mess. *Housekeeping.*

Dixon had lifted Suzanne's legs over his shoulders, ready to ram himself inside her again, when the knock on the door came. "What the fuck," he grumbled. He pushed Suzanne aside and went to the door.

"Housekeeping," the woman said, averting her eyes away from his naked chest.

"Can't you read?" he asked, pointing to the sign on the door.

"Sign not there earlier, I come back."

"Well, it's here now, and as you can see," He opened the door wider, making her flinch.

"I come back," she said, motioning to her cart.

Dixon closed the door. "Fuck." He returned to the bathroom to find Suzanne lying in a fetal position. "Great," he snarled. He got in the shower, turned on the water, drowning out the sound of her dry heaves.

Once he finished dressing, he gave Suzanne another cocktail and packed his bag. She would be dead by morning. *Time to go back to work.*

———

Dixon followed Judy down the elevator, stopping at each floor so her new employee could acquaint himself with the layout of the building. "My tenants expect their privacy to be maintained at all times. They are to be greeted like they are the most important person on the planet, however, you do not pry. If they offer information about their day, or themselves, you are expected to commit that information to memory. If Mrs. Stein in 1304 rattles on about her six ungrateful children, I expect you to listen, but that doesn't mean you share the fact that two of them are thieves, and the other four are imbeciles. I do not tolerate gossip, tardiness, or insubordination. Are we clear?"

Dixon nodded. "Yes Ma'am."

I like you, Duane. Don't fuck up, okay?"

———

Sam burst into the building, New York police at his heals. Alonso raised both hands in the air and shouted, "Hey! You just can't just bust in here —this is people's homes!"

Sam flipped open his wallet, displaying his badge. "We have a warrant."

"You let me see that warrant. He paused to study Sam's I.D. "We have rules here."

"Badge, warrant, trumps rules. We're looking for a very dangerous man. 6'2, 185 pounds, wearing a white Prada jacket. Blond hair. May appear gay."

Alonso's eyes lit up. "You mean that Duane Cooley dude? He's with Miz Judy on a tour. She just hired him."

"Where are they now?"

"I dunno."

"One of your residents is in trouble. She's pregnant for Chrissake's."

"You mean Miz Bradlee?"

"The girl's name is Sheena Bradford. Her cousin's name is Renee

Caperone. Sheena has long dark hair, early twenties. She's from California."

Alonso squinched his brow. "That's sounds like the girl, but she goes by Bradlee.

Sam turned to address Officer Vespa, the commanding officer in his group. "It's her."

"How do you want proceed?"

"Take your men and block off all the exits. No one is to come or go without my permission. You," he pointed to a muscular young officer.

"Pizzo, sir, Anthony Pizzo."

"Come with me, Pizzo."

Sam headed for the elevator. Alonso swiped his badge, and the door opened. "You gonna need this," he said, handing Sam a temporary keycard.

"Ever shot a man?" Sam turned to Pizzo.

"No, sir," he answered, "I've been on the force six years. Come close a few times. I could shoot someone if I had to."

"Today might be your lucky day."

Dixon stifled a yawn. Judy's droning about this tenant and that tenant bored him to tears. Once he had learned what he had come for, Miss Chatty Kathy had to go. "It's going to be exciting having a little one around."

"How did you—"

"Oh, the mama-to-be came home when I was speaking with Alonso. That's going to be one bea-u-ti-ful child."

"Let's keep focused, shall we?"

"I was just wondering if she requires any special attention. Suppose she goes into labor? Or needs a pickle at two in the morning?"

"Can we keep moving? I have a potential tenant coming in in an hour, I want you acclimated, so you can take your post and shadow Alfonse."

"Where does that door lead to?"

"The janitorial closet. The one next to it is the door to the stairway." Judy gave Dixon a gentle shove. "C'mon, you may as well see the rooftop garden. You'll be locking up at 10 p.m. No exceptions. Tenants tend to whine when it's time to vacate the terrace. They come up with all kinds of excuses." Judy opened the door and climbed the stairs, Dixon followed close behind. The stairwell was well insulated. No noise. He decided it was the perfect moment to pull out the knife he had stashed in waistband.

She didn't expect the knife pressed against her spine. "Is there a problem?"

"What apartment is the pregnant girl in?"

"What are you going to do to her?"

He pressed the knife harder, drawing blood.

"She's in 1308."

Dixon jammed the knife into Judy's spine as hard as he could and pulled it out.

She crawled towards the stairs and collapsed on her face.

Dixon worked fast sorting through her keyring. When he found the key marked Master, he rummaged through the janitor's closet grabbing a drop cloth, and plastic sheeting.

He rolled Judy's body in plastic, then packaged her in canvas. He wiped up blood and dragged her into the closet. He uncovered her face, soaked a rag in turpentine, and stuffed the rag into her mouth. Judy's eyes rolled back in her head. "Thanks for the tour, Judy baby."

Dixon climbed three flights of stairs and turned left. When he heard the elevator he ducked into the alcove of 1308, slipped the master key in the lock, and turned the knob. Renee appeared on the other side of the door.

"What the fu—"

Dixon held his index finger to his lips. "Shhhh. Where's Miss Bradlee?" he whispered.

Renee stepped backwards, pointing toward the bedroom. "What's– "

"Shhh. They're coming." Dixon ushered Renee into the bedroom. Sheena slept soundly.

"Tell me what is going on or I will scream."

"Miss Judy sent me. See? She gave me the key to your place. You are in danger. That detective, the one who claims he's looking out for you and Sheena's baby? He wants to take her back to Sacramento so he can take the baby."

"No—he wouldn't—"

"Miss Judy did a background check on him. He's crooked. He travels with a woman who claims she has psychic powers. Once they isolate the pregnant mother, they brainwash her into giving up the baby. If she doesn't comply—you don't want to hear the rest."

Pounding on the door made Renee jump. "How do I know you're not lying?"

"I just started this gig. If you don't want to believe me, open the door. But—you've been warned."

The pounding increased. Sheena stirred. Renee looked through the peephole. "What do you want me to do?"

"Tell them Bradlee is sleeping, and to be quiet."

Renee went to the door. "Who is it?"

"It's Detective Metzger. We need to talk."

"My cousin is sleeping—I was in the shower. Can this wait?"

"Dixon knows where you live. Do you hear me?" I have an officer outside your door. Don't open the door for anyone."

"Okay. Can I get back to my shower now? I'm dripping water on the carpet. And quit pounding on the door, you'll wake Bradlee."

Dixon whispered. "My names Duane, I'm the new doorman."

"This whole thing is insane, I need a drink," Renee said, walked over to the wet bar.

"I know, crazy isn't it? My first day on the job and all."

"I wonder why Judy didn't call to let me know you were coming."

"She mentioned a potential resident—"

Renee felt Dixon's eyes on her. "Would you like one?" she asked, glancing over her shoulder. Dixon had moved closer. "How silly of me," she said removing the corkscrew from the drawer, "You're on duty." The tiny blade wasn't enough to defend herself. Neither was the metal curlicue at the end. She felt him behind her. She picked up a bottle, swung, and missed.

Dixon slit her throat.

Sam stopped in his tracks. Why would Renee refer to her niece as Bradlee? He had called her Sheena from the beginning. Unless? Sam tiptoed to the door where young officer Pizzo stood and motioned for him to keep silent.

Dixon dragged Renee's body into the bathroom and turned on the shower. Having a cop outside the door up the stakes. If he was lucky, he could lure the cop inside. Kill him and do the ol' switcheroo. He crept into Sheena's bedroom and shut the door. No need for officer do-good to hear Sheena shriek when she realized he had found her. He slipped into her bed.

Sam tapped lightly on the door. He pressed his ear to the door and heard water running. *Perhaps I'm overreacting*. Why had Renee called her Bradlee? He listened for anything out of the ordinary. He didn't hear any variation in the sound of the water. The thrum was consistent. *The water is running, but she's not in the shower.*

Dixon dipped one hand into Sheena's tank top and fondled her breast while he covered her mouth with the other. "Hey baby," he whispered in her ear. "Miss me? Miss your baby daddy?" He squeezed her breast until she gasped. He had never realized how large her eyes were until he saw them filled with terror. He reached into his pocket and withdrew the roll of duct tape he had snagged from the janitor's closet. He heard a light rap on the door.

Sheena squirmed beneath him. She tried to scream, but the tape muffled the sound. "Tsk, tsk, tsk. You don't look happy to see me," he said, his mouth inches from her face. Tears rolled down Sheena's cheeks. "Tears of joy?" Dixon flicked them away. "I think not." His free hand wondered over the mound she had tried so hard to protect as he withdrew a piece of orange twine from his waistband. Her body shook with fear. Her arms flailed and she kicked and punched him with all her might, but she was no match for him. He bound her wrists with the speed of a cowboy roping a calf.

Sam stood very still outside the door. He closed his eyes and focused on the sounds coming from the other side of the door. Suzanne's face appeared behind his lids and all at once he knew. He drew his weapon and nodded to the young officer to do the same. "We're going in."

Sam popped a bullet through the deadbolt, grabbed the doorknob and pushed. The door swung easily and both men held their weapons ready for battle. The young officer took off towards the bathroom, while Sam checked the kitchen and one of the bedrooms. The door at the end of the hall was closed.

Dixon jumped to his feet when the door opened, dragging Sheena by the hair. Shielding his body with hers, he withdrew the knife from his waistband and held it near her neck. "You don't want to hurt our little mama now, do you?" His evil grin challenged both men. "Are you ready to risk the life of this girl and her unborn child?"

Sam lowered his weapon. "You disgust me, Dixon."

Dixon drew the knife closer to Sheena's throat. "Maybe I'll just slit her throat and kill them both myself—although I'd prefer to gut her like the pig she is—"

"Put the knife down. Let her go. It's over."

"It's over when I say it is."

"All those women. Why? You had the world by the balls—people admired you, respected you—"

"How did you find me? It was the bitch with the superpowers, right? You certainly couldn't have done it on your own."

"Suzanne led me here. She led me to Chrissy, and Patti, too. They're alive." Sam paused. He softened his tone. "I saw the photo on the wall. You were a boy."

Dixon's eye twitched. "My Grandpa built that place. Little piece of heaven, don't you think?"

"Whatever happened there doesn't justify this—let her go."

"Can't." He ran the blade across Sheena's stomach, "The baby has to go."

"Whatever twisted notion you have about this baby, it deserves a chance."

"C'mon Sam. A chance for what? You think she'll be a devoted mother? You know better. Half the whores we've busted over the years have kids in foster homes. How many find some schmuck to put a roof over their heads only to have him kick the crap out of them when he's had a bad day. Or play hide the banana with the little darlings when the ol' lady is sleeping in the next room?"

Sobs wracked Sheena's body.

"Whatever you endured as a child must've been horrendous Jim, but the killing has to stop."

"Did your psychic bitch tell you how this is gonna end?"

"No."

"Didn't think so. She's a little tied up at the moment."

"What do you know about Suzanne?"

"She's got great tits. Not a bad fuck either, but you must know that."

"Where is she?"

"What do you say we cancel this little soirée. I walk out of here. And if all goes well, I give you that information."

"Not a chance."

"Gee, that's too bad. I thought you had a thing for her."

"Release Sheena and we can talk."

"Fuck you, Sam." Dixon sliced through Sheena's neck, drawing blood.

Pizzo aimed at Dixon's head and squeezed the trigger, dropping Dixon to his knees.

"Tic-tock," he whispered, crumbling to the floor.

"No," Sam shouted, "No, no no!"

The young officer stood frozen, his gun held high. "He was gonna kill her—kill the baby, I—"

Sam refrained from blowing his top. How could he fault the kid for doing his job? They were there to save the girl, not Suzanne. "Put that thing away and Call 911,"

Sam examined Sheena's wound. "It's not deep, thank God. You're going to be just fine," he said, pulling her close. He peered over her shoulder at the body lying on the floor. Dixon's eyes were fixed on the ceiling, blood pooled beneath his head. "You're safe now, Sheena. You and your baby are safe."

"Paramedics are on their way, sir."

Sam rose, facing the young officer. "First time, officer–"

"Pizzo. Tony Pizzo, sir. Yes, I–"

"What is it?" Sam recognized the angst. It wasn't easy shooting a man."

"We saved lives today, sir, didn't we?"

"Yes, yes we did." Sam patted Pizzo's on the shoulder. "Helluva shot, officer"

Relief washed over the young officer's face.

Dixon was dead, but it wasn't over. Sam plucked a business card from his wallet. "I have another situation to attend to...If you ever need anything—"

Pizzo accepted the card. His hand trembled.

Room 1442

Sam returned to the hotel. He knew now Suzanne hadn't left him in a lurch. *Where are you?*

He raced through the lobby into the elevator, his shirt, covered in blood. His stomach clenched. He needed a clear head to see things through. *Where could he have taken her?* There had to be something on those tapes. *Tic-tock.*

He threw on a clean shirt, splashed water on his face, and grabbed his keys. On the way down to the lobby, he knocked on Suzanne's door. He didn't expect her to answer, but he stood there for a moment, hoping. When he turned to leave, he noticed the DO NOT DISTURB sign hanging on the door across the hall.

"Detective Metzger," the desk clerk stepped forward. "Can I help you?"

"I need to take a look at those tapes again."

"Come this way." The desk clerk escorted Sam into the back office. "Which day do you want to look at?"

"Show me the tape with the man who asked about the flowers."

The desk clerk typed in his password and scrolled through footage with the time codes Sam was inquiring about.

"There. Stop. Enlarge the frame. What room was this man registered in?"

"Let me look." The clerk disappeared for a moment, when he came back, he said, "1442. His name is Duane Johnson. He's still checked in."

"That's the room across from Suzanne's. Call 911 and give me a key to that room."

"Sir, I can't do that, I—"

"Duane Johnson is James Dixon, and he's dead. Now give me the key. If my partner is in there, she may already be de—we're wasting time!"

Suzanne tried to track the combat boots walking back and forth, but her vision wouldn't cooperate.

"You can't die, we're so close," he said.

Jack?

He lay down on the floor, his face inches from hers. "Breathe."

I can't Jack. I'm too tired.

"I won't let you go."

Suzanne felt her body rise. Jack, carrying her down the hill like he did when they were kids. Bumping along, laughing, so in love. She turned to tell him how happy she was, to taste his lips, but it wasn't Jack. *Sam.*

Sam found her lying on the floor, convulsing.

"Suzanne?" he checked her pupils. "Can you hear me?" She fell limp in his arms.

Sirens blared in the distance. He prayed they weren't too late.

Sam followed the ambulance to Washington Heights General Hospital, on the east side of town.

When he entered the bay where Suzanne was being examined by doctors her petite frame looked small beneath the white sheet. Her face was paler than the first time he had seen her, the night she had been shot, left for dead.

Sam introduced himself to doctors, displayed his badge, and asked for an update.

"Your friend is flying high. We're running toxicology tests as we speak." The doctor examined his watch. "I expect them back within the hour." He met Sam's eyes. "Your friend has been beaten and doesn't appear to be an addict. Can you tell me what's going on?"

"She went missing this morning. I suspect she was kidnapped between midnight and 5:00 this morning. We're here on a case."

"So, she's a policewoman?"

"No. She's a psychic."

The doctor's reaction took several moments and a series of eye-blinks. "A *psychic*?"

"Suzanne's gift has helped the department immensely. If it weren't for her, we'd still be trying to figure things out."

"Well, you can count your lucky stars you found her. She's in serious condition."

Sam choked back the lump in his throat. "Was she raped?"

"We're getting to that."

"What's your prognosis on her overall condition?"

"Can't say until we get the tox results. We've given her antidotal meds, but my biggest concern is brain damage. She has a serious concussion. Once we get her stabilized, we can get a CT scan." The doctor gently turned Suzanne's head to the left. "Her jaw doesn't appear to be broken, but I'm concerned her temporomandibular joint may be damaged, and judging from the bruising and swelling around her orbital bone, I expect fractures."

"Can she hear me?"

"She's someplace in her mind that we may not be able to reach until she comes down."

Sam took Suzanne's hand. "Hey partner. Don't stay away too long. We have work to do." Sam lifted her hand to his lips.

The doctor patted Sam on the back. "Go get some rest, let me take care of your partner."

Sam squeezed Suzanne's hand. In his mind he whispered three words he vowed never to use again.

As Sam turned to leave, the doctor said. "Before you go, I wanted to ask—who's Jack?"

———

Safe

Suzanne tumbled through space and time. Voices echoed in the caverns of her mind. Bright light blinded her. The sun? No sun in this place, only slithery things and death. She struggled to reach whatever it was that would save her from the darkness. Jack had appeared many times only to be dragged away by a fire-breathing monster. She wanted to help him, fight the demons devouring his face, but she couldn't move. *A pillar of salt. Don't look back.* Now what? She dangled over a pit of fire, her hands cramping, spasming, her grip weakening. A rose petal landed on one hand. The petal lingered there, warm, comforting. And then it was gone.

"Where am I?" Suzanne frantically scanned the room.

A red-headed nurse in eggplant colored scrubs stepped forward. "Washington Heights General. How're you feeling?"

"Where's Sam? Have you seen Sam?"

"There was a man here earlier. I didn't get his name. Handsome, salt 'n pepper hair?"

"Did he bring me here?"

"No, ma'am. You came in by ambulance." She pressed two fingers on Suzanne's wrist and glanced at her watch. "You don't remember, do you? Of course not."

Suzanne contemplated the tubes connected to the crook of her arm. "What's all this?"

"A Flumazenil cocktail. Your tox-screen came back with Rohypnol and Ketamine in your system. The Flumazenil helps reverse the effects of the Rohypnol. You must have a guardian angel. Ketamine is nasty stuff. You've been hallucinating, but the worst is over."

"I'm so tired."

The nurse patted Suzanne's hand, "You rest. I'll be right outside."

She closed her eyes. Jack stepped into view. And then they were back in the pool.

"Look at you!" he shouted. "You're doing it—you're floating!"

Suzanne felt as though she were floating on a cloud instead of water. She could feel the vibration of Jack's voice on her cheek. She turned to look at him. "I love you," he whispered. "Always have, always will." In his eyes she could see his love, and something more. *Like the first time we met.* "I have to go now, Suzanne. I'm about to start over. We'll meet again. I promise. Until then, follow your path, open your heart. I'll will be with you always, but now, your happiness is within reach. Take the love that is given, fill your mind with new memories, and never forget where it all began."

She understood. *Sam.*

Sam drove to the hospital, anxious to share the good news. While Sheena was in the hospital getting stitched up, she went into labor. Her baby boy was born two weeks early but was in good health.

When he arrived, Suzanne was sleeping. He pulled up a chair and sat, holding her hand. "I think I've fallen in love with you," he whispered in her ear.

Suzanne stirred. Her eyes fluttered. "Sam."

He brought her fingers to his lips. "I'm here. I'm right here. Always."

She closed her eyes.

She floated on sparkling blue waters. The clouds sped by. A young woman with long dark hair stood in a field of gold, Jack by her side. They faced each other, knowing. The young woman's bump had grown. Jack seemed pleased. As the woman massaged her bump, Jack vanished. Time sped up, the sun rising and setting, only to rise again. The young woman remained, her face to the sun. When she turned to go, she was no longer alone. A small boy reached for her hand. Suzanne recognized the woman from her visions. *She's safe.* Suzanne's heart filled with joy.

Destiny

Sam knocked on Suzanne's door. Two months had passed since her release from the hospital. The nightmare with Dixon was over. With Ben gone, he felt they were headed for a new beginning. *Partners*. First, and always. *Friends*. He hoped for more, but realized he needed to be patient. Fate had brought them together, his love for her would grow.

"Sam! What a pleasant surprise," she said, stepping into his arms for a hug.

"This came for you," he said, handing her an envelope.

She opened a card addressed to her from New York. The card held a photo of a beautiful baby boy. His smile was infectious. His eyes, unusual, and distinct for his age, one brown, one green. Like *Jack's*. The note read,

> Dear Suzanne,
>
> Not a day goes by that I don't think of you, and pray you are doing well. If it hadn't been for you and Sam, my baby boy would not have made it into this world. When I tell him that you were his guardian angel he reacts in a way, well, I don't know how to explain it, he doesn't just smile, he seems to understand. I am eternally grateful to you both,

and hope that one day you will meet Emmett, and see for yourself how special he is. Until then, be well, be happy, and God Bless.

Yours,

Sheena Bradford

Suzanne showed the photo to Sam. "It's him, I know it. It's Jack. He said I would see him again. I never imagined it would be like this. She held the photo to her heart. "What do you say we go for ice cream? My treat."

The End

ACKNOWLEDGMENTS

"Borrowed Time" began as a short story published in the Sisters in Crime Anthology in 2008. In 2011, I adapted my short story into a short film for "A Place Called Sacramento." Thank you to the Sacramento Chapter of Sisters in Crime, Capitol Crimes, for giving Suzanne Cash life and to Access Sacramento for providing the opportunity to show "Borrowed Time" on the big screen. I wasn't expecting my protagonist, Suzanne Cash, to stick around after the project was finished, but she did.

Psychic Linda Schooler was one of the first guests I interviewed on Paranormal Connection, a local TV program I produced and hosted for fifteen years. She not only impressed me with her psychic abilities, she impressed me with her integrity and her beautiful soul. I feel privileged that Linda allowed me to include her as a character in my book.

I've been blessed with continued support from mentor Kirk Colvin, The Eldorado Writers Guild, mentor Donna Benedict, critique partners, Michele Drier, Linda Townsdin, Tarra Thomas, June Gillam, Catherine McGreevy, and my sister Kathy, who doles out support when I need it most. I'd also like to thank one of my beta readers, Nancy St. Germain. Nancy and I have been friends since first grade and having her as a fan means the world to me.

Finishing a manuscript is a *big deal.* Thank you, Kirk and Michele, for editing, and Tarra for formatting my pages and taking on the task of all-around Project Manager. Choosing the right cover is a *big deal.* Karen Phillips, you've done it again! I am eternally grateful for everyone's incredible talent and expertise.

Thank you to my readers. It gives me great pleasure to write stories you enjoy.

Most of all, thank you to my family. Your love and support fuels my passion for writing.

Dänna Wilberg

02/11/2020

BOOK 2: MISSING

BORROWED TIME

BOOK 2 - MISSING

DÄNNA WILBERG

Contents

For the children

Fear

"I still get frightened." Suzanne Cash folded her hands in her lap. "You know—when the visions start." She'd never imagined herself in therapy, although, it wasn't as if her life hadn't warranted a little help. Her marriage was the perfect example of dysfunction...but she wasn't there to fix what was permanently broken. She was there to understand what happened to her, and learn to cope. She was tired of being afraid.

Manila folder and pen in hand, therapist Grace Simms sat forward, closing the gap between them. "You've been through a lot. One can only imagine–" she said, her tone gentle. "You were shot, left for dead, kidnapped, assaulted, drugged...I mean, seriously, Suzanne–how could you *not* be affected by what has happened to you?" Grace exhaled. "The mind has limits. Post-traumatic stress syndrome is the result of a traumatic experience. You can say it's our bodies auto-response to mental injury."

"Are you saying PTSD is causing my visions?"

"I don't know how you were able to communicate with your dead fiancé, or how you were able to lead police to a serial killer–all I can do is offer you an explanation of how your mind has responded to your experience." Grace leaned back, opening the space, allowing Suzanne to process her assessment. "How are you sleeping?"

"I'm having lucid dreams. They're eerie like the visions, but not as gruesome. Feels like the calm before the storm." Suzanne's gaze dropped to her lap. "Like something is about to happen. I just don't–" Her eyes lifted to meet Grace's. "There's a girl..."

"A girl? Can you tell me about her?"

"I wish I could. The word "missing" keeps popping up in my head like bread in a toaster." She pulled on a loose tendril of chestnut hair and twisted it around her finger. "But what does it mean? Am I *missing* something? Is the girl *missing*? Detective Metzger hasn't mentioned anything to me–I don't know what to think."

"I'm sure you'll figure it out in due time." Grace jotted a few words on her pad. "How are things going with Metzger?"

"He's well."

"Are you still seeing each other?"

"Not really–I mean, we talk. I'm not ready."

"You're following your gut–good for you. It's easy to jump into a relationship for the wrong reasons."

"I'd be lucky to have a man like Sam in my life..." She paused; her lips slid into an upward curve. "...when it's time."

"Speaking of time, this is a good place for us to stop." Grace put her pen aside, closed the manilla folder, and rose. "Would you like to make another appointment?"

"I'll call you. I appreciate your advice, Grace, but right now I'm caught between regaining my sanity and otherworldly stuff."

"I can help with your sanity," she placed a hand on Suzanne's shoulder, guiding her to the door. "Not so sure about the psychic experiences, but that doesn't mean I can't listen."

Suzanne smiled. "I have a friend to help with the psychic stuff, but she too has her limits."

Grace returned the smile. "I'm here if you need me."

That night, Suzanne teetered on the edge of sleep in her 1940s Victorian style house. Beside her bed, a clock ticked, a floorboard creaked, a cool breeze came through an open window. Downstairs, directly below her bedroom, water shushed through copper pipes; the refrigerator hummed;

ice plunked into a plastic container. Outside, quail babbled in the shrubs, owls hooted in the trees, a train whistle wailed a lonely cry. One sound no longer heard in the nightly chorus was Ben's snoring. Admittedly, she didn't miss him, or his snoring...their divorce was almost final. *Hallelujah.*

She hugged herself, shielding her heart. Her thoughts shifted to Sam, the man who cared enough to walk through hell for her. The man whose touch made her shiver. The man she wished she could commit to.

Maybe one day. That's all she could offer. At this stage in her life, she had become a student. Her quest to understand what happened to her the night she was shot, thrown into a pool, and left to die, weighed heavy on her mind. Jack, her first love, had held her head above water, saved her life...but few believed her. *Who could blame them*? Jack had died in Iraq fifteen years prior. The only person to provide answers about her experience was psychic, Linda Schooler.

Left with a superpower she didn't want did little for Suzanne's temperament. Anger, fear, heartbreak consumed her like a burning house. *How do they do it, the psychics of the world? How do they shut off the barrage of injustices bombarding their souls without warning?* And then there was the million-dollar question: *How long will this go on?* Perhaps Grace Simms was right. Perhaps she should focus on getting mentally healthy before tackling the unknown. *But how?*

She sank into a deep sleep.

In her dream, she walked down a dark, empty street, her surroundings unfamiliar. Her breath quickened. Fear gripped her hard. She ducked into an alcove of a small shop, closed due to the late hour, and waited.

Across the street, a door opened. Out came a stunning young woman dressed in a charcoal wool mini, the kind leggy girls wore with ease. Thick burgundy locks, tipped in caramel and gold escaped her red beret. Like molten lava, her hair sluiced down the back of her red leather battle jacket, and burst into flames under the streetlamp. Black boots clicked on cobblestones as she disappeared into the night.

Suzanne noted the door from which the woman came; bottle green, trimmed in ornate swirls. A brass number "6" divided two beveled glass panes. She spied the woman now in the distance. *What does it all mean*?

Her answer came soon enough when a man stepped out from the shadows. He too had his eyes on the prize.

Suddenly, a gust of wind disrupted Suzanne's dream state. She sucked air into her lungs, and pulled the covers tight around her shivering body. Light sneaked between lids still sticky with sleep. 6 a.m.? How could that be? It was just–*dark*.

She felt stiff.

She closed her eyes, letting her fatigue pull her down. This time there was no girl. No man. No dream. Just sleep.

Fun

Audra Metzger boarded a plane to Vienna.

Day one of her three-week holiday before stepping into the role of Au Pair to Marie-Élise and Alan-Pierre Duveaux, the children of prominent art dealers. The twenty-five-year-old had left Munich five years prior to pursue her love of the arts. Budapest proved to be a great place to lose oneself in a gypsy nouveau-riche lifestyle, one she felt born to live. Her long, flowing tresses now shocked with chunks of burgundy, crimson, and caramel reflected her need to feel rebellious. Imagining her stoic parent's reaction to her new look brought her joy. She knew they'd hate it, but would refrain from commenting. They'd save their commentary for Sam.

She and her brother Samson hadn't communicated in months. Good ol' Sam. No matter what he did, or didn't do, he'd always remain the golden child. He chose a different path. So be it. She denied missing him terribly by filling the void with friends, school, and the occasional "mistake." She was older now, wiser. It was *her* time to shine.

Audra managed a small suitcase through the bustle of excited travelers and navigated her way to the S-Bahn platform. The S-7 train, due to arrive in twelve minutes, would take her to LandstraBe where she would get on U-Bahn 3 and head for Karlsplatz.

Nearby, a handsome man looked her way with interest. When he suddenly retreated, she summoned his sapphire gaze to return, and he responded. She wondered his age. *Older?* Hard to tell, his shoulder length hair and gemstone eyes reminded her of a fallen angel. *Or a rock star.*

When the train arrived, she lost sight of the handsome man. So, she thought.

"Is this seat taken?"

The intensity of his stare almost made her giggle. "You're American?"

"Yes, I am." He settled in the seat beside her.

"My brother lives in California," she said, shyly.

"How nice. I know California well. Where does your brother live? We may know—"

"You wouldn't know my brother. Unless you broke the law, or something."

"I see. No chance, then. Do you live there as well?"

"Me? No, I'm from Munich. My brother watched "Dirty Harry" one too many times."

"Who?"

"Exactly. Not someone I care to talk about."

"What brings you to Vienna?"

"Holiday—I rented a flat in the museum district."

His eyes brightened. "Me too. I am anxious to see the Klimt exhibit at the Belvedere Palace."

"I'm sure you'll enjoy the display." Suddenly, she found herself blushing, sitting next to this handsome man who shared her appreciation for art.

"I'd enjoy it more if you would accompany me," he said. "Is that possible?"

The train came to a stop. She rose and picked up her small valise. She tilted her head and smiled. "We can meet at the south gate tomorrow, say one o'clock?"

"I'll be there!"

Audra hurried off the train. Before the doors closed behind her, she turned to wave and say, *"Auf Wiedersehen,"* but the man was gone.

She descended the station's dank stairwell to make her connection to the purple line. She planned to meet Britta, an old classmate, at the

Karlspaltz Café. She moved gingerly in dainty heels, avoiding the hand rail. The air reeked of stale cigarette smoke and cheap cologne. She could've opted for a clean, well-lit station, but this one provided the perfect route. The further down she went, the more indistinguishable sounds became. She didn't hear the footfall tracking her course.

When she reached the U-2 platform for the purple line to Karlsplatz, she checked the schedule board. A nine-minute wait. *Perfect.* Enough time to text Bruno, her flat-mate in Budapest. Bruno worried if she didn't check in. Sometimes she wondered if his concern was a guise for knowing where she was at all times. She knew Bruno liked to feed his sexual appetite while she was away. They had an understanding, his small hips did not belong in her jeans, skirts, dresses or panties! His love interests and playmates were not allowed on her pull-out sofa, and he was to empty the trash before she arrived home. She dearly loved Bruno, but steered clear of his wild escapades and wouldn't tolerate remnants from one of his romps.

Her fingers quickly worked the keys:

Made it to hotel, meeting Britta for a Cappuccino. Behave. XOXO

A response came within seconds:

Behave? I am not you my friend! LOL! XOXO

Audra sighed. *Yes, I live like a nun. But all that may change*...she thought about the stranger on the train. She didn't expect him to keep his word and meet her at the Belvedere, then again, a *girl can hope.*

The man standing on the Schottenring platform had no intention of going that direction. Once the train arrived for Karlsplatz, he would dart across the platform, grab a car close to hers. He loved the game. *Cat and mouse.* The glee filled moment prompted him to laugh out loud. *Not yet. Be cool, man, be cool.*

. . .

When Audra pushed through the heavy wooden door to the café, Britta rose, pounced on her friend like a playful puppy, and squealed, "Auuudraaaa!"

Audra hugged her friend tight. "I can't believe it, how long has it been?"

"Too long! Come, sit. I ordered Cappuccino's and strudel."

Audra slid into a red leather booth trimmed in hand-carved wood. Britta slid across from her and leaned forward, her heavy breasts resting on the wooden table. "Your hair! I love it! It's *gooood*." Her thick accent made "good" sound weighty and important, delicious and decadent, all at the same time.

The server brought a tray with two cups topped in foamy hearts, and a small platter of strudel dusted with powdered sugar. Audra perused the selection.

"Apple, peach, and custard, all my favorites."

"How was the train?" Britta leaned back allowing the server to place the drinks and small pastry plates on the table.

"Interesting," she replied, catching the server sneaking peeks of Britta's bosom. "Not as interesting as your breasts are to this young man." The server dropped a spoon, retrieved it, and scurried away, red faced.

The girl's covered their mouths, suppressing a fit of giggles. Britta sipped her cappuccino, and nearly choked. "Audra, you naughty-good girl, how I have missed you."

Audra squeezed Britta's hand. "I missed *you*."

"Tell me about the train. I adore the train. So many handsome men."

"You read my mind. I met this man from America. Quite handsome. I like his fashion. And his eyes." Audra bit into a pastry and moaned.

"And you gave him your number?"

"No."

"*Blödmann!*"

Audra pretended to be shocked by her friends insult at first, but then her lips spread wide. "I am not a complete prude. We arranged to meet at the Belvedere. Tomorrow, one o'clock."

Britta nodded her approval. "What is he about?"

"His hair is long, beautiful waves, blond, gold, blond, I don't know.

His eyes are blue sapphires, fit for a crown. His lips are nice. Maybe to kiss?"

"And maybe his cock will be nice to—?"

"Britta!"

"What? You don't like sex?"

Audra blushed. She conjured his image and smiled. "I will tell you if we go that far. Now tell me about you, do you have a man?"

"I have two."

"Two? Serious?"

"*Ja*. We drink, have sex, go to clubs...more drinks, more sex..."

"Both at the same time?"

Britta's plump lips puckered. Her topaz eyes glistened with glee as she nodded.

"Two? Really?" Audra reddened at the thought.

"You should try."

"The men, they are good with this?"

"Men like different. I like different. It's fun!" Britta pushed her chest forward until her cleavage popped over the top of her blouse. "I have plenty to share, yes?"

"Yes, and you *are* adventurous, but that lifestyle doesn't appeal to me. I want normal. I want a relationship, not someone just for sex."

Britta's eyes narrowed, she picked up a strudel. "You're still a virgin, aren't you?"

Audra sipped her cappuccino. "One mistake is enough."

Britta stopped mid-bite. "Who?"

"*Who* is not important. I plan to think things through before I get involved."

"This is why you have two men. Not to say at the same time, but for me, more fun!" Britta raised her cup and clinked with Audra's.

Across town, Rubio Dane slid on a stool beside Giorgi Von Graff, one of Austria's legendary playboys. His Italian-German heritage contributed to his good looks, looks that drew women to him like flies. Today, Giorgi focused on his 'Rotes Zwickl' beer, nodding to the bartender who poured another, and set it in front of Rubio. "You have something for me?" he asked.

"I think so."

Giorgi glanced at Rubio, his lips twisted into a sneer. "You *think*?"

"I'm meeting her at the Belvedere tomorrow at one o'clock." Rubio wiped condensation from his glass with a cocktail napkin. "Have I ever failed you?"

Giorgi's lips relaxed into a smile. "All right then."

"She's beautiful, you'll like her—she's your type."

Giorgi pulled an envelope from inside his cashmere coat and handed it to Rubio. "You'll get the rest when you deliver the goods." He winked at Rubio, tossed fifty Euros on the bar and walked away.

Rubio stuffed the envelope in the interior pocket of his leather jacket, pulled twenty euros from his wallet, switched it for the fifty on the bar, drained his glass and rose to leave, when he heard a smoky voice next to his ear.

"Is this seat taken?"

Rubio glanced over his shoulder. A redheaded woman in her mid-twenties with eyes the color of tumbled jade, blocked his exit.

She smiled and said, "I'm sorry, do you speak English?"

He swiveled in his chair until they were practically nose to nose. "I believe you stole my pick-up line."

"In that case, I should buy you a beer."

Her derriere fit perfect in the seat next to his. She crossed long shapely legs and placed her vintage purse on the bar. "Kitty, From Dayton Ohio. And you are?"

"Alex Mayfield, from California."

"What brings you to Vienna? Business or pleasure?"

"You can do better than that."

Kitty whispered in Rubio's ear.

"Ahhh." He squeezed her hand and smiled. "Much better."

Epiphany

Samson F. Metzger, "Chief Detective," the placard read. The idea of receiving a promotion for bringing down a serial killer was humbling. Knowing the man was once his boss? *Disturbing*.

Sam was introduced to evil at a young age. *Krampus*. He grew up with German folklore about a half-goat, half-devil that appeared around Christmas time to punish naughty German children and bring them lumps of coal, verses St. Nicolas who rewarded good behavior with gifts, and treats. *Good versus Evil*. The line was clearly drawn. And then there were men that blurred the line by managing to play both roles magnificently.

Sam pondered his boyhood and the fear associated with Krampus. He remembered festivals where the horned devil dragged his chains through the streets of Munich, his yellow eyes scouring the crowds for unruly children. Sam's father threatened to turn him over to Krampus for beheading his sister's doll in a tug of war, despite the fact that she was about to dunk the doll in the toilet for a hair wash. For many years, Sam suffered with night terrors. He hated Christmas, and for more years than he wished to count, he hated his father for instilling such fear.

His sister, Audra was never threatened with Krampus, or his dirty deeds. She was the miracle child. The pampered one, favored by St.

Nicolas. As much as he loved his sister, a part of him resented the favoritism.

Sibling rivalry lessened once Sam turned sixteen and began to exercise more independence. He and Audra grew closer. Vacations became more amiable, holidays more pleasant.

When Sam finished Gymnasium, Germany's equivalent to graduating high school in America, he chose to attend college in America. Audra never forgave him for preferring the beaches and mild weather at UCSD to the harsh winters in Munich.

Before Sam turned thirty, he had an epiphany. He realized his parents were loving in their own way, and his sister wasn't treated any better than he. Their age difference called for different measures at different stages. He came to appreciate the sacrifices his parents made for him, quit focusing on his sister's blessings, and paid more attention to his own. Unfortunately, his revelation didn't close the gap that distance had put between them, and they grew apart. He still had sketchy memories of giving Audra piggy-back rides and ski lessons.

Leaving Munich at age eighteen was more difficult than he let on to his family. It took five or more years to feel comfortable with the English language, customs, and overcome loneliness. When he turned twenty-two he joined the Sheriff's department. He jumped in, heart and soul, working ridiculous hours to prove himself. During this time, he met a girl, but he couldn't keep up with the demands of a relationship and accomplish the golden boy status to make his papa proud. Depression took its toll, and on his sprint to the finish line, he developed a limp: Alcohol became his crutch.

Sam joined AA before things got out of hand. With the help of his friend Dove Johnson, one of the finest forensic analysts he knew, he found a group that met his needs. Most of the people in his group were professionals. Doctors, lawyers, athletes, he felt his anonymity was protected, safe. Although he carried his sobriety coin with him at all times, the only person he discussed his weakness with was Suzanne. When he confessed his flaw, she didn't flinch.

He didn't plan to fall in love with Suzanne. He knew from the beginning she was married, off limits, yet his heart beat only for her. Time was a virtue, and he was a patient man. He would do anything to assure their future together. Her smile was the rainbow behind the rain.

Her kiss healed a thousand wounds. Her touch made the worst day perfect.

He often lingered in the memory of the time they made love. A weak moment, awkward in the beginning. Two warriors laying down arms. Letting go of the pain that built fortresses around their hearts. For Suzanne it had been the loss of Jack, feeling rejected, and then years of abuse from her ex-husband, Ben. For him, it was years of anesthetizing the pain he brought on himself. Blotting out images of torture and evil done to others. Senseless accidents, deprivation, and demoralization of the human spirit. Worrying he wasn't enough. And then, he held her near, and all of his troubles melted away.

He wondered, were they star-crossed lovers? Would the demands of his job, and Suzanne coming to terms with her visions keep them apart? The horror he witnessed on occasion is what she lived with in her head almost every day. How he wished he could be there for her. Hold her in his arms, protect her until the visions subsided, her sanity restored. *Soon,* he told himself daily. Soon she would be rid of her past and ready for a new beginning. He prayed he would be part of her "forever."

Audra dressed carefully for her date. Despite Britta's cajoling, she couldn't bring herself to show more skin than she was comfortable with. She wasn't a prude, but she wasn't cheap. Despite her shocking hair color, and rebellious antics, she was naïve. She didn't know this man well, and didn't want to begin their relationship with an impression that she was a tease. How she longed to be *sorglos* like Britta, but she wasn't raised to be carefree. A difference in their upbringing? Audra only met Britta's parents once, when they picked them up at school. Their laughter was infectious, their bantering, lighthearted, and fun. On the other hand, Audra's family were what Americans called "stiff." They were generous, loving people who guarded their emotions like museum curators guarded the "Ephemera" by Joseph Beuys.

Audra slipped into a plaid mini skirt, net stockings, and ankle boots. Her white sweater hugged her waistline, giving her a nice tailored look. She adjusted a red tam on her head and checked the mirror. *There. Ready*. She grabbed her coat, turned the latch on the green door to her flat and closed it tight, rattling the beveled glass inserts.

She walked three blocks to Prinz Eugen-Straße where she planned to meet the young man from the train at one o'clock. Her palms felt damp inside the pockets of her navy pea coat. For a moment she felt foolish, thinking he may not show. After all, she didn't even ask his name, nor did he ask hers. What did it matter? She came to see Gustav Klimt's work. She had been a fan since she was old enough to walk.

She had spent many summers in Vienna. It was only natural to gravitate to the places she loved as a child. One of her fondest memories was at the Belvedere Palace with Sam.

It had been a glorious day, sunny, warm, but not hot. Papa insisted on a picnic. Sam let her help carry the basket filled with meats and cheeses, bread and fresh baked goods, and bought her a ginger-orange Bionade from a vendor near the park. She remembered the way the bubbles tickled her nose, and how the sweet citrus flavor danced on her tongue. After lunch, Papa let them play near the fountains.

Sam picked a flower and placed it in her hair. "*Du siehst aus wie eine Märchenprinzessin*," he said. "You look like a fairy princess."

Sam. She remembered Krampus in the square, her flowing skirts, the tiny tiara, approval in her brother's eyes when he repeated those same words. "*Du siehst aus wie eine Märchenprinzessin.*"

But then something changed. Sam no longer found joy in Krampus. Before she was old enough to understand why, Sam moved to San Diego to begin his schooling, and she felt as though a part of her died. Tender years, spent grieving his loss, as if he were gone for good. By the time he returned to Germany for a visit, she had hardened her heart. And although she was happy to see her brother, she was reluctant to get too close. As years went by, they grew further apart. They corresponded by text, or the occasional card. Deep down inside, she missed him terribly, but was too stubborn to admit it.

Sam could be stubborn too. He never approved of her spontaneity. If she told him she was meeting a man she didn't know, he would've tried to intervene. *"Let me run his name through my data base, make sure he isn't a serial killer."* Just as the thought crossed her mind, she felt a tap on her shoulder.

"Well, hello," he said, grinning from ear to ear.

Butterflies flooded her stomach, her lips stretched into a smile. "Hello, I wasn't sure you would come."

"Nothing could keep me away." His eyes twinkled like sapphires in the sun.

She blushed, and lowered her gaze. "I don't know your name."

"Rubio."

"Audra." She extended her hand. "Pleased to meet you."

"Not as pleased as I am to meet you," he said, grabbing her wrist, and pulling her closer. "My heart is about to leap out of my chest," he said, placing her hand between well-defined muscles.

She felt thumping beneath his silk shirt and pulled her hand away. "It's chilly, shall we go inside?"

He reclaimed her hand. "May I? I'd feel better—the crowd, you know."

"Yes," she obliged, and followed close behind him. She inhaled his scent, clean, not too spicy. She noticed other women glancing their way. She felt good to be at his side.

Rubio bought two admission tickets, and moved her through the turnstile. Once inside Belvedere Palace, they stopped at the front counter to pick up headphones that would explain the art they were about to see. Audra floated from room to room enjoying each painting, its history, and the warm hand holding hers. They gazed at ornate ceilings, elaborate furniture, and sumptuous living quarters. When they reached Klimt's exhibit, Rubio removed his head phones.

"This one," he said, pointing to "Adam and Eve," a large piece depicting the nude Eve with Adam embracing her from behind. "This is my favorite."

"Why?" Audra crinkled her nose, playfully. "Do you like blondes?"

"No, silly girl, look at Adam's face. Pure bliss. He intends to make love."

Audra felt a tingle. Surely, he was not suggesting having sex on their first date? "Yes, he does look happy, however, I prefer Klimt's earlier work. The Kiss."

"Why?" his rhetorical question made her laugh.

"It seems as though the lover is more—protective," she said. "Are you hungry? There is a lovely café, we could—"

"Are you embarrassed by my observation?" he asked, reclaiming her hand.

"Why no, art is to be appreciated, not scorned."

"Would *you* have posed nude for Gustav Klimt?"

"Maybe."

He studied her face, his eyes penetrating her soul. "I don't believe you. You are pure."

"Nobody is that pure. Adam and Eve made sure of that."

"Then you are not a virgin?"

"I—"

"My apologies. I can see the question made you feel uncomfortable."

"It was a chapter in my life I choose to forget."

Rubio dropped her hand. "Let's find that café, shall we?"

Audra wondered if she spoiled the fun. Dampened his mood. Was he with her because he thought she was easy? She didn't hedge at his invitation. Perhaps she seemed too eager. *Grow up Audra. Men like sex, don't make a big deal of it. The boy who took your virginity was a boy. A lying, cheating, boy. That doesn't mean all males are alike. Rubio was sharing his view about a painting– he wasn't asking you to share his bed.*

They ordered cappuccinos, picked out pastries to nosh on, and took a table close to a large window. The view of the garden was breathtaking and reminded her of Sam. "My family came here when I was a girl. My brother and I played over there," she said, pointing to a garden circling a fountain.

"This is the brother in California?"

"You remembered."

"The cop."

"He's actually a detective. *Sherlock Holmes*."

"Not Dirty Harry then?"

"He works for the Sheriff's department in Northern California."

"Interesting. Are you two close?"

"We used to be." Her gaze, suddenly drawn to the garden, stirred emotions she fought hard to contain. She turned her focus on her date. "What about you? Do you have siblings?"

"No, I am an only child. My parents died when I was very young. I lived with my Grandmother until she passed away."

Rubio wracked his brain. Did they have this conversation on the train? Did he tell her otherwise? He couldn't remember. He told so many lies that sometimes his memory played tricks on him. "Stop me if I already—" He shifted his gaze for effect, to reel her in, extract information he needed for later. Giorgi expected him to deliver. And he would keep his promise, but first he needed to cover his ass. He wasn't comfortable snatching women with strong ties. It made things messy. Relatives came out of the woodwork to search, gather information. They vowed to find their loved one, they wanted justice. Giorgi would get nervous, make his life a living hell. As much as he detested the man, he needed him to survive.

When she placed her hand over his. The irony almost made him bust out laughing. He controlled the curve of his lips, his smile sincere. "I really like you."

Siblings

Suzanne puttered around the house, boxing up Ben's belongings. They agreed to sell the house in one year, meanwhile, he would spend that year in Camino, living with his retired Aunt Dee. He considered the arrangement his "get out of jail" card. Suzanne considered the arrangement a blessing. Her brother Steven, and sister-in-law Karen would agree. Although Ben was not connected directly to her attempted murder, he was connected to the man who shot her. *Drugs*. Ben was given a light sentence, an ankle monitor, and an iron clad restraining order. If he came within one hundred yards of her, he would go to jail.

Life should've improved without Ben, without his negativity and his outbursts. However, the visions she experienced since the incident with Jim Dixon still left her weary. Her latest vision, the girl with the different color hair, the man in the shadows, the green door, all pieces to a puzzle. She couldn't shake off the notion that something sinister was about to happen. But what? She needed to talk with her psychic friend, Linda Schooler.

"How many times have you had the dream?" Linda's melodious voice put Suzanne at ease.

"Once or twice, but I can't really call it a dream. It's more like I'm there, as an observer."

"Is the intensity the same as the last case you worked on with Sam?"

"Yes, but something is different. I don't know how to explain it, but I feel as though I know this girl, and yet she doesn't look familiar."

"Hmm, interesting. What can you tell me about the man in the shadows?"

"I can't see his face, Linda, that's what makes these visions so frustrating."

"I understand, but there is an answer for everything, you must be patient, keep an open mind. In time, the pieces will come together, and when they do, you will have your answers. Clarity comes with practice. It's like your muscles, the more you exercise, the stronger you get."

"If that's the case, I must be the wimp on the beach getting sand kicked in my face."

"*Hardly*. How's Sam?"

"Okay, I guess. I haven't seen him more than a couple of times since I was released from the hospital, months ago. We talk though"

"He's crazy about you."

"I'm not sure I'm ready to—"

"Of course not. He's not pressuring you, is he?"

"No, not at all, it's just—"

"The visions, the madness, right? I get'cha. Being psychic isn't easy."

"Easy doesn't even equate. It's like living on the edge of insanity."

"It does get better, not easier, *per se*, but you will learn to remove yourself from the emotion attached to the visions."

"Oh, Linda, I wished it all made sense."

"Look for signs."

"Signs? What kind of signs?"

"Time of day, time of year, architecture, license plates, stuff like that."

"Interesting you mention architecture. The green door in the vision is unlike anything I've seen around here. It's large, with an ornate knob in the center, flanked by two leaded glass panels."

"Sounds European."

"Europe? Europe is far away."

"Energy is limitless."

"Geezus, Linda, I hope you're wrong."

"Why?"

"I hate to fly."

Rubio offered to walk Audra to her flat. He held her hand, guarded her when they crossed the street. *The perfect gentleman*, her mother would say.

"When can I see you again?"

"I'm meeting my friend for dinner tonight—perhaps tomorrow? Or maybe you would care to join us, tonight, say eight o'clock?"

Audra felt awkward when he pulled out his cell and scrolled through his calendar. "Oh, see here, I have an appointment this evening. Tomorrow doesn't look good either. Maybe another time?"

"I would like that."

"May I kiss you?"

Audra presented her cheek. "I had a wonderful time."

His lips barely brushed her skin. "How will we keep in touch?"

"I'll give you my number?"

Rubio handed Audra his phone. She punched in the digits, and hit save. "What about a selfie?" She smiled, holding up her phone.

"No, I don't like photos of myself. May I take one of you?"

"Yes, by the door. I want everyone to know I am in Vienna. The city that captured my heart."

Rubio snapped the photo and returned her phone. "I will call you, then." He backed onto the sidewalk, turned, and walked away.

Audra watched until he was out of sight. She clicked on the photo and blew up the image. His reflection was clear in the glass behind her. She sighed. "You are *one handsome* man." She texted the photo to Britta.

Do you see what I see?

Britta texted back.

Oo-la-la!

Purchase

Rubio navigated his way back to Landstraße where he hopped on the U2 train. He rode quietly, his mind strategizing his mission. He would park his car near Audra's flat and wait for her to exit before 8:00. *It will be dark. I'll follow her to the train, invite her into my car.* He envisioned her surprise, and his response, claiming he changed his mind about joining her for dinner. Deprivan *will take seconds. Once she is unconscious, I deliver her to Giorgi. Sinchy.*

He exited the train at Karlsplatz and walked toward Casino Wein, pep in every step. He pushed through heavy ornate doors, transcending from honking horns and street noise to laughter, pinging bells, and piped-in music. He breathed in the scent of expensive cigars, perfume, cigarettes, and *money.* His heart raced with anticipation. By this time tomorrow his debt would be paid. *For now, a little fun.* He bellied up to his favorite Roulette table and placed his bet.

At 6:00 A.M., Sam awoke, groping for Suzanne's warm body. *Empty.* Another dream, yet it felt *so real.* He could almost smell her delicate scent on his skin. Her soft lips on his cheek. In reality, it had been months since they were together. He wanted to give her as much space as she needed to heal, get things settled with Ben. *Their divorce should be final.*

Sam often wondered if he had been too hard on her. Tracking a serial killer required training. She never had the luxury of attending the Police Academy. In fact, she was thrown into the mix without as much as a crash course in survival tactics. At the end of the day, he wouldn't have changed a thing. Without her help, Jim Dixon would still be on the loose—*more dead girls.* He shuddered at the thought. Without her in his life, he would've never known what it felt like to yearn, ache, *feel.*

Despite his desire to stay in bed and linger in his reverie, he had a meeting in an hour. The Sheriff's Department had received several calls from business owners claiming prostitution was on the rise in Goldorado County—they wanted to know what was being done. "They keep getting younger by the minute," one woman reported. She went on to mention that kids were too promiscuous now-a-days, and it was hard to tell junior high girls, from high school girls with their skimpy clothing and big breasts. "What the hell are they putting in our food?" she added.

Sam remembered how mature Audra appeared at fourteen, and wondered if the woman was on to something. The guys at the academy wanted to know who the "hot" chick was in the photo he kept in his wallet. He didn't envy parents raising kids in this day and age and doubted if he would ever have the chance to experience parenthood firsthand. *Dogs are nice. We'll have two, one for each of us to spoil.* He didn't know if Suzanne would agree, something to discuss with her when the time was right. For now, he was happy knowing she was still in his life.

Suzanne awoke with a start, her heart pumping too hard, every nerve in her body on full alert. "A dream," she said aloud, trying to convince her brain to back off on the adrenaline, and release some dopamine. "It was just a dream."

Still, she climbed out of bed and called Sam. "I saw her again, Sam. The same girl. I'm afraid for her."

"Whoa, slow down. Let's start over. Good morning, Suzanne. How are you?"

"Why are you doing this to me?"

"Because, you're going to have a heart attack if you don't slow down. Breathe."

"You're right. Good morning Sam, how are you?"

"I'm good. How did you sleep last night, Suzanne?"

"I know what you're doing, and it's working." Suzanne placed her hand on her chest. *Much better.*

"Good. Now tell me what you saw."

"I saw the same girl, with the colored streaks in her hair. She's with a man, who I can't identify. She likes him. He's evil. He's leading her into a trap. I can feel it, though I don't know how. I see another man. A dark-haired man. He's beholden to him. The devil's pawn. He's going to do something to the girl."

"Which man?"

A chill skittered up Suzanne's spine to the nape of her neck. She imagined Sam's hand, squeezing her shoulder. His face, too close. She shook off the image. "I didn't hear what you said."

"Which man is going to hurt the girl?"

Suzanne closed her eyes. She summoned the image from her dream. The car, crawling down a dark street— *stalking his prey.* She saw the dark-haired man, sitting behind a desk, counting cash. *That's a lot of zeros.* "The man with the dark hair is wealthy," she said. "The other man —" Suzanne paused, her eyes scanned back and forth as if she were watching an action scene on TV.

"What about the other man?"

Suzanne watched the dark-haired man hand a portion of the cash to the man she had seen with the girl. Suddenly, an epiphany hit her like a brick. "He's going to buy her."

"Oh shit." Sam plopped back down on his bed. She must be picking up on the trafficking problem, here in the county, he thought. "Do you have any idea where they are?"

"The currency, it wasn't American. Euros, I think."

"Euros?" Sam's head exploded with possibilities. "Damn, that could be anywhere."

"Belvedere. I keep getting Belvedere."

"There's the Belvedere Museum in Austria, we used to go there when we were kids." Sam felt a chill travel up his spine. "How old is the girl?"

"Early to mid-twenties."

"I need to make a phone call. I'll call you back."

Sam ended the call with Suzanne and scrolled through his contact list. He dialed Audra's number. He felt relieved to hear Audra's voice until he heard... *"You say, hello. I say good-bye. Leave a message, I've got to fly. Auf Wiedersehen."*

"Hey princess, it's your brother. Give me a call. Today. Don't worry about the time difference. I miss you." He ended the call and scrolled until he found *Dad*, clicked on the number and listened for the call to connect. He hoped to get them before bed time.

"Samson!"

"Papa, how are you?"

"Good. Your mother is here, let me put her—

"Wait dad, I need to speak with you first."

"What is it, son? You sound—"

"Where's Audra?"

"She's in Austria, she's working for a lovely family as an au pair. You know your sister—she has gypsy blood running through her veins."

"When is the last time you spoke with her?"

"Why the other—what is this about?"

"I'm not sure, and I don't want to worry you needlessly—can I have the family's name and number where she's living?"

"She's not there yet, son. She's visiting her friend. You know, the crazy one with the large—"

"Britta? Kokettieren. Flirty–"

"Yes, you remember. She's a wild one, that Britta."

"Where are they staying, do you know?"

"No. But Audra's flatmate, Bruno, may know. Give him a call."

"I will. How's mom?"

"She's right here, say hello."

Before Sam could protest, he heard his mother's sweet voice.

"Hello, is this my favorite boy?"

"Yes, mom. How are you?"

"Good," she said, "Why are you asking questions about your sister?"

"Just curious. I was thinking about her, that's all."

"Samson—a mother can tell when her son is lying."

"It's nothing, really mom. Just wanted to reach out—feeling like I've neglected her lately."

"I'm sure she would love to hear from you."

"Okay then. I'm going to track her down."

"Why don't you call her phone?"

"I did. I left a message. I just figured since I was feeling guilty, I'd make the rounds."

"Guilty, shmuilty. Just call more often."

"Love you, mom."

"I love you too, son. And when you speak to your sister, remind her she has parents that worry."

"I will, mom. Say goodbye to papa for me."

"I will. Tschüs."

Sam hung up the phone feeling sick to his stomach. Was there a connection between his sister and Suzanne's visions? He dialed Audra's cell phone once more. This time all he heard was a click.

Audra heard her phone buzz. *Samson.* "Isn't is just like you to invade my space when I'm having fun," she said, hitting the 'End Call' button. She didn't need his big brother antics right now. *Where were you when I needed you?*

She remembered the time she got tangled up with Fritchoff Meister. When she called Sam for advice, her calls went to voicemail. She was attending Realschule, about to move up to Gymnasium. Her hormones were *raging*, according to the Cosmopolitan magazine she kept under her bed, and she decided it was time to 'give it up.' Fritchoff was said to be a good lover, and she believed her sources. Bibiana, a girl from Spain, and Marta, from Cologne, couldn't get enough of his sex. They said he was very skilled at making a girl feel like a woman. What they neglected to tell her was that Fritchoff was a lug who liked to drink. And when he drank, he got very mean.

He met her at the flat where Bibiana lived with her Grandmother. Bibiana arranged for Audra to be alone with the boy while she and her Grandmother went into town. When Fritchoff arrived, he was drunk. His kisses were wet and sloppy, his penis erect. He forced her onto

Bibiana's bed, and climbed on top of her like one of those Monster Trucks she saw at an exhibition in London with her parents. His body pinned her to the mattress, and his groin smashed against her pubic bone. She fought like a hellcat. He struggled with her panties. By the time he was ready to enter her, he had gone limp. He slapped her across the face and called her names, as if it were her fault he couldn't stay stiff. She told him to leave, she threatened to call her brother, have him arrested. She went as far as dialing the phone. Sam didn't answer.

Fritchoff called her bluff. "Suck me, Bitch," he said, grabbing her by the hair. She kicked him hard until he let go. "I'll scream if you don't leave!" Just then, they heard someone pound on the wall. It was the neighbor. The timing was perfect. Fritchoff zipped quickly and ran.

Determined to have another go at losing her virginity, she chose someone less "reputable." Marc worked at the corner market, where he drove their delivery lorry on weekends. Finding the right time and the right place to rendezvous was a challenge, "*Morgon*," he'd say, *always tomorrow*.

She grew weary of his excuses; however, Cosmopolitan assured her the outcome was worth the wait. What the magazine didn't warn her about was the crush that came with the pursuit. The longer she waited for Marc to make the right moves, the more she grew to like him. When they finally made love in the back of his lorry one rainy Saturday, she believed she had fallen in love. Marc was happy to spread her legs, but had no intention of settling in longer than it took to satisfy his itch. Like her brother Sam, he aspired to a vocation that didn't include her. Cosmopolitan didn't prepare her for the heartbreak either, and she considered herself lucky that she didn't get pregnant.

Rubio seemed different. He appeared to be more sophisticated than the other boys she dated. He seemed worldly, knew how to treat a lady, not like Marc who confessed to having sex with many women in the back of his lorry while he kept her at bay. *No wonder he was always busy. Morgon.*

Sam not only felt anxious, the conversation he had with his parents tugged at his heartstrings. Audra hadn't checked in. For many years he managed his emotions with whiskey, tequila, beer, wine. Just about any kind of alcohol you put in front of him. After a while he started having blackouts, and almost lost his job. Recovery took years, but he had finally beat the urge to drink. *Until now.* He pressed his AA token in his palm. He licked his lips. *Just one.* One drink would stop the stampede in his chest. Drown the fear stuck in the back of his throat. He threw the coin across the room, and redialed his sister's number. "Goddammit, Audra! Pick up the fucking phone!"

Audra checked herself in the mirror. Looking good, she thought. Britta would be waiting at the restaurant for her. She locked the door and headed down the walk. She breathed in the crisp night air. So what if Sam weren't here to enjoy it with her...she was grown now, she didn't need him, or his approval. *About anything.* As if he were reading her thoughts, her phone rang again. This time she answered. "Who's calling?"

"You haven't lost your sense of humor, I see."

"And you dear brother haven't lost your sense of bad timing. I was about to meet Britta for dinner. Care to join us? Oh wait, you're a million miles away!"

"That doesn't mean I don't miss you."

"Funny, I can't remember what you look like."

"Audra, please–I didn't call to argue."

"Why did you call? Guilty conscience?"

"I called because I love you. And–as much as I try not to worry about my little sister, well–sometimes I can't help myself."

"You should try calling more often."

"How are you? Papa said you are working as an au pair."

"I start in three weeks. I'm on holiday. Britta and I are catching up. And what about you? Still playing Sherlock Holmes?"

"As a matter of fact, I got a promotion."

"Congratulations! Scotland Yard is lucky to have you."

"Audra, please–you know the only thing that has changed between us is air miles. I plan to visit at Christmas."

"Does Papa know? He hasn't mentioned–"

"Don't tell him. It's a surprise."

"I see. Sure. It will be our little secret. Why should Mama and Papa be disappointed when you decide not to come? Me? *Es geht mir gut.*"

"I won't let you down. I promise. *Du wirst immer meine Märchenprinzessin sein.*"

"I'm too old to be your little princess."

"Never too old."

"Sam, Britta's waiting."

"Okay. Have fun. Tell her hello from me."

"I will. Auf Wiedersehen."

"Auf Wiedersehen. And be safe. Please."

"I'm hanging up now!"

Sam chuckled. "Love you, sis." He didn't wait for her reply. He knew she loved him. He felt the pain he left behind each time they spoke. Maybe it was time to think about returning to Germany. He wondered if Suzanne would go with him. He'd ask. Soon. For now, Audra was safe. He exhaled, feeling relieved.

Sam plugged in the coffee maker, hit the 'brew' button, and went into the bathroom to begin his morning regime. A hot shower would feel good on his tight muscles. There were few people in the world that invoked physical stress. His sister was one of them. The thought of her in danger made him crazy inside. He'd kill anyone who tried to harm her. And then there was Suzanne. The affect she had on him was intense, but *different.* "Down boy," he sighed, and switched the faucet to 'cold.'

Lewis

Lewis Howard hovered over his own body, watching as doctors and nurses buzzed around the operating table like a disturbed hornet's nest. One doctor injected a long needle into his sternum, moved aside, another pounded on his chest. Another glanced at the flat line on a monitor. Just then, a surgeon entered the room, barking orders. Everyone stepped aside. On command, one nurse swabbed betadine from Lewis's clavicle to his bellybutton. Another nurse pushed a tray lined with instruments beside the surgeon.

"Scalpel."

Lewis heard him say it, and then heard a smacking sound as the scalpel hit the doctor's hand. Lewis watched as the surgeon slice him open like a Christmas pig. His chest flayed open, the surgeon inserted a metal contraption to keep his thoracic cavity stretched wide. As he reached in, and began massaging his heart, Lewis floated away.

His father and mother stood before him in an ethereal glow, arms outstretched, welcoming his arrival, their faces beaming.

"I guess I've come to a sticky end," Lewis said, looking back over his shoulder at the bloody scene below.

"Y'aven't popped yer clogs just yet," his father said.

"Me missus warned me, she did. Take it easy, she said."

"Let's give it a butcher..." The three stood observing the commotion below.

Lewis shook his head. "Not yer bog-standard death, eh?"

"Come," his father said. "Let's have a chinwag."

Suddenly...

Lewis found himself sitting at a kitchen table, his folks faffing about. He felt as though he had stepped back in time. The room was bathed in warm light. His beagle, Gingersnap, lay at his feet, panting. Just then, his neighbor, Jim walked through the door, lugging a side of beef. "Over-egged the pudding, did ye mate?" he asked, placing the beef on a wooden block. "Ye won't find a better Scotch fillet than on this joint." Lewis couldn't help but notice the ligature marks on Jim's neck were gone. The last time he saw him was the day he went barmy and hung himself.

A sad time for all, Lewis recalled. Mad cow disease brought the whole country to their knees. His own successful meat packing business, paralyzed overnight. His suppliers, neighbors and friends, lost everything.

Lewis was on his way home when he saw smoke billowing above the tree-lined lane leading to Jim's place. Odd, he thought, and decided to see if Jim was on a bender, dropped a fag, and started a bloody fire. Then he heard gunfire. Not just one or two gunshots. He heard what sounded like a bloody war. As he drove further down the lane, he saw military vehicles scattered everywhere. What he saw next etched an imprint, a never-to-be-forgotten image on his brain. Militia formed a line in front of penned animals and commenced shooting until every living cow, goat, pig, chicken, llama, and dog were dead. After each massacre, another group of soldiers dragged the carcasses to the burn pile. The stench of blood, and burning flesh made Lewis want to wretch. Jim stood alone, in shock, tears rolling down his weathered cheeks. He couldn't bear it, and vowed to take the easy way out. A week later he took his life.

The following years proved to be the most depressing times the Brits had experienced since WWII.

Dairy cows had been primarily fed *offal*, a product high in protein, consisting of animal bone and byproducts to promote milk production.

When offal was suspected to be the culprit causing bovine spongiform encephalopathy, later known as *mad cow disease*, a term coined due to the animal's abnormal behavior, there was a ban put on feeding it to cattle. But despite the ban, the disease spread at an alarming rate, escalating the death toll to 4.4 million cattle.

Lewis scraped together what savings he had to help his employees, but the coffers were running low, and once winter set in, he was afraid they'd all starve.

Although Lewis was able to procure healthy beef, and other meat products from sources in neighboring countries, news that humans were also contracting bovine spongiform encephalopathy caused meat product sales to plummet. His buyers were afraid to take a chance on importing any meat, possibly risking more deaths. At his wits end, Lewis reached out to the only man he knew that could help him, Dodi Fayed.

Dodi's father had recently purchased Harrods Department Store, which had a reputation for carrying not only exotic merchandise, but also items not available to the common market. Lewis was pleasantly surprised when Dodi agreed to meet.

Although Dodi's first purchase order was minimal, he was willing to take a risk. From that day forward, Lewis began rebuilding his business, grateful for the kindness shown to him by a man who owed him nothing. In years to come, Dodi and Lewis developed a close business relationship.

Jim patted him on the back. "Ye've never been a turnip puller, or a donkey walker, mate, always lookin' out for your pals. This time, the Lord 'imself needs ye. See that lass?" Jim pointed to a young woman standing in the distance, her long hair gleamed beneath a lamp post. Her short skirt and tall boots made her look cheeky. "She's not in the game, but she's headed for hell. Ye need to find 'er. Help 'er. These aren't punters and derelicts with a few quid, mate. These are men with heaps of dosh from makin' sport of human flesh."

Lewis squinted his eyes, taking in the sight of her. She was beautiful, with an air of innocence that made her that much more desirable. Lewis not only sensed the danger she was in, he *felt* it. He'd never laid eyes on the lass, but he knew she was German, not British. He knew the street lamp, under which she stood, was in Austria, not England. He turned to Jim. "What am I t'do?"

A surge of calamity from below took Lewis out if his reverie. "Time to go back, ol' chap," Jim said, slapping him on the back again. "Ye'll know what to do when the time comes."

A quick glance was the extent of his goodbye to his mother and father. In a blink, he was back in his body, fighting for his life.

"Again!" The surgeon yelled.

Lewis felt something like a cattle prod make contact with his heart.

"Again!"

Suddenly, he felt his heart beat. Faint at first, reminding him of the Aston Martin he bought second hand from a candle maker in Manchester. Once the car warmed a bit, she ran tickety boo. And so did he.

The next day, Lewis was commended for a jolly good outcome. Nurses and doctors popped in and out of his room to congratulate him for surviving, for coming back to life, for being a "miracle" patient. By evening, the parade dwindled. All that remained was peace, quiet, and Trudy, the love of his life.

"I saw Jim. Mum, and Dad," he confessed.

"Ye must be knackered," his wife said, reluctant to leave his side.

"And m'dog—Gingersnap was 'er name. Had 'er from a wee pup, I did."

"Ye were in surgery for six hours, luv, four of which yer heart refused t'beat."

"Tosh."

Trudy's eyes welled; her nose turned red. "'Twas a miracle the doctor didn't give up, Lew. By the grace of God 'twas four bloody hours!"

"Don't be getting all collywobbles." He reached for her hand.

She sniffed, pulled a handkerchief from her pocket, and dabbed her eyes. "Yer here now. That's what counts."

"Can't get rid of m'now, can ye?"

She brought his hand to her lips and let her tears fall.

"Jim told me 'bout a girl. She's in trouble."

"Jim never made a lick 'a sense," she said, wiping her tears.

"I saw her with me own eyes," he pleaded with Trudy, his eyes wide. "I felt it! I felt the evil lurking nearby! I–"

"Hush now. No need t'get in a tither."

"Jim said I must help 'er."

"Jim was off 'is nut, he was. Now rest. Ye need t'get better. *I* need ye to get better."

Lewis squeezed her hand. He closed his eyes, and fell in to an abyss.

———

The Debt

Rubio waited outside of Audra's flat. When he saw her emerge, he slouched down in his seat. *Pretty.* Prettier than the other girls he procured for Giorgi. She was taller too. He hoped that didn't present a problem. The containers used for transport only came in three sizes. It would be a shame to cram her into one that wouldn't allow her any movement. Although she would be heavily sedated, it was a fifteen-hour drive to the dock in Lecce, Italy, where the transport containers were transferred into shipping containers, loaded on trains, and taken to Brandisi. Giorgi said, once the ship was out to sea, the 'precious cargo' would be released to stretch and use the toilet. So why should he be concerned. His only worry should be what the *schlägers*, or thugs, would do to him if he didn't pay up.

When Audra stepped under the lamplight, he felt a moment of regret. She was the kind of girl he could've brought home to meet his mother. The fleeting feeling disappeared without a trace. Who was he was kidding? He didn't have a mother. *You are who you are.*

His car crept up alongside of Audra, window rolled down. "Would I sound too eager if I said I missed you already?"

Audra kept walking. "As I recall, I extended an invitation for you to join us."

"Then I am selfish to want you all to myself?"

"One would certainly question your motives."

"Oh, you wound me with your words, my fair lady."

Audra smiled. "I merely meant to remind you that I don't ditch my girlfriends—however, I am willing to share my time."

"Can I at least give you a lift to the restaurant?"

Audra stopped to consider his offer. "Perhaps you can give my friend a lift as well? She's there, up ahead."

Rubio's flirtatious demeanor dropped like a hot rock when he saw a woman in the distance walking towards them. What to do? He wanted to grab Audra, throw her into the car and be done with it. He had a debt to collect, a debt to pay before midnight. He pulled over to the curb. "I'd love to meet your friend, but I'm getting the feeling that you don't trust me." He paused, a smile blossoming on his face. "Or is it that you're afraid to be alone with me?"

"I'm not afraid of you, it's just–"

"I'm listening–" He hoped his smile, in full bloom now, would seal the deal.

She stepped closer to the car. "You're right. I am a bit nervous."

"Do I look like the 'big, bad wolf', or perhaps *Krampus*?"

She laughed. "No. I'm sorry. It's just–"

He raised one eyebrow.

"Okay. Yes. A ride would be nice."

"And your friend?" He nodded toward the woman still in the distance, but heading right toward them.

Audra got into the car. "That's not her," she said, "I must have been mistaken."

Rubio shook his head, his smile never wavered. He knew the woman was not her friend. She was at least sixty, and walked with a limp. "Naughty girl."

Bones

Suzanne scrolled through the Want Ads. She needed to find something to keep herself occupied, out of her head. The visions of the young woman were becoming a distraction. She couldn't get them out of her mind. She was about to jot down a phone number from the list of job ads when suddenly she felt woozy. A man's face swam in her vision like a kaleidoscope, fractured, blurry, then everything went black.

She dialed Linda Schooler.

"I'm afraid for this girl," she said, hardly giving Linda a chance to say, 'hello'.

"Whoa! Slow down."

Suzanne took a deep breath and exhaled. "Sorry. It's just that I feel something terrible has happened, but I don't know what. I saw a man, well at least he appeared to be a man...it was hard to tell, his image was shattered, like glass, or one of those tubular thing-a-ma-jigs that you look into."

"A kaleidoscope?"

"Yes. Like that."

"This is where meditation comes in, Suzanne. Quiet your mind, see if you can put the pieces together to form a complete picture."

"I hate this, Linda. This isn't a gift, it's a curse!"

"Remember the good you've done in the past. You found those girls, stopped a serial killer from killing again. When you change your perspective, the universe will point you in the right direction. Trust me."

"Where have I heard those words before?" And then it dawned on her. "That's it—she trusted him."

"See? That's what I'm talkin' about, Willis. Let it go, and it will flow."

"Gosh, Linda—I don't know where to start."

"The information will come. Let it happen, don't force it."

"I still feel like this is happening far away."

"You mentioned that before. Like the setting was in another country. Plant the seeds, let them grow."

"Easy for you to say."

"Hah! I wish. It took me years to filter out the garbage, you know, self-talk, negative chatter. You've got to learn to tune it in. Visualize getting a crystal-clear picture. Believe me, the more you fiddle with the tuner, the better reception you'll get."

"I'll try."

"If you need help, try gardening. Nothing like connecting with Mother Nature."

Suzanne hung up the phone feeling better. Linda was spot on, she needed something to focus on other than herself. A walk would do her good. She grabbed a light jacket from the hall closet, filled a water bottle, and stepped into the sunshine.

A block or so from her house, she turned to see a woman walking behind her. The woman was older, maybe sixty. She walked with a limp. Suzanne covered her ears. The cry of kittens was deafening.

Lewis, newly released from the hospital, hobbled to the window. "Ye shouldn't be up, Luv," his wife called from the kitchen.

"Ye got eyes in back of yer 'ead, now do ye?"

Trudy walked into the room, her hands on her hips. "Y'know I do–and ye 'ave rocks in yers! What do ye mean by getting up to fancy a glimpse out the window? The doctor said to keep yer rump in the chair for the next few days. Yer stitched to the brim."

"Ye know, I'm not a teetotaler. I feel like I have bees in me bum."

"Well, lucky bees, I say—how 'bout a game of rummy?"

"Ye'll beat me again, like ye always do."

"I promise to go easy on ye. Now please, come sit down."

Lewis hobbled his way back to his chair. "I can't seem to shake this feelin'."

"What feelin' is that, Luv?" she asked, shuffling a deck of cards.

"Doom." He plopped into his chair. "Ah, git ye chin off ye chest, Luv—not doom for me. It's what Jim said. The girl. Something happened. I feel it in me bones."

Lecce

Audra couldn't move. Her hands and feet were bound. Her mouth, taped. A dank smell permeated her nostrils. She felt movement beneath her. It was dark. But nothing was more terrifying than the sound of whimpering that surrounded her. At first, she thought she heard kittens, crying, mewling...then she realized, the sound was human. *Children*.

A wave of nausea hit her. A scream stuck in her throat. *Don't be a fool.* Her brother's voice entered her head. *If you vomit, you'll choke.* She certainly didn't want to do that. Wasn't that how John Bonham and Jimi Hendrix died? She remembered Sam telling her their story when she was ten or eleven. She drew in a deep breath and willed herself to overcome the nausea. *I don't want to die.*

A short while later, the movement stilled. She heard coarse voices issuing commands in *Italian*. She smelled fish. Suddenly, she was being hoisted into the air. A man said what sounded like, "that side, put it on that side, you idiot!" Her Italian was weak, so she wasn't sure. All she knew is when the container she was in came crashing down, pain shot through her hip and shoulder. She cried out.

"*Stupido*!" The man sounded like he was seething. "*Rompi la merce*!"

Merchandise? She wasn't sure that's what he said until another man chuckled and said, "*Rompilo, l'hai comprato.*" *Break it, you bought it.*

Audra heard containers slide on something gritty. *Fish, grit,* they must be near water, a port perhaps, off the coast of Italy. The cries of the children grew louder when a heavy door slammed, and chains clanked, metal to metal. And then...*silence.*

An hour or so later, she heard the chains being removed, the door was lifted, and more containers were loaded on board. Although Audra couldn't see what was going on, she could sense that the containers were filling up the space around her, the air becoming dense. A chemical smell, something used for cleaning mingled with the fish. The door slammed. The chains slid in place. The vehicle started to move.

She could tell the road was winding by the way her body sloshed back and forth. The engine labored each time the driver shifted gears. *Hills.* She listened for sounds that would identify the region they were in, whether they were headed inland or to the coast. The scent of fish grew stronger. She wracked her brain to remember her lessons in geography. Pictures formed in her mind, cities along the coastline.

She gathered from the production of her natural bodily functions that they had traveled less than twenty-four hours. Although she felt dehydrated, she had peed twice. Traveling from Austria to Italy's northern coast would've taken maybe five hours. Which meant if her estimations were correct, they were going south. Why Italy? Why the coast? *Why Rubio, why?*

Rubio stepped into the Casino Wein seven minutes before midnight. Before he reached his favorite roulette table, he was hoisted off his feet and ushered through a door leading to a room he was well acquainted with. A man only known as Ivan sat behind a heavy wooden desk counting euros.

"Either you have my money, or you are completely mad coming here. He checked his watch. "Five minutes to spare."

Rubio straightened his rumpled coat and removed an envelope from his breast pocket. "It's all there, count it."

Ivan's snarl relaxed into a sarcastic grin. "I trust you." His eyes like steel traps latched onto Rubio's. "We have an understanding you and I. If you try to cheat me, you die. Simple." He gestured to one of his goons, "Get him out of here."

Rubio felt the blow to his kidney, but he didn't go down. The man flanking his right side made sure of that, as he pushed him out the door. Rubio caught his breath and moved along. Wein wasn't the only casino in Austria. Casino Graz was 197 kilometers away. Far enough away from Ivan and his spies. He crossed the road, got in his car and pulled away. The drive would give him time to atone for his sins. *Until next time.*

Rubio was in deep with Giorgi. Rubio saw too much, knew too much.

He served as bait—the guy who did the dirty work.

When he delivered Audra to Giorgi, Giorgi seemed pleased, paid him on the spot. Rubio was still in earshot when Giorgi ordered his men to get her caged and on the truck for the midnight run. Normally, Giorgi liked to sample the merchandise, this time he didn't. Rubio wasn't sure if it was because of the time crunch, or whether he had a buyer who wouldn't accept damaged goods. He knew Giorgi could be sadistic.

'Regret,' was a word that didn't belong in Rubio's vocabulary, yet he felt guilty about Audra. *She was different.* The others were mostly runaways, orphans, losers. The clientele didn't care, as long as they were clean and didn't put up a fuss. Drugs took care of the 'fuss' part, most of the grabs didn't know where they were, or didn't care. Once they were hooked on drugs, they would do anything for their next fix. *Like trained seals, begging for fish.* Rubio knew the drill. He was once just like them. It was Giorgi who recognized his potential. It was Giorgi who changed his life. And it would be Giorgi who could make his life a living hell if he didn't do as he was told.

Rubio was six when he was taken. A woman posing as a social worker snatched him from his home in Bakersfield, California. She claimed he was being neglected, that his parents weren't capable of taking care of him.

His mom worked in a bakery; his dad was a roughneck on an oil rig in Santa Barbara. Rubio wasn't the best dressed kid in school, nor was he the worst. There were times when he didn't bring a lunch and had to rely on charity, but those times were few and far between. So, when Miss Nester came to the door and insisted Rubio go with her, he was confused. "My parents are good—they love me!" he screamed. At least he thought so, until they didn't come for him. How could they love him? If they did, they would have stopped Miss Nester from taking him to a foreign country where he was beaten, sodomized, and forced to do unspeakable things.

When Rubio was twelve, fifteen-year-old Giorgi was being introduced to adult pleasures. His father hosted a party on one of his many yachts, and procured flesh in various ages, shapes, and genders. Giorgi overheard Rubio negotiating with one of the older girls for a bite of her cake. He told his father Rubio was a smart one, pleasing to the eye, and one day the boy would work for him. Three years later, Giorgi's father purchased Rubio for five hundred Euros. He fed him, clothed him, and made him watch Giorgi transcend into adulthood. Rubio came to know Giorgi's cruelty, his idiosyncrasies, kinks, and deepest desires. By the time Rubio was eighteen, he was rounding up Giorgi's merchandise, and personal concubines. Later, Giorgi took him into the business. Like his father, Giorgi was immersed in human trafficking.

The first thing Giorgi did was get Rubio clean. He had no tolerance for druggies, or fuck-ups. However, Rubio found another addiction, *gambling*. He loved the adrenaline rush when he won, the low when he lost. Life became a roller-coaster ride. He'd won big, lost big, and ultimately became tethered to Giorgi.

Rubio convinced himself that the kids he snatched were better off. Giorgi made sure they were well fed, and groomed for pleasure. Those who did not abide by Giorgi's rules were beaten and immediately sold to other traffickers. As much as Rubio hated Giorgi, hated the business, Giorgi paid well, which afforded Rubio the freedom to destroy his own life.

Giorgi had clients all over the world—Princes, diplomats, powerful players. He supplied entertainment for high profile people from every walk of life. His "kingdom" stretched far and wide, and those who sought his services not only kept a tight lip, many of them made it possible for Giorgi to operate at an overwhelming capacity. It boggled Rubio's mind how much perversion there was in the world. Giorgi's number one rule—it wasn't his place to judge.

Rubio checked his watch. Audra should be in Lecce soon, the first stop on her long journey. He had to laugh at the irony–by morning, she'd be heading for the US. He wondered if her brother would start sniffing around once he realized she was missing, or if he even cared. The thought hardened his heart. No one looked for him. *No one cared.*

Lewis writhed in his lounger. Eyes squeezed tight, he moaned, mumbled, tossed and turned. "I can't move!" he cried. "I can't move!"

Trudy shook him awake. "Lewis! Wake up, Luv–yer havin' a mare."

Lewis' eyes rolled around in their sockets, as if searching for answers. Trudy shook him again. He awoke with a start. "Lecce!"

"A cat in a flour sack, ye are–"

Lewis took a moment to get his bearings. He swiped his face, wiping away whatever image plagued his sleep. "It's the strangest thing–"

Y'gettin' y'self all lathered up over somethin' Luv, what is it?"

"The girl–they've taken 'er to Lecce!"

"Lecce? Where's that?"

"Italy. We have t'call somebody."

"Call who? The Bill? What y'gonna tell 'em, Lew? Ye 'ad a 'mare 'bout a girl y'never met? 'They,' whoever 'they' is, 'as taken her t' Lecce?"

A tear rolled down Lewis' cheek. "She's in a god-awful place." He wiped the tear with his palm. "I keep seein' Euros, and American money. I think they mean t'sell the lass."

"Lew, let me call the doctor. Yer beginning t'scare me outa me wits."

"I don't need a doctor. I need the Vicar."

Trudy disappeared from the parlor, and reappeared with a pot of tea, her worried brow, relaxed. "I rang my sister...she 'as a friend."

"Y'didn't tell 'er I was bats, did ye?"

"No, of course not. Tess has a knowin'—she understands such things." Trudy filled each cup with tea, a lump of sugar, and a dab of milk. "She said, she'd give 'im a ring."

She met her husband's scowl with a warm smile. "It wouldn't hurt."

"It's so real, Tru." He shook his head. "Never experienced anythin' like it."

Trudy smoothed his hair, hooked a finger under his chin, and lifted his face to meet her gaze. "I believe something 'appened to ye. Not sure what. But I pray that Tess' friend can give ye the answers y'need."

———

Passion

Suzanne lingered in a hot bath. The bubbles had melted, but the water still felt wonderful on her aching muscles. She had taken a part time job at *Face In A Book*, a local book store, stocking shelves, counter work and whatever was required. Although she had only worked a few days, she enjoyed the vibe and the clientele. *I need to get back in shape*, she told herself. It had been awhile since she did any heavy lifting, or exerted herself. Psychic work didn't require muscle. At least not the kind of muscle she was used to.

She received a check from the Sheriff's department once a month, as a retainer fee. She felt undeserving each time she endorsed the back and made a deposit. She'd talk to Sam about it later, at 6 p.m. when they met for dinner.

She hadn't seen Sam in months. They spoke on the phone once or twice a week, but that was all. She knew as soon as she let him into her life, she would want him in her bed. Once she let him into her bed, there would be *commitment, ownership*. Rushing into a relationship could only lead to disaster. *He's not Ben,* she reminded herself. *Take it slow.* Even her therapist agreed. Yet, Sam held a place in her heart that she couldn't deny. *You love him.* "No, I don't," she said aloud. She let her head settle against the terry pillow and her mind wandered. It didn't take long for a vision to spoil the moment...

She could see narrow streets, lined with a myriad of interesting architecture. Modern dwellings mixed with historical refurbished, and crumbling structures. Cobblestone streets gave way to concrete roads, rail yards, shipyards, and buses. A golden sky, streaked with salmon pink, cerulean, and azure blue gave her a peaceful feeling—until a box truck barreled up the street, its gears grinding with the climb. The vision of the girl popped in and out of her mind's eye, along with the fractured image of the man she had seen in an earlier vision. The sound of kittens mewling was deafening. She covered her ears and slid beneath the water.

Sam splashed hot water on his face, squirted a dollop of shaving cream in his hand, and lathered two days' worth of stubble. Once he was clean shaven, he stepped into the shower. His heart was so happy that he burst into song. *"Does Suzanne love me? How will I know? How can I tell if she loves me so?* Just the thought of kissing her made his body react. He hit his falsetto, *"That's what it is!"* He sang a few more bars as he soaped up and rinsed.

He had waited patiently for Suzanne to agree to a dinner date. The ache in his heart did a quick recovery every time he heard her voice, but he wanted more. He wanted to relive the intimate moment they shared when they were vulnerable, needy, *irresponsible.* He'd start with a kiss if allowed, *take it from there.* He wanted it to be right between them. "Right" meant acquiescing; giving her space. Opening the door as wide as it would swing in hopes that one day she'd walk through, hang her hat, and stay awhile.

Work kept him busy, he didn't have time to wallow over *what could be.* He would take "what is," and be satisfied, regardless of the outcome. "You're in a good place," he convinced the image in the mirror. But as he combed his salt and pepper hair, he noticed more silver had crept along his temples in the last few months, and his mom's voice recited an old adage in his mind, "Every man needs a good woman to keep him young."

He planned to take Suzanne to one of his favorite places, Los Pinos, in Cameron Park, a little town in the foothills of NorCal. The Mexican cuisine was authentic, the atmosphere homey, yet elegant. It was far enough from the city to allow them time to talk during their commute. *You'll have her all to yourself.* What more could he ask for?

He wasn't expecting the phone to ring.

He towel-dried his hair, and wrapped it around his waist. "Metzger," he announced. All he heard was gibberish, a crackle. Then the line went dead. He looked at his caller ID. *Audra*. He looked at the clock. *1:19 a.m. in Vienna. Maybe she butt-dialed me*. Was she at a party? She said she was having dinner with Britta. *What's Britta's last name*? He couldn't recall. He'd wait 'til morning, try calling back again...but it was no use... unease reached the pit of his stomach. *Gonna give yourself an ulcer, buddy. She's not your little princess anymore. She's an adult. She's smart. She can take care of herself.* Why wasn't he convinced? He redialed her number. His call went to voicemail.

Suzanne dressed in a sapphire blue pullover sweater, black slacks, and black suede boots. The two-inch heel gave her just the right height. She pulled her chestnut colored hair into a sleek ponytail that settled at the base of her neck, and finished with a little mascara, pink lipstick, and a pair of silver hoop earrings.

Sam rang Suzanne's bell promptly at six. Suzanne took one last look in a mirror that hung by the door. *Why am I so nervous?* Her rosy glow was a dead giveaway. Her heart beat to a rhythm only lovers can feel, like a thousand butterflies fleeing at once. By the time she opened the door, all her senses were on full alert. When she heard his deep resounding voice utter, "Hello," her color deepened.

"Hello yourself, stranger." Heat pooled in her cheeks.

Sam remained frozen; his eyes glued to hers. "Can I just kiss you and get it over with? Otherwise I won't be able to focus on anything else, and I certainly want to enjoy the evening, you know, without staring at your lips, or imagining how incredible your body would feel against mine."

"Would you like to come in?"

He stepped inside, closed the door, and took her face in his hands. His kiss was slow, tender, loving. When he released her, he stuffed his hands in his pockets. "Sorry. I couldn't help myself you look so beautiful. Are you hungry?"

"Famished." She pulled him to her, her lips tingling at the touch of his. His scent worked its magic. Every fiber in her being wanted to take him upstairs, devour him, instead, she set him free. "It's really good to see you, Sam."

Audra assumed they had arrived to their destination. It seemed as though the truck had backed into a confined space, the outside noise, suddenly muffled by the barrier surrounding the vehicle. She no longer heard traffic, road noise, or seagulls. What came next, chilled her to the bone. The first cry came from what sounded like a toddler. Whimpering escalated into uncontrollable wails, and hiccups. The whimper lasted a few moments longer, and then Audra heard a scream, a loud smack, and a thump.

One by one, the containers were emptied. When it came her turn, her hands were bound, and a black sack was thrown over her head. "*Mossa*!" A voice demanded. Audra scooted forward, her feet navigating the space below her. Someone grabbed her arm, pulling her forward until her feet met the ground. She twisted her ankle on impact, falling forward on her knees, her palms. The floor was smooth, greasy. She smelled exhaust fumes, and more distinct odors. Fennel. Vinegar. *Finocchio marino*. She knew the fragrance well. Her mother made it often, using a variety of fennel grown along the rocky coast of Apulia, and white vinegar. She stored the concoction in glass jars, and served it with antipasto salad, or used the finocchio in a pasta dish called, *pasta con le sarde e finocchietto,* made with sardines, saffron, raisins, and *pinoles*, pine nuts. In a pinch, finocchio marina could be purchased in the *Lebensmittelgeschäfte* back in Germany, and Sam said he found it in California grocers as well, but it wasn't as good as their mother's.

Audra concluded this location was a holding center. *For what purpose?* Her pulse quickened. She wanted to call out to Rubio. *Was he even here*? She recalled getting into his car...he told her she looked nice and leaned toward her as if to give her a kiss. She closed her eyes, anticipating his lips, but instead of a kiss, he jammed a needle into her leg. She didn't have time to question his motive, the drug paralyzed her senses, and she blacked out.

Now, a meaty hand pushed her forward, she bumped into a wall.

She stretched her hands out in the darkness, only to have them knocked away from the wall, but not before she discovered the structure was rough. Puglia was known for their *trulli's*, stone structures built without mortar. Navigating Puglia took experienced travelers. It was easy to get lost in the maze of unmarked streets. She remembered going uphill, hearing seagulls, trains. No. She was closer to the coast. Lecce was known to import finocchio marina. Lecce also had ports nearby.

Where were they taking her? The others? *Children*. She felt sick. Sam had warned her of the traffickers in Cologne, Berlin, Hamburg, how they hung around the bus depots, train stations, luring young girls into prostitution. But she wasn't *dumb*. She knew to stay away from *riff raff* as Sam called them. Rubio seemed like a regular guy. He was educated, well-dressed, handsome, charming. She imagined him a little naughty, but never evil.

Audra became aware of the temperature change, and smell in the air. The fennel smell mingled with the smell of urine. Hers?

"*Tutto spento! Usa il bagno. Mettiti questi," a raspy voice said. Her handler thrust a bundle* of fabric at her chest. "*Capiche*?"

Audra nodded her head. Her clothes were wet, they needed to be changed. A wrinkled hand guided her to a toilet, lifted her skirt, pulled down her tights and panties. "Sit."

Audra obeyed, her bladder let loose, following orders. She had barely finished her business before she felt her boots being tugged off her feet. Then came her tights and panties.

"*Apri le tue gambe*," the raspy voice directed. Audra played dumb. She didn't want to open her legs, but warm water gushed upward, and Audra was caught by surprise.

"*Mettiti questi*," the raspy voice commanded. Washed clean, her boots and garments were replaced with dry panties and a loose shift. No bra, no shoes. *No running*..."Where are they taking me?" A blow to the head knocked the question from her lips. She saw stars, and hit the ground.

When she awoke, she was back in her crate, surrounded by what sounded like *mewling kittens* all around her. She wasn't the only one. The nightmare was real. She drew her knees to her chest and covered her ears. A scream lodged in her throat.

. . .

"I have to confess," Sam said, glancing from the road to Suzanne, and back again. "I didn't choose Los Pinos just for the food, which is excellent, by the way, I chose it because I wanted you all to myself, with no distractions."

"I'm happy you did. I love this drive." She turned toward him, placed her hand over his. "I missed you."

Sam couldn't contain the grin that appeared on his face. He withdrew his hand and placed it over hers. Suddenly, Suzanne pulled her hand away, drew her knees to her chest, and cupped both hands over her ears. Sam pulled off the freeway, and stopped alongside of the road.

"Suzanne? What is it? What's happening?" He slipped his arm around her and drew her close. "Let me help you. Tell me what you're seeing."

"It's dark. I can hear them, they're everywhere!"

"What are they? Describe them to me."

"I can't see them," she cried.

"Tell me what they sound like, can you do that?"

Suzanne flattened her palms against her ears. "Kittens. I hear kittens. But they're not kittens! They're–"

"What, Suzanne?" He gently implored. "You can tell me."

Suzanne removed her hands from her ears, her eyes haunted, her face pale. It was as if the word coming from her mouth was not her own. "*Children*."

Sam placed a hand on her shoulder, his tone softened, sounding hypnotic. "Breathe." Gently, he massaged her shoulder, focusing on the trigger point between the rotator cuff, and the crook of her neck.

"I'll be fine," she said, glancing at his hand, then meeting his stare. "Why does this happen whenever we're together? Why can't we just have a quiet dinner without one of these visions hijacking our evening?"

The lines creasing his forehead relaxed. "I'm beginning to feel special." The grin that followed eased her mind. *He understands*.

"I have no explanation for this one," she said, taking his hand in hers. "I've seen this girl before. It's almost as if she's been with me since my near-death experience. I have no idea what our connection is...she wasn't one of Dixon's victims. At least I'm not feeling that she is."

"We can put all of that behind us, Suzanne. Dixon is dead."

"The man I see—I sense he's another Dixon. Charming, good looking...a predator. I feel she's in danger, but I don't understand, why am I hearing kittens, or children cry? It's maddening."

"Could it be spousal abuse? So many kids get caught in the mix of anger, and insanity. One of the most difficult parts of my job as Sheriff are the 10-16 calls. You never know what you're walking into."

"I don't know. There's something about the crying. It's muffled, or indistinct. It reminds of the time I approached these kids outside of a grocery store. They had this box, and when they lifted the lid, I saw it was filled with these adorable fluffy kittens." She smiled. "Maybe the universe is trying to tell me I need a cat in my life."

"What do you say we discuss it over dinner?"

"You sure you don't want to take me home?"

"And miss gazing at you by candlelight? No way!"

"How do you always manage to make me feel better?"

"It's something I enjoy doing?" He patted her knee. "I live for these moments."

They pulled back onto the freeway, feeling as though the storm had passed. But in the back of Sam's mind, niggled the phone call he received earlier, the faint prattle and crackle before the hang-up.

"How would you feel about taking a trip with me?"

She returned his question with a salacious smile. "Don't you think we should get through dinner first?"

After what seemed like an eternity in hell, Audra heard movement outside of her crate. The chain, keeping the lid secure, slid to the floor with a clang. A small hand reached inside with a bottle of water, and a sandwich. "Toilet," the small voice said, dropping an empty plastic bag into her lap. Audra could see the barrel of the AK47 strapped to the kids back.

It had taken a few seconds for Audra's eyes to adjust to the light, but she assessed the child was male, between 10 and 12, possibly Asian. She could barely make out his features. His skin was pale, his arms seemed too thick to be female, his fingernails, bitten to the nub. Angry scars circled his wrists. The command in his voice when he said, "toilet" resonated authority that comes from fear. Audra had worked with enough children to recognize the symptoms.

During her schooling, she worked at a Grundshule near her home in Frankfurt. The children's ages ranged from 6 to 10. Once they finished with Grundshule, the kids were divided into three categories, the slower kids went to Hauptshule, Realschule prepared kids for vocational work, and Gymnasium prepared students for University. Working with children in Grundshule gave one a pretty good idea of which kids would end up where. One boy in particular stood out to Audra. *Martin.* He was frail, suffered with asthma. Bullies love to tease, ridicule, play mean tricks on him, but Martin always seemed to outsmart the best of them. He spoke quietly, 'Martin the Mouse,' they nick-named him. One day he had taken enough of their abuse. She saw his hands shake, his knees clench together, his voice took on a deep tone, it sounded tough, and strong. But Audra knew this façade was out of anger, shame, frustration, and wouldn't last long...*like this boy.*

"*Danka,*" she said to the boy, before light transcended into darkness.

"Welcome," the boy mumbled back, closing the lid.

American, she thought. *How did he get here?* Wherever 'here' was. And— *what do they intend to do with me?*

Dinner was relaxing for Sam and Suzanne, the booth cozy, their conversation intimate. Star crossed lovers converging at last. "I've never felt this way," Sam said, reaching for Suzanne's hand across the table. "I swear you've put a spell on me."

"I think witches cast spells, not psychics," she said.

"Are you sure?"

Suzanne chuckled. "Yes, I'm sure. But I do have to agree with you, this evening has been rather intoxicating."

"Intoxicating? Dear God, how much alcohol did they put in your drink?"

She could feel her cheeks warm. "Hardly enough to make me feel this good. It's you, Sam. I feel good around you."

"Good enough to go to Germany with me?"

"You were serious!"

"I was thinking about visiting my folks, and my sister."

"And here I was thinking Seattle, the Grand Canyon, San Diego—Germany is far, I don't speak the language!"

"I do. And I know my parents would love you. My sister, eh, not so sure."

"I'm flattered to be asked. Can I think about it?"

"Of course. No pressure. I thought May would be a nice time to go. It's still a bit chilly, but spring is a beautiful time of year. There are many festivals, and gardens to visit."

"Sounds lovely."

"I like to go before the tourist season."

"When you're in Germany, do you feel like you're home?"

"I haven't been back in years. The last time wasn't so pleasant. My sister and I had a falling out."

"Tell me about your sister."

"Audra is—how can I say this nicely? She has a mind of her own, and she believes life should be the way she wants it."

"Sounds like a spirited young lady."

"Somehow, I think the two of you would hit it off. You both seem to be—"

"Stubborn?"

Sam's full lips parted, revealing straight white teeth. "Finish your drink. We may be able to catch the sunset heading home."

Suzanne took a sip and pushed the drink aside. "I love a good sunset, let's go."

Sam paid the bill and escorted Suzanne out the door. Before she got into the car, she took his hand and placed it around her waist. "Before we go any farther, there's something I would like."

"Say the word, it's yours."

"A kiss. I would really like another kiss."

Sam pulled her close. His eyes seized hers, setting her on fire. His lips were gentle, sweet. "I thought you'd never ask," he whispered.

"Let's go home," she said.

Audra nibbled on her sandwich. She sipped her water, and waited. It seemed too quiet. Minutes had turned to hours. Day had turned to night. Audra could tell by the ceased activity. No more hustle bustle.

The trains became less frequent, airplanes, less frequent. She strained to hear voices. Strained to hear clues concerning her destiny. She wracked her brain, reliving her date with Rubio. The way he acted, his questions, his demeanor. *He set me up.*

Suddenly a phone rang. The person receiving the call paced back and forth, his voice loud, then soft. He spoke in a language Audra was not familiar with. It wasn't Italian. *Farsi?* Maybe. The one word she understood was "ship".

Her body shook. Tears stung her eyes, yet she didn't cry out. Wherever they were taking her, she would remain strong. She relied on Britta's sensibility to track her down when she didn't show up. To tell someone. But, *who?*

When they arrived back at the house, Suzanne couldn't get inside fast enough. Sam quickly locked the door behind him, cupped Suzanne's face in his hands and covered her mouth with his. His tongue slipped between her teeth, exploring his boundaries. Suzanne welcomed him, pressing her body against his. Together they probed and prodded, finding the right rhythm, the right amount of pressure, and thrust.

"I forgot how good you taste," he said, nibbling his way along her jaw, down her neck, and returning to her lips.

"In that case, I think we should go upstairs for a refresher course."

"Just a heads up, I'm a slow learner. This may take all night."

Suzanne took his hand, leading him up the stairs, and into her room. A nightlight glowed from the corner of the room, casting their shadows on the wall. Sam noticed the room looked very different from the time he rescued her from Ben. The bed now faced the window, where she could greet the morning sun. Pillows, in muted shades covered half of the bed. The detective in him longed to turn on the light, note the changes, but his lover side didn't dare spoil the mood. He felt like a college kid about to make love to his high school sweetheart.

Suzanne began to undress, but one hoop earring caught in her sweater. "Great," she grumbled.

"Here, let me help," he said, releasing the thread from the metal. He pulled the sweater over her head, and tossed it on the bed. His eyes feasted on the swell of flesh spilling over black lace. He bent down to kiss each mound before reaching around her back, unhooking her bra, and setting her free. "Let me look at you," he said, filling his eyes with her beauty. He removed his shirt, and drew her close, skin to skin. His kiss, gentle at first, increased in urgency. Shedding their clothes between kisses, they stood naked, holding each other so tight, their hearts beat as one.

Suzanne lifted the bedspread, sending pillows and clothes tumbling to the floor. She gasped at the giant shadow the mound created on the wall. "If that thing moves, kill it," she said in jest.

Sam laughed, easing Suzanne onto the bed, touching and tasting her, on the way down. He moved her into a comfortable position, maintaining his stride. She moaned with each stroke, each nibble, until his lips found hers, and their passion ignited.

"Please," she begged, "I want you inside me."

Sam gazed into her eyes as he prepared her for his entry. Once inside, he moved slowly, feeling her rise up to meet each thrust.

Suzanne had dreamt of this moment, but never expected to feel such ecstasy with a man she had spent so little time with. Sure, they had grown close pursuing Dixon, even had unbridled, needy sex. But this was different. As he moved inside of her, she felt as though he was healing her from the inside out. She felt loved, safe, cherished, desired, *whole*. When he whispered the words, "Come with me," she knew he referred to more than a physical release, he was inviting her to be with him forever. She cried out, answering his call, as their souls soared to great heights and exploded into the ether.

"I wasn't expecting—" Sam caught his breath and propped himself up on one elbow. He traced Suzanne's lips with his finger. She returned his gaze.

"Dessert in bed?"

"It's more than that—it's—" His eyes traveled the length of her body and back. "I never imagined—" Suzanne pressed her fingers on his lips.

"Yes."

"Yes?" Confusion creased his brow. Suzanne laughed.

"Yes, I'll go to Germany with you."

———

Vision

Lewis had no patience when it came to waiting on a woman. Trudy learned years ago that when he was ready to leave, it was time to go. No dinking around.

Waiting on her cousin, and her cousin's friend, was torture. "Y'said she'd be here at noon. It's 'alf past."

"Keep yer britches hitched. She'll be 'ere." Trudy picked up a basket filled with yarn and several gages of knitting needles. She selected a set already attached to a strand of grey wool. The clickety clack sound of the needles, and the repetitious movement, eased her mind. Two rows in, she heard the buzzer. She tossed the project back into the basket and rose. Wagging her finger she said, "Don't ye be sayin' nothin' 'bout the time. Tess is doin' us a favor."

Lewis peeked through the peephole. "'E looks pretty dodgy, 'e does."

"The two of ye can 'ave a good chin-wag in the parlor."

"And where will ye be?"

"In the garden with Tess."

"I feel like a barmy ol' fool."

"Puddle mush. Open the door before they grow roots."

Lewis opened the door and forced a smile. "Tess! Good to see y' gal. Come in."

"This 'ere's Martin Joseph, a good friend of mine."

"Welcome." Lewis ushered the couple into the parlor. "I'm Lewis, m' wife Trudy."

Trudy grabbed Martin's hand and shook it. "Thank ye for coming, my Lew 'ere's been 'avin' these dreams—"

"Not exactly dreams...more like—"

"Visions?"

"Yes. Visions."

Trudy wrapped her arm around Tess. "Let's walk in t'garden, 'ave a chat?"

Lewis gestured for Martin to sit. "Sherry?"

"None for me, thanks."

Lewis took a seat directly across from Martin. "What d'I need t'do?"

Martin's lips curved into a warm smile. "Tell me what happened."

"Well, I saw m'self on the operating table, splayed open like a prize pig. I saw me mum, and me dad...like it was yesterday. And my friend—hung 'imself he did, when the plague hit in '96. Damn shame. 'E was a good ol' chap. Lost everythin'."

"Did they speak to you?"

"Yes. They spoke of a lass. Said she's in trouble. Said they took 'er to Lecce."

"Italy?"

"Yes. I saw money. Euros. Lots of 'em. It felt as though she'd been sold."

"Did your neighbor tell you who 'they' are?"

"No." Lewis bowed his head. "Feels like I'm watchin' someone drown, and I can't swim."

"Sounds like you had a near death experience. When that happens, a person steps into the other side, where all things are revealed."

Lewis's eyes narrowed. "Don't believe in that 'ogwash."

"It's pretty far-fetched. I was eight years old when a livery truck went rogue and smashed our Fiat like a cockroach. I was comatose for three and a half weeks. When I awoke, I knew Jack Brabham won the British Grand Prix, I knew his time was 1:34.4 on lap 56, I knew that John Surtees placed second, and Innes Ireland placed third—six months before the race took place. I've seen horrific crimes weeks before they happen, but going to the police has only made me a prime suspect.

Lewis' head dropped into his hands. He covered his eyes. "I feel so helpless. Why show me somethin' I can't do anythin' about? Why torment me like this?"

"It's a bloody mystery." Martin clasped his hands behind his head. "Do you want answers?"

"Yes, but I may be pushin' dirt or bonkers before the answer reveals itself!"

"Don't beat your head. The answers will come. Do you meditate?"

"Thought that rubbish went out with John Lennon?"

Martin unclasped his hands and slapped one knee. "Rubbish is it?"

Lewis chuckled. His mood lightened a bit. "I've heard the term–not so sure I'd know how to go 'bout it."

"Go within. Be silent. Listen to your thoughts. There's plenty of books, listen-ups. You can find something that works for you, man. Relax, let the information flow." Martin leaned forward, his eyes narrowed, his pitch dropped a notch. "I walked in your shoes. After a few miles, I found my stride." Martin winked. "It helps to write your thoughts down, no matter how willy-nilly they seem."

"Does this ever go away?"

"It's not the flu. You've changed. You died; you came back. Ask yourself why? You feel helpless, I understand, but the more information you collect, the more pieces of the puzzle you'll have to work with."

"And y'think I'll get the whole picture in time?"

"Maybe. Maybe not. It may take a month–it may take years. All I know is for me, my job here wasn't finished. Perhaps I was meant to have this conversation with you, and for that reason alone I was spared. We're like one big machine. Every part is integral. I may be the cog in your wheel. Tomorrow you may be the cog in someone else's. It's the way the universe works, man."

Lewis reached for Martin's hand and shook. Although he felt a wee bit better, darkness lingered in his soul. When he rose, he felt unsteady. *Moving.* His stomach turned sour. He wanted to lie down. *Disappear.*

Audra struggled to keep the meager meal she had eaten from erupting. She never had a problem with motion sickness—until now. The crate pitched and swayed. Waves pounded the vessel. The wind howled, drowning out the cries around her. She closed her eyes and prayed. Prayed the storm would subside, prayed she wouldn't choke on her vomit, prayed she wouldn't die in her sleep.

Jack?

The phone rang, startling Suzanne out of her reverie. Her night with Sam was extraordinary. She could almost feel his touch on her skin. She clicked on her phone without a second thought, ignoring the caller ID.

"Suzanne? Suzanne Cash?"

"Yes. Who's calling?" she asked.

"It's Sheena. Sheena Bradford, do you remember me?"

"Yes! How are you? How is the baby?"

"Emmett is fine, he's cutting teeth, into everything..."

"Before you know it, he'll be asking for the keys to your car!"

Sheena laughed. She sounded good. Happy. "You're probably wondering why I'm calling," she said, her voice suddenly serious.

"Tell me." Suzanne sat up, and braced herself for what was to come.

"Emmett is starting to display—how can I put this? He has a gift. One I don't fully understand. I thought perhaps, you could meet him. Give me some insight on what to expect."

"Sheena, geez, I don't really know how it all works myself, perhaps—"

"Please, Suzanne? I trust you." She paused. "Besides, I've never had the chance to thank you in person."

"I don't know, Sheena, New York is–"

"I'm in Sacramento. I moved back. There was no sense staying after Dixon murdered my cousin. I wanted to go back to school, finish my degree at Sac State."

"In that case, I would love to get together. Unfortunately, I'm busy this week, how about next?"

"Excellent! And Suzanne?"

"Yes?"

"He says your name."

Suzanne ended the call, her mind reeling. She thought Jack was finished with her once he reincarnated, moved into a new body, a new future. Did he intend to hijack her mind again? *He's a baby. How could a baby be a problem?* Only one way to find out.

Suzanne practically jumped out of her skin when the doorbell rang. She glanced out the window. *Sam*. She ran to the door.

"You'll never guess who—" She stopped mid-sentence. Sam's face was stone-cold serious. "Sam? What is it? What happened?"

"I was hoping you could tell me," he said. "Can I come in?"

"I don't understand, what's wrong?"

"My father called this morning. Audra's friend Britta called my parents to see if they had heard from my sister. They had dinner plans three nights ago. My sister didn't show up, and Britta hasn't been able to reach her."

Suzanne's blood ran cold. Chills ran up her spine. The image of the leggy girl with crimson hair flashed across her brain.

Sam could tell by Suzanne's expression she was getting a hit. His heart stampeded in his chest; tears filled his eyes. "You saw her. You told me about the girl, you mentioned the Belvedere. Is that where you saw her?"

"I saw a young woman. I had no idea who she was." Tiny hairs prickled on the back of Suzanne's neck. "I don't know the location, it was dark, someone was following her. That's all I saw."

Sam took a step toward her. "Think Suzanne, think. There must be more!"

Suzanne flinched. Sam's intensity caught her off guard. "I had asked you if there were any missing girls, you said 'no'."

Sam took a deep breath and exhaled. "I'm sorry. How could you know?"

"Know what?"

"It's my fault, I should've followed up."

"I don't understand."

"I got a weird call from my sister's number. I thought maybe it was a mistake. I didn't follow up."

"Don't do that to yourself, Sam. Not calling back doesn't necessarily equate to a problem."

Sam nodded. He looked miserable. "You warned me. I didn't listen. I thought it was just *coincidental.*"

"You're right—what I saw may be nothing."

"No, Suzanne, you've never been wrong. You're my only hope."

Missing

Lewis stared out the window. A storm swept through London, flooding the streets, and slowing traffic to a crawl. Headlights bobbed below, smearing light in both directions. Every now and then, the wind would whistle through the trees, shaking them senseless. In the distance, bells eerily tolled from Westminster Abbey. He didn't hear Trudy enter the room.

"What'cha staring at luv?"

Lewis startled. "Damn, Tru, don't sneak up on me like that."

"For the love of muffins, yer an oily skillet. I brought y'tea, thank y'very much."

"Sorry, luv. I feel like I could jump out of me skin, these days. Like I got a grasshopper in m'knickers."

"I know, luv. Come. Sit. Tell me 'bout it. I'm a good listener."

"Wish I could explain it t'where it makes a lick 'a sense."

"Try me, luv. I promise not t'judge."

Lewis settled into a chair. He poured a dab of cream into his cup; Trudy poured his tea. He sipped gingerly, blowing between sips. "I'm afraid to close me eyes—it's like I'm trapped in a horror movie. The kind where y'feel the evil gettin' stronger, the music gets louder, and y'just know there's somethin' waitin' 'round the corner that's gonna make y'crap yer knickers, and scream like a teenage girl."

"What do y'think is 'round the corner, Lew?"

"I don't know. That's the horror of it all. I feel it, but I just don't know."

"Did Martin Joseph give any advice?"

"Humph. 'E said t'meditate. Reminds me of when the Beatles lost their minds to that Maharishi back in the day. Maybe I should get m'self stoned."

"May be fun!"

"Oh Tru, isn't it like y'to see the sunny side of things?"

"I feel blessed yer still here, Lew. There's always that."

Lew smiled for the first time since Trudy stepped into the room. "I'll figure it out luv. Somehow, I'll figure it out."

Sheena Bradford pretended to dust around Emmet's chubby legs with a feather-duster. "Does that tickle?" Emmett giggled with delight. "I talked to our friend today. She said she would love to meet you. What do you think about that?"

Emmett climbed off the coffee table and toddled to the bookshelf across the room. He navigated the books on the shelf, babbling to himself. Sheena grabbed her phone and turned on her camera.

"What'cha looking for buddy?" She moved closer to capture his expression and garble for future reference. "Can you smile for mommy?"

Sheena watched him pull each book half-way out, check the title, and push it back in. "Are you looking for Barney? Those are mommy's books, Bud, your books are down below." Emmett didn't veer from his mission. When he found what he was looking for, he pulled the book onto the floor, plopped down, pointed to one of the photos on the cover, and grunted. His expression was so intense, Sheena zoomed in.

"That's Big Ben, Em. Do you like the clock?"

Emmett opened the book, featuring landmarks all over the world. He carefully turned the pages until another photo caught his eye. He pointed and grunted again.

"That's the London Bridge, sweetie, like the song," she sang, "*London Bridge is falling down, falling down, falling down, London Bridge is falling down, my fair lady.*"

Emmett turned to another page, and another, his tiny features intent on something specific. Through the viewer, she saw his eyes light up. He pointed to the Westminster Abbey and got all excited.

A chill skittered up Sheena's spine. "Why those photos, Em? What are you trying to tell me?" He closed the book and perused the shelf. He settled on a dog-eared paperback. "Let mommy see, honey. Whatcha got there?" Emmett handed her the book.

She couldn't believe her eyes. Goosebumps gathered on her flesh. Out of all the books Emmett could have chosen, this one gave her the creeps. A girl running for her life, the title scrawled across the cover struck a nerve: "Missing."

Brotherhood

Sam sighed. "I'm sorry things didn't work out. I hope you understand." Suzanne straightened his shirt collar. Worry, and lack of sleep stole the sparkle from her eyes, and the smile from his lips. "I'll be back as soon as I can."

Suzanne walked him to the escalator, rode one floor up and stopped. Airport security wouldn't allow her any further.

"I pray you find her, Sam. And I pray that she is unharmed."

"I'll call you when I get to Austria. Let me know if you get anything, I don't care how trivial it seems, or what time of day or night. Britta is meeting me at the airport. She is going to help me trace Audra's steps." He pinched the bridge of his nose. "She said my sister met someone on the train. They met up at the Belvedere Palace–some art exhibit."

"Klimpt."

"Yes, that's the one. How did–"

"I saw the Belvedere the first time I met you. The Klimpt exhibit banner hung by the entrance. Oh Sam, if I had only known." Suzanne hung her head.

"How could anyone know?" He pulled her close. "Drive safe. I gotta go." He kissed her tenderly and waved goodbye. She was still waving when the tram doors closed. She felt as if a part of her left with him.

Art

The plane landed at Sacramento International Airport at 3:00 p.m. Passengers from all over the world snaked their way around the roped off area for their turn to have their passports stamped, and enter the U.S.

Giorgi Von Graff stood behind a woman from Salinas, chatting as if they were long-time friends, her brown eyes sparkled as he spoke.

"Where would you recommend that I dine first?"

The woman's reply dripped with snobbery. "The Fire House on 2nd Street is lovely, if you want American cuisine."

"I will take your suggestion," he said, his dazzling smile winning her over.

"There's Morton's on Capitol Mall, if you like steak and seafood."

"Yes, I do love both."

Just then, she turned to acknowledge the Customs and Border Protection Officer calling, "Next?"

"Enjoy Sacramento," she said, smiling, and scooting her luggage in front of her.

Giorgi offered to help. "May I?"

The woman blushed, and flipped her blond hair to one side. "I'm fine, but thank you."

A CBP Officer motioned to Giorgi, and he stepped up to the booth. "Reason for entering the U.S.?" he asked, his tone dry as toast.

"Business. I am an art dealer." Giorgi produced his passport. The Officer thumbed through it, lifting his gaze.

"You've made several trips this year, Mr. Von Graff. The art business must be quite lucrative."

"It can be, yes. Staying afloat requires constant attention."

"I see. And how long do you intend to stay in the U.S.?"

Giorgi handed the Officer his itinerary. "My return ticket is for one week from today. I expect to leave accordingly."

The Officer stared at Giorgi for a moment longer, then stamped his passport. Slowly, he handed the document back to Giorgi, his face transforming from stoic to friendly. "Welcome to the U.S., have a nice day. His smile vanished. "Next?"

Giorgi picked up his suitcase, and moved through the turnstile.

Outside the airport, Giorgi saw the woman he chatted up in line getting into a car driven by a familiar face. She nodded. He nodded back. Business as usual.

He hailed a cab, and gave the driver an address. "Westlake Village."

Giorgi checked into his hotel, unpacked a few items, and dressed in a charcoal suit, and white shirt. He pulled one of the many red ties from the drawer, looped it through his collar and tied a perfect knot. He examined his image in the mirror. He looked like your typical business man, as he would expect the men he was meeting to look as well, with one difference, the red tie, red ascot, red shoes they wore would speak of the brotherhood they shared.

He slipped into a cab, and instructed the driver to take him to Morton's House of Steaks.

When he entered the restaurant, he greeted the hostess with his charming smile. "I am meeting—oh there they are!" He slipped past her and joined two men at the bar.

The man wearing a red ascot slid to his left, offering Giorgi the seat in the middle. Giorgi looked down, spying red shoes worn by the man on his right. "Gentlemen," he said. "What are we drinking?"

The two men exchanged glances. Red ascot spoke up. "What do you recommend?"

Giorgi plucked the wine list from its brass holder, opened it up and began pursuing the vinyl covered pages. "I hear the red wines are the finest in this establishment. Says here, plump, juicy grapes, picked at the peak of perfection."

"Local or imported?" Red Ascot asked with utmost curiosity.

"I prefer reds from Italy." Giorgi proclaimed. "I am told shipments arrive regularly through the port of Sacramento."

"And the vintage?" Red Shoes turned to Giorgi, his lip quivering slightly.

Giorgi studied Red shoes piggy eyes. "Aged 6-14 years. Does that meet your satisfaction?"

Red shoes could barely contain his excitement. He gestured to the waiter. "We'll have three glasses of your best red wine." He rose, and gestured with a head nod. "And bring them to our table." A grin spread across his face. "Suddenly, I'm very—*hungry*."

Red ascot agreed. "Famished."

Water

Suzanne glanced at the clock. Sam had only been in the air 4 hours, and already she missed him terribly. She returned her dinner to the kitchen untouched and turned on the TV. She scrolled through the listings, hoping a program would catch her attention and take her away from her angst. She couldn't imagine the pain Sam felt knowing some monster had kidnapped his sister.

She clicked on BBC. Maybe old reruns of "Are You Being Served" would lighten her mood. Strange dialog caused her to increase the volume. It was as if another conversation was layered over the existing dialog. Did that even happen? Was it possible to dub the sound of one program over another? She listened carefully.

"I keep seeing her, Tru. Each time I close my eyes, she's there."

Suzanne turned the volume up another notch.

"I'm afraid what they'll do to her."

"Lewis, y'can't be in your right mind after what happened."

"Trudy, I saw her. Jim said she was in trouble, and she is!"

"Y'died, Lew! They had to resuscitate ye, y'lost oxygen to your brain."

"It's real, Tru, y'got t'believe me."

Suzanne dropped the remote.

Once she composed herself, she googled "near-death experiences." The list of prompts was endless. She had to narrow it down. She typed in "Lewis" near death experience. Again, pages of websites popped up on her screen. *Perhaps Lewis is British*? She typed in more key words and scrolled through the prompts, one by one. After viewing 34 websites to no avail, she found one that could be beneficial. A small article was printed in a London Journal a couple months earlier. Lewis Howard from Kensington pronounced dead for four hours after open heart surgery regains consciousness. Wife Trudy claims his survival is a miracle.

When Suzanne googled Lewis Howard, Kensington London, little came up. Beneath the same article was a photo of man in his early forties posing with Princess Diana and Dodi Fayed outside of Harrods of London. The previous article didn't mention Lewis was famous, sharing the same name had to be coincidental. For the next hour, she perused the internet, astounded at the number of people who shared her plight. One man from Russia reported waking up 3 days after he was pronounced dead, others reported hours, minutes.

Some recounted their visit in heaven, others described the depths of hell, a number of people had no recollection at all. What surprised her were how many people there were who had stories similar to hers. What the articles didn't divulge was how many came away with visions like hers. And what about Lewis? Was he out there experiencing visions of brutality? Crimes against helpless women and children? Or was he getting lottery numbers? Hitting it big on the crap tables? Her brain hurt from thinking too hard, her eyes burned, her lids felt heavy. She laid her head down on the desk and began to dream...

She dreamt she was riding along, surrounded by lush, green countryside. Sunlight dappled Sycamore trees and a sweet scent filled her senses. Suddenly she caught a whiff of something unpleasant. A burning smell. Flesh. She rolled up her car window, but it was too late. The odor permeated her nose, grew stronger by the minute. *Meat. Burnt meat.* There was no escaping it, she looked for the source. In the distance, a plume of smoke. Then came the sound, bleating sheep, barking dogs, cows, moaning in pain. Horses added to the cacophony. Gun shots rang out in succession. *Turn around.* Turn around before you reach—*the slaughter.*

Suzanne woke with a start. Her fingers hit the keyboard, bringing her computer back to life. She typed the words "slaughter in London." She got more than she bargained for.

Her screen filled with newsworthy items; MAD COW wipes out England's cattle industry. British outbreak affects about 180,000 cattle and devastates farming communities. Creutzfeldt-Jakob Disease—a fatal disease that slowly destroys the brain and spinal cord in cattle...the list went on. But what did Mad Cow have to do with Lewis, his near-death experience? And what was Lewis Howard's connection to Sam's missing sister?

"I'm tired," she said, flipping off her computer. A hot bath with scented oils seemed like a needed reprieve.

She turned on the faucet, lit a candle and turned out the light. Shedding her brushed cotton tee and faded jeans, she stripped down to bare skin, and accessed her image in the mirror over the sink. *Not bad*. Her full breasts were still perky, her stomach flat, and lean. She was one of the lucky ones who didn't contend with cellulite, and her buttocks were firm. She hadn't scrutinized herself in a long time. Her shape was never topic for conversation with Ben. But now? Now she appreciated her body, and the way it fit together with Sam's, like a puzzle piece.

She splashed cold water on her face, and blotted it dry, but her flushed cheeks remained. She wound her hair into a top-knot, secured it with a tortoise-shell pick, and stepped into the tub. The temperature was perfect. Not too hot, not too cold.

She lathered a sponge and glided it over her smooth skin, leaving a sudsy trail. She imagined Sam's lips following the trail, his hands exploring her body, cupping her breasts, massaging the crevice between her legs. She closed her eyes to relive their lovemaking. His hot kisses, finding places she had forgotten existed. His weight pinning her down as he ravished her inside and out. The way their bodies moved together in sync, puzzle pieces, made from the clay. The intensity of their climax, waves, crashing again and again upon the shore, as they clung together, their hearts beating as one. His scent, clean and spicy, still lingered on her bedsheets. She longed for his return.

She submerged deeper in the tub, rinsing the memory from her skin. She prayed for his sister's safety, but the vision that flitted through her sixth sense said differently.

The water in the tub began to pitch, sloshing over the sides. Suzanne sat up, trying to erase the image from her brain. "Nooo," she cried, hanging onto the side of the tub, but the water swelled and receded. Suzanne closed her eyes, facing the message head-on. Crying, mewling, echoed in her ears, the stench of urine, feces, and vomit assaulted her nose. Another sound, creaking, metal against metal...and then it stopped. The water stopped moving, the odors, gone, the sounds, gone, with the exception of one voice, that sounded as if it were coming from the bottom of a well. "Help me."

Audra squeezed her eyes shut, opened them, and repeated the exercise a few more times. *I'm still alive.*

The seas seemed to have calmed as they glided along. It was hot. Humid. *Somewhere tropical.* But where? They had been at sea for seven days according to the tally marks etched on her leg with her fingernail. If her geography served her right, if the ship was heading north, it would be cold. If it were headed south, they most likely would dock in the next week. If they were heading West, much longer. And if she died along the way? Who cared?

———

WAVES

Sam checked into the Lindner Hotel, next to Belvedere Palace. It was a newer property, not the hotel he remembered from childhood. He took a quick shower, changed into jeans, a coral polo shirt, and navy suede jacket he only wore when abroad. Despite the pleasant daytime temps, evenings could be cool.

He had fueled up on airplane food, Salisbury steak, mashed potatoes, and broccolini, two cups of coffee, a cheese Danish, boiled egg, and two slices of bacon. Jet lag was not an option. He texted Britta when he landed. She would meet him in the lobby in ten minutes. Time was of the essence.

"Sam?" Britta's vivacious personality was reduced to 'scared kitten.' Makeup smudged beneath her eyes indicated she had been crying.

"Britta. Thank you for meeting me," he said. Britta buried her head in his shoulder, and sobbed.

"I should've called sooner. I didn't know what to do. I thought maybe—"

Sam lifted her chin, brushed away her tears with his thumbs. "You didn't know." He slipped an arm around her and lead her to a one of the lobby's chairs. The modern design reminded Sam of Nina Levitt's work. A combination of punk and porn. Britta looked perfectly at home, her leather clad legs crossed, her bosom overflowing an electric blue bodice, her blonde hair wild and free.

"What can you tell me about the guy she met?"

"I can do better." She scrolled through her phone. "Look. It's him." Sam took the phone from her hand.

"This is the guy she went to the Belvedere with?"

"She sent me the photo after he dropped her off at her place. She thought she was a clever girl for catching his image in the glass."

Sam checked the time code on the photo, 5:53 p.m. "What time were you supposed to meet Audra for dinner?"

"Eight o'clock. I waited until Nine. I texted her several times, then I thought maybe she was busy having sex or something, so I called. Three more times. I gave up and went home. No big deal. I was happy for her. I figured she was finally—" Britta stopped when she saw Sam's expression. "She said you wouldn't approve."

"Approve?"

"*The sex*. Handsome man, lonely girl. Audra liked him."

"Send me the photo. I'm going to the police, file a report. Is there anything else you can tell me?"

"She met him on the train. I think she got off at Karlsplatz, that's where we met, the café around the corner."

"Thank you, Britta. You've been very helpful." Sam pulled 50 Euros from his wallet and stuffed it into her hand. "Grab a taxi home. I'll call you if I hear anything." Sam pulled Britta to her feet and into a warm brotherly hug. "We'll find her," he vowed.

Outside, Sam hailed a cab for Britta, and one for himself. He slipped inside and gave a command. "Take me to the police station."

"This is rather unusual, Detective," the policeman replied, his accent as thick as the mustache under his nose. "You're welcome to fill out a missing person's form, but it sounds to me that you are not sure if your sister has gone missing, or if she is holed up with her lover."

"No one has heard from her in three days. She doesn't pick up her phone." Sam swiped his hand over his stubbly face. "Do you have children?"

"Yes. And I do understand your predicament, but I see no reason to suspect foul play."

Sam pulled his phone from his pocket, and offered it to the policeman. "Have you ever seen this man?"

The policeman squinted, put on a pair of reading glasses and looked closely. "Yes. He looks familiar. Let me check." The policeman disappeared through a secured door, shutting it behind him. Sam heard voices. When the policeman returned, his demeanor had completely changed.

"I cannot help you," he said, thrusting Sam's phone back at him as if it were going to blow up in his hand. "Fill out the form, your choice."

Sam didn't argue. He filled out the meager form, and handed it back to the policeman. "Thank you," he said, looking deep into the policeman's eyes. He thought he saw a flicker of remorse. He looked closer at the policeman's name: *Irlich von Steuben.*

The temperature seemed to have dropped 10 degrees in the last hour. Sam pulled his jacket closed and zipped it half-way. The wind blew, reminding him of his childhood. Of Krampus, the Christmas devil. *Where can she be?* He saw the sign for the U-Bahn, and headed down the stairs. Even if he had to ride the trains all night, he would find this pretty boy his sister was involved with.

A taller policeman opened the door to the secured room. "What did you tell him?" he asked von Steuben.

"To fill out a form or leave."

"Good. We don't need some American Rambo sticking his nose where it doesn't belong."

"I have a feeling he's not going to quit until he finds his sister."

"We don't need Giorgi Von Graff getting wind of this. Rubio is his boy. He goes down, our tits are in a ringer."

"The detective showed me his credentials. He has dual citizenship. He can make waves."

"Well, let's make sure he doesn't."

Green Door

Suzanne woke to the phone ringing next to her pillow. *Sam.* "Hello?"

"Did I wake you?"

"What time is it there?"

"Afternoon, 3:30 p.m. Rode the trains all night looking for this guy my sister met—I just got up myself. How are you?"

"I've been getting snippets, but it's too weird to even explain."

"Try me."

"I heard a conversation going on over a TV program I was watching on the British Broadcast Channel. It was a man talking to his wife about someone hurting a girl. What are the chances of that? Get this—she mentioned his near-death experience. I hopped on Google to see if I could find anything."

"And?"

"I'm not sure. This man, if he is the same man that died, was also in a photo with Dodi Fayed, and Princess Di."

"I don't see a connection."

"There lies the problem. I drifted off for a bit and had a dream about Mad Cow Disease. I'm stumped."

"You're beautiful when your stumped."

"I think I'm blushing. How did your meeting go with Britta?"

"She said my sister was lonely, and horny."

"How was that information helpful?"

"It's been years since I saw my sister. I really don't know her that well anymore. Maybe she is shacking up with some guy."

"Do you really believe that?"

"No. The police were no help. Except—"

"I'm listening."

"The policeman I spoke to seemed to recognize the photo Audra took, but acted like he didn't."

"Send me the photo, let me take a look."

Sam clicked on the photo, and forwarded it to Suzanne. "I'll wait until it comes through."

"How is your hotel?"

"It would be better if you were here with me."

Suzanne heard the ping and opened the attachment. "This is the door I saw in my visions! This is the man!"

"What else can you tell me about him?"

Suzanne closed her eyes. Nothing. All she saw was the light filtering through her bedroom window. "I don't think it works that way, Sam." She could hear his audible sigh. "I'm sorry."

"No, no—I can't expect you to—damn, I was hoping."

"If I get anything, I'll call you."

"Yeah. Okay. Fine."

Suzanne felt his disappointment. She struggled for positive words to end the call, but nothing good came to mind, instead, a feeling of foreboding washed over her. "Be careful," was all she could say.

———

Clients

Giorgi climbed into his Mercedes SUV rental and headed for the freeway. He glanced in the mirror at his polished appearance. His clients loved him. He was their sex Santa, ho, ho, ho. *The naughtier, the better*. He catered to the twisted, insatiable, perverted, and cruel. Who was he to judge? He provided something for every palate.

He'd been doing business in Sacramento for twenty years. He serviced millionaires, politicians, celebrities, businessmen and women alike. Young, old, and in between. In his line of work, money talked. You want a fourteen-year-old virgin? Older? Younger? Girl? Boy? Dark skinned, light skinned, blue eyed, brown eyed, long hair, short hair, no problem. *I'm the candy-man*.

Soon, a fresh load of flesh would be arriving in Sacramento. The crates would be off-loaded from the ship before they reached port and were distributed accordingly. But first, he would meet with his minions, arrange for black market videos to be made in L.A. He had several buyers clamoring for their piece of the action. Those sold into the active sex slave industry would be taken to various locations, checked by doctors, and taken to their new homes. Giorgi was known for his high quality and compensated handsomely for his discretion. This shipment proved to be exceptionally profitable, with an order placed for a "babysitter" at triple the price. Rubio promised Giorgi the girl he captured fit the bill. A virgin, brunette, beautiful, nubile, and intelligent.

The buyer lived on a ranch in a rural area. He bred race-horses, owned properties all over the world, including little remote islands, he used for his escapades. When the buyer called earlier that day with a dinner invitation, Giorgi couldn't refuse. "Just a few 'close' friends," he said. Giorgi exited east on Highway 50, anticipating a very interesting evening.

Audra took small bites of the sandwich her handler threw into her crate yesterday. *Or was it the day before?* Peanut butter and jelly. Evidently, the crew hadn't considered the risk of peanut allergies. Earlier, Audra had heard a commotion. Someone screamed something about blowing up like a balloon. "

Sta esplodendo come un palloncino!"

Angry voices cursed in Italian. Then came footsteps. Keys jangled; chains dropped to the floor. A metal door squealed opened, then closed. A shushing sound, like something being dragged across the floor. Another door opened to a balmy breeze. Then came a splash. *Dead kid overboard.*

———

Transaction

Suzanne filled a kettle with water for tea and placed it on the stove. An image popped into her head of lighting the fire with a wooden match instead of the knob. The hands were not hers. Older. Steady. A phone rang, the same hands picked up the call.

"Who's this y'say'? And how do y'know me husband, Lew?"

Suzanne closed her eyes. She felt dizzy. But not round and round dizzy, but up and down dizzy. The feeling swelled, receded, then swelled again. *Ocean.*

Sam rode the U Bahn to the last stop, switched cars, and waited for the train to repeat the route. Three young girls got on, giggling, and speaking rapidly in French. Two sat down in one seat facing forward, the third sat across, in the aisle seat, facing the girls, and Sam. The car filled fast, and soon very few seats were available. The door closed, and the train began to move. Sam heard a shush and a thump behind him. A young man traversed down the aisle, struggling to keep his balance. He stopped next to the girls and gestured to the empty seat.

"*Ist dieser Platz besetzt*?"

The two girls facing front giggled. The one facing Sam slid over. The young man sat down, turned and smiled at the girl next to him.

"*Danka*," he said, flashing a dazzling smile.

Sam couldn't help but notice his eyes, the shape of his face. His hair was shorter, but there was no mistaking his eyes. Sam held up his phone, pretending to text. He snapped a photo, and compared it to Audra's. *It's him*. He watched the young man flirt, despite the language barrier. Sam refrained from jumping up and ripping out his throat. When he heard him introduce himself as Rubio, he made a note. The guy moved fast, working his magic on the young girls. By the time they reached the next stop, the spell was cast.

Sam rose and grabbed the pole next to Rubio and the girls. He nodded at Rubio, gesturing toward the girls.

"*Du bist ein Glückspilz.*" *You're one lucky guy.* Sam fixed his eyes on Rubio. "I have money. I can pay."

The girls gave Sam a dirty look.

"*Pervertieren*," one girl said to the other. Rubio laughed.

The girls turned to one another and giggled, oblivious to what he just inferred. Rubio on the other hand seemed curious.

"Pervert? Me? I have a daughter your age. This man is a pimp."

One girl looked as if Sam struck her in the face. Her eyes grew big. She grabbed her friend's hand and moved toward the front of the car.

Rubio's expression soured. "You're a cop."

"No, just a man," he replied sliding next to Rubio. "I like them a little older. Sweet. Brunettes are my favorite." Sam looked around to make sure no one was paying attention to their exchange. "I meant what I said. I have money."

"Not here," he said. "Get off at Schönbrunn. I'll meet you at Herzog's on Sechshauser Strasse in twenty minutes."

Sam winked. A sly smile spread across his face. "Maybe today is my lucky day."

Sam stepped onto the platform. He navigated his way to the staircase, and out into the open air. He turned this way and that to get his bearings before heading west. When he saw Herzog's, he crossed the street, and went inside. "*Zwei*," he said to the hostess. She grabbed two menus and led him to a corner table. "*Danka*," he said, and took a seat facing the door.

The large window provided him with an excellent view of the foot traffic outside. Sam would be able to spot Rubio quickly. Or so he thought. When Rubio came around the opposite corner, ten minutes later, Sam was surprised.

Rubio didn't greet the hostess, instead, he snapped his fingers at the bartender, who dropped his bar towel, and hustled over. *They know him,* Sam thought.

"What are you drinking, American," he asked, his cavalier demeanor bordering on cocky.

"Clausthaler," Sam replied.

"Becks." Rubio waited until the bartender was out of earshot before sharing his glib observation. "The pervert is an alcoholic as well? Interesting."

Sam's hazel eyes turned to pitch. He chuckled. "Ah, another assumption. Alcohol impedes the performance, I'm looking forward to an exciting evening."

"And what makes you think I can provide that for you?"

A cunning smile slid across Sam's face. "This isn't my first rodeo."

Rubio returned a like smile. "What do you want."

"I'm partial to brunettes. Preferably one who speaks my language." Sam leaned closer, his voice, barely a whisper, "I want to be able to understand the dirty talk, *verstehst du*?"

Rubio nodded. "Anything else?"

Sam steepled his hands on the table. "Slender, au pair, college girl, you know the type, innocent on the outside, tigress on the inside." Sam closed his eyes, his mouth relaxed into an *ahhh*, as if he was conjuring an image. When he opened his eyes, Rubio was staring. "I'm very particular, " he said, "but as I said earlier, I can pay."

Rubio leaned back in the chair. A darkness washed over him. Was it regret? Sam didn't want to speculate. His agenda was to save his sister, not heed this moron's guilty conscience. At least, not yet.

"Why not hire a prostitute?" Rubio's eyes narrowed. "There are plenty to be had."

“For the same reason I don't buy my wine at the local market.”

“I see, you are an elitist.”

“I thought I was a perverted alcoholic?”

Rubio, nodded. “Same difference.”

"And you speak very good English for a—pimp."

"Touché!" Rubio chuckled. "I consider myself more of a—" He thought for a moment, his lips puckered, "—a collector of art."

"Then we are on the same page."

"Meet me at St. Stephen's Cathedral at ten tonight. Don't be late."

"How do I know you are not setting me up?"

Rubio's eyes hardened. "You don't. Bring cash." He took a swig of beer, rose, and hurried out of Herzog's.

Sam texted Suzanne: Found the guy. Pray I find Audra.

Suzanne sat at her desk, deciphering her scribbled notes. She needed to find the man in the photo. Lewis Howard. She started her computer and began to search. UK phone book. She typed in his name, Kensington, London, and hit return. Six names scrolled across the screen. She dialed the first.

On the fourth try, she heard the familiar voice. "I'm trying to reach a Lewis Howard—he was in the meat business..."

The words echoed the voice in her head, "Ow do y'know m'husband, Lew?"

"Mrs. Howard, I don't actually know your husband, I know of him, I know he had a near death experience, I know a girl is missing...I keep seeing him, hearing his voice..."

Trudy nearly collapsed on the floor. She caught herself by grabbing onto a kitchen chair. Her voice was weak when she called, "Lew–Lew come, it's for you."

Lewis answered with a suspicious, "'ello?"

"My name is Suzanne Cash, I'm calling from America. I too, had a near death experience. I see things, hear things, they don't make sense half the time, but as I told your wife, there is a girl, she's in trouble–I need your help."

"I know what yer sayin,' woman, but 'ow can I help?"

Words tumbled out of Suzanne's mouth, faster than anticipated. "I don't know–she was in Austria when she disappeared–are you getting any visions? She's a dark-haired girl, in her twenties..."

Lewis took the phone to his chair and sat down. It seemed the weight of the world had lifted off his shoulders. "Then, I'm not daft after all."

Suzanne exhaled, "I know how you feel. I thought I was losing my mind! And then there was my dead boyfriend..." Suddenly there was silence on the other end of the phone. "Lewis? Are you there?"

Suzanne could hear the angst in his voice. "I saw me friend—'E told me 'bout the girl."

"He's guiding you from the other side. That's how it worked for me."

"I feel the need t'travel. I kept hearin' Lecce, had a bad feelin' 'bout the place. And water. It's all so strange. The missus thinks I popped me cork."

"No. You're fine. It was explained to me that dying changes your frequency, we pick up energy, thoughts are energy, so are visions. It's our job to figure out what it is we are supposed to do." She heard the quiver in his voice.

"Are they goin' t'find the girl?"

"With our help, yes they will."

"Then I'm beholden for y'ringin' me. What's next?"

"We share notes. Lecce must mean something...any ideas?"

"Lecce is a walled city, a bit dodgy if y'ask me. They say there's 2000 years of bloody history waitin' t'be discovered in the underground tunnels. She's a bloody perfect place for criminal activity."

"What about water? Is there water nearby?"

"Several ports. Brandisi is one of the largest."

"It's a start. The big question is, where are they taking them?"

"'Tis a 'them' then, is it?"

"I'm afraid so."

Suzanne texted Sam: Found my London source. He believes Audra was taken to Lecce. She may have been put on a boat.

Suzanne was about to fry herself an egg when the phone rang. She expected it to be Sam, and didn't check the caller I.D. The voice on the other end of the phone caught her by surprise. "Suzanne? It's Sheena."

"Sheena, how are you? How is little Emmett?"

"He's fine, except his behavior has been a little odd. He keeps showing me pictures, specific pictures in books. I thought it was just fascination, until he showed me a book with a missing girl. It gave me the creeps. I thought maybe you'd be able to give me some insight."

"What else did he show you?"

"The London Bridge, Big Ben..."

"Can I come and see him?"

"Of course, I would love that, when?"

"I can come now."

"Now? You're scaring me."

Giorgi woke to the sound of a rooster's crow. He surmised, by his surroundings, it had been quite the party. Breakfast awaited under an assortment of silver domes. He lifted one lid discovering a frittata made with lobster claw meat and topped with caviar. The second, Crème Brûlée French toast with golden raspberries. The last, poached eggs, displayed on a rasher of thick smoked bacon, covered in Béarnaise sauce and topped with roasted asparagus. He closed the lid and poured a cup of coffee, lifted it to his lips, reconsidered, and set the cup down.

He remembered eating a decadent dinner of veal medallions with roasted fennel and butternut squash last evening, followed by whiskey and cigars. Must've been the liquor served in the delicate cordial glass that knocked him on his ass. He vaguely remembered warm bodies crawling all over him like puppies, nipping, sucking. All of which had been recorded on video, of that he was sure. *Leverage*. They wanted to be sure all the balls weren't in his court. Although, he was sure that when it came to blackmail, he held more clout. Everything these people did was in excess. Their lifestyles, a constant game of one-upmanship. Desensitized, and soulless. Preying on the weak made them feel alive. Giorgi understood. After all, misery loved company.

Giorgi showered, dressed, and headed back to the hotel. No need to overstay his welcome. The deal was made. The merchandise would be delivered in ten days. Once the ship reached the port in Oakland, and the cargo was assessed, and stabilized, delivery would take place. Meanwhile, he'd work on his tan.

• • •

Emmett greeted Suzanne at the door, his bib, wet with drool. "He's teething, Sheena said, scooping him up and closing the door. "It's nice to see you, she said, leaning in for a hug. Emmett reached for Suzanne.

She stared into his fathomless eyes. One green, one brown. He didn't blink. He circled his arms around her neck and rested his cheek against hers.

Sheena stood slack-jawed. "He doesn't react that way with anyone." Suzanne gave him a gentle squeeze and set him down. "I don't think I'll ever fully understand the nature of our relationship, but what I do know is he is trying to tell us something."

"For sure! I can't tell you how many books he goes through a day trying to communicate. He hasn't been sleeping very well, either. I thought it was because of his teeth breaking through his gums. But now, I'm beginning to wonder."

"Right before you called, I was speaking with a man who had a near-death experience. We were comparing notes. Sam Metzger's sister is missing."

Sheena's jaw dropped. "No way! She was kidnapped in London?"

"No, Austria, actually. But Lewis lives in London."

Emmett giggled and clapped his hands. Both Sheena and Suzanne smiled. He crawled over to the book shelf. He pulled himself up, and began rummaging through the books, tossing the ones he didn't want on the floor.

"Here we go again," Sheena said, stacking the discarded books in piles on the floor. "What are you looking for this time, buddy?"

Emmett grabbed a children's version of "Noah's Ark" off the shelf. The author kept the bible theme, but instead of animals on the ark, there were children from all over the world. He opened the book to an illustration of the ark bouncing on the waves, some of the children looked delighted, their hands in the air, others looked miserable, their faces colored green with discomfort. Emmett pointed at the arc, and handed the book to Suzanne, grunting what sounded like, "Here."

Suzanne opened the book, and studied the page. "Is this where she is, Emmett?"

The boy clapped his hands. He toddled to Sheena, crawled up in her lap, and buried his head in her bosom. Every now and then he would peek at Suzanne and giggle.

Sheena wrapped her arms around him, and squeezed. "What does it mean?"

"It means Jack can still communicate with me. I believe that although he's been reincarnated into a new body, his soul remains the same. He knows things."

"Will he grow out of it?"

"I don't know. I'm new at this myself." Suzanne ruffled Emmett's hair and smiled. "He helped me find those girls–and *you*."

"Me?"

"Yes. He led me to you."

"How is that possible? He wasn't born yet?"

"I believe the reason he was so adamant to save you was because he planned to reincarnate into your womb. I saw it. He showed me."

"That's crazy."

"I know. What's even more crazy is getting help from a toddler." Suzanne clasped her hands together. "What else do you want to show me Emmett"

He climbed down from Sheena's lap and hurried across the room. He ran one tiny finger along the books on the shelf. He stopped, listened, as if a voice from another world guided him. He shook his head, his eyes flooded with tears. He ran to Sheena, and buried his head in her lap.

"Hey baby boy, what's wrong? It's okay, mama's here." Sheena glared at Suzanne. "Maybe this wasn't such a good idea."

"I'm sorry. Perhaps he's not ready to share."

"Or—he's frightened."

"Either way, time will tell."

Duty-Bound

"Have y'popped y'cork, Lew?" Trudy blocked Lew's attempt to fill his suitcase. "Y'just had heart surgery. Y'aven't completely healed. What if y'get infected, or go pear-shaped?"

"I won't be goin' pear-shaped, Tru. I need t'help the lass."

"Why you?" She pleaded. "Why not let The Bill handle it, or that woman? She knows as much as y'do about the poor girl."

"Did ye ever feel so strong about a thing that if y'don't follow through, y' won't be able t'live with y'self?"

"No, Lew. I've lived m'life on the safe side. Takin' care of m'self and the man I love. I can't imagine m'life without ye, and if that's not enough to stop y'barmy ways, y'not the man I married 52 years ago."

Lewis stopped in his tracks. "I'm <u>not</u> the man y'married 52 years ago. Somethin' 'appened t'me. And if y'can't understand, then we've gone sideways."

Sam walked six blocks to St. Stephens Cathedral. He stared up at the regal structure in awe. The "Mozart's" were busy hawking tickets for various operas. Sam stood near the entrance, and waited for Rubio. After 2 hours, he had the feeling he wasn't going to show. Fear gripped the pit of his stomach. Rubio was his only chance of finding his sister.

And now? He figured Rubio would lay low until Sam no longer posed a threat. Or perhaps he would change his route, conduct business as usual. Sam headed back to the hotel, his tail between his legs.

Suddenly, he heard footsteps, following very close. He turned to see Rubio in his wake. "What the fuck, man?"

"Did you really think I was going to show up with the goods without checking you out first? What if you were a cop?"

"Right, why didn't I think of that?" Sam curbed his anger. "Now what?"

"Meet me here in an hour." Rubio slipped him a piece of paper with instructions and an address written in black fine-point marker. "Don't be late."

Sam found a bank kiosk and withdrew 600 euros in cash, three 100€ bills, the remainder in small denominations, just for show. He folded the bills strategically, and stuffed them inside his breast pocket. If Rubio produced Audra as his evening entertainment, it would be over, if not, he needed to play along, at least until he could grab Rubio by the throat and convince him to tell him where she was. The rendezvous place was three blocks away–he had 15 minutes to kill. His last meal churned in his stomach, his senses, on overdrive. Blood coursed through his veins, thrummed in his temples. Hair prickled on the back of his neck as he neared the dingy building where his fantasy was to play out. He checked his watch. Five minutes. He walked across the street and waited.

Rubio walked briskly, practically dragging a young woman in his wake. When they slipped into the doorway, Rubio backed her against the door and held her face in his hands. Sam couldn't hear what Rubio was saying, but by the resonance of his voice, Sam imagined it was a warning.

Sam ran toward Rubio, grabbed him by the hair, spun him around, and wrapped his arm around his neck. "Where's my sister," he seethed in Rubio's ear. "Where's Audra?"

"You're a fuckin' lunatic, man. I brought what you asked for."

"I want the girl you met at the Belvedere Palace. Where is she?"

"I don't know what you're talking about!"

"I saw you. You were visiting the Klimt exhibit," Sam seethed, his forearm pressing against Rubio's windpipe.

"I don't know where she is. We had one date, that's all–I haven't seen her since."

"You're a liar." Sam tightened his grip. "Where is she?"

Rubio struggled to no avail. "He'll kill me if I tell you," he said, gasping for air.

"I'll kill you if you don't." Sam squeezed tighter.

"She's long gone, man. You'll never find her."

Sam ground his heel into Rubio's instep while tightening his grip on his neck. "Tell me where she is!"

Rubio squealed. "She was shipped out, some rich guy bought her, that's all I know!"

"Where?" Sam dug harder, this time sliding his heel toward Rubio's toes. Rubio whimpered. Sam was about to do it again when the young woman slipped behind him, and jabbed something into his back. Sam loosened his grip. He reached behind him and came away with blood on his hand. "Damn," was all he said before he sank to his knees.

"*Nimm sein geld*!" The woman shouted. Sam clutched the wad near his breast.

"Fuck the money, let's go," Rubio said, and the two took off running.

Sam dragged his bleeding body to the curb, and hailed a taxi. "Take me to the nearest hospital–I've been stabbed."

———

LACERATIONS

Sam woke up to a middle-age woman in baby-blue scrubs checking his vitals. "What—?" he asked, his voice weak.

"You came in last night with a lacerated kidney. You were rushed into surgery—you're going to be fine. The doctor should be in soon. Until then, rest. You've lost a lot of blood. Anyone we should notify?"

Sam thought a moment. "No. I'm fine," he said. No use getting Suzanne all riled until he knew the extent of his injury.

"Okay, then. The police are going to want to speak to you when you're up to it. We don't take kindly to tourists being stabbed on our streets."

Sam closed his eyes, reliving the scene. He had a few questions of his own. "I was attacked from behind. I didn't see who did it."

The nurse patted his hand. "I'll be back later to check on you."

Sam was grateful he'd booked his room for an indefinite time. No need to contact the hotel. The only one who would be concerned with his whereabouts was Suzanne. He didn't suspect Rubio would hunt him down and finish him off. Right now, he was probably pissing his pants knowing Sam was on to him. Rubio answered to a higher power. *Someone who has all the answers.* Answers that would save his sister.

. . .

Rubio dipped his hand in one embossed leather pocket and opened his phone. He tapped in a number and waited. "It's Rubio. There's a cop here from the states inquiring about one of Giorgi's purchases." He paused, spied his surroundings, and lowered his voice. "One of my girl's poked him last night. If he's alive he's probably at Vienna General." Rubio listened, nodding his head. "Yeah, well, he's your problem now. If Giorgi finds out we're both fucked."

Rubio pressed "ENDE" and stuck his phone in his pocket. He walked past the Opera House teaming with tourists. Casino Bar was calling his name. It closed at 3 a.m. He had three hours to work through his frustration. One big win and he'd hop a plane to Tahiti, cut his hair, change his name. *Change my luck.* He said too much. Either "Dirty Harry" was going to put his ass in a sling, or Giorgi would. He knew Audra was a big mistake. Girls with families were always trouble, but Giorgi didn't give him much choice, and Audra checked off every box on the list. Except one. *I hope she reaches California before they find out she's not a virgin.*

Audra pried her sticky eyes open with her fingers. Her throat felt parched. How long had she been knocked out? Loud noises bled through her comatose state. A clanking sound, followed by scraping, screeching, and a thump. The kittens were quiet. Too quiet. She wanted to call out to them. Make sure they were still there. *Still alive.*

She lost track of their route. The scratch marks blurred in front of her. From the stench assaulting her nostrils, she had lost more than a day. Once they started moving again, they would hose down the crates, open the doors, give them water, and food. How she had come to appreciate the little things.

Satan

Suzanne checked her phone. No new messages. *Where is he?* She hadn't heard from Sam in three days. Her text messages to him, left unchecked. *Something's wrong*. She closed her eyes, wishing now, more than ever, a vision would assure her that Sam was safe. *Nothing*.

"Linda, it's Suzanne."

"I know. Kinda goes with the territory."

"I'm worried about Sam. Any reason I should be?"

"I wish I could give you the answer you want to hear, but I can't. At least not without more information."

"He's in Germany. His sister is missing."

"That explains the euros you were seeing earlier."

"Yes, but he went to Vienna. I haven't heard from him since he found the guy he suspects snatched his sister."

"Have you tried the hospitals?"

"No. I didn't want to go there."

"No one wants to think the worst, but trust me, if you don't cover your bases, you're going to drive yourself nuts."

"Sage advice, once again. Thank you."

"Try connecting heart to heart. See if that works for you."

"Thank you, my precious friend. I will let you know how it goes."

"And when you find him, tell him the blood between the sons of Satan can be thicker than the brotherhood of man."

Sam swallowed two pills and a few sips of water. The pain had subsided enough to get off the intravenous meds they were giving him. "When can I leave?" He asked the pretty young nurse. She returned a nervous titter.

"No English," she said.

"*Wann kann ich abreisen*?"

"*Demnächst*."

Sam nodded. "Soon. Great. *Danka*."

She tittered again and hurried out of the room.

Sam reached for his phone. After the excruciating feat to grab it, he discovered his battery was dead. He tossed it back on the nightstand and laid his head back. Within minutes the pain killers kicked in and his eyes slammed shut. Suzanne appeared behind his lids. Her face, drawn with worry, tears filled her eyes. "I'm fine, my love. I'm going to be fine," he heard the voice inside his head say. He wanted to rush to her, hold her tight, reassure her that forever was their fate...but her face morphed into Audra's...and worry turned to terror...and tears turned to blood.

When Sam awoke, Irlich von Stuben, the policeman he saw at the station, stood over his bed, his piercing eyes lacking compassion.

"*Wer hat Sie Detective erstochen*?"

"I didn't see her face. It was dark. *Zu dunkel*."

"You came to the station. About a missing girl."

"Yes. I remember you. I was inquiring about my sister. Do you have any news?"

"*Nein*. I suggest you go home."

"Why would I do that?"

"Meddling in police business can get you hurt." He nodded toward Sam's wound. "Wouldn't you agree?"

"Where I come from, when someone is missing, we don't threaten the family...that is unless we know something we aren't sharing."

"Be careful, Detective. Krampus still roams the streets looking for those who disobey the rules."

"You have a predator in your midst, and you're okay with that?"

"I don't remember you mentioning—"

"And if I did?"

"Go home, detective. This isn't America. The streets are filled with runaways, and wayward girls who go missing every day. Frankly, I blame the parents. They are responsible for teaching them not to talk to strangers."

Sam struggled to sit up. He wanted to punch the policeman's smug face. Choke him until his sharp little eyeballs popped out of their sockets. "*Fick dich!*"

"Your passport will be confiscated in three days," he said, patting Sam's foot. He lifted his gaze, his eyes, glued to Sam's, and continued, "The blood between the sons of Satan can be thicker than the brotherhood of man." He turned to go, adding, "Feel better, detective."

Following the policeman's departure, the sweet nurse came back in to fluff his pillows and take his blood pressure. He pointed to his phone with pleading eyes, "*Hast du ein Ladegerät das ich mir ausleihen kann*?"

She nodded, and opened the drawer on the nightstand. Inside, was a chord with various phone jacks. She found the one that fit Sam's phone and plugged it in.

"*Danka.*"

She smiled. "*Krampus stiehlt jeden Tag Kinder.*"

"Where does Krampus take the children once he steals them? *Bringt sie wohin*?"

"America."

Sam rethought the warning he received from the policeman. Maybe it wasn't a threat after all. *Perhaps he was giving me a heads up.*

The Racket

"Do you speak English? *Um sprichst du Englisch*?" Suzanne rolled her eyes. Her attempt at speaking German failed on all levels.

"Very little. Can I help you?

"Do you have a patient by the name of Samson Metzger? He's an American. A German born American."

There was a moment of silence. "*Nein*. I'm sorry."

The phone went dead before she had the chance to ask any more questions. This was her fourth try. Either the operator didn't speak English, or Sam was not listed as a patient. She dialed his cell number, just to hear his voice, but before the call transferred to his voice mail, she heard a faint "hello."

"Sam? Can you hear me?"

"Hey, sorry I haven't called, my phone—"

"You're hurt."

"I keep forgetting you have that super-power."

"Dear God! What happened?"

"I got stabbed."

"When? Where? Are you all right?"

"I'm fine. Any news?"

"Yes, the man I told you about, Lewis, Lewis Howard, he wants to help look for Audra. It's a start. And it feels right. I don't know why, but—"

"The nurse mentioned America, she said children are stolen every day, and taken to America."

"Lewis thinks your sister was taken to Lecce, he said there's a port in Brindisi."

"I'll see what I can do about checking myself out of here. I'll be home as soon as I can."

"Did they arrest the woman who stabbed you?"

"How did—"

"I don't know, it just popped into my head."

"No. I haven't given the police any information. I believe they know who took my sister."

"Why would—"

"It's a racket, bigger than I imagined, a multi-billion-dollar business. Finding someone who's not on the take may be a challenge. For now, I have to have faith that Audra is still alive."

"Linda said to give you a message. She said, 'The blood between the sons of Satan can be thicker than the brotherhood of man.'"

Sam's spine tingled. "I'm coming home."

Paper

Audra's menstrual cramps kept her rolled up like one of the bugs she remembered flicking off of the benches at Belvedere park with Sam. He'd usually initiate the flicking competition, but her long slender fingers acted quickly with precision, matching his tenacity. She got him in the eye once—he got even by smashing a bug in her hair. How she wished she had taken his advice. She knew the questions Rubio asked her were inappropriate, yet she let her girlish ego override her sensible self. It had been a long time since someone as attractive as Rubio paid attention to her.

Most of her friends were what Americans called "nerds." Her flatmate Bruno knew very attractive men, but they were more interested in her fashion sense, and each other, than her. *Bruno.* She'd give the moon and the stars to be cuddled up on the sofa with Bruno, his cat Latté, and a classic Rita Hayworth movie. How she took the small things for granted, considered her life boring. Britta lived a life she envied, always a new man, a new job, a new adventure. Getting the job as an au pair and coloring her hair was the extent of her adventurous side. Her parents thought that moving to Budapest was rebellious...*what would they think of me now?*

The latch above her head opened and closed long enough to throw in an orange, a peanut butter sandwich, and a bottle of water.

"Hey!" she called. "I'm getting my period. Can I get something? For the blood? *Sangue*?"

Twenty minutes passed before the lid opened and a roll of paper towels bounced off her head. When she looked up, she caught his eyes. Brown, vacant, small. *It's him.*

"Thank you," she said. "*Danka.*"

The lid didn't slam, instead it eased down like a warm breeze on a summer night. She didn't cry. She didn't yell. She tucked a wad of paper towels between her legs, *just in case,* closed her eyes, and prayed.

When morning came, Audra's head pounded from waves slamming the ship, knocking her against one side of her cage, then the other. She was cold, achy, sick to her stomach. The drugs they mixed in the peanut butter had given her nightmares. Her body shook. Tiny lights appeared in her peripheral vision. *This is bad.*

Suddenly, the lid opened. She felt a plastic bag hit her shoulder. *Maintenance.* "First we clean, then we eat," she heard her mother say. "No, first we pee, then we clean, Mama," she said aloud. She squatted over the bag, and hoped for the best. The rocking made it difficult to aim, but she was determined to void in the bag, and not on the floor.

When she finished, she gathered wet paper towels, plastic wrap, and a water bottle, stuffed them into the bag, and knotted the top. She wondered how the little ones managed, and began to sob. Bits of conversations she had overheard from the crew suggested child trafficking. Her heart hurt for their stolen innocence, stolen humanity, for the pain they would endure *all for the sick pleasure of some deviant.* For the first time since Sam announced his vocation, she understood his calling. It was men like him that made a difference. *If only I had said, 'No' to Rubio.*

Prayer

Sam hailed a taxi, instructed the driver to take him to the hotel, where the driver would wait until Sam grabbed his belongings, and settled his bill. They would then head to the airport. However, when Sam entered his room, he discovered it had been ransacked.

"Son-of-a-bitch!" He winced as he shoved the strewn mess into his suitcase. His side ached with every move. He reached in his pocket for the small white envelope he received from the discharge nurse, tossed two tablets in his mouth and chased them down with a miniature bottle of water he grabbed from the mini-bar.

When the driver saw Sam exit the building, he jumped out, deposited Sam's suitcase into the trunk, and started the engine. "*Und es geht los*."

Sam shook his head. "Yes. Away we go."

Beneath his cool exterior, Sam was seething. The only people who knew which hotel he'd been staying in was the hospital staff, and the police. He had no doubt who trashed his room. But, why? Only one answer, the police were part of the operation, and wanted to send a message. Without allies, he was sunk. His badge, obviously, meant nothing, and he knew first hand, crooked cops felt they were above the law. Linda's words rang true, as did the policeman's warning. He was dealing with an evil so prevalent in every walk of life. It was no secret that children were being trafficked by and to world leaders, respected politicians, Hollywood's elite, and those with deep pockets. The thought made him sick.

He paid the driver, and maneuvered his suitcase through the revolving door. He followed the signs to the Air Berlin ticket desk where he produced his passport, badge, gun permit, and credit card. He opened his bag, extracted a hard Pelican case, showed the contents to the agent, and repacked the case in his bag, already missing the weapon he was forbidden to carry on board.

While waiting for his flight, Sam surveyed his surroundings with the scrutiny of a bounty hunter. A small figure, dressed in a black niqab stood by a partition, flanked by two tall figures dressed in three-piece suits. When she turned, Sam could barely see her young, sad eyes. Ten? Twelve? Sam wondered about her escorts. Were they taking her to somewhere to be sold? Was she being offered as a bride to a wealthy sheik? The thought churned his stomach, and he looked away.

Near a coffee kiosk to his left, was another young girl, her skirt so short, you could practically see what she had for breakfast. Her escort was older, tattoos, piercings, disguising his true age. He hovered over the girl as if she were his prey. If she moved further than a foot from his side, he yanked her back, and secured her wrist in a tight grip. The girl didn't object, she merely obeyed, her head hung low. Sam wanted to box the guys ears, scream in his face. How dare he treat the girl that way. Would his sister's fate be that which he was witnessing? Would some goon tether her to his side with brute force? Transport her from one buyer to the next? He closed his eyes, remembering Audra's sweet face. *Please, God...let me find her before*—he couldn't finish his prayer. The thought of someone hurting his sister paralyzed him. *I will find you*, he vowed.

Audra

"Do not lie to me Rubio," Giorgi said, his voice as tranquil as blue waters in Sardinia, Italy.

"The guy was a dick! He tried to kill me!"

"Perhaps I'll finish the job myself."

"I didn't tell him anything, Giorgi, not a goddamn thing. And I didn't stab him, Blondi did. She was trying to protect me—the guy had his hands around my throat."

"Rubio, Rubio. You fucked up. You brought me a girl with ties...a brother who is a cop no less. He's not going to stop looking until he finds her."

"He has no idea where she is—and no one is going to help him find her. In a few days, she'll be in Oakland. Then she'll be yours to deal with."

Giorgi released an audible sigh, as if he were bored. "True. And Rubio? If she gives me any trouble, I won't hesitate to have you killed. Capisce?"

"Understood."

Giorgi ended the call, and moved to the window to enjoy the sunset. His southwest view overlooked the city. Now bathed in a golden hue and glittering lights, ribbons of red and gold shimmered against the river bank. The evening was too lovely to waste anticipating trouble. Very rarely did he involve himself with the details of a delivery. That's what his minions were for. However, this one was an exception. His buyer, a long-time friend of his father's, was paying a handsome price for a virgin with a specific look. He didn't intend to disappoint his client or his father. If everyone did their job, he would get his product to the buyer, collect his fee, and go home.

Light blinded Audra's eyes for a split second before tattooed arms slipped a black hood over her head, and lifted her from her container. She committed the artwork to memory for future use. The head of a goat transfixed on a reversed pentagram had symbols on each point, but she couldn't make them out. She had seen the symbol in her history books, *the mark of Satan*. Krampus.

The man led her through a short hallway, and into a doorway, in which he told her to duck. "Don't want to bruise the merchandise," he said. "The boss would have my ass." He pushed her head down, and through the opening. He closed the door behind him, and removed the hood. His face was hidden by a mask, and when he spoke, his English was perfect. "Remove your clothes, shower, and put these on."

She turned to see a pair of black pants, and a long sleeve black T-shirt arranged on a cot, next to a pair of KEDS, a sports bra, and a pair of cotton underwear. "Yeah, not Victoria Secret, but they'll have to do," he said. "I'm going to stay right here, so don't be stupid. *Non essere stupido. Capiche*?"

Audra wanted to tell him she understood English, but the less he knew about her, the better. She did as she was told.

The water not only felt glorious on her aching muscles, she was determined to get the stench off her body, and wash her hair. She lathered, rinsed, lathered again, and rinsed until she no longer felt the filth of her own body waste clinging to her skin. The water trickling down her face, mingled with her tears. If God had heard her prayers, he kept silent. Days turned into weeks. And now?

"*Sbrigati*! Hurry up!" She heard him shout. "Your chariot awaits," he said, and burst into laughter.

She shivered as she toweled herself dry. She stepped out of the bathroom, covering herself as best she could. The tattooed man had the decency to turn around.

"This isn't my favorite gig," he said. "I spent five years in Susanville, no one wants to give a guy anything legit once he's been in that place." He sighed. "But that's not your problem. You got enough problems without worrying about me." He tapped his feet on the floor. "Yeah, I gotta sister. She's a junkie piece o'shit, but I wouldn't humiliate her either." He paused. "You done? *Finito*?"

He didn't wait for an answer. He turned as she was pulling the pants over her hips. "Lucky guy, whoever he is. You're really pretty. And older than the others. Too bad things worked out for you this way. It's strictly business. Don't take it personal or nothing."

Audra remained silent; her eyes cast to the floor.

"Let's go," he said, placing the hood back over her head. "He's waiting." The tattooed arms reached for her wrists, retied them together, and guided her to the door.

When they stepped back out into the hall, it was quiet. Too quiet. Her heart hammered against her chest. She felt as though she would internally combust. The ringing in her ears grew louder, and louder until she could no longer bear it. "Where are the children?" she screamed.

Primal

Sam's flight proceeded smoothly. A two-hour layover in Frankfort allowed him time to regroup. *Construct a game plan.* He looked forward to seeing Suzanne, hearing what she had to say about the Englishman. What a crazy situation...accepting Suzanne's visions had taken time to get used to, buying into a stranger's visions made him feel like he was back at square one. This was his sister they were talking about. Neither of them knew Audra, how could he trust the information coming from a stranger? And why were they thinking about Audra in the first place? Suzanne mentioned a girl fitting his sister's description when they first met. Premonition? And how did she find this guy so quickly? She said she heard him talking in her TV. And Sheena's baby! How did Emmett figure into the mix? *God, I need a drink.*

And as if thoughts were things, a stewardess magically appeared with a small tray filled with beverages. "Wine? Beer?" His blank stare made her repeat the question.

"Uh, I–no thanks." He reached in his pocket, grasping his sobriety coin in his hand. He needed to keep his head. As much as he wanted to go on a bender, crawl into a hole, and forget the world, now was not the time. *Evil will not prevail,* he told himself. The knot in his stomach competed with the throbbing in his side.

And yet? Evil ran rampant. He dealt with evil every day. It never ceased to amaze him the destruction and pain humans inflicted upon one another with blatant disregard. But this–selling humans–for sex, for organs, human sacrifice—*whatever*—this he would never understand. *Children.* He shuddered recalling Suzanne's vision, *mewling kittens*. How did Audra become a target for such evil? Was it her innocence? Her beauty? Did her petite frame and youthful looks fit a certain profile?

He'd never understand human smuggling. Worldwide, prostitution had become more acceptable. His beloved Germany itself had its fair share of laufhauses, brothels, and sex clubs. In fact, "Pascha," a brothel in Cologne, had been the largest brothel in Europe. Las Vegas and Pahrump, Nevada supported *legal* brothels...but that wasn't enough. There were infantophiles, those attracted to children under five years old, hebephiles, who liked children eleven to fifteen, ephebophiles, who like them older, fifteen to nineteen. They even formed their own group, "MAP," minor attracted persons. One thing he had learned in AA, pick your battles. Right now, the most important thing was to find his sister, and if it meant believing in purple dinosaurs or little green men, he would follow every lead possible.

Trust. A word he was beginning to reassess. He trusted Suzanne, he just didn't always understand her gift, *or curse, as she would put it.* He prayed that whatever the universe was imparting to her about his sister was enough to save her life.

His sorrow was so deep, he felt as though he were drowning. The only escape from his dark void was to relive the moments he had shared with Suzanne before Audra went missing. As he stared out the oval window at the nothingness below, his mind conjured the scent of her hair; the touch of her soft, smooth skin; the way her tongue tangled with his, probing with longing, as her breasts heaved against his chest. Her long legs, wrapped around his hips as he thrust inside her, gently, rhythmically, satisfying a primal hunger, and absolving themselves from any hinderances that came before.

His reverie lulled him to sleep. He awoke to an announcement from the pilot that they would be landing within the hour. *Sacramento.*

Suzanne planned to meet him at the terminal.

Filthy

"Commune with nature." Isn't that what Linda said? Suzanne wandered through the rose garden at Capital park. Squirrels dashed up and down the trees, chittering playfully. The air was crisp, and the scent of roses faint. Suzanne walked from bush to bush determining which one she liked best. Her way of not forcing the images, she desperately needed to see, to form in her mind's eye. *Relax, let your mind receive on its own accord.*

Suzanne sat down on a bench facing the capital. As the hour reached eight, more people hurried along the perimeter, heading for work. The sun, still in the east, crept over high-rise buildings, spilled along the walkway, and warmed the back of her head. She tried her best to clear her mind and focus on Mother Nature. She spotted an odd-looking bird perched on a branch to her left, and a bee buzzing around a white rose bud, tipped in pink. The grass, still wet with dew, was a myriad of tiny rainbows, and clover. It had been ages since she indulged herself in the beauty that surrounded her. She almost felt sad for the time she had lost as she appreciated what a beautiful city she lived in. She made a mental note to visit the park more often, and turned her body so she could feel the sun on her face. She winced. Too bright. She turned away, but the bright light remained imprinted on her "screen." As she inhaled, exhaled, and relaxed her shoulders, she saw tattooed arms, pushing a long-legged, petite figure into a white van. She couldn't see their faces, but somehow, she knew. *Audra*. The image told her nothing, other than the girl was alive.

"Show me more," she said aloud.

"I'm sorry, are you speaking to me?"

Suzanne's eyes flashed open. The man standing before her had a quizzical look on his face.

His smile gave Suzanne an uneasy feeling. He was movie-star handsome, with jet black hair, and violet eyes, trimmed in long lashes. He had a faint accent, but Suzanne couldn't distinguish its origin.

"No! I mean, I was thinking out loud, I guess."

"Ah," he said, a slight twinkle in his eyes. "I thought I was the only one who did that." He looked away. "Beautiful day."

"Yes," she agreed. She wanted to know more about this man, but didn't feel inclined to ask. His clothes were expensive, his tanned skin accentuated his striking features, and the ruby, blue sapphire, and clear crystal point-encrusted watch circling his wrist was the most exquisite time piece she had ever laid eyes on. It had to be a Rolex.

He followed her eyes to his wrist, and tugged at his sleeve. "My father's a jeweler. I'm an only child," he said, the twinkle returning. "Mind if I sit?"

Suzanne was stunned by his proposal. She moved to the far end of the bench, allowing plenty of space between them. "Not at all, I was just about to—"

"Please don't tell me you're leaving," he said, his voice, a cool breeze on a summer's day. She felt herself hypnotized by his gaze.

"I must. I'm picking up a friend at the airport."

"I see—girlfriend?"

"No, boyfriend, actually."

"Ah—then it would be obtuse of me to invite you for a drink this evening."

His smile challenged her better sense, but her commitment to Sam kept her strong. "Thank you, but that won't be possible."

"Are you sure? A drink with a new friend, surely there is no harm in that?"

"Harm no, more like inappropriate. It's not who I am."

"And who are you?"

Suzanne rose from the bench and smiled. "Enjoy your day." She heard him sigh as she walked past him and headed toward toward 'L' Street, where she was parked. She could feel his eyes watching her. He took her breath away, but not in a good way. He made her feel— *dirty*.

Suzanne waited in the Sacramento Airport at the bottom of the escalator, near baggage claim. Her palms were moist, her heart fluttered in her chest. Love? Or anxiety? The jury was still out. She had long forgotten what it felt like to be in love, and her relationship with Sam often led to dangerous waters. Her experience with the man in the park left her perplexed. How could anyone that good looking, invoke such an ugly vibe?

And his watch...she typed the description into Google, and was flabbergasted with the results. It wasn't a Rolex, after all. The watch was made by a jeweler in New York, appropriately named, "The Mystery," and retailed for $1,457,063.19. What was a man of his caliber doing in Capital Park so early in the morning? Was he a diplomat? He did have an accent. Perhaps he was visiting a California Senator, or the Governor, himself. Why invite her for a drink? Certainly, a man of his stature dated woman of the same ilk. Unless he mistook her for *easy prey*.

Sam's voice took her by surprise. "Suzanne!" He beelined toward her, arms open wide. As he held her tight, he whispered, "I missed you."

Suzanne hugged him tighter. "And I missed you." She broke the embrace. "How was your flight?"

"Long." He looped his arm through hers, and steered her toward "Baggage Claim."

She could tell by the way he walked that something was amiss. "What are they giving you for pain?" she asked.

"I don't remember the name of it, nothing we have here in the states. It works great, and doesn't seem to have many side effects." He checked his watch. "I fell asleep on the plane. I should have taken one hours ago."

When Sam's luggage popped out of the hopper, and onto the belt, Suzanne insisted upon lifting the suitcase off of the carousel. "I'm not helpless," Sam complained.

Suzanne rolled the suitcase toward Sam. "Is this it?"

"No, I have to go to the baggage office to claim my firearm."

Sam slapped his I.D. on the counter, along with his claim slip. Suzanne noticed when the TSA officer handed him his gun case, Sam seemed hesitant to take it, as if it were a newborn or a bomb.

Suzanne kept her feelings in check because she was familiar with Sam's moods. She had seen him struggle with impending depression mixed with determination and grit. Once they were alone, she hoped he'd open up to her. Allow himself to unleash his demons, talk about his pain. "I'm parked in the garage." She didn't wait for him to protest, she grabbed his gun case, set it on top of his suitcase, and rolled them behind her.

When they reached the car, he pinned her against the door, his mouth urgently seeking hers. When she opened her eyes, she saw the angst in his. She cupped his face in her hands. "We'll find her."

"How can you be so sure?"

The image of the well-dressed man in the park came to mind. "I have a feeling she's here. Here in Sacramento."

———

Kittens

The tattooed man struck Audra so hard, she felt her teeth rattle. She couldn't control the sobs that were long overdue. "Geezus," he said in a huff. "You can't go screaming like that!"

"Where are they?" Her voice dwindled to a whisper.

"You speak English."

"A little," she said regretting her outburst.

"The children are safe. They are being taken to their new homes."

Audra knew their "new" homes would never replace their real homes, nor were they safe. Their lives would be forever changed. She wanted to ask *why?* How could a human being do such despicable things to another, especially a child?

"We need to get going." He lifted her hood, stuffed her mouth with a wad of fabric, and tied another strip of cloth around her head to keep the gag in place. Although she couldn't see his face, his eyes shown through the small holes of the mask. They were ice blue, and no doubt matched his heart.

"Watch your step," someone growled. *A new voice.* Audra stepped down, assisted by strong hands. The hands gripped her flesh so hard, she cried out. A blow to the back of her head silenced her immediately. She wanted to scream, lash out, kick, scratch, bite, use whatever strength she had to gain her freedom, but instinct told her this wasn't the time, or the place. They were still on water. She smelled mold, fish, suntan lotion, and beer. The place she was confined to reeked of cigarettes, and body odor. She sensed she was in the cabin, surrounded by engine noises, as well as footsteps, shuffling, and laughter above her. Another language, she recognized as Spanish, spoken by three different voices. She heard what sounded like a casting reel, a high pitch squeal, and a click. Was she in the custody of fisherman? On a fishing boat. But where? Spain? Portugal? Lisbon? What did it matter? Between her bondage, not being allowed to see, and menstrual cramps, her thought was, *I want to die.*

When she awoke, it was dark. The boat rocked gently, bumping into a padded surface. It reminded her of the time she and Bruno took a river cruise down the Danube in a friend's yacht. They docked in different slips along the way, and each time they tied up, the crew threw out rubber bumpers to keep the boat from crashing into the pier. One afternoon it rained, and she opted out of the monastery tour in Bratislava. The wind picked up, rocking the boat until she felt sea-sick. The sound of the boat bumping against the rubber buoys sounded like the sound she was hearing now.

The door opened to the cabin, and she smelled food. The hood was removed from her head, then the gag. A hollow voice spoke from behind a mask. "*Mangaire.*" Audra shielded her eyes against the bright light shining in her face. She accepted the plate with her bound hands, and set it down. She held out her wrists to be untethered. She was surprised when the man obliged her wishes.

After using the toilet, she washed her face and hands, and returned to her place. The man sat waiting in the corner, texting on his phone. She could see he was young, even in the dim light. His hair, the shape of his ears, his fair skin was smooth, and firm. Audra guessed early twenties. His voice too, sounded young. She wondered if the men on the boat were illegals, working for some rich man, staying under the radar? Guys like him, like Rubio, what was their objective? Did they have goals in life? Were they addicted to something that prevented them from being upstanding citizens? Were they too lazy to enter into a vocation? Or were they just plain evil?

As if he heard her thoughts, he looked up. "*Manga*!"

Audra could barely open her mouth. Her throat was parched, emotion brewed at the surface, constricting her muscles. She felt as though she had swallowed a brick. "Water?" she asked, softly. Again, the young man granted her request. She wanted to grill him for information, but was afraid if she did, he'd punish her. Take away her food and water. She needed to regain her strength. She lifted the plastic spoon to her lips.

Her belly cramped. *Too much, too soon*. The food too spicy, too heavy. Her mind supported her ravenous state; however, her stomach didn't agree, and it all came out of her like a volcanic eruption.

"Goddammit, pig!" He shouted. He grabbed Audra by the hair, and pushed her into the muck. "Clean it up!"

Audra's stomach erupted again, this time barely missing his shoes. He danced away from her, cussing and swearing. All Audra could do was cry.

Another man banged on the door. "*Culerto*–what's up in there?" He turned the knob and barged in. "Sick."

"It's the food, man. She don't like your cookin'."

Audra buried her face in her hands and sobbed, shaking her head, "No".

"Aw, *chica–chica*. You okay?" The man bent down and helped Audra to her feet. Go lay down. We will take care of the mess."

Audra didn't refute the kind gesture. "*Grazzi*," she said.

The kind man shoved the other one into the corner. "Clean it up, and be nice to our guest. If our boss catches wind of any mistreatment of his goods, he will cut off our balls and feed them to us on a spoon—*comprendez*?"

Once the mess was cleaned up, the two men left her alone. Unmasked, untied. She stretched out on the long, padded bench, closed her eyes and fell asleep.

When she awoke, it was morning. She shivered from the cold. The sound of waves lapping alongside the boat, and the hum of the motor, indicated movement. She looked out one of the portholes. Trees. Houses. A pot of tea and crackers caught her eye across the room. A change of clothes hung over a chair. She may still be a prisoner, but at least her captors acted less like barbarians, and more like humans.

She inspected the cabin. The commode was small, old, in need of a good cleaning, but usable. A nozzle hung from a hook, with enough hose to rinse below her waist, but no more. A dirty bar of soap, and a small scrub brush occupied a rusted dish. She pushed up on the handle, water sprayed her face.

She listened to the action going on above board, debating whether to risk a shower before redressing into clean clothes. She felt the teapot. Hot. She hurried into the small cubicle, and stripped out of her clothes.

She clenched down, keeping the scream from escaping her mouth. The water was icy cold, and stung her skin. She scrubbed with such speed her body was red from head to toe. She dried herself with her dirty clothes pulled inside out, and dressed. She was done in three minutes.

She held the pot in her hands, then lifted the lid to inhale the steam. She poured herself a cup, and drank, enjoying the warm sensation traversing down her throat, into her stomach. She bit into a cracker, and spit it out. The taste was offensive. She vowed never to eat again.

"Come!" The kind man said, standing in the doorway. "Time to go."

Americano, Flat White

"His name is Lewis Howard," Suzanne said, lifting Sam's suitcase out of the car. "He has one helluva story."

"How does his story tie in with my sister?"

"You know how Jack would tell me things?"

"Yes, I remember," Sam said, his brow bunching into a frown.

"Lewis has a deceased friend that shares information with him."

"What does his friend have to do with my sister?"

"I don't know, maybe he's like Clarence, the angel in *It's a Wonderful Life.* He needs to earn his wings." She set the suitcase down on the walkway, and sighed. "I don't know, Sam," she shaded her eyes from the sun, "I'm new at this. All I can do is relate what is happening as it comes to me."

"I apologize. It's not your fault—I—"

"Sam, don't. It's the fault of the person who took her." She picked up the suitcase. "Let's go inside. You need to rest. You're as pale as a ghost."

It was the first time Suzanne had been in Sam's apartment. Her eyes roamed about the room, getting a feel for the man she knew little about, yet cared for so deeply. His apartment was sparsely furnished, warmly decorated with a few antiques. She could feel his sentiment toward his homeland by the elegant paintings, hanging on the walls. She recognized the serenity of Caspar David Friedrich's, "The Monk by the Sea," and the "The Wanderer Above the Sea of Fog." Both pieces spoke of Sam's isolation, and his reconciliation with who he had become. She knew it wasn't easy for him to face death, demoralization, and destruction every day. *And now this.*

She moved from the living room into the kitchen, impressed by his tidiness, and organizational skills. *Everything in its place.*

"Sit, make yourself at home," he said, rolling his suitcase out of sight. "Coffee?" he asked.

"Please, you sit and let me make you a cup. All you need to do is point."

"I'm not an invalid."

"No, you're a stubborn man who needs to rest. Otherwise—"

"Otherwise what?"

She could tell by his tone he wasn't one to be threatened. "Do you remember the first time I made you a cup of coffee?"

"Yes. Your husband came home, and caught us in the kitchen talking. I must admit, he had every right to suspect I had more than coffee on my mind."

She laughed. "I think a re-do is in order. Please? Let me do this one simple task?"

"You know me too well."

"I want to. I want to do more, Sam. I want to make your world right again, find your sister, catch the bad guy, and fix you coffee."

He grabbed her hand, and pulled her near. His eyes reflected the sadness in his heart. "Can you? Can you really do all that for me, Suzanne?"

"I want to," she said, placing her lips on his.

He threw up his hands and winced with pain. "Okay then," he said through his gritted teeth. "You win."

Suzanne plugged in the coffee pot, placed a filter in the holder and scooped grounds into the basket. She filled the pot with water, and poured it into the top of the machine. She pressed the "brew" button, and set the canister on the shelf. She caught a teapot out of the corner of her eye, and turned, as if the teapot had magic powers. She moved closer, touching the spout. Her hand was not her own. She removed the teapot from the shelf, and wrapped her hands around the round body. Her hands felt warm. She lifted the lid and inhaled. Although the pot was empty, she sensed the steam escaping the pot was soothing. Next to her, the water filtered through the basket into the coffee pot. In her mind's eye, she could see water streaming from a metal hose. Suddenly, she felt unsteady, and grabbed onto the counter. The rocking motion stopped.

"She's on a boat. She's safe." Suzanne turned to Sam, "She's safe for now."

"How do you know?"

"She showered. They served her tea. I saw it."

Lewis took a deep breath and exhaled. "Your ticker sounds good," the cardiologist said, as he listened through his stethoscope. He squinted at the scar on Lewis' chest. "Knittin' looks good too. You've healed quite nicely."

Lewis began buttoning his shirt. "I'm okay t'travel then?"

"No heavy liftin'," he said, "and don't be gettin' too excited over those pretty flight attendants." He winked. "I don't expect any further trouble."

"Can I ask y'somethin' Doc?" Lewis' gaze dropped to the floor.

The cardiologist stopped writing, and gave Lewis his attention. "What's troublin' you then?

"Do y'think there's an afterlife?"

"Seen some inexplainable things in my career, including what happened to you. Why do you ask?"

"I think I went t'heaven and back. Now I'm haunted by what 'appened."

The doctor's bushy brows gathered in the middle of his forehead. "What did you see?"

"Well, I didn't see the man 'imself, mind ye, but I did see me dead neighbor, and me mum and dad."

"It's not unusual to have that kind of experience, I've heard it before. But not often. Most of my patients don't die during surgery."

The doctor patted Lew's hand. "You're not off your nut, Lew, I'm sure something happened…I just can't explain what, or why."

"Thanks, doc, it's reassurin', y'know."

"You're going to live a long life if you take care. Glad to hear you're not stewin' at home." The doctor placed one hand on Lew's shoulder, easing him toward the door. "I neglected to ask, where is it you're off to?"

"America."

"*America*?"

"I'm off t'find a missing girl."

When Lewis arrived home and shared the good news with Trudy, she went into the bedroom, slammed the door and bawled for thirty minutes.

"Are y'bawlin' for m'leavin' or because y'ave to put up with m'ol' sorry arse for another twenty years?"

"Both. I can't believe 'e's lettin' y'go. What if—"

Lewis grabbed Trudy by the shoulder's and shook her. "If the good Lord saw fit t'take me 'ome, 'e had 'is chance." He lifted her chin. "Please, ease yer mind, Luv. I'll be fine." Lew picked up two sweaters from the pile of clothes on the bed. "Now 'elp this ol' chap out and tell me, the blue? Or the brown?"

Trudy pointed to the blue sweater, her eyes glistening. "Yer an 'onorable man, Lewis Howard. 'ard-headed as they come, but 'onorable all the same. But know this, if y'die in America, I will never forgive ye. And don't be thinkin' 'bout showin' up as no ghosty. Do y'ear me, man?"

Lew's lips tilted into a sheepish grin. "I'll come back as a cat, scratchin' at yer door…that way I know ye'll let me in." Trudy rushed into his arms and held him tight.

Pictures

"How many?" Sam scribbled a number on his pad. "Uh, huh, I understand. How many more are you expecting?" Perplexed, he turned to Suzanne, who was listening to the conversation. "Who does know?" His upper lip clamped down on his bottom lip, holding back the words he wanted to say. "Thank you for your time," he said, and tossed his phone on the table.

"No luck?" Suzanne rose, her hands clasped on top of her head.

Sam blew out his frustration. "Nope. The Port of Sacramento isn't set up for containers. They handle mostly auto imports, farming equipment, stuff like that."

"Lewis mentioned Italy..."

"It's like trying to find a needle in a haystack. The nurse I spoke with in the hospital didn't indicate any specific location in the states, and the cop was just as vague."

Suzanne bent down, and took Sam's hand. "We'll find her."

Sam rose, side stepping Suzanne. "The guy I just spoke to asked if I checked with the FMC, or the UNODC."

Suzanne raised her brow. "The what and what?"

"The Federal Maritime Commission, and the United Nations Office on Drugs and Crime. Evidently there's a Container Control Programme that was initiated some years back to monitor the containers coming from other countries for the very purpose of catching smugglers bringing drugs, weapons, and humans into the country. Obviously, the system is flawed."

"I have a feeling that however she arrived, she is no longer a part of the scene."

"How can you tell?"

"I just got a visual of a leaf falling from a tree."

"I pray that you're right." He pulled her close. "I have faith in you, Suzanne, I hope you know that."

"And I you. You're one helluva detective." She kissed him lightly. "We make a good team." She lifted his chin. "Tell me what I can do. Who can I call?"

"Let me check in with the office. I need to connect to some of the task forces in Sacramento and Stockton. They may have a jump on any new activity."

"Lewis Howard arrives tomorrow from London. He's just as determined to find your sister as we are."

"I'll leave Lewis to you. Meanwhile, I'll be checking with the other agencies." He smiled, and took her hand. "When I got stabbed, all I could think about was how upset you were going to be with me for not calling. I'm glad I was wrong."

"And I was sorry I didn't see it coming." She let go of his hand. "I didn't tell you about Jack."

"Jack? I thought—"

"I went to see Sheena. Emmett was showing me pictures in books... he showed me Big Ben, and a book titled, "Missing." I know it's crazy, but it's Jack." Suzanne paced while Sam listened. "He showed me Noah's Ark—he's getting images, I know it—showing me pictures is his way of communicating."

Sam shook his head. "Crazy is right. He's a baby! He shouldn't be—God!"

"I don't know if Emmett knows what it all means, and I pray that he never finds out, but at least I know that if I can't—"

"YOU found Dixon, Suzanne, not Jack."

"And you found me." She cupped his face in her hands and kissed his lips, nipping his bottom lip with her teeth. He pulled her onto his lap, and drew her closer, bending her backward into the crock of his arm. His eyes held her gaze as he took control, kissing the corner of her mouth, her jaw, nibbling her ear. Her chest pressed against his, their hearts thumping like rolling thunder. "I've never seen your bedroom," she whispered.

"I'd be happy to give you a tour."

Special Order

Giorgi waited for his turn to be seated at one of the Rio Café's deck side tables. Once seated, he ordered a vodka martini with a twist, and set his sights on his view of the Sacramento River. He smiled to himself knowing his "merchandise" arrived late the previous night. He turned at the sound of a familiar woman's voice, and nodded. The woman sashayed onto the deck. Giorgi rose and pulled out a chair. "I ordered you a martini."

"Aren't you a love," she said tilting her sunglasses, revealing chocolate brown eyes. Her blond hair, tucked beneath a wide brim hat. "What did you think of Morton's Steak House?"

"P-lease." He opened his napkin and laid it across his knee. "How is everything going?"

"One of the items was damaged in transport, but that's to be expected, given the fragile nature..." She shifted her gaze to the water. "The Vermont order has been filled, three pieces were sent to DC, seven to New York, and forty-seven to L.A." His eyes, like magnets, drew her back into his gaze.

He steepled his index fingers, and raised his brow. "And my special order?"

"Not to worry, that one is being prepped for delivery."

The waitperson brought her martini. "Are you ready to order?" she asked.

"Oh goodness, we've been so busy chatting..." The woman opened the menu and browsed the selections.

Giorgi intervened. "Bring us two of your stuffed salmon dishes. And I'll have a glass of your finest chardonnay."

"You have a choice of rice pilaf or–"

"Just salads for both. Olive oil and vinegar on the side, please."

The woman handed the menu to the girl and smiled, "Well, that settles that."

Giorgi ignored the woman's indignant look. "You have two days. Two. I expect nothing less than perfection."

"Have I ever let you down?"

Giorgi drummed his fingers on the table. "How's that lovely home in Salinas?" He checked one manicured hand, nonchalantly. "And that beautiful granddaughter of yours? How old is she now, twelve? Thirteen? Such a *tender* age.

The woman gasped. "I don't find your joke amusing."

Giorgi's dazzling smile disappeared. His eyes turned to flint. "Who's joking?"

Fizzle

Audra had lost all conception of time. Her head swam, her vision was blurry, her limbs, heavy and limp. "Am I dead?" she asked, in a voice that didn't seem to fit her mouth.

"No darlin' just a little *relaxed*." Lilly, the woman from Salinas lifted one of Audra's eyelids, then the other. She turned to the man guarding the door. "How much did you fuckin' give her?"

"I followed the instructions you gave me to a tee. She should be coming down by now."

"Don't give her anymore until I tell you to. Help me get her undressed and into the shower. I need her ready to go in an hour. I pray to God this shit wears off. Get her some coffee. No–Get her a flumazenil. And remind me to get a hold of Dave at the compound pharmacy. We're running low."

Lilly paced the room, observing Audra's behavior. "Shit, shit, shit!"

Each time she moved, Lilly's image smeared across Audra's vision. Audra struggled to focus. Her face felt frozen.

She couldn't lift her arm, or stop the man invading her space. "C'mon babydoll," he said, "time to make you all perty."

Long slender fingers pried Audra's lips apart. He placed a small lozenge on her tongue. "Close," he said. She obeyed. The tablet fizzed inside her mouth, and she wanted to giggle. She felt like a rag doll, as he tossed her onto the bed and began removing her top, her sports bra, and pants. She could feel his eyes feast on her body. He took liberty, touching her breasts as he worked. When she was naked, he lifted her from the chair, and carried her into the shower.

She melted under the hot spray, like a popsicle in summer. She looked at the bottom of the shower to see what flavor she was, disappointed she didn't see cherry-lime, her favorite.

———

Timepiece

Lew kissed Trudy one last time before pushing through the turnstile. He checked over his shoulder to see her frozen in her knickers, her eyes leakin' like a busted radiator. She waved as if he were going off to war. He waved back, hoping his smile reassured her he would return.

When he reached his terminal, he took a seat facing the window. Watching planes land and depart eased his anxiety. He hadn't flown since he sold his meat-packing company twelve years ago. Back then, he was strong, confident. *An Ace*. Now those around him thought him one sandwich short of a picnic. He was the chap that died and came back to life. *Frankenstein*.

He wasn't chuffed at the thirteen-plus-hour flight across the pond.

Sitting on the runway, he second-guessed his decision to get involved with a girl he'd never met. *What if we don't find the lass, what then*? Was he all mouth and trousers? Somewhere in his refurbished heart lie the answer. The only thing that kept coming to mind was a watch. *Gaudy. Expensive*. He hadn't had a vision of the girl in days.

———

Hungry

Suzanne reached for Sam's shoulder, but her eyes gravitated to the bandage an inch above his waist between his hip and buttocks. She startled when she closed her eyes and witnessed the knife enter his flesh. A groan stuck in her throat. Her body trembled.

Sam rolled over, wincing slightly. "Hey, what's wrong?"

"My God, Sam," she cried.

Sam brushed the hair from her face. "Talk to me," he said softly.

"Hold me," she said, burying her head against his bare chest.

Sam pulled her close, shifting his weight. His fingers massaged her neck and shoulders. He never thought he'd be one to console another person. *Until Suzanne.* He opened his heart, brushed the dust off his feelings, allowed himself to feel compassion. He wanted to surrender to love, hold her until years crumbled away, like the chalk cliffs in Jasmund National Park on Rügen Island, a place he visited as a boy with his family. *Audra.* Rocks, fossils of sea urchins, sponges, and oysters tumbled into the sea, the rugged landscape as fragile as the human condition. *Time.*

"I saw it happen." Suzanne pulled away. "I saw the knife—"

Sam reached for his wallet on the nightstand. He opened it and pulled out the most recent photo he had of Audra. He flipped it toward Suzanne. "She is what's important, not me. If I had been allowed to stay in Austria, I'd still be searching. The fact that you, and your friend Lewis, feel my sister is here is a revelation, I would have stayed in vain. I will heal. I'm eighty percent better already. But this girl—" He tapped on Audra's face, "this is the only pain that needs tending to." He exhaled his frustration. "How about some coffee?"

"Isn't that how we ended up in bed in the first place?"

He kissed Suzanne's nose. "I am not complaining."

Suzanne brewed coffee, drank a quick cup and left. Sam had phone calls to make. He started with Andrew James, a guy he met at the police academy years ago. Since then, Andrew joined the FBI in the bay area.

"Rumor has it, she was put on a ship out of Brindisi, Italy."

"Did you call Interpol, or the Homeys?"

"No, I know technically it's not your department, but I'd thought I'd start with you guys." Sam sipped his coffee. "Any reports of a human smuggling ring bringing a shipment in?"

"Geez, we get tips all the time. Let me check if there's been any activity in Oakland. If we're talking L.A. or Long Beach, I can give you the number for a friend of mine, Roger Blitz. He's a good guy. Hang on."

Sam finished his coffee listening to canned music on the other end of the line. He admired Andrew for his dedication to the bureau. It wasn't a job for sissies.

"Well, you're right, there was a report of a shipment that came in this week, however by the time we reached the docks, the containers were empty. We alerted the coast guard, but chances are the traffickers have already unloaded the goods...which means we now have to put boots to the ground, check with all our informants to find out who went where. It all takes time, my friend."

"What do you mean, who went where?"

"Some are brought to the US to work, you know, slave labor, farming, restaurants, factories...then there's sex trafficking...we check the brothels for underage kids, roust up the pimps, heat 'em up until they talk. It's like shining a light on cockroaches, they tend to scatter. But we have a really good team that gets results. How old is the girl you're looking for?"

"Twenty-five."

"Hell, her age makes it harder. She's legal. Won't be easy getting a conviction. I assume there's a missing person's report?"

"She disappeared in Austria. The authorities consider her an adult making bad choices."

"And your thoughts?"

"I know better."

"In that case, send me a profile. I'll do some digging."

Suzanne drove home, showered, and dressed in a pair of high-waisted jeans, and an almond color cashmere sweater. She twisted her hair into a long rope, and piled it on top of her head, securing the loose bun with a clip. She swiped mascara on her lashes, and painted her lips rose petal pink. She grabbed a sheet of white card stock, and a black marker from the drawer. She printed LEWIS HOWARD in neat block letters, and blew on the ink to dry. In twenty minutes, she would be meeting the man from London, whose life, like hers, had been changed forever.

While Audra's photo floated through the ether, Audra floated in and out of reality. Intermittent bursts of laughter, followed by intense paranoia, and fear. Her brain fought to make sense of her situation. *Sheisse. Where am I? Where's Britta?* She saw Britta a few minutes ago.

"Britta?" she called.

Lilly entered the room. "Britta? Is that you?" Audra repeated.

"Are you hungry?" Lilly responded, walked across the room and parted the drapes.

Audra squinted. "Britta?" she whispered.

"No, darling. I am not Britta. I'm your new best friend." Lilly snickered. "I am taking you to meet another friend. He's going to take good care of you...providing you take good care of him, that is."

The woman's words whirred in Audra's head like an egg beater.

"Britta?" She looked like Britta. Blond, busty. Audra squinted. Maybe not. The woman's nose was narrow, sharp. Witchy. Her dark brows matched her roots. Britta was blond, through and through. Audra knew, she had showered alongside Britta in *hochschule*.

The woman was talking, *English*, not German, or Viennese. Audra strained to understand. "Not Hungary, Munich."

"I didn't ask where you were from, twit," she grumbled. She brought her fingers to her mouth. "Eat? Food?" She rubbed her tummy. "Hun-gry."

Audra's gaze darted around the room. It locked onto a ceiling sprinkler, and froze. The next thing she knew, she was *moving*. Her hands and feet were bound, black cloth covered her face, and a gag kept her from screaming.

Suzanne held up her home-made sign. She spotted a man wearing a bowler hat in the distance, navigating his way to baggage claim by reading the signs along the way.

"Lewis?" Suzanne smiled, hoping she had identified the right man.

"Yes, yes of course," he chuckled, extending his hand. "Suzanne, I presume."

"Yes! So nice to meet you," she said, accepting his enthusiastic hand shake. "I'm parked in the lot," she said pointing over her shoulder. "Can you manage? Or shall I bring the car around?"

"I promised me wife that I'd accept a hand with m'baggage."

"I'd be happy to help. How was your flight?"

"I closed me eyes 'alf way across the pond. I managed a film, can't bloody remember the name of it."

"I'm happy that you chose to stay in my guest room rather than a hotel. It will give us time to talk, and perhaps figure things out."

"I 'ave to say, yer quite generous puttin' up an ol' codger such as meself. The missus, she's not so keen on the idea."

"I'm happy to do it, and if Trudy isn't comfortable with the arrangements, you can always stay at Sam's. I'm sure he wouldn't mind."

"Sam?"

"Yes. Sam is an undercover detective for Goldorado County. It's his sister that is missing."

"She's not missin', she's been taken."

Terror shimmied down Suzanne's spine. "Any idea who took her?"

Glue

Sam entered his office at noon. A handful of employees stayed behind to cover the others who went to lunch. One dispatcher, one desk clerk, one desk sergeant. They all nodded as he crossed the room.

His desk was the same as he left it. Papers piled neatly to one side of his leather mat. His coffee cup, rinsed and dried, sat approximately six inches to the left of his phone, right above his favorite pen. The calendar on the wall still on the page of the day he left. He walked over to the wall, crossed six days off the month, making note of the small notations written by his secretary, Julie. He missed an appearance at the Crab Feed sponsored by Goldorado County Search and Rescue. Bummer, it was one of his favorite events. He had planned to take Suzanne this year. The tickets were in his top drawer.

He sat down, already feeling the burn in his side. He picked up the phone and dialed the first number on the list he pulled from his breast pocket. The voice on the other end launched into a greeting, "California Department of Justice Sacramento, how can I direct your call?"

"This is Detective Sam Metzger, Goldorado County Sheriff's Department, can you connect me with someone in the human trafficking task force division?" Sam waited patiently for a voice to magically appear on the other end of the phone. He wasn't expecting a recording.

"Leave your message at the tone." He slammed the phone down on the receiver. *What to do?* He picked up the phone and re-dialed Andrew. "Hey buddy, it's Sam again...I need your help."

Sam and Andrew arranged to meet at 4 p.m., when Andrew's shift ended. Until then, Sam trolled the internet looking for suspicious ads. Sometimes trafficking was a click away. With the social media boom, criminals were able to work the system, eluding law enforcement. One just needed to know the lingo. "Puppies for Sale," "Babysitter Wanted," "Models Wanted." The possibilities were endless. The ads that piqued his attention were "Crate Trained Puppies" 4-6 weeks.

He worked an investigation back in the day where a woman in Jackson kept her children caged, and rented them out like power tools. When the Feds busted her, she had six kids ranging from five to fourteen that she trafficked for sex, slave labor, and childcare. Other than being caged, the kids seemed oblivious to the abuse. They were polite, well-mannered, and educated. The older children taught the younger ones how to read, write, spell, and do math. The mother seemed like your typical soccer mom. No one suspected, until the twelve-year-old became pregnant, and almost died behind a grocery store after trying to abort the baby herself. His drinking at the time anesthetized the horror.

Suzanne fixed a green salad with figs, feta cheese, and cucumbers. A chicken baking in the oven, dressed with red potatoes, fennel and carrots smelled divine. Lewis watched her work, but she knew his mind was elsewhere.

"Would you like to phone your wife to let her know you arrived? If I were her, I would rest easy knowing you were safe."

"Y'know the missus all too well. She's probably bit through both thumbnails by now."

"She seems delightful. Would you care to use my cell?"

"Much obliged." He said, rising from the kitchen chair. "I 'ave this 'ere gadget that works just fine." He produced a flip phone from his pocket and left the room.

When he returned from his call, his face looked relaxed, and his smile warmed Suzanne's heart. She imagined what it must be like being married, and in love. She never had that with Ben, but she felt sure if she and Sam were to marry it would be different. Then again, there were no guaranties in life. "Live in the now," Linda had said. Right *now*, she was content, but worried. "I haven't heard the kittens cry in the last couple of days."

Lew's eyes grew large. "They've parted ways," he said. "Don't know 'ow I know, but it feels right as rain t'say it."

"Do you still believe she's on the boat?"

"No," he said, shaking his head. "Can't get a clear picture. Like m'glasses need a good wipe."

Suzanne nodded. She understood. Neither of them wore glasses, and yet the images she saw in flashes weren't clear. "I'm expecting a friend to join us for dinner. Her name is Linda Schooler. She's a psychic. I don't know what I would have done without her help. She understands what we are experiencing. I believe she can help us put the pieces together.

"Glue. Huh." His attention wandered once more. "Glue," he whispered.

Rich

Audra sat alone in a room. An ostentatious room, filled with trophies. Animal heads lined one side of the room, a bookcase with metal figures, with marble columns, and wooden bases. The many fixtures hanging from the ceiling were made of deer antlers, those from young bucks. *Children*. Audra's body began to shake. The person associated with this room had no regard for life. Krampus. She was sitting in a devil's den.

Audra couldn't remember being dressed. The filmy prairie dress she was now wearing made her feel uneasy. Her long tresses, now fixed into two braids, were adorned with pink ribbons, and hung over each breast. She felt like a little girl again. *Prinzessin*. Tears rolled down her cheeks.

The smell of cigar smoke wafted up from behind her. She didn't turn to look. His voice reached her ears. Deep, gravelly. "Well, aren't you perty."

Perty. That's what he said. The kind one. But it wasn't his voice. *Coincidence? Did they know each other?* Her body stiffened.

"Don't you be afraid now, young lady. Ol' Jake is gonna take good care of you. Yes siree...*real good care*."

Audra cringed when he fondled one braid, brushing a knuckle across her breast. She could hear a wheeze coming from his chest. His breath a foul combination of cigars and gingivitis. His greying hair, thin, greasy, and long, parted down the middle, accentuating dark blue eyes. His cheeks were ruddy, his nose bulbous, like the drunks that hung out at the local pub on the corner back in Budapest. Her appearance seemed to please him. She squeezed her eyes shut. Her body trembled. "Please don't, I—" she whispered. The slap came so swift and hard, it knocked the rest of her words out of her reach.

Linda Schooler arrived just before the oven timer went off. "I'm Linda Schooler," she said, reaching for Lewis' outstretched hand. "Welcome to the US." She gave him a package.

Lewis raised the package to his nose. "Lavender soap?"

"Yes." Linda said, excitedly, her Shirley Temple dimples showing. "I hope you like it. Sometimes it's nice to have a bit of home when you're in a strange place."

"'Ow did y'know? It's m'favorite."

"She's psychic," Suzanne said. "And my mentor."

The threesome conversed over dinner, mostly recounting Lewis' near-death experience. Lewis interrupted with, "Do y'smell that?"

Linda and Suzanne exchanged glances. "Smell what?" Suzanne asked.

"Cigar smoke," he said.

Suzanne closed her eyes. "I hear gunfire, but it's from long ago."

Linda fingered the cloth napkin absently. "Yes, it feels like we're going back in time."

Lewis slipped into a trance-like state. "The lass, it's as if she's a prize of some sort."

"What else do you see?" Linda asked.

"Trees, water. Wildflowers. Purple ones." He cupped one ear. "I 'ear dogs barking...I know that bark, I do...the Queen Mum has dogs like—" He stopped, his eyes flashed open. "Huntin' dogs."

"Lupines grow wild, but it's a little early for them around here. There's water all up and down the coast," Suzanne said, clearing the table. "We have rivers, lakes streams..."

"There are areas that are less progressive, where people live on acreage so they can hunt and fish." Linda rose, assisting Suzanne with the dishes. "That may account for the hunting dogs."

"The mutts I'm talkin' 'bout are pure breeds. Set y'back a pound or two."

"Trafficking is a rich man's sport..." Suzanne loaded the dishwasher.

"Let's make a list," Linda suggested. "Cigar smoke, hunting dogs, wild flowers, trees, water—sounds like we're looking for someone who owns property, someone with money."

Suzanne called over her shoulder, "We can have Sam check to see if anyone prominent has been busted for solicitation."

Linda nodded. "It's a start. Lewis? Anything you want to add?"

Lewis thought for a moment...*that watch. That big expensive watch.* "M'mind is on trinkets. All the posh stores at the airport, I suspect. Quite fancy, they are." He cleared his throat. "Need to keep me mind focused on our girl. I feel like we need to take the *reins*." Lewis steepled his fingers. "Don't know why that word popped from me mouth. *Reins*. Huh."

Suzanne brightened. "I get it, Lewis—it's like getting the hiccups. Random words pop out of me too. It takes a bit of concentration to decipher their meaning. If I'm lucky, they come with an image."

Linda scratched her head. "I associate reins with horses, power."

Suzanne slipped back into her chair. "So far, we have wealth, property, fields, dogs, horses..."

Linda tilted her head, as if listening to someone beside her, except no one was there. "What is one thing that money can't buy?"

Suzanne spoke up. "Character."

Rumors

"Listen," Andrew said. "You didn't hear this from me."

Sam nodded. "Of course."

Andrew took a swig of beer, and set it down carefully. "This shit is deep. Real deep. We have all these task forces set up, but sometimes, it feels like we're tripping over one another. It's rare that we all show up on the same stage. Meanwhile, these traffickers are ruling the roost. I can't tell you how many botched stings I've been on. We're either too early, or too late."

"So, what you're saying is your numbers don't match."

"In a nutshell. We get a tip on a freighter coming in with a couple hundred immigrants. We don't know how many of them have paid a smuggler to bring them into the country, how many are being smuggled in to sell, all we know is once the sting is set up, we end up busting a few dozen."

"What about the tunnels? Kids? Little kids?"

"Don't believe everything you hear on social media."

"Are you saying it doesn't happen? There are no children being brought to the US as sex slaves?"

Andrew leaned back in his chair. His eyes pierced through Sam's. "Yes. It happens." He leaned forward, his jaw working back and forth. "We work our asses off to make sure it doesn't."

Sam sat up tall. "And when it does?"

"The shit hits the fan. That means someone, somewhere, dropped the ball." He leaned back again, and lowered his voice. "Or—someone's on the take."

"Say the ship comes in…how easy is it to unload the merchandise before they hit US waters?"

"Ever see one of those ships? It takes special equipment to unload the containers. It takes a huge crane. There's no way a smuggler is going to bring one of those monsters to the party."

"But if they have access to the cargo, they wouldn't need to move the container, only the contents, right?"

"I suppose."

"What's to stop them from taking some crates off the freighter and loading them onto say– a yacht, or a fishing boat?"

"They'd have to get past the Coast Guard."

"What if the Coast Guard is paid to look the other way?"

"Like I said. It happens."

"I need to know if it did."

Andrew ordered another beer. When the waiter was out of earshot, he continued, "I checked around. No one has heard anything about a girl that age. We did get a tip on some kids that were displaced when an orphanage closed down in Kyiv. They haven't been located yet, but we're working on it."

"What's the protocol? I know we bust up rings in the boonies, but I've never worked an investigation dealing with international traffickers…what am I looking for?"

"These people, men and women look like ordinary business people. You would never suspect them. Hell, there was a high-profile lawyer that just got arrested for trafficking and kiddie porn in Virginia. Most of the perps buy their way out of charges that stick, or you have guys like Epstein that would rather die than sing. It's all about money. If someone took the risk of bringing this girl to the US, she must be a prize. An expensive one." Andrew's eye narrowed, "Oh, and you left out one little detail."

"And what's that?"

"That the girl *is your sister.*"

Slashers

Audra's breath came in ragged waves. Below her, dogs jumped and barked, trying to nip at her heels. Fear paralyzed her. She hugged the trunk of a tree so tight the bark tore at her skin. A spider danced above her head, warning her to keep her distance. She heard horse hooves galloping toward her.

"Ye-haw, you sure are one scared little bunny." He said with a hardy laugh. "Bunnies don't climb trees though, where'd you learn to do that?" He steadied his horse underneath her. "Time to come in for supper young lady, and I won't be takin' "no" for an answer. There're bobcats out here, and hell, they know how to climb trees too." His belly jiggled with mirth. "Hop on," he said, his smile morphing into a serious slash. "Now."

Audra shimmied down the tree, grabbed a branch, and swung herself onto the back of the horse. The horse lunged forward, forcing Audra to latch onto the man's waist. As they rode swiftly to the house, she spied her surroundings, the terrain treacherous, and desolate. *What were you thinking–there is no escape!*

Suzanne walked Linda to the door, then showed Lewis to the guest room. "There's a bathroom across the hall...fresh towels next to the shower. Make yourself at home. Help yourself to food and drink in the refrigerator, and if you need me just call out. I'm a light sleeper."

"Yer very kind," he said. "Is there a telly I can look at for a bit. I don't think I'll be able to catch a wink just yet."

"Of course. Let me get the remote." Suzanne opened the drawer in the small table beside her sofa. "I'll fetch a throw for you, it still gets cold in here at night. I keep the thermostat down low, but if you need more heat, feel free to kick it up a notch."

Lewis stared at her as if she were talking Greek. Of course, she thought. Gadgets are different from what he is used too. She clicked on the TV, and gave him a quick lesson on how to navigate the buttons. Lewis punched the up arrow, landing on a movie channel. A western. They glanced at each other as if a miracle happened before their very eyes. Both took a seat, mesmerized by the scene unfolding before them.

A man on a horse lassoed a young squaw. She fought with all of her might to get free, but it was no use, the man's strength won out, and she was his captive. He rode back to his cabin, holding her tightly to his chest. When they arrived, she fought against him again, this time he used violent means to disarm her fury. He carried her like a rag doll into the cabin, and threw her on the bed. He climbed on top of her, and began ripping at her clothes.

"'At's not 'ow 'e's gonna take her," Lew said. "She's a prize."

"But why Audra? Why is *she* the prize? There are so many girls in California, why risk smuggling in a woman from another country?" Suzanne looked perplexed.

"From the visions I get of the lass, she's not only beau'iful, she's pure."

"I'd never seen her face until Sam showed me a photo of her." Lewis' astonished look made Suzanne smile. "It's true."

"'Ave to admit, she's been rather elusive, lately."

"I haven't gotten many hits myself. It was good to brainstorm with Linda. She grounds me, makes me feel like I'm not going crazy."

"Yeah, m'Tru is like that. But I know she'll b'glad when I'm back t'bein' m'fuddy-dud self."

"Most people don't understand what it's like to die, and come back to life. I can't say I ever felt as though I were dead...I just hung out with my dead fiancé while he scared the wits out of me. Was it like that for you?"

"Well, m'friends did all the talkin', but it was spiffy seein' me mum and dad." He laughed. "And m'dog, Gingersnap."

Suzanne walked over to the shelf above the buffet in her dining room and picked up two crystal points. "I got these at a gem shop in Folsom. Take one. Linda says they help clarify your thoughts."

Lewis held it up, inches from his nose. "Funny," he said, squinting his eyes. "I keep seeing a wrist-ticker, it's covered in these, only they're tiny. They sparkle like diamonds, but shaped like crystals. There're a few blue ones, and two red ones. Gaudy lookin', it is."

Suzanne grabbed her phone and typed in the description on google. "This watch?"

"Yes! That's the lot."

Suzanne gasped. "I saw the same watch. A man I met at the park wore one just like it. What are the chances—"

"I thought I was goin' daft."

"What if he's—"

Suzanne dialed Sam.

Sam had been roaming the streets, passing out his business card while showing Audra's photo to every Tom, Dick, and Harriet he met along the way. No luck. The angst in his throat thickened. Then his phone rang. *Suzanne.*

"A man approached me in Capital Park the other day. I didn't get his name, but he was wearing a very expensive watch."

Sam's disappointment was audible when he said, "There's a lot of rich people in Sacramento. I don't see what—"

Suzanne cut him off. "Lewis has been having visions of the same watch. It's a shot in the dark, Sam, but we just might hit a bullseye."

"Stranger things have happened. I'll stop by in the morning. I'm going to contact a friend of mine. She's a retired forensic sketch artist. Her name's Robin Burcell—a well-known local author—you'll love her."

"We'll be here."

Sam drove home, feeling hopeful. When he pulled into his driveway, he didn't see the two men standing in the shadows. When he went inside his house, he didn't see them slash his tires.

Smoke

"Mission accomplished," Lilly said, flicking a cigarette into a spray of sparks on the ground."

Giorgi flashed her a look of distain. "Are you trying to start a fucking fire?"

"What time is your flight?"

"Midnight." He turned to her, his eyes blazing. "Word on the street is that there's a cop looking for the girl."

"Impossible! No one knows she's here. We were extremely careful."

"There was a cop asking questions in Vienna. Rubio said he took care of him...evidently, he's mistaken. What no one bothered to tell me was he was an American–or better yet, that the fucking girl is his fucking sister!"

Lilly purred, "There is no way in hell the girl can be linked to you." She leaned closer. "Besides, Jake has always been good about cleaning up after himself." She reached in her pocket for another cigarette. "You can always get rid of the cop."

His expression turned dark, dangerous.

Lilly eased the cigarette from the package. "I swear on my life–I didn't know."

Giorgi's laugh chilled her to the bone. He disappeared into the night like a ghost.

Lilly lit her cigarette. With each puff, she mentally kicked herself for opening her big mouth.

Autographs

Sam examined the damage to his tires. "Son-of-a-bitch," he seethed under his breath. He dialed AAA, and used his clout to get immediate service. He hated to pull a power play but it was crucial he get to his appointment with Suzanne and Robin on time. Robin was doing him a favor; he intended to do the customary cop thing and pick up donuts—lucky for him he allowed time for a tire change.

He checked the perimeter of his house, searching for clues. All he found were two sets of shoe prints near the back of the garage. By the looks of them, the slashers wore athletic shoes. Expensive ones. He recalled the two guys he approached on K Street. They eyed him carefully before taking his card. Anyone with a cell could google his name to find out where he lived, but why do that? Where they sending him a message? *Butt out? Stay off our turf?* Could be anything. *Could be nothing.*

At 10 a.m., Suzanne heard the doorbell ring, followed by a knock.

"Sorry, I didn't hear the bell, I wasn't sure it was working. I'm Robin, Robin Burcell. Sam Metzger said to meet him here."

"Please come in." Suzanne led the way to the kitchen. "This is Lewis

Howard, from London." Lewis nodded in greeting. "Sam said you're a local author—mysteries?"

"Yes. I've published many series, and I've co-authored with Clive Cussler."

Lewis's eyes grew large. "I've read several of the books in the series, "Pirate," "The Romanov Ransom," and "The Gray Ghost." The missus gets 'em on Amazon. Fine read. Lookin' forward to the next two."

A tinge of pink colored Robin's cheeks as she smiled. "Thanks, I appreciate hearing that."

Suzanne set down four mugs for coffee. "Sam is on his way." She paused, "Someone slashed his tires last night."

Robin removed her sketch pad from her bag. "I think we can get started while we wait. Can you describe what the man looked like?"

Suzanne shrugged. "He was so good-looking, I'm not sure I have words that will do him justice."

Robin chuckled. "Do your best."

By the time Sam arrived, Robin had sketched the shape of the man's face, his hairline, eyes, and nose. She was drawing his lips when Sam squeezed her shoulder. "Hey, woman, how've you been?"

"Busy. Working on a new novel. How about you? Heard someone slashed your tires."

"May have been someone I gave my card to last night when I was showing Audra's picture around. The temps downtown are heating up —we're the bad guys."

Robin shook her head, "I sure don't miss those days."

Sam picked up the sketch and winked at Suzanne. "By the looks of this guy, I'd say I'm lucky you picked me up at the airport."

"He may be handsome, but he gave me the creeps."

"How so?"

"Reminded me of the first time I met Dixon–gave off the same vibe."

Lew peered over Robin's shoulder at the drawing and glanced at Suzanne. "Did y'tell 'im about the watch?"

"Yes, but I didn't tell him what the watch cost. I'd never seen anything like it so I googled it while I was waiting for your plane to land

—1.4 million dollars! And he was dressed casually—I can only imagine."

Sam lifted one brow. "Handsome AND rich?" He poured himself a cup of coffee and sat down. "The guy Audra met in Vienna was good looking too. Chick bait. I'm glad you were immune, Suzanne."

His eyes met hers and melted her heart. *How can he be so strong, yet so vulnerable at the same time?* She reached across the table, patted his hand, and gave him a reassuring smile. "I must not be attracted to monsters."

Sam walked Robin to her car while Suzanne stared at the sketch she drew. Lewis had a faraway look on his face. "What's wrong?"

"Wish I had m' books for Robin to sign, that's all."

Suzanne relaxed her jaw. "Once this is over, I'll make sure you get autographed copies of the whole series."

Too Late

Audra barely touched her breakfast. She knew she needed nourishment if she were to escape, yet her appetite matched her willingness to take the risk. So far all he had done was chase her through the fields, wearing a flimsy dress. This morning, he arrived in the dining room wearing a black western shirt, a red bandana, black jeans, a black hat, and eel skin boots with silver spurs. He spent the whole time talking on his phone, laughing, joking, like she wasn't even in the room. But as he left, he backtracked his steps, and issued an order. "Be dressed by ten." She glared at the clock on the mantle. She had fifteen minutes to dress.

The outfit laid out on her bed made her cringe. The buckskin shift was beautifully stitched. Fringed at the bottom, beaded at the top. She slipped out of her nightgown and tossed the dress over her head. At the foot of the bed she saw a pair of moccasins to match. *No underwear.* Two strips of rawhide, and two bands were placed next to a brush on her nightstand.

She had finished braiding her hair when there was a knock on the door.

"Ready?" The man stood in the doorway, a gleeful expression on his ruddy face.

Audra followed him out of the house and to the barn. A beautiful

Paint stood ready and waiting. "You do know how to ride, don't you?" he asked, worry lining his brow. When Audra didn't answer, he picked up the reins, and pumped them up and down, mimicking a riding motion. When she still didn't respond, anger turned his dark blue eyes dusty grey, his mouth dip down on both ends, and his nostrils flared.

She knew what she must do. Her fingertips danced along the horse's snout, her voice barely a whisper, as she cooed into the paint's ear.

The man's face brightened as he held out his cupped hands to give her a lift onto the animal's bare back. He licked his lips as his eyes traveled from her bent knee to the dark patch between her legs as he boosted her upward. Once she was mounted securely, he slapped the paint on its rear flank, and the horse took off like a bullet. Audra grabbed the paint's mane and hung on for dear life.

Sam tapped the hood of Robin's car and waved. The image she drew loomed in his mind. *Rich, handsome.* So what? There were many good-looking, rich guys in Sacramento. *He gave me the creeps*. Suzanne wasn't one to read people unless there was good reason. *Like Dixon*. A serial killer. *Who is this guy*? What does he have to do with my sister?

As he watched Robin's car pull away, he saw a green sedan drive by. He caught the passenger out of the corner of his eye, he wasn't sure, but it appeared to be one of the men he spoke to while looking for leads regarding his sister. The bandana and tattoos were a dead give-away. Why would they be following him? Unless—*they know something*.

Lilly paced her marble veranda, phone in one hand, cigarette in another. Beyond the safety of her retreat, mountains loomed in the distance. Every now and then she got the feeling she was being watched. Earlier she caught a glimpse of a light, flickering between the trees, as if the sun reflected off a lens of some sort. If there was someone out there, lying in wait, then what? And why did Giorgi blame her? She did what he asked, and as always, she was careful. *That detective has nothing to do with me.* Giorgi was no one to fuck with. If he wanted her dead, he would find a way. She puffed on her cigarette and blew smoke at the devil. "Fuck you, Giorgi. Fuck you—and your little dog too."

She didn't need this shit anymore. She was tired of always waiting for the other shoe to drop. She came from a family of crop pickers. Grew up poor in the "lettuce bowl." She worked her way up the ladder. Went from being gang-raped to smuggling girls over the border, selling them to the brothels in Nevada, and other states. She graduated to grooming young girls for Giorgi. She made sure they were healthy before turning them over to billionaires, high-profile CEOs, or diplomats. She did what she had to do to care for her aged parents, provide college tuition for her children and private school for her granddaughter. *Time to care for yourself.* How? *Nowhere to run. Nowhere to hide.*

Lilly went inside, poured herself a glass of wine, and returned to the veranda for her evening ritual. She settled into an overstuffed chair and waited for the sun to set fire to the hills. The opulence she'd become accustomed to no longer mattered. The comfort she surrounded herself with to compensate for the things she lacked suddenly felt like shoes that blistered her feet. She lit another cigarette, took a sip of wine. *Maybe I'll move to Puerto Rico.* Once again, light flickered in the distance through the trees... and she knew...*it's too late.*

Rubio

Giorgi sipped on a glass of McCallan "Reflection" scotch. A little celebratory drink. With Lilly out of the way, he needn't worry about any more fuck-ups. True, she delivered the girl to Jake. But for chrissake, she should have alerted him immediately that a detective was snooping around. Now he would handle the matter himself, like a cat, he'd toy with the detective a little, then go in for the kill.

His legion of minions, generously paid for their loyalty, were hand-picked. Ex-military, mostly. Snipers, mercenaries...psychopaths he could count on to get the job done without questioning his motives or disrupting the flow. Human trafficking was a lucrative business, one that survived the leanest periods in history. *High profit, low risk.*

Giorgi pinched his bottom lip. His men had eyes on the detective. Lilly was right, there was no way he could be linked to the detective's sister. Still, he felt obligated to protect his clients, for they were the ones who could blow the whistle...*or at least try.* He made it a point to stay away from clients who had nothing to lose. Although Jake was single, his eighty-nine-year-old mother, who was very prominent in the political arena, was still alive. She would cut off his balls with a butter knife before she would let him sully her good name. Giorgi could relate.

His grandfather began supplying factories with slave labor during

World War II. His father added commercial sex to their multi-million-dollar empire, and groomed him for succession. They preyed on the dreamers. The damaged. The desperate. He made his mark in the family empire by providing services to those pleasure seekers who were willing to pay top dollar to act out their fantasies. Millions grew into billions. He commandeered his own fledglings, like *Rubio.*

He hated to get rid of Rubio, he was his first prodigy. His father had gifted Rubio to him with the inclination Giorgi would take over the business one day, and Rubio would serve him well. Giorgi was an eager recipient; Rubio was a fast learner. Together, they learned the trade. Giorgi experienced more sex than imaginable while Rubio took notes. *Father's diplomatic immunity helped*. But lately, Rubio was more preoccupied with gambling than he was with his occupation. *Or me*. They had grown apart physically, but the occasional times they did get together were scandalous. Rubio was one of his favorite lovers. But he had disobeyed him one too many times...forced him into becoming a cop killer. And although he wouldn't personally pull the trigger, Rubio put him in the position to make the call–muddy the waters with other cops he had on his payroll. *Not acceptable.* He hit speed dial, and listened to the ring on the other end of the phone.

"Rubio," he said, his tone soft, deadly. "Is there something you forgot to tell me?"

Audra's fingers were twisted so tight in the horse's hair, they bled. Her inner thighs were chafed from squeezing the animals middle to keep from flying off as she flew through the trees, and leapt over boulders. Hoofs pummeled the ground behind her. Adrenaline surged through her veins. She felt as though her heart exploded and lodged in her throat when the lasso circled her head and tightened around her neck. *I can't breathe.*

———

KEMO SABE

Tears ran down Suzanne's cheeks as she struggled to catch her breath. Lewis stood helpless, frozen, knowing that what she was experiencing was beyond her control. An image of bleeding fingers had flashed in his own mind seconds before. Fortunately, Sam intervened.

"Breathe, Suzanne, you're safe." He folded her in his arms. "Breathe, sweetheart. Shhhh, you're okay. Talk to me."

Her haunted eyes grew large. She placed her hand on her throat, her chest heaved, "I—can't—breathe," she said, her voice strained.

"Close your eyes, what do you see?"

Her hands clutched at her neck. "A rope—" Her chest heaved harder. "There's a rope around her neck."

Lewis backed himself against the wall. Visions of burning animals swarmed in his head like bees. He could hear horses braying and the thunder of gunfire. The lass moved through his vision as if she were a ghost...her smile, sweet, loving...flowers in her hand...her dress, billowing as she moved, like a little princess. The vision shifted to an American TV program he had seen as a boy. "Butch Cavendish," he whispered.

Sam turned to Lewis, "Who?"

"The Lone Ranger—before y'time, mate. Butch Cavendish was the villain."

Suzanne collapsed into a chair, her mind reeling with snippets of Audra's dilemma. When her breathing returned to normal, she nodded. "Lewis is right. As odd as it seems, I was picking up the same vibe, only I was hearing Indians chanting."

Sam slid into a chair next to Suzanne, and clicked on his phone. "Let's look on the map, see where the horse ranches are in this area."

Audra laid under a blue sky, her hands tied above her head, her legs spread, her feet bound and staked into the ground. It hurt to swallow. Tears burned her eyes, her muscles spasmed and ached. The pounding in her chest began to subside, until a shadow swallowed the sun and loomed over her body.

A sardonic laugh cut through nature's melody, striking fear all over again. The man straddled her helpless form, arms akimbo. "Well, well. What do we have here?"

Audra swallowed her tears. She wouldn't give him the satisfaction of knowing how terrified she was of him. She knew enough psychology to know she was dealing with a sadistic monster who thrived on inflicting pain.

"Look what we got ourselves, Smoke," he said to his horse, nudging Audra's hip with his toe. "We roped ourselves a little squaw—*Pocahontas.*"

The man stepped over her body to remove a canvas bag he had tied to his saddle. Audra heard the rattle, but the sound did not compute until he dumped the contents three feet from her head. Audra's eyes were glued to the snake slithering towards her, its forked tongue navigating its course.

The man's laughter shattered her focus like breaking glass, as the snake inched closer to her face.

Audra fought waves of nausea, and the urge to pass out. The snake, about a foot from her now, decided to curl up for a nap. The man was busy on the other side of his horse, whistling an eerie tune. She slowly exhaled debating whether to move quickly, causing the snake to strike? Or pray for a miracle? She thought about the children that survived their journey to America, only to be raped, killed or tortured. Too late for miracles. Instead she prayed the temperature would drop, and the snake would wake and go in another direction.

No such luck. The man, now wearing a black mask, threw a stone, disturbing the snake. It popped its head up, and rattled its tail. *Scheisse!* Her heart beat like a washing machine filled with throw rugs on the spin cycle. A scream caught in her throat, making a squeaking noise as the snake struck inches from her right cheek. She was slipping away until a gun went off and she was suddenly covered in snake guts.

Sam made phone calls and researched leads on his laptop. Suzanne roasted a chicken, and put together a salad. Lewis excused himself from the room to ring Trudy, and have a shower.

Taking advantage of their privacy, Suzanne slipped her arms around Sam's neck, and whispered, "Hi Ho Silver," startling the both of them.

He scrunched his forehead. "Where did that come from?"

"I don't know. I merely wanted to give you a hug. The words escaped before I had a chance to think about them."

"Interesting. What does the Lone Ranger have to do with my sister?"

"My first thought is that whoever has your sister is either older...or a fan."

Sam's fingers flew across the keyboard, searching for "ranches in Northern California". The number was worrisome. "77,000. Where do we begin?"

"Perhaps you can narrow down the numbers by county."

Sam re-entered the information by county. "Better, but not great. Now all I have to do is find a way to get warrants for hundreds of ranches and farms. And that's if—"

Suzanne reached for his hand. "She's out there. She's alive, I can feel it. My heart-rate has been ebbing then soaring, as if her fear is alive within me. If your sister has the strong will you said she possesses, she'll stay alive."

"Is that you speaking? Or your spirit guides?"

"Both."

Audra's ears rang, her body shook. Her breath was ragged, labored. She thought being kidnapped was terrifying. Having a rattlesnake strike inches from your face gave the word new meaning. Urine trickled beneath her bare buttocks. She sobbed.

"Well now, lit-tle la-dy," he said. "Looks like I just saved your life. I suppose you're beholden to me now." His sadistic chuckle made her cry even harder. He undid the ties binding her feet. She was tempted to kick him in the balls, give him a reason to bash her head in with a rock, get it over with, but she was afraid she wouldn't die. He untied her hands, bound them in front of her, and yanked her to her feet. What did he mean *beholden*? He looped a rope through her wrists and fastened it to the back of his saddle. Was this what he meant by beholden? He mounted his horse and took off, dragging her behind. *I would have been better off with the rock.*

Sam closed his laptop. "I'll call my friend Rhett. He owns a helicopter, and knows the area like the back of his hand. He's been taking aerial shots for many of the real estate companies around here for years."

"I'll call Sheena, see if Emmett has shown her anything unusual lately."

Lewis looked at the floor. "Y'don't need a bugger's muddle, now do ye? What will y'ave me do?"

Sam and Suzanne exchanged glances. Suzanne spoke first. "After we make our phone calls, we'll decide. Meanwhile, you're welcome to watch TV."

Lew nodded. His shoulders slumped with a sigh. "Can y'show me again 'ow to turn it on, please?"

Once more, Suzanne instructed Lew on how to use her remote and left the room. Lew sat down with his hands in his lap. He massaged his wrists. They burned.

. . .

Sheena answered Suzanne's call on the second ring. Her eyes didn't leave her son, who had stuffed his bunny into a mesh bag, looped the drawstring over the tail of his rocking horse, and scooted around the living room, dragging the bunny behind him.

Close

Audra submerged herself in the jetted tub. The abrasions on her arms and legs burned in the chemically treated water. The bump on her forehead throbbed, the cut beneath her chin probably needed stitches. Her throat was raw from screaming, her heart battered her chest. She was trapped in a nightmare.

Suzanne tossed and turned in her bed. She was six years old. It was Halloween. She dressed in a Cinderella costume, and her brother Steven, dressed as the "Where's Waldo" character, ran to the door to greet trick or treaters. When they opened the door, they were shocked to see a grown-up dressed in a cowboy outfit, complete with silver pistols, and a bandana covering his mouth and nose. Suzanne froze. Steven ran to get their dad.

The man's eye's gleamed under the front porch light. Suzanne wished for a magic wand to make the cowboy disappear, *bibbity-boppity-boo*, but she knew why he was there. She *must* disappear. She stepped outside and closed the door behind her.

The woods were dark. She followed the crunching sound of his footsteps the best she could. She knew if she didn't keep up, she'd get lost.

On Halloween, there would be monsters combing the woods, looking for little girls like her.

When they reached a clearing, the cowboy pointed. In the distance, she saw a beautiful castle. "I am a princess—is that my new home?"

The cowboy tossed his hat up into the air, then his bandana. A dark hood obscured his face. Suzanne was amazed by the transformation, but even more amazed by the black steed that appeared out of nowhere. She turned to see if Steven witnessed the magic, but he wasn't there. *Oh yeah, he went to get dad because*—it was too late. The man lifted her onto the horse and they sped towards the castle.

Once they arrived, Suzanne realized the castle looked much prettier from a distance. Gnarly thorn bushes clawed their way up the side of the stone wall. The drawbridge was edged in sharp metal finials. The entrance reminded her of Krampus, and his evil maw. *Krampus?* Were they were riding into the devil's lair?

The man dismounted the black steed, then grabbed Suzanne by the arm and pulled her to the ground. "I don't understand. Isn't this my castle? Why are you being so mean?"

"Run little girl. Run. When I catch you, you will be my next meal."

Suzanne didn't question his directive. She ran.

"No," Lewis cried aloud in his sleep. He covered his eyes, refusing to witness the cruelty unfolding before him. The girl, chained in heavy manacles thrashed about as rats filled the chamber. A man stepped into the cell. His boots, caught Lewis' eye, deep red, made from an unfamiliar material. His intentions drew Lew's curiosity away from the boots when he turned the lass about, pulled up her dress and raped her. Oblivious to the vermin invasion around him, the man kept pumping until the girl was but a rag doll in his mitts. When he spilled his seed, he screamed like a banshee and vanished.

His friend Jim entered the cell, dressed in coveralls, and tall rubber boots. He smashed each rat with a shovel head. He glanced at Lew, regret filling his face. "The lass will be rubbish in a couple of days, be just these rats here." He went back to work, shoveling the dead rats into a heap.

Lew grabbed the bars of the cell. "What can I do, Jim?"

Jim tapped his finger on his temple. "Use what the good Lord gave ye, then. Y'got a bloody gift! 'E gave it to ye, use it."

Jim vanished, leaving Lew to observe the girl's limp body, lying in the dirt.

Suzanne gasped when she turned on the kitchen light and found Lew sitting at the table, his head resting on his folded arms. "Lew? Everything all right? Lew?"

Lew's body jerked upright. "Just a 'mare. Never had them before I—"

"Before you died?"

Lew swiped his face. "M'mind keeps playing tricks."

"Happens to me too. I had a dream that I was a child. A cowboy came to the door trick-or-treating, and I went with him. He took me to a castle—it was scary. He told me to run, that he was going to eat me when he caught me—it was awful."

"Strange, I was in a castle too. A man turned the lass bum over tea kettle, had 'is way with her, rats everywhere...then Jim came to clean up. 'E said I should use me gifts...a riddle if ye ask me."

"There has to be a message in here somewhere. Halloween, castles... how were the characters dressed in your dream?"

"The lass was dressed in rags, the man was big, dressed in a strange pair of boots, and a tunic." Lew disappeared into his thoughts while Suzanne put a kettle on the stove.

"We've had visions of someone dressed as a cowboy, an Indian maiden, and now medieval clothing...perhaps the man who is keeping Audra owns a costume shop."

"I feel like it's deeper than that. 'E likes a good game of cat and mouse." Suddenly, Lew's face turned to paste. His shoulders shook, he buried his face.

Suzanne rushed to his side. "What is it?"

"His boots."

"What about them?"

"I know now what they were made from."

Suzanne slid into the chair kiddy-corner from where he sat and placed her hand over his. Goosebumps covered her body. "The boots—what were they made from?"

"Skin. Human skin."

Audra heard the tumblers on the door lock clunk into place. She sat on the edge of the bed staring at the two white tablets next to a bottle of water. The note clipped to her pillow read: *Für den Schmerz.*

For the pain? Sadistic son-of-a-bitch. She swiped the pills up into her mouth and washed them down with water. She wasn't one to take medications. Her mother had taught them to use natural remedies. Lavender oil, turmeric, willow bark. But she didn't have access to those things. And if she died from a reaction to the two white tablets, so be it.

Audra pulled a blanket gingerly over her bruised, and aching body. As she drifted off to sleep, she thought about *Timmy*. A neighbor boy she knew growing up. Timmy took pleasure in tormenting his cat. He would pull the cat's fur, or drop it out of his second story bedroom window. Once injured, he would cuddle the cat, only to inflict more pain. Audra hated the boy's cruelty, and told his father. His father's words were equally cruel when he said, "It's just an animal."

Audra's captor must've been cut from the same cloth. The Metzger children were galvanized in good deeds, honesty, and kindness. The Metzger children were raised to respect living things, large and small. *The Metzger children are no longer children.* This place, this prison, headed by a monster who valued no life but his own, had no idea what she was capable of. All she needed was the right moment to strike, the right moment to reverse roles...from victim to victor. *If I survive the night.* The chemicals kicked into gear; her body sank further into the bed. The blankets swallowed her whole. Falling. Falling. Falling. *Auf Weidersehen Timmy. May you rot in hell.*

Castles

Sam climbed inside his friend Rhett's Bell 206B III helicopter and fastened the shoulder harness. Rhett handed Sam a headset, and started the engine. Rotor blades whirred above their heads. "Where to?" he asked.

"Let's head toward Oakland, see how many ranches are out that way."

"There's Slide Ranch between Mill Valley and Stinson Beach, that one is 137 acres, owned by the Nature Conservatory. Jerry Garcia of the Grateful Dead donated a bundle in 1970 to create a place for Bay area kids to experience nature."

Sam nodded. "It's a start..."

"You've got the N3 Cattle Ranch near Livermore. That's your largest. Seventy-nine square miles—can you imagine? San Francisco is forty-seven square miles! The guy paid sixty-eight mil for it."

Sam's interest piqued. "Who owns it?"

"William Brown bought it a year ago, why?"

"Isn't he the scientist that discovered that we all have "star" DNA?"

Rhett laughed. "No, buddy. He's a businessman from the Bay area."

"Business man. Interesting."

Sam's deadpan expression squelched Rhett's joking demeanor. "What exactly are you looking for?"

"My sister."

Suzanne and Lewis shuffled around the kitchen like two college roomies with bad hangovers. Suzanne managed toasted crumpets and coffee. Lewis preferred tea. They sat in silence, waiting for the caffeine to alert their brains it was time to wake up.

"I haven't had a night like that in a long time," Suzanne confessed. "I don't know what to make of it. Let's talk about the castles we're both seeing. There are castles in Calistoga, Pacifica, San Francisco, San Simeon..."

"They may as well be on another planet..."

"I'm sorry, you're not familiar with the area. The castles I was referring to are within 100 miles from here."

"Don't feel as though the lass is <u>that</u> far away..."

"Maybe not, but I'm not getting any hits that indicate a location."

"I'm new at this," he said, lowering his gaze. "And Jim ain't sharin' a bloody thing."

"Yeah, Jack left me in a lurch many times too." Love sparkled in Suzanne's eyes. "Eventually, I learned to swim."

"You mentioned a boy..."

"Kinda crazy, how everything happened to me. I loved Jack with all of my heart. It's been rather difficult for me to accept that he has reincarnated into–"

"What is it Lass, you've gone pale?"

"The baby, Emmett, in whom Jack has reincarnated himself, is the son of a serial killer. I sometimes wonder what he'll be like? His mother, Sheena, is a sweet girl. I pray he takes after her." Suzanne took a sip of coffee, her mind on Jack. "I can't imagine why he chose her. After all, he knew–"

"They say good conquers evil. Imagine if 'e didn't step in? Perhaps evil would've perpetuated itself...y'never know."

"How did you meet Trudy?" Lewis's face glowed with the memory. He was obviously head over heels in love.

"We were at a pub." His smile stretched lines from his face, bringing back the young man he once was. "I saw 'er sitting with another bloke–she looked bored t'tears. I never was one to scrap over a lass, but there was somethin' different 'bout 'er." He paused, letting the memory come to a simmer. "She caught me starin'...and she smiled. Ah, she was beautiful, and I told m'self, she's the one."

"What did you do?"

"I waltzed up t'her bloody table, tapped the bloke on 'is shoulder and said, "Excuse me, lad, ye happen t'be sittin' with me future wife."

Suzanne nearly choked on her coffee. "No way! What did he do?"

"The bloke got up and blackened both me eyes...and as I'm lyin' on the floor, with me ears ringin', me face bloody as 'ell, I hear an angelic voice say, "Y'better run before me future husband gets up and drops y'dead."

"That's the most romantic story I've ever heard," Suzanne said, brushing tears from her eyes.

"It's not a sad story lass, why the tears?"

"That's the kind of love I had with Jack. When he died, my heart died too...I married the wrong man on the rebound, and gave up on love completely."

"And now? The way Sam looks at ye—well, it's the way I look at Trudy. There's more love in 'is eyes than a bucket of worms at a fishin' hole. And the way you look at 'im 'as happily-ever-after written all over it."

"Do you think if you had these visions before you met your wife, you would have pursued her?"

The smile vanished from Lewis' face. "I—no, probably not. I see the pain it causes 'er. I can only pray once the lass is found—"

"It doesn't work that way."

"Does Sam know 'ow y'feel?"

"No, not exactly. I think I'm in love with him, but—"

"Doubts aren't good in a marriage."

"No. No they're not."

Sam held the binoculars to his eyes. He wasn't sure what he was looking for. They flew over ranches speckled with cattle, neatly kept dwellings, some larger than others. After two hours of searching for anything that would give pause, Sam called it. "Let's go back."

"We can try again tomorrow," Rhett said, "head east, up toward Tahoe."

Sam sighed. "We're searching for a needle in a haystack. I have no idea where they took her. All I have are a couple of psychics trying to manifest a location. And so far, they've come up short." Sam balled his fist. Tears stung his eyes.

Rhett, patted his shoulder. "Tomorrow. Same time. And every day. Till we find her."

Audra awoke groggy, disoriented. Her head pounded, her back ached. Her stomach cramped. She squeezed her knees together. She placed a pillow over her face, and screamed.

Her frustration released, she sat up, looked around the room. Something sparkly caught her eye. She eased herself out of bed and walked toward the closet. The dress hanging there was something out of a medieval movie. A style she had seen many times at festivals. She stepped to the dressing table to find the note that read:

den Kragen tragen. Bis 4 Uhr angezogen sein.

She looked at the clock. It was 2 p.m. *Two hours to dress.* When she lifted the dress off the hanger, she gasped. Attached to the back of the dress was a metal collar with a key. Tiny spikes circled the inside of the collar. *Schei*sse.

What kind of game was this guy playing? She wished he'd just kill her and get it over with instead of playing dress-up and scaring her to death. The thought made her shiver. Maybe that's what this was all about—making her so afraid that her heart stopped. He seemed to feed on her fear one minute, and rescue her the next. Was that his fantasy? Being a hero? She ran her finger along the tiny spikes. Images of blood gushing from her punctured neck made her adrenaline kick into high gear. She fought to catch her breath. She wanted to scream, but she couldn't push enough air from her lungs to make a sound. Pinpoints of light invaded her peripheral vision; her knees became weak. *Don't do it,* she pleaded with herself. *Don't pass out.* Too late. She crumbled to the floor in a heap.

. . .

Suzanne pulled up to Sheena's house and turned off the ignition. "Are you ready for this, Lewis?"

"Never met a babe I didn't take to."

They rang the bell and waited. Sheena appeared at the door, a worried look on her face setting the tone. "Come in, you're just in time."

Suzanne and Lewis exchanged glances. What were they walking into? When they saw Emmett, they understood.

"How long has he been–" Suzanne nodded toward the rocking horse with the sack tethered to its tail.

"That was yesterday's stint. Today he's been pulling at his neckline. I had to remove his teething bib–he kept twisting it, I was afraid he'd choke himself. Even then, he kept pulling at something, his face was turning red, and he was crying. It took over an hour to calm him down."

Suzanne smiled at the angelic boy, sleeping in his playpen. "Were there any marks on his neck?"

"Yeah, there were–tiny little red marks. I was thinking prickly heat, or roseola, but then it just disappeared, and he fell right to sleep."

"Lewis and I have been getting visions, too." Suzanne glanced at Emmett. "This has to be so frightening for him–for you."

"He's such a happy boy, most of the time. But these last couple of days, he's been hard to console. He's cutting his molars, I thought that explained his fussiness, but now I'm not so sure."

"Has he shown you any more books?"

"No, but he had a meltdown when I changed the channel on the TV this morning. It was some travel show, featuring castles around the world. When I changed it back, he moved really close to the screen, like he was in a trance." Sheena shook her head, "I just don't know what to make of it all."

"E's got the gift," Lew said. "Lad's seeing what we are."

Sheena's eyes grew large. "But I don't want him to be afraid—he's just a baby!"

Sheena's raised voice made Emmett stir. He rolled onto his back, and rubbed his eyes with his little fists. After a couple of moments, he sat up, and looked around the room. "'Uzanne, Wew," he said, smiling. He stood, and lifted his arms. "Up."

Sheena jumped to her feet and lifted Emmett into her arms. "How do you know Mr. Lew?"

Emmett laughed and clapped his hands. "Dim!"

"For the love of muffins–y'met m'friend Jim now, did ye?" Emmett reached for Lew. Lew snatched him up like a sack of potatoes, and tossed him into the air. Emmett giggled with delight, then he stared at Lewis lovingly, and wrapped his arms around his neck. He laid his head on Lew's shoulder.

Lew beamed. "Jim always wanted a lad of 'is own."

Sheena melted at the sight, tears rimming her eyes. "One day he'll have a dad who will love him as much as I do," she said.

Suzanne slipped her arm around Sheena. "You'll find a wonderful man, one day. And I believe Emmett will help."

Emmett wiggled out of Lew's arms. "Down."

The three adults observed Emmett's deliberate search for something to express his thoughts. First, he emptied his toy basket, and when that didn't pan out, he brought the TV remote to Sheena, and pointed to the screen.

"That show is over, Bud. Do you want to watch Sesame Street?"

Emmett slid off Sheena's lap, grabbing the remote from her hand in transit. He stood in front of the TV clicking through channels like a bored teenager on a Friday night. When he caught a glimpse of "Camelot" with Vanessa Redgrave and Richard Harris, he stopped. "Dat!" he cried.

Suzanne and Lewis sank into the sofa in unison. "What does it all mean?" she asked, questioning herself, more than the others.

"I'd say we're looking for a castle, right mate?"

Emmett ran to Lew and rested his hand on Lew's knee. His eyes, one brown, one green, held Lew's blue eyes steadfast. He touched Lew's neck with his tiny fingers. "Ouch," he said. "Ouchy."

"'E's going to hurt her neck?"

Emmett nodded. He ran back to his toys and piled them as high as he could. When he finished, he stood in front of the pile with his hands behind his back, his eyes closed. "Hot," he cried. "Hot!"

. . .

Sam arrived at Suzanne's house, mid-afternoon. When he didn't see her car, he parked and made a few calls. He checked with Michele, his dispatcher. "Thought you were on vacation?" she said, sounding confused.

"I'm back in town, but I'm working a special case. Any messages?"

"Yeah, two I gave to the desk sergeant, they sounded urgent. One was weird. I could hardly understand the guy, his accent was so thick."

"What did he say?"

"He said to tell you to mind your own f'n business, only he said the real word. I can't even begin to tell you where he was from."

"Did you get a number?"

"Yes, I did, but it won't do you any good. He made the call from a burner phone."

"Anything else?"

"No, just that the call gave me the creeps."

"Why is that?"

"I heard all this crying in the background, like he had a ton of kids. Sounded like a litter of kittens at feeding time."

Hair raised on the back of Sam's neck. "Thanks, Michele. If he calls again, patch me in. I don't care what time of day or night, hear me?"

Sam dialed Andrew. "Anything?"

"Word on the street is that a new shipment came in, but we haven't been able to get a bead on where they were taken. Anything on your sister?"

"Went scoping out the ranches from here to Oakland. Nothing suspicious. Helluva lot of places to hide a person."

"All the ranches I know of are owned by reputable people."

"There's the challenge. Know of any indiscretions? Rapes, stalking charges? Pedophiles?"

"I'll have to check the directory for specifics. There are so many fuckin' pedos in this area, it's not easy keeping up with all of them. We track the repeat offenders as closely as possible, but the ones put on probation, not so much. And with the new laws in place, we're lucky if any of them go to prison, you know that."

"Yes. I do." Sam tapped the steering wheel with his trigger finger. "The guy I'm looking for has fetishes."

Andrew scoffed, "You're kidding me, right? All these fuckers live in a fantasy world."

Sam scowled. "Right now, I need to find the one that has my sister."

"You're my first call when I hear anything, buddy. 'Til then, chin up. I put the word out. We've got eyes peeled. Let us do our job."

"Right. I'll check with you later."

Sam clicked off his phone and pounded on his steering wheel. Anger didn't accomplish a thing.

Suzanne tapped on Sam's window. She could tell he was frazzled. "Come inside. I'll fix us a meal."

Sam obeyed. Starving himself wouldn't help matters any, and any reprieve he could get from worrying, he'd take. *Weary.* That's what he felt. Desperation ravished his soul. He hadn't returned his father's calls, and he knew the anguish they were experiencing not knowing what happened to their only daughter. The daughter they doted on growing up. It would kill them to know she was in the hands of a depraved monster. Their little girl, the one they tried to protect since the day she was born. What could he tell them*? I failed?* He shook he head, trying to dislodge the thought from his brain.

Sam acknowledged Lewis with a handshake, and a nod. He couldn't bring himself to engage in small talk. His conversation with Andrew ruminated in his head amidst the message Michele relayed from the mystery caller.

His eyes followed Suzanne's every move. Every curve. The way her ponytail wagged back and forth as she busied herself with dinner. Lewis sat quietly working a crossword puzzle in the Sacramento Bee. Every now and then Lew would look to the far corner of the kitchen ceiling as if the answers were written up there.

Suzanne placed a bowl filled with fresh greens on the table, and dipped into an exaggerated curtsy, addressing Sam directly. "Did you happen to see any castles in the lands below today, m'lord?"

"I was too busy slaying dragons to notice, m'lady."

Suzanne leaned on the table, her face, inches from Sam's. "Actually, I'm serious."

His brow furrowed. "I thought you said we're looking for a ranch."

"What if this guy is into role playing?"

"That's kind of a given," he retorted. He glanced at Lew. "What am I missing?"

"Both Lewis and I had dreams about castles last night. When we went to see Sheena today, she said Emmett was fixated on a travel show about local castles. Then while we were there, he switched on "Camelot." Do you remember that movie? About King Arthur and Lady Guinevere?"

Sam rested his forehead in his hands. "Yes, but I'm getting a little confused. Are we looking for a ranch? Or a castle?" He placed his hands flat on the table and looked from Lewis to Suzanne. "It's not like someone would have both."

"Why not? Can't someone have enough land for both? Look at the Hearst castle, that place is a sprawling mecca of possibilities."

"Do you think that's where my sister was taken to–the Hearst castle? A tourist attraction teaming with people and staff?"

Suzanne lowered her gaze. Sam reached for her hand.

"I'm sorry. I'm—acting like a jerk. I know you are both trying to help, but—"

"But you don't believe us."

"It's not that I don't believe you, it's just that..."

Lewis pushed his chair away from the table and crossed his arms over his chest. "Just what, man?"

"If anyone is failing to get this right, it's me." Sam rose from his chair. "Perhaps I should go."

"Nope." Suzanne pushed him back into his seat. "We found a shack in bum-fuck-Egypt–right? We can find a castle on a ranch."

Sam lifted Suzanne hand and kissed her palm. "What would I do without you?"

"We can discuss that another time. Right now, we have to get some food into you, and then we can google all the castles nearby. Deal?"

Sam fought hard not to smile. A smile seemed inappropriate under the circumstances...yet he couldn't control the message his heart had to convey. "Deal."

. . .

Jake found Audra passed out on the floor. He glanced at the clock. Past four. Damn her for not being dressed and ready for their play-date. He had waited anxiously for her to appear in the emerald green gown. His mother had worn it to a medieval soirée years ago. Jake had rescued the dress from the pile of cast-offs sent to Goodwill.

He remembered the event like it was yesterday, even though he was six. He remembered how his mother's braided auburn hair circled her head like a crown, held in place with jeweled pins. All eyes were on her slim figure as she floated down the stairs. Men dressed in various outfits, kings, paupers, guardsman, warriors, drooling over her beauty, and the creamy white breasts that overflowed the square neckline of the dress. She was a vision. And as one satin shoe hit the marble floor, she began issuing orders. "Get the collar. Chain him up." Jake remembered thinking his mother was referring to a dog, or one of the many animals they kept on the property. *Imagine my surprise.* His mother was referring to him.

Audra reminded him of his mother at that age. Except for the color of her hair, or at least the caramel and crimson streaks, she was a dead-ringer.

"How does it feel?" he asked Audra's limp form. "I told you one day the tides would turn, didn't I *mother*?"

Jake picked the collar up from the floor. He felt the tiny points. His hand gravitated to his neck, remembering... remembering how the men lifted his mother's skirts, bent her over a chair and ravished her while he watched, chained to the chair's wooden leg, the collar biting into his neck, tearing at his flesh.

He nudged Audra's hip. "Wake up, bitch! We have a score to settle!"

Jakey

Sam, Suzanne, and Lewis hovered over Sam's laptop, scrolling through photos of castles within one hundred miles of Sacramento. Sam drummed his fingers on the table. "We don't even know if she's in the area. They could've put her on a boat, or taken her in a private plane somewhere."

"I'm no expert, but I feel like the lass is close."

"Me too," Suzanne said, kneading Sam's shoulders. "I know we can't give you an address to put into your GPS, but I think we're getting a better idea of what to search for. We know the person who has Audra lives on a ranch. The castle has me baffled, but what if it's more of an obstructed structure, like a reproduction, or miniature? Maybe it's more symbolic than a real place."

"*Maybe*? She could be locked in someone's basement for all we know!"

"You trusted me before—" Suzanne withdrew her soothing touch.

Sam turned to her, his eyes pleading. "Don't stop. Please. I'm sorry. I'm tired, snarky, and scared shitless if you want to know the truth. This is more than a job to me right now—I can't blow this. Please forgive me for being an ass."

Suzanne wrapped her arms around his stiff shoulders. "You're forgiven."

Lewis stepped away. "Time t'ring the missus."

"I think we all need a break," Sam said, closing his laptop. "We can continue this in the morning."

"It feels as though there's a lull in the storm. For now."

"We have to find her soon." Sam drew Suzanne into his arms. "I really am sorry for my behavior. I don't know what's gotten into me, taking my frustrations out on you."

"You're under an immense amount of stress. I'll let you know when you've overstepped your boundaries. Until then, kiss me."

Jake stood over Audra, his rage mixed with shame, and guilt. Deep inside, he knew she had nothing to do with his pain. He lifted her into his arms, feeling the heat from her body against his. *She's burning up.* Damn. Just his luck.

He pulled the covers back from the bed, and laid her down gently. He felt her forehead. *NG, Jakey boy.* It was too soon for her to die. He hadn't gotten his money's worth, satiated his need to punish. *How many times are you going to kill her*? "Every chance I get until she rots in her grave."

Jake went into his medicine cabinet, shook two Amoxicillin tablets into his hand and returned to the room where Audra slept. He placed the pills next to a fresh bottle of water, settled into a chair nearby and closed his eyes. It wouldn't be much fun to pretend with someone who was sick. *A cat, with a dead mouse.* No, he needed her at her best if he were to punish her properly. *Sleep, my fair lady. Ol' Jake has a big surprise for you.*

Offspring

Suzanne left Lewis on his own accord while she drove to see Grace Simms. "He's hurting."

Grace crossed one leg over the other. "That doesn't give him the right to hurt you."

"I got so used to Ben berating me, I think I became immune."

"Easy to do."

"I find myself making excuses...yet in my heart, I feel his lashing out is circumstantial, that he isn't himself."

Grace didn't interject.

Suzanne shrugged. "Or maybe Sam's stress is bringing out his true colors."

"Possibly. You did say he's a recovering alcoholic–"

"What has that got to do with anything?"

"I can't say for sure, but I imagine it's difficult for him not to anesthetize during this crisis."

"I haven't discussed it with him." Suzanne went deep within. "I won't make the same mistake twice."

"Are you falling in love with Sam?"

"I think so...but it's hard for me to allow anyone to get mixed up with this—this crazy thing I have going on. I mean—" Suzanne bit her bottom lip to stop the flow of words that validated her concerns.

"I thought he understood. After all, you helped him catch a serial killer."

"I feel like I'm letting him down. It's not like before. I don't have Jack in my head directing me. I mean he's still here, but it's different. Emmett can only communicate so much, whereas, Jack used to hijack my mind and make me see things."

"How about this guy from London? Is he any help?"

"Lewis and I are getting similar scenarios. He actually has a spirit friend who talks to him. Jim. Emmett sees Jim too. How is that for crazy?"

"Sounds pretty far-fetched, in fact I had trouble wrapping my head around the phenomenon myself at first. I had another patient who was psychic. Her warnings were very helpful. But I can relate to Sam's doubt. It's challenging to accept that another person can know things before they happen."

"So, do you think Sam and I should keep our relationship on a professional level?"

"Only you can make that decision."

"I'm not sure what will happen if we don't find his sister. It will devastate him."

"Be supportive. Help when you can. What happens is out of your hands. You didn't kidnap his sister. You're not responsible for the outcome. Her captor is."

"I hope Sam feels the same, should things go awry."

"If he loves you, he will."

Suzanne quick-stepped down the Victorian's wooden steps. When she reached the bottom step, she felt disoriented. She reached for the hand rail to steady herself.

"Are you okay, dear?"

An elderly woman parked her walker in Suzanne's path. Suzanne could see the vitality that once belonged to the woman. The words *money, power* popped into Suzanne's head. "I'm fine, Took the stairs too fast, that's all."

The woman nodded, and moved on. Suzanne went in the opposite direction. When she looked over her shoulder, the woman was *gone*.

. . .

Lewis sat frozen, staring into space. He remembered seeing his mother when he died, strangely enough...but seeing her standing in Suzanne's kitchen, fixing a spot of tea, stopped him in his knickers. "Mum?"

"'Who does that woman think she is? The queen 'erself?"

"Who Mum?"

"All those fancy gatherin's. And those poor children–the things they make them do!"

"Mum? Tell me, what woman?"

"Ye should know, Lew. Pretty is, as pretty does. That one's a fooler, she is...a bloody demon. Should've taken the child away from 'er, but nooo, she 'ad all that money."

"Mum, give me a name! I beg ye, tell me who she is!"

Lewis watched his mother evaporate before his very eyes.

Sam rang the bell and waited for Suzanne to answer. When she called, she was practically babbling.

"This is important Sam—I saw this old woman, but she disappeared. But I heard the words money and power, and then when I got home, Lewis told me his mother paid him a visit and she spoke of a woman who had power and money and—"

"Whoa—easy." Sam closed the front door behind him.

"We need t'find 'er," Lewis said, stepping into view, his voice raised a notch higher.

"How do we find out who owns land, she'd be older, prominent. Powerful."

"How prominent? How powerful? Nancy Pelosi powerful?"

"Who do you know of that stature that has committed crimes against children?"

Sam scratched his head. "The only one that comes to mind is Theresa Knorr, she's in her mid-seventies, but she's serving consecutive sentences in the women's prison in Chino. Not sure if she was rich, just know she killed two of her children, and her husband."

"This woman owns property. She's wealthy."

"Connected," Lew interjected.

"There's a retired congresswoman that came from money, but she's Asian, she doesn't fit the profile."

Suzanne threw her hands up in the air. "Who does?"

"You're saying this woman owns property, a possible castle, and hurts kids?"

"Me mum seems t'think so."

Sam shook his head. "With all due respect—"

"Dammit, Sam! We're not making this stuff up. We are both getting clues from the universe. We just need to connect the dots."

"The fucking universe needs to be a little more specific!"

Suzanne backed away. Lew stuffed his hands in his pockets, diverting his eyes from the scene unfolding before him. Sam swiped his face with his hand, as if he could erase the words he released in anger.

"I'm sorry," he said. "That was uncalled for."

"If I had a dollar for every time you've apologized lately, I'd be able to afford a trip to Paris." She folded her arms across her chest. "If you don't want to listen, then—" She lowered her gaze. "I know you're stressed, but we are not your—your—" Suddenly, she turned away, fighting her tears. A moment later, she heard the front door slam.

Sam walked a block and a half before he stopped to collect his senses. "She's right," he told himself. "I'm one huge asshole." He turned left, then right, to get his bearings. Then he headed towards the bar.

Lewis placed a hand on Suzanne's shoulder. "E's out of his wits, lass. I imagine I'd b'cheesed-off too if m'sister went missin'."

"I know he's not himself, but I don't want him thinking he can talk to me in that manner. I'm done being someone's verbal punching bag."

"Tru would've 'ad me ears boxed 'til Christmas," he said, with an affectionate pat on her arm. He checked his watch. "Time for tea. 'Ow 'bout I fix us a cup?"

Suzanne plopped into a chair and scooted herself toward the table. "He forgot to take his laptop. He'll be back."

Lewis set two cups on the table and filled them with tea. "Sugar?" he asked. Suzanne shook her head "no." "Cream?" He held up an ornate cream pitcher. Again, she nodded "no." He sipped slowly as he watched her stare at the wall. He thought about his mum, and how they would drink tea together when he was troubled. She always gave him good advice. "Who d'ye know that dresses fancy, and 'as lots of money?"

"In California, that could be anyone."

"From what me mum said, she's dishy, minted."

"Like a movie star?"

"She 'ad 'er day."

"There are several Hollywood actors that have retired in northern California...but why buy a girl?"

Lewis and Suzanne sat quietly, drinking their tea, waiting for the universe to provide the answer.

Sam stared at the glass in his hand. A double shot of Makers Mark bourbon whiskey, with a splash of water. He swirled the liquid in his glass, admiring the rich golden color. He waved the glass under his nose, inhaling the scent. But before he held the glass to his lips, he set the glass down next to the sobriety coin he had carried in his pocket for the last ten years.

He conjured the image of his first AA meeting, and how he resisted admitting he was an alcoholic. He was a cop. Cops drank. It was part of the job. Killed the pain. *That's what I need. A drink to kill the pain.*

"Drink up," the bartender said, placing a second drink in front of the other. "Your friend over there," he said nodding to Sam's left, "said this one's on him."

Sam turned to his left to see who his benefactor was, but could barely make out the man's face, sitting in the dark corner. Sam raised his glass, but he didn't drink. He plucked a twenty out of his wallet, snatched up his sobriety coin, and walked out the door.

Sam sensed the car creeping along behind him. He was still a block from Suzanne's where his gun was locked in the trunk. He opened up his phone, reversed his camera lens, and clicked a photo of the car. He wasn't surprised to see it was the same car he saw cruise by the other night.

He didn't want to incite a confrontation by turning around, and he didn't want to run. He looked for a clearing between the houses, and took a quick right, staying close to the bushes dividing the yards. He heard tires squeal. *They're pissed. Good.*

He jogged back to Suzanne's, retrieved his gun from the trunk, and went around to the back door. He peeked through the window and saw Suzanne and Lewis sitting at the kitchen table, drinking tea. He wrapped softly. Suzanne glanced at the door and rose, cautiously. Before she got to the door, she reached for something, Sam didn't see what.

"Who's there?" she called.

"It's me Suzanne—Sam."

She peeked through the window. They were practically nose to nose. He could see the turmoil of emotions in her eyes. He wanted to cry. She opened the door. He looked away. "Can I come in?"

"If you keep your apologies to yourself—"

"Promise," he said, easing past her.

"We were just having tea, would you–"

"I'm being followed."

Suzanne peeked out the window. "You must've struck a nerve."

"Yeah. Must've."

Suzanne walked past Sam, brushing against him. "We think we've narrowed it down to a few possibilities...interested in hearing what we have to say?"

Sam spun a chair around and straddled it, keeping his eye on the front door. "Shoot," he said, placing his gun on the table.

Suzanne's eyes widened, and her glance ricocheted off of Lew's. "He doesn't mean that literally."

"If I thought 'e did, I would've been shittin' me britches."

Sam exhaled. His lips tilted upwards. "I love you guys," he said.

Jake couldn't take his eyes off of Audra.

He marveled at how much she resembled his mother when she was young. *Beautiful.* Mother let him brush her hair...pour the perfumed beads into the tub. *Wash her back.* On Sundays they made pancakes, played checkers, watched movies in black and white. When he got older, they began playing dress up, spent afternoon's pretending they lived in the wild west, in a magical forest, or in medieval times. That was before the parties, before the men, before the sacrifices, and the bonfires in the woods...when she referred to herself as a virgin...when she was a good mother, and didn't thrive on other people's pain. Before she went to Hollywood and became *a monster*. She told him once, "What you see, is what you'll be." *You're so right mother. Look at me now.*

They hadn't spoken in years. His mother resided in a private care facility that catered to celebrities. She still attended star-studded functions, but always with the help of one of her well-paid aides. She no longer approved of his insatiable appetite for the depravity she introduced him to. She preferred to stay in her ivory tower, where she could deny the past, and pass judgement on the present. She cleansed her soul with charity contributions, setting up foundations for the underprivileged, while supporting her only son's twisted life-style.

JACKPOT

Rubio decided it was time to disappear. His last phone call with Giorgi made his flesh crawl. He knew that tone. *Deadly.* He had witnessed first-hand what Giorgi was capable of. Experienced his wrath once or twice himself. The most disturbing was when he bashed in the head of a fourteen-year-old Israeli boy who couldn't get a hard-on on command. When Giorgi wanted sex, he expected his partner to be ready, willing, and able. He said it was for the boy's own good. His new owner may not be as generous.

Rubio was born ready for sex, provided he didn't over indulge in drugs or alcohol. However, he recalled what happened one night after delivering a dozen prepubescent girls to a sheikh in Bahrain. Giorgi was ecstatic over the gold bars he received as payment, and pulled him into a seedy Pub, for a celebratory drink. After two beers, Giorgi became school-girl-giddy, animated, and giggly. This was not the Giorgi he was used to, and found this side fun, and entertaining. Two beers led to three, then four, and Giorgi grabbed his hand, placed it on his erection and gave Rubio a come-hither look that took him by surprise. Rubio dodged his advances claiming Bahrain was not the safest place to get drunk or horny. "Let's go back to the hotel," he remembered saying.

"You're a bore!" Giorgi spat at Rubio, making his heart race. He was used to Giorgi's Jekyll and Hyde personality, but he rarely showed that side of himself outside of a controlled environment. Public intoxication laws were stringent in Bahrain, Rubio didn't want to end up in prison.

Giorgi sulked during their ten-minute ride to the hotel. Once they were in the elevator, Giorgi slammed Rubio against the wall, and kissed him hard. "I want you," he said, "I want you to fuck me–*bad.*" Rubio came away with a fat lip, but Giorgi didn't stop there, determined to have his way.

When they entered the hotel room, Giorgi kicked the door closed behind him and began ripping at Rubio's clothes.

"Take it easy," Rubio said, shielding himself with a pillow. Giorgi's crazed-filled eyes turned pitch black. He slugged Rubio in the jaw.

"Don't talk back, bitch," he seethed in *that voice*, ripping the pillow out of Rubio's hands. Rubio relented, knowing Giorgi bested him in size and strength. Giorgi's sardonic smile was one of victory. He undressed as if his clothes were flammable, and his erection was a torch. "Take off your clothes," he demanded.

Rubio obeyed. He had dressed down to his underwear when Giorgi noticed Rubio was limp. He grabbed at the nylon briefs and pulled them down, furious with what he saw. He pushed Rubio onto the bed, began rubbing, stroking, sucking...using encouraging words on the flaccid member. "Come on, baby, you know you want to feel my tight ass around you." It was no use.

"Must've been the beer," Rubio lied.

Giorgi didn't speak. He hit Rubio so hard across the face, Rubio saw stars. When he tried to get up, Giorgi hit him again. And again. And again.

Later, when Rubio's friends asked if he had pissed off a Russian prize fighter. Rubio laughed and said, "No. Just some drunk." Those who saw Giorgi's bruised and swollen knuckles put two and two together. *Giorgi never apologized.*

Rubio dumped his top dresser drawer on the bed. He picked out a couple of his favorite T-shirts, seven pair of underwear, and four pair of socks. He opened the closet, ripped three pairs of jeans off of hangers, two dress shirts, and a jacket. He took one pair of leather boots, one pair of dress shoes, and his favorite Pumas, and tossed them next to the items he planned to take. He folded, rolled, and packed his suitcase as if he were headed on a business trip instead of escaping with his life.

One quick stop to his favorite casino. The ten-thousand crispy euros in his pocket made him feel lucky despite the hit he was sure Giorgi had out on him for not telling him about the cop. He wouldn't dare shoot him in his own casino.

First, a drink. Loosen his inhibitions, get his mind off of things. He passed the roulette tables, and a bank of 100€ slots. *What the hell*. He slipped a bill from the ruby clip he bought last week when he won the ten-thousand euros. He slid the bill in the machine and pulled the lever. The barrels spun, around and around until one fleur-de-lis settled in place. Then a second stopped next to it. Then a third. Rubio raised his eyes to the prize—JACKPOT 4,500,485.09. Butterflies swam in his stomach as the fourth and final fleur-de-lis settled in place. Flashing lights blinded him, bells shrieked like a fire alarm. Whoop. Whoop. People gathered like flies to the chaos. The numbers were no longer visible. All he saw was WINNER, *der SIEGER* flash in its place. Three attendants rushed to his side, urging on-lookers to step back. The attendants opened the machine, turned off the sirens, and began doing their inspection. Rubio's face flushed with all the attention he was getting. He could hardly believe his luck.

It took nearly an hour for the machine to be cleared. Once the inspectors were finished, Rubio expected to receive a check, but that wasn't true, because of the amount, they must contact the Glücksspielkommissar. Rubio's elation was waning fast. "I'll be at the bar," he said, pointing.

Immediately when he sat down, he became a magnet for women wanting a rich man to fulfill their dreams. The bartender picked up on his dilemma and hurried over. Rubio scowled. "Where's Franz?" He knew he could trust Franz.

"Covid." The bartender smirked. "What you drink?"

Rubio was cautious when eating and drinking out. Giorgi was notorious for hiring unscrupulous bartenders who slipped things into a "prospect's" drink. It made Rubio's job easier, but he worried about the same happening to him. *Not tonight*. Tonight, he won four-and-a-half million fucking euros. Besides, he only ordered beer on tap. "Stiegl," he said, drumming his fingertips on the inlaid wood. A couple of women hovered nearby, hoping to catch Rubio's eye. He pretended to focus on the KENO numbers on the screen above the bar. The bartender set his beer on the bar. "On the house," he said, grinning. Rubio raised his glass. "*Zum Gewinner*!" The bartender nodded, and disappeared.

Rubio guzzled down half of his beer. *Winning makes a guy thirsty.* He took a few more gulps and drained the glass. He scanned the area for the bartender. He was gone. *Shit. Guess it's not my lucky day after all.*

Two men helped Rubio off his stool. He could barely stand. His stomach cramped, he was nauseous, his head light, detached. He felt cold, as if his heart couldn't pump blood to his extremities. He couldn't catch his breath. He heard the sirens outside the casino. He knew what was coming. It wasn't the gaming commissioner. It wasn't good. *Giorgi-Porgi, puddin' pie, spiked my beer and made me die.* The oxygen mask covered his blue tinged lips. He closed his eyes. *Breathe.* Nothing came out.

D.O.A.

Giorgi got the text at 11:02 a.m. Rubio was pronounced dead at the hospital. *Heart failure due to fentanyl.* Giorgi slipped into a terry robe. Water in the pool below shimmered in the morning sun. A swim would do him good. Relieve his stress. He still had a mess to clean up. The cop was still searching for his sister. *Rubio, Rubio. I thought I taught you better than that.*

"Salvadore!" Giorgi's tone sounded chipper. "What's going on with the hemorrhoid I asked you to lance?" A woman standing near the elevator scowled, and turned her back to Giorgi while he listened to excuses on the other end of the line.

"I see," he said. "I may just have to take care of the matter myself." The woman gasped. When the elevator door opened, the woman beelined for the stairs.

Sam climbed into Rhett's helicopter, and fastened his belt. "Let's head towards Tahoe. We're looking for a ranch with a stone structure that looks like a castle."

Rhett raised his brow. "I've been photographing property around here a lot of years, Sam...nothing like that is coming to mind."

"My sources are telling me they see castles."

"There's a few around...Vikingsholm in Lake Tahoe is one, there's a couple in the bay area...Hearst Castle is another..."

Something didn't feel right. Both properties were state parks. Sam couldn't imagine his sister being held captive in such a public place. "Any you know of that aren't public?"

"No, but that's not to say there aren't any Tudor homes around."

Rhett fired up the engine. Sam watched the dust on the ground swirl below him. *Where are you, Audra? Where?* Soon they were a thousand feet up, and climbing.

Suzanne dressed in a pair of faded jeans, and a navy tank top. The temperature had reached an unseasonable high, which called for layering. If needed, she kept a sweatshirt jacket in the car. She slipped into her Nikes and descended the stairs.

Lewis was sitting at the kitchen table, reading a book he picked from her bookcase. He marked his place when she entered the room, and lifted his gaze. "I feel a little guilty seein' the sights with the lass still out there somewhere."

"We aren't going to do her any good sitting around moping." Suzanne opened the refrigerator and gathered ingredients for a picnic lunch. "Fresh air will do us both some good...and if we're lucky, our spirit guides will tell us exactly what we need to know."

Lew scratched his head. "Spirit guides, y'say–is that what they call 'em?"

"Linda gave me the low-down on spirit guides when I met her. They are heavenly beings that watch over us, help us navigate our path." Suzanne tore open a package of sliced turkey, and placed a few slices on two pieces of bread. "Mayo okay with you?"

Lewis chuckled. "Lass! If y'didn't know–we put may-o on everythin'!" He closed the book with a clap. "A spot of mustard would b'nice, too."

Suzanne finished the sandwiches, packed an apple for each of them, a bag of chips to share, and two bottles of water. "Let's go," she said, holding the door open for Lew. "Tell me if you get tired. I wouldn't want to be the one to tell your wife I ran you ragged. I promised her I would make sure you took it easy."

"Tru worries 'erself. I feel fine."

"I thought we'd head to the Preston Castle in Ione. It was a boy's reformatory at one time. People say it's haunted. There's a ranch nearby...are you ready for this? It's called N*everland,* I wonder if it was named after Michael Jackson's place?"

"Maybe." He closed his eyes. "Could be we're steerin' the cart up hill."

"I feel drawn to the castle, and you're right, we may not find Audra there, but we may get closer to the truth."

Suzanne parked the car in the visitor's lot and turned off the ignition. The castle loomed ahead of them. "Gives me the willies. How about you?"

"Them poor children," he said, sadness erasing any hint of amusement from his face. "Y'neglected t'tell me 'ow they died."

"I'm not sure—what are you getting?"

"It's more what I'm feelin'," he said rubbing his arms to ward off trepidation. "Like m'bones are broken." He clamped his hands over his ears. "They're screamin', I can 'ear 'em."

Suzanne started the engine, and put the car in reverse. "I'm sorry I brought you here," she said, tears filling her eyes.

Five miles down the road, Suzanne pulled over. "Are you all right?" she asked, swiping tears from her cheeks.

"It stopped." His head bounced her way. "Did y'feel it too?"

"I felt your pain."

"What kind of world are we livin' in? They beat 'em, starved 'em, neglected 'em when they was sick...bloody monsters, they was."

Suzanne bent forward, resting her forehead on the steering wheel. "I didn't pick up on anything that had to do with Audra, did you?"

"No. But I'm feelin' whoever has 'er experienced pain as a child."

Suzanne closed her eyes. Stone walls surrounded her. Rats crawled beneath her feet. She was frightened, cold. Her lips quivered as she pleaded for her life...a sinister laugh echoed in the dark, dank prison; his words poison to her ears...*how does it feel? How do YOU like it–mother?*

. . .

Jake reached his breaking point. The girl was bought to fulfill his fantasies, work out his animosity toward his mother. Twenty-four hours had passed since he found her lying on the floor. He felt her forehead. *Burning up*. Fuck. He sat her up, her head lolled to one side. He opened her mouth and forced a pill down her throat, following up with a water chaser. She didn't choke. *Thank God for small favors.*

He eased her back down. No sense wasting more time watching her sleep. He had animals to tend to, he hadn't eaten...*she'll come around when she's ready*, he surmised. *Something mother would say.*

Jake locked the door behind him. On his way outside, he stopped in the kitchen, and grabbed a box of cereal from the pantry. He hopped into his golf cart, and headed for the stone structure situated near the edge of his property.

His mother had the tower built for his seventh birthday. One of her rich "boyfriends" financed the endeavor. The guy was a sick fuck with more money than grains of sugar in a ten-pound bag. It seemed everything he touched turned to gold. The guy's parents had adopted him when he was in middle-school, left him millions when they died. Jake's mother confided that the guy landed an acting gig and made bank, winning an award for best supporting actor. As his fortune grew, so did his quest for excitement. That's where mom came in.

She was willing to role play—he was willing to pay. *Little did he know who he was playing with.* The man "accidentally" fell from the top of the turret to his death before the project was complete. Jake always wondered whose idea it was to dig a 200-foot hole in the center of the turret. His mother told police she assumed he was digging a well. When she turned on the waterworks, devastated over the tragedy, the police also fell...*fell for her lies.*

The only thing his mother ever said to him was, "Jake, you could have waited until after I married the bastard."

A year later, she married Mitchell, who added his contribution by expanding the structure. The additions included two more turrets, a bailey large enough for his mother to host events during summer months, a barbican to add strength to the structure, a drawbridge that opened over the seasonal creek running through the property, and a porticus, the metal gate that kept intruders at bay.

When it was finished, the miniature design rivaled medieval castles worldwide, and Mitchell's untimely death left his mother filthy rich.

From the beginning, the castle had been one of his mother's best kept secrets. *Her own personal torture chamber.* Few people knew the castle existed, and the ones who did, didn't dare tell for fear of being connected to the unmentionable occurrences that took place there. In winter months when deciduous trees dropped their leaves, the structure was barely visible from the air. Come March, overgrown trees and shrubbery hid the structure from sight.

Jake flashed on her next husband. *Now, there was a piece of work...the man was ten years younger, a narcissist, and very cruel.* If anyone had an ill effect on his mother, it was Gerald. Gerald fucked anything with two legs, *including her son,* and was the only one who made her cry. She took roles doing explicit love scenes to make him jealous, instead, he increased his sexual activities.

Jake was twelve when Gerald died an unfortunate death. His mother was in Europe on a film shoot. Gerald took advantage of her absence and made sexual advances toward Jake. Jake didn't want to play "horsey." A fight ensued. Jake picked up a shovel. When the police arrived and saw the condition Jake was in, they deemed the incident self-defense. Jake wasn't charged, but he was put into foster care until his mother returned to the states. When she arrived, she acted mortified, glad Gerald was dead. To think someone violated her baby boy...the performance, her best yet. *Hypocrite.* She'd been buying children from Giorgi and abusing them for years. Her and her rich friends...*Now, it's her turn to pay.*

First, he needed the girl to recover, be a worthy adversary. He paid handsomely for her, spending his mother's blood money to finance his escapade. *Why not? She taught me well. Use, abuse, hide the bodies...*

Giorgi stripped out of his swim trunks, poured himself a drink, and clicked on the TV. He wasn't expecting to see his face plastered across the screen. He picked up his phone.

"Chris, my man. Have a jet ready for me at—" he paused, checked the time on his phone, "six-thirty."

He ended the call and made another. "Put Antonio on," he

demanded. He waited a few seconds before issuing his second order. "Get rid of the problem—now—do you hear me? I don't care what you have to do—do it." Giorgi hung up, mumbling under his breath, "Fuck."

Sam pulled onto Suzanne's street, when he noticed her car wasn't in the drive. He kept going, heading for home. He wanted to shower, shave, change his clothes. He felt like a rumpled mess. Inside and out.

Rhett flew him up to Tahoe, around the lake, and into Reno. They made several sweeps over Emerald Bay State Park, Vikingsholm Castle, and the Rubicon Trail. Nothing. *Where are you*? He asked himself repeatedly. One clue. *Just give me one clue*. He wasn't even sure Audra was in Sacramento. The more he thought about it, the sillier the notion became. Of all the places in the world, what are the chances she'd land in his backyard. *Suzanne has never been wrong*. Was it enough to trust her now? *You have no choice*. Trusting people wasn't one of Sam's virtues. Meeting Suzanne allowed him to get in touch with emotions he didn't realize he possessed. If there were anyone in the world he should trust, it was she...and yet...he was a cop. A detective. It was in his DNA not to trust. He needed to try harder to understand her gift and the sacrifice she was making to help him. *If only the girl wasn't my sister*.

Steaming water trickled down his body, his eyes and mouth shut tight against the spray hitting his face. He blinked water from his thick lashes. Let the air out of his lungs. He scrubbed away the ache in his limbs, the pain in his soul. Thirty-six messages from his dad waited in his voicemail. He didn't have the courage to listen. He failed them. *Failed them all*.

He turned off the water. He couldn't drown his sorrow. He tried. The water turned cold. He stepped out of the shower. Face the music. He toweled his body, and put on his favorite sweat pants. He wandered around the house, procrastinating, prolonging the inevitable. He finally picked up the phone.

"Hallo, Papa." Sam sank into a chair adjacent to the living room window. He watched the car crawling up the street, toward his house. He didn't have to think twice, he hit the floor just before a spray of bullets sent glass raining down on him.

His father's voice, barely audible in the distance, scolded. "Sam! *Was ist das für ein Geräusch?*"

Sam reached for the phone that flew from his hand when he dove for cover. "Dad, that noise was—a disturbance outside—I'll call you back."

Sam ended the call and dialed 911.

"What's your emergency?" the dispatcher asked.

"I'd like to report a drive-by shooting..."

Giorgio hurried up the steps of the Cessna Citation X+. First stop, MIA, *appropriate*, then from Miami to VIE. By the time Metzger's death hit the airwaves, he'd be in Vienna's finest hotel sipping champagne from an Austrian crystal flute. The resemblance in the drawing of the wanted man he saw on TV was too close for comfort. What gave Giorgi leeway was his clothes. The man on TV didn't seem the type to afford a Tom Ford T-shirt or Stuart Hughes suits. He used the on-line check-out, pre-ordered a cab to the airport, and didn't plan on being seen in public for the rest of the duration. Once he was home, he could breathe easy. No one knew who he was, except for Lilly, and she was no longer a problem. His minions, knew him as Cody Smith. Most of his clients knew him as "John." No last name necessary.

It was Giorgi's job to know everything about his clients, not the other way around. Most of the time, he handled deliveries from afar... *Jake's purchase required a personal touch.* Jake's mother, Adrianne, was Giorgi's father's client for many years.

In that time, only once was there any suspicion of wrong-doing. Giorgi, only twelve years old, helped his father, Tito, with a pick up in Croatia. It was right before the country won its independence in 1995. *That* job proved to be trouble. Giorgi befriended a boy in the town square, named Filip. He gave him chocolate, and a Rubik's cube. Then, he lured the boy into an ally where one of Tito's men was waiting.

Filip was brought to the US with dozens of other misplaced orphans, who were sold to Jake's mother, Adrianne. When the boy was taken to the castle with the rest of the kids, Adrianne did a head count, and a quick critique to choose the best for herself. Filip was overlooked.

Filip, unhappy with his fate, made a run for it. He got as far as a truck stop six miles from Adrianne's ranch. He told a highway patrolman he escaped the ranch...the highway patrolman filed a "found juvenile" report and went in search for an interpreter to translate the boy's story.

When the highway patrolman dispatched a patrol car to the ranch, Adrianne denied ever seeing the boy, which was half-truth. The policeman filed a report, only stating he had interviewed Adrianne, and found nothing suspicious to corroborate the boy's story. Somehow, the story leaked to the press, and the reporters took liberty turning the film star's situation into a smear campaign. Adrianne threatened to sue for defamation of character, and the matter was dropped.

Giorgi knew they couldn't connect him to the cop's sister's disappearance, and yet, there he was, or at least his likeness, on national TV. *Fucking Rubio.* It was all his fault.

Sam swept up the glass, and waited for one of his guys to deliver a sheet of plywood from Home Depot. He expected the hitmen to return. He'd be waiting.

Robbie Platz pulled his pick-up into Sam's driveway forty minutes later. Sam opened the garage, and the two men slid the plywood off the bed, and into the house. Twenty minutes later, the hole was temporarily patched.

Sam escorted Robbie to his truck, gun in hand. Robbie departed safely, and Sam returned to the house. He dialed his father.

"Sorry, Papa."

"What is going on, Samson? Where are you? Where is Audra?"

"I'm back home, Papa. I don't know where Audra is. I went to Vienna, met with Britta, the police..."

"It's not like her not to call."

"I know Papa. I'm doing my best to find her."

"I know you are son. What can your mother and I do to help?"

"Be there in case she finds her way home. If I find anything out, I will call you. Give Mom a hug for me." Sam hung up the phone. It rang in his hand.

"Suzanne." He poured a glass of water from the tap, and straddled a kitchen chair. "What's up?"

"Anything new?" she asked.

"Someone shot out my front window. Luckily they missed." He sounded glib. Inside, his stomach churned.

"You're kidding!"

"Wish I was. You were right—I hit a nerve—I just don't know whose."

"Lewis and I both believe the person who has Audra is rich."

"No shit."

"More sarcasm? Let me guess, the next two words out of your mouth will be I'm sorry."

"You ARE psychic!"

The click on the other end of the phone hit Sam like a slap in the face. He redialed her number. The call went to voicemail.

"Suzanne—okay, I'm not sorry. I'm being an ass, there's no excuse. I promise not to apologize until I can assure you that I'm finished being an ass, because I don't know when that's going to be. It could be a week, a month, a year—who knows? All I ask is that you don't take it personally. I'm frustrated, pissed, a little fucked up in the head right now, and you are the only person I know who understands what its like to feel so fucking helpless. Don't come here, it's not safe. I'll call you tomorrow. Forgive me. Please."

Suzanne listened to the message. Tears filled her eyes. She wanted to believe Sam was different, that he was the one. Stress changed people, brought out the worst. *Lord knows you're not perfect.* "Give it time," Grace's words of wisdom rambled in the mix. Her therapist was right. *Focus on the things you can control.* It wasn't her place to "fix" Sam, or control his behavior. It was her job to make sure she didn't get swept away with the undertow.

Lewis made himself comfortable in front of the television. The shows were much different from home. Intense. Dramatic. Americans lacked humor. He changed the channel. He was getting quite good at navigating his way through the myriad of stations. He stopped between each channel to get a gist of the story before moving on to another. He landed on a classic movie channel, the plot thin, but a particular actress caught his eye. Beautiful. She swooped down the stairway, revealing long shapely legs, and a heavy bosom through filmy material flowing behind her. The man waiting at the bottom of the stairs was mesmerized as well. Until...he removed a pistol from his breast pocket, took aim, and put a hole in her heart before she reached the last step.

Lewis watched in horror as the woman transformed into a wolf, howling, and thrashing about...but as the animal took its last breath, it transformed back into the beauty again. The man checked her pulse, brushed her hair back from her eyes, and lifted her into is arms.

Suzanne startled him. "Isn't that what's-her-name?"

"The wolf or the actress?"

"She used to be quite popular. She's got to be in her eighties."

"I don't fancy 'er. She's beautiful, but wicked."

"Wicked?"

"Twisted."

Suzanne watched the credit scroll down the screen. "Adrianne Darr." She googled the name in her phone. A list of movie posters filled the screen. Suzanne advanced to Wikipedia. "Says here she's originally from this area. She lived in Hollywood for many years before returning to her roots. She bought a 27,000-acre ranch in Northern California, where she lives with her son, Jacob Levitz."

"A litt-le over 42 square miles. That's a kingdom."

"There has to be county records."

"Indeed."

"Why do you think she's wicked?"

"Did ye not see 'er turn into a she-wolf?"

"I thought you meant the guy was a wolf. She wasn't a wolf. He shot her because she cheated on him."

"No, Lass! She turned into a bloody werewolf after he shot 'er, and she turned back t'human again."

"Lewis, I've seen this movie several times. That's not what happened."

"Then I'must be flippin' m'lid."

"No, no. Let's think about this...there must be a reason you saw her as a wolf."

"Bugger if I know."

"Wolves, castles, cowboys...what's do they have in common?" Suzanne refreshed her phone. It was all right there. "Adrianne Darr...

"Pistols and Petticoats," Medieval Warriors," "Queen Wolf," "Felicia and the Fairy Princess," "Mother, May I," a story of a woman obsessed with her son..."

Suzanne googled the name again. This time adding a current date. "Well, forget Adrianne Darr. She was last seen being wheeled on stage to speak in her hometown in Burbank, California."

"What 'bout 'er son?"

"Jacob Levitz..." Suzanne plugged the name into her search engine. Jacob Levitz was a common name. She retyped his name with actress Adrianne Darr. One listing came up. She turned the phone toward Lewis, and sighed. "It's an obituary."

"Do ye 'ave a PRO 'ere?" Suzanne's brow furrowed. "A place where they keep records...we call it the PRO in London."

"Public records office."

"We can check 'is death and 'is Mum's property."

"Who needs psychic powers when you can do old fashion detective work?"

"'Ave ye heard from Sam?"

"No, not yet." Her shoulders dropped. "I'm sure he's busy."

Lewis nodded, flashed her a sympathetic smile. "Sherlock 'olmes in the mornin' tis, then."

"Yes. Tomorrow's another day."

Audra tossed and turned in her feverish state. She was ten. Mama, Papa, and Samson were in a festive mood. It was dark...the streets, filled with families celebrating All Saints Day. A Ferris wheel in the distance terrified her. She broke away from her family and hid in the stairway leading to the church basement. She could hear her name being called, but she refused to answer, and cupped her hands over her ears. All around her, "Au-draaa, Auuud-raaa!" Perspiration beaded her forehead. She felt as though a stick had lodged in her throat. She drew her arms tight across her knees and hugged them to her chest. *If I'm very still, they won't find me.* She didn't want to ride the Ferris wheel. She didn't want to fall to her death.

She listened to her name being called for several minutes before she felt the hand on her head. *Sam.* "Audra, you don't have to hide," he said.

"I won't let anything happen to you." She crouched closer to the stone wall. *Liar.*

Sam parked a few houses down from Suzanne's, his eyes glued to her bedroom window. He slouched down each time a car went by. Whoever wanted to scare him, or wanted him dead, had driven by her house...had followed him here. There was no guarantee she wouldn't be their next target.

———

D.O.A.

Suzanne greeted the sun. She couldn't sleep. An elusive butterfly. A word on the tip of her tongue. A detail she couldn't grasp. She had an inkling of something important just outside her reach. She revisited her memories at the Preston Castle...*horrible what happened to the children there*. The energy thick, disturbing. *Neverland Park. Nothing alarming*. What then?

Her encounter with Sam? She would have to dig deep to understand how she felt about that. He was already rooted in her soul. Their love must be nourished properly or the possibility of love would die. She worried about his safety. She had the dreadful feeling someone wanted Sam dead.

A golden ray fell across her lap and stretched across the kitchen floor. She wished she could summon him to her side. Together they would begin the day. Figure it all out. Instead, she heard Lewis' soft shuffle enter the room.

"Yer up early lass, couldn't sleep?"

"Nope. Something's bugging me, I can't quite figure it out. How about you? Did you sleep well?"

"Like a wee babe–except for the movies playin' in m'mind. "'Aven't been in so long..."

"That's it!" Suzanne grabbed her phone. She typed Adrianne Darr images into Google. The photos that popped up on her screen ranged from the early seventies to the early two-thousands. "Look at her, Lew! Who does she remind you of?"

Lew took the phone from Suzanne and studied the images. His jaw dropped. "Bugger the Pope—why didn't I see this last night? The earlier photos are a spit 'n image of the lass."

"I'm calling Sam." The phone rang in her hand. "Sam? I–"

"I need to speak with you in person. Can I come by?"

The knock on the door came two minutes later. Sam appeared with a tray of coffee, and a bag of pastries. "I couldn't find scones at this hour, Lew, hope you're okay with Danish and doughnuts."

"I'm fancyin' the looks of that jelly roll," he said smiling.

Suzanne remained guarded. Sam kept his distance, physically, at least. His eyes followed her through the kitchen as she gathered plates and napkins. He noticed the dark shadows beneath her eyes. He probably had a set to match. *Neither one of us has slept.*

"I want to show you something," she said, thrusting her phone in his face.

Sam squinted at the photos. "Who–"

"Adrianne Darr. She acted in cowboy movies, medieval movies, themes Lewis and I have been seeing...*and* she owns 27,000 acres in Northern California."

Sam's eyes widened. Hope washed over his scruffy face. "I would have never—"

"Lew suggested we go to the public records office for answers. Adrianne had a son, Jacob Levine. According to Google, he died in 2015."

Sam checked his watch. "Their office doesn't open until nine. Let me see what I can find out...meanwhile, I need to move you both to a safe place."

Suzanne tilted her head. "Something you want to share?"

"A couple of goons shot out my picture window last night. They've been following me ever since I showed Audra's photo around town. They know I come here. It's not safe for you to stay here."

Suzanne's pitch lowered a notch, as if another entity was speaking through her, "They're protecting their interests, Sam—they're sex traffickers."

"All I know is I have to find my sister."

. . .

Jake rose early. He had dismissed his staff, two weeks off with pay, the customary time it took for him to exhaust his playmates and dispose of them. During that time, he tended to his menagerie of animals. He didn't worry about his house guest. A micro-tracking device inserted under her left shoulder blade, a place she couldn't easily reach, kept her from escaping. The electrified fence installed around the perimeter of the property served to keep his animals and his guests in check. Surveillance cameras were installed throughout the 42 square miles.

All it took was one child to escape before all precautions were taken to make sure it never happened again. His dear, sweet mother saw to it that the property remained a safe haven for her devil-worshiping, and extravagant hunting parties she hosted back in the day.

When Adrianne turned seventy, she had a stroke, and required more care than her lifestyle on the ranch allowed. She moved to L.A., where she planned to remain until her death, leaving Jake to carry on in her absence. His idea of a good time wasn't inclusive. He put his own obituary in the paper. The only people he had regular contact with were three orphaned staff members, and Giorgi Von Graff, his supplier.

His mother's attorney paid all the bills, including the food, feed and essentials ordered by his housekeeper, and delivered weekly. In the years he had been flying solo, Giorgi mixed it up, sending him different ages, sexes, and races. Jake had improved his hunting skills, come to grips with his feminine side, and learned to appreciate the sinful depravities his mother and her companions indulged in regularly. The only time he entertained was when Giorgi came to town. Giorgi provided the invites, background checks, and anonymity contracts.

Jake didn't consider by the time he reached his mother's age, the money used to fund his excursions would be gone. He didn't plan that far ahead. Resentment coursed through his veins. Being denied a normal life, he cursed his existence...*and the girl lying in the other room*...the girl who looked like his mother before she destroyed his life. *The virgin.*

———

Roleplay

Sam, Suzanne, and Lewis bellied up to the counter at the recorder's office. "Last name Darr, D-A-R-R, first name Adrianne," Sam said.

A curly haired woman with a toothy smile replied, "Isn't that the name of that actress? Geez, is she still alive?"

"That's what we're here to find out."

"Well, if she owned property in Sacramento County, I should have it." The woman refreshed her screen, typed in her passcode, and Adrianne Darr's name. "Nothing here. Are you sure that's her real name?"

"Try Adrianne Levitz," Suzanne said.

The woman typed away. "Hm, nothing under Adrianne Levitz either."

Sam released a heavy sigh. "There has to be a way we can cross check the counties..." Sam produced his badge.

The woman glanced from one face to another, "You can find so much online these days, have you tried searching the internet? I would think with your *credentials*, you'd have access to whatever you need."

"Thanks for your time," Sam said, his smile glib. The woman's pursed lips said a lot about her willingness to help. Flashing his badge may have been overkill. He was out of his district. His title held little weight in Sacramento. *Wedding crasher.*

. . .

Sam drove down the hill to Folsom. "Early Toast" was calling his name. The host seated the threesome by the window furthest from the door at Sam's request. He would be able to keep an eye on the parking lot. So far, he hadn't noticed anyone following him since they blasted out his window the night before.

He opened his laptop. "Order what you want...everything is great. The orange juice is fresh squeezed." He busied himself logging into a program he used to access driver's licenses. He typed in Adrianne Darr. Nothing.

Suzanne and Lewis exchanged glances. Lewis leaned forward, his expression blank. "Do ye have angels nearby?"

Sam scanned his surroundings. "None that I know of."

"Ye should look harder, Jim says."

Sam raised an eyebrow. "Angels? I don't get it."

"I don't either." Lew lowered his gaze and opened the menu. "Don't suppose they serve bangers and mash..."

Suzanne interjected. "There's a town called Angel's Camp–it's quite a distance from here–hour and a half's drive."

Sam's fingers flew across the keyboard. "There's a lot of open land out there, it's worth checking out." He clicked on the plus icon to enlarge the map, and angled the screen toward Suzanne and Lewis. "see anything?"

Suzanne moved closer to the screen. "I see a lot of acreage–but nothing is standing out."

Sam moved the screen around and resumed his search. "She must go by another name. There are no DMV records for Adrianne Darr. What was the son's name?"

The waitress brought coffee. Suzanne took a sip. "Levitz, Jacob." They paused their conversation to give the waitress their full attention. Suzanne ordered a veggie omelet and orange juice, Sam held up two fingers, Lewis ordered poached eggs, a bran muffin, and juice.

"She must've filed marriage certificates," Suzanne said, holding her mug with two hands. The warmth felt good. *Cold.*

"Which one is Darr's son?" Sam asked, sharing the screen.

"Google his name with hers. You should see the obituary, but there weren't any photos."

Sam leaned back, clasping his hands over his head. "You're right. No photo. Without a photo, I'm stuck. There's fifty-seven Jacob Levitz's listed on the DMV site." He continued typing. "Twelve are either dead or driving on an expired license, eighteen are due to renew this year, twenty-seven renewed in the last two years." He slapped his hands on the table. The silverware bounced and clattered. "Damn."

"What about Darr's agent?" Suzanne asked. "He must know her real name."

Sam input the info into Google search. "Oliver Higgins. Died October 12, 2018." Sam slid his laptop to one side.

The waitress set a plate before him, then Suzanne, and Lew. She smiled at Sam. "Be back with toast. Ketchup? Hot sauce?"

"More coffee, please," Suzanne told the waitress. She then placed her hand on Sam's. "What about fellow actors?"

Sam scrolled through articles, photos, and movie clips. All of the movies Adrianne starred in pre-dated the eighties. Few had co-stars younger than her, which meant very few were still alive, and those that were, may not remember. He kept scrolling. "Well, I'll be damned."

Lewis and Suzanne froze, mid-bite. Suzanne slid into Sam's side of the booth. "Good news?"

Suzanne read aloud. "Boy accuses actress Adrianne Darr of holding him prisoner on her Calaveras County ranch." Her eyes rose to the heavens. "Thank you, Jim." She smiled at Lew. "Angels Camp is in Calaveras County."

Jake set Audra's breakfast tray on the dresser. He could see from where he stood that there was little change. He clamped his hand over her forehead. *Hot.* Her skin was clammy, her hair wet. He rolled her to one side, and felt the heat from her back. The antibiotic wasn't working. Dark shadows circled her long lashes, her cheek bones protruded from her face. Her lips, cracked and dry, had not uttered a word in days.

Unnerved, Jake lifted one lid, then the other. The girl's pupils were dilated. Her condition seemed grave, but Jake refused to be alarmed just yet. *Not your first rodeo.* He had witnessed his mother in this condition many times. He knew what to do.

Audra dreamt she was seven. Christmas day. *My sled.* Sam insisted she ride with him down the hill to make sure it was safe. She refused. She wanted to ride solo. The snow was *icy*. She flew down the hill unaware that the bottom had been bathed in sunlight all afternoon. *Hot?* The snow had turned into a slushy pond. She lost control, plunging in *arsch* first. The water was cold. *So cold.*

———

WATER

Sam slid behind the wheel, Suzanne took the passenger side, Lew took the backseat. "Calaveras County Sheriff's department promised to get back to me. The dispatcher vaguely recalls rumors of the ranch being haunted, satanic rituals, animal sacrifices, but nothing about pedophilia."

"But they gave you an address, right?"

"I need a warrant to step one foot on the place."

Suzanne raised her brow. "You'd think they'd be eager to help."

Sam pulled onto the freeway heading east. "You'd think. Got the feeling I stirred a hornet's nest." Sam peered into the rearview-mirror at Lew. He looked peaked. "You okay, Lew?"

"We'd better shake a leg. The lass rode 'er sled into the pond."

Lew's words kicked Sam in the gut. The memory flashed through his brain with lightning speed. "Did you see something, Lew?"

"Ol' Jim's nickin' m'thoughts. That's what 'e said."

Sam glanced intermittently into the rear-view mirror, reliving the memory as he spoke. "St. Nicholas brought Audra a sled for Christmas when she was seven. I took her to Camp King Oberusel so she could try it out. I wanted to ride with her on the first run, but she insisted she wasn't a *säugling*. A baby. And due to *my* immaturity, I let her go."

Suzanne's curiosity piqued, "Was it steep? Did she get hurt?"

Sam shook his head. "No, she made it down the hill just fine... however, the sun had melted the snow at the bottom of the hill, and she landed in a substantial puddle." He chuckled wistfully. "She was soaked." He glanced at Suzanne. "We never thought to bring a change of clothes, and the heater in the car sucked. She shivered all the way home."

"D'ya know t'meaning of it all?" Lewis asked.

"Not sure," Sam said. "All I know is that my parents weren't happy. Audra came down with pneumonia and almost died."

Jake dunked Audra repeatedly under water as if he were dredging chicken in an egg wash. Vivid recollections of past experiences numbed his brain.

The first time his mother took Adrenochrome, she had a reaction. Despite her concerns, friends encouraged her to indulge. It didn't take much convincing. Jake begged her not to do it, but in hindsight, she probably took it in spite of him. It was her way of getting back at him for ruining her perfect body. For aging her prematurely, for his need to be breastfed, or lifted out his urine-soaked bed. He learned at an early age to be seen and not heard. By the time he was ten, he served his purpose convincing the children his mother purchased to cooperate in the "games." He kept them from revolting by sneaking food and water into the cages while his mother fucked three or four guys in the bedroom, in the name of the Prince of Darkness.

When Jake turned thirteen, he was initiated into the coven. His proof of allegiance to Satan was to kill his only friend. His dog, Patches. A dog that wandered onto the property, suffering from mange. Jake hid Patches in the castle, nursed him back to health. Instead of decapitating the dog, like he was supposed to, he put Patches in a pillow case, and stashed him in the back of a grocery delivery truck, in hopes the dog would find a good home.

Jake grew up in a secret garden, denouncing God, defiling His creations, and serving the woman who detested his very existence. Was Karma in play? He desired to seek revenge through this virgin—purchased for an obscene amount of money—money that could have sustained him for five years.

He dunked Audra once more, pulling her up by the hair before she drowned. He wanted a replica of his mother...and that's exactly what he got. In his mind, he had performed this same ritual on his mother many times. How easy it would be to lose sight of his goal. *Drown the bitch, right here, right now.* No. He had other plans. He wanted her to taste the fear his mother had instilled for most of his life. He wanted her to scream, shake until her bladder let loose, until fear squeezed the air from her lungs, and made her heart feel as though it were about to explode. And once he caught her, he would fuck her until her eyes rolled to the back of her head, humiliate her until she cried for mercy. And THEN he would kill her. *Die,* something he wanted to do every day of his miserable life.

Babytalk

Sheena phoned her pediatrician. "Emmett's fever went from 104 to 100 in a matter of minutes, should I be concerned?" Sheena listened, her eyes on her toddler, snuggled in a chair with his favorite blanket, a stuffed horse, named "Brownie," a book about a jumping frog named Joe, and a T-shirt with a skull, a guy named Kurt bought her when they attended the Calaveras County fair her freshman year in college. She thought it odd that he dug it out of a bag of clothes she packed for Hospice a week ago. "No, I didn't give him anything. He doesn't seem to have another tooth coming in...uh, huh, uh, huh. Okay." Sheena hung up the phone.

"Well, buddy, Dr. Colasanti said if you're not better by tomorrow to bring you by for a visit. What do you think?" Sheena felt Emmett's forehead. "You feel a lot cooler, baby. Let's take your temp." Sheena held a digital thermometer to her son's forehead. The thermometer vibrated. "99.1," she said. "That was a fast recovery," she said, kneeling by his side. "What's going on?" she asked, more out of curiosity than concern.

Emmett threw the horse and frog off the chair. He twisted the T-shirt, and grunted, pulling it until his face turned red.

Sheena sat back on her heels, watching her son traverse through emotions he wasn't equipped to handle. Frustration, and fear reflected in his heterochromatic eyes made her heart break. "C'mere, Buddy," she said, lifting him into her arms. She held him close and whispered, "Mommy loves you."

Jake carried Audra back into the bedroom, where he towel-dried her hair, pulled one of his mother's flannel gowns over her head, lifted her into bed, and covered her in a down comforter. "I'll give you one more day," he warned, "then…well, as mama once told me, 'you'll just have to buck up bucko.'"

"Officer Tom Jensen, Calaveras Sheriff's department calling for Sam Metzger," the voice announced over the car speaker, when Sam picked up.

"Speaking," he said.

"I understand you're trying to obtain information on Darr Ranch."

"It's detective Sam Metzger–I have reason to believe a woman is being held captive on the Darr ranch."

"Ohhh. Really? And what makes you think that?"

"I have my sources. I was told I'll need a warrant. I'm on my way to the courthouse as we speak."

"You're wasting your time. Mrs. Darr no longer lives on the ranch."

"And her son?"

The officer cleared his throat. "Well, detective, I believe Jacob died a few years back…"

"I wasn't able to find records of his death."

"The place hasn't been occupied in—"

"What can you tell me about the boy that claimed to have escaped from the ranch?"

"Geeeez, that was years ago. Seems the kid was a runaway. There was no evidence to substantiate his accusations."

"Do you happen to know Adrianne Darr's real name?"

"Hm, that's not her real name? I wasn't aware of that. Always knew the place as the Darr Ranch."

"What do you know about a castle on the property?"

"Where are you getting your information from?"

"Are you saying there is no castle?"

"I'm saying I haven't been out there in years. Been no reason to."

"How about an address? I can check for myself."

"De-tec-tive, why would you want to waste tax-payers money? I told you, there's nothing out there."

"With all due respect, I'd like to see for myself. Address, please?"

"Really, detective, I–"

"Officer Jensen, is there a problem?"

"Maybe you better stop by the station before you head to the courthouse. After all, you are out of your jurisdiction."

Jake turned on the monitor and left the room where Audra slept. She felt cooler to the touch, but her temp rose two points from the time he retrieved her from her ice bath. He was hungry. Soup sounded good. The girl could use nourishment as well.

When Jake's phone rang, it startled him. He dropped the spoon he was stirring with into the soup. Hot broth scalded his skin. "Mother fucker!" He threw the phone across the room, shattering the device into tiny pieces. Officer Jensen's call went unanswered.

LULLABY

"I'm here to see Officer Jensen," Sam said, reaching into his pocket and producing his badge. The woman behind the desk squinted, withdrew a pair of reading glasses from the edge of the pencil holder, and took another look.

"Well," she said, country slow, "Ya just missed him."

"How can I reach him? It's important."

The woman made a clicking sound with her tongue, and called over her shoulder to a man sitting at the back of the room. "Leonard? C'mere, would'ja?"

Leonard eased his way up to the desk. "Can I help you?"

"I spoke with Officer Jensen earlier regarding the Darr ranch. I need an address." Sam spun his badge around to face Leonard.

"Something happen that I'm not aware of—*detective*?"

"We have reason to believe a missing girl may be held captive there."

"I doubt it. That place is a fortress...been abandoned for years...ever since Ms. Darr went into a home. Poor dear, first her son, then her health..."

"Funny, I can't seem to find any information on Jacob's death, there are no records pertaining to Ms. Darr's property, no DMV records..." Sam pierced Leonard's good ol' boy persona with his cold stare. "Seems like Ms. Darr has something to hide."

Leonard blinked a few times, collecting himself. "You know how it is with those Hollywood celebrity types...they do their best to protect their privacy."

"I only want to take a look, my lead may be nothing...but I do have an obligation to the tax-payers to serve and protect their best interest, and right now a young girl is missing."

Leonard side-stepped to a computer, clicked a few keys, and hit enter. "I don't see any recent missing person reports," he said, his features twisted into a stink face. "When was the report filed?"

"Two weeks ago, in Vienna Austria."

"What the hell she do—swim here?"

"She was smuggled here by a human trafficker."

Leonard shifted his weight. "You don't say?"

"I don't expect you to keep up on international trade, I just want an address so I can collect my paycheck with a clear conscience."

"It's customary to forward information to the different counties. Sounds like this is personal, you being from Goldorado County, and all," he said, taunting Sam for a rise.

"Personal?" Sam sneered. "Very."

Leonard lowered his gaze to the computer, his finger's poised on the keys. "What's the girl's name?"

"Audra," Sam said, his tone sharp, tempered steel. "Audra *Metzger*."

Audra's breath echoed in her ears. The metronome in her chest beat at the lowest point of the spectrum. In her mind, her eyes were open, her cheeks inflated with air, her lips sealed tight. *Go to the light*, the voice inside her head urged. However, her soul differed. She heard her Oma's sweet voice recharging her spirit with "*Guten Abend, gut Nacht*," a lullaby she sang when Audra was a little girl: "*Guten Abend, gute Nacht, mit Rosen bedacht, mit Näglein besteckt, schlupf unter die Deck: Morgen früh, wenn Gott will, wirst du wieder geweckt, morgen früh, wenn Gott will, wirst du wieder geweckt*." Tomorrow morn, if God wills, you'll awake once again. *Tomorrow morn, if God wills, you'll awake once again.*

. . .

When the fist pounding and handle jiggling stopped, Jake grabbed his shotgun and charged out the door. "What the fuck are you doing here? How did you get in?"

Officer Jensen leaned against the cruiser, a toothpick hanging from his thin lips. "Thought you outa know some detective from Goldorado County is about to pay you a visit."

"You don't know how to use a phone?"

"Called you three times. You didn't pick up."

"Must've been indisposed."

Officer Jensen spit the toothpick from his mouth. "That's what he's coming to talk to you about. Seems he's got his tighty-whities in a bunch over some missing girl."

Jake's eyes narrowed. "I have no idea what you're talking about. Now get the hell off my property before I—"

"Before you what, Jake? Call the cops?" Jensen's cocky smirk disappeared, he stood erect, and took one step forward. "Well, well, what do we have here?"

Jake raised the barrel of the gun, his head swiveled to the right, catching a glimpse of the girl hanging on to the front door handle before she collapsed in the doorway. He turned back, cocked the lever on the shotgun, and blasted Officer Jensen to the ground.

Jake swept the girl up by the arms. He dragged her to the bedroom, hoisted her onto the bed, removed a pair of hand-cuffs from the nightstand, and latched her to the bedpost. He didn't have time to chase after her, *at least not now*.

He grunted, lifting Jensen's limp body into the cruiser. He slid behind the wheel and sped across his property heading northeast towards the castle. He reached in his pocket for his trusty fob. *Shit*. He jumped back into the vehicle and sped back to the house. He left the cruiser running as he sprinted into the house, grabbed the fob, and sped off again. If Jensen wasn't yanking his chain, the detective could arrive at any minute. He needed time to get back and hide the girl.

He clicked one button on the fob to open the drawbridge, the second opened the portcullis. Once in, a lever, hidden behind one of the stones opened a trap door leading to an underground garage. There, Jake swapped the cruiser for a golf cart, jumped in and raced for home.

When he entered the house, he heard the buzzer go off for the perimeter alarm. *Show time.*

Sam received more information from the local grocer than he did from the police department. Seems everyone in town knew where the Darr ranch was. *Everyone but the police.*

The trio wound down Highway 16, through Angels's Camp, and picked up 108. The Darr Ranch covered both Calaveras and Tuolumne Counties. Their instructions were to look for a rusty windmill past New Melones Lake and make a left. Take the narrow-unmarked road to the end and take a right. After that, good luck. "Darr ranch has better security than Ione prison," claimed an elderly gentleman with a bushy beard. Sam's curiosity was piqued.

Lew opened his window and stuck his head out. "Ol' Jim is doing a jig. 'E says life is a stage, not t'fall for any bunk."

"Sounds like Jim and Jack missed their calling...they should've been detectives."

Lew chuckled. "'E means well."

Suzanne chimed in, "Jim's right. I get the feeling our presence is expected. Time to hide the bodies, is what Jack would say."

"Leave the police work up to me," Sam said, his voice laced with sarcasm. "I'm a professional."

At the end of the dirt road, Sam turned right. They bumped along until they stumbled upon a thirty-foot chain-link gate, attached to thirty-foot fencing trimmed in razor wire. Sam picked up a stick and poked the fence. As expected, a strong electrical current zapped the stick into a cinder. Sam pressed the button on the call box to the right of the gate. After a moment. he heard a voice.

"Ola'."

"My name is Detective Sam Metzger. I'd like to come in and speak with you."

"*No Inglés.*

"*Ven a hablar.*"

"What do you want? I'm just the housekeeper."

"I want to come in and speak to you. It won't take long, I promise."

Sam heard the gate buzz, and pushed the handle. Suzanne and Lewis stood by the car waiting for Sam's signal to advance, but he held up his hand to halt. He unlatched his holster, then the safety clip, when he heard, "Bring your friends. Leave the gun on the hood of your vehicle."

Sam obliged. He figured he was being watched, and had planned ahead. He waved to Lewis and Suzanne, who were also prepared with bullet proof vests beneath their clothing. Just in case. It was highly unusual to involve civilians in police work, but he needed them to help find his sister.

The sprawling residence in the distance belonged in the Hollywood Hills. The dry fountain centered in the circular drive rivaled those in Europe, with its rearing white marble equine figure, eyes wide, flaring nostrils, open jaw. Sam remembered his teachings about the Four Horseman of the Apocalypse. The white horse represented the *anti-Christ.*

Suzanne shivered. "I don't like this place," she whispered. She peered over her shoulder at Lew, who had slowed his pace. "You all right, Lew?"

"Been better," he huffed.

The girl tucked away in one of the secret soundproof chambers his mother had built for her escapades gave Jake time to don a pair of glasses, and remove his front partial. He had darkened his greying hair with the spray color his mother used on set in her hay-day, switched his bloody Tommy Bahama shirt for a Led Zeppelin tee, his Guess jeans for a pair of paint stained board shorts, and jammed a feather duster in his back pocket. *Ready.*

He paced back and forth in front of his surveillance monitor. The detective appeared to be in good shape. He could almost smell the woman's fear. The man who lagged behind reminded him of the drunks that staggered around the house during one of his mother's soirees. Actors, producers, directors, politicians...clergymen...influential men and women who got their jollies worshipping Satan, participating in orgies, defiling children, then returning to their high-profile positions and their sainthood on Monday, making decisions for the masses, making cash donations to one cause or another. The do-gooders of the world. *Mother.*

Jake opened the front door, confronting the detective with his abrasive demand. "Show me your badge."

Sam produced his badge. "May we come in?" He nodded toward Lewis. "My friend here could use a glass of water. He went through open-heart surgery recently."

Jake laughed. "Gee, shall I make lunch too?"

Suzanne stepped forward and smiled. "Just the water—please."

"Wait here."

Sam pressed tape strips on the inner and outer door handles, flipped the film side over each strip, and stuck them back in his pocket. Jake returned with the water.

"Okay, state your business. I have this big-ass house to clean before six tonight. I'm meeting friends at Olive Garden. The five-dollar meal deal ends at nine, and I have a long drive."

"Where is the owner?"

Jake rolled his eyes. "I'm hired by an agency. They don't tell me shit." He placed his hands on his hips. "Anything else?"

"I'd like to come in and look around."

"Correct me if I'm wrong, but every cop show I've watched on TV indicates you need a warrant."

"Only if you have something to hide."

"Did you not hear me? I'm busy! I've already spent too much time. I could've had one of the bathrooms cleaned!"

"A girl is missing."

"And you think she's here?" He laughed. "And how do you suppose she got in?"

"I could review the surveillance tapes..."

"And I could lose my job. Get a warrant." Jake pushed the door closed; Sam stopped it with his foot. Jake flung it open. "What?"

"I'll be back," Sam said, his eyes, lethal. "And I will kill anyone who hurts her."

Jakes pupils dilated. Sam took one step back as the door slammed. He did an about face. "What do you think?"

Suzanne and Lewis spoke in unison. "She's in there."

. . .

Suzanne's brain buzzed with images, fragments of Audra's face, and a room she had seen years ago in a movie with Jodie Foster. *Panic Room*. But this one was different...this one was made for–*kittens*.

Lewis's head began to spin. He bent down and put his head between his knees. "I feel sick."

"Is it your heart?" Suzanne leaned over the front seat. "Tell us what to do. Do you need a hospital?"

"It's me stomach. I dunno. Came on so quick."

Sam put the car in reverse. "I'm taking you two back to the house."

"You need us," Suzanne protested.

"I need a swat team!"

"She's in a safe room." Suzanne closed her eyes, then opened them. "In the back of the house. There's no door."

"How do I get in?"

"It'll come to me." Suzanne squeezed her eyes shut. The bumpy road made it difficult to concentrate. "I can see the room—"

"I need more!" Sam snapped.

Suzanne clicked her seatbelt, and faced forward. She swallowed her anger, and focused on Audra. "Call the FBI."

"I have no proof."

"You will when those fingerprints match Jacob Levitz's."

"If."

She whipped her head to face him, her eyes flashing. "You can either be a pessimist, or an optimist—you can't be both."

Sam checked the rear-view mirror. Lewis glared back. "You're right." Sam stopped the car. He selected a number on his phone and hit send. A man's voice responded with a greeting on the other end. "Andrew–Sam. I need your help."

Andrew buzzed Sam, Suzanne, and Lewis into his office. "It's the best I could do," Sam said, handing Andrew the prints.

Andrew led the trio through a maze of cubicles into a brightly lit lab. "We just need something to match the prints to our data base. If he has publicly announced his demise, and is posing as someone else, we may have enough...but I'm not going to blow smoke, buddy, it's highly unlikely the FBI will step in."

Sam raked his salt and pepper hair with his fingers. “What about the lack of cooperation from the local P.D.?”

“She’s there,” Suzanne piped in. “Lew and I both felt it.”

Andrew gave Suzanne the once over. “I’m sorry, I didn’t catch your name.”

“My name isn’t important. A young woman’s life is at stake. She doesn’t have much time. And now that her captor knows we know, there’s no telling what he’ll do.”

“The place is the devil’s playground.” Lewis said, “There’s children everywhere,” he added. “Dead children.”

Andrew squinted at Lew. “How do you know that?”

“Jim told me.”

Andrew clapped his hands together. “And where is this Jim? I would love to know where he gets his information.”

Lew shuffled his feet. His desperation vented Suzanne’s way. “This wanker isn’t going to help us.”

Suzanne tapped Sam’s shoulder. “Lew’s right, we’re wasting precious time. Let’s go.”

“I’m sorry I got you involved in this mess, Lew.”

“Ye didn’t put the visions in m’head now, did ye lass?”

“It’s difficult getting the police to believe you. I encountered the same resistance when Sam and I worked together before.” She sighed in resignation. “Sam is very good at his job. I sometimes feel I am more of a hindrance than help, but if we keep working together, we may eventually synchronize.”

“If I was wearin’ ’is shoes, I’d be bonkers. The lass isn’t well. She needs t’be found soon, or she’ll die.”

Sam peered over Andrew’s shoulder. The technician processed three partial prints of the tape. The computer program scanned through millions of prints, searching for a match. The program stopped, prompting a name, address, and DMV photo. “Here we go,” Andrew said, hitting the print option. He hit continue, and waited for the printer to spit out the first profile. He briefly studied the document and handed it to Sam.

THOMAS WAYNE JENSEN
DL: B7726693
DB: 06-24-81
ADDRESS: 15224 Peach Blossom Rd.
Angels Camp, Ca. 95732
ORGAN DONOR X

Sam pointed at the screen. "That's the officer who wouldn't cooperate."

"Okay, I'll admit something stinks, but is it enough?" Just then, the program stopped again, prompting another name.

JACOB LEE LEVITZ
DL: N/A
DB: 09-23-62
ADDRESS: 666 LEVIATHAN WAY
ANGELS CAMP, CA. 95732

"Check out the address!" Andrew scooted his chair to the side.

Sam moved closer. "The sign of the devil, and the gatekeeper of hell."

Andrew scrolled down. "These finger prints were obtained from a mortgage company. Jacob's name was entered on the title to the property twelve years ago, but—" He scrolled down further. "The property was taken over by a firm, Mammon and Asmodeus. Now that's creepy."

Sam shrugged. "Sounds Greek to me."

"You don't know your bible, buddy. There are seven demon brothers, seven sins. Lucifer, pride, Mammon, greed, Leviathan, envy, Satan, wrath, Asmodeus, lust, Beelzebub, gluttony, Belphegor, sloth. They used three of the names right here, I'm sure somewhere they've used them all."

Sam raised his brow. "Why make it so obvious?"

"That's their way. In our face. I went to a Catholic school. I know this shit."

Sam nodded. "Do we have enough to get a warrant?"

"I can do even better..."

Tears poured down Suzanne's cheeks. Terror ripped at her soul. She could almost feel his hot breath in her ear. "How do you like it?" he said. Suzanne looked down; blood droplets bloomed on the front of her blouse. She couldn't move her feet. Shackles burned her wrists...the stampede in her chest reached her ears, the top of her head throbbed, ready to burst. The car door slammed, and she screamed.

Lewis grabbed her shoulders. "Calm down lass, be still."

Sam held her face in his hands. "Suzanne, it's not real. Breathe."

She looked haunted. "Oh, it's real...Very real."

"Our experience didn't go as planned," Jake said, as he positioned Audra's body on the altar. He held her feet in place with a thick leather strap, shackled her wrists to heavy gauged iron chains above her head. "I wanted to play... just like we used to...only I wanted to scare you this time. You always got to be the villain. I always got locked inside the castle, while you watched them do things to me from your throne. You watched them hunt me down– rape me–you heard my screams–and you did *nothing*."

Jake stripped naked and donned one of the red satin robes he pulled off a wooden rack bolted to the wall. He laid an assortment of daggers near Audra's feet. He smoothed damp hair back from her feverish forehead. "We could've had fun...why did you have to get sick?" He kissed the tip of her nose. "Do you remember when I had chicken pox? That's the only time you showed any concern...any compassion. I always envied the children you brought here. At least you put an end to their misery."

Audra couldn't find her way through her mental haze certain she had entered the gates of hell. Her flesh burned. Her bones felt broken. When she opened her mouth to scream beetles scurried down her chin, tickled her neck, marched between her bare breasts down to her belly. She couldn't see them, but she knew where they were headed...they would climb inside her, lay their eggs. The image triggered *Belvedere Gardens*;

she was five. Sam picked a flower and placed it in her hair. She was so happy, so proud of her flower, she was a princess. Suddenly, dark clouds gathered overhead, the wind blew wicked and fierce. A beetle escaped from the flower and perched on her cheek. Paralyzed with fear, she screamed for Sam, but he was gone.

Open Sesame!

Andrew gave the signal. Thirty men dressed in S.W.A.T. gear spread out. Two men installed a cut-off switch, disarming a large section of the electric fence. Using heavy-duty bolt cutters, they removed a chain link panel. The other twenty-eight men checked weapons, and set up surveillance equipment. Once inside the property, the men scattered, taking positions around the perimeter of the house. Several engaged drone equipment to scan the property for a heat source.

Sam kept his phone open to receive Suzanne and Lewis' assessment. "The castle is hidden toward the back of the property," Lew said. Sam gave a directive to Andrew, who in turn dispatched men accordingly.

Sam and Andrew approached the front door to the house and found it unlocked. The two men split up; guns drawn. "Clear," Sam announced into the mic attached to his headset. "Going upstairs,"

Andrew went from room to room, finding each one empty. Sam inspected a statue of a horned figurine with angel's wings, strategically placed on a crescent shaped table between two rooms. He found a button on the bottom of the base, and pressed it, aware that he may have opened Pandora's Box.

Inside the room to his left, a panel slid open, revealing a stairway. He cocked his Glock 17, and proceeded with caution. When he reached the fifth stair, he saw the contents of the room below. A bed, an end table with a ballerina lamp, and a wall decked with chains, shackles. A printed poster, one would expect to see in a pediatrician's office, depicting growth measurements hung on one wall.

Next to the poster, Sam saw a metal cart with a tray. He stepped in for closer inspection...scalpels, rubber tubing, a tooth extractor, and an assortment of wire speculums for keeping one's eyes open. He revisited the bed. The sheets were rumpled, making Sam believe his sister had been in the room, perhaps when they paid Jake a visit earlier. He smoothed the sheet, imagining Audra's life essence on his fingertips.

"Metzger!" Andrew shouted, "Come up here."

Sam left his apprehension in the room and jogged upstairs to meet Andrew.

"Couple of things I want you to see," he said, leading Sam down a long hallway. "Let's go in here first."

Sam whistled low as they walked into an elaborate looking conference room. "Geezus." His stomach churned as he spied the artwork on the wall. Children being violated by adult figures wearing animal heads, men dressed as bunnies, sodomizing toddlers, scenes of torture, and blasphemy. Crosses hung upside down. On a credenza at the far end of the room was a painting of thirteen adults, dressed in red robes. Sam zeroed in on a petite figure, a woman, with a small naked boy kneeling at her feet, a metal collar attached to a chain, around his neck.

Andrew came up behind him. "I'm not a profiler, but I've read about these cases. A child who has been a victim of so-called satanic ritual abuse forms an attachment to the abuser when it's someone they rely on for their survival, like a family member, a neighbor, clergymen, or any trusted adult." Andrew pointed to the petite figure in the photo. "In this case, Jake's mother. I'd say this guy most likely has suffered displacement, and is acting out the evil that has been done to him under the guise of Satanism or some other cult."

Sam shook his head, sickened by the thought. "You said there is something else you want me to see?"

Andrew patted Sam on the back. "Yeah, c'mon." He escorted Sam to a room the size of a master bath filled with monitors. Each monitor, assigned to a particular area, revealed activity. The men saw the S.W.A.T.

team in action. Sam wondered how many of these rooms there were. Andrew pointed to a wall made of stone. "Do you see what I see?"

Suzanne left Lewis alone in the car. She walked over to the missing fence panel. She closed her eyes summoning Audra's face. Her mind's eye produced a woman who could've passed for Audra's double. One woman's soul, tormented, the other's soul void of redemption.

Suddenly, a sharp pain pierced the bottom of Suzanne's foot. Blood filled her mind's eye. She heard chanting, the voice summoning the beast. Fear clutched her heart in a tight squeeze. Lights danced in her periphery. She collapsed on the ground.

Lewis sat in the backseat of the car feeling useless. "Bugger me, Jim," he whispered. "You said find the lass. Now what—sit on me arse while the police grope in the dark? Give a chap a lift, ol' friend. Where is she?"

The hair on Lewis's arms stood up. Visions swam in his head. Castles, demons, daggers, and blood.

Sam and Andrew radioed the team. They directed the drone operator to where they had seen the castle on the monitor. Their drone operator zoomed in on an area toward the back of the property. Mindful of cameras and traps, the duo took off running. Dogs, barking in the distance, sounded stationary, as if they were penned. After about a mile, they caught a glimpse of the castle, nestled between sequoias, shrubs, ferns, and berry bushes. The lush greenery muffled their footfall as they ran toward the structure. But what they hadn't figured out was how to get in.

Lewis helped Suzanne to her feet. He grabbed a bottle of water from the car, uncapped it, and brought it to her lips. "Slow and easy, lass."

Suzanne bent over, her hands on her knees. "This is the part that sucks. I can feel her pain, and I can't do a damn thing to help her."

"Take another sip, we'll figure it out."

Suzanne snapped at him, "You got any brilliant ideas? I sure don't."

She stood erect, swiping her hands through her hair, her tone softer. "Now who's getting testy?"

"Don't ye start apologizin' now. Audra's in the castle. I see her, she's lying on a stone slab, shackled. He's performin' some kind of a ritual."

"We can't go in there," she said. "The S.W.A.T. team has direct orders to–"

"Y'got yer phone. Call Sam, tell him I see a footbridge on the north side of the buildin'. Jim says everythin' is hidden in plain sight."

Sam led Andrew and his team to the north side of the castle. There, they found the footbridge, just as Lew described. Once inside, they examined the stone blocks for buttons and levers. After a thorough search, they found one that opened a stone panel leading to a stairway. The men split up, filing down dank narrow hallways. Sam and Andrew took the stairs leading to an underground garage where they found a police cruiser with Officer Jenksen's dead body inside. Beyond that, an iron grate blocked the entryway to what looked like a tunnel.

"Hold the light," Andrew commanded, extracting a small case from his vest pocket. He chose two picks, stuck them inside the lock, working his magic. When he heard the locking mechanism click, he twisted the shaft releasing it from the body. He discarded the lock, and unlatched the grate. They followed the tunnel at a quick pace, checking the walls for inconsistencies. The tunnel veered to the right, taking them into the heart of the castle. Sam followed Andrew, tapping on the walls. After fifty feet they heard a hollow *thud*.

Audra opened her eyes in disbelief. *I must be dead.* She saw the devil hovering over her naked body, anointing her with her own blood. His eyes, burning hot coals made her think of paintings she saw at the Belvedere castle depicting chaos, pillars of fire, demons swarming sinners, devouring their souls. Here, there was only one demon. Perhaps the rest were on holiday? Or maybe her sins were unworthy. She had never felt the need to go to church, which was always a strike against her when arguments ensued with her parents regarding her independence.

"I'm a good girl," she murmured. She never imagined she'd end up in hell. Yet, *here I am.*

"You were never a good girl, Mother." Jake said flatly. "Look at what you created? The devil's spawn." His laughter echoed inside the chamber. "And now you get to feel my wrath."

Jake ran the tip of the dagger between her breasts. "I remember begging you—begging you to play with me, begging you to love me, begging you to make them stop. Do you remember what you told me?" He yanked Audra's hair, forcing her to face him. "You told me pain tempers a soul. You said if I learned to enjoy the experience, that one day I would enjoy inflicting pain on others. Well, you got your wish. Now it's *your* turn."

"I am NOT your mother," Audra cried. "I could never be so cruel," she sobbed.

"Cruel? Is that what you call what you and your friends did to me? To all those children?" Jake shook his head, his tone adamant. "Torture, mother. I'd call it *torture.*"

Suzanne's eyes scanned the room as the observer. Audra, chained as Lew had said, was conscious, and pleading for her life. The man stood over her, a dagger poised in his grip. Behind him, a rack of red satin robes, hanging from hooks. To the left of the table, she saw a stone wall, shifting her sight to the right, *a door.* She imagined Sam on the other side. *So close.*

Sam ran his hand along the vertical seam, feeling for anything that would serve as a latch, or lever. Nothing. He pounded on each stone block until he heard a thud. He lit the area with a flashlight, discovering one corner of the stone was worn. Slipping his fingertips beneath the worn area, he discovered a lip, and pulled. The stone cover opened, revealing a pin pad.

Andrew peered over Sam's shoulder. "Appears to be a mechanical keypad. Step back." Andrew produced a gadget the size of a flip phone and held it over the keypad. "19-1-20-1-14, there we go." The door opened. "Works on an alphabetical sequence."

"What did you spell?"

"Satan."

Jake whipped around, facing Sam and Andrew, their guns drawn. He moved closer to Audra, placing the dagger at her throat. "Stay back, or I'll kill her!"

Andrew stayed back. Sam stepped forward, dropping his gun to his side. "You don't want to do that Jake. Your mother would be so disappointed."

"You know nothing about my *mother*."

Sam swept the room with his open hand. "You spend a lot of time down here, Jacob? Mom set you up with your own little torture chamber? Is that why you faked your death?"

"*She* was the devil, not me!"

"Prove it," Sam said. "Put the knife down. Move away from the girl."

Jake pressed the dagger further into Audra's flesh, drawing blood. Sam raised his gun, and shot one round, grazing Jake's ear. "The next one will hit between your eyes."

Jake dropped the knife, and crumbled to the floor. Sam grabbed a robe from the hook, covered Audra, unlatched her shackles, and gathered her into his arms. Andrew handcuffed Jake, and read him his rights.

The S.W.A.T. team left their posts and gathered by the front of the castle. Audra was put on a stretcher, and taken to the ambulance waiting by the house. Sam dialed Suzanne. "She's safe. Audra's safe."

Suzanne heard relief in Sam's voice, through a strain of tears. Her own eyes shed tears as she hugged Lewis. "She's on her way to the hospital. Sam will call us later."

Lewis threw his hat in the air. "Did ye hear, Jim?" he cried to the heavens. "The lass is safe!"

Andrew eased Jake into a squad car, and slid in beside him. "You don't seem like the type of guy to get your hands dirty, Jake, who got the girl for you?"

"I don't know what you're talking about. The girl found me. I didn't find her."

"That's not true. The girl was kidnapped from Vienna, and brought all the way here, just for you."

"How do you know that?"

"A little birdie told me. And they put a hit out on my buddy." Andrew touched Jakes injured ear. "This is nothing. Wait 'til the boys in prison find out what you are—they are going to have one helluva good time with you, Jakey boy." Andrew sighed. "That is unless you want to share a name with me."

"Ask my mother."

"It would be so much easier coming from you."

"I only know him as Giorgi."

"Giorgi. That's a start."

Angels

Audra peeked under the bandage between her breasts. No stitches. She laid her head against the pillow, when she heard a knock on the door.

Suzanne entered, along with Lewis, carrying a vase filled with a colorful bouquet. "I hope you don't mind our visit. Lewis is headed back to London tonight, and he wanted to meet you before he left."

"Jim didn't tell me how beau'iful ye were, lass. I'm chuffed it all worked out."

"We're all happy you're going to be okay. Sam said they're treating you for pneumonia, and a bladder infection, but you'll be fine in a week or two."

"My brother told me how you both were instrumental in finding me." A smile brightened her face. "Thank you both."

"You're welcome. I can't help but wonder if there were—"

"Others? Yes." Audra's eyes welled with tears. "I don't know what happened to them. I was taken off the boat separately."

"Your brother is an excellent detective. He will do what he can. After all, he found you, didn't he?"

Sam arrived on cue. He kissed Suzanne on the cheek, shook Lew's hand and went to Audra's side. "*Wie geht es meiner kleinen Prinzessin?*"

"Your little princess isn't so little anymore."

Sam leaned forward and kissed her nose. "You will always be my little princess." He patted her knee. "I called mom and dad. They are relieved to say the least. I also called Britta, she was a big help. She told me about the guy you met on the train."

"Rubio."

"Yes. I'm looking into these traffickers further."

"There are others, Sam. Children. Little children."

"Yes. Andrew is working on that." He turned to Suzanne and Lewis. "I have my friends here to help as well...we'll find them."

Lew's smile faded. "Find the angels, ye'll find the children."

Giorgi

Giorgi drove to his favorite flat in Salzburg, overlooking Hellbrunn Schlöss, a pleasure palace with trick fountains built in 1612 for prince-archbishop Markus Sittikus. Georgi's father had taken him to the palace when he was a child. He pointed out how humans indulged in different forms of pleasure. "Wet T-shirt" contests of yesteryear. A fornication playground. He said Master architect Santino Solari was brilliant, commending him for mixing fun and lust under the pretense of rest and relaxation. It was all there...man's appetite for all that is forbidden under God's rule, and yet Solari was commissioned to build the Salzburg Cathedral. His father claimed he was not ashamed of his profession, after all, it was not he who originated the idea.

He thought about how good it felt to be alone. Being in the U.S. gave him *agita*, and he'd been home a few hours when he heard Jake was arrested. His minions took him out before he had a chance to talk. At least that's what they claimed. The detective, the girl's brother had eluded them, but he had to trust they didn't fuck-up with Jake, and since there had been no sign of trouble, he felt assured the job was done. None the less, it never hurt to lay low.

Giorgi removed his kidskin boots and Alpaca socks. He unbuttoned the top two buttons of his Loro Piana Vicuña polo about to pull it over his head, when he heard a knock on the door. *No one knows I'm here.* He sat quietly on the edge of the bed, commending himself for remembering to latch the security chain. However, his penthouse suite was only accessible with a keycard. He got up and peeked through the fish-eye lens. *What is he doing here?*

Policeman Irlich von Steuben stood outside Giorgi's hotel room, anticipating the browbeating he would receive for daring to invade Giorgi's privacy, and worse, breaking protocol. Von Steuben knocked again, sensing the suspect's surprise, and anger, at the intrusion even before he opened the door. He was correct in his assumption.

"What the fuck do you want? How did you find me? How dare–"

Sam stepped into view. "Don't blame him, he was merely following orders." Sam gestured to the group of FBI agents blocking each end of the corridor. Sam smiled, like a shark, about to take a bite of something tasty. "I'm Detective Samson Metzger, the brother of the girl you had Rubio kidnap for Jacob Levitz. It will be my pleasure to see these men take you into custody." He paused for effect, "Oh, and by the way, we found the kids that were taken to...*Los Angeles*."

Giorgi's face paled. "I have no idea what you are talking about. There must be some mistake."

"No mistake." Sam nodded to the agents. "One thing the devil can never seem to grasp...the world is filled with angels..."

That morning, the L.A. Times reported:

INTERNATIONAL SEX TRAFFICKING RING EXPOSED—47 CHILDREN RESCUED

Three Arrests Include Hollywood Actress, Her Son, and Austrian Kingpin!

Following tips from Sacramento's Police Department, the FBI infiltrated a human trafficking ring selling children ages 2-17 for sex.

The sting began with the rescue of a young woman abducted in

Vienna and sold to 89-year-old-actress Adrianne Darr's son, Jacob Levitz, for sex.

Ms. Darr has been implicated in past procurements and subsequent murders of sex trafficking victims. Levitz's arrest led the L.A. police department to assist agents in rescuing 47 children from a warehouse near L.A.'s garment district at 3 a.m. yesterday.

Officials also arrested the head of the multi-billion-dollar operation, Giorgi Von Graff, in Salzburg.

Detective Samson Metzger, of the Goldorado Sheriff's Department claimed the tip that lead them to Los Angeles, the "City of Angels," was truly divine.

Return

Trudy greeted Lewis with open arms. "I knew y'd come back t'me, Luv."

"Can't say I'm not chuffed t'be back." He held her tight, kissing the top of her head. "One day, I'd like t'go back t'America...see the sights...together."

"Did y'get rid of yer demons?"

"For now. We got the bloody thugs that took the girl, but I can't say the visions won't 'appen again. Suzanne said dyin' changes a bloke. I believe she's right."

Trudy patted his chest. "At least it didn't change what's in 'ere."

"If anythin'," Lew said, "m' heart grew bigger."

"Oh dear, I almost forgot." Trudy rushed out of the room and returned with a heavy box. "This arrived for ye yesterday."

Lew sliced the box open with a butter knife and hurried to examine the contents. Joy washed over his face. "For the love of muffins," he said, pulling six books written by Clive Cussler and Robin Burcell out of the box. *All signed by the author.*

Sheena peeked in on Emmett. *What a day,* she thought. Emmett's fever returned to normal out of the blue. He was sleeping soundly, which he hadn't in weeks. His tiny hands rested beneath his cheek, his features relaxed. "Sleep, my little angel," she whispered.

———

AMEN

Morning drizzle disappeared revealing blue skies, and sunshine. "This is it," Sam said, leading Suzanne to an iron gate. Sam handed two tickets to the young lady at the door, and ushered Suzanne to the counter to pick up headphones for tours of the lower and upper floors of the Palace.

The couple strolled through the halls admiring frescoes painted by Carlo Innocenzo Carlone, Marcantonio Chiarini, and Gaetano Fanti, just as Audra had months earlier. Sam slipped his hand in Suzanne's, "This is where the Austrian State Treaty was signed in 1955, by Leopold Figi."

"I want to see, "The Kiss," Suzanne said, her lips finding his for a brief connection.

"The Klimt exhibit is in upper Belvedere. We can go there now if you like," he said, his eyes focused on her mouth.

"It's all so beautiful, I can only imagine growing up with all this culture at your fingertips."

"Wait until you see the gardens. We can get a good look from the balconies on the second floor, but you must experience the scent, and the beautiful arrangements with a cappuccino or a picnic lunch."

"Sounds like heaven," she said, leaning closer. "I feel like I'm dreaming."

Sam wrapped his arm around her and drew her close. “I aim to please.”

When the couple finished their tour, they stepped outside into the afternoon sun, cappuccinos in hand.

“This is our favorite spot,” he said, nodding toward a rose garden, filled with colors fit for Monet.

Their scent perfumed the air, and Suzanne breathed deeply to capture their essence. “I could stay here forever,” she said, taking a seat on a bench nearby. “I can see why this would be such a special memory for you and your family.”

As if Suzanne’s words manifested Audra, and the Metzgers, the couple saw them heading toward them. Sam greeted them with quick hugs, and the excitement of one about to show off a new car. “Mama, Papa, this is Suzanne.”

The Metzger’s extended their hands to shake Suzanne’s, but Audra intercepted by rushing in for a hug. “I’m so happy to see you!” Suzanne returned the hug enthusiastically.

Suddenly, clouds gathered overhead, the sky bruised with dark masses, swirling with thunder and lighting. Suzanne held Audra tighter. Over the girl’s shoulder, Suzanne could see the reason for the sudden change. Giorgi Von Graff, strutted toward them, a black crow perched on his shoulder. His eyes, glowing hot coals, his smile, a maw of razor-sharp teeth.

Closer.

Sam sheltered his parents under both arms. The wind blew in gusts so powerful the roses were stripped bare.

Closer.

Fear bubbled in Suzanne’s throat, thwarting her effort to scream.

Closer.

She tried with all her might.

Closer.

She could feel the heat from Giorgi’s body.

Closer.

Inches away.

Perspiration trickled down her brow. She clutched Audra tighter, opened her mouth wide, and pushed the air from her lungs. Finally, the sound escaped with a loud shrill.

"Suzanne!" Sam shook her shoulders. "Suzanne, wake up, it's not real."

Suzanne gasped for air. "I saw him, I saw Giorgi!"

"Giorgi's in prison, he's not going to hurt you, or anyone else again."

Sam lifted her chin, his lips brushed her eyelids, her nose, and settled on her mouth. "It's over, sweetheart. Everyone is safe."

"I had a dream...it was beautiful. We were at the Belvedere Palace, we saw all the magnificent artwork, you were showing me the gardens, we were drinking cappuccino, your parents and Audra showed up...and then...he was standing there, like the devil."

"He's evil all right," Sam said, snuggling Suzanne into his arms, "but I assure you, *he's just a man*."

The End

Acknowledgments

Borrowed Time 2 – Missing is based on facts, half-truths, and mostly fiction. When I began writing the book, I was on a Mediterranean cruise. I knew where I was going with the story, but something was missing. Literally! That's when the universe handed me a gem. The real-life Lewis Howard and his wife were seated at our dinner table. When Lewis began to tell me about his near-death experience, I knew the story was meant to be written, and he was the missing element I was looking for. And although I took some liberty with his account of what happened to him, the majority of what I wrote is true. Thank you, Lewis Howard, you are forever etched in my heart.

Another aspect of this book that is true to my heart is the subject matter. Human trafficking is *real*. I witnessed first hand the seduction of young girls near the train station in Cologne, Germany. My experience was not an isolated incident—it happens in your backyard, and all over the world. I would like to express my gratitude to my traveling partner, Beatrice Gregory, for being my sounding board and voice of reason when the incident broke my heart.

My gratitude to undercover agent Andrew (who remains anonymous), not only for answering my questions about human trafficking in Sacramento, California, one of the hottest trafficking spots in the United States, but for risking his life every day to eradicate crime where he can, and for rescues he has performed with his team. I also want to thank the fabulous author, Robin Burcell, for agreeing to be a character in my book. I am grateful to my friends, Noreen and Linda, who supply me with information to investigate, and psychic friend, Linda Schooler, for listening to me ramble and for her unwavering support.

Before I thank my writing community, I would like to thank my readers. Your support, reviews, feedback, and compliments have meant the world to me. *I write for you.* Special thanks to Nancy St. Germain for waiting patiently for this release!

To my critique group, Tarra, Michele, Linda, June, Cathy, Cheri, your support and suggestions have been more valuable than you know. To the El Dorado Writers Guild, thank you for your excellent feedback. I thrive on your expertise.

I am truly grateful to my talented cover artist, Karen Ann Phillips. You rock girl! To Tarra Thomas, my editor and formatter, thank you for putting up with my last-minute changes and all my "was's." I am also grateful to my talented author friend, Terry Shepherd, for whipping up extraordinary trailers and promos for my books at the drop of a hat. You kill it, my friend. I am blessed to have all of you, wonderful people in my life!

As always, I'd like to thank my family for their love and support. They are my joy, and the fuel that keeps me going. Special thanks to my sister, Kathy Partipilo, for being my tough and loving critic.

Lastly, I'd like to thank my late Mother for encouraging me to write and for being *my* angel.

BOOK 3: MIND GAMES

BORROWED TIME

BOOK 3 - MIND GAMES

Infinity Books

DÄNNA WILBERG

Contents

Dedication

This Book is Dedicated to "The People"
Free Your Mind

PROLOGUE

"The most beautiful experience we can have is the mysterious. It is the fundamental emotion that stands at the cradle of true art and true science."

—Albert Einstein, 'The World As I See It'

Dallen Foster plastered himself against the bathroom wall, his brow dripping sweat, his hands cupping his ears. Deafening high pitched chirps and obscure messages warping his brain. Next came the visions. Small children gathered in a park. Hundreds of them. Their little faces filled with joy.

Banging his head against the tiled surface he prayed, *make it stop.* But hurting himself and reaching out to God didn't deter the signals pummeling his brain. His body jerked forward and raced for the door. *Work to do.*

His lavish apartment once served as a respite, a reward for his ambitious nature. A successful internet business afforded him 3000 square feet of the finest furnishings money could buy, an enviable art collection, and a bird's-eye-view of Golden Gate Park. He once entertained family, friends, and gorgeous women. He attended mass on Christmas and Easter. But those times were gone. Padlocks, alarms, and motion detectors stood vigil over a life he didn't choose. It was as if Dallen Foster no longer existed. He had moved to Sacramento, obsessed, possessed, working for *them*.

Dallen gathered supplies for his mission. One AK-47, six magazines, a black hooded sweatshirt, a can of spray paint, and a balaclava. *Check*. He stuffed everything inside a duffel bag and zipped it closed. He reached in a chest of drawers, picked up the pouch he received in the mail that morning, and removed the contents. "One pill makes you larger, and one pill makes you small. And the one that *they* give you will put an end to it all." No sense dwelling on the obvious. Once the job was done, so was he. He inserted the pill in his shirt pocket, grateful he didn't have to eat a bullet, or blow the back of his head. However, he wasn't guaranteed an open casket. *Lucky me.*

For months he warred against the voices, feeling at times he'd won. Feeling as though *he* was in complete control of his mind, and that the messages weren't real. Rationalizing, if he slowed down and eliminated stress, he'd be fine. It seemed the more games he played on his computer or his phone as a distraction, the worse it got. Sanity wasn't something he'd ever questioned. Until now.

When the phone rang, he answered without hesitation. "I'm ready," he said.

"Do you know where you are going?"

"Yes."

"Do you have everything you need?"

Dallen patted the small object in his shirt pocket. "Yes."

"Good. And the message you will leave?"

The mnemonic acronym "FANBOYS" danced in his head with a little tune. He sang, "Fanboys, Fanboys, Fanboys carry the fan. Fanboys, Fanboys, the boys who have a plan."

———

Paris

The clicking sound of Suzanne Cash's heels resounded on narrow Parisian cobblestone streets. Upon her approach to the entrance of the Monterosa Hotel, on Rue la Bruyère, she noticed a discarded bouquet leaning against a trash receptacle. Her eyes were drawn to the bouquet, like a fruit fly to a sticky treat. She loved flowers, and from what she could see, the bouquet was exquisite. *Why throw them away?* She stooped down to examine the beautiful blooms and spotted a thin gold band with a small solitaire diamond circling one bent stem. When she touched the ring, her noetic faculties kicked in—she felt *anger*. The words "Why her?" assaulted her brain, launching her back to another time, another place. *Jack*. Suzanne pictured her teenage self, and *Jack, kissing another girl...betrayal.* Suzanne dropped the bouquet and dashed inside the hotel, shaking the memory from her mind. *I'm past the hurt, past the blame. I'm with Sam now. Happy.*

Even psychics deserve a vacation, she reminded herself. But as the elevator rose to the fifth floor, she couldn't push the foreboding feeling from her gut. Her inner voice pleaded with the universe, *Leave me in peace.*

She entered her room, immersed in sunlight, frilly pillows, and charm. She felt as though she walked into *Vogue* magazine, and at any moment a French model would return and claim her space. Cheerful pinks, fuchsias, lime green, and black gave the room a nostalgic 70's vibe. Floral paintings complemented modern furniture and a brightly colored headboard. A white bedspread, with a black and white striped coverlet, reflected light coming through tall windows facing the street. Suzanne slipped out of her shoes, sat in a molded plastic chair near the window, and rubbed her sore feet.

She let her mind drift to Montmartre and her climb to see the Sacre-Coeur Basilica. She had set out early that morning to purchase a piece of art to take home as a souvenir, but became so overwhelmed with her choices, she decided to wait for Sam's arrival in hopes he would help her decide. Instead, she mastered the 300 stairs it took to reach Sacre-Coeur. She closed her eyes, reliving the breathtaking view in her mind. The Eiffel Tower, the Pantheon, Montparnasse Tower, Bois de Vincennes, Basilica of Saint Denis, and Buttes-Chaumont. *Top of the world.* The next two weeks would be spent exploring those sites with Sam. She longed to see Moulin Rouge up close, experience French cafés, and dine al fresco at the world's finest restaurants.

An offensive smell diverted her attention, and she stood to peer out the window. Across the street, on a windowsill a few floors above hers and to the left, sat a young woman smoking a cigarette. Her dark pageboy cut and red lipstick made her look mysterious. One long fish-net-covered leg dangled over the edge of the sill. Suzanne was enthralled with her blasé demeanor until the young woman began singing a haunting tune. Her voice echoed between the buildings. The words she sang gave Suzanne chills.

> Fanboy, fanboy, le garçon qui porte le éventail. Fanboy, fanboy, le garçon qui a un plan.

Visions surged through Suzanne's third eye; the bouquet left to rot in the street, the diamond ring, *a broken heart*...death, destruction. *Not again.* She headed for the bathroom, determined to stop the madness pummeling her brain. What would her psychic friend Linda Schooler tell her to do? *Breathe.* She took several deep breaths. *Let it go.*

Once the tub filled with water, Suzanne gathered her auburn tresses into a top knot and stripped out of the deep blue sundress that complemented her sapphire eyes. She languished in warm water scented with essential oils, relaxing her body and soul. She was on the verge of dozing when she heard sirens. The foreboding feeling she had earlier returned. The shrilling sound made the hair on the nape of her neck stand up.

Suzanne quickly dried, threw on a robe, and went to spy on the emergency vehicles gathering across the street. Below she saw the reason for the calamity. The young woman she saw earlier in the window lay twisted on the cobblestone street, blood pooling around her dark hair.

Suzanne gasped. Images swirled in her head. Snakes hissed, wings fluttered, hearts beat out of sync. Masked faces appeared, disappeared, only to reappear again. Eyes, large, not human loomed in the background. *What does it all mean*?

Suzanne instinctively knew the girl had acted on her own volition. Was she depressed? Did the flowers belong to her? Had she reached a point of desperation? Was her heart broken beyond repair? *What made her take her life?* Suzanne shuddered. Answers eluded her. *Too late.* There was nothing she could do. Her heart felt heavy. She knew something was wrong and yet...

A knock on the door stopped the verbal lashing going on in her head. She pressed her cheek to the door.

"Who is it?"

"Who are you expecting?" he asked, his voice low, seductive.

The response created a welcome visual. Salt and Pepper hair, hazel eyes, a lean, stocky build with lips that melted her butter. "Sam!" She opened the door and flew into his arms, holding him tight. "I thought you weren't coming until tomorrow?"

"That guy we arrested for elder abuse was arraigned a day early, so I changed my flight—what's going on out there? Traffic is in one big snarl."

"A woman—a young woman fell to her death." Suzanne pulled Sam inside and shut the door. "I saw her right before—" Suzanne gasped for air. Her words stung her throat. "I was in the bath when it happened. I can't be sure. One minute she was smoking a cigarette—the next she was lying in the street like a mangled doll."

Sam drew her near, crushing her in his embrace. He kissed the top of her head, working his way to her forehead, temple, and cheek. "I'm so sorry you had to witness that."

Suzanne related the day's experience, seeing the flowers, the visions, the eerie tune. "It gave me the creeps. I couldn't listen." Tears filled her eyes. "I walked away."

"You couldn't have known, sweetheart," he said leading her to the bed. "Sit. Would you like me to get you a cup of tea? A glass of wine?"

Suzanne opened the sash on her robe, and let the garment slide to the floor. No words were needed. Sam could tell by the fire in her eyes what she needed most.

Their lovemaking progressed from passionate kisses to bittersweet sex, Suzanne relieving her pain and frustration, Sam wanting to please. He hadn't seen this side of her and didn't know what to think, her hunger insatiable as she mounted him and took control. Admittedly, she gave him a run for his money, but deep inside, he knew what she was doing. *Punishing herself.* She blamed herself for not saving the girl. The curse of her gift was not being able to fit the pieces together all at once. He flipped her over, pinning her beneath him. He kissed her eyes and the corner of her mouth, slowing down the rhythm of each thrust. She tossed her head from side to side, her breathing heavy. When she cried out, he took her to a place of ecstasy and joined her there.

**

The next morning, they lingered in the hotel café, drinking cappuccinos and eating croissants. Suzanne shredded hers, her focus on the destruction, rather than the taste. Sam caught her attention. "Where would you like to start today? The Louvre? Notre-Dame?"

"I—" She lowered her gaze, gathered the crumbs on her plate into a heap, and pushed her plate away. "Let's hop an excursion boat, take a trip down the Seine. It's a beautiful day for that, don't you think?"

Sam was surprised at her change of heart. "Sounds like the perfect plan."

"I want to see everything at once!"

He reached for her hand. "I don't know if I can make that happen, but I'll try." He brought her hand to his lips. "Ma Cherie."

Suzanne and Sam ordered an Uber to take them to the Ponte Alexandre III, an ornate bridge connecting the Champs-Élysées quarter with those of the Invalides and Eiffel Tower. From there, they walked down to the water, where they bought tickets for one of the River Limousines.

"I have never seen such beauty," Suzanne exclaimed, turning in all directions as they rode down the Seine. "Look!" She pointed to the Eiffel Tower as it came into view.

"We'll come back at night. The lights are not to be missed." Sam drew her closer. "The first time I saw the tower lit up, I dreamt of a moment like this. Cruising down the Seine, with my girl at my side. I didn't even know you then, but somehow I knew when it happened, it would be perfect." He kissed her lips. "And it is."

Suzanne beamed with joy. Every inch of her was elated, wrapped up in such an exquisite moment. Every inch, except one. That one little spot, niggling at her like a pesky fly buzzing around her head. An inkling, telling her it wasn't over. An intuitive nod, telling her trouble was on the horizon. *It's just begun.*

**

Back at the hotel, Suzanne and Sam changed for dinner. "Zip me up, please," she said, presenting her back to Sam. His warm fingertips lingered at the base of her spine. As he slid the zipper midback, goosebumps gathered on her flesh. "The reservations are for nine?" She asked, pivoting on one black patent leather pump until they were nose to nose. His eyes darkened.

"You have something else in mind?"

She snickered. "Yes, but I'm a patient woman."

"And if I'm not a patient man?" He lifted her chin and kissed her lips. A soft moan escaped his throat.

She nuzzled his neck. "Five hundred dollars apiece for tickets," she whispered in his ear. "I can wait."

"I suggest you quit teasing me then and finish dressing." He patted her behind, sending her into a fit of laughter.

"We can resume later."

"Promise?" He held her close and danced her around the room.

"I promise."

**

Twenty minutes later, the Uber arrived, transporting them to the other side of town. A fine mist lingered in the air, carrying with it a myriad of fragrances, typical of Paris: cigarette smoke, perfume—and a hint of Lavender. They waited in line, soaking up the atmosphere, the bright red windmill, neon lights, white puffy clouds against a blue-black sky. Suzanne was in awe. "It's surreal—prettier than any painting, she said, waving her hand to the beauty before her, "It's remarkable."

"Paris dans toute sa splendeur," he said, grinning from ear to ear. "Wait until you see what's inside."

As the crowd shuffled in, Suzanne snapped photos with her phone. The ornate lobby, the tables surrounding the stage, bottles of French Champagne awaiting the guests. Tiered seating with heart-shaped wrought iron railings, glass partitions, trimmed in mosaic cut mirrors. Suzanne absorbed as much beauty as possible as they were escorted to their seats by a handsome, bare-chested dancer dressed in tails.

They dined on pan-roasted veal tenderloin, whipped carrots with cumin, crispy polenta, and feta cheese, in a simple sauce. For dessert, Suzanne ordered a chocolate and caramel tart with roasted peanuts, and cacao crumble. Sam ordered mousse made with creamy soft cheese filled with fresh strawberries, topped with granola with seeds and cereals.

When the house lights lowered, small, red-shaded lamps dotted the room, like stars in the sky. Sam grabbed Suzanne's hand. She smiled and touched his cheek. "I'm so happy," she said. As the spotlight lit the stage, and the music began, Sam slipped his arm around her shoulders. She settled against him to watch the show.

Scantily dressed women filed onto the stage, adorned in plumes of feathers, rhinestones, and sequins. Canned lights flooded the stage in various colors syncing with the music. The costumes reflected the changing colors, adding to the mood. Long, lean bodies, some bare-breasted, some wearing jeweled tops, or sequined jackets performed high-kicks, back flips, and the splits. When new faces gathered for the can-can, the crowd went wild.

As the dancers finished one act, another began, initiating thunderous applause and wolf whistles from the audience. When the show ended, Suzanne and Sam jumped to their feet, clapping like mad.

"I can't believe what I just witnessed," she said, walking beside Sam toward the door. "That is the most magnificent show I have ever seen."

"There are many exquisite shows in Paris, but Moulin Rouge has always been a favorite."

"Did your family visit Paris often?"

"It was only a 5 1/2-hour train ride on ICE from Munich. When my father had an unusually stressful week at work, he'd call my mother and say, 'Pack up the children, we're going to Paris!'"

"I can only imagine what it was like growing up surrounded by all of this amazing artistry." She turned to catch one last glance at the red windmill and bright lights as they slipped inside their Uber. Suddenly, a pain stabbed her left temple.

Sam looked concerned. "Are you ok?"

"Must've been the strobe lights in the last act. I'll be fine." She glanced out the window, pressing two fingertips against the pain. She didn't see the silhouetted figure climb up on the sixth-floor apartment railing above the BALI sign, next to Moulin Rouge. Moments after they drove away from the curb, the figure launched himself into the air, a swan dive plunging him 100 feet to his death.

**

Suzanne and Sam exited the Uber in front of their hotel. "Would you like to walk for a bit, Suzanne? Get rid of your headache?"

Suzanne stood motionless. *The flowers.* She stepped off the curb and walked towards the trash receptacle. The bouquet was still there. Suzanne reached for the tiny gold ring. When she held it in her hand, the pain in her head grew sharper.

"Suzanne? What is it?"

"I don't know." She held her hand out. "Something about this ring is haunting me, and I don't know why."

Sam examined the ring. "I can tell you one thing for sure—it's not real."

"Isn't trash picked up daily?"

"The flowers were next to the recycle container, that gets picked up bi-weekly." He handed the ring back to Suzanne. "Let's go inside."

Sam's energy level dropped. Suzanne could feel it. Was he disappointed that their perfect evening was ruined by her headache? Or wanting to know more about the ring? His mood shift matched hers. She felt like crying. *Why?*

"I wish I could turn it off, Sam," she said stepping into the elevator.

"I wish I could turn it off for you," he replied.

"I ruined the evening, didn't I?"

"Never," he said, caressing her shoulders. "I know how that zipper works." He winked. "And I have just the thing for that headache of yours."

As if he waved a magic wand, she felt better. He had a way of performing magic on her soul.

Sam hung the "Ne Pas Déranger" sign on the handle, turned the lock, and chained the door.

He ran a warm bath filled with bubbles, grabbed two glasses, and filled one with chilled champagne. "Let me help you out of this sexy dress," he said, reaching behind her.

Suzanne stepped out of her dress slowly, inviting Sam to appreciate her black lace bra and thong. "Do I need a little more glitz and a few feathers to entice you?"

Sam's hazel eyes smoldered to a deeper shade of green. He found her lips and answered her question with his kiss. His hands roamed her body as he removed her black lace. Once she was immersed in bubbles, he handed her a glass of champagne. He undressed, filled his glass with Perrier, and eased himself into the tub across from her.

"Un toast à une soirée parfaite, avec la femme parfait."

She laughed. "You know my French sucks."

He held up his glass. "A toast to a perfect evening with the perfect woman."

They clinked glasses. "To the only man who knows my heart."

**

The next morning Sam and Suzanne joined the other hotel patrons for a light breakfast buffet. Coffee, pastries, and juice. Each table was decorated with a vase of fresh flowers and the morning newspaper.

Sam opened the paper and sipped his coffee while Suzanne devoured a chocolate-filled croissant. "Anything interesting?"

Sam's cinched brow was a dead giveaway.

"Sam?"

Sam flipped the newspaper around to face her. The picture on the front page needed no interpretation. Police surrounded a body, lying in the street. On-lookers pointed to the building next to the Moulin Rouge. Some covered their mouths in horror. Some cried. The headline read: Deux Suicides en Deux Jours!

Suzanne felt dizzy. She handed the paper back to Sam. "This is just the beginning."

"Why do you say that?

"It's not just happening here," she said, her tone flat.

Sam took out his phone and searched the word suicides and the current date. He was shocked to learn there were 67 in the past two days alone. He turned the screen toward Suzanne. "What's going on?"

"All I know is that there will be more, and not all the circumstances will be cut and dry. There will be other victims as well."

"Lemmings?"

Suzanne rolled her eyes. "Lemmings don't commit suicide."

"I saw it happen in a Disney movie. It was something I couldn't unsee for a long time."

"The filmmaker forced the lemmings off the cliff. It isn't their nature to jump." Her words struck a chord. "That's it! It's not in their nature. These suicides are being orchestrated somehow."

"How can that be?"

"You don't believe me?"

"It's not that—"

Suzanne lifted one brow. "Not what?"

"Hard to wrap my head around some sinister force causing people to jump off of buildings."

Suzanne leaned back, her eyes blazing. "We haven't seen the worst of it yet."

———

Dancing with the Devil

Roger Salvo, CEO of InnerVibes Corp. sat behind his desk, hands steepled in front of him. Every time he pressed "send" he had hoped it would be his last—however, *Once you dance with the devil, "they" own you, mind, body, and soul.*

He had always been a techno-geek. In high school, he learned how to infuse subliminal messages into different modalities using an antiquated technique developed by James Vicary in 1957. When Vicary flashed pictures of Coca-Cola and popcorn during a movie, refreshment sales began to skyrocket. Vicary's technique had caused significant controversy, but as the advertising world blossomed, various ad agencies were known for peppering TV commercials with lures, enhancing piped-in-music with subliminal messages, and implanting print ads with sexual innuendos. Roger studied the science and psychology of subliminal suggestion on every level. Just about the time the Federal Trade Commission cracked down on the frequency and use of such techniques, Roger joined the military.

Having served in Desert Storm as an intelligence officer, Roger was able to put his talents to good use. He was an integral part of an operation in Riyadh, Saudi Arabia, using what they called a "Silent Subliminal Presentation System" invented by a guy named Oliver M. Lowery. The operation took control of the FM radio transmitters, broadcasting subliminal signals that instilled fear, anxiety, and negative emotions into the listeners, thus causing mass disbursement. Little did he know he was being groomed for something more sinister.

When he returned to the States in 1992, he married his high school sweetheart, Rebecca, the daughter of a California Senator. They bought a home, started a family...Life was good until three and a half years ago when he was invited to a party on a mega yacht docked at Pier 39 in San Francisco. Rebecca was in Florida, presiding over her grandmother's failing health. She convinced him to go to the party without her by stating, "I know you loathe parties, hon, but think of your career—all of California's elite will be there." In closing, she said that he should be flattered by the invitation.

As always, his wife was right. The guest list included Government Officials, Hollywood moguls, A-list musicians, and a host of cover girls, and models. Not a big drinker, he opted for a microbrew served by a big-busted Spanish beauty who could melt snow with her brown eyes. The next thing he knew it was dawn, he was put in a dingy and transported back to shore. It wasn't until a month later when he received a Federal Express package containing disgusting, compromising photos of him with a six-year-old boy, that he realized his life was over. Guilt and shame held him hostage, but a group of powerful players had him by the balls. His only escape from their grip was death.

The first time he received instructions, for their so-called "experiment," Roger thought he could buy his freedom. He followed their instructions to a "T," implementing knowledge gleaned from good 'ol Oliver Lowery's mind-altering subliminal carrier technology, using a very low, or high, audio frequency that delivered desired intelligence into the brain via loudspeakers, earphones, or piezoelectric transducers. Roger designed a program that would infiltrate a popular video game with negative, degrading, despairing language to be drilled into the psyche of the player. However, when he began seeing a rash of suicides pop up in the news, he felt sick. So much for racking up good karma. *What goes around, comes around.* The dubious words stuck in his head like a mantra.

The orders he received next were more disturbing than the first. His instructions, convince the listener of a selected frequency inserted into a specific song to commit murder, and then kill themselves. *No mess.*

When he balked at his orders, he received more photos, this time, his loving wife, mother of three honor roll students, chairman of the Soroptimist Club, pillar of the community, in a compromising position with the family dog. He had no idea how they got to her or when, but they may as well have stabbed him in the heart. He had no choice but to obey.

The pattern was becoming clear. These experiments served as a distraction from something bigger going on in the government, and the implementation was becoming as effortless as downloading an update on a cell phone. He had no idea when or where the "experiments" would take place, but what he did know is that if he didn't pay the piper, his family was doomed.

Roger thought about going to the police or the media, but who could he trust? The powers that be had him by the short hairs. It would take someone large and in charge to blow the whistle. Someone influential, like the President. But that notion came and went. *Puppet masters rule the world.* There were minions like him everywhere, laying down code, collecting a paycheck. *Trying to survive.* Each time he heard of a mass shooting, he wanted to rip out his heart. Washington, Scotland, Azerbaijan, Belgium, France, Israel, Italy, Spain—their reach global, their intent deadly. The agenda was far more sinister than he had imagined.

In his younger days, Roger had listened to Jim Morrison and his warped messages; however he hadn't dwelled on the lyrics like so many others did. Knowing a little something about the MK-Ultra, aka Monarch Mind Control, he suspected "they" controlled a good portion of the industry, and he wondered if it were true that the singer was one of their musical weapons unleashed on an unsuspecting public. Allegedly, Morrison's mission was to influence the wayward, lead them into a web of destruction with his devil-like timbre, hypnotic music, and dark poetry. And who couldn't relate to Bob Dylan? *The line it is drawn, the curse it is cast.* Disney, himself, was an informant for the F.B.I. and had dealings with the CIA, and was said to have used his family-friendly movies to control the minds of children. The most blatant use of control was the MK Ultra "Kitten" program. Young women bending the minds of the masses with their debauchery, dressed as famous and popular animation characters, donned in skintight animal prints to signify their "Kitten" programming, implementing every satanic symbol in the book.

Roger had two children. He could only protect them to a point. He preached regularly the importance of getting off their phones, iPads, computers...spending more time in nature, playing sports, volunteering their time,. But once grown, they were out of his sight, and he felt helpless to save his kids from "them." Back then, *eleven and thirteen were prime ages for the devil's work.* Now, watching two-year-olds twerk on TikTok made him feel he didn't stand a chance against the evil taking over the world.

His target age for detonation was 18-30. One of the programs he wrote, many years ago, trolled chat rooms for disgruntled males seeking revenge, those being bullied, or enduring unfavorable family dynamics. The program used algorithms and untraceable bots to interact with the person, thus feeding them poisonous messages.

Mnemonics and "vibrational frequency" were key in getting the person to do "their" bidding. Thoughts and emotions possess their unique wave frequency with a distinctive pattern. His program overrode the pattern by creating instability in the existing wave and allowing a new preprogrammed wave to take over. It was, and remained, a one-on-one procedure. Since then, new and improved methods had been developed. Advanced technology introduced artificial intelligence into the mix, and he prayed his knowledge would one day become obsolete. But would they let him live? *Tried to run, tried to hide—Break on through to the other side.*

**

Carousel

Before leaving Paris, Suzanne penned a couple of postcards to send home, one to her brother Steven and wife Karen...one to Linda Schooler.

Suzanne told them both how blessed she felt to be in one of the most beautiful cities in the world, and how she looked forward to flying to Vienna the next day, but first, the moment she had been waiting for... *Sam and I will be visiting the Eiffel Tower tonight for our finale. I can't wait to see the lights!*

"Ready?" Sam appeared in the bathroom doorway, a towel wrapped around his small hips. "I just need to get dressed. I'll be done in five."

"Anyone ever tell you that you're a tease?"

"Me?" He grinned. "Now you on the other hand..."

Suzanne dropped the postcards on the nightstand and stepped into his arms. She inhaled his clean scent, as he embraced her. "I hate to leave Paris."

"We'll come back. Maybe for Christmas. You'd love the decorations." She pressed her body closer.

"Yeah," she said, her breath quickening, "I think I'd like—"

His kisses turned her words into soft purrs, his bare skin ignited her fire. She wiggled out of her sandals and mini-dress, and collapsed on the bed, pulling him with her. He unhooked her bra, flung it across the room, and began exploring her breasts with his lips and tongue. Next came her lace thong. As he kissed his way down to her belly, her moans turned to sighs. By the time he reached her sweet spot, she surrendered to his magic. He whipped the towel from his waist, lowered himself on top of her, and eased himself inside.

Gazing up at him, she realized, no one had ever taken her to the heights of passion the way he had. No one cared for her the way he did. No one made her heart sing the way that he did. The way he looked at her, touched her...the feelings he invoked whether they were in bed or on a bus...a tear slipped from the corner of her eye, and rolled down her cheek.

"What's wrong? Am I hurting you?" he asked.

"No. Quite the contrary. I think I'm falling in love."

He kissed her with such passion, she raised her hips wanting to consume him with her love, but instead, he stopped and rolled to one side.

She felt her stomach pitch. "Did I say something wrong?"

His smile radiated, making his face look flush. He wiped the tear from her cheek. "I'm—I—"

She pressed two fingers to his lips. "You don't have to say a word. I shouldn't have blurted that—"

His mouth came down so hard on hers, she lost her breath. "I've been fantasizing about this moment for so long, and now that it's here, I'm lost for words."

"Sam, there's no need to—" He stopped her protest, covering her mouth again with his.

"I love you," he said between kisses. "I've loved you since the first night I saw you in the hospital when you were shot. I loved you the night we had stress sex in that hotel in New York and deemed it a mistake. I loved you when you called me on my shit when my sister was missing. I love you now, tomorrow, and the next day...so please, don't apologize for giving me hope that you might feel the same."

Suzanne held him until their hearts beat as one. When he slipped back inside of her, it was more than passion that connected them, it was a gift that true lovers share.

**

Sam handed the Uber driver a ten Euro tip as they arrived at Jardin du Trocadéro, located in the 16th arrondissement. He kept his eye on Suzanne, whose face lit up like signage on a marquee. "Come on, let's walk," he said, reaching for her hand. "We have time."

They strolled along open space toward the Fountain of Warsaw, a long basin with twelve column-like water features, twenty-four smaller fountains, and ten arches. The beauty was never-ending. Beyond the fountains were more water features, and beyond that—the magnificent Eiffel Tower, now lit in preparation for the light show to come.

"It's mesmerizing," she exclaimed, as white lights twinkled on the tower like a million fireflies. Sam draped his arm around Suzanne, and she snuggled against him. "Thank you."

"Oh, but there is more..."

"How can you possibly top the Eiffel Tower? Or this enchanting evening?"

"I made reservations at Jules Verne restaurant, it's on the second floor of the tower."

Suzanne's eyes grew large. "You are *full* of surprises."

Sam checked his watch. "We have 45 minutes—do you still want to walk? Or shall I call an Uber?"

"I want to absorb every nuance. Let's walk."

**

The Maître D' greeted Sam and Suzanne and assigned a host to escort them to a window-side table overlooking the city. Suzanne was awed by the view. "How high are we?"

"410 feet. The tower stands 1,063 feet from top to bottom, and only 906 feet are accessible by the public. Quite incredible, don't you think?"

Suzanne leaned closer to the window to get a better look, but immediately shrank back, reigning in her feeling of falling. "I'm famished," she said.

"We are fortunate to have Frédéric Anton, a triple Michelin-starred chef preparing our meal," he said, pretending to twirl a mustache. "I recommend the seven-course tasting rather than the five to take full advantage of the culinary experience."

"Great advice, I wouldn't know which of these delectable items to eliminate. The Langoustine is making my mouth water." Suzanne closed her menu and looked nervously out the window."

"Suzanne? Everything okay?"

"I would love a cocktail."

Sam signaled the waiter and ordered a glass of their best French champagne. Suzanne noticed the waiter's bright red bow tie, and his long blond hair. Sam was talking, but her eyes were on the young man whose eyes bore through hers. A chill skittered down her spine. She looked away and focused on Sam.

"I would love to join you," he said. "But..." He reached for her hand across the table. "Have I told you how good you are for me?"

Suzanne's cheeks warmed. "I'm glad to hear that, I hope you always feel that way."

When they finished dining on a brilliant bouillabaisse consommé, crab, caviar, sea bass with green peas and mint, and langoustine ravioli, the waiter arrived with expresso and dessert.

"I've never tasted food like this. This strawberry-rhubarb tart is out of this world." She explored her palette with her tongue. "What am I tasting? A liquor?"

"Chef infuses the meringue with elderflower, and Zephyr gin. Try mine." Sam offered Suzanne a spoonful of chocolate soufflé with chocolate nib ice cream. She accepted the spoon with moans of pleasure. "Taste the gavotte," he said, handing her a cookie, "it's like a crispy crepe." Suzanne took a bite, closed her eyes, and moaned again.

"We must ride the carousel, it's an after-dinner tradition," he added.

They finished their coffee, paid the bill, and headed toward the elevator. The ride down was romantic with the city lights sparkling below. Sam swept Suzanne's hair to one side and kissed her. "I'm so glad I got to experience Paris with you."

Butterflies filled Suzanne's stomach. She had never dreamed of the joy she experienced with Sam. Compatibility while working together was one thing, and lord knows it wasn't always perfect, but getting to know him in a non-working environment showed a side of him she wanted forever. Years of broken promises and suppressed misery led to now, and she was grateful for every moment.

"This way," he said steering Suzanne toward the carousel. A slight breeze made the stroll comfortable, as they talked about art, their favorite songs, and Suzanne's anticipation about meeting his family in Vienna. When they arrived at the carousel, Sam bought two tickets. "I haven't been on here since I was a kid," he said, his smile contagious. "Few know this is my all-time favorite place in Paris."

He led Suzanne to the upper deck of the carousel and lifted her onto a white steed with flaring nostrils and a colorful harness. When the soft calliope music began to play and they started to move, Sam removed a small black box from his pocket. "I think you know how I feel about you, Suzanne, and if I didn't believe you felt the same way, I wouldn't be standing here, with sweaty palms, and a heartbeat that would rival Bill Elliot's NASCAR record...I love you, Suzanne. I want to spend the rest of my life with you, side by side, in the trenches, at the kitchen sink, and in our bed. I promise to be the best husband I can for you, I am great at folding laundry, cleaning my chin stubble out of the sink, and I always put the toilet seat down." He bent down on one knee. "Will you marry me?"

Suzanne's gaze was fixed on Sam's face as the carousel finished its second rotation. She opened her mouth to profess her love and accept Sam's proposal until a magnetic force drew her attention away from him and fixated on the figure perched on the railing of the Eiffel Tower's second-floor balcony. *Long blond hair, bright red bow tie.* The magical moment shattered to smithereens as she watched the figure plummet to the ground.

**

Joseph

Joseph Ernest Martin unloaded his gear in the auditorium, and began setting up his booth with a lavish display of purple draping; a small reading table dressed in gold lamé and purple satin; two ornate chairs; a six-foot pull-up poster; a sign-in book for his daily roster; and a stack of his books, "The Compass Guide to the Quest Tarot." Twice a year, the Unified Church in Marin County hosted a psychic fair, and Joseph was in high demand.

Normally, he'd be singing Italian ballads to a few of the other psychics and Tarot readers, but today he was troubled. It was his ritual to stop for a cold brew coffee with a double shot of expresso, and extra sweet cream foam on the way to the event. However, a traffic jam near the Mill Valley train station, where he planned to be one of the early birds at the Positive Vibe coffee shop, had crimped his desire. Seeing the flashing lights ignited his spidey senses, and he received a hit from the universe on the issue at hand. *Suicide.* He said a prayer, and flipped a U-turn and got back on Highway 1.

The incident struck a chord all day. He felt there was more to the story than what he predicted the news would report that evening. He pictured a diagram of the brain, dissected into color-coded compartments. Something was amiss. The diagram was lit up like a Christmas tree, something one would expect to see if a person were receiving shock treatments. His friend, Linda Schooler came to mind. *I wonder if she's having the same experience?*

Joseph went about his day, reading client after client, the image of the brain, niggling in the recess of his mind. Each client he saw gave off a vibe he hadn't witnessed collectively before. Fear and anger bubbled below the surface in every person he read, despite their calm exterior. Questions about their future, current boyfriend, girlfriend, or spouse elicited the most worrisome card to appear in the reading. *The ten of swords*. An image of a man lying face down with ten swords in his back. The meaning, past or present, referred to betrayal, suffering, a natural disaster, *a loss*. By the end of the day, Joseph was drained.

**

"Linda!" Joseph squinted at the sun. The sound of Linda's voice brought back fond memories. "It's Joseph, it's been ages, how are you?"

"Gosh, you've been on my mind," she replied, in her melodious voice.

"Had a weird experience, wanted to pass it by you, see if you're getting crazy hits..."

"Like birds dropping out of the sky?"

"More like people walking in front of trains."

"Oh no, that's never good."

"The ten of swords came up in all of my readings the other day. I have never had that happen before."

"What do you think it means?"

"Not really sure. I've got this image of an illustration of the brain stuck in my head. And someone used the Mill Valley train station for their exit clause the other day. The news eluded to the possibility the person was on drugs and not paying attention to the crossing signal, but I'm feeling otherwise."

"Interesting...I have a friend, Suzanne Cash...she might have insight into what's going on. I can arrange for a meeting once she gets back from Europe. Sound good?"

"Any friend of yours is a friend of mine. I would love to meet her."

"Okay then, I'll give you a buzz when she gets home. Meanwhile, be careful out there, and if you come to any conclusions, call me."

Joseph felt relieved. Linda grounded him. Friends for over twenty years, they did many psychic fairs together. He didn't bond with everybody, but from the get-go, he loved her spirit, integrity, and her delightful sense of humor. If this Suzanne was anything like her, he could count on adding another chair at his table.

Linda

Hearing from Joseph was always a treat, but today their conversation put a spin on what she had been feeling herself. *Birds falling from the sky*. The mere thought gave her chills. Her readings were always more personal, one-on-one, directed toward personal growth. She was adamant about keeping her clientele circulating, not wanting anyone to become dependent on the information imparted to her by the universe. She felt it was her calling to *assist* those stuck in a rut, not to drive the bus. *Free will.*

Linda walked out to her garden. Her tomato plants had grown two feet since she planted them. The blossoms that sprouted during the warm spell indicated an abundant summer crop. She bent down to affix a stray bean shoot to one of the six poles inserted in the bed for them to climb. As she traveled down the rows of vegetables that would soon be ready to harvest, she was drawn to the sky. More chemtrails, she thought, dismayed with the chemicals that would taint her crop. A random dizzy spell gave her pause. She grabbed a nearby hoe to steady herself. Just then, a blackbird whirled itself into her kitchen window. The **BAM** startled Linda to the point that she wobbled, and pitched forward. Her saving grace was the hoe that prevented her from landing on her head. *What the heck?* She moved toward the window expecting to see the injured bird floundering in the grass...but there was *nothing there.*

Rattled, she went back inside. A glass of water, and a few words with her Amazon parrot, Big Bird, would settle her nerves. "Hey, pretty bird," she called out, filling a tumbler with filtered water. "Hey pretty bird" echoed from the other room. She looked up, noticing the imprint the bird had left on her window. *I didn't imagine it.* Joseph's words came to mind...*ten of swords.* She mouthed a prayer of protection to herself. "Dear heavenly father, I pray that you watch over mankind, protect us from evil, and guide us with your grace. Amen."

In all the years Linda had been connecting to God, Jesus, and the universe, rarely had she encountered the opposition. The only dirt she played in was her garden. She didn't entertain thoughts of the devil, or evil, not wanting to feed the beast. *Birds falling from the sky.* She placed her hands over her heart. *There's no other explanation.*

The Tiff

"Got everything?" Sam gathered their suitcases by the door.

"I hope so." Suzanne peeked under the bed to make sure she packed all of her shoes.

"Our Uber should be here momentarily. I'll get our bags. Take your time."

"Sam—" Suzanne grabbed his arm. "How long are you going to stay mad at me?"

Sam released her hand. "I'm not mad, Suzanne. I'm disappointed, concerned. I'm having a five-year-old reaction to my thwarted proposal." He kissed her cheek. "I know it wasn't your fault, I just need to process what happened. It doesn't change the way I feel about you, it's just—"

"You're not sure you want to marry someone who attracts disaster?"

"Your words, not mine." He swiped his face with his hand. "When I met you, your visions had nothing to do with me—then when my sister was abducted, I—"

Suzanne's gaze dropped to the floor. "I think I should go home."

"Please don't. We can work it out—"

Suzanne's gaze turned to flint. Her sapphire eyes, cold. "I'm not so sure."

**

The ride to the airport was brutal. Suzanne's eyes stung from holding back tears. Sam remained resolute. His lips a tight slash, as his fingertips drummed on the middle console in the back seat of the Mercedes. Even the Uber driver felt the tension. Not a word was spoken.

When the driver reached the Beauvais-Tillé Airport, Suzanne waited until Sam sorted the luggage before she dropped the bomb. She returned her bags to the trunk and addressed the driver. "Take me to Charles De Gaulle. I'm going home."

Sam returned his bag to the trunk as well. "Charles De Gaulle it is, then. *WE* are going home."

**

Sam purchased two one-way tickets to Sacramento and joined Suzanne at the bar. She sat twirling a long-stem glass filled with what smelled like gin. Sam slid beside her and ordered a seltzer with lime.

"I've never proposed to a woman before. I wasn't anticipating rejection."

"It wasn't rejection, Sam—I couldn't—"

"You ran."

"I saw him—he looked like a bird, dropping from the sky!"

"You could've told me."

"You could've asked."

"I thought you were running from me."

"I was running from—*myself.*"

"I'm sorry."

"You're sorry! I ruined the whole trip." Tears flooded her eyes. He placed his hand over hers.

"It's bad isn't it?"

"The word epidemic pops into my head." She turned to face him, her features strained. "This is only the beginning...and I have no idea where it's coming from."

"What do you mean by 'it'?"

Suzanne raked her fingers through her hair. "I don't know how to explain it. Don't you see? I don't get a manual with this shit. I feel, I see, I hear, but none of it makes sense to me until the universe does a reveal." She glanced at him, her brow pinched tight. "Do you understand?"

"I'm trying."

"Are you? Do you think I wanted to spoil the moment, a moment that I can't take back? I love you. Yes, I would love to be your wife, but not like this. Not with this glass wall between us."

"You're right, perhaps we need more time to figure things out." He draped his arm around her shoulders and kissed her temple.

"People are dying, Sam, and I've been given a front-row seat. The hits are going to keep on coming. And I don't get to say how or when. And if you're going to take it personally every time it happens—"

"You don't think it's just a coincidence? That the victims were depressed? That they needed professional help?"

She shook her head. "No. I don't."

"What do you think caused them to jump?"

She closed her eyes. The words *while you were sleeping* zipped through her brain on a film reel. She met Sam's confusion with more of her own. "That was random. I just saw these words, like they're a film title or something."

"Let's look it up." Sam opened his phone and Suzanne typed in the words. "Look—" He held the phone so they both could see. "It's a TV series. Hong-Ju is haunted by premonitions in her dreams..."

"She can see into the future—she sees those who are going to die." She took Sam's phone and scrolled through the episodes. "Hmph. There's my validation."

"Validation of what?"

"More people are going to die. Look!"

Sam agreed—the series dealt with the topic at hand. "As a cop, you know I want facts, details, descriptions. It's my job to fix things, catch the bad guys. Make the streets safe again—not piss in the wind. My hands are tied unless you can provide me with a lead, Suzanne. It hurts me to see you suffer with these visions and experiences. I'm not an empath, but my heart is linked to yours now, and I'm aware when it skips a beat. Tell me how I can stop acting like a jerk, and help you."

"I wish I could. This is bigger than both of us. This isn't a 'him' or a 'her' doing this—it's a "they". She squeezed her lids shut. "I see an eye among the stars." She opened her eyes. "It sees all."

"Like a satellite or something? Do you think the victims were tied to a space project? I know guys that can run a check."

"I know you had your heart set on Vienna—"

"Yes, but if you don't want to stay, I can always change our return flight."

"I need to know that if I fall, you'll be there to catch me. This psychic stuff scares the hell out of me, and I don't know from one moment to the next what's going to be thrown at me."

Sam crumpled up his cocktail napkin. "If you're willing to put up with my petulance..." He lowered his gaze and jutted his bottom lip.

Suzanne initiated a truce. "I'll never understand how men can be so tough one minute, and gooey the next." She leaned in for a kiss.

"Our Ryanair flight leaves in a little less than two hours from Beauvais Airport. Do you want to try and catch it? Or would you rather go home?"

She placed her hand over his. "I'll go wherever you decide."

Actors Wanted

Lizzie Brecker dressed her 4 1/2-year-old daughter, Ainsley, in a bright yellow sunsuit, and pink jelly sandals. "Why are we always running late?" she asked, fastening a tiny turtle clip in Ainsley's blonde curls.

Ainsley shrugged. "I dunno."

"Preston and Charlotte are probably at the park, waiting for us," she mumbled, grabbing a ball cap from the coat hook by the door, and unbolting the lock. "Don't forget your backpack," she said. "You all ready to have some fun?"

"Yes, Mommy," Ainsley replied all smiles.

Lizzie helped her daughter into her car seat, tossed the little backpack, and a canvas bag containing an extra change of clothes, and snacks in the back. "If you get cast for this production, it's going to be a long day," she said and slipped behind the wheel. Despite her energetic demeanor, something in her gut didn't feel right. For the first time since she enrolled Ainsley at the Synchronicity Agency, she felt uneasy. *Paranoid.* She blamed the feeling on her hormones. Her period was late. Garret would be pissed. He warned her that using a condom wasn't the best choice for birth control, but she insisted it was better than taking a pill.

Her mind, muddled with unpaid bills, the impact of having another child on their already crimped lifestyle almost made her blow a stop sign. A man in a white pick-up truck laid on his horn.

"Jesus, get a grip!" she said.

It wasn't Garret's fault bookstores were folding all over the country. They felt fortunate he was able to pick up a trucking job to tide them over until he could finish his Masters and get a teaching job. Meanwhile, he gave up his passion for photography, which she thought was weird. He got hired to do a shoot that paid well. He said it wasn't "his thing," and dropped it. When she asked him about it again, he shrugged it off.

"I don't know, kiddo," she said, glancing at Ainsley through the rear-view mirror. "Is the world going crazy? Or is it just me?"

**

Emma Sagorski was busy inputting information into her computer when an email alert popped up on the screen. *Actors Wanted*. She'd been dabbling in the arts since fifth grade but never found the courage to give up her day job as a business analyst for WebCorp Designs to pursue her dream.

She'd almost given up acting after a job she had taken a few years ago, a modeling gig. All she had to do that night was look beautiful, mingle. The yacht was impressive, the guest list even more so, but the night turned into one she hadn't anticipated. Things she witnessed haunted her still. She tried telling a few friends what happened, but no one took her seriously. She figured it wasn't in their DNA to believe people were capable of such *evil*. Some days, she had a hard time believing it herself.

Emma twisted her long blonde hair around her fist, a nervous habit she couldn't seem to break. She dialed the number below the ad and listened to the phone ring several times. "Hello. You have reached Synchronicity Studios. Please leave a message."

"Hello, my name is Emma Sagorski. I'm calling about the acting job. Please call me at 555-622-0064." Emma ended the call and went back to her work. Within seconds, the phone rang.

"Emma, hi! This is Regina from Synchronicity Studios. We got your message, and we are so grateful that you called. We had three actresses flake on us at the last minute. We are still short two for a shoot this afternoon. Are you free?"

"Why sure, I–"

"Are you familiar with Discovery Park?

"In Sacramento?"

"Yes. You'll be checking in with Mr. Jay. He'll give you your instructions."

"Okay, but I live in the Bay Area—"

"Can you be there by 4:00?"

"Sure. What kind of role is it?"

"Let me get back into that screen–I just started working here. My second job–I have a debt to pay."

Emma listened to the silence on the other end of the phone until Regina popped back in.

"Hmm, says here it's a docudrama. The tagline reads: California rallies for stricter gun control laws after madman opens fire on unsuspecting families in park. Extras needed for victim roles."

"Thanks," Emma said. "I like to know what I'm walking into. Had a bad experience once."

**

Roger Salvo pushed away images of suicides, snipers, Unabombers, black bags filled with destructive weapons. *I'll find a way out*, he thought, picking up the photo on his desk. *Rebecca,* the love of his life. *Still as beautiful as the day we met.* His family meant the world to him. He would do anything to protect them, but he needed the madness to end. After all, technology had changed, soon his talent would become obsolete. W*e could change our names, leave the country. Start anew.* He dared not say it aloud. *They may be listening*. Just then, his cell phone rang. *Rebecca?* It was as if she were reading his mind. "Hey, babe. I was just thinking about you–"

"We must be on the same wavelength," she said. "I just heard our favorite song on the radio, and suddenly I got this wild idea. What do you say we pick up a bottle of Hour Glass Cabernet, a loaf of French bread, some of that brie with truffles you like and go to Discovery Park for a little picnic?"

"Sounds—*romantic.*"

"Not sure how romantic it will be, I went past the park earlier, there must be a family event going on—the park is crawling with kids—but it's such a beautiful day, and well, for some reason I feel *spontaneous*!"

He reached for her photo, trying to remember the last time they spent quality time together. "What did I do to deserve you?"

"You know what they say–what goes around, comes around."

How he loved her laugh.

Vienna

"It's like I imagined it to be." The Belvedere Palace gardens were in full bloom. Suzanne twirled around to face Sam's parents. "Germany must be as beautiful?"

"Yes, but Vienna has always been a favorite." Beatrice Metzger smiled. "We picnicked here at least twice a year when Samson and Audra were children. They always loved playing near the fountains."

"Did I hear my name?" Sam rushed toward his sister and spun her around. Giggling, she cried, "Let me go! Suzanne—help!"

Suzanne's heart was full. She hadn't been part of a family since her parents died. Her brother Steven and his wife Karen cared, but they lived a different lifestyle than she had become accustomed to since her near-death experience. Living with them during her recovery became awkward. When she left, they slowly distanced themselves. Once she and Ben were divorced, Steven felt better about giving her plenty of space. She watched the interaction between the Metzgers, craving the closeness they shared.

Audra put an arm around Suzanne's shoulders. "How is my favorite psychic?"

"Oh pish," she said making light with a wave of her hand. "How have you been?"

"Good! I was able to redeem myself with the family that hired me as an au pair. They are really sweet people, and I love the children. So fun. Smart. They like me, too."

Suzanne and the Metzgers strolled through the gardens, enjoying the sunshine and seventy-plus-degree weather. Sam's father had hardly spoken a word. She wondered if he disapproved of Sam's relationship with someone who heard voices and experienced visions.

They walked over to the Art Corner Restaurant for a nice lunch. Suzanne enjoyed Weiner schnitzel with roasted potatoes and a green salad with roasted beet dressing.

Sam's father opened up. "I never thanked you properly for helping Sam find Audra." His eyes were wet with emotion. "Sam has told us so much about you, I feel as though we are friends." He cleared his throat. "At least I hope so."

Suzanne patted his hand. "Of course, but you must know, this so-called gift of mine can become inconvenient at times. It's not something I can control." She smiled. "At least not yet. I'm working on it."

Sam's mother raised her water glass. "To Suzanne." Sam, Audra, and Frank followed suit. Suzanne blushed. After the botched proposal, Suzanne wasn't sure she deserved the warm welcome. She raised her glass. The sun reflected off the cut crystal fracturing the light, and casting a prism on the white tablecloth. A glimpse of an oncoming train flitted through the colors, bursting into white light. Suzanne set her glass on the table and pressed her fingertips to her temples, stopping the flow of blood to her brain.

Sam intervened. "You okay?"

"Yes," she lied. "The sun..." She shielded her face from the light. "It reflected off the glass and..." It was Beatrice who moved her chair, blocking the direct sun shining in Suzanne's eyes.

"There, dear. Better?"

"Yes, thank you." She touched her nose, checking to make sure it wasn't growing.

"What do you do for work?" Frank Metzger asked, casually dipping his bread in the gravy on his plate.

"I—I," Suzanne sputtered.

"Suzanne works with me, Dad. She consults for the Goldorado Sheriff's Department."

"I see, do you have children?"

"No. I don't," she said, casting her eyes downward. "Regretfully so," she added, glancing at Sam. "Time got away, as they say. I wish I had met your son in my youth. My life would've been so different."

"In what way, dear?" Beatrice asked.

"Mother!" Audra rolled her eyes. "Sam, make them stop!"

Suzanne chuckled. "It's fine. Every parent wants the best for their children."

Audra huffed. "We're adults now, capable of making our own decis —" Audra stopped mid-sentence.

"Thanks, kiddo," Sam squeezed Audra's hand. "Mom and Dad mean well."

"Yes. I'm sorry." Audra rose, dropping her napkin on her half-eaten dinner. "I need to use the restroom. Excuse me."

Suzanne popped out of her seat. "Excuse us both—I'll join you if you don't mind." She looped her arm through Audra's.

Sam sighed. "I'm glad we could meet today," he said, glancing from one face to the next. "I want you to love Suzanne as much as I do."

Beatrice tilted her head, a smile spreading across her face. "She's very pretty. If she makes you happy, we will learn to."

"Yes. Your mother is right. We are indebted to her."

"It's not like that, Dad. She expects nothing from you—except that you treat her like a normal person. And hopefully your daughter-in-law one day."

Beatrice clasped her hands together her elbows resting on the table. "I didn't see a ring. Are you two making plans?"

"I bought a ring. I'm waiting for the right moment." He looked away, remembering what happened when he proposed. He wondered if he would ever get past that moment. The body falling, the cries from those who witnessed it. He knew Suzanne was suppressing the horror she felt. Three suicides in three days. He moved his food around on his plate but barely took a bite. *What's next?* He pasted a smile on his face. "How do you feel about coming to the States?"

Beatrice and Frank exchanged concerned expressions. Sam banged his fork down on his plate. "What is it, Mom, Dad?"

"We were hoping you would marry here, that's all," his mom said. "Can't Suzanne's family come here?"

"We're jumping the gun here. She hasn't even—" Suzanne placed a hand on Sam's shoulder, feeling the tension in his muscles.

"I may have to learn to speak German," she said, kissing him on the cheek. "I am in love with this culture."

"Our home is 15 kilometers from Frankfort," Beatrice said, "a little town called Salzbach. Frank and I have lived there since Audra left for college. You must visit one day."

Suzanne saw a small lake, with flowers. "The arboretum, it's beautiful."

Beatrice held her hand to her chest. "How did you—"

"I see things. I'm sorry, I shouldn't have blurted that out."

"No, no, dear, you're fine—it's just that—" Her voice dropped to barely above a whisper, "Do you have any idea where I misplaced my mother's ruby ring?"

**

"They hate me." Suzanne shrugged out of her cranberry- colored blouse and unzipped the side zipper on her floral skirt. She stepped out of the garment and tossed it on the bed. "Face it, Sam, your parents will never accept me." She unhooked her bra and flung it next to the pile she was accumulating on the bed. "It's what I do, isn't it? They think I should be working at carnivals, with a paisley do-rag, a red velvet skirt, a floral vest, and—and crystal beads?"

"Sounds more like a gypsy—"

"Exactly! All I need is a crystal ball, and I'll be in business. How much should I charge?" She flung herself onto the pile of clothes and buried her face. Her shoulders shook.

"Suzanne, sweetheart, don't say that." He sat beside her, massaging her shaking shoulders.

She turned and flicked his hand away. "You! You're laughing!"

"It *is* rather comical, don't you think?" He caressed her cheek. "You'll have to forgive my mother. She's old school. It doesn't matter who you are, what you do...I'm her son. She's got this notion that no one will ever be good enough for me. Or Audra. But I do know once she gets to know you like I do, she'll be like butter."

"I liked it better when they were grateful and less speculative of me becoming your wife."

"Since we're on the subject, get dressed. I'm taking you somewhere special. Where the universe can't find you."

**

A train ride and three and a half hours later, Sam grabbed Suzanne's hand and sprinted toward the entrance to Schloss Hellbrun. He pointed to a hotel across the street. "That's where Georgi Von Graff was arrested for human trafficking."

"You brought me all the way here to show me that?"

"No. Come." He led her toward the ornamental gardens.

When she saw the structure she gasped, "Is that what I think it is? The gazebo from 'Sound of Music?'"

"The very one."

Suzanne ran ahead like a little girl chasing a butterfly. When she entered the gazebo, she twirled around. With outstretched arms, she sang, "Something in my youth or childhood..."

"I must have done something good," Sam replied. He took her hand and knelt, the velvet box clutched in his hand. Suddenly black birds pummeled the glass, startling Sam and Suzanne, making them run. Sam shoved the box back into his pocket. "I can't fuckin' believe this!"

They stood in disbelief as the birds slammed into the gazebo. "Let's get out of here," he said, reigning in his disappointment, for a second time.

**

"Why birds?" Suzanne bit into her apricot strudel.

The coffee shop they had ducked into provided them with the creature comforts they needed to sort things out.

Sam scrolled through his phone. "Says here that blackbirds will swarm to confuse or escape a predator. Something could have startled them."

"I didn't see anything, did you?"

"What are you thinking?"

"I'm not getting anything, except sharp pains in my head. Like a jolt of electricity." She shook her head. "It comes and goes."

Sam sat back, crossed his arms. "All I know is that something is preventing me from delivering my finest proposal to you." He grinned. "Think that's an omen?"

Suzanne licked powdered sugar from her lips. "I'm so sorry. You're right, the timing has sucked both times." She took another bite, powered sugar coating her upper lip. "For the record, I'm dying to see the ring you picked out."

Sam sipped his cappuccino. "Is that so?"

"I can't imagine anything more romantic than being proposed to in the gazebo from Sound of Music. I love that movie, especially when Christopher Plummer sings to Julie Andrews."

Sam chuckled. "I don't sing."

"Not even in the shower?"

"That's different, no audience."

"We could change that." All that was missing was the canary between her teeth. Her eyes sparkled, her lips puckered ever-so-slightly. "*Que sera, sera*. I haven't received messages from the Beyond or any place else. *I* propose we enjoy our couple of days in Vienna, and let God handle the bad guys."

"Who said anything about bad guys?"

"You don't still think the suicides were voluntary, do you?"

"What makes you think they weren't?"

"I—my gut says otherwise."

"Are you getting hits?"

"Well possibly, but not like the other times."

Sam steepled his fingers on the table. "What kind of bad guys would force someone to commit suicide? And why? What would be their purpose?"

"To prove they can," she blurted out.

"But why?"

"Remember Pinky and the Brain?"

"Yeah, the genetically altered lab mice that wanted to take over the world." Sam pondered the prospect. "Again, who would do such a thing?"

Suzanne laid her fork on her plate and picked up her cup. "I don't know, but what else could it be?" The image of the discarded flowers in Paris rose to her third eye. Were the flowers and the ring a premonition of her own proposal gone wrong? Or was there more to it? She assumed the young woman was distraught...*maybe not*. "And the birds—what was that all about?"

Sam tilted his head and shrugged. "If we're going to catch the next train back to the hotel, we better get going." As he rose, he noticed the security camera in the corner of the room. *Cameras everywhere. What if?*

No Way Out

Roger watched the 6 o'clock news. Another mass shooting. This one hit close to home. The camera panned Discovery Park, revealing flashing lights, chaos. The lens zoomed in on a mother in a ball cap as she wept, holding one pink jelly shoe. *We were just there.* He turned up the volume.

The anchor, Valerie Blix shoved the microphone into a young woman's face. "Valerie Blix, CBN news, tell us what happened—where were you when shots were fired?" The camera moved in for a close-up. The young woman twisted her long blonde hair around her fist. She stared at the ground, her eyes wide. "I—I was jogging—" Her shoulders trembled, tears welled in her eyes. She let go of her hair, smoothed it out, and started twisting all over again. "I heard a pop—you know, like a firecracker. Then I heard the screams."

Valerie's tone sharpened, going in for the kill. "And what did you see?"

"I saw this little girl—she had turtle barrettes in her hair—suddenly she dropped to the ground and her two little friends screamed." The young woman released her twisted hair and faced the camera. "I pray to God she's not—" The young woman buried her face in her hands and sobbed.

Valerie reclaimed the mic and camera. "There you have it, folks.

Several people have been shot—some of them children. The gunman has not, I repeat, has not been apprehended. I'm Valerie Blix, CBN, reporting from Discovery Park—back to you, John."

Roger reached for the remote and clicked the "off" button. His stomach churned. Acid rose in his esophagus. His heart pounded in his chest. "I'm not responsible." *I am not responsible.* He peeked out his living room window. *No one there.* Rebecca would be home soon. Upon hearing the news, his wife's subconscious would alert her something was amiss...She'd blink a few times, give him that *I know what you did* look, and leave the room without uttering a word. Even if she thought it, she'd never accuse him of being a monster...that was *his* tune...*Berate, besiege, and belittle.*

Minutes later, Rebecca blew in carrying plastic bags filled with more things she didn't need. *Retail therapy?* Her beautiful face, void of emotion, made him wonder. She dumped the bags on the kitchen table, bee-lined to the bathroom, and slammed the door. Roger waited, his elbows resting on his knees.

When she reappeared, he called out, "Hey babe—in here"

"Why are you sitting in the dark?" she asked, tossing her red hair to one side.

"A lot on my mind. Did you hear about the shooting at the park?"

"Do you want barbequed chicken? Or would you prefer I throw it in the air fryer?" She cupped one hand over her ear, then the other. "Do you hear that?"

"Hear what?"

"I can make a salad." She gave her head a quick shake as if trying to clear her ear, the same blank expression glued to her face, until...

Here it comes. Roger braced himself for "the look". "Something wrong, Bec?"

"My ear keeps ringing." She yanked on her earlobe. "Mind chopping a little red onion for the salad?"

Again, Roger wondered what suggestions were being plugged into Rebecca's subconscious. She wasn't herself, and he knew how subliminal messaging worked, he helped design the program. The ringing in her ears...*V2K.* He and Rebecca both were part of the remote neuro network. Their thoughts stored on the supercomputer in the sky. All the puppet masters needed to construct a bio-signature was to glean neurons from their DNA. Like fingerprints, energy was unique to each individual. Once the profile was established, "they" had carte blanche over a person's beta waves, and could manipulate the sequence any way they saw fit. Many nights Roger awoke from nightmares so real he couldn't tell if he was asleep or awake. And poor Rebecca, how many nights had she awakened screaming? He felt like a hypocrite, trying to console her, but what else could he do? She had no clue she was part of a social experiment, or that he was being held hostage by the same people who put bread on the table and the Cadillac in the garage.

He took several deep breaths, and tapped on his forehead, willing himself to reclaim an alpha brain wave state. Alpha, Theta, and Delta were harder to manipulate. He knew in a beta state he worried, loathed himself, gave in to his addictions to food, alcohol—he stayed in fight, flight, freeze mode. In beta mode he was susceptible...*his every thought—monitored by them.* He assumed "them," the National Security Agency's Signals Intelligence Division, used Electro-Magnetic Frequency Brain Stimulation for Remote Neural Monitoring and Electronic Brain Link. He didn't know if a reset was that simple, but he had to try. *Vibes up. I'll do whatever it takes.* He'd find a way for them both to go "secret."

**

Dallen Foster followed his orders to a "T." *Once out of sight, shed mask immediately, deposit into small trash bag. Deposit weapons and duffle bag into large trash bag. Drop small trash bag into dumpster behind Granite Bay Community Center. Take large trash bag home.* No one paid any attention to him or suspected a thing. *In the clear.*

Once home, he kicked off his boots, popped open a peanut-butter stout, and turned on his 80" TV. Ringing in his ears justified the "Fan Boy" song stuck in his head. "Fanboys, Fanboys, Fanboys carry the fan. Fanboys, Fanboys, the boys who have a plan." He clicked through channels oblivious to what he was looking for, until...he froze. "Missy Walker reporting for KNCY news...tragedy hit Sacramento California earlier this afternoon when a gunman opened fire at Discovery Park, killing 17 people, 5 of them children."

The camera cut to flashing lights, and a host of professionals talking in small groups, collecting evidence, measuring, and marking the space between bodies. Missy's solemn voice narrated over the footage.

"Police only have a vague description of the gunman, claiming he wore a ski mask that hid his features, and battle fatigues with no markings. Several witnesses claimed the shooter was 6 feet tall, with an athletic build, others say he was short, slight, and wore a military uniform. Police are still collecting evidence in hopes they will obtain more information. Residents are encouraged to come forward with any and all information pertaining to the shootings. Again, as of this minute, police have no suspects. Missy Walker, KNCY."

Dallen stared at the TV in disbelief. "What the fuck is this world coming to?"

The ringing in his ears grew louder and louder. He clamped his hands over his ears. *One last step.* He reached into his pocket. *One pill makes you larger, one pill makes you small, and the one that* **they** *give you will put an end to it all.* Dallen popped the pills in his mouth, washing them down with a swig of beer.

The ringing stopped—*so did his heart.*

Auf Wiedersehen

The next morning, Suzanne and Sam said their goodbyes to Sam's parents and Audra at the train station. Sam had no regrets. Overall, the visit was wonderful, and despite his folk's cool composure toward Suzanne, he knew they would love her as a daughter once they were officially engaged and a wedding date was set. Audra was already a fan, no convincing needed. She clung to Suzanne as if they were long-lost sisters, which made him happy. The bond between him and his sister returned quickly, and for that, he was grateful. Nevertheless, Audra had a lot of healing to do, and he promised to be by her side all the way, even if from a distance.

He gave Audra one last squeeze. "I'll Facetime you once we get home."

His mother moved in next, and Sam lifted her off her feet. "Put me down," she cried. Wrinkles gathered around faded blue eyes, reminding him how little time they had left together. He set her on her feet. "Ich liebe dich, mama," he said, kissing her cheek.

"I love you too, son," she said.

His dad started with a handshake, and ended with a stiff hug. "Good to see you, son." He turned to Suzanne. "A pleasure meeting you, dear. Again, my gratitude for saving my daughter."

Suzanne extended her hand, and was surprised when he grabbed her face and kissed her forehead instead. Sam's mother touched Suzanne's cheek. "Auf Wiedersehen, dear. Take good care of my son." Suzanne nodded, lost for words.

The train took them directly to the Air Berlin terminal, where they took the escalator to the second floor, and checked in. With an hour to spare, they browsed in the shops.

"Linda would love this," Suzanne said, picking up a cut crystal bird, but just as quickly decided against her choice and set it down. "That was freaky."

Sam peered over her shoulder. "Not the one?"

"No, it's perfect, but holding it made my stomach flip."

Sam slid his arm around her waist. "Weird."

"Very." Yet she was drawn to the crystal bird, and again, placed it in her hand. This time she saw a bird flying toward her, its eyes black, gleaming orbs. Its sharp beak opened emitting a screech so loud inside her head, her hands flew up to cover her ears. The crystal bird crashed to the floor, shattering into tiny glass shards.

The twelve-hour flight gave Suzanne time to regroup, relax, reflect. A myriad of thoughts swept through her mind. She reviewed her encounter with Sam's parents. She still wasn't sure where she stood. They seemed to like her, *just not for Sam.* She wished her own mother was there for reassurance.

She pictured her teenage self, sitting on the kitchen counter while her mother cleaned green beans from the garden. Whenever Suzanne said anything derogatory about herself, her mother would pop a green bean in her mouth to make her stop. Her mother persisted until Suzanne laughed her troubles away. Memories of such times had been tucked away, *with my first-grade report card, photos from my dance recitals, my high school diploma*. It was easier that way. She and her brother, Steven, vowed not to tear off scabs that took months to form after their parents were tragically killed in a car crash. She felt her mother's presence from time to time...smelled her perfume...caught herself sounding like her mother when she laughed. She saw the likeness of her dad in Steven, but they both kept silent. Now she doubted their decision to bury the pain. *Memories are all we have*. The point was to let them fade until their loss no longer hurt. And yet, now that she was older, she felt holding their memories in her heart allowed her to keep them close.

Suzanne wondered what Steven would think about her and Sam, together, planning a future. He never did come to grips with what he referred to as her 'woo-woo' stuff, and gave her crap about jumping from the flame into the fire when she told him she was divorcing Ben. *I hope you're getting divorced for the right reasons, and not so you can cozy up to that detective.* His words really hurt. Suzanne and Steven didn't talk much after their altercation. *Time to bury the hatchet.*

She'd come bearing gifts. A beautiful leather briefcase and a case of Dreissigacker Organic Riesling for Steven. For his wife, Karen, a strand of Mallorca pearls, and a buttery soft, handstitched purse in teal, her favorite color. *Maybe invite them for dinner, include Sam, call a truce.*

For Linda, she opted for a 6" Hofbauer crystal butterfly, instead of the bird. She pictured the delicate winged creature on Linda's window sill, catching the morning light. Having been gone two weeks, she suddenly felt homesick.

She turned to Sam, studying his profile. His patrician nose, soft lips, cleft chin, and thick black lashes. A twinge of excitement dallied between her knees. She rested her hand on his upper thigh. He caught his breath, lifting the corners of his mouth, revealing his dimples.

"How long before we land?" She asked, her voice low, and sultry.

He glanced at her hand and eased up to her gaze. "We could always sneak into the lavatory..."

Her hand inched closer to his crotch. "Why didn't I think of that?"

**

Sam, grinning now, laid his hand on top of hers. "We could get arrested." Her wicked smile put thoughts in his head, which in turn, directed his blood flow elsewhere. As much as he wanted her, losing his badge was a high price to pay. *But, oh,* he thought, *what a delightful way to break the law.* He brought her hand to his lips. He wanted to suck on her fingers, make her squirm. "Miss Cash, you are quite the tease."

"Tease?" Her eyes narrowed. "Wait until I get you home."

He lifted her chin, kissing her softly. "I cannot wait until 'forever' begins.

Run Lizzie Run

Lizzie Brecker, still holding on to her daughter's pink jelly shoe, was escorted to an ambulance near the edge of the taped-off area where the shooting occurred. She couldn't help but be awed by how realistic the set looked, from the medical personnel to the police officers and newscasters.

"Mommy!" Ainsley popped her head out from the white sheet covering her face.

"We'll drive you back to your car, Ma'am," said the paramedic, closing the door.

Lizzie hugged her daughter tight. "You lost your shoe, and a nice lady found it." She slipped the pink jelly on Ainsley's right foot. "Good job falling down, sweetie. You were a natural!"

Ainsley grinned, pleased with herself. "Can we stay and watch?"

The paramedic piped in, "Sorry sweetie, closed set—but you were fantastic." She put two fingers to her forehead, closing her eyes. "I see ice cream in your future." She opened her eyes in time to catch Lizzie's eye roll.

"Maybe after dinner," Lizzie said, patting her daughter's hand.

**

Lizzie noticed some of the other actors being dropped off in the distance. She wondered why they were all spread out. "Hey, I'll bet your daddy's home." But Ainsley ignored her, already distracted by her tablet. "Yep," Lizzie muttered and entered the freeway.

Garret's truck was parked in the driveway when she arrived home. The tailgate was down, he was loading garbage bags into the bed.

"Hey handsome—what doing?"

"Get Ainsley, and get in the house. *Now.*"

Lizzie bristled. How dare he talk to her like that, but seeing the way he was tossing the bags around, she sensed his urgency and did as she was told.

"What's—" Garret put his pointer finger to his lips. He grabbed a sheet of notepaper off the pad by the phone and began writing:

They're listening. Don't say a word. Stay calm. Go pack your things. I have blankets, pillows, towels, Ainsley's favorite toys, her clothes, shoes, and the cash I've been stashing since Ainsley was born. I'll grab my stuff next. Please play along, no matter what I say, okay?

Lizzie's eyes filled with tears, as she nodded slowly. "Hey, we had a great day. Our baby girl was a Rockstar!"

"That's great," he replied, his tone less than impressed. "You told me you were going to take that shit to Hospice today."

"I—"

"You what? I wanted that shit out of here weeks ago—months! You've been holding on to your mom's stuff, all the baby crap you've accumulated over the years. I'm tired of it, Liz. I want it gone! Now!" He kissed his fingertip, and pressed it to her lips."

"Fine! What do you want me to say?"

He winked his approval. "Nothin'. I'll do it my damn self." He wrote on the paper:

Finish packing. Meet me at Applebee's off Highway 50 and Cameron Park Drive.

"What about the bags in the closet," she asked, acting annoyed. "Did you get those too?"

"No—I didn't."

"They're too heavy for me, can you—"

"Dammit, Liz," he said walking toward the bedroom, "You gotta stop collecting so much shit. You know I like a tidy place, not all cluttered with tchotchkes, and every damn drawer stuffed to the hilt."

She followed him down the hall. "Can you just get the bags without bitchin'?"

Ainsley poked her head out of the bathroom. "Mommy, Daddy, are you mad?"

Lizzy gathered her mini-me in her arms. "No, Sugar Plum, we were discussing something—too loud?" Ainsley jutted her bottom lip and nodded her head. "Aw, sweetie, Mommy's sorry. C'mere." She squeezed her once more. "Wanna help Mommy bring some clothes to Hospice?"

"What's Hotspice?"

"Hospice is a place where you bring items you don't need anymore so they can sell them and help sick people."

"I wanna help sick people."

Lizzie stooped to Ainsley's eye level. "And what do you say—since you did such a good job today—we get that ice cream we talked about?"

"Yay! Ice cream!"

Garret exhaled. "Sorry, I was so cranky, Bug. Daddy had a rough day at work."

"It's okay, Daddy. We love you."

"I'm glad of that, hon, cuz Daddy loves you and Mommy very much."

**

Once the truck was fully loaded, the Breckers drove separately to meet up at Applebees.

As they jumped on 50 East, heading for Lake Tahoe, Garret and

Lizzy remained silent. The last thing Lizzy grabbed was the pad of paper off of the kitchen counter. She wrote:

I'm scared.

Garret turned on the radio. He glanced in the rear-view mirror, out the side window, and back to Liz. Under his breath, "Me too, sweetheart. Me too."

———

Emma

Emma Sagorski slipped her key in the ignition of her 2019 Honda Accord and listened as the car roared to life. She leaned toward the radio, listening. *Hissss.* She banged on her dash. The hissing sound continued. She checked the car's vitals: Engine pressure: *good.* Temperature gauge: *normal.* She turned the radio on. The hissing stopped. "Huh," she muttered to herself. She pressed the NAV button and programmed her journey home. She punched the pre-set button to her favorite country station, buckled her seatbelt, and drove away.

Minimal traffic put her at ease. She thought the shoot went well. Her interview role with the TV anchor, believable. *Quite the production.* Seemed so real...and yet...*that's showbiz.* She cranked up the volume and sang to Blake Shelton and Gwen's latest hit. "I've always been a rollin' stone..."

Suddenly her head buzzed. Her ears rang with a piercing high pitch sound. She exited the freeway at 59th Street and blew through a stop sign. She tightened her grip on the steering wheel, feeling as if she had lost control. She couldn't have been more correct as she involuntarily turned right at the corner, squealing on two tires. She jammed her foot on the brake bracing herself, but the car picked up speed. Screaming at the top of her lungs, the car burrowed its way past Mrs. Maggio's oleander bushes, through her front window, through her living room, kitchen, and out the back door, crashing into the cinder block wall. The last thing Emma heard was...*game over*.

**

Mrs. Maggio clutched her heart. *Breathe,* she told herself. *Surely someone called 911*. Her eyes—drawn from the gaping hole that was once her back door to her parakeet, lying still inside his crushed wire cage.

She shuffled around the cage to where the Honda's blinking tail lights flashed red, mimicking her heartbeat. Ringing in her ears. She couldn't tear her eyes away from the lights. Her heart, now pounding in her chest. *Faster.* She imagined a red balloon, filling up with air. *Faster.* Latex, stretching to its limit. *Faster*. Exceeding capacity until...***Boom.***

Something Worse

Joseph propped his feet up on his leather ottoman, a plate of homemade ravioli resting on his lap. He sipped his chianti, set it down, and picked up the remote. Brad was out of town. TV would fill the void. He clicked on the local news. Big mistake. Flashing lights behind the blonde anchor reminded him of the incident at the train station. But this was no suicide. *Worse.* A gunman went on a killing spree. Joseph changed the channel to discover more of the same, but this station cut to another scene, one he couldn't resist watching.

"Mrs. Elanor Maggio died of a heart attack after this car..." The camera panned to the house. "Driven by an unidentified young woman, came crashing through her house." As the camera zoomed in on the path of destruction, Joseph noticed the birdcage on the floor. His hair prickled the back of his neck. "Mother of God—this was no accident."

He set his plate aside, closed his eyes, and said a prayer of protection. The sensation he felt was almost the same as rolling up the windows in his car while driving 70 miles per hour down the highway—the sound of air sucked out the window, ears popping, the ringing that follows.

**

Linda turned on her computer. A little writing would take her mind off the unsettling feeling she had carried around all day. Poetry required creativity, concentration, being in a space where ideas flowed. She took a deep breath and exhaled. The candle, burning nearby, scented the room with sweet basil, and vanilla. Her hands rested on the keys…she began.

Skies of blue, now steely grey
A feather in the wind.
A yellow kite, a whispered prayer,
To thee, I truly send.
Thou may be brave, with sword and stone,
And heart may be of gold,
But evil lurks in hearts of men,
More than earth can hold.

Linda bowed her head. She knew thoughts were things. A person could just as easily manifest disaster as they could well-being. If she lingered in this dark place, let disturbing thoughts dance in her soul, she may as well open the door for the devil and invite him in.

She saved the poem, deciding to try another day, and checked her mail instead. The screen went to her home page, revealing headlines for the latest Yahoo News. Her breath caught in her throat when she saw the car smashed against the concrete wall. Below that image was another…crime tape, flashing lights, and a woman holding one pink jelly shoe.

Linda slammed her laptop shut. "No!" she cried. "God is good. Satan is a liar!" She held her hands high. "The light of God surrounds us —the love of God enfolds us—the power of God protects us—the presence of God watches over us—wherever we are, God is. Amen." Her arms dropped to her side. She imagined a plane, falling from the sky. "Not falling. Landing." The corners of her mouth rose in earnest. "She's home. Suzanne has arrived home, safe."

Sweet Home

Lights shimmered below, reminding Suzanne of Christmas lights during the holidays. Sam leaned against her, enjoying the view.

"Hard to believe," she said. "Less than twelve hours ago we were in Germany."

"I know flying isn't your favorite thing to do, but I hope we can do it again soon. I can't imagine not having you as my traveling companion."

"Sacramento is so pretty at night, a landscape of glittering jewels."

"Glad to be home?"

"Almost. We need to land first."

Sam chuckled. "Okay, I'll retract that question until I have you in bed."

Suzanne clipped his mouth with hers. "In that case, I can think of better things to ask me."

"Such as?"

"Not sure...but the answer is yes."

**

Sam dropped Suzanne's bags inside the front door. They were both exhausted from the long flight and then getting stuck in traffic for over an hour. "Want me to take these upstairs to your bedroom?"

"Yes, please. I want to check my messages. I'll be right up." Suzanne flipped the kitchen light on and pressed the play button on her answering machine. After eight hang-ups and three robocalls, she heard Linda's sweet voice...

"Suzanne, Suzanne-a-dan-na, it's Linda Schooler calling...hey, I have a friend I would love you to meet. Weird stuff going on, birds on the brain, or else I'm just being a bird brain, not sure which...anyhow, thought we could put out heads together, see what flavor Jell-O oozes out. Hahaha. You know me, love to keep things light. Talk to you soon. Bye."

Sam came up behind Suzanne, and she jumped. "Sam! Geez, don't sneak up on me like that."

Sam looked at his stocking feet. "Wasn't intentional."

"Sorry, I'm so jumpy."

"It's called PTSD—and I understand. Won't let it happen again. Promise. Next time I'll bang pots and pans, or whistle to get your attention so I don't startle you."

"That was a message from Linda. She mentioned 'birds'...said weird stuff has been going on...think the same things are happening here?"

"I just checked my messages, too—Kelly, our dispatcher, mentioned a mass shooting today at Discovery Park. That must've been why traffic was backed up."

Suzanne rushed over to the TV and turned it on. "We missed the news at 10, but the 11 o'clock news starts in a few minutes."

Sam glanced at his watch. "I should get going. I'm expected back in the office tomorrow...and I'm sure you could use some sleep. You didn't get any rest on the plane."

"I suppose you're right. Call me tomorrow?"

"Absolutely," he said. His kiss was tender, his hands caressed her arms, back, and waist, eventually cupping her face. "Thank you for making my dreams come true. I had a wonderful time with you, and can't wait to do it again."

She held him tight, oblivious to the prompt leading into the news. It was Sam who broke the embrace to listen. "...as we take you live to Discovery Park."

The anchor, frozen in place waiting to be cued from the control room, finally spoke, drilling each word into the ears of the viewers. When the anchor finished her shocking announcement, the station cut to a b-roll of the earlier chaos. The anchor continued her summation...

"So far as we know, six are dead, two of them children, and of the seventeen wounded, several remain at the hospital in critical condition. Names have not been released and the public needs to be aware—the gunman is still at large." The camera cut back to the anchor. "Eyewitnesses have reported conflicting descriptions of the shooter, making it difficult for police to profile a suspect. Anyone with information is encouraged to contact the Sacramento Police Department as soon as possible. Back to you..."

Suzanne's mouth hung open. Her eyes were stuck on the stream of images before her. Sam massaged her shoulder. "What's going on? What are you getting?"

Suzanne flashed a look his way. "It's not true."

"You think they know who it is and they're not telling us?"

"No! I mean it's not true. It's..."

"Let's sit down, discuss this..."

Suzanne walked to the sofa and eased down as if she were in a trance.

Sam sat beside her. "Are you okay? Can I get you a glass of water?"

The haunted look in her eyes answered his first question. He started to rise, but she pulled him back down. "I'm fine, it's just—"

"I agree, something weird is going on, but what?"

"I'm not sure, Sam. I saw the little pink jelly shoe in that woman's hand, and I got a flash of them fleeing. There's a man with them. Husband, father...he's afraid."

"Afraid?"

She placed her fingertips on her temples, squeezing her eyes shut. "I see mountains...desolation. They're hiding from something."

"Not some*one*?"

"Yes, but I feel like they're being tracked by some*thing*."

"Do you think the man in your vision is the shooter?"

"No."

The next report on the news rattled Suzanne to the core. The clip of a car that had smashed into a house—"two people dead—"

Suzanne's lips began to move. "One from a heart attack, the other from the crash."

Sam's eyes grew large. "How did you—?"

"She was there, Sam. The woman in the car was at the park."

Sam exhaled. "Suicide?"

"No, I don't believe so." She closed her eyes for a moment. "I sense fear, struggle. It's as if the crash was against her will."

"What the hell is going on, Suzanne?" He stood, pacing the room. "First the suicides in Paris...now this? Has the world gone crazy? Or is there something more sinister at play here?"

"Color me crazy, but I'm getting a feeling there is another force behind this mass shooting besides the shooter. I see faces—vacant eyes—"

He swiped the scowl off his face with his hand. "Let me see what's going on around here. I'll get back to you tomorrow."

"What do you think we should do?"

"I can't keep poking my nose into another department's territory—but if you're getting hits, we certainly can't keep the leads to ourselves." He kissed her once more, this time more perfunctory, than passionate. "Sleep well. Everything's going to be okay."

Suzanne locked the door behind him and went up to bed. She wasn't ready for another investigation, but perhaps she didn't have a choice. *When the universe calls...*

She eyed her suitcases in the corner. *Tomorrow.* She grabbed a long T-shirt out of the drawer and stripped down to her panties. She gave her face a quick wash, brushed her teeth, climbed into bed, and had just turned out the light when she heard her mother say, "It's a cross, Suzanne. It belonged to my mother. It's yours now, I want you to have it." Was it coincidental that her mother had been on her mind all day?

Suzanne launched herself out of bed and rummaged through her closet until she found a small striped box. Inside, beneath her diplomas, dance recital photos, and various trinkets from her childhood was a pink velvet pouch. She emptied the contents into her palm and went into the bathroom. The bright light made the tiny cross sparkle. Immediately upon hooking the clasp, she felt better.

Get Down to It

Joseph broke his nail-biting habit when he was thirteen. He hadn't so much as nibbled, *until now*. He didn't watch the news, as a rule, *until now*. He limited himself to one glass of wine a day, *until now*. He yearned for his husband Brad to be by his side to ease the unsettling feeling of doom that had come over him the other day when that twenty-three-year-old man walked in front of an oncoming train.

Joseph had queried his spirit guides to help him untangle the minutia clouding his vision. If it wasn't the Eiffel Tower, it was a woman smoking a cigarette, a bouquet of flowers, the gazebo from the movie, "Sound of Music" ...*crazy*. Being alone with his thoughts was never a problem...*until now*. He picked up the phone.

"Linda, it's Joseph. Am I calling too late?"

"Too late to save the girl in the movie I'm watching!" She laughed. "To what do I owe the honor?"

"Brad's out of town. I'm giving myself an ulcer over a young man I don't even know."

Linda chuckled. "Perhaps you better explain..."

"Oh no, it's nothing like that—heavens no. Brad and I are happier than bugs in a rug—I'm referring to the young man who walked in front of the train."

"I didn't see a thing on the news about him."

"I'm not surprised. I caught the blip they considered coverage."

"I would have expected the media to have a field day with the young man's choices. Drugs?"

"I don't think it was drugs."

"What then?"

"Not sure. I keep seeing him. His vapid expression doesn't fit the drug scenario. He's like a zombie—possessed. His aura is *fragmented*.

"It's funny when you say that, I get that impression when I see these kids with their faces glued to their phones, or their tablets. We're transforming kids into zombies every day with all the modern technology available to them."

"I agree. Mother's little helpers used to be drinking a gin and tonic in the afternoon, or popping a valium—now they have electronic babysitters."

"What's really bothering you?"

Joseph chuckled. "Never call a psychic unless you're prepared to give it up."

"Dang tootin'."

"I have a feeling, and I could be wrong, but it feels to me that he was murdered."

"Wow. How did we get from zombies to murder?"

"My spirit guides never fail me, Linda—"

"Walk me through your theory, then."

"Have you ever read anything about people missing in Alaska?"

"I heard some blame the disappearances on the aurora borealis."

"Yes! They believe the electromagnetic force from the aurora borealis is affecting people's brains, making them transform into zombie-like creatures who are compelled to search for the light source in the wilderness, and consequently, get lost."

"They're not finding any remains."

"True," Joseph said. "I've also read that the government has a facility in Anchorage with equipment that has been able to imitate the aurora borealis, and control the weather by aiming electromagnetic signals into certain areas."

"Why would the government harm the very people they are hired to serve?"

"Linda, Linda—because they can. Because we are specimens under their microscopes. They've been experimenting with mind control for decades!"

"Wow. Just wow."

"I know. That was a lot to dump on you, I'm sorry." He paused. "Maybe I should've fixed myself a hot fudge sundae instead of robbing you of your peace of mind."

"Ice cream sounds really good right about now." She chuckled. "But seriously, what are friends for? I'm glad you called to discuss this with me...I've been sensing an evil presence myself. I had a blackbird fly into my window the other day...when I went to rescue it, it vanished...and yet, when I went inside, the bird's essence was on the window." A nervous titter later, "The poor thing hit so hard, I was surprised he didn't break the window." She sighed heavily, "What I'm trying to tell you is I know what I saw—there is no way the bird flew away unscathed. I felt an evil force at work. Whether an electromagnetic field was at play here, I'm not sure, but it was something...and it's more powerful than we can imagine."

After he ended the call, Joseph opened the freezer door and stared at the container of Ben and Jerri's Vanilla Bean. His diabetes was finally under control after nearly losing the battle. A strange voice in his head taunted, *do it, do it*. "No!" he said, slamming the freezer door. "You don't get to win."

**

Linda scooped a perfect ball of vanilla ice cream into a small glass dish and garnished it with a handful of fresh raspberries and a dollop of whipped cream. Her conversation with Joseph put her in a mood. Ice cream fixed a lot of things, according to her nine-year-old self. Being a grown-up sucked sometimes. This was one of those times. She held no responsibility regarding Joseph's issue, believing we choose our agenda prior to our incarnation, and Joseph chose to be bothered by the young man's death. It was God's job to help him through the experience. Her role was to be supportive. His lesson, not hers. Or so she thought. She had to admit when it came to evil, she was a— "Scaredy cat," she mumbled. She did a quick taste. *Yep, ice cream cures almost anything*. Feeling better she called out, "Hey pretty bird."

"Hey pretty bird," echoed from the next room.

"What do you think about your feathered friend crashing into the window the other day?"

Silence.

"Do you think he flew away—and I just missed it?"

Silence.

Linda resumed her position in front of the TV and hit play. Suddenly Big Bird began to squawk. Linda hit pause, dropped her spoon in the dish, and went to investigate. Big Bird's beak was partially open, his pupils tiny pinpoints. His chest heaved.

Linda opened the door to his cage and stroked the parrot's lemon-yellow head. "What's the matter, my friend?"

"Scaredy cat."

Linda held Big Bird close to her chest. "It's okay, buddy. It's okay."

Lizzie in the Sky with Diamonds

Lizzie, Garret, and Ainsley rolled up to a cabin nestled among white firs and Jeffrey pines. Lizzie rolled up her window, cutting off the heavenly scent. Ainsley, asleep in the backseat, allowed Lizzie a few minutes to digest their predicament. Garret had said little, and what he did say was cryptic, and made no sense. Before they even hit the freeway, he had removed the SIM cards from both phones and disconnected the GPS on the dash.

Garret turned off the car and settled sideways in his seat against the door. His face looked even paler in the moonlight, his eyes haunted, his voice sullen when he spoke. "I never told you what really happened on the yacht that night when I was hired to take photographs."

"I figured you didn't want me to know...but that night changed you. I figured you met someone."

"I'm sorry you felt that way...believe me, it was nothing like that." He took her hand in his. "I'm so sorry if I made you feel that way—I just didn't know how to talk about it."

"Talk about what, Gar? It's been over three years."

"I was afraid. I'm still afraid—even more so now."

"What happened?"

"That shoot you went on today—they're saying it's real."

"It was a re-enactment, they said it was to be used as a training video for emergency personnel—they do those all the time. It's called 'crisis' acting."

"I saw the news footage before it hit the airwaves. It was sent to me in a text. The woman the news anchor was interviewing? I met her on the yacht. Now she's dead."

"What are you saying?"

"The photos I took were blackmail photos, disgusting photos of men having sex with children. That woman was there, she witnessed what happened, she was drugged, gang raped, and now she's dead."

"Garret, you must be mistaken. We went to a legitimate gig. Ainsley was a little Rockstar! Why are you doing this to us?"

"Not me, Lizzie, *them*. They're going to kill us too—I know it."

"This isn't funny, or cute, or any adjective I can think of. We are your family—whatever sick notions you have—keep us out of it."

Garret grabbed her arm. "Don't you understand? These people are powerful! They don't let people walk away from their dastardly deeds, Lizzie—they sent me that video as a warning!"

"Everybody's angry," Ainsley cried from the back seat.

Lizzie unbuckled her seatbelt and reached back to stroke her daughter's leg. "Shhhh, baby. We're not angry. I'm sorry if we were talking too loud." Lizzie glared at Garret. "Isn't that right, Garret?"

"Yeah, sorry Bug." He opened his door. "Daddy's gonna check out our new digs. I'll be right back."

"Mommy, where are we?"

Lizzie shook her head and mumbled under her breath. "Hell, if I know."

"Mommy said a bad word."

"Mommy's probably gonna say a lot of bad words, sweetie." She sighed. "You're right, I'm not setting a good example. I'm sorry."

"I'm hungry."

"Me too, my darling...as soon as daddy gives us the all clear, we can fix a couple of PB&J's—would you like that?"

Garret appeared at the door. Ainsley's face brightened. "Daddy!"

Garret waved when he heard Ainsley call him. One of the things Lizzie could be sure of was the bond they shared. As far as *their* relationship, Lizzie was on the fence. She had no idea what was going on, or whether she could trust the man she had stood behind, supported, and loved all these years. Her main concern was their daughter.

Once inside, Lizzie made good on her PBJ promise. Garret helped unpack the essentials they needed for the night. Blankets, pillows, PJs for Ainsley. Lizzie unpacked the rest of the food items, bathroom necessities, a bottle of "19 Crimes" wine, and the Daves—David Bowie, David Grey, and Dave Matthews. Wine cut her vocabulary in half. Music soothed her soul. Then she remembered the life inside her and went into the bathroom, locked the door, and cried.

Ainsley snuggled next to Garret on the couch. "Why is Mommy crying?"

"I think she's practicing for an audition. How did you do today?"

"It was okay. Mommy said I did good."

He plastered her bangs back with his hand and lifted her chin until their eyes met. "I'll bet you were the best kid on the set." He kissed her forehead and released her bangs. "I love you, Bug. Always remember that, okay?"

"I love you, too, Daddy."

Garret clicked on the TV. Before he could navigate the channels, a lead-in for the midnight news caught Ainsley's attention. Look, Daddy! That's my shoe!

**

Garret tapped on the door, expecting permission to enter. When his wife didn't reply, he checked the door to find it locked. "I'll be out shortly," Lizzie snapped. He listened to the toilet flush, water splashing, a thud, and a rustling sound on the other side of the door until it opened, revealing the tear-stained face he loved.

"I'm sorry." He braced his left arm against the door jam. "This is all my fault."

Lizzie's gaze dropped to the floor. She tightened her lips to a slash. New tears sprang from her eyes as she lifted her gaze to meet his. "I'm pregnant. His jaw dropped. Color drained from his face. Lizzie turned and slammed the door.

Steven

Suzanne opened one eye, shielding her face from the morning sun blaring through her bedroom window. Her phone vibrated on the nightstand. She squinted at the clock. "Crap!" She threw the covers aside and sat up, rubbing her left temple. "Hello?"

"I woke you, didn't I?"

"Linda! I'm up. I'm up. How are you?"

"Go back to sleep, but first, tell me—are you free today? I need to meet with you."

"Gosh, how can I go back to sleep now? Is it secret stuff? Or can you give me a hint—what's going on?"

"That's what I need to speak to you about. Crazy shit, can I say shit?"

"Go for it."

"Crazy shit is going on. I have a friend, a psychic who is also experiencing crazy shit. Boy—four shits in a row—that's how bad this feels."

"I can stop by around 2 o'clock—does that work?"

"Yes. Let me see if my friend can get here too, he lives in the Bay area."

"Great! See you at 2 o'clock. And Linda?"

"Yes?"

"The bird did hit the window, but it wasn't real—whatever *that* means."

**

Suzanne showered and dressed in a pair of jeans, a white tank top, and red flip-flops. After dressing up every night in Europe, it felt good to put on her "play clothes," as her mom would've called them. *Mom again.* Suzanne hadn't thought about her mom this much in years. "Mom?" She looked around the room. "Are you here?" She smelled 'Muguet du Bois', her mother's favorite perfume. "I don't know why you're here," she said, her eyes misting, "but I'm glad you are. I miss you. I know I've been burying every good thing you brought to my life, but—I hope you understand—first Jack, then you and Dad—I just couldn't—" Suzanne sat on the bed, tears streaming down her face.

**

At 1:30 sharp, Suzanne drove to Linda's. She called her brother Steven on her way.

"Well, I'll be damned, if it isn't my little sister."

"Hi Steven, how are you?"

"I could be dead, for all you care."

"Guilt? Really?"

"You need money?"

"No, Steven, I don't need money. I called to see if you and Karen want to come over for a barbeque on Saturday?"

"Loverboy gonna be there?"

"Sam—yes, Sam will be there, do you have a problem with that?"

"No. Just wondered how much beer to bring, that's all."

"Sam doesn't drink. Besides, I planned on providing the beverages, any requests?"

"No, that's okay, you know what I like—right? You still remember?"

"Yes, but I did forget what an ass you can be when you want to."

"Touché. What time? Karen misses you—God knows why?"

Suzanne laughed. "Because she knows what a loving, devoted sister I am."

"What time?"

"Six. And Steven?"

"I knew there was a catch."

"Not at all. I just wanted to tell you that Mom's been visiting me."

"No kidding." After a pregnant pause, "Tell her 'hi' for me."

**

Linda answered the door promptly at two. "Come, come."

"It's getting warm out there." Suzanne inhaled. "I smell baked apples."

"I made a pie."

"I brought you a gift." Suzanne handed the small bag to Linda. "I found it in Germany. It had 'you' written all over it."

Linda lifted the crystal butterfly from the wrapping and held it up to the sunlight streaming through her window. "It's beautiful, I'll cherish it always." She gently set it on her windowsill, just as Suzanne imagined she would.

"Is your friend coming?"

"Yes. He'll be here shortly. I'm anxious for you to meet him, we've been friends for years. He's a very gifted young man."

"How did you meet?"

"Psychic faire in Sacramento—he rescued my sign-up sheets when they went flying across the parking lot. I had my hands full. My juggling act needed work."

"I can't imagine doing fairs."

"I couldn't either, but after I came to grips with my gift, I studied hard to make it happen. My way of giving back—bringing light where there is darkness."

"That must be a good feeling. I get all the ugly stuff."

Linda rose. "Hold that thought." She went to the door and returned with a handsome young man in tow. "Suzanne, this is Joseph, Joseph Ernest Martin. Joseph, Suzanne Cash."

Suzanne took Joseph's offered hand. "Pleased to meet you."

Joseph sniffed the air. "You didn't!"

"I did. But I used coconut sugar—better for your innards."

Joseph hugged Linda so hard her face turned red.

Suzanne sat on a kitchen chair. "Linda tells me you are psychic as well..."

"Yes—did she tell you about my disturbing experience?"

"No. She didn't." Shivers ran up Suzanne's arms. "What happened?"

Joseph launched into his story about his coffee ritual, and the young man stepping in front of the train."

"You're pale," he said. "I didn't upset you, did I?"

"Three young people committed suicide while we were in Paris." Suzanne watched Joseph's eyes grow large. "While we were in Salzburg, a flock of blackbirds attacked the gazebo we were standing in."

Linda glanced at her window. "This morning you told me the bird hit the window, but it wasn't really there, what did you mean by that?"

"I'm not sure."

Linda recapitulated the story. "A bird slammed into my window, but when I went to investigate its condition, it was gone. I thought I was hallucinating, but then when I came in the house, I saw an imprint on the glass where it hit."

Suzanne's jaw dropped. "That's crazy!"

Linda threw up her hands, "That's what I said, crazy shit."

Joseph clasped his hands together. "Something strange has been going on for a long time, but lately, people seem so disconnected. I heard somewhere the suicide rate was way up."

"You're correct," Suzanne agreed, "the suicide rate is up, but why? Is it depression? Or is there another driving force?"

Joseph pushed himself away from the table and crossed his legs. "Have you ever heard about HAARP?"

"No, what is it?"

"It stands for High-frequency Active Auroral Research Program. The facility claims to be researching the ionosphere, but rumor has it they are doing more than that. They use a high-powered, high-frequency instrument that 'is able to'—Joseph demonstrated air quotes—'temporarily excite an area of the ionosphere to study the results.'"

"They're making weather?"

Joseph nodded. "Essentially."

Suzanne cinched her brow. "Good way to depopulate."

"It's also been rumored that they are experimenting with electromagnetic frequencies. 3000 people a year go missing in Alaska."

"And you feel this HAARP is responsible?"

Joseph shrugged. "What makes a person walk out the door during dinner in the middle of winter without a coat? There are stories of people getting up in the middle of a meal, walking out the door, never to be heard from again."

Suzanne and Linda exchanged glances. Suzanne spoke. "I'm sorry, I respect your opinion, but I can't imagine—" Audra's image flashed across Suzanne's mind, carrying with it the evil done to her, and the children delivered to the U.S. in cages for wealthy, powerful people to abuse and exploit. She bowed her head. "Maybe I can." She met his gaze. "Rumors and stories aren't facts. We need more information."

Joseph leaned back in his chair. "Agreed, but what does your gut tell you?" Linda leaned forward to catch every word.

Suzanne placed her palms flat. "I believe sinister powers are at play here. What I saw didn't make sense to me at the time I witnessed it, and it makes no sense to me now. I was being shown the suicides for a reason, I'm just not sure what to do about it."

Linda chimed in, "What did Sam say about the suicides?"

"Well besides spoiling two proposal attempts? He's concerned."

Linda's smile returned. "Did he get down on one knee, like in the movies?"

"He tried so hard to make it a perfect, romantic gesture...the first time he tried to propose we were on the carousel beneath the Eiffel Tower when one of the waiters we had at dinner did a swan dive off the balcony of the Eiffel restaurant. Sam didn't see it happen, I did. The second time we were attacked by blackbirds."

Linda zeroed in on Suzanne's left hand with a sympathetic sigh. "Oh, dear."

"It's ok," Suzanne said. I had a premonition that it was going to be spoiled—which I realized after the fact of course."

Joseph changed topics. "We know the statistics on the suicide rate have gone up."

"Considerably," Linda agreed, "but the blame is falling on the Covid-19 pandemic, isolation, grief over losing loved ones, losing jobs. Be hard to prove it's anything else."

Joseph shook his head. "You're right, Covid covers all the bases... *fear*. Fear can bend minds faster than any instrument."

Suzanne tilted her head. "And the shooting last night?"

Linda's 'deer in headlights' expression pre-empted, "Yeah, what the 'F'?"

Joseph slapped his hand on the table. "Are people losing their minds?"

Suzanne chimed in, "I had the impression that the people reported dead, aren't really dead. And then to top it off, one of the witnesses interviewed on the news drove her car through a house and killed the homeowner and herself. What are the chances of that happening?"

Linda shuddered, still stunned, "Crazy shit."

Joseph shook his head. "The plot keeps getting better and better."

"You're right," Suzanne agreed. "The world is beginning to read like one big thriller novel."

For This, I Pray

Lizzie lay in bed, staring at the back of Garret's head, boring holes into his brain, compelled to pummel his back, spit out the angry words swimming in her head. *How dare you sleep while I carry the weight of our situation on my tired shoulders?*

The pitter-patter of tiny feet brought her to her senses.

"Mommy, I can't sleep."

"C'mere, Lovey," Lizzie whispered. She drew Ainsley close to her breast. "Comfy?" She felt Ainsley's soft curls brush her clavicle and inhaled her sweet scent. *Dear God*, she prayed silently, *please keep my—* she reached down, placing her hand between her firstborn, and the child growing in her womb, please *keep my babies safe. Amen.*

**

Sam had spent the previous day catching up; attending meetings, returning phone calls, addressing urgent matters regarding personnel, new hires, and an officer accused of unnecessary roughness. By the end of the day, he was spent, proud of himself for staying focused on his work, and not dwelling on what Suzanne was dealing with. By the time he dialed her number, it was late.

"Hey," he said, his lips curving upward at the mere sound of her "Hello."

"I would ask how your day was but—"

"But?" He asked, shuffling through his mail.

"I can feel—never mind," she said, changing the lilt of her tone. "How was your day?"

"Productive—did you feel otherwise?"

"An image of Brutus and Popeye came to mind."

"Interesting..."

"The guy has anger issues...he needs help."

Sam thought about the situation with Officer Spence, the man accused of breaking an arrestee's nose for spitting on him. There would be a hearing...until then, Officer Spence was put on leave. Sam knew Spence felt justified. *So out of character*. "Anything else?"

"Yes. I hear bees."

"Bees?"

"Yes, bees. He's not thinking straight."

"Interesting you would pick up on that..."

"Is everything all right?"

"Besides craving a slice of honey-sweetened lemon meringue pie? Can I tempt you to join me?"

"It's nine o'clock!"

"Is that a "no"?" Sam heard her catch her breath and smiled.

"I'll be right over."

"Great! I'll pick up a couple of slices at the Buttercup Pantry. I'll meet you in the Catholic church parking lot at Highway 50 and Bass Lake Road in thirty minutes. We can eat pie and gaze at the stars."

**

Suzanne swapped her cotton nightshirt for an oversized cotton T-shirt, a pair of navy cargo pants, and flip-flops. She grabbed a sweatshirt jacket from the coat rack on her way out the door. The days were warm, but the nights were on the cool side, reminding her of sleeping outdoors, campfires, and s'mores.

As she drove up the hill, she swiped at her clavicle. "Of all things..."

she said, brushing away something that tickled. She placed her hand on her stomach, imagining a life inside her. "No," she said aloud. "We've been careful." But the feeling didn't dissipate with her conviction. A little girl with curly hair whispered in her head, M*ommy's gonna have a baby. Daddy's mad.*

Suzanne pumped her brakes. Her speedometer read 78mph. "Whoa. Damn!" Her heartbeat slowed along with the car. "I hate this!" she cried. The little girl laughed and skipped out of her mind. Suzanne's eyes drifted to the new cell tower to her right. 5G, faster, better, *deadly*. Bees. *Take the bees and lock them up, lock them up, lock them up. Take the bees and lock them up, my fair lady.*

Suzanne took the Bass Lake exit, turned left at the light, and followed the road up the hill to the next light. So many changes had transpired in the last couple of years. More homes and even more cell towers. *Progress.* She shook off impending doom and swerved into the first tier of the parking lot flanking the church. The view, spectacular, the rendezvous, exciting, the love she felt was a shield protecting her mind, body, and spirit. The headlights ahead confirmed it. *Sam.*

"You made great time," he said. Placing a paper bag on the hood of his car, he went to work opening two clear containers. He handed one to Suzanne with a plastic fork.

Suzanne walked to the edge of the pavement, admiring the lush green trees, and glittering lights below as she ate. "It's beautiful—do you come here often?"

"Before the housing boom, the drug dealers used this area as a storefront. Down there," He said, pointing to a clearing across the road below. "that was the party pit."

She looked up, "So many stars."

"Happy you came?"

"I missed you," she said, feeding him a forkful of lemon dessert. He returned the gesture, kissing her lips between bites.

"I met a friend of Linda's today. Joseph Martin, another psychic."

"Wish I had been a fly on the wall."

"He was interesting, indeed. He mentioned a facility in Alaska, HAARP, ever heard of it?"

"I've heard conspiracy theories..."

"Yes, I'm not sure I want to entertain the thought of the government sending out electromagnetic frequencies that control people's thoughts."

Sam swallowed another bite. "Sounds far-fetched..."

"And yet—I'm learning how tainted the human race can be."

Sam drew her into his arms. "Don't go down the rabbit hole, Suzanne, there must be an explanation for what is happening."

"You're right. How do you feel about children?"

"Other peoples?" A sly smile slid across his face. "Suzanne?"

"Oh—it was just a question. I got a hit on the way here. I have no idea what it means."

"I'm listening..."

"A little girl's voice"—she said, "'Mommy's gonna have a baby, Daddy's mad.'"

Sam released his hold, his smile faded. "Doesn't sound good."

"No." Suzanne flashed a brief smile. "And what's with all the cell towers lining the freeway?"

"Progress?"

"Why do I feel like I'm being watched?"

"If I had all the answers—"

"Kiss me," she said, caressing his arm. "I want to go where they can't find me."

Sam circled one arm around Suzanne's waist, his hand sliding to the small of her back, his other hand cupping the back of her head. "That I can do."

**

Sam drove home contemplating Suzanne's comments about the cell towers, the rapid growth...the little girl's voice...her question about children. *Slow down, buddy. First comes love, then comes marriage, then comes Sammy with a baby carriage.* Audra teased him with that adage when she saw him holding Gerta Von Dyke's hand—he was fourteen, Audra was six. Although love arrived later than expected, when Suzanne mentioned children, he got excited. He wondered if she sensed his disappointment when she referred to someone else.

But if he were being honest, they weren't ready to commit to raising a family. *Hell, I'm still waiting for the right moment to propose. Again.*

Sam turned on the radio to redirect his thoughts. He listened to the commercial claiming he had a friend in the diamond company, followed by a healthcare company raving about their maternity services. Odd, he thought. But when "You're Having My Baby" began to play on his favorite oldies station, a weird sensation traveled up his spine. He drove past the cell tower perched on top of the wooded hillside, recalling Suzanne's words: "Why do I feel like I'm being watched?"

**

Suzanne switched the dial to a podcast. Conspiracy theories didn't interest her, but this one caught her attention. A former CIA Agent, discussing the National Security Agency using EMF Brain Stimulation for Remote Neural Monitoring and Electronic Brain Link in their neurological and bioelectric research. "The NSA can actually get inside a person's brain and program it to do their bidding," he said, in an altered voice Suzanne assumed was to protect his identity. "They have been using these techniques since the 1950s," he said, "But of course with advanced technology, they are literally able to monitor what you are thinking, and alter your thoughts."

Suzanne thought of the visions she had experienced since her near-death experience, the images, and words that popped into her head without permission. *What if?* What if she were being used as a pawn? No. *Impossible.* How would "they" know about Jack? About the love they shared? Their hopes and dreams as young lovers? And what about Dixon? Did they know he was a serial killer? Did they orchestrate the plot to catch him? Rescue those girls? And what about Sam? *Is he part of the plot?* She switched channels.

"Well, I think I'm going out of my head," sang Little Anthony and the Imperials. Suzanne turned off the radio.

"This is nuts," she said. She noticed another cell tower up ahead. "Or is it?"

**

After a quick shower, Suzanne climbed into bed. Her pillow held Sam's scent, and she inhaled, wishing he was beside her, his body warm, firm against hers. She closed her eyes, imagining his heart beating against her chest, his tender kisses, soft whispers telling her what he wanted to do to her, for her. Heat pooled between her legs. She wanted him inside her. She wanted him forever. Her body melted into her mattress, a delicious wave of satisfaction overcame her to the point where she felt dizzy. The room began to spin. She picked up the phone ready to dial Sam when she heard the high pitch coming from the device. She pressed his number into the keypad, but the signal grew louder. Her phone went dead.

"I was at fifty percent last time I looked," she mumbled. She opened her nightstand drawer, stuck her hand inside, and groped for her charger. Suddenly the phone came to life. A voice startled her announcing that her call could not be completed as dialed. Tiny bumps skittered from head to toe, making her shiver. A high pitch ring pulsed in her left ear. The words, "Don't fuck with us," came out of nowhere. Her body jerked out of bed. Paranoia washed over her as she looked around the room expecting another worldly being to step out of the shadows and strike her dead, instead, she heard a small voice say, "Mommy, why do we have to stay here?"

**

Sam threw his keys in the dish by the door and began unbuttoning his shirt. He flipped a light in the kitchen, illuminating the sterile environment. He poured himself a glass of water and downed it all at once. He poured another. Since he and Suzanne parted ways in Cameron Park, he felt an unquenchable thirst. Every station he turned on the radio played beer, Captain Morgan, or Jim Beam commercials. The rhetoric bordering on ridiculous, but at the same time, eating at his soul. He reflected on the moments in Paris, and Germany when he wanted so badly to join Suzanne in a glass of wine or share a beer with his dad. Temptation was an ugly beast, one he thought he had tamed once and for all...and yet all he had on his mind since he got onto Highway 50 was how much he wanted a drink. He drank the second glass of water as quickly as the first. He slammed his glass on the counter like a drunk demanding another shot. His head buzzed. His body heavy. His spirit drowning in self-pity. He shook his head, like a wet dog. *What the fuck is going on?* A voice inside his head replied, "Want to quench that thirst buddy boy? Take your gun, put it in your mouth and pull the trigger." Sam searched the room as if someone were pulling a prank.

Sam covered his ears. "Not today, asshole."

Sentinels Everywhere

Lizzy rummaged through the boxes they packed, unloading their meager fare into pine cabinets. She was happy she grabbed the extra gallon of milk she bought at the store the day before the acting gig. Ainsley would be waking to a routine bowl of cereal keeping a semblance of normalcy.

"Mommy, why do we have to stay here?" She asked between spoonfuls of Honey Nut Cheerios.

"We're on kind of an adventure, hon. Didn't you like waking up to all these beautiful trees? Feels like we're in an enchanted forest, like in Sleeping Beauty."

"Is there going to be a witch?"

"I don't think so, but Daddy is out gathering wood, and he's really good at finding humongous pine cones. I bet you can help him later." Lizzy dropped her hands from her hips, wrapped them around Ainsley's head, and planted a kiss on the child's forehead. "Would you like that, Bug?"

"Can we hunt for frogs? I would like my very own prince."

Lizzy chuckled, "Me too, babe, me–" Lizzy heard the door slam. Garret removed his boots, letting them drop to the floor.

"I could also look for a princess hidden amongst the pines," he snarled.

"I was kidding."

"Were you, now? Do you think I like this?"

"Garret, please don't–I was telling Ainsley how good you are at finding pine cones. She said she's more interested in finding frogs–what do you think? Any chance of finding a frog or two?"

Garret moved toward his daughter with apologetic eyes. "How's my girl this morning?" He kissed the top of her head, flashing a crooked smile at his wife. "It's a pretty day. Go for a hike later?"

Lizzy rested her crossed arms on the yellowed Formica counter and shrugged her shoulders. "Sure. Sounds like fun."

Garret squeezed Ainsley and left the room. Lizzie followed, her words hushed, "Do we have a plan?"

"Not yet."

"Our money can only go so far..."

"Don't you think I know that?" he snapped.

Lizzy flinched and backed away. "I'm–I'm not blaming you."

He sighed and swiped his hand over his unshaven face. "I know, babe." She stiffened as his arms encircled her. He hugged her tighter and whispered, "I love you, don't ever forget that."

"I try to believe that but–"

"Try harder. We have another baby coming. He's gonna need all the love we have to give."

Lizzy released his hold on her. "He? Since when?"

"Since I made a deal with God." He shrugged. "It's a guy thing."

Lizzy melted into his arms. "Let's go take that walk before I float away."

**

Ainsley skipped ahead, her blonde curls catching the golden rays filtering through the trees. Lizzie held Garret's hand. The scent of pine, the slight breeze, and the warmth of the sun gave her a momentary feeling of peace. But then Garret dropped her hand and stopped walking. He shielded his eyes from the sun and pointed toward the sky. The fear that loomed in the back of her mind lurched forward to steal her serenity. She looked up to see the cell tower nestled between the pines. She glanced at Garret. His eyes connected with hers. He rushed to grab his daughter and whispered something in her ear. He gestured for Lizzy to return to the house.

"We can't hide here forever, Gar, we need a plan."

He thumbed through his phone. "I can't tell if they're tracking us."

"From the cell tower?"

"Who knows what's up there? Cameras? Listening devices? Heat sensors?"

"Now you're acting paranoid. Why would the government spend all that money—go through all the trouble to track someone like us?"

"I saw their faces, Liz—I know who they are. One of the guys ran for state senator for Pete's sake. Actors, musicians, pop stars—the list goes on. These people are under *someone's* thumb. And then there's the voice—"

"What voice?"

"I didn't tell you because I didn't want you to worry—or worse—commit me."

"What are you talking about?"

"Shortly after I did the gig on the yacht, I started hearing a voice in my head. At first, it was berating, condescending, telling me I was a loser. Then it became suggestive, aggressive, telling me I'd be better off dead."

Lizzy dropped into a chair and covered her ears. "Don't! I can't listen to this."

"I've been fighting it off the best I can." Tears welled in his eyes. "Sometimes I thought the voice was right. You and Ainsley would be better off."

"Don't you EVER say that again—do you hear me, Garret Brecker?" She rushed into his arms and buried her head against his shoulder and sobbed.

"Shhhh, now. I don't plan on doing anything stupid. I just wanted you to know." He tilted her chin to meet his gaze. "There's more to this than we know. We need to work together."

"What can we do?

"Pray."

**

Ainsley sat on the bedroom floor, her tiny legs tucked beneath her. She hummed an uncharted melody as she dressed her baby bear, Tilly, in a purple T-shirt, and green paisley overalls. Every now and then she'd stop, hug Tilly, and reassure the bear in her bravest voice, "Everything will be all right."

FLOWERS

When Suzanne's cell rang, she picked up immediately. "Linda—everything okay?"

"Yes, fine. I thought I'd invite you to lunch today. Fly by the seat of our pants, take in a movie in Folsom, or hang out at a nursery. One can never have too many flowers.

"Sounds wonderful! Thai Paradise isn't too far from the Palladio Theater, or Green Acres."

"See ya at 11:30."

Suzanne turned on the shower, undressed, and stepped in. Her thoughts conjured the bouquet of flowers she discovered by the trash can in Paris. She wondered if sometimes she made too much of things, or that her mind was stuck in crazy mode. "No," she said into the warm spray, "I'm not crazy." The flowers haunted her. The ring, fake as it was, was significant. She needed to decipher the message, that's all. When she closed her eyes, she saw trees. Tall pines stretched for miles. She heard a little girl hum, her voice, like an angel's. She imagined the girl, blonde curls, holding something, mumbling loving words. Suzanne opened her eyes. The humming remained.

Suzanne sensed danger. A prickling sensation covered her wet skin. "Talk to me," she whispered. The humming stopped.

She dressed, combed her wet hair, and twisted it on top of her head.

A little mascara, and she was good to go. The floral sun dress she bought in Paris was perfect for their outing. She slipped into a pair of hot pink flip-flops, grabbed her purse, and headed for the door. As she put her key into the lock, she froze. *Sam*.

She dialed as if it was a life or death matter, the weight of the feeling crushing her from the inside out. When he answered, she felt relieved. "Everything okay?"

"I think so, why?"

"Not sure, I panicked for some reason, like you were hurt. Glad you're okay."

"I'm fine, but I had a peculiar night."

"What happened?"

"Hard to explain. Closest I can come to a description is snakes trying to nest in my head."

"Wasn't getting snakes—more like life or death."

"Suicide?"

Suzanne's stomach dropped. "Sam? What's going on?"

"Last night, coming home, all I could think of was guzzling booze. Then I felt like a loser. Went downhill from there."

"I'm on my way to meet Linda, but I can cancel, we can talk?"

"I'm fine. We can talk later. I did an exorcism."

"God, Sam. I can't believe we're having this conversation."

"I'll drive up your way tonight. We can have dinner."

"Only if I can do the cooking."

"Deal, only if you let me help."

"Deal."

**

Suzanne's mind felt fractured like she was being pulled in too many directions. Paris, the little girl, Linda, Joseph, and now Sam. She needed to ground herself if she was to keep her sanity.

She parked next to Linda's truck and went inside. Linda's cheery face instantly eased her mind. They hugged, ordered two Thai ice teas, coconut-lime soup with chicken, and a side order of jasmine rice to share.

Suzanne recapped her conversation with Sam, how she knew something was wrong before she called, the little girl's voice, and how disturbed she felt hearing it. Linda listened patiently, her smile never wavering.

"Do you think there's a connection?"

"Do you? You've been at this longer than I—I'm not sure what to think. Everything that has happened is so ludicrous."

"I agree. I have never encountered the likes of what I have been getting lately either. Is Sam a religious man?"

"I don't know. We've never discussed religion. Why?"

"Prayers for protection can't hurt."

"We're having dinner, I'll ask."

"I sense that he's very pragmatic, but it doesn't hurt to have God in your corner. He's one of the good guys."

"I'll let him know." Suzanne reached for Linda's hand and squeezed it. "Thank you for listening. It's not easy having this stuff rummaging around in your head."

"Out of clutter, find simplicity. From discord, find harmony. In the middle of difficulty lies opportunity."

"Einstein?"

"Yes. A cluttered mind requires more energy."

"I wonder if that's the goal?"

"Who's goal?"

"Good question. But keeping that in mind, I will figure a way to declutter."

Linda tapped two fingers on her forehead. "Defrag your computer."

"Exactly. Any suggestions?"

"Hold your glass in your hand, feel the cool glass against your palm. Feels good doesn't it?"

"Yes, especially on a hot day."

"Be present. The soup warms our insides, nourishes our bodies. The rice provides texture, reminding us that we are dimensional beings. Focus on the here and now. Be one with your space, your actions, the sensations that surround you, body, mind, and spirit. Let your thoughts find their way to a place of peace, and tranquility. Select each thought you want to address when the time comes to do so...until then, let each thought have its own resting place in your head. Don't allow them to collide, or rush into one another."

Suzanne brushed a stray hair from her cheek. She let her fingertips linger on her skin. “I think I get it.”

“Good. Have some more soup.”

Suzanne ladled chicken and broth into her bowl. “I saw a forest.”

“What kind of forest?”

“The trees looked like the pines in the Sierras.”

“And the association?”

“Not sure.” Suzanne elaborated on the little girl’s voice she had heard. “I’ve heard it a couple of times now.”

“I’m sure when it’s time, the universe will reveal the correlation. Until then, try and keep your channels clear.”

“Speaking of which, what do you think of all the cell towers going up?”

“It makes me sad to think that the bees are dying off, whether 5G is to blame or not, I’m not sure...but this I know...everything is made of energy...and cause and effect is a real thing.” Linda sighed. “Progress.”

“I don’t know why I’m so bothered by it all of a sudden.”

“Don’t let yourself be consumed by your thoughts. Breathe. Let go, let God. The answers will come.” She patted Suzanne’s hand. “I like that you saw trees, that must’ve been a pleasant sight.”

“It almost made me dizzy.”

“Oh no. Dear. Do you think the little girl is in the forest? Possibly lost? I remember when I was a girl, living in Canada, my parents took me and my sister camping at Jasper National Park. Not thinking, I took off chasing some furry creature and got turned around. My parents searched for me for over an hour.” Linda chuckled, “Got my b-u-t-t warmed for that one.”

“You’re right, but she said something like, “Mama’s having a baby, and daddy’s mad.”

“Gee, Suzanne, not sure what to make of it. More will come. Give your mind a rest. You’ll see.”

**

Sam drove to the courthouse. Officer Spence would be going in front of the judge for breaking Liberty Johnson’s nose during an arrest. Court was in session when Sam slipped in the door.

"He was out of his mind, your honor. He resisted arrest and kept coughing and spitting on me. Hard to put food on the table when you got Covid."

"Did you know Mr. Johnson to have Covid, Officer Spence?"

"He had symptoms, your honor. He was coughing, he was burning up when I helped him up off the ground."

"Did he say he felt sick?"

"No, your honor. He said he was covered in bees."

"How did Mr. Johnson's nose get broken, Officer Spence?"

"He came at me, I blocked him with my elbow."

"According to an eye witness, you were angry…"

"Yes, your honor, that part is true. Mr. Johnson wouldn't come peacefully. He was displaying irrational behavior, I believed this behavior to be drug induced, and as I stated, he seemed sick. But that didn't diminish his strength, or his belligerence towards my partner and me."

The judge shuffled through his papers. "Mr. Pickler, would you approach the bench?"

A slight man in a baggy suit approached the bench. The court reporter took the man's oath. The judge eyed the witness over his spectacles. "Sir, you claim you saw Officer Spence break Mr. Johnson's nose—care to explain what you saw?"

"Geez your honor, it was dark. I just saw the cops all over Lib. When Lib, Mr. Johnson, got up, that cop right there," he said, pointing, "did something, cuz next thing I know, Lib, eh, Mr. Johnson, was holding his face and bleeding all over the place."

"How far away were you from Mr. Johnson?"

"He was on the grass, I was on the road."

"Ten feet away? One hundred feet away?"

"Thirty, forty?"

"Close enough to be certain Officer Spence hit Mr. Johnson?"

"Well, he was yellin' at him!"

"Did you see Officer Spence hit Mr. Johnson?"

Mr. Pickler scratched his head, blinked a few times, and turned to look at his buddy, Liberty Johnson. "Sorry, Lib. I guess I can't be positive, I just know they told me Lib was bleedin' really bad, and then that cop wrestled him to the ground and cuffed him."

The judge leaned forward. "Who told you Mr. Johnson was bleeding?"

"You know, the guys who tell me stuff all the time."

"Where can we speak to these *guys*?"

"They're up here," he said, pointing to his head. "They're in my head."

Adrenaline surged through Sam's body. His ears began to ring. The judge tapped his gavel, dismissing the charges against Officer Spence. The courtroom was also dismissed. Sam caught Spence on the way out.

"Means the world to me, you being here, sir."

"Glad things worked out. Hope this serves as a wake-up call to rein in that temper of yours."

"Yes sir."

"Spence? How often does this happen? How often do you hear perps talking about bees, and hearing voices in their heads?"

"All the time, sir."

"Any particular area?"

"Mostly along the corridor. They do drugs under the viaducts, get all crazy."

"Just curious, any cell towers close by?"

"As a matter 'a fact, they put up a couple new ones between Missouri Flat and School Schnell Road."

Sam patted the officer on the back and took leave. He drove along Highway 50, looking for the towers. Conversations he had with Suzanne played on his mind. She mentioned bees—she had never met Spence, yet she knew he had anger issues. She also questioned the towers. Was it even possible to transmit signals that would cause people to hear voices? And if it were true, how could he prove it? *Everyone would think I'm nuts.*

Despair

Roger Salvo drove down Interstate 80, his beloved at his side. He glanced over at her, noticing her face was void of emotion. "Glad to be getting away?" he asked.

She turned to him, her smile radiant. Hopeful. "Yes. We haven't been to Napa in ages."

"Anywhere in particular you want to stop first?"

"V. Sattui—I want to pick up a few bottles of Angelica for the holidays."

"The holidays?"

"Christmas will be here before we know it."

Roger nodded. "Okay, hon. V. Sattui it is." He focused on the road, despair creeping up his chest, causing a lump in his throat. Christmas was months away, and Rebecca didn't drink sweet wine. When they woke that morning, she begged to take a ride to St. Helena to visit her favorite consignment shop, claiming she felt dumpy in her current wardrobe. Roger thought it was an odd request, seeing as her wardrobe was filled with expensive, tasteful, designer clothes, and second, she had been knocking around in workout clothes from Target for the last year or so. She wasn't one to fuss over her clothes. She looked stunning in anything she put on. But it was a lovely day, not too hot, so he agreed to take the drive.

"How would you feel about moving to another country," he asked.

"You mean leave the kids? Live off the grid?"

"The girls can come too. We can find something in the Swiss Alps, or buy an island in Tahiti."

Her face twisted into an ugly scowl. "You know damn well they'll find us."

**

Suzanne drove into her driveway. Lunch with Linda was never an 'eat and run' ordeal. They never did make it to the nursery, or the movies. Instead, they managed to close the place down. Thai Paradise stopped serving at three to regroup for the dinner hour, however, they allowed Linda and Suzanne to remain immersed in conversation. When she checked her watch, it was after four. Sam said he'd be over at six. She had picked up two porterhouse steaks, asparagus, two gigantic mushrooms, and two nectarines for grilling. She had an hour to freshen up and dress, and an hour to prepare dinner. After a quick shower, she put on a pair of pink lace panties and a matching bra, that barely covered her breasts. Her tanned skin made the color pop, and she imagined Sam's reaction when she stripped out of her strappy paisley swing dress. She twisted her hair into a knot and fastened it in place with a pink pearl butterfly clip. "There," she said, twirling in front of her full-length mirror. Sam made her feel beautiful, no matter how she dressed. Perhaps that's why she made a special effort to look her best.

She gathered ingredients for a salad—mixed greens, cucumber, dates, feta cheese, pecans, olive oil, and raspberry balsamic. She chopped the cucumber, dates, and pecans, added them to the feta and greens, and set the bowl in the fridge to chill. The dressing came last after the rest of the meal was grilled. "Alexa," she said, "launch Keener 13 radio." Alexa obeyed, and soon Suzanne was dancing to Martha and the Vandellas.

The doorbell promptly rang at six. She greeted Sam at the door, accepting his offering of flowers, and a bottle of wine. "I hope this is a brand you like," he said, kissing her cheek.

"Perfect, thank you." She inhaled the bouquet. "The flowers—they're beautiful." She peeked between the stems. *No ring.*

"I had an interesting day," he said.

"Do tell."

"The officer I told you about—the one who broke his perp's nose—you were right, he *does* have anger issues, however, the judge decided it wasn't his fault. The perp resisted arrest, and in the scuffle, Spence blocked a hit, and nailed him in the nose with his elbow."

"Accidents happen."

"The interesting part was when the witness testified, he claimed he was told his friend was bleeding by voices in his head."

"I imagine that made him an unreliable witness."

"That's right. Spence claims he gets calls from people living along Highway 50 all the time that are hearing voices."

Suzanne dropped a butter knife, startling herself. "Let me guess—there are 5G towers nearby."

"Yes. But that doesn't mean the towers are the source. Could be drugs, could be these people are so far removed from reality, they keep their own set of friends in their head."

"What about Spence's anger?"

"He needs to get some help with that, but at least he knows he'll be held accountable. I won't have bullies working for me."

Suzanne kissed Sam's cheek. "Want to help me set the table?"

"Be happy to. How was your day?"

"Linda and I solved the world's problems over lunch. To use her expression, 'Some weird shit going on.'"

**

After a sumptuous dinner, Sam cleared the dishes. Suzanne loaded the dishwasher. She poured herself a glass of wine and instructed Alexa to play Sadé radio. Sam came up behind her and buried his face in her hair, as they swayed to the music. When he turned her around to face him, she could feel the heat coming from his groin. She pressed her pelvis against his.

"I think we can let the rest of this go until later," she said, taking a deep breath to inhale his scent.

He maneuvered her across the kitchen toward the stairs, his tongue exploring her mouth. He watched her take each step, her hips tilting from side to side. She could feel his eyes wandering her backside as she reached the top of the stairs. Without turning around, she slipped the straps of her dress down her shoulders, and let her dress fall to the floor. She stepped out of the material and turned to face him.

He devoured her with his eyes, his lips. He eased her down on the bed, covering her body with his. "God, you're so beautiful," he said, as his eyes captured hers. He began to move, stimulating her senses, and every nerve in her body.

When their kisses escalated to a frenzy, she helped him shed his clothes. He, in turn, unhooked her bra, and slid her panties down, following the progression with his mouth. He lingered between her legs, making her moan. When he was satisfied that she was ready for him, he slipped inside of her.

"I love you," he declared over and over again, touching and tasting every part of her body within reach. When she cried out, he quickened his pace, bringing them both to ecstasy.

Satiated, they collapsed side-by-side. "I think I worked off that delicious meal we just ate."

"Me too," she said, cuddling close.

"Hmmm," he said, running a finger across her breast. "That means there's room for dessert."

**

Suzanne's body melded against Sam's, his soft snoring, a comfort to her. More and more his company eased her mind, felt like home in her heart...*where love lives*. She pressed her cheek to his shoulder, and he sighed in his sleep. Part of her wanted to wake him, make love one more time, the other part relished holding him close while he slept. She wanted to step inside his dreams, see herself there, see what their future held. She wanted to synchronize her heartbeat with his, breathe as one. She shuddered at the thought of spending one day apart—until the sound of a gunshot echoed in her brain, shattering her thoughts into tiny bits that rained down from the sky, and into a deep dark well of despair.

**

Roger signed the register at the hotel desk and waited for the keys to their room. Rebecca's idea. A romantic interlude, after a day of shopping, wine tasting, and sightseeing. When they reached Sonoma, the sun had faded from pale orange to crimson, to grey. "Let's get a room," she said. "The wine made me horny. I can't think of anything else other than fucking you six ways to Sunday."

Roger knew this wasn't his wife talking. At least not the wife he knew. Rebecca could get frisky, but she never swore, was never crude. She'd show him she wanted sex with a display of affection. A long kiss. Nibbling his ear. He knew the signals. What he didn't know was these new signals. He couldn't see inside her head. But they could. They picked up the algorithms of her breathing, eye movement, heartbeat. Her thoughts came next, strip them bare, replace them with their own agenda. He knew the drill.

Rebecca barged into the room like a college kid late for a frat party. She tore off her clothes, tossed the pillows on the floor, and laid spread-eagle on the bed. "Do me," she insisted. Roger wanted to cry.

"Baby, how about if we slow it down a tad? Let me get my shoes off, at least."

Rebecca blinked. "You used to be so—so—"

"So young?"

She blinked again. Her eyes became vacant. Suddenly, she shivered. She hid her nakedness under the coverlet, placed her head on a pillow, and fell asleep.

**

Roger awoke that morning in limbo. Rebecca lay next to him. Naked. He caressed her shoulder, causing her to stir. She peeked under the covers discovering her nakedness and lashed out at him.

"What did you do Rog? Why am I—" She wrapped herself up in the covers and stomped into the bathroom, slamming the door behind her.

Roger heard her weeping. He assumed she felt ashamed. After a minute he went to her, his voice soft as butter. "Bec, honey, can I come in?" He didn't expect an answer, nor did he expect the door to be locked. A vow they made to each other when things began to get crazy. *No locked doors.*

"I did it again, didn't I?" she cried. "Right? I got drunk and turned into some cheap whore?"

"Honey, you were tipsy, we made love, it was wonderful."

"Wonderful is when I remember being kissed. Not waking up feeling like I fucked a fire hydrant."

"I'm sorry if I hurt you, you *were* a little wi—"

The door swung open. "Are you saying I did this to myself? Really?" She extended her leg, exposing bruises on her inner thigh. "I did THIS to myself?"

Roger hung his head. It was his fault. He's the one who got them into the mess they were in. He's the one who helped create the technology they used to punish him by hurting Rebecca, by turning her into a deranged nymphomaniac at their will. He wouldn't be surprised if the escapade was recorded somehow to be used against them at a later date. "I'm sorry, my love. I never meant to hurt you."

She flinched, her eyes fluttered, she appeared confused. She closed her robe and pointed to the heap of bedding on the floor. "What are those doing in here?"

"They're soiled. Let's leave them here for the maid."

"Oh. Yes. Good idea." Rebecca smiled. "Where shall we go for breakfast?"

**

Linda answered her door at 7 p.m. Her client seemed agitated, in a hurry to get through the door. Linda rolled her shoulders, deflecting the man's negative energy.

"Tea?" She asked, escorting him into her "reading" room.

"Nah," he said, plopping down in one of her velvet chairs.

Linda cleared her energy field with a silent prayer, took a few deep breaths, and smiled at her client. "What would you like to address this evening?"

"I lost my fucking job. I'm not sure what comes next—how I'm going to provide for my family—whether I should even be here."

"Here? Speaking with me?"

"No. On the fucking planet, period."

The man's negative energy was powerful, his aura was fuzzy, frazzled. Linda closed her eyes. She pictured a woman, her grey hair swept up into a French twist, her body soft, doughy. She was knitting a mile a minute. 'I didn't give birth to a weakling,' the woman said. 'Tell him to "buck up bucko.'

Linda wondered how to convey the woman's disparaging words without pouring salt into the man's already wounded ego. Her father had lost his job once. Not being able to pay the bills stripped him of his dignity. Fortunately, he found a job that suited his vocation as a welder, with better benefits to boot. "Sometimes God closes a door, and opens a window," she said. "My dad was fired once—the job he found was ten times better." She summoned another thought. "I see a woman knitting."

Linda watched the emotional transformations on the man's face. Disbelief, discernment, disgust. "My mother knits. That's all she does," he said. "Sits in front of the TV, clickety-clack, clickety-clack all day long."

"Your mother lives with you?"

"Yes." His eye-roll gave Linda a glimpse of their relationship, however, she wondered why she thought the woman was speaking from the other side. She closed her eyes once more...

This time a bus came to mind, followed by the word, Oklahoma. "I'm getting Oklahoma, are you planning a trip?" She saw a group of people posing for a photo. "Relatives or friends living there?"

"Nope."

A mill manifested behind the group of people. Christmas decorations hung on the lampposts. "I'm seeing a mill, my guides are indicating a job opportunity in December, does that make sense?"

He chuckled. "I don't see myself moving to Oklahoma, Linda."

"I'm just the messenger."

Linda wrapped up her reading at eight. The images and messages she received weren't accepted by her client in the manner in which they were given. The man's mind was made up. He was angry over what had happened, he wanted to wallow a bit and seemed determined to prove her wrong. Her goal was to diffuse any thoughts of him harming himself. In the end, she felt he was prideful, but prudent.

The original vision hung around longer than she expected. A message within a message. "Buck-up bucko," she said aloud. The man hadn't elaborated on his relationship with his mother, but Linda got the clear sense that it was strained.

Flipping through channels, Linda found a comedy with Steve Martin. She settled back in her chair, and let laughter jiggle her thoughts into a better place.

An hour later, she woke with a start. Chills ran up her spine. Clackety, clack, clackety clack. An old woman's words sizzled in her head, "Only a damn fool would move to Oklahoma."

Sunshine

"I had an ugly thought last night," Suzanne said, pouring Sam a cup of coffee.

Sam checked his watch. "My staff meeting isn't until nine—care to share?"

"Actually, I was thinking about you when it happened. I—gosh, how do I explain?"

"Spit it out. You can tell me anything, you know that, don't you?"

"I heard a gunshot."

"While you were thinking of me?"

Sam observed the way she white-knuckled the mug in her hands, her eyes misty. "I'm sure it's just a manifestation of everything that's occurred in the last few weeks. You've been under a lot of stress."

Suzanne nodded. "You have a point. I'm not an expert at interpreting these psychic hits, all I know is that thought in particular bothers the hell out of me."

"I'll be fine, don't worry. I subscribe to something Ronald Reagan once said: "Evil is powerless if the good are unafraid.""

"Good words to live by—now go, before you're late."

He cupped her face in his hands and kissed her lips. "I love you."

She kissed both of his palms. "Call me."

Sam hesitated. His eyes searched hers. She knew what he was waiting for, but something inside of her couldn't let go of the words he longed to hear. She hugged him tight, hoping her heart conveyed the message. "Stay safe."

**

Suzanne tidied up her house, took a shower, and fixed herself a cup of tea. Outside, the weather was pleasant, and she took refuge on her back porch. She closed her eyes, sensing her surroundings. Fresh-cut grass, oleanders, lemon blossoms, car exhaust, fabric softener, glue, and magic markers, gave way to fragrant pines, *sunshine. She smells like sunshine.*

**

Lizzy opened a pouch filled with glitter sticks, glue, and magic markers. Ainsley had drawn an outline of a tree and was ready to color it in. Lizzy put her arm around her daughter's small shoulders and squeezed. "You smell like sunshine."

Ainsley looked skeptical. "Sunshine doesn't smell."

"Oh, yes it does. She lifted a hunk of Ainsley's hair and waved it under her nose. "Smell."

"That's my hair, Mommy, not sunshine."

Lizzy pointed to the sky, "Baby, the sun is what makes your hair smell so good." Lizzy sniffed her hair, her neck, her cheek. "Yep! That's sunshine, all right."

Ainsley shrugged off the sniffing assault, giggling. "Mommy—stop—I'm coloring."

"Okay, if you don't smell like sunshine...you must smell like stinky feet."

Ainsley laughed harder. "Like Daddy's?

Lizzy laughed, and whispered, "Don't let Daddy hear you say that!"

Not far away, Garret watched his wife and daughter's playful banter. He had to admit, being in the outdoors had been good for all of them. *But where to go?* He thought about Colorado. *Not far enough.* Oklahoma? He could change his name, get a job working in one of the mills. *They'd find you.* Wyoming? They could search for a piece of land, live off the grid, *homestead*. He was glad he had the foresight to take their savings out of the bank months ago. Thirteen thousand wouldn't get them very far, but it was something. He would let their house go into foreclosure, figure out a way to start again. His heart hurt knowing they would have to change their appearance and cut Ainsley's beautiful curls. *Whatever it takes to stay alive.*

**

Suzanne tried to focus on the message she was receiving. *Where are you?* Her inner voice inquired. *What do you want to tell me?* Nothing. "I can't help you if I don't know where you are or what you want," she said, aloud.

After a few minutes, she gave up and went into the house. She had to keep reminding herself throughout the morning that she was a vessel, and that God was at the helm. *Tahoe.* Perhaps a ride up the hill would clear her chakras. She texted Sam to apprise him of her plan. On the way back, she planned to stop at Apple Hill, check out their vegetables. Steven and Karen would be coming for dinner soon.

**

She drove through Placerville, admiring the small town's charm, and ambiance. It had been a while since she explored the gold country. She wanted to visit the new Batia Winery. She heard the wine was amazing, and that they had music performances a couple of times a week. A great place to go with friends, if she had any that imbibed. Perhaps she'd invite Steven and Karen to go some time. Her mother's voice invaded her thoughts. *He misses you*. "I've been right here, Mom. I can't help it if he can't accept what I've become."

The next eighty miles up the mountain were smooth sailing. Suzanne arrived on Tahoe's south shore and looked for a place to park. Linda had told her being by water would charge her batteries, serve as a conduit for any messages the universe wanted to convey. She was ready.

She walked down to the pier, the sun warming her bare shoulders. Dark glasses shielded her eyes, but the glare from the water was intense and made her think of Jack. It was August...

She was lying in the pool on a raft, water droplets, sparkling diamonds on her skin, as the sun drenched her in golden light. When she looked up, Jack was staring at her. The sadness in his eyes conflicted with his cocky smile. "Is that all you do? Lay in the pool all day, communing with Sun Gods?"

"If you join me, we can commune together."

...That was the day he told me he was leaving for boot camp. In retrospect, she knew he was never coming back.

Suddenly, a flock of blackbirds flew overhead, piquing her curiosity as they danced in the sky in perfect formation. She watched in awe as the birds changed directions and patterns, tightly synchronized as one. But then, a weight descended upon her soul, and she lifted her glasses, daring the sun to blind her from her anticipation to no avail. Her horror grew as the murmuration disbanded into chaos, and birds began falling from the sky like rain.

**

Shook up, Suzanne ran for her car and headed west to Sacramento. By the time she reached Apple Hill in Camino, her heart was once again beating at a normal pace. With another sixty miles to go, she stopped at Boa Vista Orchard, picked up apple cider for salted caramel martinis, apple beer for Steven, and an assortment of veggies to grill. She felt as though a zombie had taken over her body. She couldn't shake the image of the birds dropping into the water, no matter how hard she tried.

**

When she arrived home, she turned on her computer and typed, *birds falling from sky*. Different websites offered several possibilities. *Predator?* She didn't see anything larger flying near the birds, then again, it was bright. *Magnetic field?* Did something disturb their magnetic field, causing them to crash into one another? She watched several videos of birds falling from the sky in Mexico, and Oregon, India. Then moved on to a strange illness, killing songbirds in Indiana, Ohio, Kentucky, Washington D.C., Pennsylvania, Delaware, West Virginia, Virginia, and Maryland. These birds experience neurological symptoms.

Ornithologists stumped. *Interesting*...but nothing conclusive, and she wasn't getting psychic hits one way or another. *It's a mystery.* She scrolled down until another title caught her eye. 5G Causing Birds to Fall from the Sky.

Suzanne finished an article on 5G trying to assimilate what she read and correlate the information with what she had experienced. Experiments to control brain activity in mice, no mention of these same experiments being done on humans. Nothing made sense, yet it all seem to fit together with what was happening. And how did the little girl fit into the mix? Was she part of the shooting at the park? Suzanne conjured the pink jelly shoe she saw the woman holding on the news the day of the mass shooting in the park. Suzanne wondered...why did she have the impression it wasn't real? And what about the suicides in Paris, and birds disappearing, and dropping from the sky?

She poured a glass of iced tea and went to her mailbox. As she sorted through her mail, a tune wafted through her brain, whimsical, lyrical—*Fanboys, Fanboys, Fanboys carry the fan. Fanboys, Fanboys, the boys who have a plan.* She shuddered, nearly choking on her tea. Her stomach burned, she felt woozy, and behind her eyes, all went black. Two words broke through the darkness. *He's dead.*

**

The News

Although Linda considered herself a Christian, she preferred Buddhist temples to church. She loved Jesus, however: she was certain the serenity she felt upon entering a Temple came from a previous lifetime. She visited often, especially when in need of solace. She wandered through the garden, mentally conversing with Bonsai trees and exotic flowers. She raised her face to the sun to feel the warmth of God's touch on her skin. Peace. Love. She pictured tranquil waters, light dancing around Asian lily pads, lotus blossoms embracing the sky with outstretched arms. She felt centered. Fulfilled.

She let her thoughts drift to Suzanne and her angst. Linda prayed. She prayed for clarity, protection, and love. Next, she prayed for Sam. She could read his heart, and she knew his struggle. He was a man of honor, justice. Suzanne was his solace.

She prayed for Joseph. She asked God to grant him willpower and resilience. He too struggled at times—she knew that from being his friend for so long. He was dear to her, and she wanted the best for him. She knew he was troubled by the young man who died on the train tracks, and she prayed for resolve. The man was in God's hands now, Joseph couldn't change the man's fate, even if he tried. Linda found it disturbing that Suzanne witnessed the same scenario. She surrounded all the troubled souls on the planet with white light and prayed for spiritual wisdom.

**

Joseph stood out on his balcony, a glass of Conundrum red wine in his hand. The sun was setting over the Bay, red and orange shards crushing cobalt blue. Coq au vin in the oven, and Ben in the shower, gave him a few minutes to reflect on his day. He had read two difficult clients and worked on creating a book cover for a friend who was writing his memoir. Joseph was pleased with the way the cover turned out, using his creativity brought him joy.

The readings he did earlier disturbed him. His first client couldn't keep from looking at his phone. When Joseph asked him politely if he would please put it away, the man snapped at him. When Joseph calmly explained that he was cheating himself out of getting the full benefit of his reading, the man told him to fuck off. His second client misconstrued everything he said. She could only see doom in every positive card he drew. *Even Ben seems to be a little cantankerous.* Joseph chalked up their shortcomings to Mercury being in retrograde. *Brush it off.*

Just then, Ben appeared bare-chested, wearing a pair of plaid pajama pants. He finished towel drying his hair and slung the damp towel around his neck. "Hey," he said, his words a love note. "Dinner smells *a-maz-ing*. Need me to set the table?"

Joseph stepped inside and into Ben's arms. "What I *need* is a hug."

**

Sam turned off his kitchen light, brought his plate filled with a grilled T-Bone steak, a baked potato, and fresh broccolini into the living room, and turned on the TV. With the hectic day he had, the last thing he needed was more negativity, but before he could change the channel, he got sucked into the lead-in. "A man believed to be the Discovery Park shooter was found dead in his apartment this afternoon."

He took bites of food during the commercial break. When the news resumed, he set his plate down and turned up the volume. "Dallen

Foster's dead body was discovered this afternoon after a neighbor complained about an odor coming from the apartment adjoining his." The anchor tossed the spotlight to another anchor in the field. The camera panned the area as a petite Asian woman gestured toward the Spanish-style building in the background. "Police are not divulging exactly what was found inside Foster's apartment, only that they have reason to believe the man may be responsible for last week's mass shooting at Discovery Park. After speaking with neighbors, we have learned that Mr. Foster was new to the area, and kept to himself. Back to you."

Sam flipped channels to see if the other stations were reporting the same information. He dialed Suzanne. "Turn on the news. See if you pick up on anything."

**

Suzanne wasn't expecting the reaction she got from watching the news clip. She closed her eyes and felt the man's tortured soul standing nearby. So close, that if she reached her hand out, she would be able to touch him. His image appeared behind her lids; he was younger than she had expected; twenty-five at best. His energy wasn't evil, it was—*sad*.

Suddenly bombarded with visions of the suicides in Paris, Suzanne shook her head, attempting to clear the tragedies from her mind. "Sam?" She paced her living room floor. "Sam, I think the suicides in Paris are somehow connected to this man. I don't know how, but I sense, Dallen Foster was a victim as well."

"The man opened fire on a crowd of kids—how could he be the victim?"

"I don't believe he acted on his own volition—just like those people who jumped off buildings in Paris, or the young man Joseph told me about, the one that walked in front of a train."

"I agree, it doesn't make sense." Silence came between them for a beat, and then, "Did you have dinner?"

"I made a salad. I wasn't very hungry. You?"

"I grilled a steak. I should've invited you over. We could've discussed this over a nice meal."

"How sweet, but it's just as well. I plan to take a hot bath and go to bed. My head hurts from thinking so much."

"I agree, it's been a long day. I'm sure Sac P.D. has everything under control. I was surprised to see the man is dead, that's all. They didn't say how he died, either. Normally, all details of a case are kept under wraps until the official reports come in. How they pinned the shooting on this guy so quickly has me baffled." Sam sighed. "Okay, my beautiful Suzanne—get some rest. We can talk tomorrow."

"I'll look forward to your call. Good night, my love."

Suzanne proceeded as planned—eased into a hot bath, sat back and relaxed, closed her eyes, and let her sensory experience begin. She had learned that water conducted energy, allowing messages from the universe to flow into her brain. Dallen Foster, the man with the sad face appeared virtually behind her third eye, this time even more of an enigma. She saw him in school, bright, attentive. As a young man, gregarious, successful, the life of the party. Suddenly, the image dispelled into darkness. She saw him alone, paranoid, a shell of his former self—*a vessel*. She knew what they would find when they looked for his cause of death. *Suicide*.

Far Away

A smattering of cumulous clouds against an azure blue sky guided the Breckers along Emerald Bay Road to the Aisle Gas station, where they picked up a map, two coffees, a small carton of milk for Ainsley, three "freshly made" breakfast sandwiches, and a package of Oreo cookies. Garret paid for the fill-up with cash and headed westbound for Highway 50. The crisp temps couldn't compete with the warmth the threesome bestowed on each other. It could have been fear or the collective consciousness that had brought them together, but from the moment they closed the cabin door behind them, they functioned as a unit. Gone were the whining, bickering, blame, and anger. It was as if they were on an adventure. A planned vacation. *With one exception.*

"Mommy? Do I have an auntie Suzanne?"

Lizzie twisted around in her seat to face her whimsical, yet wise four-year-old. "No, I'm sorry Sweet Pea, Daddy and I are only children." She smiled. "We have a couple of cousins, but no Suzanne. Why?"

"The lady who talks to me in my head—that's *her* name."

Garret and Lizzie exchanged glances. Garret adjusted the rear-view mirror, centering his daughter in its frame. "What does the lady say to you, Bug?"

Ainsley slurped her milk through her straw before answering. Her eyes shown big, and blue. "She wants to know where I am?"

**

"Time to fire up the grill?" Sam washed his hands and grabbed a kitchen towel. He stood behind Suzanne and kissed her neck.

"Uh, huh. The ribs are marinating in the fridge—and if you don't stop, my brother may walk in here to find us making love on my mother's walnut dining table."

The doorbell rang.

Sam laughed. "At least we would have gotten a warning."

She grazed his lips with hers on the way to the door.

"Suzanne!" Steven gushed. "Sam, nice to see you. Suzanne, you're flushed. Karen, you remember Sam?" Steven pushed passed everyone and headed for the kitchen. "Smells like mom's cooking," he called over his shoulder.

"Of course, I remember you," Karen said, moving in for a hug. Don't pay any attention to my husband. He's half Irish, three-quarters bull-shit, and one-eighth jerk."

Suzanne wrapped her arm around Karen, guiding her toward the kitchen. "It's been a while—I've missed you."

"I can't remember the last time I was in this house."

"Me neither," Steven piped in. "Love what you've done to the place."

"I haven't done—"

"I was referring to garbage you got rid of—you know—Ben? The ex?"

Sam chimed in, "I guess it's easy to judge a person until you walk in their shoes."

"C'mon Sam. Ben was a loser—we both know that."

"I was referring to your sister. Divorcing Ben was her decision to make—in her own time."

Karen played referee. "What can we do to help?"

Suzanne flashed her a grateful smile. "I was about to make a salad—Sam, will you please get my brother a beer?"

Suzanne shifted gears, doling out a chopping board and knife to

Karen, while keeping a close eye on her brother. *Who does he think he is?* The answer came quickly, from an unexpected source.

He's always acted like a Neanderthal over other men's attention towards you. He's just like your dad.

Mom?

You can tell him I'm here, but I doubt he will believe you.

"Steven? Mom's here. She said you're acting just like Dad."

"Yeah, right," he said.

Sam diffused the situation by commandeering Steven's help outside until Steven popped his head back in to say, "I felt her Suz! She grabbed my goddamn ear!"

**

The evening progressed nicely. Steven curbed his sarcasm and engaged in a lengthy conversation with Sam over sports. By the time they sat down to dinner, Suzanne felt as though a weight had been lifted, and she was surrounded by love.

Dipping her hands into a sink of sudsy water, Karen said, "Tell me about Paris."

Suzanne scraped off a dinner plate and set it on the sink to be rinsed. "It was lovely. Breathtaking. Enchanting. Romantic."

"But?"

"But what?"

"I know you, Suzanne. You're leaving the rice out of the pudding."

"It wasn't perfect...there were...interruptions."

Karen's eyes sparkled, "What kind of interruptions? Did you get caught doin' it in public or something?"

Suzanne's jaw dropped. "No!" She blushed. "That would've been something, though."

"What happened?"

"Let's see, three people jumped to their death, Sam's proposal was ruined by one of them, and then once again in Salzburg by a flock of blackbirds that swarmed the gazebo we were in—the one from *Sound of Music*, no less—need I say more?"

Karen reached for her hand. "I didn't see—" Suzanne stepped back.

"There's nothing to see. He hasn't—" She took a deep breath and exhaled. "Things happen for a reason."

"I'm so sorry. Clearly he loves you. I bet he's waiting for another opportunity to ask. I'm sure you've both been busy since you got back."

"Karen, have you noticed anything strange lately?"

"Strange doesn't begin to describe what's going on in the world. People are angry, distracted, rude...I mean, no one knows how to communicate anymore—everyone is too busy looking at their phones. It's creepy."

Suzanne nodded, and drifted away in her thoughts for a moment, staring out the window, into her backyard. And then the little girl appeared, her once long blonde curls, now short, and brown. Her smile appeared the same, but her eyes revealed a sadness. A loss. When she saw Suzanne watching, she quickly turned away. And disappeared.

Suzanne stood frozen in her thoughts. *What are you running from, little one? And where are you going?*

"Suzanne?" She felt Karen's hand on her shoulder. "What is it? You're as stiff as concrete."

"Just lost in thought, I guess." Suzanne wiped her palms on her faded jeans. "Let's go see how the boys are doing."

**

Outside, Sam and Steven seemed to be involved in a serious conversation. One they quickly aborted when they noticed Suzanne and Karen walking towards them.

"We didn't mean to interrupt," Karen said, placing her arm around Steven's shoulder.

Steven gave Sam a sharp glance and slipped his arm around Karen's waist. "No worries, just guy talk, right Sam?"

Sam's demeanor relaxed, "Yeah. Two beautiful ladies? I'd say more of a distraction than an interruption." He leaned forward and planted a light kiss on Suzanne's temple.

"I'm calling bullshit." Suzanne chuckled. "What were you two talking about?"

Sam raised his brow and gestured toward Steven. "I relayed some of our experiences in Paris. Your brother has different theories on what happened, that's all."

"I'd love to hear them, Steven, care to share?"

"Not really, but I would like another beer." He broke away from Karen and walked toward the house. "Can I get anyone anything?" He asked.

Suzanne's brow creased. "What just happened?"

Sam shrugged. "He's having trouble processing your situation."

"My *situation*? What exactly does that mean?"

Karen interjected. "You know how your brother is, Suzanne. I think he refuses to believe in anything he can't control."

Suzanne's shoulders slumped. "Yeah, I guess you're right, but he's going to have to accept the change because I'm stuck with it."

Changes

Tears rolled down Lizzy's cheeks as the scissors bit into Ainsley's blonde curls. Once the task was finished, she picked up the pile of hair, sifted it through her fingers, and sobbed. The fuckers responsible for tracking them had no right to rob them of something so sacred, so precious as their daughter's crowning glory. She opened the box of brown hair color with jerky, angry motions. She wanted to scream out loud, but the walls were thin in the cheap motel outside of Silver Creek Junction, Utah.

They had driven all night, her patience worn thin, her heart heavy. More tears fell as she smeared brown goop on her daughter's little melon. Ainsley hummed a song she learned in Bible School when she was three. *Jesus loves me, this I know...*

Ainsley wrinkled her nose. "Am I going to look like Trevor?"

"Who's Trevor?"

"You know, Mommy. Trevor from my school?"

Lizzy had forgotten about school. The fee automatically would be taken out of their account on the first of the month. There was no way to cancel without leaving a trace. "No sweetheart. You're going to be Ainsley in here—" she placed her hand over Ainsley's heart, "but on the outside, you're going to be different. Like you're playing the part of another little girl, with short brown hair. Do you want to pick out a name for the little girl you'll be playing?"

"I like Belle. Can I be Belle?"

"I think that's a beautiful name. How about Belle Louise? It has a nice ring to it, don't you think?"

"Louise?" She tilted her head. "Can I be Belle Suzanne Benton?"

"Why Suzanne?"

"She's my friend."

"Where do you know this Suzanne from, again?"

"Mommy, I told you. She's behind my eyes." She pointed to the middle of her forehead. "Right here."

"Like Grandma?"

"No," Ainsley said. "Grandma visits me from heaven. I can see her..."

"Where does Suzanne live?"

"Sacramento."

"How do you know that?"

"I can see the tower from her backyard—just like ours."

"What does she look like?"

"She's pretty, like you, Mommy."

A chill skittered up Lizzy's spine. She always knew her daughter was special. Bright, intuitive. She had even accepted that she was able to see her deceased mother. But this—what if all this time "they" were fucking with her baby's head, the way they fucked with hers? And Garret's? *How can I be sure of anything, anymore?*

**

When the phone rang, Suzanne woke from a deep sleep.

"Uh oh, I disturbed Sleeping Beauty, didn't I?"

Suzanne squinted at the clock. 10:02. "Linda, no, no. I should've been up hours ago."

"I just wanted to say 'hi', see how your dinner party went last night."

"It went well. My brother still thinks I'm nuts, but my mother showed up and squeezed his shoulder—something she did when we were kids."

"When he was naughty?"

"Mostly when he wouldn't shut up. He had a tendency to talk a mile a minute at the wrong times. Like at school, or church."

"It's nice that you went to church."

"Yeah." The tune, "Jesus Loves Me" sung in an angelic voice played behind her words. "We went to a quaint little neighborhood church until the city tore it down."

"At least you and your brother are talking again, that's important."

"Yes, I agree." The tune got louder. Suzanne could see the small mouth singing the lyrics. The picture expanded, and the little girl's face appeared. "Linda, I keep seeing that little girl. She doesn't *appear* to be in peril, and yet I feel that she is."

"How so."

"In the beginning, I saw her with long blonde curls. Now she has short brown hair."

"Have you checked for abducted children?"

"No. I feel that she is running away, but she's happy. It seems to be an adventure of some sort."

"Time will tell. Do you know where she is?"

Suzanne closed her eyes. "I see an arch. A natural arched rock formation."

"Get on your computer. See if you recognize it anywhere."

"Oklahoma keeps popping into my head."

"Funny. Mine too. I was doing a reading for a client the other day, and Oklahoma came up."

"It's a start."

"Sometimes the images we get are puzzle pieces. You just gotta work 'em until they fall into place."

"Linda, you watch the news, did you see they found the man they suspect was responsible for the shootings at Discovery Park? His name was Dallen Foster."

"To be honest, I only get my news online. It seems less manipulating. And even then, I have to get past the theatrics."

"I was wondering what your take—"

"I don't feel he was entirely responsible. In my mind, I'm seeing the title, *Walking Dead*, that show about zombies."

"Me too. What do we do about it? How do we find the truth?"

**

Roger sat behind his desk, arms tucked behind his head, staring into a blank screen. He could hear his beloved wife tossing random things into the trash can. It all started with an expired can of soup. Then came boxes of expired pasta, Jell-O pudding, items that didn't outlive their good intentions. By the time Roger excused himself from the wreckage, she had dragged one of the 32-gallon trash cans from the garage into the middle of the kitchen floor. She'd been at it for over an hour. Each item followed by a battle cry and a "Fuck you!"

His project was due in two days. His mouse lay dormant next to his keyboard and the stack of schematics mapping out his next task using cerebral cortex cloning, which entailed identifying emotion signature clusters, taking the undesirable personality traits from one source, and implanting them into the targeted host using Extremely Low Frequency (ELF), a *subradio frequency*, pulse modulated microwave remote mind control technology. In other words, he was to provide a program that would turn a normal human being into a killing machine, like the poor sucker who massacred the adults and children at Discovery Park. What the poor slob would never find out, because of the well-designed post-suicide clause, was that he missed more people than he hit and that somehow the news omitted those minor details. Roger suspected half of Sacramento's population was part of the "Hive Mind" project, using an assortment of mass mind manipulation programs that allowed decisions to be made without protest. Democracy being stripped away, right under the noses of the people who felt justified in exercising their rights, casting their votes, fighting for the underdog. People who slept well, ignoring the takeover poisoning their air, and their dream state—admonishing anyone or anything that posed a warning to the contrary.

Roger knew it was all a masquerade. He was reminded of the Eloi, and the Morlocks in H.G. Wells' *Time Machine*, a movie where a time traveler visited the future through a time-traveling machine. The Eloi, a human species, oblivious to emotion, concerned with nothing except their own rudimentary needs and self-indulgence; the Morlock, a species that worked to provide comfort for the Eloi, but in truth the Morlock controlled the Eloi, and raised them as their food supply. A prime example of utopia, and dystopia. *Eventually, all control will lie in the hands of the puppet masters.* Roger's only way out was to put his family into the car, close the garage door, and turn on the gas.

A crash, coming from the kitchen, brought him back to his senses.

**

Joseph planted himself in a wooden chair behind a wooden table and began sorting through a stack of newspapers. His goal was to find articles pertaining to the young man who walked in front of the train the week before. The image haunted him, and as much as he meditated, requested and prayed for guidance from his spirit guides and God himself, his quandary remained unresolved.

Linda and Suzanne spoke of an epidemic...people, birds, off-kilter... caught in a web of an unexplained superpower...mind control. Whatever means took the young man's life, Joseph needed to understand. And he needed to come to terms with his obsession over the young man's demise.

After scouring through thirty-seven newspapers, he finally found what he was looking for. A name to go with the face that haunted him. Testimony from David L. Harmon's mother, Nola, to the press. "David was a quiet boy. He loved to read, listen to podcasts on scientific discoveries. He always had his earbuds in. Maybe he didn't hear the train coming." The next paragraph read: "He planned to finish his bachelor's degree in science this year. He wanted to work as an engineer for Honeywell in Clearwater, Florida, and eventually work his way into the NASA program on Merritt Island. He said he'd find me a little apartment nearby. David loved his family. He was kind, a gentle soul, always upbeat. I can't imagine why he would take his life, especially that way. His uncle Bill was a railroad engineer. He had shared how people did themselves in by walking in front of trains, and he knew the toll it took on his uncle Bill every time it happened, and he felt bad for him." The short article ended with a GoFundMe link and funeral plans.

Joseph pushed himself away from the table. He was right. David L. Harmon didn't walk in front of that train. He was pushed. Not by *someone*, but by *something*.

**

The morning sun made its way west until it hid behind the trees in Suzanne's backyard. After her conversation with Linda, she needed to shake off the doom and gloom by doing something productive. First, she looked up rock formations on her computer. There was a natural rock bridge in Virginia, a beautiful rock formation in Tufa Towers, California, Spider Rock, Arizona, Devils Tower in Wyoming, and several arches in Utah. As Suzanne scrolled through the list, a couple seemed similar to her vision, but none of them were exact. When her stomach reminded her it was empty, she powered down her computer and treated herself to a cup of coffee and a piece of rye toast.

After a quick shower, she drove to the nursery in Jackson and wandered through plants, trees, and piles of brick. She came home with two mature tomato plants, six Crazy Love rose bushes bursting with "double color-soaked blossoms," and purchased two pallets of brick to be delivered in ten days. She always wanted to carve a path and install a brick walkway from the back step, to the garden flanking the back fence. "My own yellow brick road," she said, drawing her eyes from the beginning of the path to the end, where the Tower Theater landmark stood sentinel in the distance.

Feeling drained from digging, and lugging five-gallon containers from her car into the backyard, Suzanne stripped out of her sweaty clothes in the laundry room and headed for the shower upstairs. Her foot had hit the first step when the doorbell made her jump. *Shit. Now what*? If she stepped any further to the right, she would be in line with the sidelight window to the right of the front door. If she moved to the left, she could be seen through the sidelight on the left. If *I stay still, they'll go away*. Not so. Pounding came next...then...

"Suzanne?" Sam's voice.

"Sam? Are you alone?"

"Yes, I am, are you?"

"Yes. But I'm naked. Can you give me a minute?"

No answer.

"Sam?"

"Yes?"

"What are you doing?"

"Wishing I had x-ray vision."

"No need." She unlocked the door, grabbed his hand, and led him inside.

**

The water was warm, soothing. Sam's kisses sent pleasurable sensations to every part of her body. They both lingered under the spray, exploring each other as if it were the first time. "We're wasting water," Sam whispered in her ear.

She twisted the faucet, stopping the flow, her hands finding where they left off. "I'll wash if you dry."

"Deal."

She soaped up his body, making him squirm.

"Not fair," he groaned.

Her eyes twinkled as she performed her final scrub. "You can thank me later."

**

As promised, Sam did the drying, making sure every crevice was moisture free. Except for one. "I prefer that part of you wet," he said, as he wrapped the oversized towel around her. He carried her to the bed, threw back the covers, and crawled in beside her. He held her close, alternating between kneading her buttocks, and her breasts. Her body rose, and she wrapped her long limbs around his waist, her words welcoming him inside.

Their love dance lasted long enough to build momentum, each of them prolonging their release. When the moment came to let go, they both cried out in ecstasy. When the final wave crashed to the shore, they lie exhausted in each other's arms.

**

"Make it a double," Sam mumbled in his sleep. The bar was dark, dank. Cigar and cigarette smoke clung to the walls from years gone by. A buxom bartender wiped the lackluster wood with a shredded cloth that smelled like urine. "If ya want another yur gonna hafta speak up. I'm not a mind reader ya know."

Sam slammed his fist on the bar. "Make it a double," he barked, loud and clear. "Did'ja hear me *that* time, bitch?"

Her mouth opened wide. Sam saw beetles scurry in and out. Her tongue lashed out with a hiss. She slammed a glass filled with whiskey in front of him and grinned. "That's more like it, *Sam*."

He threw back the whiskey in one gulp. *Sam. How does she know my name*?

She hoisted herself up onto the bar and slithered close to his ear. "Everyone knows your name, Sam. *Everyone*."

Sam woke with a start. His chest heaved in and out, his breath, shallow, ragged. Suzanne grabbed his arm.

"Sam? What's wrong? Are you okay?"

Sam sat up. "Man, I can't remember the last time I had a nightmare."

Suzanne jumped out of bed and came back in a moment with a glass of water. "Drink this," she said, "It will make you feel better."

He shoved her hand away. "I think I've had enough to drink for one night."

"It's water, Sam."

His eyes searched hers. "It felt so real."

"But it wasn't. This is real. You here, with me, in my bed, drinking a glass of water."

"In my dream it was—"

"Whiskey."

"How did you—"

"First thing that popped into my head. And didn't you say you were being inundated with liquor commercials the other night?"

"Yes. But how do you explain the dream I just had?"

"And how do you know you're having a dream?"

"I just told you—"

The Tower Theater's image loomed in her head, a beacon of hope. "Whatever you saw, it's not real."

Sam stared at her. Her expression was steady, compassionate, loving. "Do you know something I don't?" he asked.

"I know you struggle with alcohol, or at least you did in the past. I know that weird shit is going on, preying on our weaknesses. You yourself said you haven't had a nightmare in ages. Let me guess...the bartender was eager to serve you."

"I'm the one who—"

Suzanne raised one brow. "Think hard."

"No, I guess you're right. She manipulated me into ordering another by—"

"Pushing your button."

"Yes."

"Whoever 'they' are, it's their mission to get to you."

"You know how crazy that sounds?"

"I do—and I can't explain how I receive the messages I get or see what I see, but somehow, I don't think it's the same." She paused. "The word 'cloning' comes to mind."

FATE

Rebecca appeared in the doorway to Roger's office, dressed to the nines. "Going somewhere?" he asked. "It's kind of early to go clubbing, isn't it?"

Rebecca assessed her reflection in the glass doors of Roger's ten-foot bookshelf. She stared at her face as if it wasn't her own, tugging at her cheeks with her fingertips. She blinked away whatever image stared back at her. "Rog,—baby?" She pivoted on one black patent heel. "Do you think I'm pretty?"

Roger rose from his desk. "Yes," he said, crossing the room until they were nose to nose. He locked his eyes on hers, placing a gentle hand on each slender shoulder. "I think you are the most beautiful woman on the planet." He wrapped his arms around her and held her close. "How about if we change into something more comfortable, and I take you to lunch?"

She stepped back. "You're not even dressed!" Her plump lips spread into a pirate's smile. "We can't have you gallivanting in your boxers, now, can we?"

"No. Let's both change." He parted the blinds with two fingers. "Looks pretty warm out there. Shorts and a T-shirt sound comfy—what do you think?"

"And sandals. These shoes hurt my feet." She removed her stiletto heels and tucked them under her arm. "Or flip-flops."

"Yes," he said, kissing the top of her head as he guided her out of the room. "Let me shut down my computer, I'll be right there." He watched her walk down the hall towards their bedroom. When she was out of sight, he returned to his screen, saved his work, engaged the security commands, and shut down. Inside, his stomach churned acid. His heart beat a little too fast. His eyes panned the room. "Don't worry," he whispered to the unseen force in the room, "I'll make my deadline. I always do."

**

Sam and Suzanne held hands as the waitress at Mayahuel Restaurant led them to a table in the outside courtyard facing K Street. It was early for lunch, but Sam managed to take time out of his busy day to be with her. He wanted to make the magic last as long as he could before returning to work. He sat with his back to the wall, facing the street. It was a cop thing. He watched couples file in, enjoying the day, others absorbed in one another or their meal. One couple piqued his interest. The man was dressed in shorts and a T-shirt. His wife wore a loose tank, capris, and flip-flops, which seemed normal, except for the bright red lipstick that colored her lips. He watched as the couple finished their meal at a table adjacent to theirs.

As Suzanne perused the menu, Sam's eyes were glued to the couple. The man, oblivious to his stare, quietly pleaded with the woman beside him. She stared straight ahead, as if his words fell on deaf ears.

"What are you going to have?" Suzanne asked, nudging him with her elbow. "Have you even looked? Or has the woman at the next table captured all of your attention?"

"Sorry. The cop in me is running amuck."

"What's wrong?"

"I don't know yet. Just a feeling."

Suzanne followed his gaze. What she saw gave her a start. The woman's head pixelated. A noose circled the man's neck. "Definitely trouble."

Sam called the waiter over. "I'll take their check," he said, nodding toward Roger and Rebecca. The waiter looked surprised. He leaned in.

"Are you sure?" he whispered, "they both ordered ribeyes. And several drinks."

Sam nodded. "Yes, I'm sure."

The waiter returned with the other couple's bill. As expected, it was over one hundred dollars. Sam produced his charge card and slipped it inside the pocket of the leather check folder.

After returning with Sam's card and receipt, the waiter stopped at the couple's table to inform them the bill was taken care of. Sam received the response he had hoped for when the couple rose and headed his way.

"How very kind of you," Rebecca slurred.

Roger stiffened. "Name's Roger—do I know you?

"No. The name's Sam Metzger. Sheriff's department, Goldorado County." Sam shook the man's hand. He could feel Roger's nerves humming beneath his skin. "This is my partner, Suzanne Cash. She's my psychic investigator."

Roger stepped back. "Am I in some sort of trouble?"

"No, no. We were just having lunch. Wanted to do something kind, pay it forward, so to speak."

"Roger Salvo. My wife Rebecca. We were doing the same—beautiful day and all. You're a ways from home, aren't you?" Sam dropped his customer copy of the receipt. Roger caught it midair and returned it to Sam.

"Good catch—I seem to be all thumbs today." Sam inserted the receipt into his wallet. "Suzanne lives out this way. We love the food here." Sam directed his focus on Rebecca, who was now teetering at Roger's side. "You okay, Ma'am?" he asked.

Rebecca smiled. "Sure. Peachy."

Roger's discomfort became visible. "We best be going. Thank you for lunch. I'll be sure to pay it forward, myself."

Sam slipped a business card into Roger's palm. "Always happy to make new friends in the area," Roger nodded, pocketed the card, and ushered his wife away.

Sam sat back down, encouraging Suzanne to do the same. "What did you get?"

"I'm curious, how did you know there was anything to 'get'?"

"Just a hunch. What did you see?"

"The woman isn't in her right mind, and he's trapped."

"Well, now I have his prints." Sam patted his pocket. "We shall see if there is anything to know about this guy."

Suzanne shook her head. "What an interesting day."

"Still have an appetite?"

Suzanne grinned. "Absolutely!"

**

Roger hurried back to his car, Rebecca in tow. The sound of her flip-flops echoing in the concrete parking structure fell in sync with his heartbeat. He could feel his blood pressure rise. His face felt clammy, his palms, sweaty. His gaze darted in all directions. Someone was watching. "Rebecca, get in the car." He opened the passenger door. As she pivoted her body, her foot slid off her shoe, and she stumbled and dumped the contents of her purse onto the ground. As he scurried to collect the items, he caught a glimpse of a man standing across the way. *Holy fuck.* It was one of the men from the yacht. Roger recognized him. He had watched the waitress serve him the drink that knocked him on his ass and ruined his life. *First the cop, now this guy.* Suddenly he felt his days were numbered. He pretended he didn't see him. "Here you go, baby," he said, depositing Rebecca's belongings back into her bag.

Using only his peripheral vision, he took in as many details about the man as he could. He got behind the wheel, backed out of his parking space, and let out a sigh of relief. Rebecca reached for his crotch.

Roger took a deep breath and put her hand back in her lap. "Not now, baby. Wait until we get home."

**

Owen Westford waited until Roger was out of sight before he walked to the end of the row and got into his car. He had hand-picked Roger that night on the boat. Owen knew from military projects he had worked on that Roger's talents were priceless. Owen's ambition knew no boundaries. Roger provided the means; Own provided the ways. The powers that be understood enough about the weapons they procured, but they were too busy playing war games to notice Owen's obsession for control. Once he was elected Governor, there would be no stopping him. California would serve as a pit stop to the top.

Name Game

Lizzie Brecker, now Amy Lynn Benton, stared out the window, oblivious to the scenery speeding by. Morning sickness forced them to make various stops along the highway, stops that could've been avoided if she wasn't six weeks pregnant. Ainsley, now Belle Suzanne, quietly played with her new art supplies in the backseat. Garret sat silent, stone-faced, eyes on the road. She prayed silently to end the nightmare they were trapped inside. She prayed to return to normalcy. She prayed for her little girl's curls to be long, and blonde again, and for the strange little girl in the backseat to be her sweet Ainsley once more.

"I hate this," she said to no one.

Garret, now Peter Boyd Benton glanced her way. "I thought five hundred dollars was pretty cheap for all three of us, don't you?"

"Providing they're legit. The driver's licenses look pretty good, but who knows, there's all that info stored on the magnetic strips, isn't there? I mean there's no way we can get through security at the airport."

"I kept our old ones just in case. The guy said the one strip is just a repeat of what's on the front of the license. The second strip can only be read by specific scanners, which retailers don't have. Once we open a bank account with the matching social security numbers, we should be good."

"I would think trust would be more costly. At that price, how do we know we can trust what he said to be true?"

"The names, other than Ainsley's, or Belle, are already attached to the socials. Belle's birth certificate is a fake, but no one really checks further than to see if it matches our names. Once she's registered in school, we'll have more substantial records for her. We'll find a place that is more concerned with good character than the money in your wallet or your credit score."

"What about the baby? We have no insurance."

"Babe, please don't worry. Let's take things one step at a time." He reached for her hand. "Am-y." His sheepish grin won her over. She placed her hand in his.

"Can I call you Pete?"

"Yes, m'am."

**

Ainsley couldn't keep up with the conversation her parents were having in the front seat. The motion of the car made her sleepy, and she had worn herself out climbing on the rocks while Mommy threw up. Daddy told her the rocks were a natural arch, made by God. She thought it looked like a rainbow, covered in red mud. She closed her eyes, manifesting the image behind her lids. She wanted to share it with Suzanne.

**

Suzanne stripped her bed, and gathered the linens for the wash. She turned on her favorite radio station, Keener13, and cranked up the volume. Music always made work more fun. Keener played tunes she remembered her parents listening to on CDs. The disc jockey's voice was comforting. She felt her mother's energy. *I loved that song*, she heard her mother say. The Alan Parsons Project sang *Eye in the Sky*. But now, as an adult, Suzanne thought the lyrics sounded... *suspicious.*

Closing her eyes, she imagined herself as a little girl, dancing in the living room with her mom. "We had fun," she said aloud. "Not always, but the good times were the best." A virtual hug brought tears to her eyes. "I miss you, mom. I really do."

She closed the laundry room door and went into the kitchen. About to head out the door to water her rose bushes, she heard the little girl's voice calling her name. When she closed her eyes, she saw the same vision she had seen the day before. *The stone arch*. Suzanne smiled. She could see a sign, *Canyonlands National Park*.

Suzanne clicked on her computer and googled the new information. Sure enough, the arch vision she received from the little girl matched the pictorial on the Moab, Utah website. "I am the eye in the sky, I can read your mind," she whispered.

She dialed Linda.

"I found out where she is!" she blurted.

"Goodie, goodie. That's great news."

"She's communicating with me, Linda. That's a first. She's alive, and she's sending me pictures."

"Kids are very intuitive. She trusts you."

"I'm glad, but I don't understand why."

"We chart our earth experience before incarnating into this lifetime. You must be in the same soul group. She knows she can count on you for help if she needs it. In turn, she is showing you a facet of your gift you were meant to discover."

"Sam and I had an interesting lunch. A couple sitting nearby set off all kinds of red flags."

"Red lips?"

"How did you—"

"Popped into my head. You subconsciously sent me an image."

"Dang, that's cool. What else do you see?"

"When I close my eyes, the image gets fuzzy."

"Yes. The poor woman was out of her mind."

"Was there a man? Dark hair? Handsome?"

"Yes. Do you see a noose around his neck?"

"I'm not sensing suicide, more like he's stuck. I see a large boulder on his back, weighing him down. I also see another man. This one is as evil as they come. He speaks with a forked tongue. He's in shadow."

"We just saw the man and woman. Sam was very clever in collecting the man's prints."

"Sam is a wonderful detective, what is his interest in the couple?"

"He's not sure. I'm not sure why I picked up on her state of mind, or his for that matter. It was very strange."

"Do you think there's any connection to the little girl?"

"I don't know." Suzanne stuffed one hand in her pocket. "Have you heard from Joseph?"

"It's been a few days. I'll give him a call. See if he's had any hits."

"I feel as though we're all groping in the dark. I have no idea if all these fragments belong in one picture, or are just that, fragments that will lead us nowhere."

"Shush, Missy. Have faith."

"If you say so, meanwhile, I have a little girl to track."

**

Linda dialed Joseph. His answering machine picked up. Linda wasn't surprised. "Joseph Ernest Martin, it's Lin-da. We've been thinking about you, and wondering what you're up to." She chuckled. "Wondering if you have any pieces to add to our puzzle? I like the corner pieces, myself. Okay. Call me!"

Unease crept into Linda's psyche. Just then, the phone rang.

"You have got to stop leaving me cryptic messages, Ms. Schooler. What did I miss?"

"Nothing huge. Just a missing girl, a suspicious couple, and a boogieman. Take your pick."

"I went to see David's mom."

"The train guy—you found out his name? You found his mom?"

"He was a victim. I know it. I found an interview his mom did with a local newspaper reporter. She said her son was happy. He had goals. One thing that struck me was she mentioned David always had earbuds in, and that he was an avid podcast listener. What if—he was listening to a directive to walk in front of that train?"

"That's beyond my comprehension. Enlighten me"

"It's stuff I've been reading about for years, Linda. Electromagnetic frequencies—programmed into subliminal messaging through digital means. We already know our phones keep track of everything we do. It wouldn't surprise me if they are not only *collecting* information; they are influencing how we *think*, what we *do*."

"Gotta tell you, I'm having a hard time wrapping my head around what you're saying but considering the advancements in technology, it wouldn't surprise me...but *why*? Why would someone *do* that?"

"Wish I had an answer for you. All I know is David did not walk in front of that train on his own volition."

"How do you prove he didn't?"

"I don't know."

**

Linda tended to her parrot, Big Bird while questioning him about life. "Why do people intentionally hurt other people? Why can't we share the planet? Love one another? It was God's plan, what went wrong?"

Big bird listened intently, cocked his head, squawked, and said, "Bullshit."

Linda gave the bird a kiss on his beak. "You naughty bird, I love you so much."

Big Bird fluffed his feathers. "Awww."

With Big Bird settled back in his cage, Linda sat down at her computer. She typed in "Artificial Telepathy". The first article to pop up was from a Facebook group in Sacramento. "Why are we seeing so many drones at all times of the day and night?" Linda clicked on the link and perused through the comments. Basically, the Sac P.D. were using drones for surveillance in crime-ridden areas, making it safer for the officers *and the criminal.*

She clicked on another link; a patent filed for artificial telepathy. Best she could glean from the application was that the patent-pending device would be inserted into a human receptor allowing that person to communicate with another connecting device, such as a phone or a computer, 'hands-free', and without detection of any apparatus, like headphones. Linda shook her head. What was the world coming to? And yet, she lived in a realm where dead people communicated with the living, and angels and spirit guides imparted information through audio and visual means. How could she deny mankind had caught up with its own natural abilities to capitalize and control others?

By the time she closed her laptop, she had read testimonies from people who felt targeted by mysterious forces that not only were able to read one's thoughts via their smart devices but were able to communicate with them as if they were inside their heads. *But why cause someone to commit suicide?*

Were they testing the limits of their control? Linda wondered.

Deliberation

Sam's day concluded with a sting operation targeted at a group of high schoolers who had banded together and built a meth lab in one of the girl's grandmother's basement. The grandmother had taken the girl in when her mother was arrested for drugs a year ago. The grandmother had mentioned to a waitress at Sweetie Pie's Café how frustrated she was with all the foot traffic that came with her good intentions—people coming and going all hours of the day and night. The waitress mentioned the conversation to her sometime boyfriend who had recently joined Goldorado's Sheriff's Department as a deputy and was looking to score a few points. The deputy's ambition incited an investigation that led to a bust.

Once everyone was booked, and escorted to the appropriate facility, Sam called it a day. He wanted to drive straight to Suzanne's, take her in his arms, and let go of his stress. But part of that stress included her—or at least why he felt compelled to procrastinate on his marriage proposal. He wanted to wake up to her every morning, share her bed, her life. He reminisced over their lunch date, and how well they worked together. His instincts, her psychic intuition, great chemistry. So why couldn't he put the damn ring on her finger and be done with it? Were his thoughts about falling off the wagon making him feel unworthy? Since he met her, he had been struggling with denial. Justifying his drinking by blaming it on his job. Trying to convince himself that things were different now, that he could have a drink socially without jumping off the deep end.

He stopped at a mini-mart. *Maybe just a beer.* He'd start with one. Test the waters. If his plan failed, he'd be back at square one, and possibly lose Suzanne along with his sobriety.

After thirty minutes passed, he went inside, bought a bottle of water and a pack of gum, avoiding the beer section altogether. She was more important to him than a beer.

"I need to speak with you," he said, feeling relieved at the sound of her voice on the phone.

"You okay?"

"Yeah—are you busy?"

"I was finishing up some laundry—what's wrong?"

"Nothing. I need to have a conversation with you, but I'd rather talk face-to-face."

"Sure—yes. I'll leave the door unlocked."

**

Sam stopped at Yum Yum Dumplings in Cameron Park and picked up dinner for two. When he arrived at Suzanne's he had rehearsed what he wanted to say a million times in his head.

He knocked once and opened the door. "Suzanne? It's Sam," he called out.

"Hey—" she replied, hidden behind a stack of jeans. "Make yourself at home, I'll be right down."

Sam unpacked their dinner and set the table for two. He found a candle in a drawer, a holder in her china cabinet, and a book of matches beside her stove. He lit the candle and turned to see her standing in the doorway, smiling with delight.

"Wow. This is a nice surprise. Twice in one day? You're going to spoil me." She rushed into his arms. Her long lashes brushed his cheek as she found his mouth, and kissed his lips. "I'm so happy you're here."

"Sit. I need to get something off my chest first." Suzanne's puzzled expression made him rethink his strategy, but the nagging voice inside his head convinced him to proceed. "I've been sober for years—you know that. What I need to know from you is whether you're okay with that, or whether you feel cheated that I can't enjoy a beer or a glass of wine with you—because it sure bothers me."

"Sam—I thought we were clear on this. Your drinking is no more of an issue than if you had a milk allergy or were gluten intolerant. Some people don't jive with certain things, and I get that. Do I wish things were different? Maybe a smidge, but we do okay together, don't we? Is it a problem for you that I enjoy a glass of wine now and then?"

"No. I wish I could join you, but I know I can't. Or at least I've convinced myself that it's not worth taking the chance of losing you."

Suzanne settled into his lap and wrapped her arms around him. Her eyes said it all, but her lips confirmed. "I love you. I'm not going anywhere."

"I'm happy to hear it," he said, "because I have another question for you." He reached into his pocket and came away with a small black velvet box.

Suzanne jumped up, her hands plastered to her chest. "Sam—really?"

He rose and took her hand. Before he slipped the ring on her finger, he got down on one knee, "Will you be my wife?"

"Yes," She said, tears pooling in her eyes. "I thought you'd never ask."

Just Plain Tired

Lizzie and Garret crawled into the queen-size bed, Garret faced the door, Lizzie faced the wall. Ainsley was sound asleep on the sofa bed across the room. The ache in Lizzie's heart grew as large as the canyons they had crossed in Denver. She wanted her own bed, her own clothes, her backyard, the smell of her plug-ins, and Alexa on command. She missed her friends, coffee klatches, auditions, and acting. She missed the pile of shoes in the basket by the front door, she missed baking cupcakes for Ainsley's pre-school, and afternoon drives to the park. She missed her husband's touch and laughing out loud over stupid things one of them said. She missed the love they shared before that night. That awful night on the boat when their lives changed and created a nightmare they couldn't escape.

"You comfortable?" He asked, his breath warm in her ear.

"Not really," she said, her focus glued to the ceiling. She had learned to neutralize her emotions by putting up a wall. A wall she knew he wanted to tear down, but only when it suited him. Now was one of those times. She could feel his intention in his groin as he pressed himself against her. "I'm really tired, Gar."

"Pete. Remember? I'm Pete, you're Amy, Belle is asleep." He snuggled closer.

"Okay, Pete. Amy is tired. Part of the first trimester in case you forgot."

Garret moved away with a huff, punching his pillow into shape. "Fine," he grumbled. "Fuckin' fine."

**

On the road again, with another day's travel, the threesome did their best to remain civil. Ainsley's boredom was to be expected, and no matter how much they explained the situation, the four-year-old couldn't grasp their dilemma. Garret was still brooding over Lizzie's rejection, and Lizzie was just plain tired of it all.

Facing an uncertain future added to everyone's anxiety. Measuring words worked for the first couple of hours, but as the scenery changed from majestic to mundane, and truck stops thinned to uncomfortable proportions, snarky comments became the norm.

"We can get out here if you're sick of our whining," Lizzie said.

"Can you give me a break? I didn't see the sign back there. I know she's gotta pee. What do you want me to do?"

"Try thinking of someone else instead of yourself for a change."

Ainsley whimpered in the back seat. "Stop fighting."

"We're not fighting, bug. We'll find a place for you to go potty—can you hang in there a bit longer for Daddy?"

"Okay, Daddy." Ainsley directed her attention to miles of prairie land. The reflection in her window reminded her she was no longer the little girl who lived in Sacramento. Her only connection with her past was Suzanne, the nice lady she saw in her head. She forced the thought to the forefront of her brain and conjured the image she wanted Suzanne to see, then she pushed it out into the ether and waited for a response.

**

The diamond on Suzanne's finger sparkled in the sun. "I can't believe it," she said to Sam. "It's so beautiful."

"You're beautiful," he said. He backed her against the kitchen sink and devoured her lips. "And tasty."

"And you're going to be late for work."

"How would you feel about moving up the hill?"

Suzanne scanned the room. "And give up my house? I grew up here, Sam."

"I understand, but once we're married, we will have to reside in Goldorado County if I'm to keep my job."

Suzanne's face clouded over. "I forgot about that."

"You can keep the house—turn it into an Airbnb?"

"I'll think about it. Now scoot, before you don't have a job to go to."

**

Suzanne took the breakfast dishes to the sink. Lost in thought, she saw the little girl's face reflecting in her window. She smiled at the sight. "There you are—I've missed you." The little girl smiled broadly. "Where are you now?" Suzanne closed her eyes. Flat land, wheat fields, and wildflowers appeared in her third eye. "I don't know where you are, but I'll find you." The girl's image dissolved, leaving Suzanne feeling a loss.

Again, she went online, attempting to match up her visions with images she googled. Not knowing why she was seeing the little girl perplexed her. The girl was somehow connected to the shooting at Discovery Park, but as far as Suzanne could tell, she was alive. *One jelly shoe.* And yet, considered fairly new to her psychic abilities, Suzanne had no logistical way of deciphering her visions, other than researching that which seemed plausible. She Googled prairies and came up with several Midwest states. If the little girl was in Utah, she must be heading east. Wheat fields and wild flowers stretched from Nebraska to Ohio, from Kansas to Michigan. There was no telling where she was now without a sign or a landmark. Suzanne would have to wait for another clue. *And then what?* She didn't sense the girl was in any danger. *Not yet, anyway.*

**

Owen Westford checked his inbox for the encrypted document sent by Roger Salvo. *Right on time.* Owen downloaded the doc on a thumb drive, and inserted the thumb drive into his private computer. A copy of the document would be sent to a secret, classified organization that would determine where the program would be used. Their last project, the shooting at Discovery Park, was meant to put the fear of guns in the minds of every California citizen. When hearts bled, people united, laws got passed. Ba-doom. Owen enjoyed tying up loose ends. Sending Emma Sagorski crashing into that old woman's house was fun—a technique he was still perfecting.

Owen had his agenda. *He who holds the key rules the world*. He was out to gather people he could manipulate into doing his bidding. He had used mind control on colleagues, constituents, and Hollywood starlets. It was easy. 5G and hyperspectral surveillance imaging, along with facial recognition software made connecting with his victims a breeze—that's how Special Ops tracked down Osama bin Laden. Owen's team rose to the top of the heap for creating the imaging software used for that job. But most government work bordered on the mundane. Owen preferred doing his own research when it came to bending minds. For example, the suicides in Paris. Making random people do the—*unthinkable.*

He loved to fuck with people's heads. They had no idea what was happening to them. Dallen Foster thought he was losing his marbles. What made him an interesting target was his ego. Foster never dreamed someone outside himself would have the knowledge to conquer his thought process, immobilize his common sense, override his conscience, turn him into a killing machine.

Garret Brecker was another story. Owen underestimated the guy. He had him by the balls, involved his wife and kid in the Discovery Park incident, followed up with a discreet threat, and then 'poof' he was gone. *No sweat.* Finding him would be a piece of cake. Owen 'fingerprinted' all of his minions right off the bat.

In the 70s, MKUtra subproject 119 was scrapped when Congress got wind that the CIA was experimenting with unsuspecting individuals, controlling their minds. Since then, the CIA was careful not to call attention to their findings. People like him and Roger didn't officially exist. And hence, a broader range of sophisticated and advanced equipment made it possible to control more than a handful of minds in undisclosed labs. Now, they were able to control the masses through electronics. *God Bless smart devices.*

Roger Salvo was brought into the fold against his will, *his 'will' left intact.* Owen needed him firing on all cylinders. Roger was an expert at creating the blueprints for their shenanigans; Owen provided the commands. Roger answered to the piper; and unfortunately, he had no idea who the piper was—or that the jobs he did weren't always for the government. Owen had skillfully covered his tracks. Together, they had successfully ruined lives for over a decade.

For now, Owen had to focus on Roger's obsession with jumping ship, directing Roger's wife's overzealous libido, and the new guy he saw Roger talking to at Mayahuel. *The cop.* The woman sitting with the cop wouldn't be easy. Her brain waves didn't register the same way other people's did. She seemed to have a shield protecting the frequencies he needed to access to gain control.

Getting inside the cop's head would have to do for now.

**

Garret drove into Hardesty, Oklahoma just before dusk. The detour to Optima Lake proved to be a waste of time. The lake was barely a puddle, reminding him of Folsom Lake when it was at its lowest. Multiple burn scars around Optima Lake caused Garret to rethink his decision to set up camp. Storm clouds crept toward them from the West. They'd be sitting ducks should lightning strike and start another blaze. Or worse. Tornadoes are more deadly at night. Decision made, he followed East Highway 54 until he saw a half=dome structure marked Round Top Hamburgers and Pizza. Without seeking approval, he veered left and swooped into a parking space.

"We had pizza last night," Lizzie said, her tone sharp.

"The sign says they have hamburgers too."

"I don't know Gar—*Pete*, can't we just do a drive-through?"

"Well, A-my. I don't see one, do you?"

She hopped out of the vehicle, shielded her eyes from the sun, and surveyed the area.

"I'm hungry, Daddy."

"Me too, Bug. Let's wait 'til Mommy comes back from the dark side."

"Dark side? I thought we were in Okyhoma."

"We are Bug, but the dark side is where Mommy goes when she doesn't get her way."

Lizzie shot daggers his way. "I don't see anything close by. How far are we from our destination?" She climbed back into her seat and slammed the door.

"We don't have a solid destination from here. We can head for Oklahoma City tomorrow, there are plenty of oil rig openings there—but I was hoping to stay off the grid, grab a local paper, find a handyman job or something."

"I can look into elder care."

Garret smiled. "Teamwork." He reached for her hand. "That's the only way we're going to survive this—"

Lizzie lowered her gaze to their hands locked together as one. She was too weary to argue. She squeezed his hand. "You're right. Let's go check out some Okyhoma pizza."

———

Witching Hour

Roger tore the blankets off his sweat-soaked body and wobbled into the bathroom. He checked his forehead for a fever. *Clammy*. He'd been a mess ever since he saw the man he recognized from the yacht in the parking lot the other day. *The man who stood behind the waitress who offered me the drink that knocked me out.*

He knew 'they' were watching, controlling Rebecca's behavior, creating Pavlov's response in him. He was happy his daughters were away at school. From what he could tell, they were fine. Rebecca's withdrawal from the prestigious clubs she had belonged to for years raised questions from longtime friends, but those who knew her suspected she was experiencing mental issues, and were too polite to ask more questions than necessary. Other friends regarded Rebecca's overzealous sexual behavior and flirtatiousness as a threat to their marriages.

He examined his bloodshot eyes in the mirror. He was afraid to think, knowing every thought, every inkling, every brain fart could be tracked. His only shot at overcoming his fear was to fight fire with fire.

He turned off the bathroom light and climbed back in bed. Rebecca moaned, sliding her hand up his leg and settling on his crotch. She began massaging, gently at first. He held his breath, trying to diffuse the sensation heading for the medial orbitofrontal cortex in his brain by visualizing a shut-off valve. When her attempt to arouse him failed,

Rebecca turned over and began to snore. He glanced at the red numbers luminating nearby—*3:30 a.m.* Three hours until his alarm would sound...and his nightmare would begin all over again.

**

Sam tossed and turned, and while in his dream state, he staggered down an abandoned street. He noticed the silhouette of a woman at the corner up ahead. Her sheath skirt hugged her hips, the slitted side revealed one long leg. Her stiletto heels gleamed beneath the sodium light; her face in shadow. As Sam approached, he could see her long hair, cascading over ample breasts. Closer, her red lips invited him to participate in sin.

"I'm engaged," he said, thwarting her efforts to draw him in.

"I'm married. What does it matter?"

"It matters to me," he replied.

"For now, but flash forward, when the whiskey claims your virtue, and your dick is the only voice you hear, you'll jump at the chance to fuck a woman like me."

"Fat chance," he slurred.

She grabbed his arm and pressed her body against his. Her jade eyes flashed with fury as she checked his hardness with her fingertips. "Liar," she spat. "You want me—and you know it." She raised her skirt, forcing his hand between her legs.

"*Suzanne*," he moaned, exploring the moist flesh thrusting against his palm.

"Suzanne? You're all the same!" she cried shoving him hard and sending him sprawling on his ass.

Sam awoke on the floor, gripping the side of the bed. He struggled for a moment, gasping, his heart pounding. He settled his back against the bedrail and waited for his pulse to return to normal. *What the hell*? He swiped the perspiration from his brow. Never had he experienced a dream so realistic, or frightening. He conjured the couple he and Suzanne met at Mayahuel and mentally compared the woman to the woman in his dream. One and the same. *But why*? He was drawn to her from the get-go. Couldn't take his eyes off of her, even though Suzanne was nearby. He didn't think it was a sexual attraction—now he wasn't sure. *Those red lips.*

He felt tempted to call Suzanne. He wanted to hear her voice, tell him it was a dream and nothing more, but the idea was insane. He would wake her, rob her of her peace of mind to appease his guilty conscious.

He grabbed his laptop and googled Roger Salvo.

Baby, Baby

Heartburn. Lizzie swallowed hard, forcing the acid back down her esophagus only to have it erupt, and scald her throat. *Worst part of pregnancy.* She massaged her belly. The best part of pregnancy was the life sleeping soundly inside her womb. She reflected on the heartburn she had with Ainsley and the full head of hair she possessed from day one. Small price to pay for the beautiful curls her daughter had flaunted proudly for the last four years. Lizzie's eyes misted over recalling Ainsley's tresses lying on the bathroom floor in that cheap motel.

Lizzie wondered what her unborn child would be like. Boy? Girl? She knew from conception Ainsley was a girl. This time she wasn't so sure. Nor was she sure about making an appointment with an O.B., when or where her child would be born. So many things to be settled. She still couldn't accept their situation or the severity of getting caught in a web of lies. She had been raised to be honest, truth was gospel, and being who God made you to be was something to be proud of. Her parents would be rolling in their graves if they knew the predicament she was in. *Mama loved Ainsley's curls.* Daddy didn't take to Garret right away, said he lacked grit. *He's tryin', Daddy. He's tryin' really hard to protect his family.*

**

Ainsley skipped from one shadow to the next, trying to keep up with her mother's stride. California weather was different. Okyhoma felt hot, sticky. She wanted to tell Suzanne about her new home and the new baby, but she wasn't sure how to do that. Her mother settled on a bench in front of a big building. Ainsley couldn't read the big blue letters, but she knew from the way people walking past them were dressed that there were doctors inside.

The four-year-old closed her eyes and began a search inside her mind for Suzanne. And then she saw her, standing in her yard, watering roses.

Ainsley projected her thoughts, as if she were holding a normal conversation, and waited for Suzanne to respond.

"Hello, Suzanne—your flowers are pretty." Ainsley squeezed her eyes tight, hoping to expedite an answer. She knew when Suzanne laid the hose down and closed her eyes too, that she would respond.

"Hi," she said. "Can you tell me your name?"

"Ainsley is my real name, but Mommy calls me Belle now—that's my new name.

"What's your last name?"

"I forgot. I have to ask Mommy."

"Where are you?"

"Okyhoma. It's really hot here."

"I'll bet—are there a lot of cows where you are?"

"No, mostly cars."

"Are you okay? Are you safe?"

"Yes, but Mommy's going to have a baby, and Daddy needs to find a job."

Just then Lizzie tapped her daughter on the shoulder. "Belle? Belle, what are you doing?"

"Talking to my friend, Mommy."

Lizzie looked around, thinking perhaps she missed something. "Honey, I don't see anybody."

"She's in here, Mommy," Ainsley said, pointing to her head.

"Does your friend talk back to you?"

"Yes. I told her about the baby. She smiled really big."

Lizzie refrained from losing her cool, but the concern in her tone was evident, causing the little girl to shrink back when she asked, "What else did you tell her?"

**

The temperatures that week had been brutal, burning some of the lacy edges on Suzanne's sherbet-colored roses. She had snipped a few stems to add fragrance to her bouquet of white hydrangeas, and peonies, when a sound wafted past her thoughts, heightening her senses. She closed her eyes and listened. The sweet little voice had returned, and Suzanne's inquiry began, collecting puzzle pieces. *Ainsley. Belle. Okyhoma. Baby.* If only she could tap into the little girl's mother's thoughts, she would be able to assess the predicament they were in. *Why change names?* Suzanne could sense they were on the run, but why? Snippets played in her mind, a yacht, the dark-haired woman from the park, a camera flash, click, click, click. Horrific images came flooding back to her. *Paris*—the woman lying in the street; the man jumping from the balcony in the building next to Moulin Rouge, the waiter, diving off the Eiffel Tower. *Somehow there's a connection.*

She glanced down at the flowers gathered at her feet and shuddered. Almost a replica of the bouquet she saw discarded in front of the hotel in Paris. The only thing missing was the fake diamond ring. She held up her left hand, contemplating the ring Sam slipped on her finger only days ago. Intuitively, her eyes were drawn to her bedroom window. The figure standing beside the filmy curtain was as clear as day. *Mom.*

**

Garret drove up in time to witness the scolding Ainsley was getting from Lizzie. He recognized his wife's 'bitch' posture, chin up, shoulders squared, brows touching, lips tight against her teeth, warm blue eyes transformed into Alaskan icebergs. He honked the horn, breaking the tension. His baby girl looked relieved.

"Hey—why the boo-boo faces?"

"Does this look like a boo-boo face to you?" Her teeth were clenched, her head lowered like an animal in strike mode.

Garret cocked his head. "Nah. That's your pissed-off face." He winked at Ainsley and swept her up in his arms. What's wrong?"

"Mommy doesn't want me talking to my new friend, Daddy."

"*Mommy* doesn't want you blabbing to the world where we are, that's all, Punkin'." She touched Ainsley's cheek. "I get scared, that's all."

Garret and Lizzie exchanged glances. He could see tears forming beneath her lashes. "Mommy's right, Sweet Pea, we're on a secret mission. We can't tell anyone where we are. Not even your new friend."

"Okay, Daddy."

**

Linda gathered a clean pair of knit pants, her favorite Moody Blues T-shirt, and clean undergarments. She grabbed a bottle of shampoo from the cabinet beneath the bathroom sink and set it on the edge of the tub. She turned on the faucet and undressed. The cool water felt good on her skin after hours of laboring in the hot sun. Weeds were picked, debris removed from pots, and a week's bounty collected in various baskets to share with neighbors. She said a silent prayer, thankful that her health allowed her the luxury of maintaining a garden.

She poured a dollop of shampoo into her hand and lathered it into her hair. Eyes squeezed tight, a face flashed behind her lids. A man. His thin face, smug. Devious. Linda hurried to rinse the soap from her eyes so she could open them and banish the uneasy feeling she got with the vision. *So much for a relaxing shower.*

She toweled herself dry and dressed. Despite the heat, goosebumps gathered on her flesh. A high-pitched ring pierced her left ear. The words, you can run, but you can't hide scrolled through her brain like a ticker tape.

"Suzanne? Linda."

"Hey—I was going to call you."

"Funny how that works—say, any more contact from your little girl?"

"Yes—that's what I wanted to speak with you about—she reached out to me. They're in Oklahoma. They've changed her name. It was Ainsley, now it's Belle."

"I got a download—a message from a man I'd never want to meet in person—he said, 'You can run, but you can't hide.'"

"What do make of it?"

"I don't know, girly girl, Suzie-Q. Someone is up to no good—we just need to figure out who."

"Any more dead birds?"

"Not that I know of. Has Sam found out anything? I'm seeing an 'R'."

"I'm still thinking about that couple we met at Mayahuel..."

"And?"

"His name started with an 'R'—Roger."

"And Sam was fixated on the woman with red lipstick?"

"Ah, yes, that bright red lipstick. Sam thought she was being trafficked—but it turned out to be the guy's wife. Strange couple for sure."

"What did the man look like?"

"He was about 6'1, athletic build. Dark colored hair, grey sideburns, dark eyes."

"The man I saw was thin, weasel-type features, beady eyes, pointy noise, small mouth, weak chin. His hair was closely cropped, brown I think. He had this look on his face—entitled, above the law. He gave me the creeps."

"I don't know how to connect the dots, Linda. What I experienced in Paris and Austria has nothing to do with the little girl I keep seeing... or does it?"

"If her family is on the run, perhaps the man in my vision has something to do with it."

"How do we go about getting answers?"

"Let go, let God. Ask and you shall receive."

"I wish it were that easy."

"It is."

A moment of silence settled between them, until, "By the way, Sam finally asked me to marry him. We're officially engaged."

"What—when?"

"The other night. He'd been struggling with a proper proposal."

"Did he just hand you the ring and say, 'Here'?"

"I had to remember that he tried so hard to make his proposal perfect, first in Paris, then in Salzburg. It was fine. I'm happy with the way it worked out."

"When's the wedding?"

"Oh—I'm—we're in no hurry. Getting engaged was stressful enough."

"Of course."

"I mean—we will marry eventually—just not right now."

"I get it."

"Why am I hearing speculation in your tone?"

Linda chuckled. "You both are afraid of disappointing one another. You don't want to repeat your mistakes, and he doesn't trust himself."

"You must be psychic."

"Yes, and I also have some of the prettiest tomatoes you've ever seen—wants some?"

"Love some! I'll be right over."

**

Joseph moved his mouse toward the curve of the woman's jaw and clicked. Red hair tumbled past her jaw, down her shoulder, and over her breast. He grabbed a set of luscious red lips and dragged them to the blank area beneath a nose. Joseph pressed 'save' and moved back to assess his creation. There was something about her that gave him pause. She seemed familiar. Every man's dream? Perhaps, but he wasn't 'every' man. His dream guy left the toilet seat up and snored like an elk in heat.

"Is this the cover art?" Brad plopped into the bright yellow cantilever chair flanked by two Etienne prints. "Those lips."

Joseph sighed. "This isn't where I was going with this—I had envisioned blonde, smoky eyes, pouty pink lips."

"Far from it."

"I know. I wonder if Bridget will freak out."

"Did you read Bridget's book first?"

"I read some of it—enough to know the woman on my screen is inappropriate—but for some reason, I kept going."

"She's intriguing, someone you know? Someone you did a reading for?"

"Nope. Never saw her before. She crept into my head, and now I can't unsee her."

Brad came behind Joseph and massaged his shoulders. "I've known you long enough to know that she has a place in your life—just wait. The pieces will fall into place. Now—what do you say we go have lunch and take in a movie?"

Joseph saved the file once more and powered down his computer. The woman's image stayed with him. *Why?*

**

When Suzanne arrived at Linda's, she instantly felt grounded. Linda greeted her with her warm Shirley Temple dimpled smile. "I made us some ice tea," she said ushering Suzanne inside. "It's so dang hot, I considered sprinkling popcorn on the patio to see if it would pop."

"My roses are miserable. I put up some shade cloth, I hope that helps."

"This heat is a game changer. I often think about what Joseph said about the HAARP machines the government uses to experiment with the ionosphere..."

"I can't even entertain the thought—though with technology being what it is—who's to say it's not possible?"

"Right? History has shown us that humans are capable of great atrocities."

"Aren't you in a cheery mood!"

"I guess when you see an ominous face in your third eye while you're taking a shower you've been looking forward to, it makes you a bit cranky." Linda waved her hand in front of her face as if she were swatting a fly. "There. All gone."

Suzanne relaxed into laughter until they both felt better. "Who *chooses* to be psychic?" Another round of giggles brought them more relief.

Linda served iced tea, and pieces of homemade, strawberry rhubarb pie. Mid-bite, Linda grabbed Suzanne's hand. "Dang! Let me see that beautiful gem you're wearing, Missy."

Suzanne proudly extended her hand, showing off her engagement ring. "I love the setting. Sam certainly knows my taste. Simple, elegant, but *sturdy*."

"Never seen anything like it. Did he have it designed?"

"Possibly—I didn't ask—he wouldn't have been able to answer me anyway—my mouth was stuck to his for the next hour."

"Oh, funny. It looks to be a designer ring. I love the thick band, and the bezel setting holding that huge diamond. The word 'bezel'—derived from a French word I believe. The settings date back to the 1600s. Interesting choice."

Suzanne blushed. "I must admit, it is pretty spectacular. The man that comes with it is pretty spectacular too." She scooped up the last forkful of pie into her mouth, but she couldn't contain her smile.

"Have you told your brother?"

"No, not yet. Mom knows. She paid me an unexpected visit this morning."

"Do tell..."

"I was out in the garden—I saw her watching me from my bedroom window. My ring was sparkling in the sun—she nodded and smiled. I heard her say, "Congratulations, he's a fine man. He'll find them."

"He'll find them? 'Them' as in the little girl?"

"I'm pretty sure that's who she was referring to."

"You said the little girl paid you a visit this morning, how did she seem?"

"Fine. Happy. She's excited about having a sibling. I can't get a bead on the parents though."

"Or, what if she's *not* in danger."

"Why would her parents change her name? Move to Oklahoma? I feel it in my bones, Linda. They're running from something or someone. There's a connection between that woman who drove her car into that house in Sac, and the little girl who was supposedly injured or killed at Discovery Park."

"You know when people die, they get stuck on this side of the street sometimes. They either have unfinished business, or can't let go of the human experience, but you said she isn't a spirit."

"I had a moment this morning when my experiences in Paris came flooding back. I feel as though I'm being redundant, but it seems everything that is going on is connected in some way."

"It wouldn't surprise me. When I saw that man's face, like I told you on the phone, I got the creeps. He's a key ingredient in the soup—but I also feel the man you mentioned..."

"Roger? The man we met at Mayahuel?"

"Yes, him—there's a connection there." Linda closed her eyes. "If R is Roger, he's facing away from the image of the man I saw—hmm. Possible that R doesn't know the man—or—could be that R is a victim too."

"I definitely felt something disconcerting about the wife. Those lips —and the pixilation—like she wasn't real."

Linda cocked her head, "Pixilated...like her mind is missing, not in control of her being. Could she be brainwashed?"

Suzanne's jaw dropped. "Wow, that's it! I need to call Sam."

**

When the temps went up, tempers flared. People became irritable. Sam did his best to keep his cool, but sometimes he got rattled. Short. Pissed off. He hadn't slept well, his dream of the woman with the red lips still played on his mind. It wasn't like him to dwell. His head hurt. A faint buzz in his ear—another distraction. But it took Mrs. Anochek leaving her baby in her car while she went into the QuickMart to buy smokes, lottery tickets, and a large soft drink to set him off.

"What the hell is wrong with people?" he shouted. Connie, one of his dispatchers flinched. Robert, the desk sergeant on duty coughed and excused himself, leaving Sam standing in the middle of the room fuming.

When the deputy who arrested Mrs. Veronica Anochek entered the building, he lowered his gaze.

"What the hell happened? Is the baby going to be okay? Did you follow the paramedics to the E.R.?"

"Yes. Johnson is still there. The baby is going to be fine. They gave him IV fluids and oxygen. The mom was taken to the hospital for a psych evaluation. She's a mess.

"Drugs?"

"No, I don't think so, but she was definitely in la-la land." The deputy perched one butt cheek on a nearby desk. "She totally ignored the flashing lights and the paramedics—tried getting in the wrong car. She seemed genuinely confused. It took a few minutes before she realized she left her son in the car. She thought he was home with her mother-in-law who was visiting from Chicago. She said the cigarettes and lottery tickets were for her, and the soda was for her nephew who was mowing the lawn." He shook his head. "It was kinda spooky—as if she were having a bad dream."

Sam shivered. "Geezus." Red lips briefly hijacked his senses. He shook off the memory. "I'll take the report when you finish writing it up. I want to follow up. What's the baby's name?"

The deputy took a pad from his shirt pocket and flipped through the pages. "Lukas. Lukas Anochek. Eleven months." The deputy stood erect. "Good thing someone saw the kid—another few minutes and he wouldn't be alive to see his first birthday."

"Good work." Sam grabbed his keys. "I'm heading to Marshall Hospital. Call me on my cell if you need me."

Sam jumped into the driver's seat, turn on the ignition, and cranked up the AC. He was still doing a slow burn. Something about this case reminded him of Paris, Austria—people behaving strangely, and he wanted to know why.

**

"Metzger." Sam's tone was harsh.

"Bad day?"

"Suzanne—I didn't even look. I'm driving."

"I only need sixty seconds. Linda and I were discussing that woman we met at Mayahuel. She was simply dressed, but her make-up was overdone, impulsive, and she practically looked through us when her husband was talking to us. We think she's being brainwashed."

"I can see why you'd make that assumption, but by whom? Her husband? I looked him up. Zip."

"There has to be a record of him somewhere."

"I got bigger problems right now. A woman wigged out, left her eleven-month-old baby in her car while she went shopping at QuickMart."

"It was 104 degrees out today!"

"No kidding. Luckily someone called 911. The baby is going to be okay. I'm on my way to Marshall to speak with the mom."

"I think when this day is done, you're going to need a hug or two. Or three."

"Sounds good, my love. I'll call when I'm on my way."

Sam felt better simply hearing her voice. She had a knack for calling when he needed her most. He let out a big sigh. He couldn't control the world. He couldn't prevent people from committing crimes, or making stupid mistakes...all he could do was try and understand that the human condition could be frail, and God worked in mysterious ways. Ying and Yang. Right and wrong, black and white. The duality of man's existence—there has to be one to have the other.

When he entered the hospital, he stopped at the ER to check on the baby. Relief washed over him when the ER nurse reported the infant remained in stable condition. Sam inquired about the mother.

"She's with her son. Psych is on its way. You have an officer keeping an eye on them both." The nurse smiled, "I'm not a psychiatrist, but I am a mom. Sometimes things get crazy—I can't tell you the things I forgot to do—not excusing or condoning—she just doesn't seem like the irresponsible type."

"Why do you say that?"

"I've been a nurse for forty years—I know irresponsible when I see it. Besides, the doc is checking her for an ear infection. She was complaining about a sharp pain, and buzzing in her left ear. Could have something to do with her absentmindedness."

"Fever?"

"Nope. Just pain and buzzing."

Sam's blood ran cold.

**

"Nights in White Satin" played on the radio while Suzanne prepared shrimp salad to go on buttery croissants. She chopped celery, and Redtail jumbo shrimp, into a bowl with Spike seasoning, and mayo. She put the salad in the fridge and made a green salad with fresh cucumbers and tomatoes from Linda's garden. She poured herself a glass of her homemade sangria.

The evening cooled down to a bearable eighty degrees, and a slight breeze kicked up. She took her glass outside and sat in one of her Adirondack chairs. She drew her legs beneath her and closed her eyes, letting the Moody Blues seep into her soul, and the wine relax her mind. Besides the mystery of the little girl, despite all the violence and unrest in the world, she was in a good place. She peeked at her ring sparkling in the last glimmer of sunlight. *Blessed*. She felt blessed. Her years with Ben had been filled with heartache. If her lungs hadn't expanded and contracted, she wouldn't have known she was alive half the time. She intended to make up for the years she had squandered in a miserable marriage.

She knew her brother would take a little more convincing before he accepted Sam into the fold. He was starting to warm up to the idea of them being a couple, but now they were engaged, now it was serious.

"Don't let him spoil things for you dear."

Startled, Suzanne spilled her drink. "Damnit Mom! You scared me."

"Sorry, Suz. I forget."

Suzanne could barely make out her mother's face in the fading light. She wiped up the spill with the bottom of her shirt and took a swig from her glass. "Do you like him, Mom? If you were still here, would we have your blessing to marry?"

"I knew from the moment he stepped into your hospital room when you were shot, that he was meant to be with you. You two have many lifetimes together. This time you get to love each other as man and wife."

"How do you know all that? Do they tell you those things when you die? And where's Dad? Is he watching over me too?"

"Yes, and no. He's busy with other tasks right now, but he knows what's going on with you. He checks in more with your brother—although Steven has no idea. Your brother needs guidance once in a while too, you know."

Suzanne laughed. "He'd be horrified if he knew Dad—"

"Who would be horrified? If Dad knew what?"

Suzanne jumped, spilling her wine once more. This time she gave up and poured the rest of the contents into the grass. "Sam! You scared the livin'—"

"Sorry, I heard you talking—I didn't mean to scare you."

Suzanne rushed into his arms. "Hi."

"Who were you talking to?"

"Mom. She was telling me my Dad visits my brother—can you imagine?"

Sam laughed for the first time since he woke that morning. He squeezed her tight. "I love you. Please don't ever change."

Suzanne stepped back and tugged at the spreading red stain. "Can I at least change my shirt?"

He assessed the red blotch. "Better get that rinsed out."

"Make yourself at home. I'll be right down."

**

Sam wanted to follow her up the stairs, help her out of her shirt, her bra, jeans, and panties, but he decided to forego his desires until she gave him the green light. He didn't want her to feel that sex was their only common interest. He wanted to understand her fully, her thoughts, her dreams, her gift. Knowing her deceased mother was in the picture made him feel a bit uneasy, as if he were in a position to be judged. Could she see into his dreams?

"Hey—how was your day? You seem—distant. I thought for sure you would've volunteered to help me undress," she said.

He snatched her up in his arms and swung her around as if to prove her wrong. "If I did, I wouldn't have been able to stop myself from removing all of your clothes and ravishing every inch of your beautiful body."

"Duh!"

Sam laughed. He held her tighter. His kiss was tender. His eyes held hers. "I am so in love with you—but I need to talk to you—I need to—"

"What's wrong? You sound so serious."

Suzanne led him outside to an Adirondack loveseat. "Sit."

Sam obeyed. Words tumbled in his head. Where to begin? "I've been having really strange dreams lately, and I wanted to share them with you because they don't make sense to me."

"I'm listening."

"In my dreams, I'm drinking. At first, I thought it was because I feel bad that we can't share a glass of wine—but then it escalated. It was as if

I were being cajoled into putting a gun to my head." He watched Suzanne's face pale, and he wondered if he should continue. She took his hand in hers without a word. "Last night I dreamt about the woman we met at Mayahuel."

"The woman with the red lips..."

He chuckled. "Yes. She was coming on to me—I told her I was engaged—she didn't care—it was as though she was there to ruin things for me—for us."

"As I mentioned on the phone, Linda and I discussed her this afternoon. We feel as though she is a victim. They both are. She and her husband. We got the impression they are tied to the incident at the park, and the little girl I keep seeing."

"But why am I—"

She cupped his face in her hands. "Whatever is happening is affecting us all. It seems we are under a spell—the suicides—the mass shootings—the bizarre behavior—" She pressed her fingertips to her temples. "I don't know how, but I believe it's all tied together—and all those cell towers are making it possible to control people's thoughts, somehow."

"If that were even possible, what would be the motive?"

"Million-dollar question."

He kissed her nose. "Please tell me that you won't give up on me."

"Sam! How can you think such a thing?"

"I have a feeling that things are going to get ugly, and I don't want to lose you."

She kissed his lips. "Never."

"One more question."

"Ask me anything."

"Does your mother like me?"

Suzanne hugged him tight. "She said we are a match made in heaven."

Evil Lurks

Roger keyed in his password and clicked on his email. The morning sun streamed through wooden slats creating a pattern on the cream-colored walls of his office. He leaned back in his chair contemplating what looked like jail cell bars sprawled across the room and wondered if the gods were mocking him, or if jail was truly his fate.

He clicked on the first document and shuddered. His instructions—create code to manifest severe psychosis in a thirty-five-year-old male that would cause him to kill his thirty-four-year-old pregnant wife and four-year-old daughter. Roger pounded on his keyboard as his eyes darted around the room. "You've got to be fucking kidding me!" He buried his head in his hands and cried.

"I won't do it—do you hear me, motherfucker?" he sobbed. "Kill me! Kill us all—I won't do it!"

Rebecca screamed from the other room.

**

Garret jammed the gas nozzle into the beat-up 1986 blue Ford pick-up he purchased for $800 cash, plus two days of labor putting in a high-tech sprinkling system for a farmer in Medicine Park. With a population of 416 people, Garret's California accent turned heads, making him feel uncomfortable, but luckily, the folks in Medicine Park resembled "left-over hippies," and by the end of his first day on the job, they welcomed him and his family into the fold.

One of the guys, Jason, lived adjacent to the cabin Garret (Peter) rented, and referred him to a friend of his who owned a painting company. Jason's girlfriend, Joy, worked in daycare, and gave Lizzie (Amy) names of families looking for nannies in Lawton. In less than two weeks, The Breckers, now Bentons, established themselves in Medicine Park, no questions asked.

Their story was that their home burnt down during the Cal fire, and they lost everything, including a dog named Fuzz. And although it wasn't the truth, Garret felt the story gained more sympathy because of the dog. Kids and pets were at the heart of this town, and they felt they lucked out, yet Garret was vigilant in keeping their true identity secret, and remained on high alert.

He questioned Ainsley's "imaginary" friend. He didn't like the idea of his little girl sharing their identity with anyone, and yet how could he expect her to phase out of her true self into this make-believe person they created for her with no repercussions. "It's for her own safety—for our safety!" he reminded Lizzie when she defended Ainsley's right to seek happiness in her mind. But that was the part that scared Garret the most—someone accessing her mind without consent. His angst wasn't unwarranted. The dream he had the previous night proved he had a lot to fear.

He had awoken drenched in sweat. His heart galloped. His skin tingling from remnants of the night terror. He was on a yacht, snapping photos of the elite. He had just finished taking pictures of what appeared to be a young woman scantily dressed in a pink pinafore posing with a sheik. When he expanded the print, he could tell she was no older than fourteen. A man stood in the background critiquing his work, his face in shadow.

"Follow me," the man said. "There's more."

This time Garret entered a room so dim he could only make out two shapes. One small, one larger. Once his eyes adjusted to the dark, he could see a child and a woman—both were naked. He could feel the vein in his neck pulsating, he felt clammy and cold. When the man flipped a switch on the wall, the bright lights revealed his wife and daughter. They didn't appear to be frightened, on the contrary, their eyes were taunting as their bodies moved in grotesque positions. Ainsley bared her teeth. Lizzie's tongue slithered out of her mouth and danced toward his face to a hypnotic beat. The fleshy beast parted his lips and slithered down his throat in search of his heart. It squeezed so hard, he felt himself lose consciousness, until Ainsley began to laugh in a shrill voice, the sound coming from something spawned in the bowels of hell.

He sprang out of bed, disturbing Lizzie's sleep. "What's wrong?" she slurred, her voice still raspy with sleep.

"Nothing," he lied. "It was just a dream."

She held out her hand. "I'm sorry. Come back to bed."

Garret climbed under the covers. Lizzie scooted close, spooning his backside. "I love you," she whispered, and he wanted to cry. She hadn't spoken those words so freely in so long, and yet, a little voice inside his head screamed, *Liar!*

His first instinct was to turn over and grab her by the throat. But then he heard a ringing in his left ear, and he knew. *They found us.*

**

Suzanne rubbed sleep from her eyes. She struggled to hang on to the vision that stole her respite. She grabbed a pad of paper and the pen she kept on the nightstand, per Linda's suggestion, and began to write.

> *yacht*
> *deep cavern, dark*
> *serpent's tongue*
> *the girl*
> *TROUBLE*

Her recall was foggy, jumbled. The essence of the dream hung between her conscious and subconscious mind. She sat on the edge of the bed and closed her eyes, summoning the scenario to surface. What she saw was a small hand reaching out of the darkness, what she heard was *'help me!'*

Suzanne took a deep breath and blew out. Once again, she dived into her mind to extract the clues she needed to make sense of what was happening. Energy swirled behind her third eye bringing forth knowledge and clarity. *He's going to kill them both.* A jolt of energy hit her hard. *He's going to take his own life, and no one will ever know.* Know what? *Why he killed them*? Or know *he's not to blame*?

"You should get more rest," her mother's voice scolded.

"Mom, not now. I must find her. Do you know where she is?" Suzanne glanced around the room, hoping to catch a glimpse of her mother's ectoplasmic form. "Mom?"

"She told you. Listen."

"I don't have time for riddles, Mom. She's in danger—the little girl is in danger!"

"Don't fret dear. Just listen."

Suzanne threw a pillow at the wall and bounced off the bed. "Fine. I'll find her myself."

**

Suzanne pondered the girl's whereabouts over coffee and toast. "What's with all the riddles?" she asked aloud. Since her accident, her world had been full of riddles. Fragments, fractals, a word here, an image there. Linda had explained how universal law worked, and yet she couldn't grasp why everything had to be so freaking hard. She wasn't trying to save herself—or was she? *Look for the lesson.* Linda's teachings hit her like a ton of bricks.

Was she that little girl? Had she felt as though she lived in a make-believe world? Is that why her mom showed up? To help her heal by helping another little girl in pain? But I had my brother—I had Steven. *You never faced the truth.*

Suzanne brought her coffee outside, where the world could see her, witness her existence...Where she could feel part of the pulse of life. The dream and her mother's words weighed her soul. *Rise above it. Be one with the clouds.* Linda's words, rescuing her from despair, once again.

Suzanne set her cup down and unclenched her fist, extending her arms, palms up. "I am asking God, please, place your blessing in these humble hands to find the girl. To bring her to safety. To unleash the hold of Satan, and return this family to your grace, to their heavenly father and mother."

The breeze picked up, the smell of roses filled her nostrils, a butterfly landed on her knee. "I am your servant," she whispered. "I pray for your divine guidance." A bee buzzed by, and her tears fell like rain.

**

Sam barely made it to work on time. His internal clock had been on the fritz since they returned from Europe. As many times as he had navigated through various time zones, not once had he struggled to bounce back.

On his way in, he switched stations three times to avoid the blatant ploy for his attention. "I don't want your stinking rum, I don't want your nasty beer, I don't have to drink no more, so keep your shit away from here," he sang, to an 80s tune he couldn't remember the name of.

He was agitated. The woman with the red lips sauntered into a wonderful dream he was having about Suzanne, robbing him of his sleep, nipping at his sanity. He must've shut off the alarm somewhere between his third shot of whiskey and her unzipping his pants—with her teeth. *I digress.*

He had found a Roger Salvo listed on a military roster back in the late 80s. The kid in the photo, wet behind the ears, saluting a flag, bore a close resemblance to the man he met at Mayahuel. After a deeper dive into Roger Salvo's military records, he discovered the kid in the photo disappeared. Sam couldn't find a death certificate...had he been recruited into the secret service? *But then why would he offer his name when we met?* Perhaps Roger Salvo wasn't his real name. Through more digging Sam discovered a photo from the Sacramento Bee's archived Society page. A wedding photo of Rebecca Blane, daughter of current senator Richard Blane, and good ol' Roger Salvo, C.E.O. of InnerVibes Corp, posed in complete bliss. Suzanne flashed across his mind. *She'll be every bit as beautiful a bride, if not more.*

Focus.

Sam had a full slate. Three unsolved murders in the county, two drug busts, 140 pounds of the country's number one villain, fentanyl, and two Ukrainian girls trafficked out of a good Samaritan's summer home. The world was going crazy, and he felt he bought a ticket to ride. Suzanne was his solace, but even she was affected by this unexplained, unfathomable mystery.

Sam entered the station in time to witness a fisticuff between Officer Spence and a recruit, John B. Wright. Sam burst between them as if he were parting the Red Sea. "In my office!" he barked.

The two men looked at the back of Sam's head, both slack-jawed, then at each other, as if they had awoken from a trance.

Sam gently closed the door behind them. He moved past the men and eased himself into his chair. The silence was deafening. And then he spoke, his voice as calm as a deep blue sea.

"What is our job here?"

The two officers replied in unison. "To protect and serve, sir."

"This isn't high school. Or the ghetto. Or Jedediah's Karate Dojo. So tell me, what the fuck is going on?"

The men exchanged shameful glances. "Must be burnout," Spence said. "It was my fault. I have a big mouth sometimes."

Sam's eyes grew large. "Sometimes?"

Spence grinned, breaking the tension in the room.

Sam wasn't amused. "I have a good mind to suspend you both," he said.

Spence stepped forward. "You have every right to, sir, but I ask that you don't. If anything, send us to the gym where we can work off some steam. I don't know about you, but there's so much strange shit going on, I can't sleep. I feel like someone has hijacked my brain, like those zombies you see on TV. I need some time off, but you know yourself, we're shorthanded."

"Yeah," John interjected. "Seems like the bad guys are winning."

Sam steepled his hands beneath his chin. "Either of you having strange dreams?"

**

Owen Westford sipped on his Blue Lagoon cocktail, the blue Curaçao liqueur made from Laraha, a bitter orange fruit grown in the Caribbean. The sun, now high in the sky, tanned his coconut-oiled skin, as he lazed by the pool, without a care in the world. His dirty deeds on autopilot for the time being.

Earlier that week, he sent Roger Salvo his instructions. He'd teach that twit, Garret Brecker that he can't escape. Although he hadn't pinpointed his location, he had tapped into his brain waves and stirred up some unpleasantries. *What a world.* His network of minions, increasing in numbers by the minute. He was able to clone the cop's frequency the day he stalked Roger and Rebecca at Mayahuel. He added his secret sauce to the cop's brain waves. How he loved toying with Rebecca, and how he loved watching Roger do the herky-jerky every time he did.

Owen didn't mess with Roger's mind too much. Instead, he took advantage of his ability to see the world through Roger's eyes by tapping into his visual cortex using quantum mechanics, and an AI program that tracked and recorded Roger's every blink. Owen had to admit, this feature was one of his favorites that Roger himself helped develop. He had watched Rebecca spread her legs, perform her magic on Roger's dick...he could almost feel her luscious lips on his own as they closed in for a kiss...but watching the book fly across the room during Roger's hissy-fit over taking out Garret Brecker and his family disturbed him. Fortunately, he knew how to handle Roger. *So much blood.*

Owen had watched as the paramedics lifted Rebecca onto the gurney, her face pale. One guy pierced her hand with a large needle, while another pressed on her carotid artery. Roger sent the schematics posthaste. Now, all Owen had to do was locate the family and proceed. But not today. Today he wanted to relax, take it easy. He looked forward to the lobster cocktail he ordered while he enjoyed his drink and listened to the surf.

**

"Steven," Suzanne blurted into her phone. "Steven, Sam and I are engaged—I wanted you to know."

"As if my day wasn't stressful enough," he replied.

"Really? You're not happy for me?"

"Thrilled!"

"You're lying. Mom said you'd give me a hard time."

"Mom?" he scoffed. "What—are you two hanging out?"

"Something like that. She's been around a lot lately. Jealous?"

"Hardly. Tell her I said 'hi'—and while you're at it, tell her I don't dislike Sam per se, I just don't trust him."

"She already knows."

"Well—I'll be goddamned."

"What do you say we go to that new wine-tasting place in Placerville—Batia? I've been wanting to check it out. Their wine has great reviews, and they have music on Friday nights. I know Karen would be game—"

"What about Sam? I thought he doesn't drink?"

"He doesn't. That doesn't mean he can't enjoy himself. C'mon, it would be fun. We can celebrate."

"Let me talk to Karen and get back to you." Steven paused. "Are you really happy with this guy?"

"Extremely. I've had a hard time believing it myself—being happy, that is. It's been difficult trying to remember what being happy was like. Ever since Jack—"

"How can you be happy if you're still thinking about Jack?"

"It's different. I can think about Jack without feeling empty. Since I fell in love with Sam, Jack is just—a memory."

"What time on Friday?"

"Six o'clock. I'll reserve a table."

"Okay." More silence. "I just want the best for you, Suz."

"Mom said that too."

"I miss her."

"Try reaching out—and Steven?"

"Yeah—"

"She said Dad is around you all the time."

"Huh—and here I thought those were my farts I smelled."

"You're disgusting."

"I know." After a beat, he said, "Suz?"

"Yeah?"

"Congratulations."

Suzanne smiled to herself. Her mother's perfume lingered in the air.

"I love you, big brother."

"Love you too, baby girl."

Medicine Park

What Garret valued most about Medicine Park was the lack of cell towers. Residents didn't mind the lack of service—they were more about getting together, face-to-face. They weren't big on social media, selfies, or texting. They enjoyed barbequing, telling stories, playing cards, strumming on the guitar, or full-out jam sessions. No one talked about their day at the office—it was all about how their tomatoes were growing, whose dog boinked whose.

Lizzie enjoyed the company of the women. She learned how to bake bread, weave jute, make jewelry out of old spoons. Ainsley was happy, playing with the few kids her age, Star, Phoenix, and Arlo. They made chalk drawings on the sidewalk, shared a tire swing, spit watermelon seeds, and ran in sprinklers. They ate homemade popsicles and drank Kool-Aid. There was even a penny candy store that sold items Garret had heard about from his parents. Life was good...until the dreams became more frequent. The buzzing in his ears—louder.

The disconcerting sounds in his head were a constant reminder of the squirrel that ate its way into his parent's attic when he was about thirteen. Everyone in the house would freeze when they heard the scratching noise coming from above. His dad would storm out of the room like Elmer Fudd in the Bugs Bunny cartoons swearing a blue streak. They all listened for the thump of the retractable ladder hitting the linoleum floor in the pantry, and his father's heavy breathing as he seethed, "I'm gonna kill that bastard."

Dreams of his wife and daughter—memories of the vermin in the attic, chewed on his brain cells leaving little piles of debris...and much like his father, the intrusion scratched away at his self-control...filling the empty spaces with rage.

**

Ainsley saw him coming toward her, his face bunched up like a used grocery bag, paint speckles stuck to his skin. Her first instinct was to run. But she hadn't done anything wrong, her mom would've told her if she did. She stood stuck in the moment, trying to figure out why he was so mad.

He stopped a few feet away, swiped his hand over his face, and walked into the house.

She climbed up on the rusty swing set that divided the yard next door and closed her eyes. She pictured Suzanne's garden, and settled her thoughts there, where she felt safe. When Suzanne appeared, she wasn't alone. Another woman was beside her, a woman with the same colored hair. She appeared to be kind, and Ainsley sensed that she loved Suzanne a lot.

When Suzanne turned her way, Ainsley waved.

"Who you waving at, Bug?"

Ainsley's eyes flew open. "Shooing a knat." The lie stung her tongue. Her mother's golden rule came to mind. *Truth or soap*. Ainsley learned the hard way. But she wasn't sure what was going on with her dad. It seemed every day he was different, and she didn't trust him. She saw hate in his eyes, and she was scared.

She heard Suzanne's voice call to her, but she couldn't answer. Her dad didn't want her talking to her imaginary friend anymore. He wanted her to play with her new friends—but they didn't understand how much she missed her old house, her toys, and the smells of the flowers that she loved to collect in the summer for the pretend salads she fed to her baby dolls. She was tired of being Belle. *I want to go home*.

Her dad stirred the dirt around with his worn-out Keds. "Mama's fixin' dinner, you hungry?"

Ainsley shook her head *No*. "Push me, Daddy."

Garret moved behind the swing, grabbed the thick wooden seat, raised it over his head, and let go. Ainsley squealed. "Daddy! Not so high!" Her chin trembled, tears flooded her eyes. She prayed he wouldn't catch her on the rebound and send her flying to the moon. As soon as it was safe, she dragged both feet in the dirt, creating a cloud of dust.

"Goddammit, Belle," he shouted.

When she jumped off the swing, she saw his wrath. "You shouldn't have pushed me so high," she cried. "And my name is Ainsley!"

**

Lizzie ran to the kitchen window when she heard the shouting. She saw the little brunette head bobbing toward her. By the time she reached the backdoor, her baby girl was running at full speed. "Mommy," she cried, flinging herself into Lizzie's arms. "I hate him—I hate Daddy, he tried to make me fall off the swing."

Lizzie glanced Garret's way. His expression lacked compassion as he brushed past them both and slammed the door.

**

"Is that true?" Lizzie's hushed tone didn't hide her anger.

"I pushed her a little too hard. It's not as if I was tryin' to *kill* her for fucks sake."

"You frightened her, she's just a little girl."

"Right. See if I offer to push her on the swing again—and she needs a refresher course on why we're here, and what's gonna happen if they find us—if they haven't already—shootin' off that big mouth of hers."

"Do you hear yourself?"

"I can't help it. I feel like I got a swarm of bees in my head, and I can't keep us safe unless everyone does their part."

"She's four!"

"Yeah, well she's not gonna see five if they find us."

Lizzie's anger rose to a fevered pitch. Words blasted out her mouth, pelting him one at a time. "**Don't—ever—say—that—again**."

**

Sacramento's heatwave didn't fare well with Suzanne's designer roses. They required constant care. Her inexperience with the variety she chose kept her online, and outside, determined to keep them alive. She wasn't alone. Her mother hovered nearby.

She felt a prickle at the back of her neck. A sweet scent followed, and she turned to seek the source. "It's her," she said, aloud.

"It's who?" her mother questioned.

"The little girl I told you about, don't you remember?"

No answer.

"Mom?" Suzanne removed her gardening gloves. "Mom, she wants to come home."

"That's not what I'm here for, Suzie. I'm here for *you*."

"This *is* for me—she needs my help." Suzanne felt cold air waft past her. "Mom?" Nothing. She closed her eyes and summoned the girl, hoping to connect. *Something's wrong.* The feeling, strong this time. The little girl's fear came through loud and clear.

Suzanne gathered her clippings into a canvas bag and dumped them into a compost bin. She picked up her gardening tools, cleaned them with the hose, and laid them on her patio to dry. She wanted to call Sam but thought better of it. He was overloaded at work, and adding her problems to the mix seemed selfish. *I can do this*, she thought.

A glass of iced tea, and a piece of avocado toast, and she'd be up for the task of finding the little girl on her own. She brought her plate to the kitchen table and grabbed her laptop. *Sam*. That's what he would do. He would google his clues until a picture began to form. Her advantage was harnessing universal energy to help in the process. She washed down her last bite of toast with a sip of tea and got to work.

She reviewed her list of first impressions. "Yacht." She closed her eyes and waited for another impression to coincide with the first. A word Sam used while in Paris came to mind...she had asked him where he was going...he replied, "Das klassifiziert ist." *That's classified*. "What has that got to do with a yacht?" She closed her eyes again, this time she saw a yacht slicing through blue waters.

Her fingertips hovered over the keyboard. She Googled the words *yacht* and *classified*. Thirty-two sites appeared on the screen. "Nope, I'm not taking a cruise," she said, clicking through minutia. The last site had an image of a huge yacht, the sun shimmering in its wake, bikini-clad beauties and men in suits raising a glass, EINGESTUFT painted in gold letters adorned the stern. She googled the word. Her scalp tingled when she read the German translation. *CLASSIFIED.*

The next words she focused on were cavern, deep, and dark. A pair of eyes greeted her behind her closed lids. *Who are you?* she asked telepathically. His eyes were filled with hate. She saw the letter G float across the image. "Where are you?" she asked, aloud. She saw a white walking bridge, beautiful waterfalls that invoked a smile. "Now we're cookin'."

She didn't have to search for the meaning behind 'serpent's tongue', the evil spoke for itself. When she closed her eyes, she saw two figures, one larger than the other, feminine energy. A squirrel scampered into view, its teeth, razor- sharp. She opened her mind, stretching it as far as it would go. A baseball bat. A swing set. *Blood.*

Suzanne prayed for the objects in her vision to be blessed, *let them do no harm.* She asked for protection for the little girl and her family, knowing trouble was the last word on her list. She prayed that she would find them before trouble paid a visit. In her gut, she knew, trouble was on its way.

Party-line

Linda waved when she saw Joseph come through the door. Joseph was dressed in a scarlet shirt and black slacks. A scarlet and black stripe tie completed the ensemble into his classy, 'signature look'.

"Wow, it's just lunch," she said giving him the once-over.

He gave Linda a quick squeeze before he slid across from her. "I did a TV interview this morning—I didn't have time to change."

"How did that go?" she asked.

"Wonderful. I got to talk about crazy stuff, and the host sat glued to every word."

"What was the topic?"

"Mind control."

"Shut up—really?"

"Yes, it was quite an interesting topic."

"Did he have good questions?"

"Yes—and actually, it was his choice of topic."

"Dang. When does it air? I wanna see it."

"I'll let you know."

"What was your favorite part?"

"Talking about H.G. Wells, his interest in AIs, and how his novels were so prophetic."

"I've only read a few, but now that I think about it, you're right—crazy stuff, indeed." Linda picked up her menu and browsed the selections.

Joseph ordered them both Thai iced tea while they decided on a dish. "How's your friend?"

"Suzanne?"

"Yes. Has she figured out how to use her superpowers yet?"

"She's working on it. How about you? Have you figured out why that young man walked in front of a train?"

"No. I just know it wasn't his nature to do so, and speaking with his mother helped validate my suspicions."

Linda's expression conveyed her sympathy before asking, "What else is going on? How's your graphic design biz?"

Joseph let out a hardy laugh. "I just did a book cover for a client. I created a redhead with lips that would make Angelina Jolie lovers drool."

"Sounds sexy."

"Right? The only issue is that the protagonist in the book is an awkward middle-aged blonde." Joseph leaned across the table, closing the gap between them. "The thing was, Linda—I could not stop myself from creating the character that way—I was possessed."

"What did your client say?"

"She stared at the drawing for what seemed like forever—then she lowered her glasses, cleared her throat, and said in a stern tone, "Joseph—did you even *read* the damn book?" Which is what Brad asked me when I showed him the draft."

Linda covered her mouth, suppressing a laugh. "So, did you make her blonde?"

"I did the drawing over, but I couldn't let go of the redhead." His eyes grew large. "I have her hanging on my wall."

Linda couldn't contain herself, laughter bubbled up and over. "What did Ben say?"

"Oh, I don't think he felt threatened. *Although*—I gotta say—those lips! Marone!" Joseph's mirth suddenly changed to concern. "The thing is, Linda, I've never had that happen before. I'm serious. That redhead had me under some kind of spell as if she were meant to be drawn."

"Interesting you should say that. Suzanne met a woman, a redhead, and she mentioned her red lips. I wonder if there's any connection?"

"I know that energy has changed since the pandemic. I can feel it. It reminds me of the telephone party lines from back in the day—at any given time someone could pick up the phone and listen to your conversation. Everyone knew everybody's business, and behind the scenes, someone was controlling the switchboard."

"Party-line on steroids?"

"We all know *someone*," he said, using air quotes, "is listening, and we just accept it because we really don't know who that *someone* is...we figure a ginormous computer in Timbuktu is spitting out algorithms, and that our information is safe. But what makes us think that if information can be extracted through algorithms, the same concept can't be used to reverse the process? And *put* thoughts in our heads?"

Linda's jaw dropped. "Are you saying that some unforeseen entity caused that young man to kill himself?"

"His name was David. And until that day, according to his mother, he appeared to be happy. So yes, I'm saying it's possible."

**

Linda drove into her driveway just as the sun was setting behind her. Her conversation with Joseph had her reeling. *Frequency*. Invisible to the naked eye. *Seeing is believing*. And yet, as Joseph mentioned during their conversation, humans were surrounded by the most astounding technology, and the average person didn't care *how* they were able to video chat with a person clear across the world, only that it was *possible*. And now that the internet was the information highway, anyone hungry for information, entertainment, or attention, was glued to a device twenty-four-seven. Few people were aware of the changing technology had on nature. Few people cared. Changes were blamed on fossil fuel and global warming, while the airwaves were being inundated with waves of every length imaginable. She didn't claim to understand, nor did she have any idea how to bring about change—what she knew was a bird hit her window and disappeared, and people were dying in unforeseeable circumstances, and in unexplained ways. *And who knows what else?*

The idea that there was a "they" behind it all was difficult to fathom. And yet, in history, the most horrendous wars were orchestrated by man, human trafficking dated back to the pharaohs, and a host of other crimes against humanity happen right under our noses—so why not an invisible enemy?

**

Ice melting in Roger's drink left condensation on his desktop. He opened the bottle of scotch and refilled his glass half full. He held up the glass, examined the contents against the fading light, and took a big swig. *My glass will never be half full again.* He drained the glass dry and checked his watch. Visitor hours would be over soon, and Rebecca would wonder why he wasn't there.

Guilt surged through every bone in his body as his mind replayed the scene in the kitchen that day. Her scream. The knife on the floor. The look of disbelief on her face as blood spurted from her neck. The 911 call.

She's lucky to be alive.

Roger considered himself fortunate the paramedics on duty that night were trained to deal with severe self-inflicted wounds. Once Rebecca was settled in ICU, Roger went home and got to work. By 2 a.m., he had completed the required task. Three people would die. *Them or us.*

**

Lizzie couldn't sleep. She felt trapped in a Stephen King novel, her husband morphing into a person she no longer recognized. He had very little interaction with them since Ainsley accused him of trying to make her fall off the swing. He moped around with a scowl on his face, and when he did interact with either of them, he was short- tempered. He had stopped shaving, and his hygiene suffered as well. He spent hours in the shed throwing an ax against a doubled sheet of plywood he brought home from one of the construction sights he was working on in Lawton.

A big housing boom kept everyone working long hours. The painting company Garret worked for got the bid. Garret got a raise, which would have made him happy but the owner was no longer able to pay him cash, and Garret (Peter) was nervous about using his fictitious social security number to collect his pay.

She said she'd see if she could nanny for an additional child to increase their income while he either found another job or took less for working side jobs through his current employer. "What do you want me to do?" she asked.

"I don't give a fiddler's fuck what *you* do. I'm not risking getting caught."

"Then don't—but stop taking your bad mood out on us."

She searched for a glimpse of her husband behind his hateful eyes. He was in there *somewhere*. "I'm trying to help."

Ainsley wiggled under Lizzie's arm and held onto her mother's waist. She stared at the man before her. The man she once adored. "Tell him to go away," she said, her voice smaller than she was.

Lizzie squeezed her tighter, "Sweetheart, we don't talk to Daddy that way."

"He's not my Daddy. He's that man."

Lizzie flashed a nervous smile at Garret. "I think we're all under a lot of stress." She held her belly, protecting the life inside from the possibility of an ugly situation.

Garret didn't budge. His jaw worked, grinding his teeth. He didn't speak. His eyes rose to the ceiling. A single tear ran down his cheek.

She relaxed her hold on Ainsley. "Honey, go to your room," she said. Ainsley made a wide berth between her and her father. Her eyes watching his. When she was out of sight, Lizzie sat on a kitchen chair.

"Sit. Let's talk this out." Garret didn't move. "Please."

After a few moments, he eased himself into the chair opposite of hers. She reached for his hand. Tell me what's going on. You are not yourself, and you're scaring me, and your daughter.

"I don't feel like myself."

"Tell me what's wrong—how can I help?"

"You can stay the fuck away from me."

"Is that what you really want? Or is that what you're manifesting in your mind? Would it be easier for you if we're gone? Out of your life? Is that what you want?"

He leaned close, his eyes piercing her heart. "What I *want*—is the both of you *dead*."

The Man Without a Soul

Sam wrapped twice on Suzanne's door, a bouquet of flowers held behind his back. When she answered, he presented them with a smile. "For my love."

Suzanne beamed. "You're the sweetest—thank you."

He closed the door behind him and drew her into a lingering kiss. "I promise to keep the flowers coming once we're married."

"Oh, so these aren't I want to get into your pants flowers?"

"Do I need to bring flowers to do that?"

"Not at all," she said pressing her body against his. She whispered, "Are you hungry?"

"Famished." He devoured her lips as his hands roamed her backside. "Are you?"

"Absolutely," she replied, between moans. Suddenly, she heard crying and pushed away from Sam.

"What's wrong?"

She closed her eyes, allowing the universe to deliver the message. She saw Ainsley face down, crying into her pillow. Suzanne's inner voice reached out. *Are you hurt?* The little girl searched the room.

"Can you see me?" she asked.

Yes. I can see you. Are you okay?

My Daddy wants to kill us, she replied, telepathically.

Tell me where you are. I will come and get you.

The bad man will see you, she said. *He's in my daddy's eyes.*

Suzanne shivered. When she opened her eyes, Sam was staring at her.

"Everything alright?"

"The little girl is in trouble Sam, we have to find her—she said her dad is going to kill her!"

"Slow down. Did she say where she is?"

"No. She said the bad man is in her daddy's eyes. He must have something to do with possession, or—or—" She rubbed her temples with her fingertips until her thoughts became clear. "Mind control. Someone is controlling her father's mind—that's why they fled."

"We need to know where she is before we can help her."

Suzanne closed her eyes urging the girl to return. Instead she saw another face. A thin face. *A man without a soul.*

Crybaby Bridges

Suzanne's phone rang, disrupting her sleep. She glanced at the clock. *6:30 a.m.* "It's early Linda—what's wrong?"

"There's a turkey vulture perched on the telephone wire outside my house."

"Aren't they too heavy?"

"Yes, but that's not what's disturbing me...he has a blackbird in his beak."

Suzanne blinked away the carnivorous image. "And your take?"

"This mind control thing is bigger than any of us can imagine."

"I agree, but there has to be a source. From what I've read, anyone can alter frequencies using quantum physics. I don't claim to understand how it works—all I know is that I have a scared little girl who claims her father is going to kill her."

"I'm getting waterfalls."

Suzanne sat up. "So did I—and a white walking bridge. I googled it —nothing hit home."

"Did you try Oklahoma?"

"Yes. My pulse rate increased when I read about the Crybaby Bridges. The urban legend fits in with the mind control theory—women who have either jumped or driven off these bridges with their babies. Supposedly the bridges exist all over Oklahoma."

Linda's voice dropped. "I can't imagine—"

"I had a disturbing dream the other night about the little girl. Her father was forcing medicine in her mouth, then she was swinging on a swing...and he came up behind her and hit her in the head with a baseball bat."

"I just got chills. What parent would do such a thing?"

"She came to me last night when Sam was here—she said her daddy wants her dead."

"We need to work harder at locating where she is."

"Linda? Can you come here? I'll fix some breakfast—we can search together."

"I'm on my way."

**

By the time Linda arrived, Suzanne had made a batch of French toast, a fresh pot of coffee, and had the table set for two. Together they pooled resources to come up with a plan.

Linda finished her last bite and said, "I have a friend that used to travel through Oklahoma back in the day when he serviced copy machines. He's a history buff, he may be familiar with the bridges there."

"Growing up," Suzanne said, "we stayed on this side of the Rockies, I have no knowledge of the Midwest states, but I feel that they picked a location that is remote, almost—*dated*."

Linda's attention strayed for a moment. "I'm getting 'houses.'"

"As in neighborhood?"

"Yes, but not quite." Linda's eyes scanned back and forth as if she were reading text. "New. New homes. Surrounded by fields. And something to do with—Jesus." She paused, her eyes misting over, then, "Google it."

Suzanne typed in Jesus, new homes, and Oklahoma and waited for the screen to fill with answers. "Well, there's a lot of new construction, an ad for a new Jesus movie, but no cigar on that word combo. What else?"

Linda cocked her head one way, then the other, as if listening to two different conversations. "Try the word 'holy'."

Suzanne's fingers flew across the keyboard. "Bingo! There's a Holy City in Lawton, Oklahoma."

"But no waterfalls or white footbridge?"

Suzanne clicked on the images of Holy City. "Nope—but looking at the images, they seem far away, more as in future than distance."

"What else is close to Lawton?"

Suzanne clicked on a map of the area and zoomed in. "Coral Crossing, Taupa, Cache, Fort Sill..."

Linda moved closer to peer over Suzanne's shoulder. "Where do we begin?"

"I wish I knew."

Suddenly Linda jabbed the screen with her index finger, "Looky, looky, Linda gets a cookie!"

Suzanne enlarged the map. Northwest of Lawton, above Indiahoma Wye was a town called Medicine Park. "In my dream, the little girl's father was forcing her to take medicine! Linda, you're a genius!" She typed the name into the search bar and held her breath. If they were right, there would be waterfalls and a white walking bridge. Sure enough. "I need to call Sam—and book a flight."

**

Sam sat in the back of the courtroom as Veronica Anochek stood before the judge. From where he sat, he could see her shoulders shake, and could only imagine tears streaming down her face. Her one small indiscretion, leaving her unattended child in the car, cost her custody for the time being. Veronica's lawyer had begged the judge for leniency, which he granted by way of foster care for the baby for three consecutive months while Veronica underwent a psychological evaluation, and therapy. At the end of one month, she would receive weekly visits, after three months, if all went well, her baby would be returned to her.

The situation made Sam's heart sick. If she were under the same spell that everyone else in the county seemed to be, it wasn't justice served, it was another point for the devil. On the flip side, she was lucky her baby lived.

He was on his way back to his office when he received Suzanne's message. He had learned that when she got excited, there was no better time to share her news than the present. "Hi sweetheart, I got your message. Let me see if I can clear my schedule—I can't let you go alone —we're partners, remember?"

"Of course—but it's imperative we go now, Sam. I really fear for her safety."

"Book the flights, I'll see what I can do."

"I already did. I'm psychic, remember?"

"And my work?"

"My spirit guides assured me everything would work out."

"Great! What time are we leaving?"

"5:45. I'm already packed. I can run by your place and grab your things if you don't have time—"

"That would be great. I'll ring the landlord to let you in."

"How did I get so lucky?"

"I was thinking the same thing."

**

Bags beneath Garret's eyes were a tell-tale sign he was functioning on little sleep. His conscious effort to keep his temper in check took more energy than expected. The dreams he'd been having were violent and evil. He didn't trust himself to share a bed with Lizzie and slept on the sofa in the living room. If in fact his brain were being scanned for a weak spot, they found it. His family. Despite his actions of late, he loved them more than life, and if it came down to him or them, he would rather die than cause them harm. But there was an ugliness festering below the surface, changing his thoughts sporadically, randomly, to loathing, hate, and *murder*.

He watched his beloved and his pride and joy through the kitchen window. Lizzie's baby bump protruded from her Rolling Stones T-Shirt as she pushed Ainsley on the swing. They acted as if they didn't have a care in the world. He felt isolated, shut out of their happy place, and he had no one to blame but himself. The infestation in his head grew as well, and the baseball bat next to the swing set gave him twisted ideas. He could almost see the two of them lying on the ground, their heads a bashed-in bloody mess. He licked his bottom lip, the way he did when he had a brilliant idea.

**

"Daddy's spying on us," Ainsley said.

When Lizzie turned, she saw his grim face in the window. "He's just jealous because we're having fun, that's all. She waved for him to come out and join them.

He shook his head 'no'.

"So be it," she said, "we can have our own fun."

"Why does he want to kill us, Mommy?"

"Baby! Don't say such a thing—your father would never—" Lizzie gathered Ainsley in her arms and squeezed her tight.

Ainsley wasn't convinced as her eyes gravitated to her father's blank stare. "I think we better hide the baseball bat."

**

Now or Never

Once they were buckled up, and the plane headed for the tarmac, Suzanne relaxed and said, "I can't thank you enough for coming with me. I know how busy you are at work—" She placed her hand over Sam's.

He lifted her chin. "You've never proved me wrong. I believe we'll find the little girl—and get a bead on out what's going on."

"Linda saw a turkey vulture sitting on the telephone wire behind her house snacking on a blackbird. She interpreted it to mean that the little girl is small potatoes compared to what is really going on."

"We can only take one thing at a time. Let's find the girl and go from there."

Suzanne snuggled close. "Any more dreams?"

"Not lately, but I see people at work acting more strange than usual. Angry, foggy, indifferent. Can't explain it—no one can."

"Having my Mother pop in is comforting, but at the same time, I wonder, why now? She never showed herself before."

Sam chuckled, "Makes me feel a little self-conscious when we're making love."

"Really? I hadn't noticed."

"I keep one eye open waiting for her to appear—"

Suzanne gave him a playful jab. "I'm sure she'd rate you as a ten."

"I don't remember my parents having sex—they must've waited until Audra and I were gone."

"They must've done it when you were seven—your sister wasn't born from an immaculate conception—unless you're keeping something from me."

"I swear, I never once heard a thing. No moans, or gratifying outbursts of any kind."

"Am I too loud?"

He gave her a sideways glance. "You let me know I'm doing my job satisfying you—I wouldn't change a thing."

"Good, because I couldn't contain myself if I tried."

Suzanne steered her attention toward the window. Sunbeams danced upon the clouds, lighting them to a brilliant golden-orange glow. Their beauty reflected in the bodies of water below, the scene ethereal and serene. She wanted to capture the image and keep it forever in her heart. Being with Sam filled her to overflowing with a love and appreciation for all that was good in the world. She lingered in the thought until the flight attendant handed Sam a Scotch and soda.

"There must be some mistake, I didn't order a drink," he said, perplexed.

"Compliments from the Captain," she said, flashing a dazzling smile.

"Please thank the captain for me, but I can't accept." He dug his sobriety coin out of his pocket and held it up for her to see. Her eyes glazed over, and she walked away.

**

When the plane landed, the couple waited their turn to exit. Sam was hoping to see the Captain, thank him for the gesture, but he didn't expect the exchange to happen. He had felt Suzanne's body go rigid when she witnessed the incident unfold. Her demeanor changed from bliss to apprehension, and yet she hadn't expressed herself as such. So, when she stopped dead in front of him to stare at another passenger, Sam's attention was at full alert.

After a moment, she slipped back into a cool mode and moved

forward. Once they were free from the cluster of passengers deplaning, Sam took her aside.

"What was that all about?"

"I'm not sure," she said, trying to maintain composure, but Sam could see fear in her eyes.

"Did you know that man?"

"No. It's hard to explain—"

"Try me."

"Evil comes in all shapes and sizes. He—" She collapsed into an empty chair. "I saw Hitler. Not him per se, but a man equally murderous. I saw the discarded bouquet from Paris, the suicides, the mass shooting in the park..."

"You think he's responsible for the suicides?"

"They weren't suicides to him. They were an *experiment.*"

**

Lizzie kneeled beside the bed with Ainsley, their hands folded in prayer. "God bless Mommy, and my friend Suzanne. Please show her the way to my house so she can save us from Daddy."

"Honey, look at me—"

Ainsley opened her eyes, at Lizzie's command. "Why don't you call me by my name anymore, Mommy?"

"I do—"

"You call me Honey, Sweetie, Bug, Baby—but not Ainsley or Belle."

"Oh, Bug, I wish it were that simple." She cradled Ainsley in her arms. "I love you so much, and I love your name, I picked it out special for you before you were born...but now, we have to use different names, and it breaks my heart to say it...so when I call you those other names, in my mind, I AM calling you Ainsley, only without saying it." The shadow creeping across the floor startled them both, and they bolted upright. "Geezus, Pete—you scared me."

"What have I told you both about using our real names?"

Lizzie swept her hand around the room. "There's no one here. We were having a heart-to-heart."

"They can hear you."

"Really? Then hear this—FUCK OFF—LEAVE US ALONE!"

Garret reached for Lizzie's throat. Ainsley kicked his hand away. "Don't hurt my Mommy," she screamed.

Garret swatted his daughter's foot away from him.

"I hate you!" she cried.

Garret blinked a few times as if his daughter's words didn't compute. He did an about-face and left the room.

Lizzie gathered her baby girl close to her breast and whispered in her ear, "We have to leave here. Tonight."

**

Three hours, and Eighty-four miles later, Sam and Suzanne parked the car at their "Tiny" rental. A full moon lit their way from the car to the front door. It was 2:15 a.m. "This looks intriguing," he said, his tone laced with humor. "What exactly is this place?"

"It's a tiny house. All the hotels were booked. I was lucky to find it. We have it to ourselves for a week."

"Good, because I don't think anyone else would fit."

"I think it's charming. There's a lovely view, and besides, what better way to find the little girl than to be nestled in between half of Medicine Park's population?"

"Is it bad to mix business with pleasure?"

"You're lucky it's too late to explore." She stepped from the tiny kitchen into the bedroom, unbuttoning her blouse.

"I never considered myself lucky until I met you," he said, undoing his pants. He eased her onto the queen size bed— his feet touching one wall, her knuckles hitting the other when she threw her arm over her head.

"I could get used to this tiny house," she said between giggles.

"You'd have to add Arnica to your daily regime."

"People would think you're abusive with all the bruising I'd incur."

"Especially when you let out one of your mating calls."

In response, she pressed her body to his, extolling his appreciation with a low growl. But before he could enter her sacred space, the tiny house began to shake.

"Shhh," Sam whispered. He bounced out of bed and into the pants puddled on the floor. He grabbed his gun from the locked case in his duffle bag and padded to the door.

"Who's there?" He called.

"It's Jason, your neighbor. I saw you pull in a while ago. Your running lights are on."

Sam tucked the gun in his waistband and opened the door to a long-haired man in his forties. He stepped outside and peered around the corner. "Thanks, man. It's a rental. Guess I'm used to my car lights going off automatically." He stepped back inside and felt around the tiny kitchen counter for the keys. He shut the door behind him.

"Okay, cool. Goodnight." As Jason walked toward a larger tiny house across the way, he turned to Sam. "And don't worry about the—uh-hum—noise. We're all friends here."

Sam was glad Suzanne wasn't in earshot of the man's comment. She would've turned fifty shades of red. He unlocked the car door, reached for the toggle switch to turn off the lights, wondering why he hadn't noticed they were left on. Once the lights were off, he realized the brightness of the moon diminished the car's beams. Returning to the tiny dwelling, he surveyed the area. Besides the tiny house Jason occupied, there were two, small one-story-houses about thirty yards away with shared space between them. Sam's attention froze on the swing set in the middle of the yard.

"Suzanne, wake up." Sam nudged her gently. "There's a swing set in a yard close by, come take a look."

Suzanne wrapped the sheets around her and stepped outside. The moon cast shadows on the swing set making it seem ominous. "I'm not picking up anything." She closed her eyes and opened her mind. She saw a room full of shadows, a closed window. She heard the little girl's laughter echo in the recess of her mind. As the laughter faded, Suzanne realized, "She's gone!"

"Now what?" Sam swiped his hand across his chin.

"I'm exhausted. I say we get some sleep and regroup in the morning."

**

Lizzie had climbed out the bedroom window and crept between the tiny houses with Ainsley in tow. The folded piece of paper in her back pocket was her only hope. It contained the phone number of a safe haven for women she had seen on a flyer hanging on the wall in the dressing room of the Goodwill store in Lawton. She considered it an omen.

All she needed to do was get to a pay phone.

The duo ducked into a gas station less than a mile out of town. Lizzie deposited four quarters into the phone slot and dialed the number she had written down the day before.

"Holy Springs," announced a sleepy voice.

Lizzie cleared her throat. "I need help. My husband has threatened our lives."

"Where are you now?"

"A gas station on Highway 49, right on the border of Medicine Park."

"And where is your husband?"

"At home, hopefully still asleep. We snuck out a window."

"Who are you with?"

"My four-year-old daughter."

"Are you on foot?"

"Yes."

"I'll be there in twenty minutes. Look for a red Jeep. My name is Melissa."

Lizzie sighed in relief. Ainsley held onto her waist, her eyes half closed. "C'mon, Bug, let's wait over there, behind those trash bins. Melissa is coming to get us.

**

Lizzie snuggled Ainsley close to her breast. She conjured memories of when she was a baby and the love she and Garret bestowed on their bundle of joy. She fast-tracked through the years stopping to enjoy moments shared...traveling to gigs, dance recitals, and modeling jobs. Ainsley loved being on stage. Her aptitude for remembering lines far surpassed her age.

Although Garret's family focus had waned over the years, she never doubted his love for his baby girl. In fact, until he took the photography gig on the yacht, his daughter was his world. *We both were*. The anger she felt toward him since then was perhaps unwarranted. He didn't do anything wrong. *He never was a good communicator*. But the fear... wondering if he was going to snap and kill them both...*I won't do it*. She had another life growing inside of her to protect as well.

She never imagined her life turning out this way. Hopefully, they would be safe at Holy Springs, and Ainsley wouldn't carry the scar from some monster's evil doing.

Lizzie didn't fully comprehend the magnitude of danger they were in, mostly because she didn't want to. She wanted to return to a peaceful, happy existence, but she knew it wasn't possible. She added another layer of worry—*what will he do if he finds us*?

**

Garret stirred. The woman with the luscious lips beckoned him. "I have something to show you," she said. He followed her into the jaws of hell.

Lizzie and Ainsley danced, holding something between them. *The baby*. Garret woke, gasping. He sat on the edge of the sofa trying to clear his head. *What the fuck*. He moved his head from side to side, popping the kink in his neck. He went to the sink, poured a glass of water, and drank it down. He leaned against the counter glaring at the bedroom door.

A sensation sizzled in his brain like marinated steak on a barbeque. He imagined the door, breathing in and out. He shook his head, but the illusion didn't dissipate. As if under a spell, he walked to the door and grabbed the knob. The knob didn't budge. Locked? He tried again. No luck. His ire rose, and he pounded the door with his fists.

"Godammit Lizzie, let me in!" Realizing he said her real name made him even madder. "Open the fucking door," he bellowed. Silence. He pressed his ear against the door. "Not a creature was stirring, not even a —" He slammed into the door with all his might. "—mouse!" The door sprung open. His eyes adjusted to the dark. The room was *empty*.

**

Owen Westford relaxed in a hotel three miles from Fort Sill, Oklahoma, watching HBO, and sipping on a dry martini. His laptop, charging on the nightstand, shut down for the night, his clothes hung neatly in the closet. His mission was nearing completion. It was late. *Tomorrow's another day*. He had his personal tracking devices in place. If Garret or Sam had looked up in the sky, they may have seen Owen's secret weapon winking at them.

Garret's brain wave activity had registered at a level Owen strived for. Roger's handiwork paid off. Despite his reluctance to participate, Roger was the best in the business. If Owen was a sentimental slob, he'd cut the man some slack. But "squirm" was the name of the game. He knew the game well...hazing in college, ridicule in the military, labeled a skinny dweeb...but now he had "more politicians dancing with the devil than Cardi B," he said aloud. Celebrities, politicians, billionaires, even the Pope had succumbed to his bidding. The more experimenting he did under the government's secret cloak, the more power he acquired. When the time was right, he'd rule the world.

He tossed the rest of his martini down the hatch and grimaced. *God, how I hate cheap hotels*.

**

Garret jumped into his truck, madder than a hornet. *Fuckin' bitch*. He slammed his palm on the steering wheel and peeled out of his drive. The moonlight made the world seem surreal. The landscape, he observed, resembled one of those 3D slides that came with the View-Master he had as a kid. He was surprised at the recall. The fissures in his memory rivaled LaPaz, Arizona...but every now and then, normalcy slipped between the cracks and happiness crept in.

He kicked up gravel and squealed onto Highway 49, and drove past the first gas station, slowing down to scan the parking lot. Nothing unusual, a semi gassing up, a family in a red jeep pulling out in the opposite direction...*probably stopped for snacks or a bathroom break*. His heart ached. He stepped on the gas and headed for Lawton.

**

As soon as Lizzie and Ainsley jumped into Melissa's red Jeep, she had them tuck their hair beneath ball caps she provided to match her own. "Just a precaution," she claimed.

Lizzie held her breath when she saw Garret's truck slow down in front of the gas station. "That's him," she whispered. The door locks clicked into action.

Melissa gave the directive. "Stay calm. Look at me and laugh. And you, pint size, in the back seat there—grab that stuffed pig I brought for you and lay your head down on the door like you're going to go to sleep. We're going to pull out nice and slow—like we have all the time in the world." Melissa looked in the rear-view mirror. "Thank you, Lord. He's going the other way."

Lizzie couldn't hold back her tears.

Melissa patted her hand. "I know how you feel—you probably love the guy—but the important thing is getting you and that beautiful little girl of yours to a place where he can't find you. We can sort out your feelings and logistics once you're safe.

Ainsley closed her eyes, but she wasn't pretending to sleep...she wanted to show Suzanne her new stuffed pig. She needed to see Suzanne's face. She needed to know Suzanne was there for her because deep down, she knew they were never going to be safe as long as that man was in her daddy's head.

Hide and Seek

An image of a swing set in the moonlight seeped from Suzanne's subconscious into her dream. The swing was moving, *unattended*. A man's face loomed behind the scene, his eyes crazy with fear, and anger. A red jeep sped through the scene, with a stuffed pig in the rear passenger window. Another man lurked in the shadows. Suzanne sat up with a start.

"What is it, hon?" Sam reached for Suzanne, careful not to startle her.

"I saw their faces—the little girl's father—the man on the plane. I saw their faces in my dream. That's never happened before."

"That's great, sweetheart, I know you struggled with seeing faces."

"I wonder if the man on the plane is the man in the father's head—the little girl mentioned him."

"Hard to say—we can check it out in the morning unless we go window peeping in our birthday suits."

"I saw a red jeep. Don't know what that means.

"Yet." Sam kissed her shoulder. "I have faith in you. You'll figure it out."

One kiss led to another. "You gave me my wings Sam. I think love has raised my frequency."

Sam laughed as he pressed himself against her thigh. "Yeah, mine too."

**

Two wooden Adirondack chairs served as the perfect place for Suzanne and Sam to spy into the neighbor's yard over coffee. The eastern exposure made it plausible to wear dark glasses, and their vigil less obvious. Loud noises came from the house they had their eye on, and they waited patiently for the responsible person to show his face.

"Let's act touristy and go over there—ask for a recommendation where to eat breakfast."

"And if he's as deranged as you claim? He could blow one or both of us away without batting an eye."

"Look—it's him." Suzanne waved. The man didn't wave back. He gave a curt nod and climbed into his truck. Suzanne rose against Sam's protest, and ran towards Garret's truck, catching him by surprise.

"What the fuck, lady?"

"I'm sorry, we just got into town last night, and I—*we* were wondering if you could tell us where we can find a good breakfast spot?"

"I'm no fuckin' tour guide." He put the truck in reverse. "Do you mind? I'm late for work."

Suzanne backed away from the truck and into Sam. Sam saluted Garret, his gaze fixed on him as he backed out of the driveway and took off in a hurry down the street. "He was wearing painter's coveralls. He's going to work," she said.

"I'll take a look around his house. You keep watch. Let me know if you see anyone coming."

Sam disappeared around the corner. Suzanne took cover under a tree. She fanned her face, pretending to enjoy the beautiful weather. When Sam didn't return, she opened her phone to check the time. Twelve minutes had gone by, her heartbeat ticked off every second.

Finally, Sam reappeared and sat next to her.

"You had me worried—I was afraid you broke in—or worse."

"Back door was unlocked—appears Daddy drank his breakfast—the kitchen counter was littered with beer cans." He brought her hand to his lips for a quick reassuring kiss. "From what I could see, the bedroom at the back of the house was trashed. No blood, no dead bodies, thank goodness. I saw a couple of dolls, girl's clothing, 4T, mom's clothes—you're right. They took off."

"Where could they be?"

He lowered his sunglasses. "Let's take a look around town—get a feel for the people. See what this town's law enforcement department has to offer."

Suzanne nodded, "Maybe someone took them in."

"There's always that possibility."

**

Suzanne followed Sam's lead. They walked the small strip of quaint shops, gauging the local vibe, ending up at a café for a quick breakfast.

"You and breakfast seem the perfect combination," he said.

"Although dessert is my weakness."

His devilish smile confirmed her preference. "One of these days we should discuss a wedding date. My mother keeps leaving hints on my voicemail. And Audra wants to know if we've decided on a color scheme yet."

"We've only been engaged a short while. Isn't it too soon to think about a wedding?"

"Do you have reservations about getting married this year? Do you even want a big wedding? I know you and Ben didn't—"

Her thumb gravitated toward her ring finger, adjusting the band in place. "I would love to marry in a church, but not sure about a big wedding. I really don't have that many friends to invite—Steven and Karen are my only family. What about you?"

"I'd be happy with small—but it's what you want."

"I want to find the little girl—and go home. Then I want to kidnap Linda and go dress shopping. I think once my mind is clear, I can focus on a wedding. I love the snow. We could get married in Lake Tahoe."

"Sounds romantic." He kissed her hand.

She looked around the room. "I feel like we've stepped back in time."

Sam followed suit, taking in the long-hair, colorful garbed patrons.

"I didn't experience the sixties, but I have a feeling, it was much like this."

Suzanne closed her eyes for a moment. "I'm not picking up on anything." Her eyes veered beyond the café's picture window to the Wichita Mountains. "She's out there somewhere."

**

Lizzie wrapped her arms around Ainsley's small frame, instinctively lifting the little girl's hair off her neck. Her hair had grown a couple of inches since the beginning of the nightmare they were trapped in. "He's not a bad person. I don't know what happened...well I do, but I'm afraid to talk about it. They may be listening."

Melissa glanced at June, the administrator at Holy Springs. "You said your husband threatened your life. What happened?"

"He hasn't been himself." Lizzie let go of the tears she had been holding back since they climbed out of the bedroom window and ran for safety. "I don't know how to explain it without sounding crazy."

June handed her a tissue. "We're here to help, not to judge."

"Do your best," Melissa chimed in.

"Mommy—don't," Ainsley pleaded.

"We're safe, baby. Daddy doesn't know where we are." Lizzie held her daughter tighter. "We're both afraid of what he'll do if he finds us."

June steepled her hands together. "We pride ourselves on safety and anonymity here. What we need to establish is how much danger you are in, and how much help you will need."

"I don't know—I'm still trying to process this."

Ainsley broke away from her mother's grasp. "Suzanne is gonna find us—she'll keep us safe."

Both women sought Lizzie's reaction to her daughter's outburst, but Lizzie was too stunned to speak. June leaned forward, touching Ainsley's hand. "Who is Suzanne, honey? Is she your auntie? Or a friend?"

"She's my friend. And she can see me—and I can see her. She knows my *real* name."

Lizzie covered her face with her hands. Her tears came harder now, her body shook. "I don't know what to say." She dried her tears with her palm. "I'm so tired."

Melissa stood up. "Perhaps we can talk later after you've rested."

Lizzie nodded. "Yes. I'd like that."

**

Garret climbed down from the ladder, a bucket of paint in one hand, gripping the metal rungs with the other. He felt like a zombie. The beer had deadened his senses earlier, but now he felt like he had bricks in his pockets. Each step, an effort. His head throbbed, his mouth, dry. If only the structure he was painting was higher, he'd do a backflip and end it all. *Do it*, the voice inside his head cajoled. "Shut the fuck up!" he screamed.

The momentary silence gave him the opportunity to defrag. He imagined Lizzie's smile, his daughter's laughter. *Where are you?* He wanted the nightmare to end, but not by taking his life, or theirs. He wanted back into the body that fell in love with his wife, the body that made love to her, the body that created his daughter, and the baby on the way. He wanted to feel Lizzie's lips on his. He wanted to hear her voice convincing him that happiness was theirs, and that no one could ever take away their love. *Love conquers all.* But then his fists balled up, blood pooled in his cheeks, and a slow burn crept up the back of his neck and he knew...*someone has to die.*

Sovereignty and Buffalos

The door closed behind Linda's last client. The reading drained her. Questions about war, God, and sovereignty. It seemed lately fear occupied the minds of her clients. Very few asked, "Will I get the job? Will he call me? Is my mother at peace?" A shroud of darkness fell on the lightest of hearts. Confusion, isolation, and doom was the new consensus—*"I feel like I'm dying...sometimes I wish I was dead...life has been drained from me...life isn't worth living."*

She put a kettle on for tea and turned on her TV. Twenty minutes until her favorite program started allowed time to make a turkey sandwich. She toasted two slices of sourdough bread, peeled off two lettuce leaves, and sliced a tomato from her garden. A light smear of mayo, and she was good to go. A few minutes into the program, she received a universal hit. *Buffalo.* She could smell them, feel the heat from their fur-clad bodies, hear their heavy hooves pounding a dusty trail. She put her sandwich on the snack tray, and let her mind roam free. *Children.* Cobblestone streets. Marching...

She didn't know what it all meant, but the sensations were strong, and she knew she was blessed with a puzzle piece. The question: *Where does it fit?*

Linda knew Suzanne and Sam had flown to Oklahoma to find the little girl. Even before they left, Linda had prayed for clarity. Buffalo, children, marching...how much clearer could it get? She texted the three words to Suzanne oblivious to the time difference.

LINDA

BUFFALO, CHILDREN, MARCHING - MAKE SENSE TO YOU?

**

Joseph leaned back in his office chair. His eyes settled on the picture hanging on the wall of the redheaded woman with the luscious lips he had drawn for his client's book cover. He had made adjustments, possessed by the mystery of her essence, and the hold she had on his psyche. He had redrawn the woman's eyes after Source had shown them with eagles centering her pupils and one of her red hair tendrils in the shape of a snake. Her chin marked defiance, and her pug nose was now slightly off-center. He added one dangling earring in the shape of a man, hanging upside down, beneath his head, a long red slash.

When Ben entered the room, his jaw dropped. "Well isn't she creepy?"

"I know. And I can't take my eyes off of her. There's a message behind this augmentation...I'm trying to figure it out."

"Does she have anything to do with that kid who stepped in front of the train?"

"No, I don't think so—it's deeper than that."

"Come to bed Joe, it's late."

Joseph couldn't deny the power behind the woman's eyes, or the tune that played over and over in his head. *"Fanboys, Fanboys, Fanboys carry the fan. Fanboys, Fanboys, the boys who have a plan."*

Little Red Jeep

Garret perused the streets of Lawton, searching for his wife and daughter, crazed, and sleep deprived, his skin spattered in paint. Rage surged through every fiber of his being. And yet the tiniest spot of his heart held onto the love he once knew. "You can't take that away from me," he sang under his ragged breath.

He saw a red jeep drive past him, and like a bull in an arena, he turned his truck around and charged toward the vehicle. The jeep rolled to the side of the road. Garret jammed his truck in park, and flew out of the driver's seat, ready to do battle. The Jeep's driver, a woman with brown curly hair, reached for a shotgun from the passenger seat and aimed it at his head.

"You gotta problem?" she asked, her finger on the trigger.

"I'm looking for my wife, my little girl."

"What's that got to do with me? You nearly ran me off the road."

"I saw your Jeep, last night, pulling out of the gas station in Medicine Park."

"So what—it's a free country last time I checked."

"I thought maybe—"

"Well you thought wrong asshole—now get in your truck and get the hell out of here before I blow your head off."

Garret didn't argue. He imagined steam coming out of his ears, but he bit his tongue. He hopped in his truck and drove away.

Melissa made a call to June. "Make sure you keep Lizzie and her little girl out of site. I think I just had the pleasure of meeting the husband—and he ain't too friendly."

**

Owen eased himself into the hotel pool. His Rolex watch looked garish perched on the pea-green tile trim. The pool was empty. He made sure of it. *A tilt, tilt here, a tilt, tilt there, here a tilt, there a tilt, everywhere a tilt, tilt.* All it took was the right frequency, transmitted from a satellite to a 5G tower nearby. He had Roger to thank for that one. He designed the exercise for a mission in Iraq. Owen snagged it for his own pleasure, had Roger reprogram the software to cause temporary aquaphobia in a designated area. The dumb shit had no clue why he was given the order, he just did what he was told. *That was then.* Lately, Roger questioned his directives, even refused his latest order. He was to locate Garret Benson and program his brain to kill, as he did with Dallen Foster. Benson would kill his wife and daughter, and then himself. So far, they were all alive.

Strong-willed subjects were able to resist to a point. Owen knew this, was even fascinated by their resistance. Mind games weren't perfect. Resistance remained an enigma. Why were some people so easily swayed, like Roger's wife Rebecca, while others were difficult to control? The billion-dollar question. Garret was deteriorating, Owen had checked his progress on his laptop over coffee. *He's getting ready to crack.*

**

Garret had never faced the barrel of a gun before. He wondered if all the open-carry states had chicks driving around with shotguns in their front seats. *You're not in California anymore, buddy-boy.* He laughed out loud at the irony. At least here he could *see* the enemy. The thought triggered his memory of what he observed that night on the yacht again. *The waitress. The drinks. The man standing behind the waitress. Who was he?* At the time Garret didn't think anything of the man's presence, but now, he wondered.

It hurt to think.

He never was much of a drinker. A few beers with the boys, one or two with pizza on a Friday night, during Super Bowl, that's all. He couldn't believe he went through a twelve- pack before breakfast. *It's her fault*. He'd deal with her once he found her, and he *would* find her. For now, he needed to gobble a handful of aspirin and close his eyes for a bit. Painting all day in the hot sun drained the starch out of him. He needed to have a clear head when he went back out to hunt for his wife and daughter.

From the time he closed his eyes, he regretted it. Colored spots danced behind his lids forming a face. Her face. *Traitor. We were supposed to be in this together*. Her lying eyes, *reptilian*, her lying lips opened to *fangs and a serpent's tongue.* He knew touching her skin would scorch his fingers. The image sizzled in his brain momentarily, then gave way to another vision. Two bodies, clinging to one another, mother and child, twisted in death. *Amy? Belle? Where are you?*

**

Melissa led the prayer at dinner, welcoming newcomers into the fold, asking the good Lord for protection, "Please watch over our flock." Followed by a chorus of "Amen" and a procession through the food line. Chicken fried steak, lima beans, okra, mac 'n cheese, and biscuits.

Ainsley wrinkled her nose. She cupped her hands over her mouth and whispered in Lizzie's ear, "Mommy, what is that stuff?"

Lizzie put a spoonful of each item on her daughter's plate. "It's called southern cookin', and we are so grateful for the culinary experience." Ainsley rolled her eyes. "Eat what you can, baby." Ainsley took her plate and joined another little girl her age at the end of a long wooden table.

Melissa took Lizzie aside. "I don't want to alarm you, Liz, but I ran into a man who just might be your husband. 'Bout five-eleven, dark hair, little scar on his chin—drives an 'ol beat-up, blue pick-up truck?"

Blood drained from Lizzie's face. "Where? Does he know where we are?"

"No, Ma'am—scared him off with my Winchester Repeater. Daddy gave it to me for my sixteenth birthday. We haven't parted company since." Melissa filled her plate saying, "I made sure he didn't follow me. You're safe."

"Thank you. I—I never—"

"No one does, Darlin'. Look around you. First, it's a slap, then a black eye, and before you know it, you're running for your life." Melissa steered Lizzie toward the table.

"Garret has never hit me. This whole thing is insane."

"Sure honey. I know, but I saw the crazed look in that man's eyes. There's no tellin' what he'd do if he found you."

Lizzie's appetite tanked. She moved her food around on her plate. She wanted to believe her husband was under some evil spell, and once it was gone, they could return home, see their family and friends, get their lives back. She couldn't imagine living out the rest of her days, raising her daughter, moving from shelter to shelter. She glanced at Ainsley, catching her eye. Ainsley stabbed an okra with her fork, opened her mouth, and held the fork high like she was about to swallow a fish. She took a bite, turned to her mother, and rubbed her tummy. Lizzie's angst evaporated. *Everything will be alright.*

**

Suzanne and Sam sat outside, cold drinks in hand, watching Garret swing on the swing. At one point, he swung so high, he almost flew over the bar. He dragged his feet, came to a complete stop, and started over.

"He's mad," Suzanne said in a hushed tone.

Sam nodded. "Possessed."

"I got a text from Linda. She sent three words, buffalo, children, marching."

"We saw buffalo driving in from Lawton." He opened his phone and tapped his map icon. "There's a military base nearby, Fort Sill. Could be an orphanage near the base, or a safe house."

"Before we left, I was seeing the word, holy. There's a Holy City nearby too. There's a connection."

Just then, Garret flung himself to the ground. He lay in the grass, his arms and legs splayed. Sam made a beeline for the yard.

"Hey man, you okay?"

Garret rose, brushed himself off, and faced Sam. "Yeah, long hot day, the cool grass feels good." He extended his hand. "Peter Benson. Pete."

"Sam. My fiancé, Suzanne."

Without warning, Garret ran toward Suzanne, his hands balled into fists, screaming, "Where are they? Where's my daughter?"

Sam grabbed the back of Garret's shirt and spun him around. "What the hell do you think you're doing?"

Color rose in Garret's face as he poked his finger toward Suzanne. "It's her! She's the one putting ideas in my little girl's head."

Sam stepped in as a barrier. "You're wrong, man. We came here to help."

Garret froze, stunned. "Who are you?"

Suzanne spoke. "We know you're running from someone, from something. You're being controlled."

"You must be crazy—where's my little girl?"

"Ainsley? Or Belle?"

Garret's machismo deflated. His body crumbled to the ground, his pain escaping his soul in heart-wrenching sobs. "It was a job. I knew I shouldn't have done it, but we needed the money."

Sam squatted down beside him. "What happened?"

"I can't tell you," he cried, "they'll kill my family."

"I'm a cop. I can't help you if you don't tell me. We didn't come this far to judge—your little girl is in danger."

Garret wiped his eyes. "I don't know how they do it, my head hurts, I feel like I'm losing my mind." He hung his head. "I have dreams of killing them—my wife, my little girl, and the baby." He raised his eyes pleading with Sam, "I can't control it—I don't want to live."

Sam wrapped his arm around Garret and helped him up. "C'mon, man, let's go inside and talk this out."

Garret ran his head under the kitchen fawcett, and dried himself with a wad of paper towels. "It started with a gig, on a yacht. I was hired to photograph the guests, politicians, celebrities, billionaires, or so I thought."

"When was this?"

"After our daughter was born."

"What happened?"

"One guy gave orders to another man, who in turn gave them to me, but he was always there, lurking in the shadows. I never got a good look at his face."

"What kind of photos was he asking you to take?"

"Disgusting photos. Damaging photos. The victims were drugged, then positioned in precarious positions with children, animals, people of the same sex...you name it."

Sam scrolled through his phone to a file with saved photos. "Recognize this couple?" He handed the phone to Garret with Roger and Rebecca's photo displayed on the screen.

Garret dropped the phone. Sam caught it mid-air. "I take it that was a yes?" he said.

Garret's face paled, his voice barely a whisper. "Yes. He was on the yacht that night. I photographed him with a little boy. It made me sick."

"Did you know who he was?"

"No. But I got the impression he was someone important. The big cheese left the room when he came in. He told the guy who was doing the posing to make sure he got home safe and sound."

"What about his wife?"

I see her in my dreams...or should I say my wife—she morphs in and out of her image. It's those red lips I see."

Sam understood. "What else can you remember?"

"There was a woman—she was an actress I think, she walked around making small talk. She—she was the woman who drove into a house the night of the Discovery Park shooting. I saw her in the news footage. She had been at the park."

"Interesting. Anything else?"

"My wife and daughter were at the park too."

**

Owen took one last bite of steak and shoved the plate aside. He plugged his earphones into his laptop and cranked up the volume. What he heard was music to his ears. His voice recognition program found a matched pattern from an interview conducted at the Discovery Park shooting. "Hello, Lizzie." He checked the coordinates on the map. Six miles east of Fort Sill. *Smart lady.* Garret must've rubbed her the wrong way. However, she wouldn't be an easy access, the location she was in was guarded like Fort Knox. "Well," he said aloud, leaning back in the chair, "decisions, decisions." He had intended for Garret to kill Lizzie and Ainsley, then kill himself. He had no choice but to reverse the process. He clicked on "operation red lips," dragged the program onto Garret's profile picture, and hit 'play'. He brought his arms up behind his head, "Boy, I feel like God!" He waited for the frequency to sync up inside Garret's head, before he whispered into the microphone, "Fanboys, Fanboys, Fanboys carry the fan. Fanboys, Fanboys, the boys who have a plan."

**

Garret was once again imprisoned by his nightmare. Held down by his evil wife and daughter. Their claws tearing at his flesh. Their teeth gnashing between red lips. He couldn't cry out. He wanted to die. End the mnemonic beat echoing in his brain. *Fanboys*...fight the demons. *Fanboys.* The power is yours. *Fanboys carry the fan*...the knife is in the drawer...*Fanboys. the boys who have a plan*... one good slice to the jugular, *do it now, man*.

**

Sam and Suzanne observed as Garret tossed and turned on the sofa. It was late, they were both tired, but didn't feel comfortable leaving Garret alone. Sam, being more vigilant, sat erect, eyes wide open, his gun, resting in the holster strapped to his chest. She felt herself fade from the room on and off, trying so hard to stay awake. At last, her body surrendered, and gave way to sleep...

She saw herself in front of stone outcroppings, and structures that seemed to date back to Christ. The crude landscape bore crosses and inscriptions. In the distance, she saw buffalo roaming the land. She heard the little girl's laugh and searched for her whereabouts. "Hello," she called out. The little girl came into view, waving from a ledge above an arched entry.

"I'm so glad you came," she said, her little voice echoing.

"I've been looking for you, and your mom. Can you show me where you are?"

"The bad man is in Daddy's head. We ran away."

"I know sweetheart, that's why I'm here in Oklahoma. My friend Sam is here too. He's a policeman. We want to get you to a safe place."

"Mommy says we *are* in a safe place. Safe from Daddy. I don't like the food. It's yucky."

"What else can you tell me?"

"Melissa has a red jeep, and Miss June loves Jesus. A lot."

"I'm in Medicine Park, can you remember that?"

"Okay. I'll tell Mommy."

Just then, commotion and loud voices tore Suzanne from a deep sleep. She saw Sam and Garret arguing in the kitchen. Garret was brandishing a butcher knife. Sam held his gun and pointed at the man's chest.

"Stop!" Her scream distracted the men long enough for Sam to knock the knife out of Garret's hand. "What are you thinking?"

Garret rubbed his wrist. "There's no way out."

Sam holstered his gun. "In the morning I am taking you to the Fort Sill Army Base. That's the only place I can think of that can protect you. Until then—where do you keep your tin foil?"

———

Holy City

The rules were: everyone had to work. Whether it was babysitting, kitchen duty, housekeeping, or volunteering at the gift shop in Holy City, there was always a job to do. Since Lizzie and Ainsley were new to the area, Lizzie didn't feel there would be any threat volunteering for the gift shop. No one knew them. It was a remote area teaming with tourists. There was plenty for Ainsley to do to keep busy, opening packages, sorting items, and she had her little pig from Melissa to keep her company. *Besides, it will do us good to get away for a bit, focus on something other than fear.*

Once the small school bus was loaded, June drove to Holy City. Upon arrival, Lizzie and Ainsley were in awe. "Can I pet the buffalopes, Mommy?"

"I'm not sure if they would like that as much as you would, but we can ask."

"Okay, Mommy." Ainsley skipped ahead and grabbed June's hand. Lizzie could hear the excitement in her daughter's voice. When June looked over her shoulder laughing, Lizzie knew it was a 'no go' and shrugged.

Ainsley stomped back to her Mom, tears in her eyes. "Miss June said they're too dangerous." Her pout continued. "Everything is too dangerous. I wanna go home."

"We need to help out today, Bug. These kind people are helping us. We need to help back. Dems da rules." Lizzie noticed Ainsley wasn't listening. Her focus was on the entry to the city. "See something interesting, hon?"

"It's Suzanne. She knows we're here."

Lizzie panicked. "What do you mean, Bug? What did you tell her?"

"Nothing, Mom. She just knows."

**

Sam called ahead to Fort Sill, explained his position, the situation, and received a polite rejection. "Surely you have a brig you can keep him in until we can get him back to California."

"There's been no crime, sir, and he's a civilian."

"Is there any place you can think of that we can get him the protection he needs?"

"Sorry sir, not really." There was a pause. "Have you checked Holy City?" They're kinda out there in the middle of nowhere...Not sure if EMF waves would penetrate rock or not."

"Thanks for your help." Sam hung up the phone, his attention directed at the pathetic creature slumped over the counter with tin foil wrapped around his head. "Well man, looks like we're going for a ride."

Suzanne piped in. "What did they say?"

"The army can't help us. The staff sergeant I spoke to recommended Holy City."

Suzanne's jaw dropped. "That must be the place I saw in my dream. We can't go there."

"We don't have many options."

Garret lifted his head, his eyes, steely orbs. "That's where she is, isn't it? You saw my daughter there."

Suzanne measured his anger, wishing she hadn't said anything. "It's more of an omen. Something bad will happen there."

Sam checked a map on his phone. "We can't trust that whoever is behind this won't find you and instill a directive to kill. I'm going to call the Sheriff's office and see if I can keep you behind bars until we can figure something out. For your sake, as well as your family."

**

Owen jammed his laptop into his suitcase. *What the fuck.* He had checked his equipment, there were no glitches, no hiccups, yet he had lost Garret *and* his family. He was counting on the 'get in, get out' method he'd grown accustomed to—he was not happy. He knew the vicinity where Garret was staying, but the signal was weak. His only reprisal was the cop. Seeing him and the dark-haired woman on the plane gave him pause. He wasn't counting on them to come to Garret's rescue. How did they suspect he was in trouble? *Must be the woman.* He smiled. It had been a while since he programmed a female. *This is going to be fun.*

**

Roger dreaded opening his laptop every morning. Dreaded it so much that he'd sit at his desk for at least half an hour procrastinating. He'd sort paperclips, clean his nails, read the news on his cell phone... anything to avoid "they."

Rebecca had taken on a new hobby...sitting in front of her vanity mirror, painting her lips red. He had given up trying to make her stop—she had wiped off and reapplied lipstick so often that her mouth was swollen, cracked, and bleeding.

When the inevitable came, the time when he could not avoid facing his orders for the day, he opened his laptop and prayed he would not have to hurt another soul. But it was no surprise. Like war, there'd be collateral damage. World leaders were notorious for shedding blood, he should be immune to their treachery by now. And yet...

He clicked on the secured email he received at 5:32 a.m. *Somebody must be traveling.* The only time his orders were issued outside California's time zone was when nefarious acts were being inflicted in other parts of the world. This time, Roger was told to create a pattern for schizophrenia for a female with a side order of incontinence. *That's enough to slow a person down.*

Roger went to work, ignoring the grunting sounds coming from the other room. Hours later, when he finished, he hit the send button and went to check on Rebecca. She had moved on from her lips to powdering the scar on her neck.

"Rog, honey? Why did you do this to me?" She asked, as if she were inquiring about the weather. Rog, honey? Is it going to rain today? He rushed to her side, enfolding her in his arms.

"I'm sorry, baby. I never meant to hurt you." He kept his eyes open so as to not relive the horror of her standing in the kitchen with a butcher knife in her hand.

Buzzards

Linda swallowed her last vitamin, finished her tea, and headed outside to do some weeding. The morning was still cool enough to work out back without dragging her electric fan onto the patio. Her fatigue level was minimal, her energy soared. *It's a good day.*

She donned her gardening gloves, picked up her spade and foam kneeling pad. *Here I come, ready or not.* She lowered herself to the ground, praying her sciatic nerve would behave. She dug around her tomato plants, extracting the pesky growth choking out their roots. The sun felt warm on her back. A slight breeze cooled her neck, blew curly tendrils away from her face. She prayed as she worked, thanking Jesus for the privilege of tending the soil.

Suddenly, the breeze stopped, the sun's warmth disappeared. An ominous feeling came over her. She looked up to see a kettle of turkey vultures circling overhead. She rested her palm on the spade's handle and eased herself up off the pad. She could see her parrot, Big Bird, through the kitchen window, perched at the top of his cage, freaking out. "Oh dear," she said and hurried into the house.

Not sure what to think about the Buzzards, she decided to observe from the safety of her kitchen—until one broke free from the flock and came dive-bombing toward her. Terrified, she backed away from the window, rolling Big Bird's cage as she moved. Shielding her eyes, she covered the cage with her body as the vulture came crashing through the glass.

**

Joseph stayed in bed that morning with a migraine. He hadn't had one since he went on a gluten-free diet years ago. His face felt flushed, yet he didn't have a fever. He tuned into what his body was trying to tell him. Flu? No. Cold? No. Stress? Possibly. Having crazy dreams that drained his energy while he slept didn't help. He thought about Linda, and his body went rigid. Something was wrong, he could feel it. He grabbed his cell.

"Linda?" She was in tears. "Linda, what's wrong?"

"A bird—my window—there's glass everywhere. On the floor, in Big Bird's cage, in my hair. It's everywhere."

"You know you just rhymed, don't you?"

Linda half-laughed, half-cried. "And isn't it like you to crack a joke when I'm over here in shambles?"

"I felt something was wrong. I'm glad I called. What can I do to help?"

"If you were closer, I'd hand you a broom. I'll have to call someone to board up the window."

"Do you want me to come and stay with you until it's replaced?"

"What about Brad?"

"He's in San Diego this week. Your timing is perfect."

"Thanks, I owe you."

"Nah, what are friends for?"

Linda hung up the phone and grabbed the broom. Suddenly, she felt something brush the back of her leg, and she screamed.

The turkey vulture glared at her with one eye. Its talons clawed at the air, one wing stretched and twitched, stretched and twitched. Blood oozed from the bird's mouth. Linda knew what she had to do.

**

By the time Suzanne got Linda's call, they were on their way to Holy

City. "I called to warn you," she said. "Evil is headed your way—big time!"

"We're on our way to Holy City. I saw it in my dream. We just dropped off Garret—they're holding him at the Lawton County jail. We're hoping to find Lizzie and Ainsley."

"I'm at the Vet. A turkey vulture broke in through my kitchen window this morning. He didn't steal anything but left one heck of a mess. The Vet says he has a concussion and a broken wing. He also said he's never heard of such a thing."

"I'm so sorry, Linda."

"I got the most ominous feeling before it happened. I feel evil is very close to you. Please be careful."

"Are *you* going to be okay?"

"Joseph is coming over, and I have a repair guy coming this afternoon."

"I'm glad you won't be alone. I'll keep in touch."

"Suzanne, spirit is giving me a message for you—keep your head on straight. Nothing is as it seems."

**

"Owen checked his email. *Thanks, Buddy*. The expediency with which he received Roger's program indicated Owen was back in the driver's seat. *Small, but mighty*, his Dad used to say. He clicked on Roger's message and got to work.

First, he located Sam, finding him would be the easiest way to access Suzanne. Roger's voice recognition software was so sophisticated, Owen was able to get a sample of Sam's voice off of YouTube. With facial and voice recognition programs he and Roger developed anonymously back in the day, the government could find anyone, anywhere. Roger perfected a frequency pattern identifier, which got pooh-poohed in Congress and shelved years ago. Owen found it useful. It didn't take long to locate his target. She was sitting next to Sam in his car. He aimed the signal at his target, aligned the sensory pattern, dialed in the code, and pressed 'send.'

Owen watched the graphs on his monitor, waiting for Suzanne's brain waves to emanate the signal. Something was wrong. An error came up on the screen. ABORT TARGET. Owen hit the reset button. "Let's try this again." But this time he received another error. SUBJECT NOT COMPATIBLE.

**

A sharp piercing sound came out of nowhere. Suzanne grabbed her head. She hadn't slept well the night before, her water intake was lacking, and her stress level was off the charts. "I need a sandwich or something."

Sam laced his fingers through hers, "Sure. You okay?"

"Had a sharp pain—it's gone now. Linda said to keep my head... now I'm wondering what that means..."

"We have to focus on one thing at a time. If Garret hadn't tried to slug that officer, we'd be babysitting a psychopath. Let's get you a sandwich, find the girl, and get back to California. I need to have a heart-to-heart with Roger Salvo."

"I want to know who that man on the plane is."

"You really think he's a piece in the puzzle?"

"I do. There was something about him, it was as if he had no soul."

"I meet soulless characters every day..."

"It was more than that, Sam. He didn't look at me, he looked through me." She faced the window, let the scenery ease her mind. The wide-open space, the mountains, dark plumes filling the sky. "It's going to rain."

"I see a drive-thru, will that suffice?"

"Yes, even better. I think eating may help, I have this high pitch ringing—"

"I've had that too. Usually before I start craving alcohol."

"Did you bring the tin foil?"

Sam chuckled. "I didn't think I'd need it."

"If I start acting crazy, set me straight."

He patted her hand. "Hopefully the ringing is due to the weather change."

Suddenly it occurred to her. "That man on the plane—he wasn't looking through me, he was looking past me—at you. He was looking at you!"

Accuracy Rate

Accuracy Rate

The gift store shelves were restocked with religious artifacts, T-shirts, postcards, and hand-made items from local Indian tribes. Lizzie and Ainsley had spent most of their day in the backroom unpacking the items, while the other volunteers brought them to the front of the store.

Ainsley kept popping her head out of the stockroom door despite Lizzie's warning. "Bug, please, I need you to mind me. Stay away from the door. Mommy doesn't want you getting hurt.

"I'm waiting for Suzanne."

Lizzie sighed, choosing her words carefully. "Baby, Suzanne lives in California, remember?"

"I know Mommy. But she's here. I feel it."

Lizzie checked the time. "We're supposed to meet Miss Melissa in ten minutes. Can you help me open this last package? I think it's a toy."

Ainsley skipped over to Lizzie and fell to her knees. "She knows where we are."

Lizzie stiffened. "Honey, I know you like Suzanne, but what if she's not the person you think she is...like that preschool teacher you had last year, remember how we thought she was so nice when you started school, and then after a few months she wasn't so nice anymore..."

"Mrs. Wren."

"Yes. Mrs. Wren. And remember what Mommy told you? How we need to get to know someone better before we know if they are friends?"

Ainsley's chin rested on her chest, her eyes cast down to the floor. "Yes."

"Lizzie stroked her daughter's hair. "Sweetie, Mommy doesn't want you to be disappointed or hurt, do you understand that?" Ainsley nodded. "Mommy wants you to be safe—and I think if I had the chance to meet this Suzanne, I might think as highly of her as you do—but for now, we have to be very careful who we talk to."

**

"How much further?" Suzanne wadded the paper from her taco and tossed it in the paper bag on her lap, and took a sip of Sam's soft drink.

"Twelve miles," he replied. "Feeling better?"

"I'll feel better once we're there, it's five minutes to three already."

"It's not much further."

"My insides are fidgety. We're going on my visions—she could be anywhere."

"I think your accuracy rate is pretty damn good."

"It's imperative we find them. Even with Garret locked up, I fear for them."

"We'll be there in fifteen, twenty minutes."

"Then what?"

"We get them on a plane back to California—keep them at your place until we can figure out the source."

"What about Roger? Do you think he's responsible for all of this?"

"If he's not, he damn sure knows who is."

**

Melissa skidded her red jeep to a stop, stirring a plume of dust. "C'mon, you two, we have to skedaddle."

Lizzie shielded her daughter. "What's the hurry?"

"Got a call from a friend of mine who works at the Sheriff's office in Lawton. He looks out for the women in the shelter. He said a guy matching your husband's description was brought in by a detective from California."

"Then we're safe."

"Hard to know for sure. They're holding him on an attempted assault charge. He swung at an officer, but if he makes bail, he'll be released. Jerry, my friend, knows you're here. It's just a matter of time before your husband gets wind of our shelter." Mother and daughter hopped into the car. Melissa smiled at Ainsley over her shoulder. "Hey angel face, did you have fun?"

Lizzie lowered her tone, "I don't understand what a detective from California would want with my husband—he's not a criminal."

"Forgive me for sayin'—this is the guy who wanted to bash your head in with a baseball bat. That doesn't make him a saint in my book." She glanced at Lizzie, "Listen, it's our job to keep you safe. That's what we do."

Ainsley pressed her face to the window, looking for buffalo when a car went whizzed by. "It's Suzanne! Mommy I saw her, I saw Suzanne! We have to go back!"

Lizzie twisted in her seat. "Baby, it's probably someone who looks like your friend. Remember, Mommy said she's in California?"

"It was her, I saw her."

Lizzie rubbed her temples. The buzzing in her head reminded her of a time she was skiing in Lake Tahoe. It was foggy, she wanted to get in one last run. She came up on another skier and swerved, turning her head as she hit a tree. She saw stars, heard a high-pitched sound in her left ear for days. She could hear Ainsley whining about something, her words, needles in her brain. "Shut the fuck up!" she screamed, holding her head.

"Calm down," Melissa said. "That's no way to speak to a child."

Lizzie's body shook. She reached for the door handle and pushed. The door was locked.

Melissa edged to the side of the road and stopped. "Listen, we all have bad days. This is just a wrinkle compared to what's gonna happen if your husband finds you. Now, can we please keep it safe until we get back to the shelter? We can have a cup of Joe, talk about our feelings... you *will* get through this."

Lizzie blinked a few times. Ainsley sobbed quietly in the back seat. "Go away, bad man. Go away."

**

Suzanne whipped her head around. "Sam! That's the Jeep I saw in my dream!"

"Look," he pointed ahead, "Holy City."

Sam drove into the visitor's lot. Suzanne bolted out of the door before he had the gearshift in Park. A shaft of sunlight split the black clouds in two, forcing her to shade her eyes. "In my dream, she was right up there," she said pointing to the ledge left of the arched entryway."

"A little dangerous, wouldn't you say?"

Suzanne faced Sam, expressing her revelation. "Exactly. That's the message. She's still in danger."

"C'mon let's go check things out."

"No. She's not here."

"How do you know?" An eagle flew overhead, riding an airwave. Suzanne followed the bird with her eyes.

"I just do."

**

Ainsley laid across her bed, her arms crossed beneath her chin. She had skipped dinner, storytime, and her bath. She brushed her teeth against her will, and dressed in her favorite nightgown. Despite the pep talks and apologies, she remained sad.

"Are you going to pout all night? The other kids are catching lightning bugs over by the Eagle Park sign. Wanna go see?" Lizzie threw a pair of socks that were rolled into a ball, missing Ainsley's nose by an inch. Ainsley didn't flinch. "How long are you going to stay mad at me?"

"You never listen to me."

"Bug—that's not true."

"Why couldn't we go back?"

"Miss Melissa thought we'd be safer if we didn't."

"Miss Melissa is mean."

"Now Bug, that's not how we talk about people, especially people that are trying to help us."

"But she was there, Mom. Suzanne was there."

Lizzie's ire rose a notch as she poked Ainsley's shoulder for emphasis. "How many times do I have to say it? Suzanne is in California!"

"Mommy you're hurting me."

Lizzie lowered her face, inches from her little girl. "That's nothing compared to what I'm going to do to you if you don't shut up about Suzanne."

Ainsley covered her head with her pillow to muffle her cries. Her Mommy wasn't herself, *like Daddy*. The bad man took both of her parents. Only one person she could count on. *Suzanne—help me. Please.*

**

Suzanne sat under the stars with Sam. A breeze carried the scent of white petunias from a planter nearby. "I hear her crying out to me," she said. She leaned back in the chair, closing her eyes. "That eagle I saw earlier. It means something, I don't know what."

Sam nodded toward the neighbor's place, "Why don't we go pick Jason's brain."

"This is why you're the perfect partner."

"Comes with the territory. I rely on your intuition."

Suzanne looped her arm through Sam's. "My gift is made stronger by your love and support."

Sam rapped on Jason's door. Jason answered, a beer in one hand, a hotdog in the other. "Hey, man, what's up?"

"Got a minute to chat? We're wondering about the eagles around here."

Suzanne smiled. "I saw one at Holy City today, I was hoping to get more info on their habitats."

"Eagles, huh?" He took a swig of beer. "Man, the only eagles I know about are the rock group and the Eagle Amusement Park that's been closed for years." He looked away as if trying to capture the memory. "I was just a kid when it shut down. Signs still there...rumor has it the mansion is occupied by ghosts."

Sam glanced at Suzanne. "Ghosts?"

"Yeah. I think they're squatters myself. No one ever goes out that way—so why not?"

"You've been a great help. Where is this amusement park?"

"Off Highway 62." I wouldn't go wandering around there at night. There's a lot of snakes over that way. Used to be an exhibition at the park. I guess when they closed down, they let 'em all go. The mansion is still standin'. Creepy."

"Thanks, man, we'll check it out in the morning."

"Sure I can't offer you folks a beer?"

Sam hesitated. Suzanne noticed the glitch in her fiancé's expression. He shivered before answering. "No thanks, Jason. I'm a—a—"

"How well do you know the family that lives over there?" She pointed toward Garret's house."

"Pete? He's okay. Keeps to himself. That kid of theirs is sure cute. Don't talk to Amy much. I ran into her at the Goodwill store recently. She was coming out of the dressing room, didn't even say 'hello,' she asked me if I had a pen."

Suzanne's expression puzzled "That's all?"

"Yeah, she went back into the dressing room, came back out, and handed me the pen. Not a thank you, kiss my ass, or adios."

"Was Gar—I mean Pete with her?"

"Naw, he works during the week. I had a dentist appointment in Lawton, just stopped in GW to pick up a couple of paperbacks." He finished his beer with one gulp. "I love to read—mysteries, mostly."

"Thanks, you've been most helpful."

"You folks ask a lot of questions for tourists."

Sam shrugged. "What can I say, we're from California."

"That explains it."

Good Will

The Goodwill store opened at 9 a.m. Suzanne and Sam arrived at 8:52 a.m. "I have a good feeling about this," she said.

"I could get used to this town," he said. "Everyone is so friendly."

Immediately after the doors opened, Suzanne made a dash for the dressing rooms.

Sam looked around the store, acting nonchalant until a few minutes later, when Suzanne came up behind him.

"Look what I found." She clicked on the photo she took in the dressing room of the poster hanging on the wall.

"Holy Springs Shelter. I'll be damned. Nice work."

"Call the number—see if they're there."

"Sweetheart, even if they are, whoever answers that phone is sworn to secrecy. I think what we need is a visit to the Sheriff."

"Without proof, what is he going to do?"

Sam thought for a minute. Suzanne's apprehension didn't go unnoticed. "You want to call and tell them you're in trouble, don't you?"

"Now who's psychic?"

"Is that why my head hurts?"

"He's grasping at straws."

"Who?"

"That man, whoever he is."

"Only one way to find out. Make the call."

**

Melissa got the call at 9:15 a.m., interrupting her morning ritual: Hazelnut coffee, extra cream, two sugars, and a chocolate glazed donut. She popped the remainder of the donut into her mouth, and hopped into her jeep, coffee sloshing out of her cup.

June stepped out from one of the cabins, hands on hips. "Where you off to?" she called.

"Goodwill for a pick-up—hold down the fort."

June's face screwed into a disapproving scowl. "We don't have any more room!"

"We'll make it work. She can bunk with Lizzie and the girl."

"Whatever." June waved a sign of dismissal and went back inside.

Melissa left the dirt road adjacent to the rusted Eagle Park sign and headed for the highway.

**

Suzanne paced in back of the Goodwill store, keeping her eye out for a red Jeep. When she saw it barreling through the parking lot, she took a deep breath. She hadn't cried in so long that she wasn't sure she remembered how. She pinched her cheeks, thought of the one memory that could invoke emotion. Sam in the hospital in Germany, *with a stab wound in his kidney*. She hadn't heard from him in days. She took the memory from the past and applied it to the present. *What will I do if I lose him to another criminal act?* Tears streamed down her face. *Ready*.

"Sue?" Melissa opened the passenger door. Suzanne slid inside. "I'm Melissa. Let's get you somewhere safe—we can talk then. You okay? You're not hurt?"

Suzanne shook her head 'no', the tears flowing more effortlessly. The thought of the little girl having to endure this endeavor made her sad. Melissa patted her hand. "This too shall pass," she said. "Where you from?"

"Chicago," she lied. *Sue? Chicago?* She abhorred lying and knew as soon as she found the little girl and her mother, she'd come clean.

"You'll meet my partner, June. We've been running the shelter for eighteen years...since her husband beat the snot out of her in back of a bar in Toledo and left her to die. I just happen to take the wrong exit and needed to turn around...that's when I saw her crawlin' towards the road." She drummed on the steering wheel with her thumb. "We get a little money from the state, not much. Most of our funds come from donations, and Holy City shares some of their donations with us, in return, we volunteer in the gift shop." She glanced at Suzanne. "Just so you know."

Guilt seeped into Suzanne's consciousness. "Maybe this is a bad idea."

"Like I said, we'll have a cuppa Joe and talk things out. We want to help."

"Do you take in everyone who calls?"

Melissa gave her a side glance. "We try to take in those who need help."

"How do you keep the husbands and boyfriends away?"

"We don't give out the address to anyone, first of all, and second, the Sheriff in Lawton is a friend. He keeps the boys away from the yard if you get my drift."

Melissa glanced in her rear-view mirror. "What's your boyfriend drive, Sugar?"

"A Subaru. Why?"

"Just curious. There's a white SUV following us."

Suzanne reacted with a fearful glance in the side mirror. "No," she lied, again. "That's not him."

**

Sam allowed enough distance between him and the red jeep so as to not alarm the driver. He slowed, sped up, making it seem as if he was distracted, and not focused on a pursuit. When the Jeep turned on its blinker, he sped up, and veered around the Jeep, passing on the right. Once the vehicle turned, he flipped a U-turn and continue at a stalker's pace. He made note of the Eagle Park Amusement Center sign in the foreground, expecting the next roads leading to their destination to be as rural as they get. He was right. Up ahead, a single-lane-road wound through the bones of what had once been a popular attraction for locals and tourists. To the left, and about a mile up the road, he could see a large structure and *the red Jeep*.

He decided to wait until Suzanne had time to establish a connection before making an appearance.

**

Melissa ushered Suzanne into a small office space with two high-back chairs a credenza with a Keurig coffee maker, a selection of coffee pods, non-dairy creamer, a mishmash of ceramic mugs, and a bowl filled with Hershey's kisses. "Help yourself. I'm partial to Hazelnut, myself."

Suzanne smiled halfheartedly, "No thanks, I'm good."

Melissa opened her drawer, produced a couple of tea bags, and tossed them toward Suzanne. "I keep forgetting to put those out."

Suzanne picked up a bag. "I haven't had Jasmine tea since my mother passed. Thank you."

"How long have you been with this guy? What's his name—"

"Sam."

"Tell me about him."

"He's handsome, kind..."

"Melissa lifted one brow. "They all are sweetie...till they're not. What happened? What made you call us?"

"We went over that on the phone. He got violent. Started screaming at me. I was afraid, and I don't know anyone here."

"How long have you two been together?"

"About a year." Suzanne held up her left hand. "We recently got engaged."

"Why didn't you go to a hotel? Book a flight home?"

"I was afraid—I saw your poster—I thought—" Suzanne lowered her tear-filled gaze. "I thought calling you was the right thing to do."

Melissa sighed. "Let's give it 24 hours. Give you some time to think about your goal. Get a good night's sleep." Melissa finalized the meeting by opening the door. "Let me show you to your room. I hope you don't mind sharing."

June called to Melissa and Suzanne as they were exiting the office. "Can I speak with you, please?" Melissa excused herself.

Suzanne's ears perked up. She heard them say something about a woman named Lizzie, and a little girl. Melissa waved the woman off with the flick of a wrist. "I'll take care of it," she said. She noticed Suzanne listening and turned her head to conceal her words. It didn't matter, Suzanne got the gist of what was said by her body language. Melissa didn't expect Suzanne to last more than a day, and she was right.

"Sorry," Melissa said. "I had planned on having you share a room with another woman and her child, but it seems there's a problem. Have a seat over there," she said pointing to a room filled with comfy furniture and a flat- screen TV. "I'll be back."

Chills crept from Suzanne's arms to her scalp. She could feel the little girl's energy and her fear. Suzanne closed her eyes. When she opened them, the little girl stood before her. "I knew you'd come," she said, rushing into Suzanne's arms.

**

Lizzie shook her head vehemently, "I don't give a shit who you are, she's my kid, and I will discipline her the way I see fit. She's MY daughter, and if I want to knock her fuckin' head off, I will—I am her MOTHER!"

Melissa tightened her lips. "We can't have this behavior here, Lizzie. If you can't control your temper, I will have no choice but to report you to the proper authorities."

"Go fuck yourself," she said gathering what little she had brought with her when she escaped from Garret's wrath. Her head hurt. Even her silver dental fillings seem to vibrate. She wanted to lash out like a mad dog, foam at the mouth, howl at the moon. She checked her fingernails to see if they were growing into claws. She wadded the small bundle of clothes tight to her breast and made haste.

Down the hall and to the right she stopped in her tracks. "Leave her alone, bitch—get away from my kid!"

Suzanne held Ainsley tighter. "They got to you too."

"You have no right—" Lizzie grabbed Ainsley's arm, but Suzanne shifted her weight to protect the girl.

"We found Garret. He's in jail—it's for his own good."

"Who are you?" Lizzie clenched her fist, ready to strike. "What right do you have— "

"Mommy, don't! It's Suzanne, my friend!"

Lizzie's face went blank, her hands flew up, and she squeezed her head as hard as she could. Ainsley screamed and threw her arms around her mother's waist. Suzanne threw her arms around them both, envisioning white light filled with positive energy enfolding them, raising their vibration, consuming them in love.

**

Owen slammed his fist on the desk. An error blinked on his laptop screen, followed by SYSTEM FAILURE: FREQUENCY NOT COMPATIBLE.

———

Half-Truths and Shot Guns

Sam heard the double click before he knocked on the door. He looked up at the surveillance camera, smiled, and waved. The double barrel greeting was no surprise.

"What do you want?" June stood her ground, shotgun aimed between Sam's eyes.

He produced his badge and ID. "Detective Samson Metzger, Goldorado Sheriff's Department, I'm here with concerns for the Brecker family. Garret Brecker, or as you may know him, Peter Benson, is locked up in Lawton for assaulting an officer, but his wife Lizzie, and daughter Ainsley are in deep trouble."

June lowered the gun. "What kind of trouble?"

"Someone is trying to kill them, or to be more concise, someone is trying to get them to kill each other."

June chuckled. "And how do you propose they'll do that?"

"If I can speak with them, we can sort out the details."

Suzanne appeared at the door, peering over June's shoulder. "June, he's not lying. Check with your friend in Lawton. It all sounds crazy, but it's the truth. That's why we're here."

June lowered the shot gun. "You have five minutes before I call the Sheriff myself."

Ainsley huddled with her mother and Melissa in the day room.

Lizzie, shaken to the core, clung to her daughter like plastic wrap. "I would never hurt you," she repeated over and over between kissing the top of her daughter's head. Stunned, Melissa remained silent.

Suzanne led Sam into the room, making introductions as she joined Lizzie and Ainsley. Sam's gentle demeanor put them at ease.

"We suspect the source is coming from California, but we don't know exactly how the frequency is being transmitted. We know the headaches, the ringing, and buzzing noises are symptoms of being controlled. Behavior changes, anger, violence, and death by different means are a result of the patterns being transmitted to the brain."

Lizzie grabbed Suzanne's hand. "You stopped it—you stopped me from hurting my daughter—how?"

All eyes gravitated toward Suzanne. "I'm not sure," she said. "Linda told me a long time ago that by raising my vibration, I would be able to conquer evil. If you think of it in musical terms, the devil can't hit notes that the divine can."

Lizzie squeezed Ainsley tight. "Is that why my baby can see you?"

Melissa piped in, "I guess I don't have to worry about where you're going to sleep tonight, Su-*zanne.* Are you really from Chicago?"

"Half-truth. I was conceived there."

Lizzie detached herself from Ainsley to stand before Sam. "What can we do? How do we stop it?"

Sam placed his hands on Lizzie's shoulders. "We need to find the source."

**

Owen stepped onto the plane heading back to California. The emails he sent Roger, filled with venom, went unanswered. "What the fuck?!" At risk of breaching security measures, he'd have to wait until he was off the plane to deal with the matter. *You'll pay, mutha-fucka.*

———

Weather or Not

Roger rested his chin on his closed fist. Black clouds loomed outside Rebecca's hospital room window in addition to his bleak mood. *I wonder if they control that too.* He didn't doubt it. If they could control a person's mind, why not the weather? *It's all about frequency.*

He interrupted his pity party long enough to glance at his wife. Tubes snaked from her slender arms to bags of fluid hanging from an IV pole. Her neck and face were bandaged like a mummy. While he was busy playing Mr. Destructo in his office, Rebecca was sculpting a couple of new features on her face and neck with a callus remover she found in her pedicure kit.

After emergency surgery to reattach her lips and repair the gaping hole in her neck, a twenty-four-hour psych evaluation was ordered, and Rebecca was moved to UC Davis' psychiatric ward for observation. Roger claimed she had succumbed to incremental depression over the years...he thought the last incident, when she had slashed her throat with a butcher knife, was the tip of the iceberg. He didn't dare tell them she was being controlled by an anonymous source lest he find himself in the bed next to her.

He was weary. Defeated. And at the moment, safe. The hospital's

WIFI was self-reliant. Because of the nature of their equipment, any outside electrical interference was controlled. *I wish we could move in.* Just then his phone buzzed. He stared at the text. *Fuck you.*

**

Linda woke up feeling apprehensive. The man with the slender face plagued her dreams. His beady eyes drilled holes in her brain, filling it with worms, pincher bugs, and beetles. Brown stalks grew out of every orifice until she resembled a caricature, shaped like a tree. Her gnarly branches reached with maleficence for the sun peeking out behind dark clouds in the sky. But then the clouds parted, the sun's rays bathed her in light, and green leaves sprouted from her tree-like limbs.

She knew illusions came from the brain's interpretation of information being fed into the source. She delved into its manifestation. The tree represents growth, life, family. Worms aid in tilling soil. Pincher bugs are scavengers that feed at night. Beetles are diverse, sacred, they defend themselves using their hard-exoskeletal design. The sun represents enlightenment, Jesus, *the son of God*. A bible verse came to mind, John 1:5...God is light, and in him is no darkness at all.

**

Joseph tore the picture of the woman from his wall. Her tempting lips, tempting him no longer. He felt a sense of freedom, a release that weighed heavy on his chest. He dialed Linda, and put the phone on speaker...

"Linda! I'm calling to check on you. Any more birds?"

"No birds. Dreaming about trees, and bugs now—how 'bout you? How're those hot lips?"

"I'm removing them from my wall as we speak?"

"Oh? Change of heart?

"Ben wants to renew our vows. I'm so in love."

"Interesting. No more weird feelings?"

"No, but I have to admit, I *was* kind of depressed. Those lips were a distraction, for sure, but last night when Ben surprised me with a special dinner and proposed we renew our vows, he lifted me to a higher plane. Love conquers all, right?"

"I think you're on to something there, my friend. Any visions of a thin-faced man?"

"No visions per se, but I'm getting the word 'desperate'."

In the Same Boat

Owen circled Roger's house three times. Three days had gone by. Roger hadn't returned his texts or responded to the emails Owen sent during his layover in San Diego on the way back from Oklahoma.

Since Owen returned, he spent hours poring over schematics, trying to figure out why his program was malfunctioning. He had lost connection with Garret, his wife, and the cop. He needed Roger's expertise, even if it meant revealing his identity. He planned on posing as a messenger. He would commiserate with Roger, pretend to understand the nature of the beast, even pretend to be *in the same boat*.

**

Sam had been staking out Roger's house since they had returned two days prior. Lizzie and Ainsley were staying with Suzanne. Garret was released on bail but had to remain in Oklahoma until his court date. Sam was able to help him purchase equipment that would scramble any frequency directed at his house, and hopefully protect him from further attacks.

His conversation with Roger in Rebecca's room at UC Davis was enlightening and frightening at the same time. Roger revealed his participation in the government's secret programs, and how he received his directions from an unknown source. He showed Sam the texts, and although Sam was unable to track the number, his gut told him that desperate people resort to desperate measures.

Suzanne prepared him for any nefarious mental persuasions with a prayer of protection. He felt as if he were a priest going up against Beelzebub. He went so far as to stop at a religious store and buy a cross.

He ran the plate on the car watching Roger's house. Government plates belonging to Owen Westford, a high-ranking technical engineer with the CIA. Sam made a few calls, confirming his suspicions, that Westford was acting on his own behalf.

Sam removed his gun from its holster, held it to his side, and approached the vehicle. He tapped on the window, startling Owen. "Step out of the vehicle." Owen held up his middle finger and started the car. Sam aimed his gun at the front tire and squeezed the trigger, pivoted his upper body, shot the back tire, and aimed the gun at Owen's head.

"You must be fuckin' nuts! Do you know who I am?"

"You're not Jesus Christ, and I am here to see that you are no longer able to play God."

Resolution

Garret stepped off the plane and hurried to meet Lizzie and Ainsley at the bottom of the escalator near baggage claim. Suzanne, Sam, Linda, and Joseph witnessed the happy reunion.

Sam, Garret, and Joseph chatted while the girls excused themselves to the restroom.

"Are you sure it's over?" Garret asked.

"Owen Westford has hired a shrewd lawyer, and the government will need to assess the damages. To prosecute, they will have to either admit or deny their involvement with the programs he was using. It's going to be tricky, but I feel once the media gets hold of this information all hell will break loose, and he will be tried for the deaths he caused, and of course, you will have to testify against him.

Garret looked relieved. "What about the other guy?"

"Roger Salvo?" Sam nodded. "He'll be indicted. His wife Rebecca will testify on his behalf. She's been through hell."

"I see a room filled with bars," Joseph said, "but they're shadows... I'm feeling his sentence will be much lighter than Westford's.

**

Suzanne and Sam drove the Breckers to Lizzie's aunt's house and said their goodbyes. Ainsley teared up. "You won't forget me?"

"Never! And once you're settled, I bet Mom will let us have a lunch date."

Lizzie hugged Suzanne and Linda tight. "We can't thank you enough."

Suzanne's eyes misted over. "You have a very special little girl...her gift is what saved your life."

"See Mommy, I told you Suzanne was nice. She can have a baby in her tummy too!"

Suzanne placed her hand on her abdomen. "Maybe someday," she said.

Sam jumped in giving hugs and shaking hands. Linda and Joseph departed. As Sam and Suzanne headed to the car, he said, "I heard you say something about lunch—are you hungry?"

Suzanne slipped her arm around Sam's waist, her eyes filled with love. She gave him a nudge. "*Very.*"

THE END

Acknowledgments

Borrowed Time 3 – Mind Games is based on facts, half-truths, and mostly fiction. With so much controversy in the world, it has become a challenge to distinguish fact from fiction. And in the end, who *really* knows? I thought it would be interesting to write about Mind Control, incorporating information presented by both sides of the coin, and adding my own two cents. I find it curious when I think of something random, like a cleaning product or a favorite food, the item appears on my phone, a TV commercial, or a radio ad. This manifestation has been blamed on coincidence, algorithms, big brother, and "them". But what is the real truth? What do we really know about 5G? And why *are* birds falling from the sky?

First, I would like to thank my readers. Your support, reviews, feedback, and compliments have meant the world to me. Thank you, Nancy, Kathy, Linda, Beatrice, Renee, Melanie, Debbie, Tanya, Cindy, Beth, Barbara, Marie, Pat, and those who are true fans and wait patiently for each new release. *I write for you.*

My gratitude to the truth-seekers out there, who risk it all to enlighten those willing to listen. I am grateful to my friends Noreen and Linda who supply me with information to investigate, and psychic friend, Linda Schooler, who permits me to take liberty with her character, who listens to me churn these stories in my head, and always lends her unwavering support. Thank you to Joseph Ernest Martin for sharing information with me over the years, and for agreeing to be a character in Mind Games.

To my critique group, Tarra, Michele, Linda, and June, your support and suggestions have been more valuable than you know. To the El Dorado Writers Guild, my mentor Kirk, Erin, Sandra, Nolan, Ellen, Carol, and others who have provided excellent feedback, I thrive on your expertise. Thank you to my Sisters in Crime group, Capitol Crimes, and to Beatrice Gregory for being an excellent traveling partner. Our adventures inspire me to write.

I am truly grateful to my talented cover artist, Karen Anne Phillips. You rock girl! To Tarra Thomas, my editor and formatter, thank you for putting up with my last-minute changes and for not freaking out when I forget which file is which! I am also grateful to my talented author friend, Terry Shepherd, for his kind words, generosity, inspiration, and for doing an amazing job narrating my stories into audiobooks. You kill it, my friend. I am blessed to have *all of you* wonderful, brilliant people in my life!

Lastly, I'd like to thank my family, Don, Ashleigh, Erika, and Olivia for their love and support. You are my joy, and the fuel that keeps me going. Special thanks to my sister, Kathy Partipilo, for always being my tough and loving critic.

April, 2023

Resources

"Mind control, as the name states, empowers a person, entity, or device, to change or alter human thoughts. In warfare, nothing could be more powerful than the ability to alter the thoughts of your enemies. In government, mind control would amount to the most powerful method of human slavery."

PrepForThat: Jim Satney April 23, 2018

Learn More:

1. Government accidentally releases mind control documents - PrepForThat

https://prepforthat.com/government-accidentally-releases-mind-control-documents/

2. DARPA's Secret Mind Control Program: Our Thoughts Won't Be Our Own (anomalien.com)

Sneak Peek

Here's a preview of the opening action in Suzanne Cash's next adventure. Her paranormal connections link her with victims of a vicious cartel with designs on controlling California's economic and political future. With wedding plans in full swing, will Suzanne and Sam be able to decode and act on one of the most challenging cases of their careers? Borrowed Time: Book 4 - Golden State: Coming in 2024!

Borrowed Time: Book 4 - Golden State

Chapter 1
Visitors

Death. Darkness. Voices crying in the night. Growling dogs. Rows and rows of greenery...Suzanne Cash winced and flailed in her sleep. Fear made her cry out. "Dear God, make them stop!"

She awoke, drenched.

Sitting up at the edge of the bed, she collected herself, breathing in and out to slow her heartbeat. Being psychic took its toll on her, mind, body, and soul. Three months had gone by since her last encounter, but it seemed she no sooner found reprieve from one situation, another took its place. Dreams filled with horror, yet she couldn't pinpoint a reason for them. *3A.M.* The witching hour. She needed at least two more hours of sleep.

Her psychic friend, Linda Schooler's remedy for times like these took the edge off: *Positive thoughts.* She and Sam were making plans to marry. *Life is good.* And yet burying herself under the covers couldn't get rid of the chill she felt in her bones. *Something bad is going to happen.*

As her body relaxed back in a dream state, she repeated a mantra in her head. *I am safe. I am loved. I am protected by the angels and spirit guides that surround me.* She eased into her alternate universe and began a new story...

It was December...the winds whipped into a frenzy. Drifts of snow collected along the Highway 50 corridor. *Late!* Sam was waiting. She glanced into her rearview mirror. "Mom, you look lovely—doesn't she Dad?" *If only.* The emptiness she felt was enough to turn the car around and head back down the hill. "Life is but a dream," her mother sang.

Suzanne punched her pillow into a mound, and wriggled into a comfortable position. She peeked at the glowing numbers taunting her from her nightstand. 3:18 A.M. "What's the use?" She slid out of bed, flipped on the bathroom light, and caught a glimpse of herself in the mirror. "Well, don't you look lovely?" Suddenly, her self-assessment came to a halt. She froze. Standing behind her was a dark-haired woman, her arms stretched out, her feet bare.

Suzanne spun around. "Who are you? And what are you doing in my bathroom in the middle of the night?"

"No sè."

Suzanne sighed. "I don't know either."

When Suzanne needed advice, she dialed her psychic friend Linda for advice. "She was Mexican, or Spanish. What little Spanish I remembered from high school allowed me to move her toward the light."

Linda clicked her tongue on the roof of her mouth. "Interesting the visitation would present itself after your dream."

"I was thinking about that, she did seem unsettled, and her clothing, or lack thereof gave me the impression her death was an atrocity." Suzanne followed with a wisp of an idea. "I feel like she was running from something, or someone."

"Let it go, see what comes to you."

"Yeah. Hopefully I'll get some answers before bedtime—but hey—what do you say we have lunch tomorrow? I'd like to go through some bridal magazines with you."

"Oh gosh, I'd love to, but I've got an appointment at the Front Street Animal Shelter tomorrow. I think it's time for me to get another dog."

"Did you have one in mind?"

"I fell in love with a Brittney Spaniel pup. She's adorable."

"Sounds terrific. Another time then?

"Come here. I'll fix lunch. You can meet my new dog."

"I'm warning you—my mother may tag along."

"I thought—"

"Yes. She's on the other side—but for some reason she's been hanging around. In my dreams, in my bedroom. It's kind of daunting. Especially when Sam is over."

"Woo! I can only imagine." Linda gave a whistle, her bird mimicked her in the background. "I hear your phone beeping—Sam right?"

"You must be psychic! It is, I'll talk to you tomorrow." Suzanne clicked over to the other line. "Hi Handsome."

"Hi Beautiful, I was wondering if you're available tonight. Short notice, but I'd love for you to come to my house, I—*we* were invited to a barbecue."

"Sounds fun, what time?"

"See you at 6."

Suzanne hung up, feeling elated. But when she went to place her phone on the charger, she noticed a cold air pocket in the kitchen. She checked to see if she had left the freezer door open. *Nope*. She stood still, waiting to see if the chill in the room manifested into an entity, and it did. Five of them.

Coming in 2024 from Dänna Wilberg!

www.ingramcontent.com/pod-product-compliance
Lightning Source LLC
Chambersburg PA
CBHW060820310726
48980CB00002B/350
* 9 7 8 1 9 5 5 1 7 1 4 8 9 *